# The Qur'an

# Islam's Holy Book *Verses*

An Easy To Read English Version

**Akhtar A. Alvi, P. E.**

# Contents

Edition 2. 00

eBook ISBN: 978-1-963974-55-3
Paperback ISBN: 978-1-963974-56-0
Hardback ISBN: 978-1-963974-57-7



Edition 1. 00
Published in August, 2020
By
www. 24by7Publishing. com
ISBN: 978-81-947356-3-2

## DEDICATION

I dedicate this book to my family:

| | |
|---|---|
| • Spouse: | Late Razia A. Alvi |
| • Grandparents: | |
| – Maternal: | Zainab Bibi and Wali Muhammad |
| – Paternal: | Jivi Bibi and Khushi Muhammad |
| • Parents: | Barkat Bibi and Muhammad Hussain Alvi |
| • In-Laws: | Chirag Bibi and Rehmatullah Shah |
| • Auntie and Uncle: | Sardaran Begum and Ali Muhammad Alvi |
| • Paternal Auntie and Uncle: | Beernisan Bibi and Khushi Muhammad |
| • Sister: | Kishwar |
| • Brothers: | Anwar, Sarwar, and Zafar |
| • Cousins: | Rashid, Suria, and Rukia |

God please bless their souls and reward them paradise.

# ACKNOWLEDGMENTS

My thanks to:

- Late Razia Alvi, the love of my life and life-partner for 50 years. She encouraged me to do this translation. I am grateful to her for her patience with me during the 11-year effort, when her health was fragile. She has passed away on March 13, 2019. I miss her. God please:
    - bless her soul and reward her paradise.
    - allow us to live together in paradise.
- Our family friends, Parveen and Akhtar Shah, for encouraging me to do this translation.
- Our grandsons, Jibril and Musa, for their review to confirm that the translation was simple and concise.
- Family-friend Attorney Faisal Shah, for his review to say: *With regard to your interpretive translation of the Koran, I finally had a chance to sit down and read your letter and sample excerpts. I admit, I was quite impressed by your effort. I also understand and appreciate your motivation for the project.*
- Shakil Ahmad Qureshi, Ph. D., and his colleagues at Aabroo Educational Welfare Organization, Lahore, Pakistan, for reviewing the excerpts of the book and commenting: I have added value in writing this book. It should be published.
- My friend Timothy L. Triplett and younger son Anwar A. Alvi for their editing.
- Naveed Ahmad Malik for the graphic design.
- Rizwan Alvi, our elder son, and his Photographer, John Kernick, for my portrait.


Akhtar A. Alvi, P. E.
maaalvi@gmail. com

## WHY THIS TRANSLATION?

I have translated the Qur'an in English for four reasons:

1. For filling the void of "An Easy To Read English Version" of the Qur'an in concise and simple English for a layman, without scholarly discussions and explanations. People are busy making a living and are short of time.
2. I needed an electronic copy of the Qur'an for researching God's characteristics to write my book: *Understanding God And His System.*
3. I am a Muslim, born in a Muslim-Family and a Muslim-Country, Pakistan. I have been educated in Muslim-Schools. Why I have not understood the Qur'an all my life? I have done this translation to help Muslims, like me, and non-Muslims to understand the Qur'an for practicing it in their lives.
4. For helping the non-Arabic speakers to understand the Qur'an.

During the 1950s, I was a teenager in Pakistan. One day, I asked my father: Is there a God? He said: Yes, but did not give me a reason or a proof. Not satisfied with his answer, questions about God have been on my mind all my life: Is there a God, if yes:

- Where is He?
- What:
    - is He Like?
    - does He do?
    - has He done?
    - will He do?
- How does He do it?

For example:

- On a hot summer day, the farmers pray to God for making rain for their crops. At the same time, the owners of the ice-making factories pray to God for the days to be hotter for selling more ice. Between the competing prayers of the farmers and the factory owners, what does God decide and how does He decide it?
- During 2023, the world population has reached eight billion. Every moment of a person's life, the person has needs, wishes, and desires. According to the Qur'an, God knows about everyone's needs, wishes, and desires, and decides about them.
  How does God decide about them? Is He making decisions by

pushing billions of buttons at the same time?

For earning a living, I worked for 46 years. During these years, the questions about God have been on my mind. During:

- 1964-1970, I taught Civil Engineering at the University of Engineering & Technology, Lahore, Pakistan.
- 1970-1975, I developed irrigated agriculture and hydropower for the Government of Benue Plateau State, Nigeria, West Africa.
- 1976, with the love of my life and life-partner, late Razia, and two sons, Rizwan, 20 - month, and Anwar, 6-week old immigrated to the United States of America.
- 1979-1981, I taught at the Louisiana State University, Baton Rouge, USA. There, I, also obtained a second Master of Science Degree in Civil Engineering. Earlier, I had obtained a Bachelor of Science Degree and a Master of Science Degree in Civil Engineering from the University of Engineering and Technology, Lahore, Pakistan, in 1964 and 1970 respectively.

In the United States of America, I have worked for:

- The manufacturers and exporters of sprinkler irrigation equipment as a project design engineer.
- Texaco and Enron, two large oil and gas companies. I managed their projects for engineering design, construction, and environmental compliance.
- The U. S. Department of Commerce – EDA (Economic Development Administration), as an Environmental Officer and a Civil Engineer for 11 years, 1999-2010. I retired in January 2010.

Upon retirement, I started researching about God. The subject is vast and a lot has been written about it. After my initial research, I looked into the Qur'an ; read its English translations; and found:

- Most of the translations are difficult to understand, because they are verbose, literal translations.
- The translations have grammatical errors. The same verse has been translated by authors in the present and future tenses.
- The translations are not concise. Some authors have used Arabic words and explanatory notes. These break the reader's chain of thought and make comprehension difficult.

Examples of the comparative translation are attached.

For my understanding of the Qur'an ic view of God, I needed an English translation of the Qur'an in concise, simple, and easy to understand English. Not finding such a translation, I have done this translation.

God's characteristics are scattered throughout the Qur'an. I needed an electronic copy of the Qur'an's translation in English. That is the second reason why I have done this translation.

For over 60 years, I have not understood the Qur'an. I have wondered:

- How many Muslims are in my situation?
- If I, an educated Muslim, have not understood Islam's holy book, how can we, the Muslims, expect the non-Muslims to understand it?

For helping the Muslims and the non-Muslims to understand the Qur'an is the third reason why I have done this translation.

During 2023, the world population has reached eight billion. About 0.5 million are Arabic speaking. For over 7.5 billion non-Arabic speaking people, the Qur'an is needed in the languages they speak. That is the fourth reason why I have done this translation. God willing, this *an easy to read English version of the Qur'an* will be published in other languages also.

Akhtar A. Alvi, P. E.
maaalvi@gmail. com

# COMPARATIVE TRANSLATIONS

## Literal, Verbose, and Confusing Translations
## Verse 2:177

Author 1. It is not benignancy that you turn your faces around in the direction of East and West; but benignancy is (in him) who believes in Allah, and the last day , and the Angels, and the book, and the Messengers, and brings wealth in spite of his love for it (Or. offers out of love for Him) to near kinsmen, and the orphans, and the indigent, and the wayfarer, and the beggars, and (to ransom) necks, (i. e. captives "slaves") and keeps up the prayer, and bring the Zakat (mandatory charity), (i. e. pay the poor-dues) and they who fulfill their covenant when they have covenanted, and the patient (ones) in misery and tribulation, and while in violence; (i. e. during fighting) those are (they) who act sincerely, and those are they who are the pious.

Author 2. It is not Al-Birr (piety, righteousness, and each and every act of obedience to Allah, etc. ) that you turn your faces towards east and (or) west (in prayers); but Al-Birr is (the quality of) the one who believes in Allah, the last day , the Angels, the book , the Prophets and gives his wealth, in spite of love for it, to the kinsfolk, to the orphans, and to Al-Masakin (the poor), and to the wayfarer, and to those who ask, and to set slaves free, performs As-Salat (Iqamat-as-Salat), and gives the Zakat (mandatory charity), and who fulfill their covenant when they make it, and who are As-Sabirin (the patient ones, etc. ) in extreme poverty and ailment (disease) and at the time of fighting (during the battles). Such are the people of the truth and they are Al-Muttaqun (pious - see V. 2:2).

Author 3 It is not righteousness that ye turn your faces to the East and the West; but righteous is he who believeth in Allah and the last day and the angels and the Scriptures and the Prophets; and giveth wealth, for love of Him, to kinsfolk and to orphans and the needy and the wayfarer and to those who ask, and to set slaves free; and observeth proper worship and payeth the poor-due. And those who keep their treaty when they make one, and the patient in tribulation and adversity and time of stress. Such are they who are sincere. Such are the Allah-fearing.

Author 4. Righteousness is not that you turn your faces toward the east or the west, but [true] righteousness is [in] one who believes in Allah , the last day , the angels, the book , and the Prophets and gives wealth, in spite of love for it, to relatives, orphans, the needy, the traveler, those who ask [for help], and for freeing slaves; [and who] establishes prayer and gives zakah; [those who] fulfill their promise when they promise; and [those who] are patient in poverty and hardship and during battle. Those are the ones who have been true, and it is those who are the righteous.

Author 5. It is not righteousness that you turn your faces towards the East and the West, but righteousness is this that one should believe in Allah and the last day and the angels and the book and the Prophets, and give away wealth out of love for Him to the near of kin And the orphans and the needy and the wayfarer and the beggars and for (the emancipation of) the captives, and keep up prayer and pay the poor-rate; and the performers of their promise when they make a promise, and the patient in distress and affliction and in time of conflicts-- these are they who are true (to themselves) and these are they who guard (against evil).

Author 6. It is not righteousness that ye turn your faces Towards east or West; but it is righteousness- to believe in Allah and the last day , and the Angels, and the book , and the Messengers; to spend of your substance, out of love for Him, for your kin, for orphans, for the needy, for the wayfarer, for those who ask, and for the ransom of slaves; to be steadfast in prayer, and practice regular charity; to fulfill the contracts which ye have made; and to be firm and patient, in pain (or suffering) and adversity, and throughout all periods of panic. Such are the people of truth, the Allah-fearing.

Alvi. Turning your faces toward the east or the west is not righteousness. Righteousness is to:

- believe in God, the last day, the angels, the holy book (the Qur'an ), and the Prophets;
- give your wealth, in spite of its love, to relatives, orphans, needy, travelers, and to those who ask for help;
- free slaves;
- establish prayer;
- give Zakat (mandatory charity);
- fulfill the promises you have made; and
- be patient in poverty, hardship, and during battle.

These are the true believers and righteous.

# COMPARATIVE TRANSLATIONS

## Conflicting Grammatical Tense
## Verse 3:9

Author 1. Our Lord, surely You will be gathering mankind for a Day, (and) there is no suspicion about it; surely Allah will not fail the promised (Appointment).

Author 2. Our Lord! Verily, it is You Who will gather mankind together on the day about which there is no doubt. Verily, Allah never breaks His Promise".

Author 3. Our Lord! Lo! it is Thou Who gatherest mankind together to a Day of which there is no doubt. Lo! Allah faileth not to keep the tryst.

Author 4. Our Lord, surely You will gather the people for a Day about which there is no doubt. Indeed, Allah does not fail in His promise. "

Author 5. Our Lord! surely Thou art the Gatherer of men on a day about which there is no doubt; surely Allah will not fail (His) promise.

Author 6. Our Lord! Thou art He that will gather mankind Together against a day about which there is no doubt; for Allah never fails in His promise. "

Alvi. Lord, surely You will gather mankind on a Day (of Resurrection) about which there is no doubt. Certainly, God does not break His promise.

# COMPARATIVE TRANSLATIONS

## Too Many Arabic Words and Explanations
## Verse 5:100

An Author. Say (O Muhammad SAW). "Not equal are Al-Khabith (all that is evil and bad as regards things, deeds, beliefs, persons, foods, etc. ) and At-Taiyib (all that is good as regards things, deeds, beliefs, persons, foods, etc. ), even though the abundance of Al-Khabith (evil) may please you. " So fear Allah much [(abstain from all kinds of sins and evil deeds which He has forbidden) and love Allah much (perform all kinds of good deeds which He has ordained)], O men of understanding in order that you may be successful.

Alvi. Say: The evil and the good are not alike even though a lot of the evil may impress you. O men of understanding, be mindful of your duty to God so that you may succeed.

# COMPARATIVE TRANSLATIONS

## Differing Translations
## Verse 6:20

Author 1. Those to whom We have given the Scriptures recognize it as they recognize their [own] sons. Those who will lose themselves [in the hereafter] do not believe.

Author 2. Those to whom We have given the Scriptures (Jews and Christians) recognize him (i. e. Muhammad SAW as a Messenger of Allah, and they also know that there is no Ilah (God) but Allah and Islam is Allah's Religion), as they recognize their own sons. Those who destroy themselves will not believe. (Tafsir At-Tabari)

Author 3. Those unto whom We gave the Scriptures recognise (this revelation) as they recognise their sons. Those who ruin their own souls will not believe.

Author 4. Those to whom We have given the book know this as they know their own sons. Those who have lost their own souls refuse therefore to believe.

Author 5. Those whom We have given the book recognize him as they recognize their sons; (as for) those who have lost their souls, they will not believe.

Author 6. The ones to whom We have brought the book recognize it (just) as they recognize their sons. The ones who lost their (own) selves, so they do not believe.

Author 7. Those to whom We have given the Scriptures recognise him, that is, Muhammad (s), by the descriptions of him in their Scriptures, as they recognise their sons; those, of them, who have forfeited their own souls do not believe, in him.

Alvi. Those to whom We, God, have given the Scriptures (Jews and Christians) recognize God's oneness as they recognize their children. But those who have lost their souls do not believe.

# AUTHOR REQUEST

The objective of this book is a presentation of the Qur'an, Verses, in concise and simple English, for an easier understanding and practice in daily life. Accordingly, I am requesting the readers to help me in improving it, by suggesting simpler words, shorter sentences, and correct grammar. I can be reached at: maaalvi@gmail. com.

Akhtar A. Alvi, P. E.
maaalvi@gmail. com.

# CHAPTER 1

# THE OPENER

**Name:** The Opener
The Qur'an has 114 chapters. This is the first chapter.

**Verses:** Seven

**Summary:**

- Description of God's characteristics.
- Prayer of humans for God's guidance in living their lives for success in the worldly life and the life hereafter.
- Rest of the Qur'an is God's answer to the prayer.

**By Verse**

1:1.* In the name of God, the compassionate**, the merciful***.
1:2. All praise is for God, Who is the Lord of the worlds;
1:3. the compassionate, the merciful;
1:4. the owner of the Day of Judgment****.
1:5. God, we worship You alone and only Your help we seek;
1:6. guide us to the straight path;
1:7. the path of those whom You have favored, not of those who have incurred Your wrath or have gone astray.

**Chapter 1, Verse 1.*

***Who loves unconditionally.*

****Forgives when requested.*

*****That Day, God will end the universe and call all humans before Him to decide everyone's eternal life based on a person's deeds in the worldly life. The good deeds will land a person in paradise and the bad deeds will land a person in hell.*

# CHAPTER 2

# THE COW

**Name:** From Verses 67-73.

**Verses:** 286. It is the longest chapter in the Qur'an.

**Summary:**

- Characteristics of God, believers, disbelievers, and hypocrites.
- Stories of:
    - Prophet Adam and Satan.
    - The construction of the Kabah (God's house at Mecca), including the change in direction during prayer.
    - The argument between King Nimrod and Prophet Abraham about God.
    - Prophet Abraham asking God to show him how He gives life to the dead.
    - Prophet Ezekiel, who wondered how God will bring the fallen township to life after its death.
- History of Jews, including God's favors on them, saving them from Pharaoh's atrocities, and their misbehavior. God urges them to follow Prophet Muhammad.
- Instructions for organizing the new Muslim community at Medina:
    - Establishing formal prayer, praying during battles, fasting, paying Zakat (mandatory charity), making pilgrimage to God's house in Mecca, and fighting in God's cause.
    - Marriage to disbelievers.
    - Murder and its compensation.
    - Wills, spending of wealth, and giving charity.
    - Orphans and use of their property.
    - Sexual relations with wives during fasting and their menstruation.
    - Writing of agreements and having witnesses.
    - Unlawful eating.
    - Wine and gambling.
    - Divorce, dowry, remarriage, children's breastfeeding, providing for the widows and the divorced women.
    - Money lending and interest.

## By Verse

In the name of God, the compassionate, the merciful:

2:1. Alif, Lam, Meem (are Arabic letters).

2:2. There is no doubt in this book, the Qur'an. It guides those who fear God,

2:3. believe in the unseen, establish prayer, and give in charity from what God has given them,

2:4. believe in what has been revealed to you, Prophet Muhammad, and to other prophets before you, and are certain of the life to come after this worldly life.

2:5. Such people are rightly guided by their Lord and will be successful.

2:6. As for disbelievers, whether you, Prophet Muhammad, warn them or not, they will not believe.

2:7. God has sealed their hearts and ears. He has placed a covering over their eyes. They will be punished severely.

2:8. There are some who say: We believed in God and the last day, but they do not really believe.

2:9. They try to deceive God and the believers, but they deceive no one except themselves, though they do not realize it.

2:10. There is a disease in their hearts that God has increased. They shall be severely punished for their lying.

2:11. When it is said to them: Do not make mischief on earth; they reply: We are but peace-makers.

2:12. Surely, they are mischief-makers, but they do not realize it.

2:13. When it is said to them: Believe as others believe; they reply: Are we to believe as fools believe? They themselves are surely the fools, but they do not know it.

2:14. When they meet with those who have believed, they say: We too have believed. But when they are alone with their evil companions, they say: Surely, we are with you; we were only mocking.

2:15. God mocks them, and let them sin and wander blindly.

2:16. These are the ones, who have exchanged guidance for misguidance, but their bargain shall bring no gain, and they are not on the right path.

2:17. Their example is that of a man who started a fire, and when it lighted up what was around him, God took away the light and left him in darkness; like that they cannot see.

2:18. They are deaf, dumb and blind, and will not return to the right path.

2:19. Another example is of a dark-cloud rainstorm with thunder and lightning, in which they put their fingers in their ears at the sound of every thunderclap for the fear of death, but God, has encircled these disbelievers.

2:20. The lightning snatches away their eyesight. When it flashes they walk; but when it darkens upon them, they stand still. If God willed, He could have taken away their hearing and sight. Surely, God is able to do all things.

2:21. O mankind, worship your Lord, Who created you and those before you, so that you may become righteous.

2:22. It is God Who has made the earth a bed for you and the sky a canopy, and sends down rain from the sky to produce fruits for your livelihood. So when you know this, do not set up rivals to God.

2:23. If you are in doubt about what We have revealed to Our servant Muhammad, then produce a chapter like it. Call upon your helpers beside God to assist you if you are truthful.

2:24. But if you cannot, and surely, you will never be able to; then fear the fire which has been prepared for the disbelievers. Its fuel shall be men and stones.

2:25. O Muhammad, give good news to the believers who do good deeds. They shall live in gardens with water flowing under them. Whenever they shall be given a fruit to eat, they shall say: That is what we used to have; but it will be something similar. They shall have pure spouses and will live there forever.

2:26. God is not shy of giving the example of an insignificant thing like a mosquito or a larger creature. By the example, the believers know that it is the truth from their Lord, but the disbelievers say: What did God intend by this example? By giving examples, God guides many and misleads many. But He misleads none except the evildoers.

2:27. Those who break the agreement with God after confirming it, split apart what God has ordered to be joined, and make mischief on earth, will be the real losers.

2:28. How can you disbelieve God? It is He Who gave you life when you were lifeless, will make you die, will bring you back to life, and then you will return to Him.

2:29. It is God who has created for you what is on earth. Then He turned to the sky and created seven heavens. He knows all things.

2:30. Think about when your Lord said to the angels: I am going to appoint a deputy on earth. They said: Will You appoint someone who will cause mischief and shed blood, while we praise and sanctify You? God replied: I know what you do not know.

2:31. God taught Adam the names of all things. Then He placed the things before the angels, and asked them: Tell Me the names of these if you are right.

2:32. The angels replied: Glory to You, we have no knowledge except what You have taught us. In reality, it is You who is perfect in knowledge and wisdom.

2:33. God said to Adam: Tell the angles the names of the things. When he did, God said: Did I not tell you that I know the secrets of the heavens and the earth, and what you disclose and hide?

2:34. Then We said to the angels: Bow down to Adam; they did except Satan. He refused and showed arrogance.

2:35. God said to Adam: You and your wife Eve live in paradise and eat from it plentifully what you like, but do not go near this tree; otherwise you will transgress.

2:36. Satan tempted them to go near the tree to get them out of garden and from their condition of happiness. We, God, said to them: Go down to earth, some of you are enemy to the others, and for a time you will live there, and have your means of livelihood.

2:37. Then Adam learnt words of repentance from his Lord and repented. His Lord accepted his repentance, because Lord accepts repentance often and is the merciful.

2:38. We, God, said: You all go down from here; and if My guidance come to you, those who will follow My guidance shall have no fear and grief.

2:39. Those who will disbelieve and deny Our revelations will be companions of the fire. They will live in it forever.

2:40. O Children of Israel, remember My (God's) favor upon you, and fulfill your covenant with Me and I shall fulfill Mine, and fear Me alone.

2:41. Believe in My revelations, which confirm your Scriptures (Torah and Gospel). Do not be the first to reject them. Do not sell My revelations for a small price, and fear Me alone.

2:42. Neither mix the truth with falsehood, nor knowingly conceal the truth.

2:43. Establish prayer, pay Zakat (mandatory charity), and bow down with those who bow down in worship.

2:44. You order others for righteousness but why do you forget to practice it yourself, though you read the Scriptures? Have you no sense?

2:45. Seek God's help with patience and prayer, though seeking help with patience and prayer is difficult except for the humble ones,

2:46. those who think that they shall meet their Lord and they will return to Him.

2:47. O children of Israel, remember My favor which I bestowed upon you, and I preferred you over other nations of the world.

2:48. Fear the Day of Judgment when no one will be of service to anyone else; no pleading or ransom for freedom will be accepted from anyone; nor the guilty shall be helped.

2:49. Remember when We, God, delivered you from the people of Pharaoh, who oppressed you severely. They killed your sons and spared your daughters. This was a great trial for you from your Lord.

2:50. Remember the time when We parted the sea for you to pass through it safely and drowned Pharaoh's people while you were looking on.

2:51. Remember when We appointed 40 nights for Moses. In his absence, you made the calf a god for worship. You did wrong.

2:52. Even then, We forgave you so that you might be grateful.

2:53. Remember, when We gave Moses the Scriptures, the Torah, and the criterion of miracles, and of right from wrong, so that you might be guided.

2:54. Remember when Moses said to his people: You have wronged yourselves by worshiping the calf. So repent to your creator, God, and slay those who do wrong. That will be the best for you in His sight. Then God forgave you, because He accepts repentance often and is most merciful.

2:55: Remember when you Israelites said to Moses: We will not believe you until we see God with our eyes; so a thunderbolt struck you while you were looking on and you fell dead.

2:56. Then We revived you, so that you might be grateful.

2:57. We gave you the shade of clouds and sent down manna and salva (edibles and quail) for you saying: Eat the good things We have provided for you, but you rebelled. They harmed themselves, not Us, God.

2:58. Remember when We God said: Enter this city and eat freely from it, but enter the gate with humility asking for repentance. We will forgive your sins and increase the reward of those who do good.

2:59. But the wrongdoers changed Our words. So We sent upon them a punishment from the sky because they disobeyed.

2:60. Remember when Moses prayed for water for his people. We told him to strike the rock with his staff. Thereupon, 12 springs gushed from it and each group knew its drinking place. Then We said: Eat and drink from what God has provided, but do not spread mischief on the earth.

2:61. Remember when you Jews said: O Moses, we cannot always eat one kind of food. Call upon your Lord to provide us what grows on earth, green herbs, cucumbers, garlic, lentils and onions. Moses replied: What! Would you exchange what is good for what is worse? Go to a city and you will have there what you have asked for. Humiliation and poverty were brought down upon them. They deserved God's wrath, because they disbelieved in God's revelations, killed the Prophets unjustly, disobeyed, and exceeded the limits.

2:62. Whoever among Muslims, Jews, Christians, and Sabaeans believes in God and the last day, and does good, will have his reward from his Lord. There will be no fear and grief for him.

2:63. Remember the time when We raised the mountain of Sinai over you ( the Israelites) and took a promise from you saying: Hold firmly the book We have given you and bear in mind what it contains, so that you may guard against evil.

2:64. But even after that, you turned away. If it had not been for God's favor and mercy upon you, you certainly would have been among losers.

2:65. You have known those who exceeded the limits of Saturday / Sabbath*. We said to them: You become monkeys, despised and hated.

**Saturday is the Jews' holyday for rest and worship.*

2:66. We made their punishment an exemplary punishment for them and for their succeeding generations, and a lesson for the God-fearing people.

2:67. Remember the time when Moses said to his people: God commands you to sacrifice a cow. They said: Are you joking with us? He replied: I seek God's protection from being ignorant.

2:68. Then they said: Ask your Lord to make clear the cow's details. Moses replied: He says that she should be neither old nor young, but of middle age. Now, do as you have been commanded.

2:69. But they asked: Please ask your Lord to make clear the cow's color. He replied: God says that the cow is of deep bright yellow color, pleasing to look at.

2:70. Again they asked: Call upon your Lord to make clear to us because all the cows are alike, and if God wills, we will be guided.

2:71. Moses answered: God says that it is a cow neither trained to plow the soil nor to irrigate the fields, one free from fault with no spot upon her. They said: Now you have given an accurate description. So they sacrificed her, though they did not want to do it.

2:72. Remember the time when you Jews killed a man and disagreed about it. But God brought out what you were hiding.

2:73. We, God, said: Strike the dead body with a part of it. Thus, We brought the dead to life to show you My signs so that you may understand.

2:74. Even after that, your hearts hardened as rocks and even harder. There are some rocks from which springs gush; some split open for water to flow from them; and others tumble down for fear of God. God is not unaware of what you (Israelites) do.

2:75. Believers, do you hope that the Jews will believe in your faith, while some of them have been hearing God's word, understanding it, and changing it knowingly?

2:76. When the Jews meet the believers they say: We are believers too. But when they meet each other in private, they say: Must you tell them what God has revealed to you so that they would present that against you before your Lord? Have you no sense?

2:77. Do not they know that God knows what they hide and disclose?

2:78. There are illiterates among them who do not know the book but depend upon what they hear from others and guess.

2:79. Woe to those who write the book with their hands and then say: This is from God; so that they may sell it for a small price. Woe to them for what their hands have written and what they earn.

2:80. They say: The hellfire will not touch us except for a few days. Ask them: Have you received God's promise which He would not break? Or what you say about God you do not know?

2:81. Those who do evil and are engrossed in sins are inmates of the hellfire, where they will live forever.

2:82. But the believers who do good deeds are dwellers of paradise, where they will live forever.

2:83. Remember when We, God, took the promise from Israel's children for not worshiping anyone except God, doing good to parents, relatives, orphans, and the needy, speaking kindly to people, establishing prayer, and paying Zakat (mandatory charity). But you broke the promise, except a few, and paid no attention.

2:84. And remember when We took your promise of not shedding each other's blood and turning out each other from your homes. You gave this promise solemnly and witnessed it.

2:85. But you killed one another, evicted your own people from homes, and helped others against them sinfully and aggressively. If they came to you as captives, you ransomed them, although you were forbidden to evict them. So do you believe in a part of the book and disbelieve in another? What could be the punishment for those who behaved like that except to be disgraced in this life and severely punished on the Day of Resurrection? God is aware of your deeds.

2:86. These are the ones who have bought the life of this world in exchange for the hereafter. Their punishment will neither be lightened nor will they be helped.

2:87. We gave Moses the Scriptures, the Torah, sent Messengers after him, gave Jesus, the son of Mary, clear proofs and strengthened him with the holy spirit. But whenever a Messenger came to you whose message you did not like, you became arrogant, called some of them liars, and killed some.

2:88. They say: Our hearts are covered up and we do not need your guidance. No, God's curse is on them because of their disbelief; they believe in so little.

2:89. And now when a book from God, the Quran, has come to them which confirms what they have, and have prayed long for victory against the disbelievers. God's curse is on the disbelievers.

2:90. Miserable is the price for which they have sold their souls. They deny the revelation which God has sent down, grudging that God would send down His favor upon whom He wills from among His servants. They have drawn on themselves wrath upon wrath. Humiliating punishment is for the faithless.

2:91. When it is said to them: Believe in what God has revealed, they reply: We believe in what has been revealed to us. They disbelieve in what has been revealed since then, even though it is the truth and confirms their Scriptures. Ask them: Why then did you kill God's Prophets if you are in fact believers?

2:92. Moses brought you clear proofs, but in his absence you worshipped the calf and committed sin.

2:93. Remember when We, God, made an agreement with you and raised the Mount Sinai over you saying: Hold firmly what We have given you and be obedient. You said: We have heard but disobey. Because of your rejection of the promise, worship of the calf was made to sink into your hearts. Tell them O Muhammad: If you are faithful, how strange is your faith that commands you to do evil.

2:94. Say to them: If home in the hereafter with God is for you alone to the exclusion of other people, then ask for death if your claim is true.

2:95. But they will never ask for death because of the sins they have already committed. God knows the wrongdoers.

2:96. You will find them greediest for life, even more than the disbelievers. Every one of them wishes for a life of 1,000 years. But such a life by no means will remove them from punishment. God sees what they do.

2:97. O Muhammad, tell them: Whoever is Angel Gabriel's enemy should know that he has revealed the Qur'an to your heart by God's command. It confirms the holy books that came before it and provides guidance and good news to the believers.

2:98. Whoever is the enemy of God, His angel Messengers, Gabriel, and Michael should beware that God is the disbelievers' enemy.

2:99. We, God, have sent down clear revelations to you; no one would deny them except the disobedient.

2:100. Has it not been that every time they made a covenant, some of them threw it away? The truth is that most of them did not believe in it.

2:101. When God's Messenger came to them confirming their holy book, some of them threw the book behind their backs as if they knew nothing.

2:102. The Israelites followed what the devils fabricated against Solomon's kingdom. But Solomon did not disbelieve. It was the devils, who disbelieved. They taught people magic and that which was revealed to angels Harut and Marut at Babylon. The angels did not teach anyone without saying beforehand: We are only a trial, so do not disbelieve by learning magic. Yet they learned from them about causing separation between a husband and his wife, although they could not harm anyone except by God's permission. But people learned what harmed them and did not benefit them. They certainly knew that whoever purchased the magic would not have any share in the happiness of the hereafter. They sold themselves for evil, if they only knew.

2:103. If they had believed and guarded themselves against evil, God's reward would certainly have been better, had they but known this.

2:104. Believers, do not say to Prophet Muhammad, raina (attend to us), but say undhurna (look after us), and listen. The disbelievers will be grievously punished.

2:105. The disbelievers among the people of the holy book and the idolaters dislike that God sends down any good thing to you, Prophet Muhammad. But God chooses to whom He wills for his mercy. God is very generous.
2:106. If We, God, repeal any revelation or cause it to be forgotten, We replace it with a better one or similar to it. Do you not know that God has power over all things?
2:107. Do you not know that God has the kingdom of the heavens and the earth, and you have no guardian or helper beside Him?
2:108. Would you, believers, question your Prophet Muhammad as Moses was questioned? Whoever exchanges faith for disbelief has certainly strayed from the right path.
2:109. Many Jews and Christians enviously wish to turn you (the believers) back to disbelief after you have believed and the truth has been made clear to them. Forgive them and be patient with them until God brings about His command. God has power over all things.
2:110. Establish prayer and give Zakat (mandatory charity). Whatever good you do for your future, you will find it with God. He sees what you do.
2:111. They say: No one shall enter paradise unless he is a Jew or a Christian. That is their wishful thinking. Say to them: Bring your proof if you are truthful.
2:112. On the contrary, those who submit to God and do good works will have their reward from Him. They shall have no fear and grief.
2:113. The Jews say: The Christians do not follow the truth; and the Christians say: The Jews do not follow the truth. Yet they both read the Scriptures. Those who have no knowledge say the same. God will judge their differences on the day of judgment.
2:114. Who is more unjust than he who prevents mentioning of God's name in places of worship and strives to ruin them? It is not proper for such people to enter them except in fear. They shall be disgraced in this world, and severely punished in the hereafter.
2:115. The east and the west belong to God. Whichever way you turn, there is God. He is everywhere and knows everything.
2:116. The Christians say: God has taken a son. He is above such things. The fact is that whatever is in the heavens and on earth belongs to God and all are obedient to Him.
2:117. God is the originator of the heavens and the earth. When He decides for something to happen, He only says: Be, and it happens.
2:118. The ignorant say: Why does not God speak to us or a sign comes

to us? Those before them said the same thing. Their hearts are alike. But We, God, have clearly shown the signs to those who have firm faith.

2:119. O Muhammad, We have sent you with the truth, a bearer of glad tidings and a warner, and you shall not be answerable for the companions of the blazing fire.

2:120. O Muhammad, the Jews and the Christians will not be pleased with you unless you follow their religion. Say: God's guidance is the only guidance. If you were to follow their desires after all the knowledge has come to you, you will have no helper or protector from God.

2:121. Those to whom We, God, have given the Scriptures and read it as it ought to be read, they believe in it; and those who disbelieve it are the losers.

2:122. O children of Israel, remember My favor which I have bestowed upon you, and I have preferred you over the people of the world.

2:123. Guard against a day when no soul shall avail another, no compensation will be accepted from anyone, nor anyone's pleading will benefit anybody, nor will they be helped.

2:124. Remember when God tried Abraham with His commands, which he fulfilled. God told him: I will appoint you mankind's leader. Abraham asked: And of my progeny? God replied: My promise does not apply to the wrongdoers.

2:125. We made the Kabah, the grand mosque at Mecca, a place of assembly and security for mankind saying: Make the station of Abraham, where he prayed, a place of prayer for you. We took the promise from Abraham and Ishmael to keep it clean for those who would go around it, and visit it for meditation and worship.

2:126. Remember when Abraham said: Lord, make it a city of peace and provide fruits to its people who believe in God and the last day. God said: I will provide disbelievers an enjoyment for a short while, but I will drive them to the punishment of the hellfire, which is an evil destination.

2:127. Remember when Abraham and Ishmael raised the foundations of Kabah, the grand mosque at Mecca, they prayed: Our Lord, accept this service from us; You are the all-hearing, all-knowing.

2:128. Lord, make us submissive to You and raise from our offspring a nation that will submit to You. Show us the ways of worship and forgive our shortcomings; surely, You are the forgiving, the merciful.

2:129. Lord, send them a Messenger of their own who shall recite Your verses to them and teach them the holy book and wisdom, and purify them. Surely, You are the mighty, the wise.

2:130. Who but a fool will turn away from Abraham's religion? We have chosen him in this world, and He will be among the righteous in the hereafter.

2:131. When his Lord said to him: Submit; he replied. I have submitted to the Lord of the universe.

2:132. Abraham instructed his children to follow the faith, and so did Jacob saying: My children, God has chosen this faith for you; hence, die only in this faith.

2:133. Were you present when death approached Jacob and he asked his children: Who will you worship after me? They replied. We will worship your God and the God of your fathers, Abraham, Ishmael and Isaac; the one God, to Whom we have surrendered.

2:134. They were a people who have passed away. They will have what they earned and you will have what you have earned. You will not be questioned about what they did.

2:135. The Jews say: Become Jews and you will be rightly guided; the Christians say: Become Christians and you will have the true guidance. Say to them: No, we follow the religion of Abraham, who was truthful and non-idolater.

2:136. Believers say to the Jews and the Christians: We believe in God and in what has been revealed to us, and was revealed to Abraham, Ismail, Isaac, Jacob, and their descendants, and to Moses, Jesus, and other prophets. We make no distinction between them, and have submitted to God.

2:137. If they believe as you have believed, they are rightly guided. If they reject it, they will be differing strongly. God will suffice to defend you against them. He hears everything and knows everything.

2:138. Take God's color (religion, Islam). And who can color better than God? We worship Him.

2:139. O Prophet, ask them: Do you argue with us about God, who is your and our Lord? We shall both be judged by our deeds. We are devoted to Him alone.

2:140. Do you say that Abraham, Ismail, Jacob, and their descendants were Jews or Christians? Ask them: Do you know better than God? Who is more unjust than he who conceals a testimony that he has received from God? He is not unaware of what you, Jews and Christian scholars do.

2:141. They were a people that have passed away. They will have what they earned and you will have what you have earned. You will not be questioned about what they did.

2:142. The foolish will ask: What have made the Muslims change the direction they used to face during prayer (towards the Aqsa Mosque in Jerusalem)? Tell them: The east and the west belong only to God. He guides whom He likes to the right path.

2:143. We have made you, the believers, a just community so that you may witness over mankind, and your own Prophet Muhammad may witness over you. We appointed the direction you used to face during prayer* to make evident who would follow the Messenger and who would turn upon his heels. In fact, it was a difficult test except for those whom God guided. God would have never caused you to lose your faith. Indeed, God is kind and merciful to mankind.

**Muslims used to face towards the Aqsa Mosque in Jerusalem, but God changed it towards the grand mosque (Kabah) at Mecca.*

2:144. We have seen you turning your face towards heaven for guidance. We shall make you turn your face towards a direction during prayer which you will like. Turn your face during prayer towards the sacred mosque at Mecca. Wherever you are, turn your face towards it in prayer. Those who were given the Scriptures (Jews and Christians) know that it is the truth from their Lord. God is not heedless of what they do.

2:145. Even if you bring every sign to those who were given the Scriptures (Jews and Christians), they will not follow you for facing towards the holy mosque at Mecca during prayer. Neither you will follow the direction they face during prayer, nor will any of their sects follow the other's direction for facing during prayer. If you follow their desires after the knowledge has come to you, you will surely be among the unjust.

2:146. The Jews and Christians recognize the place that has now been designated for facing during prayer as they know their children. But some of them conceal the truth knowingly.

2:147. This is the truth from your Lord, so never doubt it.

2:148. Everyone turns to a direction in prayer. Therefore, try to excel one another in doing good deeds. Wherever you are, God will bring you together. God has power over all things.

2:149. Whichever way you depart, turn your face toward the sacred mosque Kabah at Mecca at the prayer time. Indeed, it is the truth from your Lord. God is not unaware of what you do.

2:150. Whichever way you depart, turn your face toward the sacred mosque at the time of prayer; and wherever you are, turn your faces towards it, so that people shall have no accusation against you, except those who are unjust. Do not fear them; fear Me (God), so that I may complete My favor to you for guidance.

2:151. We have sent you your own Messenger Prophet Muhammad, who recites Our verses to you, purifies you, and teaches you the holy book (the Qur'an ), wisdom, and what you do not know.

2:152. So remember Me (God) and I will remember you. Thank Me and do not be ungrateful.

2:153. Believers, seek help through patience and prayer. God is with the patient.

2:154. Do not say that those who are killed in God's cause are dead. They are alive, but you do not understand that life.

2:155. We will test you with fear, hunger, and loss of wealth, lives, and crops. Give good news to those who persevere patiently.

2:156. In calamity they say: We belong to God and we will return to Him.

2:157. Lord's blessings and mercy will be upon them. They are rightly guided.

2:158. The Mountains of As-Safa* and Al-Marwah* are among God's symbols. There is no sin in walking between them during pilgrimage to God's house. He who does good of his own accord, God recognizes it favorably.

**These are contiguous to the sacred mosque Kabah at Mecca.*

2:159. God and those entitled to curse will curse those who conceal the clear proofs and the guidance We have revealed after We made them clear in the Scriptures.

2:160. But I, God, will accept the repentance of those who repent, make amends, and reveal what they concealed. I am generous in accepting repentance and showing mercy.

2:161. The curse of God, angels, and mankind is on those who reject faith and die rejecting.

2:162. They will live under curse forever. Their punishment will neither be lightened nor will they have relief from it.

2:163. Your god is one God. There is no god but He, most gracious, most merciful.

2:164. In proof of that for the thoughtful people, there are signs in God's:

- creation of the heavens and the earth,
- alternation of the night and the day,
- sailing of the sea ships for benefiting mankind,
- sending of the rain from the clouds that gives life to the

lifeless earth,

- spreading of all kinds of animals on the earth,
- changing of the winds, and
- moving of the clouds between the sky and the earth.

2:165. There are those who take others equal to God for worship. They love them as they should love God. But believers are stronger in love for God. The wrongdoers will realize when they will see the punishment that all power belongs to God and He is severe in punishment.

2:166. When they will see the punishment, the leaders will disown their followers and cut off their relationship.

2:167. The followers would say: If we had a chance to live, we would disassociate from them, as they have disassociated from us. God will show them their regretful deeds. They will not have a way to come out of the hellfire.

2:168. O mankind, eat what is lawful and good on earth. Do not follow Satan's footsteps, because he is your sworn enemy.

2:169. Satan entices you to evil and immorality and to say about God what you do not know.

2:170. When it is said to the disbelievers: Follow what God has revealed; they say: No, we will follow what our forefathers did. But their forefathers lacked wisdom and were not guided.

2:171. The disbelievers are like the animals who hear nothing but shouts and cries of their shepherd. They are deaf, dumb, blind, and understand nothing.

2:172. Believers, eat the good things We have provided you and be grateful to God if you worship Him.

2:173. God has forbidden you to eat dead animals, blood, swine flesh, and what has been dedicated to someone other than God. However, there is no sin if one is forced to eat these by necessity but does not intend to sin or exceed the limit. God is forgiving and merciful.

2:174. Those that conceal God's revelations in the Scriptures for a paltry price will swallow nothing but fire. On the Day of Resurrection, God will neither speak to them nor purify them. They will have a painful punishment.

2:175. They have exchanged guidance for error and forgiveness for punishment. They are bold in pursuit of the hellfire.

2:176. God has revealed the truth in the Qur'an. But, those who disagree with it have gone too far in disbelief.

2:177. Turning your faces toward the east or the west is not righteousness. Righteousness is to:

- believe in God, the last day, the angels, the holy book (the Quran), and the Prophets;
- give wealth, in spite of the love of it, to relatives, orphans, needy, travelers, and who ask for help;
- free slaves;
- establish prayer;
- give Zakat (mandatory charity);
- fulfill promises; and
- be patient in poverty, hardship and during battle.

These are the true believers and righteous.

2:178. For believers, the payback for murder is decreed: If a free man commits a murder, he should be killed, so should be a slave for a slave, and a female for a female. But if an affected brother pardons a murderer, then grant him blood money per common law, and the murderer should pay him with gratitude. This is your Lord's concession in mercy. After this, whoever will exceed the limits shall be severely punished.

2:179. O people of understanding, there is life for you in avenging someone for a wrong or criminal act. It is hoped that you will avoid breaking this law.

2:180. When death approaches you, you should distribute your wealth by will* equitably to your parents and relatives. This is a duty upon those who guard against evil.

**In Chapter 4, the distribution to parents and relatives has been fixed.*

2:181. It is sinful to alter the will after hearing it. God hears and knows all things.

2:182. If anyone suspects partiality or wrongdoing on part of the person who left the will, and makes settlement between the affected parties, there is no wrongdoing on his part. God is forgiving and merciful.

2:183. Believers, fasting is made obligatory for you as it was for those before you, so that you may guard against evil.

2:184. Fasting is for a certain number of days. If someone is sick or on a journey, he should fast on a like number of other days. Those who can fast with hardship, but do not, may feed one poor person, but feeding more than that by one's free will is better. However, fasting is better for you if you knew.

2:185. The Qur'an was revealed in the fasting month of Ramadan. It provides guidance to mankind with clear teachings and distinction between the right and wrong. Therefore, whoever is present in the month should fast. But whoever is sick or is on a journey should fast a like number of other days. God desires ease for you, not difficulty. He desires that you should fast for the whole month, glorify His greatness, and thank Him for guiding you.

2:186. O Prophet Muhammad, when My servants ask you about Me, tell them that I am close to them. I listen to and answer the prayer of every petitioner when he calls to Me. Therefore, they should listen to My call and believe in Me, so that they may be rightly guided.

2:187. On nights during the fasting month, sexual intercourse with your wives is permitted. They are your garments and you are their garments. God knew that you were deceiving yourselves. He has pardoned you and has removed this burden from you. Now you can associate with them, and seek what God has decreed for you. Eat and drink until you can distinguish between a white thread and a black thread in the light of the dawn; then complete your fast till the night appears. Do not associate with your wives while you are in retreat in the mosques. Those are limits set by God, so do not break them. God makes clear his signs to men that they may learn self-restraint.

2:188. Do not usurp one another's property, nor bribe the judges so that you may take a part of others' property wrongfully.

2:189. O Muhammad, they ask you about the moon's phases. Tell them: They are for people to fix the dates and the periods for the pilgrimage. Righteousness is not entering your houses* from their backs, but righteousness is to guard against evil. Enter your houses by their doors. Observe your duty to God so that you may be successful.

**The pagan Arabs used to enter their houses from the back after putting on clothes for pilgrimage and also after returning from pilgrimage.*

2:190. In God's cause, fight those who fight you, but do not attack them first. God does not love the aggressors.

2:191. Kill the disbelievers who fight with Muslims wherever you find them. Drive them out from where they drove you out. Persecution is worse than killing. Do not fight them at the sacred mosque of Kabah at Mecca until they attack you there; but if they attack you, kill them. Such is the payment for the disbelievers.

2:192. If they stop, know that God is forgiving and merciful.

2:193. Fight them until there is no more oppression and worship is acknowledged to be for God. But if they stop, then there should be no hostility except against oppressors.

2:194. Respect a prohibited month* if it is also respected by the enemy. But retaliation is permitted for violations of all prohibited things. So if anyone assaults you, assault him in the same way. But fear God and know that God is with those who avoid breaking the limits.

**Four months of the Arabic lunar calendar were considered sacred and no fighting was allowed in them. Rajab (the 7th month, was for visit to the grand mosque), Zul-Qad (the 11th month, before the month of pilgrimage), Zul-Hajj (the 12th month for the pilgrimage), and Muharram (the first month after the month of pilgrimage) were reserved for keeping peace for the pilgrimage. As Arabs were cheating to fight with others during these months, God allowed the Muslims to retaliate if attacked in these months.*

2:195. Spend your wealth in God's cause. Do not destroy yourself with your own hands. Do good; God loves the doers of good.

2:196. Complete the pilgrimage and the Umra* to the sacred mosque at Mecca for God. If you are prevented from continuing the journey, offer to God whatever sacrifice you can afford, but do not shave your heads until the offering has reached its destination. But if someone among you is ill or has an ailment of the head, he should compensate by fasting or almsgiving or sacrificing. During peaceful times, whoever performs the Umra* before the start of the pilgrimage should offer sacrifice if one can afford. But he who cannot afford should fast for three days during the pilgrimage and for seven days when he returns home, completing ten days. This is for him whose house is not near the sacred mosque. Be careful of your duty to God, and know that God is strict in punishment.

**the informal pilgrimage.*

2:197. The months of pilgrimage are known. If one decides to perform the pilgrimage, he should abstain from sexual intercourse, obscenity, and quarrelling during these months. God knows whatever good you do. Take provisions for the pilgrimage journey, but the best provision is the right conduct. Fear Me O men of understanding.

2:198. During pilgrimage, there is no sin in seeking bounty from your Lord by trading. When you return from Mount Arafat near Mecca, stay at Masharil-Haram, the holy monument in Muzdalifah between Arafat and Mecca, and celebrate God's praises. Remember Him as He has guided you when you had gone on the wrong path.

2:199. Then depart from the place where all pilgrims depart and ask God's forgiveness. He is forgiving and merciful.
2:200. When you have completed the pilgrimage rites, praise God as you used to praise your forefathers, but with greater fervor. There are some who say: Lord, give us abundance in this world; but they will have no share in the hereafter.
2:201. There are others who say: Lord, give us what is good both in this world and the hereafter, and protect us from the hellfire.
2:202. They will have their reward in both worlds for what they have earned. God is swift in accounting.
2:203. Celebrate God's praises during the appointed days of 11th to 13th of Zul-Hajj, the pilgrimage month. But if one hastens to leave from Mina in two days, there is no blame on him, and if one stays on, there is no blame on him, provided his aim is to do right. Fear God, and know that you shall be gathered before Him.
2:204. There is someone whose views about the worldly life may please you, and he even calls God to witness about what is in his heart; yet he is your deadliest enemy.
2:205. As soon as he leaves you, he spreads mischief on the earth and destroys crops and animals. God does not like mischief.
2:206. When it is said to him: Fear God, his arrogance leads him to more crime. The hell, an evil resting-place, will settle his account.
2:207. There is another type of man who gives his life to earn God's pleasure. God is full of kindness for such devotees.
2:208. Believers, submit to God whole-heartedly. Do not follow the footsteps of Satan, who is your declared enemy.
2:209. If you deviate after clear proofs have come to you, then know that God is mighty and wise.
2:210. Are they waiting for God to come down to them in shade of clouds with angels for their fate to be settled? All questions go back to God for decision.
2:211. Ask Israel's children how many clear signs We have sent them. But if anyone, after God's favor has come to him, exchanges it for disbelief, then God is strict in punishment.
2:212. The life of this world is attractive to the disbelievers. They ridicule believers. But the righteous will be superior in rank over them on the Resurrection Day. God gives in abundance to whom He is pleased with.
2:213. In the beginning, mankind was one community, but it changed. God sent it prophets to give good news to the followers of the right path and to warn those who went away from it. And He sent with

them the holy book (the Qur'an ) with the truth to judge their differences. No one differed over the holy book, except those who were given it after clear proofs came to them. They differed out of jealousy. God guided those who believed in truth concerning their differences. God guides to a straight path whom He wills.

2:214. Do you think that you will enter paradise without facing trials that were faced by the believers before you? They met poverty and hardship and were so shaken up that their prophet and his followers cried out: When will God's help come? They were told that God's help was near.

2:215. The believers ask you, Prophet Muhammad, as to what they should spend in charity. Say: Whatever you spend should be for the parents, relatives, orphans, needy, and traveler. Whatever good you do, God knows it.

2:216. Fighting is decreed for you while you dislike it. You may dislike a thing which is good for you, and like a thing which is bad for you. God knows while you do not know.

2:217. O Muhammad, they ask you about fighting in the prohibited month. Say: Fighting in that month is a grave offence; but far worse in God's sight is to prevent others from God's path, to deny Him, to prevent access to the sacred mosque, and to drive out its worshippers. Persecution is worse than bloodshed. They will not stop fighting with you until they turn you back from your faith if they can. If anyone turns back from the faith and dies in disbelief, his works will bear no fruit in this life and in the hereafter; he will be companion of the hell and will live there forever.

2:218. In contrast, the believers, who have left their homes for God and have fought in His cause, can hope for His mercy. He is the forgiving and merciful.

2:219. O Muhammad, they ask you about drinking and gambling. Say: There is great harm in them, and some benefit for people; but the harm is greater than the benefit. They ask you how much they should spend. Say: That which is in excess of your needs. God makes His signs clear to you to think,

2:220. both about this world and the hereafter. They ask you about orphans. Say: The best thing to do is what is for their good. There is no harm if you live together with them, as they are your brothers. God knows the one who means harm and the one who means good. If God wished, He could have made it hard for you. He is powerful and wise.

2:221. Do not marry the disbelieving women, until they believe. A believing slave-woman is better than a disbelieving woman, even though she may attract you. Do not marry your women to the disbelievers until they believe. Likewise a believing slave is better than a disbeliever, even though he may attract you. The disbelievers invite you to the hellfire. God, by His grace, invites you to paradise and to forgiveness. He makes His signs clear to mankind that it may pay attention.

2:222. They ask you about menstruation. Say: It is an unclean state; keep away from women during it; and do not approach them for sex until they are clean. Then you may approach them as God has prescribed for you. God loves those who turn to Him in repentance and keep themselves clean.

2:223. Your wives are your fields. Go to your fields as you please. Do good works for your future. Fear God and know that you will meet Him. Give good news to the believers.

2:224. Do not swear in God's name against doing good, acting rightly, and making peace among people. God hears and knows everything.

2:225. God will not question you for the unintentional oaths, but will for the intentional ones. God is forgiving and tolerant.

2:226. There is a four-month waiting period for those who swear not to have relations with their wives. But if they return to normal relations, God is forgiving and merciful.

2:227. If they have decided upon a divorce, know that God hears and knows everything.

2:228. Divorced women shall wait for three menstruation periods. It is unlawful for them, if they have faith in God and the last day, to hide what God has created in their wombs. Their husbands have the right to take them back in that period, if they wish for reconciliation. The women have rights similar to the rights of men, but men have status over them. God is powerful and wise.

2:229. A divorce is only permissible twice. After that, the wife should either be retained honorably or let go with kindness. It is not lawful for men to take back anything they gave to their wives, unless they both fear that they would be unable to keep the limits decreed by God. In that case, there will be no blame on either one of them if she would give something to be released from the marriage bond. These are the limits decreed by God. Do not cross them. Those who cross limits are the wrongdoers.

2:230. If a husband divorces his wife for the third time, he cannot remarry her until she has married another husband, and that husband has divorced her. There is no harm if they remarry, provided the woman and her former husband think that they can keep the limits set by God. These are the limits set by God, which He makes clear to those who understand.

2:231. When you divorce women and they have completed their waiting period, either take them back honorably or release them with kindness. But do not keep them to harass them. Whoever will do that would certainly wrong himself. Do not make joke of God's verses. Remember God's favor upon you that He has sent down to you the Qur'an and wisdom for your instruction. Fear God and know that God knows all things.

2:232. When you divorce women and they complete their waiting period, do not prevent them from marrying their prospective husbands if they agree in a lawful manner. This instruction is for those who believe in God and the last day. This is more virtuous and purer for you. God knows while you do not know.

2:233. Mothers shall breastfeed their children for two complete years if the mother desires to complete the term of breastfeeding. The father will bear the cost of their food and clothing according to his means. No one shall be burdened greater than one can bear. Neither a mother nor a father shall be harmed because of the child. The same duty falls upon a father's heir. If by mutual consent consultation, they both desire to wean the child; there will be no blame on them. If you wish to have your children nursed by a foster-mother, there is no blame upon you as long as you pay her fairly what was agreed upon. Fear God and know that God sees what you do.

2:234. After the husbands' death, the widows shall keep away from men for four months and 10 days. When they have fulfilled their term, there is no blame on you for what they do with themselves in an honorable manner. God is well aware of what you do.

2:235. There will be no blame on you if you make an offer of marriage indirectly or hold it in your hearts. God knows what is on your mind. Neither make a secret contract with them except in a lawful manner, nor resolve on the tie of marriage till the prescribed term is fulfilled. Know that God knows what is in your hearts, therefore fear Him. God is forgiving and patient.

2:236. There is no blame on you if you divorce women before touching them or fixing the dowry. However, give them a suitable gift, the wealthy according to his means, and the poor according to his means. This is an obligation upon virtuous.

2:237. If you divorce them before touching, but after fixing the dowry, give them half of the dowry, unless they forgo it, or the husband forgoes his half as the marriage tie is in his hands. The forgoing of the man's half is closest to righteousness. Do not forget to show kindness to each other. God sees all your deeds.

2:238. Guard strictly your habit of prayers*, including the middle (Asr, late afternoon) prayer. Stand before God in devotion.

**Muslims have five daily prayers: Fajr, before sunrise, Zohar, in the afternoon, Asr, at late afternoon, Maghrib, at sunset, and Isha, approximately an hour after sunset, before going to bed.*

2:239. If you fear an enemy, pray on foot or on horseback. When you are in security, remember God in the manner He has taught you, which you did not know.

2:240. Those who die and leave widows behind should provide in their will a year's maintenance and a residence for them. If they leave on their own, there will be no blame on you for what they do in an honorable way. God is powerful and wise.

2:241. For divorced women, reasonable maintenance should be provided. This is a duty on the righteous.

2:242. Thus God makes his revelations clear to you that you may understand.

2:243. Have you not considered those Israelites who left their homes in thousands for fear of death? God said to them: Die; then He gave them life. God is kind to mankind, but most are ungrateful.

2:244. Fight in God's cause, and know that God hears all and knows all.

2:245. Who will give God a good loan so that God will repay him many times more? It is God who gives wealth and poverty. You shall all return to Him.

2:246. Have you not heard about what the Israelites' leaders asked one of their prophets (Samuel) after the death of Moses? They said: Appoint a king for us, and we will fight in God's cause? He asked: What if you refuse to fight when asked to do so? They replied: Why should we not fight in God's cause when we have been driven out from our homes and separated from our children? But when they were ordered to fight, they turned away, except a few. God knows the wrongdoers.

2:247. The Israelites' prophet said to them: God has appointed Saul as your king. But they replied: How can he be the king while we deserve it more than him; and he is not even rich? He said: God has chosen him over you and has gifted him abundantly in knowledge and body strength. God gives His authority to whoever

He wills. God is all-inclusive and all-knowing.

2:248. Their prophet also told them: A sign of his kingship is that you will get back the boat containing the relics left by the families of Moses and Aaron, as an assurance of security from your Lord. It is under angels' protection. That will be a sign for you, if you are true believers.

2:249. When Saul started with the army, he said: God will test you at a stream. Those who will drink its water except a sip will not go with my army. But they all drank from it, except a few. When he crossed the river with the faithful, they said: We have no power to fight against Goliath and his forces. But those who were convinced that they would meet God, said: How often, by God's will, a small force has overcome a big one. God is with those who steadfastly persevere.

2:250. When they met Goliath and his soldiers, they prayed: Lord, give us endurance, plant our feet firmly, and give us victory over the disbelievers.

2:251. By God's will, they defeated them. David slew Goliath. God gave him power and wisdom and taught him what He willed. If God did not defeat some by others, the earth would have been full of mischief. But God is kind to his creatures.

2:252. O Muhammad, these are God's verses which we recite to you in truth. Indeed, you are one of Our Messengers.

2:253. God raised the rank of some Messengers over others. He spoke to Moses and raised the status of others. He gave clear miracles to Jesus, the son of Mary, and strengthened him with the Holy Spirit. If God willed, those succeeding them would not have fought one another after clear proofs had come to them. But they disagreed among themselves; some believed and others disbelieved. If God wanted they would not have fought one another, but God does what He intends.

2:254. Believers, spend from what We have provided you before the day arrives when there will be no bargaining, friendship, and intercession. The disbelievers are the wrongdoers.

2:255. There is no god but Him, the ever-living and self-sufficient. Neither slumber nor sleep overtakes Him. Whatever is in the heavens and on the earth is His. Who can plead with Him without His permission? He knows what is visible and invisible to humans. They can comprehend only that part of His knowledge which He allows. His kingdom extends over the heavens and the earth, and their preservation does not tire Him. He is the most high, the great.

2:256. There is no compulsion in religion. The right course has been made clear from the wrong course. He who rejects false gods and believes in God will hold a firm hand that will never break. God is all-hearing, all-knowing.

2:257. God is believers' guardian. He takes them from darkness to light. The disbelievers' guardians are false gods, who lead them from light to darkness. They are companions of the hellfire, in which they will live forever.

2:258. Have you not heard of Nimrod who argued with Abraham about his Lord because God had given Nimrod kingship? Abraham said to him: My Lord gives life and death; he replied: I give life and death too. Abraham said: God brings up the sun from the east, you bring it up from the west. The disbeliever was bewildered. God does not guide the wrongdoers.

2:259. Consider the example of the Prophet Ezekiel who passed by a fallen and ruined township (Jerusalem). He said: How will God bring it to life when it is dead? God made him die for 100 years; then He revived him. God asked him: How long have you been away? He replied: A day or a few hours. God told him: You have been away for 100 years; yet look at your food and drink; they have not rotted. Look at the bones of your donkey. We will make you a sign for the people. We will bring the bones together and cover them with flesh. When it became clear to him, he said: I know that God has power over all things.

2:260. Also consider when Abraham said: Lord, show me how You give life to the dead. God asked: Have you no faith? He replied: I have, but I would like to reassure my heart. God said: Take four birds, train them to follow you, put each of them over the hills, and then call them. They will fly to you swiftly. Know that God is mighty and wise.

2:261. The example of those who spend their wealth in God's way is like a seed which grows seven ears, each with a 100 grains. God multiplies His reward for whom He wills. God is very generous and all-knowing.

2:262. Those that spend their wealth in God's cause and do not follow up their charity with taunts and insults will be rewarded by their Lord. They shall have no fear and grief.

2:263. A kind word with forgiveness is better than charity followed by insult. God is free of all wants, and He is most patient.

2:264. Believers, do not make giving of your charity worthless by reminders of your generosity and insults, like those who spend their wealth for showoff, but believe neither in God nor in the last day. They are like rock covered with soil. When rainstorm falls on it, it leaves it bare. They will gain nothing from what they have earned. God does not guide disbelievers.

2:265. But those who spend their wealth seeking God's approval and strengthening their souls are like a garden on high ground. When a rainstorm falls on it, it yields double crop. Even if it is not hit by a rainstorm, a drizzle is sufficient for it. God sees all what you do.

2:266. Would any one of you; when old with young children, like to have a garden with palms and vines watered by streams, hit by a whirlwind fire to burn it? Thus, God makes His signs clear to you that you might think.

2:267. Believers, give in charity the wealth you have earned, and what We have brought for you from the earth; but not the worthless things which you would not accept yourself. Know that God is free of all wants, and is praiseworthy.

2:268. Satan threatens you with poverty and invites you to miserly conduct. But God promises you His forgiveness and abundance. God cares for all and knows all things.

2:269. God gives wisdom to whom He likes. Whoever receives wisdom receives great wealth. But only those with common sense learn from these things.

2:270. God knows what you spend or pledge in charity. The wrongdoers have no helper.

2:271. Giving charity publicly is good, but giving it to the poor in private is better. That will do away some of your sins. God is aware of what you do.

2:272. O Muhammad, it is not your responsibility to set people on the right path. God guides whom He wills. Whatever charity you give is for your own good for seeking God's pleasure. It will be paid back to you in full, and you will not be wronged.

2:273. Those who are occupied with God's cause and are unable to travel in the land for trade or work deserve special help. An ignorant person considers them self-sufficient because of their modesty, but you can recognize their need by their looks. They do not ask people for charity. God will know of whatever you will give them.

2:274. Those who give charity by day and night, in private and in public, will be rewarded by their Lord. They will have no fear and grief.

2:275. Those who take usury (high/compound interest) will stand before God on the Day of Resurrection as touched by Satan and driven to insanity because they say that taking of usury is like trading. But

God has permitted trading and forbidden the taking of usury. Those who will stop after receiving God's direction shall be pardoned for what they did; their fate will be in God's hands. Those who will repeat the offence will be companions of the hellfire. They will live in it forever.

2:276. God does not bless lending money on usury, but blesses acts of charity. God does not love an ungrateful sinner.

2:277. The believers who do good works, establish prayer, and give Zakat (mandatory charity) will have their reward with their Lord. They will have no fear and grief.

2:278. Believers, fear God. Give up the balance of usury due to you if you are believers.

2:279. If you do not, then be warned that God and His Messenger will wage war against you. If you repent, you may have your principal. Neither the borrower nor you will suffer loss.

2:280. If the borrower is in hardship, grant him respite till he is able to repay. But if you forgive the loan as charity, that is better for you if you only knew.

2:281. Fear the day when you will return to God. Then every soul will be compensated for what it earned, and no one will be treated unjustly.

2:282. Believers, when you take a debt for a specified period, write it down.

- Let a scribe write it justly. No scribe should refuse to write it as God has given him the gift of writing. So let him write and the debtor dictate, fearing God and leaving nothing out of it.
- But if the debtor is of limited understanding or is weak or unable to dictate himself, let his guardian dictate for him justly.
- Get two male witnesses; if not available, select a man and two women from those whom you consider suitable witnesses. If either woman would err, the other will remind her.
- Witnesses should not refuse to witness when called upon to do so.
- Do not fail to write whether it is a small or a large debt with its specified term. That is more just in God's sight, ensures accuracy in evidence, and prevents doubts. However, if it is an on-the-spot transaction, there is no

blame upon you if you do not write it. But take witnesses when you conclude a contract.

- No scribe or witness should be harmed. If you will do so, you will commit a sin. Fear God, Who teaches you and knows all things.

2:283. If you are on a journey and cannot find a scribe, then a security deposit should be taken. If one of you entrusts another, then let the trustee discharge his trust fearing God, his Lord. Do not conceal testimony. Whoever conceals it, his heart is sinful. God knows what you do.

2:284. Whatever is in the heavens and on earth belongs to God. Whether you show or hide what is on your minds, God will call you to account for it. He forgives whom He pleases and punishes whom He pleases. God has power over all things.

2:285. The Messenger Prophet Muhammad believes in what has been revealed to him by his Lord and so do the believers. They believe in God, His angels, books, and Messengers. They say: We make no distinction between His Messengers; we have heard the message and obey it; Lord, we seek Your forgiveness; and we shall all return to You.

2:286. God does not impose upon any person a duty beyond his ability. He will enjoy the reward of what good he has earned, and suffer for the bad he has earned. Believers, pray: Lord, do not punish us if we forget or make a mistake. Do not lay on us the kind of burden You laid on those before us. Do not impose upon us a burden for which we do not have the strength to bear. Pardon us, forgive our sins, and have mercy upon us. You are our protector. Help us against the disbelievers.

# CHAPTER 3

# THE FAMILY OF IMRAN

**Name:** From Verse 33.

**Verses:** 200

**Summary:**

- The chapter is similar to Chapter 2, The Cow.
- Fundamental truths about God, revelation, death, and the life-after-death.
- Invitation to Christians and Jews to accept Islam.
- Births of Mary, Jesus, and Prophet Yahiya, John the Baptist.
- Instruction to Muslims for establishing virtue, eradicating evil, giving charity, following righteousness criteria, and prohibiting usury.
- Lessons from the battles of Badr* and Uhud*.

**The first and the second battle between Muslims and their enemies were fought at Badr and Uhud respectively. Muslims won the first battle, but lost the second.*

### By Verse

In the name of God, the compassionate, the merciful:

3:1. Alif, Lam, Mim (are Arabic letters).

3:2. God! There is no god, but Him, Who is living and sustains everything.

3:3. O Muhammad, God has revealed the Qur'an to you with truth. It confirms the Scriptures that came before it. He sent down the Torah to Moses and the Gospel to Christ for guidance to mankind.

3:4. God has sent down the criteria of the right and wrong. Those who disbelieve in God's revelations will be severely punished. God is powerful and capable of taking revenge.

3:5. Nothing on earth or in the sky is hidden from God.

3:6. It is God who shapes you in the wombs of your mothers as He pleases. There is no god but Him. He is all powerful and all wise.

3:7. O Muhammad, it is God who has revealed the Qur'an to you. Some of its verses are precise in meaning and form its foundation, and others are figurative (metaphorical; not literal). Those in whose hearts is disbelief follow the figurative verses, seeking to mislead and to give them their own meaning. But none knows their meaning except God. Those firmly rooted in knowledge say: We believe in them, they are from our Lord. No one will grasp the message except the men of understanding.

3:8. They pray: Lord, let our hearts not go off the right path after You have guided us. Grant us Your mercy. Indeed, You are the giver of bounties without measure. You will never break Your promise.

3:9. Lord, You will surely gather mankind on a day about which there is no doubt.

3:10. The disbelievers' wealth or children will not help them against God. They will be fuel for the hellfire.

3:11. The disbelievers' fate will be no better than that of Pharaoh's people and those before them. They denied God's signs and He destroyed them for their sins. He is strict in punishment.

3:12. O Muhammad, say to the disbelievers: You shall be defeated and driven into hell, which is a miserable place to live.

3:13. There was a sign for you in the two armies that met in combat*. One was fighting in God's cause and the other was of the disbelievers. The believers saw the disbelievers twice their number. But God supports with victory to whom He wills. There is a lesson in it for those with sight.

**At Badr, near Medina. The enemies of Islam from Mecca, came to fight the Muslims. Their objective was to defeat the Muslims for stopping them to spread Islam. This was the first battle between the Muslims and their enemies. The Muslims were 313 and the Meccans were a 1,000. More battles were to follow. The Muslims won.*

3:14. Mankind is tempted by the love of women, sons, gold and silver, fine branded horses, cattle, and crop-land. These are the enjoyment of the worldly life, but God has the best return with Him.

3:15. Say: Shall I tell you what is better than these? God will reward the righteous with gardens watered by running streams. They will live there forever with virtuous wives and God's pleasure. God watches over His servants.

3:16. They say: Lord, we have indeed believed, so forgive our sins and protect us from the punishment of the hellfire.

3:17. They are patient, truthful, and obedient. They spend in God's way and pray before dawn for God's forgiveness.

3:18. God has testified that there is no god but Him. So do the angels, and the knowledgeable humans, with truth and justice, that there is no god but Him, the all-mighty, the all-wise.

3:19. The true religion with God is Islam. Those who were given the Scriptures (Jews and Christians) did not differ, except out of jealousy, after knowledge had come to them. Whoever disbelieves in God's verses, He is swift in calling to account.

3:20. O Muhammad, if they argue with you, say to them: My followers and I have submitted to God. Then ask those who were given the Scriptures (Jews and Christians) and to the illiterates: Have you submitted yourselves to God? If they have, they are rightly guided; but if they turn away, your duty is only to convey the message to them. God sees what His servants do.

3:21. Give news of a painful punishment to those who disbelieve in God's revelations, kill the Prophets wrongfully, and also kill those who teach just dealings with mankind.

3:22. Their works will bear no fruit in this world and in the hereafter. They will have no helpers.

3:23. Have you not considered those who have been given a portion of the Scriptures? When they are invited to God's book to settle their dispute, some of them turn away and decline arbitration.

3:24. This is because they say: The hellfire will not touch us but for a few days only. Their forgeries have deceived them in their own religion.

3:25. What will they do when We shall gather them on a day about which there is no doubt? That day every person will be paid in full what one has earned, and no one will be dealt unjustly.

3:26. Say: O God, owner of the kingdom, You give kingdom to whom You will and take kingdom away from whom You will. You honor whom You will and humble whom You will. In Your hand is all good. Indeed, You have power over all things.

3:27. You make the night to pass into the day, the day into the night, bring forth the living from the dead and the dead from the living, and give sustenance to whom You please without measure.

3:28. The believers should not take the disbelievers for friends than believers. Whoever does that, shall have no help from God, but will be pardoned if it was in self-defense from them. God warns you to fear Him. All shall return to Him.

3:29. O Muhammad, tell them: God knows what you hide in your hearts or reveal it. He knows what is in the heavens and on earth, and has power over all things.

3:30. The day will come when every person will be confronted with the good or evil he has done. He will wish that there was a great distance between his evil and him. God warns you to fear Him. He is full of kindness to those who serve Him.

3:31. O Muhammad, tell mankind: If you love God, follow me; God will love you and forgive your sins. God is forgiving, merciful.

3:32. Also tell them: Obey God and the Messenger. But if they turn away, then God does not love the disbelievers.

3:33. God chose Adam, Noah and the descendants of Abraham and Imran* above all the people.

**Imran was the name of the father of Moses and Aaron; and also the name of Mary's father and Jesus' grandfather.*

3:34. They were descendants of one another. God hears and knows all.

3:35. Remember when Imran's wife said: Lord, I dedicate the child in my womb to Your service. Accept it from me. You hear and know all.

3:36. When she delivered the baby, she said: Lord, I have delivered a girl. God knew what she had delivered. The male is not like the female; I have named her Mary; protect her and her descendants from Satan, the outcast.

3:37. God graciously accepted her, made her grow in a good manner, and put her in Zechariah's care. Whenever he visited her in her chamber, he found food with her. He asked: Mary, where does this food come from? She replied: This is from God. He provides to whom He wills without limit.

3:38. Thereupon, Zechariah prayed: Lord, grant me a good offspring. You hear all prayers.

3:39. When Zechariah was standing in prayer in the chamber, the angels told him: God gives you good news of a son, to be named John. He will confirm God's word, will be honorable, chaste, and will be a prophet among the righteous.

3:40. Zechariah said: Lord, how will I have a son when I am old and my wife is barren? He was told: God does what He wills.

3:41. Zechariah said: Lord, give me a sign. He was told: Your sign is not to speak to anyone for three days except by signs. Remember your Lord much and praise Him morning and evening.

3:42. Remember when the angels told Mary: God has chosen you, purified you, and chosen you above the women in the world.

3:43. O Mary, be obedient to your Lord, bow down, and worship with the worshippers.

3:44. O Muhammad, these are the unseen things which We have revealed to you. You were not with the temple's priests when they cast lots to decide who from them should be Mary's guardian. You were not present when they argued about it.

3:45. The angels said to Mary: God gives you good news of a word from Him. His name will be Messiah (Jesus), the son of Mary. He will be honored in this world and the hereafter and will be among those near to God.

3:46. He will speak to the people in his childhood and in manhood, and be one of the righteous.

3:47. She said: Lord, how shall I have a child when no man has touched me? The angel said: Such is God's will. God creates what He wills. When He decrees a matter, He only says it to be, and it happens.

3:48. God will teach him the Scriptures (the Torah, the Gospel), and wisdom.

3:49. And will make him a Messenger to Israel's children. He will say to them: I have come to you with a sign from your Lord. From clay, I shall make a bird's form. I shall breathe into it and, by God's permission, it shall become a bird. I shall cure the blind and the leper, and give life to the dead by God's permission. I shall tell you what to eat and what to store in your houses. Indeed, in that is a sign for you, if you are believers.

3:50. I have come to you to confirm the Torah that was revealed to you before me and to make lawful some of the things forbidden to you. I have come to you with a sign from your Lord, so fear God, and obey me.

3:51. God is my Lord and your Lord, so worship Him. That is the straight path.

3:52. When Jesus found disbelief in Israel's children, he said: Who will be my helpers in God's cause? The disciples said: We are God's helpers and believe in Him. Bear witness that we have submitted to Him.

3:53. Lord, we believe in what you have revealed and follow Your Messenger Jesus Christ, so write us down with those who bear witness.

3:54. The disbelievers planned against Jesus, but God planned too. God is the best planner.

3:55. Remember when God said to Jesus: I will recall you by causing you to die, raise you up to Me*, and purify you from the disbelievers and make your followers superior to the disbelievers until the Day of Resurrection. Then you all will return to Me, and I will judge your differences.

**Scholars differ about the nature of raising up, whether it would be physical or in spirit and soul. I think it is in spirit and soul.*

3:56. I will punish the disbelievers with severe punishment both in this world and the hereafter, and they will have no helpers.

3:57. As for the believers who did righteous deeds, God will reward them in full. God does not like the wrongdoers.

3:58. What We are reciting to you are revelations full of wisdom.

3:59. In the sight of God, Jesus is like Adam. He created Adam from dust, then said to him: Be, and he was.

3:60. This is the truth from your Lord, so do not doubt it.

3:61. O Muhammad, if anyone argues with you about Jesus after the knowledge has come to you, say: Let us get together and gather your and our sons, women, then pray to God for His curse on the liars.

3:62. This is the true account. There is no one who has the right to be worshipped except God. He indeed is the all-mighty, all-wise.

3:63. If they turn away from accepting the challenge, then surely God knows the mischief-makers.

3:64. O Muhammad, say to the people of the Scriptures (Jews and Christians): Let us come to an agreement that we shall worship none other than God, associate no partner with Him, and not take others for Lords beside Him. If they turn away, then say: Bear witness that we have surrendered to Him.

3:65. O people of the Scriptures, why do you argue about Abraham while the Torah and the Gospel were not revealed until after him? Why do not you understand?

3:66. You have argued about matters of which you have some knowledge, but why do you argue about which you have no knowledge? God knows, you do not.

3:67. Abraham was neither a Jew nor a Christian. He was an upright man who had surrendered to God. He was not an idolater.

3:68. Surely, the nearest to Abraham are those who followed him and this Prophet Muhammad and those who believe. God is believers' guardian.

3:69. O believers, some from the people of the Scriptures wish to mislead you. They mislead only themselves, but they do not understand.

3:70. O People of the Scriptures, why do you disbelieve in the revelations of God, while you know they are true?

3:71. O people of the Scriptures, why do you mix truth with falsehood and knowingly conceal the truth?

3:72. Some people of the Scriptures say to each other: Pretend to believe in the morning what has been revealed to the believers, but reject it in the evening, so that the Muslims may abandon their religion.

3:73. They also say: Believe no one except the one who follows your religion. O Muhammad, say: Right guidance is from God. Do not believe that anyone can receive which you have received (the revelation), or that they would argue with you before your Lord. Say: All reward is in God's hand and He grants it to whom He wills. God cares for all and knows everything.

3:74. God selects for His mercy whom He wills, and He is the possessor of infinite reward.

3:75. Some people of the book (Jews and Christians), if entrusted with a great amount of gold, will readily return it; others, if entrusted with a single silver coin, will not repay it unless you constantly demand it. They say: There is no blame on them to betray and take the properties of the illiterates Arabs because God allows it. But they tell a lie against God and they know it.

3:76. Whoever fulfills his promise and guards against evil is surely loved by God.

3:77. Those who exchange the agreement with God and their oaths for a small price will have no share in the hereafter. God will not speak to them, look at them, or purify them on the Day of Resurrection. They will have a painful punishment.

3:78. There are some among them who twist their tongues in reading the Scriptures, so that you may consider it to be a part of the Scriptures. They say that it is from God, while it is not. They tell a lie against God while they know it.

3:79. It is not possible for a man whom God has given the book, wisdom, and Prophethood to say to people: Worship me rather than God. On the contrary, he would say: Worship God by virtue of your study and teaching of the book.

3:80. Nor would he instruct you to take the angels and prophets as lords. Would he order you to disbelief after you have submitted to God's will?

3:81. Remember when God took the promise from the Prophets saying: I have given you the Scriptures and wisdom. A Messenger will come to you confirming what is with you, you must believe in him and support him. God asked: Do you agree and accept this commitment? They said: We agree and accept it. He said: Then bear witness, and I bear witness with you too.

3:82. After that, whosoever will turn away from the promise will be defiantly disobedient.

3:83. Do they seek a religion other than God's, when all creatures in the heavens and on earth, willing or unwilling, bow to His will, and will be brought back to Him?

3:84. O Muhammad, say: We believe in God and what is revealed to us;

in what was revealed to Abraham, Ishmael, Isaac, Jacob, and his descendants, and in what was given to Moses, Jesus and other prophets from their Lord. We do not discriminate among them and have submitted to Him.

3:85. Whoever desires a religion other than Islam (submission to God's will) shall not be accepted from him, and he shall be a loser in the hereafter.

3:86. How will God guide those who reject faith after accepting it and acknowledging that the Messenger Muhammad was true, and that clear signs had come to them? God does not guide unjust people.

3:87. Their punishment will be the curse of God, the angels, and the mankind.

3:88. They will live under it forever. Their punishment will neither be lightened nor delayed.

3:89. Except for those who repent after that and do righteous deeds. God, surely, is forgiving and merciful.

3:90. Who reject faith after they accepted it, and then persist in their disbelief, their repentance will not be accepted, because they have gone off the right path.

3:91. Those who rejected faith and die, their offer of ransom of as much gold as the earth contains will not be accepted. There will be a painful punishment for them, and they will have no helpers.

3:92. You will not attain piety unless you spend in charity what you love. God is aware of what you spend.

3:93. All food was lawful for Israel's children, except what Prophet Jacob made unlawful before the Torah was revealed. O Muhammad, say: Bring the Torah and read it, if you are truthful.

3:94. Then after that, whosoever shall invent a lie against God shall be a wrong-doer.

3:95. Say: God has spoken the truth; so follow Abraham's religion. He was an upright man and was not an idolater.

3:96. The first house of worship ever built for mankind is at Mecca. It is a blessed-place and a center of guidance for the mankind.

3:97. In it are clear signs; the place where Abraham used to pray; whoever enters it attains security. Pilgrimage to it is a duty from God for those who can afford the journey. But if anyone denies faith, God is self-sufficient and does not need any of His creatures.

3:98. Say to the people of the Scriptures (Jews and Christians): Why do you reject God's revelations? He is witness to what you do.

3:99. Say: O followers of the Scriptures, why do you prevent believers from God's way and seek to make it crooked while you know it is straight? God is not unaware of what you do.

3:100. Believers, if you follow some of those who received the Scriptures, they will make you disbelieve after you have believed.

3:101. But how can you deny faith when God's revelations are recited to you, and the Messenger Muhammad lives among you? Whoever holds firmly to God will be shown a straight path.

3:102. Believers fear God as He should be feared and do not die except in submission to Him.

3:103. Together, hold firmly God's rope and let nothing divide you. Remember God's favors upon you. He brought your hearts together when you were enemies and you became brothers by His favor. He saved you when you were at the edge of the fire's pit. Thus God makes clear His revelations to you that you may be guided.

3:104. Let a nation spring from you that invites to goodness, commands right conduct, and forbids indecency. Such people shall surely be successful.

3:105. Do not be like those who became divided and differed after clear proofs came to them. Those will have a great punishment.

3:106. On the Day of Resurrection, some faces will be bright with joy and others darkened. Those with darkened faces will be asked: Did you reject faith after accepting it? Then taste the punishment for rejecting faith.

3:107. Those with bright faces will be in God's mercy and will live in it forever.

3:108. These are God's revelations. We recite them to you, O Muhammad, in truth. God wants no injustice to His creatures.

3:109. Whatever is in the heavens and on the earth belongs to God. All matters go back to Him for decision.

3:110. You are the best community that has been raised for guidance to mankind. You command right conduct, forbid indecency, and believe in God. Had the people of the Scriptures (Jews and Christians) believed, it would have been better for them. Some of them are believers, but most are evildoers.

3:111. They cannot cause you serious harm. If they will fight you, they will turn their backs and flee. They will not be helped.

3:112. God has put them under humiliation wherever they may be, unless they make an agreement of protection with God and the mankind. They have drawn God's anger and put themselves under destitution, because they disbelieved in God's verses, killed the Prophets unjustly, disobeyed, and exceeded the limits.

3:113. They are not all alike. Some people of the Scriptures stand up for the right, recite God's verses during the night, and prostrate in prayer.

3:114. They believe in God and the last day, command what is right, forbid what is wrong, and hasten to do good. They are righteous.

3:115. Whatever good they do its reward will not be denied. God knows the righteous.

3:116. The disbelievers' wealth or children will not be of any use against God. They are companions of the hellfire, in which they will live forever.

3:117. The likeness of what they spend in this life is that of an icy wind which strikes and destroys the harvest of a people who have wronged themselves. God has not wronged them, but they have wrong themselves.

3:118. Believers do not be intimate friends with others than your own people. They would spare no pains to ruin you and wish you hardship. Hatred has already appeared from what they have said, and what their hearts conceal is far worse. We have certainly made clear to you the signs, if you will use reason.

3:119. You love them but they do not love you, even though you believe in the entire Scriptures. When they meet you, they say: We believe. But when they are alone, they bite their fingertips in rage at you. Say to them: Die in your rage. God knows what is in the hearts.

3:120. If good touches you, it grieves them; but if harm strikes you, they rejoice at it. If you are patient and fear God, their plot will not harm you at all. God understands what they do.

3:121. Remember when you, O Muhammad, left your family in the morning to post the believers at their stations for the battle of Uhud*. God heard all and knew all.

**Near Medina. The second battle was fought there between Muslims and their enemies. Muslims lost it.*

3:122. When your two parties were about to lose courage, God was their ally. The believers should put their trust in God.

3:123. God had already given you victory at the battle of Badr* while you were few in number. So fear God, perhaps you will be grateful.

**Near Medina, where the first battle between Muslims and their enemies was fought. Muslims won it.*

3:124. Remember when you, O Muhammad, said to the believers: Is it not enough for you that your Lord should help you by sending

down three thousand angels?
3:125. Yes, if you remain patient and conscious of God, and the enemy was to attack you suddenly, your Lord will reinforce you with 5,000 battle-equipped angels.
3:126. God made it a message of hope for you and an assurance to your hearts. Victory comes from God alone, Who is the all-mighty, all-wise.
3:127. God might cut off a flank of the disbelievers or suppress them so that they turn back disappointed.
3:128. It is not for you, O Muhammad, but for God to decide whether to forgive or punish them. They are wrongdoers.
3:129. And to God belongs all that is in the heavens and on earth. He forgives whom He pleases, and punishes whom He pleases. God is often forgiving, most merciful.
3:130. Believers do not take usury by doubling and multiplying it. Fear God that you may be successful.
3:131. Fear the hellfire, which has been prepared for the disbelievers.
3:132. Obey God and the Messenger Muhammad that you may be granted mercy.
3:133. Hasten to earn forgiveness from your Lord and a paradise, as wide as the heavens and the earth, prepared for the righteous.
3:134. The believers give charity in prosperity or adversity, restrain anger, and forgive people. God loves those who do good deeds.
3:135. If they do an evil or wrong themselves, they remember God and ask forgiveness for their sins. Who can forgive the sins except God? They do not knowingly persist in what they have done.
3:136. Their reward will be God's forgiveness, and gardens watered by running streams. They will live there forever, an excellent reward for the righteous.
3:137. Many nations have passed before you. Travel through the land and see the end of those who denied the faith.
3:138. The Qur'an is a clear statement for mankind and a guidance and instruction for those who guard against evil.
3:139. Do not lose heart or despair. You shall have the upper hand if you are believers.
3:140. If you have received a blow at the battle of Uhud, the disbelievers have also received a similar blow at the battle of Badr. We give such variation in fortunes to mankind by turns, so that We may know the true believers and choose the witnesses of righteousness. God does not love the wrongdoers.
3:141. And by this test God wanted to sort out the true believers and

destroy the disbelievers.

3:142. Do you think that you would enter paradise without God testing those of you who fought hard in His cause and remained steadfast?

3:143. You did indeed wish for death before you met it. Now you have seen it with your own eyes.

3:144. Muhammad is but a Messenger. Many Messengers have passed away before him. If he was to die or be killed, would you turn back on your heels to disbelief? He who turns back on his heels will never harm God. God will reward the grateful.

3:145. No person can die unless God permits. The time of death has been pre-fixed. Whoever desires a reward in this world, God will give it to him; and whoever desires a reward in the hereafter, God will give it to him. God will surely reward the grateful.

3:146. Earlier, many prophets and their followers have fought in God's way. They never lost heart if they met disaster in God's way, nor did they weaken or give in. God loves those who are steadfast.

3:147. All that they said was: Lord, please forgive us for our sins and excesses, establish our feet firmly, and help us against those that resist faith.

3:148. Therefore God gave them the reward in this world and the excellent reward in the hereafter. God loves those who do good deeds.

3:149. Believers if you would obey the disbelievers, they will drive you back to disbelief and you will be losers.

3:150. But God is your protector and He is the best helper.

3:151. God shall cast terror into the disbelievers' hearts, because they associate partners with God, for which He had sent no authority. Their home will be hell, a miserable home for the wrongdoers.

3:152. God had certainly fulfilled His promise to you when initially, with His permission, you were killing the enemy until you faltered, argued about your duty, and disobeyed the Prophet's order after He had shown you that which you love, the booty. Some of you desire this world, and others desire the hereafter. God let you be defeated at the battle of Uhud to test you. He has already forgiven you. God is gracious to the believers.

3:153. Remember how you fled and climbed the mountain without looking aside at anyone while the Messenger Muhammad was calling you back from behind. So God repaid you with distress upon distress to make you learn a lesson not to grieve for which you lost or what had befallen you. God is well aware of what you do.

3:154. Then after the distress, God sent down security upon you. Drowsiness overcame some, while others worried about themselves, thinking wrongly and foolishly about God, and asking: Have we a hand in implementing the affair? O Muhammad, say to them: The affair is wholly in God's hands. They are concealing what they will not reveal to you. They say: If we had anything to do with the affair, none of us would have been killed here. Tell them: Even if you had been in your houses, those decreed to be killed would have gone to the place of their death. It was so that God might test what is in your hearts and purify your hearts. God knows about your innermost thoughts.

3:155. Those of you who turned back on the day the two armies met at the battleground of Uhud, it was Satan who caused them to run away from the battlefield because of some of their sins. But God has already forgiven them. God is forgiving and patient.

3:156. Believers, do not be like the disbelievers who say of their brethren when they travel or engage in fighting that had they been with us, they would not have died or been killed. God makes this to be an intense regret in their hearts. God gives life and causes death. God sees what you do.

3:157. And if you are killed or die in God's cause, His forgiveness and mercy are far better than all that they amass.

3:158. Whether you die or are killed, you will be gathered before God.

3:159. O Messenger, it was God's mercy that you dealt with them gently. Had you been harsh and hard-hearted, they would have broken away from you. Ignore their faults, ask God's forgiveness for them, and consult them in affairs of administration. When you have taken a decision, put your trust in God. God loves those who trust Him.

3:160. If God is your helper, no one can overcome you. If He abandons you, who is there who can help you after Him? Therefore, the believers should put their trust in God.

3:161. NO Prophet will take illegally a part of war booty. Whosoever will take unlawfully, he will come with it on the Day of Resurrection. There, every person will be compensated for what it earned, and no one will be dealt unjustly.

3:162. Is he who follows God's pleasure like him who has earned God's displeasure? His home is hell, a miserable destination.

3:163. God distinguishes between the two. God sees what they do.

3:164. God certainly has done a great favor to the believers that He has sent among them a Messenger from themselves, who recites them

His verses, purifies them, and teaches them the Qur'an and wisdom; although earlier they had been in evident error.

3:165. Why is it that when a disaster struck you at the battle of Uhud, although you had struck the enemy with one twice as great in the battle of Badr, you said: From where does this come? O Muhammad, tell them: You yourself have brought it upon you. God has power over all things.

3:166. What struck you on the day the two armies met was by God's permission so that He might test the believers.

3:167. And that God might test the hypocrites too. It was said to them: Come, fight in God's cause and defend yourselves. They said: Had we known that there would be fighting, we would certainly have followed you. That day, they were nearer to disbelief than to belief. They say what is not in their hearts. God knows best what they conceal.

3:168. Those, who sat at home, said of their brethren: If only they had listened to us, they would not have been killed. Tell them: Then avert death from yourselves, if you speak the truth.

3:169. Never think of those who have been killed in God's cause as dead. They are alive with their Lord, receiving provision from Him.

3:170. They rejoice in God's reward and in receiving the good news about those who have not yet joined them, they have nothing to fear and grieve.

3:171. They rejoice in God's favor and kindness, and in knowing that God will not waste the believers' reward.

3:172. For those who answered God and the Messenger's call, even after being wounded, and do right and refrain from doing wrong will have a great reward.

3:173. The hypocrites said to them: A great army has gathered against you, therefore, fear it. But this increased their faith, and they said: God is a sufficient protector for us.

3:174. They returned with God's blessings and grace. No harm touched them. They followed God's pleasure. God's rewards are infinite.

3:175. Satan caused you to fear from his supporters. Do not fear them. Fear Me if you are believers.

3:176. Let not the conduct of those who rush to disbelief grieve you. They cannot harm God at all. God's plan is to assign them no share in the hereafter. There will be great punishment for them.

3:177. Surely, those who have bought disbelief instead of faith shall do no harm at all to God. They shall have a painful punishment.

3:178. Let not the disbelievers think that Our postponement of their punishment is good for them. We are postponing the punishment so that they may increase in sinfulness. For them is a humiliating punishment.

3:179. God will not leave the believers in the current state. He will separate the wicked from the good, but will not do so by disclosing to you the secrets of the unseen. For that, God chooses from His Messengers whom He pleases. So believe in God and His Messengers. If you believe and fear God, there is a great reward for you.

3:180. Let not those who greedily withhold the gifts of God think that it is better for them. Rather, it is worse for them. What they withhold will be hung by their necks on the Day of Resurrection. The heritage of the heavens and the earth belongs to God. He is aware of what you do.

3:181. God has heard those who have said: God is poor and we are rich. We shall record it and their killing of the Prophets unjustly, and say to them on the Day of Judgment: Taste the punishment of the hellfire.

3:182. This is because of what your hands have earned. God is not unjust to His servants.

3:183. To those who say: God has directed us not to believe in any Messenger unless he shows us a sacrifice consumed by heavenly fire, ask them: Messengers came to you before me with clear signs and with what you asked for, then why did you kill them, if you speak the truth?

3:184. O Muhammad, if they deny you, so were other Messengers denied before you, who came with clear proofs, written ordinances, and the enlightening holy books.

3:185. Everyone will taste death. You will be paid your full compensation on the Day of Resurrection. He who will escape from the hellfire and admitted to paradise will have attained success. The life of this world is deceptive.

3:186. You will surely be tested in your possessions and in yourselves. You will hear much wrong from those who were given the Scriptures before you, and from the idolaters. But if you persevere and ward off evil, then that will be a determining factor in all affairs.

3:187. Remember when God made an agreement with the people of the Scriptures to make their teachings clearly known to mankind, and not to hide them; but they threw them away behind their backs, and sold them for a little price. They made a wretched bargain.

3:188. Do not think those, who rejoice for what they have done and like to be praised for what they have not even done, and as if they are safe from a painful punishment. They certainly will be severely punished.
3:189. The kingdom of the heavens and earth belongs to God. He has power over all things.
3:190. For the men of understanding, there are signs in the creation of the heavens and the earth and the alternation of the night and the day.
3:191. They remember God standing, sitting, and lying on their sides, and reflect on the creation of the heavens and the earth, saying: Lord, You have not created this without purpose, glory be to You, and save us from the punishment of the hellfire.
3:192. Lord, whoever you will admit to the hellfire, indeed, You will disgrace him. For the wrongdoers, there shall be no helpers.
3:193. Lord, surely we have heard a preacher calling us to the faith, saying: Believe in your Lord. We have believed. Therefore, Lord, forgive our sins, cover our evil deeds, and make us die with the righteous.
3:194. Lord, grant us what You promised us through your Messengers and do not disgrace us on the Day of Resurrection. Indeed, You never break Your promise.
3:195. Their Lord accepted their prayer, saying: I will not deny any man or women among you the reward of their labor. You are related to one another. Those who emigrated or were expelled from their homes, suffered persecution, and fought and were killed in My cause, I will most certainly forgive their sins and admit them into the gardens watered by running streams. That will be their reward from God. He has the best rewards.
3:196. Do not be deceived by the disbelievers' activities throughout the land.
3:197. It is a small enjoyment for them. Ultimately, they will live in hell, a miserable place for rest.
3:198. For those, who keep their duty to their Lord, are gardens watered by running streams. They will live there forever. That will be a welcome gift from their Lord. What God has in store is better for the righteous.
3:199. There are some among the people of the Scriptures who believe in God, in the revelations to them and you, and in bowing in humility to God. They do not sell God's revelations for a small gain. They will have their reward from their Lord. God is swift to take account.

3:200. Believers, be steadfast in patience, show courage to fight against the disbelievers, be ready to do your duty to God, always fear Him, so that you may succeed.

# CHAPTER 4

# THE WOMEN

**Name:** From Verse One.

**Verses:** 176

**Summary:**

- Theme:
    1. New Ways: To comply with the new moral, cultural, social, economic and political ways in place of the ones of the pre-Islamic period. These are in continuation of those given in Chapter 2, The Cow.
    2. Bitter Struggle: To cope with the bitter struggle that was going on with the unbelieving Arabs, the Jewish clans, and the hypocrites who were opposing Prophet Muhammad's mission of reform.
    3. Promoting Islam: To promote Islam in the face of bitter opposition of evil powers by capturing more and more minds and hearts.
- Women: Treatment, justice, number of wives, dowry, punishment of illegal sexual relations, types of women prohibited for marriage, marriage with slave girls, corrective measures for disobedient women, and arbitration in family disputes.
- Orphans: Orphans and management of their property.
- Distribution of inheritance.
- Prohibition of drinking.
- Punishment for murder.
- Prayer: Obligation at prescribed times, during travel, and in state of war. Ablution with clean soil.
- Dealings with people of the Scriptures, hypocrites, non-belligerent clans, and pre-Islamic alliances.
- Aftermath of the battle of Uhud, preparation for armed conflict, fighting for the oppressed, and migration.
- Respect for one another's property and trade.
- Settlement of disputes.
- Distinction between the intentional idolaters and the helpless believers.
- Jesus: Death and trinity.

- God's dealings with the Prophets and Satan. Worship of other than God is an unforgivable sin.
- Relations with God and fellow human beings. Fate of believers and disbelievers. Obedience of God's Messenger is God's obedience.
- Reporting of important news to responsible persons.
- Response to greetings.
- There is no escape from death.
- Slander, false charges, uttering of evil words, investigation, and secret counsel.
- The Qur'an's message and authenticity.

**By Verse**

In the name of God, the compassionate, the merciful:

4:1. O mankind, fear your Lord, Who, from a single soul, and from its kind, created its mate, and from both spread many men and women on earth. Fear God, in Whose name you claim the rights from one and another and avoid violating the ties of relationship. God is ever watching over you.

4:2. Give orphans their property. Do not exchange their valuables with your worthless things, and do not consume their property by mixing it with your own. That surely is a great sin.

4:3. If you fear that you would not be able to treat orphan-girls justly, then you may marry other women of your choice, two, three or four of them. But if you fear that you would not be able to treat them equally, marry only one or a slave-girl you may own. That will be better to avoid injustice.

4:4. Give women their dowry willingly. But if they give you back some of it on their own, take it as lawfully yours.

4:5. Do not give the weak-minded orphans the property God has given you for their maintenance; but feed and clothe them from it, and speak to them kindly.

4:6. Test orphans' abilities until they reach a marriageable age. If you find them of sound judgment, hand over their property to them. Do not consume it excessively and quickly anticipating that they will grow up soon. Whoever is self-sufficient as a guardian, should refrain from taking a fee. Whoever is poor, should take what is reasonable. When you hand over their property, have witnesses in their presence. God takes sufficient account of your deeds.

4:7. Both men and women are legally entitled* to a share from what their parents and relatives leave behind, whether the property is small or large.

**The verse was revealed as a repudiation of the pre-Islamic practices in which women and children were not given an inheritance.*

4:8. If relatives, orphans, and needy are present at the division of inheritance, give them a share also, and speak to them kindly.

4:9. Those disposing of an estate should have the same fear as they would have for leaving a helpless family behind. They should fear God, and speak words of comfort and justice.

4:10. Those who consume orphans' property unjustly, fill their bellies with fire. They will burn in the flames of hell.

4:11. God's orders for distribution of your inheritance are:

- For children, a male's share will be twice of a female.
- If daughters only, two or more, their share is two-thirds. If one daughter only, her share is a half.
- For parents, each has a sixth share if the deceased left children. If there are no children and the parents are the only heirs, the mother has a third. If the deceased left brothers or sisters, the mother has a sixth.
- The above distributions shall be after complying with the deceased's will and paying for his debts.
- You do not know whether your parents or children are more beneficial to you. But these are God's orders. He is all-knowing, all-wise.

4:12. And:

- Your share is a half in what your wives leave, if they leave no child. But if they leave a child, you get a fourth.
- Your wives' share is a fourth in what you leave, if you leave no child. But if you leave a child, they get an eighth.
- If the deceased has left neither parents nor children, but has left a brother or a sister, each one gets a sixth. But if there are more than two, they share in a third.
- The above distributions shall be after complying with the deceased's will and paying his debts provided no loss is caused to anyone.
- The distribution is ordered by God. God is all-knowing and most tolerant.

4:13. God has set these limits. Whoever obeys God, and His

Messenger, will be admitted to the gardens watered by running streams. They will live there forever and that will be a great success.

4:14. Whoever disobeys God and His Messenger and breaks the limits, will be admitted into the hellfire to live there forever. That will be a disgraceful punishment.

4:15. If any of your women commit illegal sexual intercourse, take the evidence of four witnesses from among you against them. If they testify to the allegation's truth, confine them to their houses until they die or God finds another way for them.

4:16. Punish the two persons who committed this crime. If they repent and do good deeds, leave them alone. God is ever accepting repentance and is the most merciful.

4:17. God accepts the repentance of only those who do wrong in ignorance and repent soon afterwards. He will forgive them. He is the all-knowing and all-wise.

4:18. But God will not forgive those who do evil until death comes to them and they say: Now we repent. Also God will not forgive those who die disbelievers. He has prepared painful punishment for them.

4:19. Believers, it is not lawful for you to inherit the widows of your deceased relative against their will. You should not treat them harshly in order to take back part of the dowry you gave them. If they committed adultery, punish them. Live with them in kindness. If you dislike them, it is possible that you dislike a thing and God brings you a lot of good through it.

4:20. If you want to divorce one wife to wed another and you have given the former a great amount of dowry, do not take back anything from her. That would be improper and grossly unjust.

4:21. How could you take it back while you both have intercourse with each other and entered into a firm contract?

4:22. Do not marry the women your fathers married, except what has already happened. That was an immoral, hateful, and evil way.

4:23. Marriage is forbidden to your mothers, daughters, sisters, father's and mother's sisters, brother's and sister's daughters, foster mothers who suckled you, foster sisters who suckled with you, mother-in-laws, step daughters under your guardianship, who were born to your wives with whom you have intercourse, but there is no sin on you in marrying their daughters if you have not had sexual intercourse with your wives, their mothers, and you want to leave them to marry their daughters, the wives of your sons by blood, and two sisters at the same time, except for what has already happened. God is often forgiving and most merciful.

4:24. You are prohibited to marry married women except the war-captive slave-women you own. This is God's decree for you. All other women are lawful to you, provided you seek them in marriage by giving them dowry from your property, desire virtuous character and not unlawful intercourse. For enjoying marriage with them, give them their obligatory dowry. However, there is no harm in consensual compromise for the dowry. God is ever knowing and wise.

4:25. Whoever cannot afford to marry a free believing woman, he can marry a war-captive believing slave-girl he owns. God has full knowledge of your faith. You being from the same community, marry them with their guardian's permission and give them their fair dowries, provided they are virgin, have not committed unlawful intercourse, and do not have secret lovers. But once they are married, if they commit adultery, their punishment is half that of a free unmarried woman. This allowance is for those who fear committing sin, but self-control is better for you. God is forgiving and merciful

4:26. God wishes to make clear and show you the ways of the righteous people before you, and to accept your repentance. God is all-knowing and all-wise.

4:27. God wishes to forgive you, but those, who follow their lusts, wish you to deviate far away from the right path.

4:28. God desires to lighten your burden because man was created weak.

4:29. Believers, do not consume one another's property unjustly; rather trade it by mutual consent. Do not kill one another. God has been most merciful to you.

4:30. Whoever will commit such acts of aggression and injustice shall be thrown into the hellfire. That is easy for God.

4:31. If you avoid the major forbidden sins, We will forgive your lesser sins and admit you to an honorable place, paradise.

4:32. Do not wish for the things God has given to others. Men and women will be rewarded for their labors. Request God for His generous reward. God has full knowledge of all things.

4:33. We have appointed heirs to inherit the property left by parents and relatives. Also, with whom you have made a pledge, give them their due. God is witness over all things.

4:34. Men are managers of women's affairs, because God has made some of them excel others, and men spend their wealth to support the women. The righteous women are obedient. They guard men's rights in their absence because God wants them to guard those rights. As for those women from whom you fear disloyalty and ill-conduct, advise them first, next refuse to share their beds, and lastly beat them lightly. If they return to obedience, take no further action against them. God is most high and great.

4:35. If you fear a breach between a husband and his wife, appoint an arbiter from his family and another from her family. If they desire reconciliation, God will cause their reconciliation. He has full knowledge of all things.

4:36. Worship God and do not associate anyone with Him. Show kindness to parents, relatives, orphans, needy, the related and nonrelated neighbors, companions, travelers, and the slaves you own. God does not love the arrogant and boastful.

4:37. God does not love those who are miserly and direct others to be miserly and conceal what God has rewarded them. We have prepared a disgraceful punishment for the disbelievers.

4:38. And God does not love those who spend their wealth for show off, do not believe in God and the last day, and are friends with Satan, who is an evil companion.

4:39. What harm would it have done them if they believed in God and the last day and spent from what God has given them? God has full knowledge of their deeds.

4:40. God does not do injustice even of an atom's weight to anyone. If there is a good action, He multiplies it and gives a great reward from Himself.

4:41. What will the disbelievers do when We will bring a witness from every nation and call upon you, O Muhammad, to testify against them?

4:42. On that Day (of Judgment), those who rejected faith and disobeyed the Messenger Muhammad will wish that they were buried in earth. But they will not be able to hide anything from God.

4:43. Believers, do not offer prayers when drunk; wait till you can understand what you are saying. Likewise, do not offer prayers when unclean because of a sexual discharge until you have taken a bath, except when you are travelling, and if you are sick, are on a journey, have answered the nature's call, you have sexual contact with women, and cannot find water, take clean soil, wipe it over your faces and hands. God is ever pardoning and forgiving.

4:44. Have you not considered those who were given a portion of the Scriptures? They purchase error and wish you to go off the right path.

4:45. God knows believers' enemies well and He is sufficient for protection and help.

4:46. Some Jews take words out of context and say: We hear, but disobey; give ear but not hear. They say that by distorting their tongues and defaming the religion. If they had said: We hear and obey, hear us, and look at us, would have been more upright and better for them. God has cursed them for their disbelief. They do not believe, except a few.

4:47. O Jews and Christians, who have been given the Scriptures, believe in what We have revealed (The Qur'an ), which verifies what you already have, before We distort your faces and turn them backward, or curse you as We cursed the violators of Sabbath/Saturday. God's commandment is always executed.

4:48. God does not forgive the worshipping of other gods beside Him. But forgives whom He pleases for other sins. He who associates anything with God has certainly fabricated a tremendous sin.

4:49. Have you seen those who claim themselves to be pure? God purifies whom He wills. Injustice will not be done to them in the least.

4:50. Look, how they invent lies about God. That of itself is a flagrant sin.

4:51. Consider those who have been given a portion of the Scriptures. They believe in idols and false gods, and say to the disbelievers that they are better guided than the believers.

4:52. God has cursed them and no one will help them.

4:53. Have they a share in the kingdom? If that were so, they would not have given a trifle to anyone.

4:54. Are they envious of others because God has given them bountiful? If so, let them know that We gave Abraham's children the book, wisdom, and a great kingdom.

4:55. Some believed in Prophet Muhammad and some did not. The hellfire is sufficient for them.

4:56. We will drive the disbelievers of Our verses into hellfire.
Every time their skins will be burned, We shall replace the skins for them to taste the punishment. God is all powerful and wise.

4:57. We will admit believers, who do righteous deeds, to gardens watered by running streams. They will live there forever. They shall have purified wives. We will admit them to a cool shade of paradise.

4:58. God commands you to hand over the trusts to those who best fit to discharge them. If you judge between people, judge justly. God gives you excellent instructions. God hears and sees all things.

4:59. Believers, obey God, the Messenger, and those in authority among you. If you disagree about anything, refer it to God and the Messenger, provided you believe in God and the last day. That in the end is better and more suitable.

4:60. O Muhammad, have you seen those who pretend to believe in what has been revealed to you and to those before you? They seek the judgment of false gods for their disputes, though they were commanded to reject them. The Satan wishes to lead them away from the right path.

4:61. When it is said to them: Come to what God has revealed and to the Messenger, the hypocrites turn away from you.

4:62. But how do they behave when a disaster strikes them because of what their hands committed? They come to you swearing by God that they intended nothing but goodwill and conciliation.

4:63. God knows what is in their hearts. Be patient with them but warn them and give them advice that may reach their souls.

4:64. Tell them that We sent Messengers to be obeyed by My will. If they had come to you when they wronged themselves and asked God's forgiveness, and you had asked forgiveness for them, they would have found God forgiving and merciful.

4:65. But I swear by your Lord, they will not have true faith until they make you judge their disputes, and accept your decisions with full submission without any reservation.

4:66. Had We ordered them to sacrifice their lives or to leave their homes, only a few would have done it. Had they done that, it would have been better for them to strengthen their faith.

4:67. We would have given them a great reward.

4:68. And We would have guided them to a straight path.

4:69. Those, who obey God and the Messenger, will be in the company of God's favored ones: The Prophets, saints, martyrs, and righteous. They are the best companions.

4:70. This is God's reward. He knows well how to reward you.

4:71. Believers, be on your guard. Either march in groups or in one body.

4:72. There are some among you who linger behind. If disaster strikes you, they would say: God has favored us that we did not accompany them.

4:73. But if God blesses you with good fortune, they would say – as if there had never been any friendship between them and you: Oh we wish we had been with them to receive a good share of the fortune.

4:74. Let those who exchange the worldly life for the hereafter fight in God's cause. Whether they die or conquer, We shall richly reward them.

4:75. Why should you not fight in God's cause for the helpless men, women, and children, whose cry is: Our Lord, rescue us from this town (Mecca) whose people are oppressors; and send us a protector and a helper.

4:76. Those who believe fight for God's cause; and disbelievers fight for the cause of idol-gods. Fight against the allies of Satan, whose strategy is weak.

4:77. Have you seen those who were told to hold back from fighting, establish prayer, and pay Zakat (mandatory charity)? When fighting was prescribed for them, some of them feared man as much as God or even more. They said: Lord, why have You prescribed fighting for us; could You not grant us a delay for a short period? Say to them: The enjoyment of this world is short; the hereafter is better for those who fear God; and you shall not be wronged in the least.

4:78. Death will overcome you wherever you may be, even if in fortified towers. If a benefit comes to them, they say: This is from God; and if a misfortune befalls them, they say: This is your, Muhammad's, fault. Say: All is from God. What is the matter with these people that they fail to understand anything?

4:79. O man, whatever good comes to you is from God, but whatever misfortune befalls you is from yourself. We have sent you, O Muhammad, to mankind as a Messenger. God is your all-sufficient witness.

4:80. He who obeys the Messenger obeys God. But for those who turn away from you, Prophet Muhammad, We have not sent you as their guardian.

4:81. They say to you: We are obedient to you. But when they leave you, some of them plot against you at night. God records their plots. Therefore, leave them alone and rely upon God. God is your sufficient guardian.

4:82. Do they not reflect upon The Qur'an ? Had it not been from God, there would have been many contradictions in it.

4:83. When good or bad news come to them, they spread them around. Had they referred them to the Messenger and to other leaders, they would have drawn right conclusions from them. Were it not for God's grace and mercy upon you, all but a few of you would have followed Satan.

4:84. Therefore, fight in God's cause. You are only accountable for yourself. However, urge the believers to fight. It may be that God will restrain the might of the disbelievers. God is stronger in might and punishment.

4:85. Whoever joins in a good cause will have its reward. Whoever joins in an evil cause will share its burden. God has power over all things.

4:86. When someone greets you, return the greeting with an equal or a better one. God takes account of all things.

4:87. None has the right to be worshipped but God. He will gather you all on the Day of Resurrection, about which there is no doubt. Whose word is truer than God's?

4:88. Why are you divided about the hypocrites when God has cast them off because of their bad deeds? Would you guide those whom God has sent off the right path? You will not be able to guide whom God has sent off the right path.

4:89. They would like you to disbelieve like them, so that you may be all alike. Do not befriend them until they have emigrated in God's cause. If they do not, seize them and kill them wherever you find them. Do not take them as friends or helpers,

4:90. except those who seek refuge with your allies or come over to you because their hearts forbid them from fighting against you or their own people. If God wanted, He could have given them power over you, and they would have fought against you. Therefore, if they withdraw from you, do not fight against you, and offer you peace, God forbids you to harm them.

4:91. You will find another kind of hypocrites who desire security from you and their people. Every time they are called back to disbelief, they yield to it. If they do not withdraw from you, and neither offer you peace, nor stop their hostilities against you, then seize them and kill them wherever you find them. In their case, We have given you clear authority.

4:92. A believer should not kill another believer except if it happens by mistake. He that accidentally kills a believer should free a believing slave, and pay compensation to the deceased's family, unless the family declines it freely. If the deceased was a believer from your enemies, the penalty is the freeing of a believing slave. If the deceased belonged to your allies, compensation should be paid to his family, and a believing slave be freed. For those who find this beyond their means, they should fast for two consecutive months for seeking God's repentance. God has all knowledge and wisdom.

4:93. Whoever kills a believer intentionally, his punishment is hell. He shall live in it forever. God will be angry with him, curse him, and prepare a painful punishment for him.

4:94. Believers, when you go to war in God's cause, distinguish between friend and foe. If someone greets you with a salutation of peace, do not say to him: You are not a believer. If you seek worldly gain, God has abundant rewards. You too were like that, but Gad favored you; therefore, distinguish carefully. God is aware of what you do.

4:95. Believers, who stay home other than the disabled, are not equal to those who strive in God's way with their wealth and lives. God has honored those who strive with a rank higher than those who stay home. God has promised reward to both, but those who strive have a better reward,

4:96. of higher rank, forgiveness and mercy. God is ever forgiving and merciful.

4:97. Those who wronged their souls by staying in the enemy land and hiding their faith out of fear, the angels will ask them when taking their souls: What was wrong with you? They will reply: We were oppressed in the land. The angels will say: Was not God's earth spacious for you to emigrate? Their refuge will be hell, an evil destination.

4:98. As for the helpless men, women and children who are weak and lack means of migration,

4:99. God may pardon them. God is ever pardoning and forgiving.

4:100. He who emigrates in God's cause, will find many places on earth for refuge and a lot of resources for livelihood. Should he die as a refugee for God and His Messenger, his reward becomes God's obligation. God is ever forgiving and merciful.

4:101. There is no sin for shortening the prayer if you are on a journey and fear that the disbelievers may attack you. The disbelievers are your open enemies.

4:102. O Muhammad, when you are leading the faithful in prayer in a state of war, let one party stand in prayer behind you while carrying their arms. When they have prostrated, they should go to the rear for the other group that has not prayed, to come forward for praying behind you while being on their guard carrying their arms. The disbelievers wish that you neglect your arms and baggage so they could suddenly attack you. There is no blame upon you for putting down your arms if you are troubled by rain or are ill, but be on guard. Indeed, God has prepared a humiliating punishment for the disbelievers.

4:103. When you have completed the prayer, remember God standing, sitting, and lying down. When you are out of danger, re-establish regular prayer. Prayer has been decreed upon the believers to be performed at specified times.

4:104. Do not be weak hearted in pursuing the enemy. If you are suffering hardship, so are they, but you have hope from God, while they have none. God is full of knowledge and wisdom.

4:105. O Prophet, We have revealed the Qur'an to you with the truth that you may judge between people by God's guidance. Do not be an advocate for the deceitful.

4:106. Seek God's forgiveness. God is forgiving and merciful.

4:107. Do not plead for those who deceive themselves. God does not love the dishonest and sinful.

4:108. They may hide their crimes from people, but they cannot hide from God. He is with them when they plot by night about matters that He does not approve. God has knowledge of what they do.

4:109. You may plead for them in this life, but who will plead for them before God on the Day of Resurrection, or who will then be their defender?

4:110. Whoever does evil or wrongs himself, but then seeks God's forgiveness, will find God forgiving and merciful.

4:111. Whoever commits a sin commits only against himself. God is the all-knowing and all-wise.

4:112. Whoever commits an offence or a sin and then accuses an innocent man with it will bear the guilt of falsehood and a flagrant crime.

4:113. O Prophet, if it was not for God's favor and mercy upon you, a party of them had plotted to mislead you. They only mislead themselves and cannot hurt you at all. God revealed to you the Qur'an and wisdom, and taught you what you did not know.

God's favor upon you has been great.

4:114. There in not much good in people's secret talks; except if someone advises to give charity, and to do right or bring reconciliation among people. Whoever does that seeking God's approval, God will give him a great reward.

4:115. But whoever opposes the Messenger even after guidance has been clearly shown to him, and follows a path other than that of the believers, We shall leave him in the path he has chosen, and land him in hell, an evil refuge.

4:116. God will not forgive idolatry, but will forgive whom He pleases for other sins. Whoever associates anything with God, has strayed far away from the truth.

4:117. Instead of God, they worship female goddesses and pray to rebellious Satan.

4:118. God has cursed Satan for he has said that he would take a portion of God's servants.

4:119. He would mislead them, create sinful desires in them, will order them to slit cattle's ears, and to tamper with God's creation. He who chooses Satan than God for his protector ruins himself beyond redemption.

4:120. Satan promises them and arouses sinful desires in them, but Satan's promises are nothing but deceptions.

4:121. The Satan's followers refuge will be hell, and they will find no escape from it.

4:122. But believers who do righteous deeds will be admitted to gardens watered by running streams. They will live there forever. It is God's true promise, and whose word is more truthful than God's?

4:123. The final result shall not be according to your wishes or that of Jews and Christians. Whoever does a wrong, will be paid in return for it, and besides God he will not find a protector or a helper.

4:124. If anyone does good deeds, whether male or female and have faith, will enter paradise, and the least injustice will be done to them.

4:125. Who can be better in religion than the one who submits himself to God, does good deeds, and follows the way of Abraham, who was true in faith? God chose Abraham for a friend.

4:126. Whatever is in the heavens and on earth belongs to God. He surrounds all things.

4:127. People consult you concerning women. Say: God has instructed you about them and what has been revealed to you in the Qur'an concerning the orphan girls. You do not give what is prescribed for them while you desire to marry them. Concerning the helpless children, you should deal justly with orphans. Whatever good you do, God surely knows it.

4:128. If a wife fears ill treatment or desertion from her husband, there is no blame on them for an amicable settlement between them. A settlement is better, even though humans are swayed by greed. If you show generosity and keep away from evil, God is well-acquainted with all that you do.

4:129. You may try but will not be able to treat your wives equally, however much you may try. Do not turn altogether away from one leaving her suspended. If you do good deeds and keep away from evil, God is ever forgiving and merciful.

4:130. If you separate, God will compensate you both from His abundance. God cares for all and is wise.

4:131. Whatever is in the heavens and on earth belongs to God. We instructed the Jews and Christians who were given the Scriptures before you and now instruct you also to fear God. But if you reject that, know that whatever is in the heavens and on earth belongs to God. He is free of need and is praiseworthy.

4:132. Whatever is in the heavens and on earth belongs to God. He is sufficient to carry through all affairs.

4:133. If He pleases, He could destroy you all and replace you with others. God has the power to do that.

4:134. Whoever desires the reward of this world should know that God has the reward of both this world and the hereafter. God hears and sees all things.

4:135. Believers, stand firm for justice as witnesses before God, even if that may be against you or your parents, or relatives. God can better protect than you whether the person is rich or poor. Do not be led by passion to avoid justice. If you distort your testimony or refuse to give it, God is well aware of what you do.

4:136. Believers, have faith in God, His Messenger, the Qur'an, He has sent down upon His Messenger, and the Scriptures He sent down earlier. Whoever disbelieves in God, His angels, books, and Messengers, and the last day, has certainly gone far off the right path.

4:137. Those who believe, then reject faith, then embrace it, deny it again, and grow in disbelief, God will neither forgive them nor guide them to the right path.

4:138. Warn the hypocrites of a painful punishment,

4:139. for befriending disbelievers instead of believers. Do they seek honor from them? All honors belong to God.

4:140. God has instructed you in the Qur'an not to sit with those who deny and ridicule God's verses until they talk about something else, otherwise you will become like them. God will surely gather the hypocrites and the disbelievers in hell.

4:141. The hypocrites watch your fortunes. If God gives you a victory, they say: Were we not with you? If the disbelievers are victorious, they say to them: Were we not mightier to fight against you, even then we protected you from the believers? On the Day of Resurrection, God will judge between them and you. He will never let disbelievers triumph over believers.

4:142. The hypocrites try to deceive God, but it is He who entraps them. When they rise for prayer, they stand up lazily. They pray for show off to the people and remember God a little.

4:143. They waver between belief and disbelief and are not on either side fully. O Muhammad, you will not be able to guide whoever God has left off the right path.

4:144. Believers, do not befriend disbelievers instead of believers. Would you give God a clear evidence against yourselves?

4:145. The hypocrites will be cast at the bottom of hell. There will be no one to help them.

4:146. Except those who repent, mend their ways, hold fast to God, and are sincere in their religion to God, they will be with the believers. God will grant the believers a great reward.

4:147. Why should God punish you if you are grateful and truly believe? God is appreciative of your good deeds and knows all things.

4:148. God does not like the undignified speech unless by the one who has been wronged. He hears and knows all.

4:149. Whether you do good openly or in private or pardon those who wronged you, know that God is ever pardoning and is all powerful.

4:150. Those who disbelieve in God and His Messengers, and those who separate God from His Messengers say: We believe in some Messengers but not others. They seek to adopt a way between belief and disbelief.

4:151. They are truly disbelievers. We have prepared a humiliating punishment for them.

4:152. In contrast to them, God will certainly reward those who believe in God and His Messengers and do not discriminate between the Messengers. God is ever forgiving and merciful.

4:153. The people of the Scriptures (Jews and Christians) are asking you, Prophet Muhammad, to bring down a book to them from heaven. Indeed, they asked Moses for an even greater miracle to show them God. A thunderbolt struck them for their wrongdoing. They worshipped the calf even after clear signs had come to them. Even then We forgave them and gave Moses a clear authority.

4:154. When We made an agreement with them, We raised the Mount over them*. We said to them: Enter the gate bowing humbly, and do not violate the limits on Sabbath (Saturday). We took from them a solemn promise.

**It means the agreement was made at the Mount's foot.*

4:155. But they broke the agreement, disbelieved in God's revelations, slayed the Prophets wrongfully, and said: Our hearts are hardened. It is God Who has set a seal upon them for their disbelief. They shall not believe, except for a few.

4:156. They denied the truth and uttered a great falsehood against Mary.

4:157. They said: We have killed Jesus, the son of Mary, God's Messenger. They neither killed him nor crucified him, but it appeared so to them. Those who disagree about it are also in doubt. They are not sure that they killed him, except conjecture. For certain, they did not kill him.

4:158. But God raised Jesus up to Himself*. God is mighty and wise.

**Scholars differ about the raising up, whether it was physical or in spirit and soul. I think it was in spirit and soul.*

4:159. There is no one among the people of the Scriptures (Jews and Christians) that will not believe in Jesus before his death. On the Day of Resurrection, Jesus will be a witness against them.

4:160. God made certain good foods unlawful for the Jews which were earlier lawful for them because of their wrongdoing and hindering others from God's way,

4:161. and for practicing usury while they were forbidden from it, and cheating others of their property. We have prepared a painful punishment for the disbelievers among them.

4:162. We will give a great reward to those who are well-grounded in knowledge, believe in what has been revealed to you, O Muhammad, and what was revealed before you, establish prayer, give Zakat (mandatory charity), and believe in God and the last day.

4:163. O Muhammad, We have sent revelation to you as We sent revelation to Noah and the Prophets after him. We sent revelation to Prophets Abraham, Ishmael, Isaac, Jacob and his descendants, Jesus, Job, Jonah, Aaron and Solomon. We gave David the Psalms.

4:164. We have told you about some Messengers, but not others. We spoke to Moses directly.

4:165. We sent Messengers for giving good news and warnings, so that people would not have a plea against God after the coming of Messengers. God is mighty and wise.

4:166. God bears witness to which He has revealed to you (the Qur'an ). He has sent it down with His knowledge and the angels bear witness to it, though God alone is sufficient as a witness.

4:167. Those who disbelieve and hinder others from God's way have wandered far from the truth.

4:168. God will not forgive those who reject faith and do wrong; nor guide them to the right path,

4:169. except to the road to hell, wherein they will live forever. That is ever easy for God.

4:170. O mankind, God's Messenger Muhammad has come to you with truth from God. Believe in him; it will be better for you. But if you reject faith, know that to God belongs all what is in the heavens and on earth. God is all-knowing and all-wise.

4:171. O Christians, do not exceed the limits of your religion. Speak nothing except truth about God. The Messiah (Jesus, the son of Mary), was only God's Messenger and His word, which He sent to Mary, and a spirit from Him. Therefore, believe in God and His Messengers, and do not say: There are three (Christian Trinity). Desist from it, and it shall be better for you. God is only one God. God is above having a son. Whatever is in the heavens and on earth is His, and He alone suffices for their protector.

4:172. The Messiah Jesus never looked down upon being God's servant, nor do the angels who are nearest to Him. Those who look down upon worshiping Him and take pride in it will be gathered before Him to answer.

4:173. Then God will reward the believers who do good deeds, and enrich them from His abundance. But He will severely punish those who look down upon worshiping Him and take pride in it, and they will find none beside God to protect or help them.

4:174. O mankind, you have received your Lord's clear evidence. We have sent you a clear light.

4:175. Those who will believe in God and hold fast to Him, He will admit them to His mercy and grace, and guide them to Him on a straight path.

4:176. They consult you about the inheritance of a childless person. Tell them God's instructions: If

- A man dies childless, but has a sister, she will have half of his estate.
- A sister dies childless, her brother will be her sole heir.
- There are two sisters, they will have two-thirds of his estate.
- He has both brothers and sisters, the share of each male will be that of two females.

God makes His instructions clear to you for not erring. God knows all things.

# CHAPTER 5

# THE TABLE

**Name:** From Verse 112.

**Verses:** 120

**Summary:**

1. Commandments and instructions for Muslims' religious, cultural, and political life:

    - Rules for pilgrimage to the holy mosque (Kabah) at Mecca.
    - Lawful and unlawful food. Abolition of the pre-Islamic restrictions.
    - Taking food with the people of the Scriptures (Jews and Christians) and marrying their women.
    - Washing and bathing for praying and using soil when water is not available.
    - Punishment for rebellion, disturbance of peace, and theft.
    - Drinking and gambling.
    - Breaking of an oath and law of evidence.

2. Admonition to Muslims:

    - Stick to justice.
    - Guard against the wrong behavior of the people of the Scriptures (Jews and Christians).
    - Steadfastly obey God and His Messenger to avoid the evil consequences which befell Jews and Christians who had violated God's instructions.
    - Observe the dictates of the Qur'an.
    - Avoid the hypocrisy.

3. Admonition to Jews and Christians:

    - Warning against wrong attitude and invitation to follow the right way.
    - A detailed invitation for the Christians. The errors of their creed of Trinity.

**By Verse**

In the name of God, the compassionate, the merciful:

5:1. Believers, fulfill your obligations. It is lawful for you to eat animals' flesh except those described in the following verse. Hunting is forbidden during pilgrimage to Mecca. God decrees what He desires.

5:2. Believers, do not violate the holiness of the ceremonial acts decreed by God, the sacred month, the sacrificial animals, their garlands, and those going to the sacred mosque for seeking their Lord's grace and pleasure. Once your pilgrimage has ended, you are free to hunt. Let not the hatred of those who debarred you from the sacred mosque incite you to retaliate. Help one another in goodness and piety, but not in sin and aggression. Fear God, because He is severe in punishment.

5:3. You are forbidden to consume:

- the dead animal,
- blood,
- the swine flesh,
- the animal on which a name other than that of God has been invoked,
- the strangled animal,
- an animal beaten to death, killed by a fall or gored to death, or eaten by wild beasts, except when you found it alive and slaughtered it, and
- something sacrificed for idols.

Also forbidden for you is drawing arrows for luck, which is a sinful act. This day:

- The disbelievers have lost all hope of defeating your religion. Do not fear them; fear Me (God).
- I, God, have perfected your religion for you and completed My favor on you by choosing Islam as your religion. Therefore, follow the prescribed limits of lawful and unlawful eating, but he, who is compelled by hunger to eat what is forbidden, but not willfully, will find God forgiving and merciful.

5:4. O Muhammad, they ask you about what has been made lawful for them. Say: All good things are lawful for you, and what you have taught the hunting birds and animals to catch by training them as God has taught you. Eat what they catch for you by pronouncing God's name on it. Be careful of your duty to God. Surely, God is swift in accounting.

5:5. This day, the following have been made lawful for you:

- all things good and pure,
- the food of the people of the book (Jews and Christians) and your food for them, and
- marriage to chaste women, both from believers and the people of the book (Jews and Christians), when you give them their dowries, live in honor with them, do not commit fornication (sex between unmarried partners) and become their secret lovers. Whoever rejects faith, his labor will be fruitless. In the hereafter, he will be among the losers.

5:6. Believers, when you get ready for prayer, wash your faces, hands and arms to the elbows, wipe heads, and wash feet to the ankles. If you had sex, take a bath. But if you are ill, or on a journey, or have answered nature's call, or have been in sexual contact with women, and do not find water, take clean soil, rub it on your faces and hands. God does not wish to burden you, but to make you clean and to complete his favor on you, so that you may be grateful.

5:7. Remember God's favor upon you and the agreement He made with you when you said: We hear and obey. Fear God. God knows your hearts' secrets.

5:8. Believers, stand firm for God, become just witnesses, and do not let the hatred of others prevent you from being just. Act justly; justice is next to piety. Fear God. God knows what you do.

5:9. God has promised forgiveness and a great reward for the believers who do good deeds.

5:10. Disbelievers who deny God's revelations will live in hellfire.

5:11. Believers, remember God's favor upon you when He restrained the hands of those who wanted to harm you. Fear God. The believers should put their trust in God.

5:12. God made an agreement with the Israelites and appointed 12 leaders among them. God said: I am with you; if you establish prayer, give Zakat (mandatory charity), believe in My Messengers and assist them, and give a good loan to God, I will forgive your sins and admit you to gardens watered by running streams. But after this whoever disbelieves shall stray from the right path.

5:13. Because they broke the agreement, We have cursed them and hardened their hearts. They have changed the words of the Scriptures and have abandoned a good part of the message that was sent to them. You will find them deceitful except a few of them. But bear with them and pardon them. God loves the kind.

5:14. We also made an agreement with the Christians, but they too have forgotten most of the message that was sent to them. So We have planted the seeds of animosity and hatred among them until the Day of Resurrection, when God will tell them about what they did.

5:15. O people of the Scriptures (Jews and Christians), Our Messenger, Prophet Muhammad, has come to you, who makes clear to what you used to conceal from the Scriptures, and he overlooks most of your faults. A light and a clear book (the Qur'an ) from God has come to you.

5:16. With it, God will guide those who seek His pleasure to the ways of peace and will bring them out of darkness into the light by His will, and will guide them to a straight path.

5:17. Those who say that Christ, the son of Mary, is God, are blasphemous. Say: If God decides who could prevent Him from destroying Christ, the son of Mary, or his mother, or everyone on earth? To God belongs the kingdom of the heavens and earth and all that is between them. He creates what He wills, and He is able to do all things.

5:18. Jews and Christians say: We are God's children and His beloved. Ask them: Then why does He punish you for your sins? In fact, you are His created human beings. He forgives whom He wills, and punishes whom He wills. God has the kingdom of the heavens and earth and all that is between them. All will return to Him.

5:19. O people of the book (Jews and Christians), Our Messenger has come to you for making things clear to you, after an interval during which no Messenger came, lest you would say: No one came to us to give good news and to warn us. But now a prophet has come to you to give good news and to warn you. God has power over all things.

5:20. Remember when Moses said: O my people, remember God's favor upon you when He raised prophets among you, made you kings, and gave you what He had not given to any other people.

5:21. O my people, enter the holy land which God has assigned to you. Do not turn back, or you will be ruined.

5:22. The Jews said: O Moses, mighty people live in this land. We will not enter it till they are gone. Only then we shall enter.
5:23. Thereupon, two God-fearing men whom God had favored said: Attack them through the gate, and when you have entered it you shall surely be victorious. Rely on God, if you are believers.
5:24. They said: O Moses, we will not go in as long as they are there. Go, your Lord and you, and fight. We will stay here.
5:25. Moses cried: My Lord, I have power only over my brother and me, so separate us from these rebellious people.
5:26. God replied: This land will be forbidden for them for 40 years, during which they will wander on earth. Do not grieve for these rebellious people.
5:27. Tell them accurately the story of Adam's two sons (Abel and Cain). Each offered a sacrifice. It was accepted from Able but not from Cain. Cain said to Abel: I will surely kill you. Abel replied: God accepts sacrifice only from the righteous.
5:28. If you stretch your hand to kill me, I shall not lift my hand to kill you, because I fear God, the Lord of the universe.
5:29. I would let you add my sin to your sin and thus live in hell. That is evildoers' reward.
5:30. His ego prompted Cain to murder his brother Able; he killed him and became one of the losers.
5:31. Then God sent a crow who scratched the ground to show him how to hide the dead body of his brother. He said: Shame on me that I was not even able, like this crow, to hide the dead body of my brother. He repented.
5:32. Because of that, We decreed for Israel's children that whosoever killed a person except for murder or for creating disorder in the land, it shall be regarded as if he had killed all mankind, and whosoever saved one life, it shall be as if he had saved all mankind. But majority of them continued to commit excesses in the land even after Our Messengers came to them with clear signs.
5:33. The punishment of those who wage war against God and His Messenger, and spread mischief in the land is that they should be killed or crucified or their hands and feet cut off from opposite sides, or exiled from the land. That is their disgrace in this world, and there will be a heavy punishment for them in the hereafter,
5:34. except those who repent before you apprehend them. You should know that God is forgiving and merciful.
5:35. Believers, fear God and seek means to please Him. Strive hard

for His cause, so that you may be successful.
5:36. As for the disbelievers, if they had everything on earth and much more to give as ransom for punishment on the Day of Judgment, it would not be accepted from them. There would be a painful punishment for them.
5:37. They will wish to get out of the hellfire, but will not be able to come out. Their punishment will be everlasting.
5:38. As for the thief, male or female, cut off their hands as an exemplary punishment from God for their crime. God is powerful and wise.
5:39. But whoever repents after his wrongdoing and reforms, God surely will forgive him. God is forgiving and merciful.
5:40. Do you not know that to God belongs the kingdom of the heavens and earth? He punishes whom He wills and forgives whom He wills. God has power over all things.
5:41. O Messenger, do not grieve for those who hasten unto disbelief; the men who say with their tongues: We believe, but their hearts have no faith, and the Jews who listen to the lies of others and pay no heed to you. They change words of the Scriptures and say: If this be given to you, take it; if not, be beware. You cannot help a man whom God doomed into sin. God will not clean their hearts. They will be disgraced in this world and punished in the hereafter.
5:42. They listen to falsehoods and take anything forbidden. If they come to you O Muhammad, either judge between them or turn away from them. If you turn away from them, they cannot harm you. If you judge between them, judge justly. God loves those who act justly.
5:43. But why do they come to you for decision when they already have the Torah containing God's judgment? Yet they are turning away from it, because they are not believers.
5:44. We revealed the Torah containing guidance and light. The Prophets, who submitted to God, and the rabbis and scholars, who were entrusted with God's Scriptures and were its witnesses, judged those who are Jews by the Torah. Do not fear the people but fear Me (God), and do not sell My verses for a small price. Whoever does not judge, by what God has revealed, is a disbeliever.
5:45. In the Torah, We decreed for them: A life for a life, an eye for an eye, a nose for a nose, an ear for an ear, a tooth for a tooth, and a wound for a wound. But if any one forgoes the retaliation by way

of charity, it is an act of making amends for him. Those, who fail to judge by what God has revealed, are wrongdoers.

5:46. After those prophets, We sent Jesus, the son of Mary, confirming what was already revealed in the Torah. We gave him the Gospel that contained guidance and light, and confirmed what preceded it in the Torah as guidance and instruction for the righteous.

5:47. Let the people of the Gospel (Christians) judge by what God has revealed in it. Those who do not judge by that are evildoers.

5:48. We have revealed to you, O Muhammad, the Qur'an with truth. It verifies the Scriptures that came before it and guards them. Judge between them by what God has revealed, and do not follow their desires to be away from the truth that has come to you. For every one of you, We prescribed a law and a way of life. If God wanted He could have made you all one nation, but it is His wish to try you by what He has given you. Therefore, try to excel one another in good deeds. All of you will return to Him and He will tell you about what you differed.

5:49. O Muhammad, judge between them by what God has revealed. Do not follow their desires, and beware of them, lest they tempt you away from some of what God has revealed to you. And if they turn away, know that God intends to punish them for their sins. Most of them are wrongdoers.

5:50. Do they wish to be judged by the pagan laws? But who is better than God in judgment for a people who are firm in faith.

5:51. Believers, do not take Jews and Christians as friends. They are friends of one another. Whoever among you is their friend is indeed one of them. Surely, God does not guide the wrongdoing people.

5:52. You see that those with the disease of hypocrisy in their hearts are racing to woo the Jews and Christians. They say: We are afraid a misfortune may strike us. Perhaps they will repent their hypocrisy when God will bring you a victory or makes His will known.

5:53. Then the believers will say: Are these the ones who solemnly swore by God that they were with you? Their deeds will become worthless, and they will be losers.

5:54. Believers, whoever renounces the faith, God will produce others He will love and they will love Him, who will be humble towards the believers, strong against the disbelievers, will fight in God's way, and will not be afraid of the critics' blame. That is God's grace which He bestows on whom He wills. God is all-embracing and all-knowing.

5:55. Your only friends are God, His Messenger, and the believers who establish prayer, give Zakat (mandatory charity), and bow down in worship.

5:56. Those who seek the friendship of God, His Messenger, and believers should know that God's followers are sure to be victorious.

5:57. Believers, do not seek the friendship of the disbelievers and of those who were given the Scriptures before you and they ridicule your religion for sport. Fear God, if you are true believers.

5:58. When you call for prayer, they ridicule it for amusement. That is because they do not understand.

5:59. Say to the Jews and Christians, do you disapprove of us for no other reason than that we believe in God and the revelations that have been sent down before us? Most of you are rebellious and disobedient.

5:60. Then say: Shall I tell you who will receive God's worse penalty? It is those whom God has cursed, He became angry with them, and made them apes, pigs, and slaves of the false gods. Their situation is worse and it leads away from the right path.

5:61. When the Jews and Christians come to you, they say: We have believed. But they come with disbelief and leave with it. God knows their hidden thoughts.

5:62. You see many of them competing with each other in sin and wickedness, and eating what is unlawfully gained. Certainly, what they do is evil.

5:63. Why do not their rabbis and religious scholars prohibit them from speaking sinful words and eating what is unlawfully gained? Certainly what they are doing is evil.

5:64. The Jews say: God's hands are tied. No, tied are their hands and cursed are they for what they say. His hands are free and He spends as He wills. What your Lord has revealed to you has surely increased rebellion and disbelief in many of them. We have put animosity and hatred among them till the Day of Resurrection. Every time they ignite the fire of war against you, God extinguishes it. They spread mischief on the earth, but God does not like the mischief makers.

5:65. If Jews and Christians believe and fear God, We will remove their sins and admit them to the gardens of pleasure.

5:66. If Israelites and Christians follow the Torah, the Gospel, and what their Lord has revealed to them, they will enjoy happiness from every side. Some among them are on the right path, but most are on the evil path.

5:67. O Messenger, proclaim what has been revealed to you from your Lord. If you do not, you will fail in delivering His message. God will protect you from the people. He does not guide the disbelievers.

5:68. Tell Jews and Christians: You shall not be guided unless you follow the Torah, the Gospel, and what your Lord has revealed to you. What has been revealed to you, Prophet Muhammad, from your Lord will surely increase the wickedness and disbelief of many of them. But do not grieve for the disbelievers.

5:69. Whoever from the believers, Jews, Sabaeans*, and Christians, believes in God and the last day, and behaves righteously, will have nothing to fear or to grieve.

**an ancient South Arabian people, modern-day Yemen, believed to be the biblical land of Sheba*

5:70. We made an agreement with Israel's children and sent Messengers to them. But whenever they did not like a Messenger's message, they either rejected him or killed him.

5:71. They thought no harm would come to them. They were blind and deaf. God forgave them, but many of them again became blind and deaf. God is watching over their deeds.

5:72. The Christians surely are disbelievers who say: God is the Messiah, the son of Mary. The Messiah himself said: O children of Israel, worship God alone, my Lord and your Lord. Whosoever associates a partner with God, God has forbidden paradise for him and he will live in hellfire. Evildoers will have no helpers.

5:73. They are certainly disbelievers who say: God is one of the three in Trinity. There is but one God. If they do not stop from what they are saying, surely the disbelievers among them will be severely punished.

5:74. Will they not repent to God and ask for His forgiveness? God is forgiving and merciful.

5:75. The Messiah Christ, the son of Mary, was but a Messenger. Many Messengers passed away before him. His mother was a truthful woman. They both ate food. See how We make the revelations clear to the Christians, but see how they ignore the truth.

5:76. Ask them: Will you worship someone besides God that can neither harm nor benefit you? It is God who hears and knows all things.

5:77. Say to the Jews and Christians: Do not exceed limits in your religion beyond the truth and do not follow the desires of a people who went off the right path, misled many, and strayed from the right path.

5:78. David and Jesus, the son of Mary, cursed those Israelites who disobeyed and exceeded the limits.

5:79. They did not prevent one another from wrongdoing. Their deeds were wretched.

5:80. You see many of them making friends with the disbelievers. Evil indeed is what their souls have prompted them. They have incurred God's wrath and they will live in suffering forever.

5:81. If they believed in God, the Prophet, and what was revealed to him, they would not have befriended the disbelievers, but many of them are defiantly disobedient.

5:82. You will find the Jews and those who associate others with God have the most enmity towards the believers. The nearest in affection to the believers are those who say: We are Christians. This is because there are priests and monks among them who are not arrogant.

5:83. When they listen to what has been revealed to the Messenger, you see their eyes overflowing with tears because they recognize the truth. They say: Our Lord, we have believed, so write us down among the witnesses.

5:84. Why should we not believe in God and the truth that has come to us, and why should we not earnestly desire that our Lord count us with the righteous people?

5:85. And because of what they said, God rewarded them with gardens watered by running streams to live there forever. This is the reward of those who do good deeds.

5:86. But those who disbelieve and deny Our revelations are companions of hellfire.

5:87. Believers, do not forbid the good things which God has made lawful for you. Do not exceed the limits. God does not like those who exceed the limits.

5:88. Eat the lawful and good things that God has provided for you. Fear God, in Whom you believe.

5:89. God will not punish you for what is frivolous in your oaths, but He will punish you for breaking the oaths that you earnestly pledge. For making amends for a broken oath, feed 10 needy persons with what you normally feed your families, or cloth them, or free a slave. But whoever cannot afford that, he should fast for three days. That is for making amends for a broken oath. Protect your oaths. God makes clear to you His revelations that you may be grateful.

5:90. Believers, note that alcohol, gambling, alters for idols, and drawing arrows for luck or decisions, are Satan's works. Avoid them so that you may be successful.

5:91. Satan wants to create enmity and hatred among you with intoxicants and gambling, and to prevent you from God's remembrance and prayer. Will you not abstain from them?

5:92. Obey God and the Messenger, and abstain from these things. But if you pay no attention, then know that Our Messenger's duty is only to convey the message clearly.

5:93. There shall be no blame on those, who believe and do good deeds, for what they may have eaten, as long as they abstain from the unlawful things, believe, and do good deeds; and are also mindful of their duty to God and believe in Him; fear Him, and do good. God loves those who do good deeds.

5:94. Believers, God will test you through the game that your hands and spears can hunt, so that He may know who fears Him unseen. He that would exceed the limits after this will be painfully punished.

5:95. Believers, do not kill game while on pilgrimage. Anyone doing so intentionally will compensate by bringing an offering to the holy mosque (Kabah at Mecca), of a domestic animal equivalent to the one killed, as judged by two just men among you; or by feeding the needy or its equivalent in fasts, so that you may know your action's consequences. God has forgiven for what has happened in the past, but if there is a repetition, God will punish you. God is exalted and is the Lord of retribution.

5:96. The game from the sea and its use as food for you and the seafarer is lawful. But forbidden is the game from the land as long as you are on pilgrimage. Fear God to Whom you will be gathered.

5:97. God made the Kabah* the sacred house, a place of security for people, and also made sacred the months, the sacrificial animals with their garlands, so that you may know that God has knowledge of what is in the heavens and the earth. God knows all things.

**Kabah is a small, cubical building in the courtyard of the great mosque at Mecca. It contains a sacred black stone.*

5:98. Know that God is severe in punishment, but is forgiving and merciful.

5:99. The Messenger's duty is only to convey the message. God knows what you reveal and hide.

5:100. O Prophet tell them: The evil and the good are not alike even though a lot of the evil may attract you. Be mindful of your duty to God O men of understanding, so that you may succeed.

5:101. Believers, do not question about things which, if made known to you, would distress you. But if you ask about things when the Qur'an is being revealed, they will be made known to you. God will forgive you for this. God is forgiving and gracious.

5:102. Before you, some people asked such questions, and lost their faith because of that.

5:103. God has not instituted superstitions like a bahirah*, a saibah*, a wasilah*, or a ham*. But the disbelievers have invented a falsehood against God, and most of them have no understanding.

**In the pre-Islamic period, the Arab idolaters considered four types of camels as sacred and were dedicated to their gods. Such camels could not be ridden, or made to carry any load, and the she-camels could not be milked for human consumption. These camel were marked with slit ears, and they were allowed to water and graze freely wherever they wanted:*

- *Bahirah was a she-camel that gave birth to five young ones, the fifth of which had to be a male.*
- *Saibah was a she-camel that was consecrated to gods voluntarily by its owner as a thanksgiving offering for overcoming illness or protection on a journey.*
- *Wasilah was a she-camel that gave birth to seven female young ones consecutively. If at the seventh birth she bore a pair, male and female, those were also let loose.*
- *Ham was a male camel who fathered seven young ones.*

5:104. When it is said to them: Come to what God has revealed and to the Messenger; they say: Sufficient for us is that which our forefathers followed; even though they knew nothing, nor were they guided.

5:105. Believers, you are responsible for yourselves. If you follow the right guidance, no harm will come to you from those who have gone off the right path. All will return to God, and then He will tell you of what you did.

5:106. Believers, when death approaches you and you make a will, take two just men among you as witnesses, or two outsiders, even non-Muslims, if you are traveling through the land and the death strikes you. If you doubt their honesty, detain them both after prayer, and let them swear by God saying: We will not exchange our oath for a price, even for a near relative, and we will not withhold testimony which we are giving for the sake of God, otherwise, we would be sinful.

5:107. If it is found that those two lied under oath, let two others from those who are trustworthy and have a lawful right to represent the affected parties stand in their place. Let them swear by God: Our testimony is truer than their testimony, and we have not exceeded the limits of our duty, otherwise, we would be wrongdoers.

5:108. They will likely be true witnesses for fear that their oaths may be contradicted by others. Be mindful of your duty to God. God does not guide the rebellious people.

5:109. One day, God will assemble the Messengers and ask them: What response did you receive for your teachings to the mankind? They will reply: We have no knowledge; indeed, it is You who knows about the unseen.

5:110. God will say: O Jesus, the son of Mary, remember My favor for:

- supporting you and your mother with the Holy Spirit,
- you for speaking to the people in the cradle and in maturity,
- teaching you the Scriptures, wisdom, the Torah, and the Gospel,
- you for making the shape of a bird from clay and breathing into it for becoming a bird with My permission,
- you for healing the blind and the lepers with My permission,
- you for bringing the dead to life with My permission, and
- restraining Israel's children from killing you when you came to them with clear proofs, and the disbelievers among them said: This is obviously magic.

5:111. Remember when I inspired the disciples for believing in Me and My Messenger Jesus. They said: We have believed and bear witness that we have submitted to God.

5:112. Remember when the disciples said: O Jesus, the son of Mary, can your Lord send down for us a table spread with food from heaven? Jesus said: Fear God, if you are believers.

5:113. They said: We wish to eat from it, be stronger in faith, know that you have indeed told us the truth, and be its witnesses.

5:114. Jesus, the son of Mary, said: Lord, send down to us a table spread with food from heaven to be a feast for us, and a sign for those to come after us, provide for us the means of livelihood, and You are the best provider.

5:115. God replied: I will send it down to you, but whoever among you will disbelieve after that, I will punish him with a punishment as no one has been punished.

5:116. Then God will say: O Jesus, the son of Mary, did you say to the people to worship you and your mother as gods besides Me? He will answer: Glory to God; how could I say that to which I have no right? If I had said it, You would have known it. You know what is in my heart, but I cannot tell what is in Yours. You alone know what is hidden.

5:117. I told them what You commanded me to say: Worship God, my Lord and your Lord. I was a witness over them as long as I was among them, but after You passed me away from the world, You have been watching over them, and You are witness of all things.

5:118. They are Your God's servants. It is for you to punish or forgive them. You are the mighty and wise.

5:119. God will say: This is the day when the truthful will benefit from their truthfulness; they shall have gardens watered by running streams to live in them forever; God is pleased with them and they with him; this is great success.

5:120. God has The kingdom of the heavens and earth and what they contain. He has power over all things.

# CHAPTER 6

# THE CATTLE

**Name:** From Verse 136, 138, 139, and 142.

**Verses:** 165

**Summary:**

- God's characteristics and refutation of idol-gods.
- The life-after-death and the Day of Judgment.
- Superstitions.
- Admonition, warning and threats to the disbelievers.
- Principles for building an Islamic society, including giving charity on the harvest day.
- Prophet Muhammad's mission, limitations of his powers, attitude towards believers and disbelievers, and encouragement to continue the mission.
- Prophet Abraham's story and its relation to Prophet Muhammad's mission.
- Proof of Prophet Muhammad's Prophethood, and right guidance.
- A comparison of the teachings of the Torah and the Qur'an.

**By Verse**

In the name of God, the compassionate, the merciful:

6:1. Praise is for God, who created the heavens, earth, darkness, and light. Yet the disbelievers' equate others with Him.

6:2. It is He who created you from clay, and decreed a term for you to live in this world and another in the next life, yet you are still in doubt.

6:3. He is God in the heavens and on earth. He knows what you hide, reveal, and earn.

6:4. Yet every time a revelation came to the disbelievers from their Lord, they ignored it.

6:5. Thus, they denied the truth, when it came to them, but they shall learn the consequences of their mocking.

6:6. Can they not see how many generations We have destroyed before them? We had made those generations more powerful on earth than you by sending down abundant water from the sky and giving them flowing rivers. We destroyed them for their sins and raised other generations after them.

6:7. O Muhammad, even if We had sent down to you a book written on paper and they had touched it with their hands, the disbelievers would have said: This is nothing but obvious magic.

6:8. They ask: Why an angel was not sent down to Prophet Muhammad? If We had sent down an angel, their fate would have been decided at once, and they would not have been given time for repentance.

6:9. If We had sent down an angel, We would have sent him in human form, which would have confused them in what they are already confused about.

6:10. O Muhammad, before you, other Messengers were ridiculed. But those who ridiculed them met the fate of ridicule.

6:11. Say to them: Travel through the earth and see what the end of the disbelievers was.

6:12. Ask them: To whom belongs what is in the heavens and on earth? Say: To God, who has decreed mercy for Himself. He will surely assemble you all on the Day of Resurrection, about which there is no doubt. Those who have lost their souls will not believe.

6:13. To God belongs all that exits in the night or day. He hears all and knows all.

6:14. Say: Should I choose a protector other than God? He is the creator of the heavens and the earth. He feeds all and is not fed. Say: I am ordered to be the first to surrender to Him and not be an idolater.

6:15. Say: I shall never disobey my Lord because I fear the punishment on the Day of Resurrection.

6:16. On that day, if the punishment is averted from anyone, it will be due to God's mercy. That will be a great success.

6:17. If God gives you adversity, no one else can remove it, but Him. And if He gives you good fortune, know that He has power over all things.

6:18. He has full power over His servants. He is all-wise and all-knowing.

6:19. Ask them: Whose testimony is most reliable? Say: God is witness between us. This Qur'an has been revealed to me for warning you and whom it reaches. Do you really swear that there are other gods beside God? Say: I do not testify to that; He is the only God, and surely I deny other gods beside Him.

6:20. Those to whom We have given the Scriptures (Jews and Christians) recognize the oneness of God as they recognize their children. But those who have lost their souls will not believe.

6:21. Who is more unjust than he who invents a lie against God or denies His revelations? Indeed, the wrongdoers will not succeed.

6:22. The day when We shall gather the idolaters, We shall ask them: Where are your gods about whom you talked about?

6:23. They will not argue, but will say: By God, our Lord, we did not associate other gods with You.

6:24. You shall see how they will lie against themselves and how their invented gods will fail them.

6:25. Some of them listen to you. But We have made them hard of hearing and covered their hearts lest they hear and understand your words. They will not believe in Our signs even if they see them. When they come to argue with you, the disbelievers say: This is nothing but stories of earlier people.

6:26. They keep others and themselves away from truth. By doing so, they destroy none but themselves, but they do not understand.

6:27. If you could see them when they will be made to stand before the hellfire, they will say: If we could return to life on earth, we will not deny the signs of our Lord and be among the believers.

6:28. But what they concealed will become clear to them. Even if they were sent back on the earth, they would revert to what was forbidden. Indeed, they are liars.

6:29. They say: There is no other life than the life on the earth, and we will not be raised to life again.

6:30. If you could see them when they will be made to stand before their Lord, He will ask them: Is this not real? They will reply: Yes, our Lord, it is. Then He will say: Taste the punishment because you disbelieved.

6:31. Those who deny that they will ever meet with God are losers. When the Hour of Resurrection will come upon them unexpectedly, they will say: Alas, we neglected it. They shall carry the burden of their sins on their backs. Unquestionably, heavy is the burden they are carrying.

6:32. This worldly life is but a sport and a pastime. The life in the hereafter is better for the righteous. Will you not understand?

6:33. O Muhammad, We know what they say grieves you. But they do not call you untruthful, it is God's revelations that the wrongdoers reject.

6:34. Other Messengers before you were rejected. But they bore their rejection and persecution patiently until Our help came to them. No one can change God's decisions. You have already heard of those Messengers.

6:35. If their rejection is difficult for you to bear, then if you can, seek a tunnel into the earth or a ladder to the sky to bring them a sign. Had God willed, He would have given them guidance. So, do not be ignorant.

6:36. Only those who hear will respond; as for the dead, God will bring them back to life. They will return to Him.

6:37. They ask: Why has no sign been sent down to Prophet Muhammad from his Lord? Say: God certainly has power to send down a sign, but most of them do not understand.

6:38. All animals on earth and all birds that fly with their wings are communities like your own. We have not neglected anything in Our book. They will be gathered before their Lord.

6:39. Those who deny Our revelations are deaf and dumb living in darkness. God sends off the right path whom He wills, and puts on a straight path whom He wills.

6:40. Ask them: If God's punishment comes upon you or the Hour of Resurrection suddenly overtakes you, who will you call other than God for help? Answer me if you are truthful?

6:41. No, on God alone you will call. If He pleases, He will remove your distress and you will forget your idols.

6:42. Before you, We sent Messengers to other nations. We put them through poverty and hardship so that they might humble themselves.

6:43. When Our punishment came to them, why did they not humble themselves? Instead, their hearts hardened, and Satan made attractive to them what they were doing.

6:44. When they forgot the warning they had received, We opened the gates of good things for them, until, suddenly in the midst of their enjoyment of Our gifts, We called them to account and they plunged into despair.

6:45. So the evil doers were eliminated. Praise be to God, the Lord of the universe.

6:46. Ask them: If God took away your hearing and sight, and put a seal on your hearts, who other than God could restore them to you? See how We explain our revelation to them, yet they turn away.

6:47. Ask them: If God's punishment came to you suddenly or openly, will anyone be destroyed other than the wrongdoers?

6:48. We send Messengers only to give good news and to warn. Those who believe and mend their ways shall have nothing to fear or

to grieve.
6:49. But those who deny Our revelations shall be punished for their defiant disobedience.
6:50. O Muhammad, tell them: I do not claim that I have God's treasures, know the unseen, or am an angel. I only follow what is revealed to me. Ask them: Is a blind and the one seeing alike? Can you not think?
6:51. Warn those who fear for being gathered before their Lord that there will be no protector and mediator besides Him, so that they might become righteous.
6:52. Do not send away those who call upon their Lord, morning and evening, seeking His favor. You are neither accountable for them, nor they are accountable for you. If you were to send them away, you would be a wrongdoer.
6:53. Thus We have tested some of them by comparison with others so that they should say: Are these whom God favors among us? Does God not best know who are grateful?
6:54. When those who believe in Our revelations come to you, say to them: Peace be upon you. Your Lord has taken upon Himself to show mercy. If any one of you does evil in ignorance, then repents and mends his way, he will find God forgiving and merciful.
6:55. Thus We explain the revelations in detail to expose the criminals' way.
6:56. Say: I am forbidden to worship those on whom you call upon instead of God. Say: I will not follow your desires; otherwise I would have strayed from the right path.
6:57. Say: I have received clear evidence from my Lord, yet you deny it. That which you desire to hasten is not in my power; the decision is for God only. He declares the truth and is the best judge.
6:58. Say: If I had the power to hasten which you challenge, the matter would have been decided between you and me. But God best knows the wrongdoers.
6:59. He has the keys of all that is hidden; none knows them except Him. He knows what is on land and in the sea. Not a leaf falls without His knowledge. There is no grain in the earth's dark depths and no green or dry thing that is not written in a clear record/book of God.
6:60. It is He who makes you sleep at night like dead, knows what you did during the day, and then rouses you up for completing the

specified term of your life. You shall return to Him, and He will tell you what you did.

6:61. God has full power over His servants. He sends guardian angels to watch over you, who take away your soul when death approaches you. They never fail in their duty.

6:62. Then all His servants return to Him, their true Lord. Unquestionably, His is the judgment, and He is swift in taking account.

6:63. O Muhammad, ask them: Who saves you from the dangers of the land and the sea, when you call upon Him humbly and secretly saying: Save us, and we will certainly be grateful.

6:64. Say: God saves you from these dangers and every other distress, yet you associate other gods with Him.

6:65. Say: God has the power to send punishment upon you from above or from beneath your feet, or to divide you into quarreling factions for causing you to suffer from one another. See how We explain Our revelations in various ways so that they may understand.

6:66. Your people have rejected the Qur'an though it is the truth. Say: I am not responsible for your affairs.

6:67. With time, every prophecy shall be fulfilled, and you shall come to know of it.

6:68. O Muhammad, when you meet those who mock Our revelations, withdraw from them until they start talking about something else. If Satan causes you to forget this, leave the wrongdoing people as soon as you remember.

6:69. Those who fear God are not responsible for the disbelievers, but only to remind them so that they may guard against evil.

6:70. Avoid those who take their religion as play and amusement and are seduced by the worldly life. Warn them lest their sins destroy their souls. They will have no protector and mediator beside God. Should they offer every possible ransom, it shall not be accepted. Those are the ones who are given to destruction for their sins. They shall drink the boiling water and be severely punished for their disbelief.

6:71. O Muhammad,

- Ask them. Are we to:
  - ➢ call on idols which can neither benefit us nor harm us?
  - ➢ turn upon our heels after God has guided us,

like those whom Satan has enticed to wander around the earth, although their companions call them to the right path saying: Come to us?

- Say to them: Surely God's guidance is the true guidance, and we are commanded to submit to the Lord of the universe.

6:72. We are commanded to establish prayer and to fear Him. We shall be gathered before Him.

6:73. It is God who created the heavens and the earth in truth*. On the day when He will say: Be, and it shall be. His word is the truth. His shall be the kingdom on the day when the trumpet** shall be blown. He knows the visible and the unseen. He is all-wise, all-knowing.

**created in true proportions for a purpose.*

***The trumpet shall be blown for every creature to die and to end the world.*

6:74. Mention about Abraham who said to his father, Azar: Do you take idols as gods? I see that surely you and your people are obviously in error.

6:75. Thus We showed Abraham the phenomena of The kingdom of the heavens and earth so that he would become a firm believer.

6:76. When night came, Abraham saw a star. He said: This is my Lord. But when it faded in the morning light, he said: I do not love those that disappear.

6:77. When he saw the moon rising, he said: This is my Lord. But when it disappeared, he said: Unless my Lord guides me, I shall surely go off the right path.

6:78. Then when he saw the sun rising, he said: This is my Lord; this is greater than the star and the moon. But when it disappeared, he said: O my people, indeed I am free from what you associate with God.

6:79. I have turned my face toward God who created the heavens and the earth, and believe in truth. I am not an idolater.

6:80. Abraham's people argued with him. He said: Do you argue with me about God, who has guided me? I do not fear your idols; they cannot harm me without my Lord's will. My Lord has the knowledge of all things. Will you not be warned?

6:81. Why should I fear your false gods when God has not allowed you to worship them? Which of us has more right to salvation?

Answer me if you have knowledge.

6:82. Those who believe and do not mix their belief with injustice will have salvation and are rightly guided.

6:83. That was the argument We gave Abraham against his people. We raise in rank whom We will. Your Lord is the all-wise and all-knowing.

6:84. We gave Abraham Isaac and Jacob as descendants and guided them as We guided Noah before them. Among his descendants, We also guided David, Solomon, Job, Joseph, Moses, and Aaron. We reward those who do good deeds.

6:85. From his descendants, We guided Zechariah, John, Jesus and Elias, who were righteous.

6:86. And guided from his descendants, Prophets Ishmael, Elisha, Jonah, and Lot. We elevated all of them over other creatures.

6:87. We chose many from their fathers, descendants, and brothers for Our service, and guided them to a straight path.

6:88. This is God's guidance by which He guides whom He wills from His servants. Had they worshiped other gods beside Him, their deeds would have been useless.

6:89. Such were the people whom We gave the Scriptures, authority, and Prophethood. If their descendants deny them, We will entrust them to a people who believe in them.

6:90. O Muhammad, those were whom God guided. Follow their guidance. Say: I do not ask you for any reward for it; it is only a reminder to the mankind.

6:91. They do not give due credit to God when they say: God has not revealed anything to a human. Ask them: Who revealed the Torah which Moses brought as a light and guidance to mankind? You have written it on parchments, showing some parts and concealing most. By it, your fathers and you were taught what you did not know. Tell them: God revealed them. Then leave them to amuse in their vain discourses.

6:92. Like the Torah, the Qur'an is a blessed book which We have revealed. It confirms what was revealed before it, so that you may warn the people of the mother city (Mecca) and those who live around it; those, who believe in the life to come, will believe in it and maintain their prayers regularly.

6:93. Who is more wicked than the one who invents a lie about God or says: It has been revealed to me; while nothing has been revealed to him. Or the one who says: I will reveal the like of what God has revealed. If you could see the wrongdoers during the agony of death while angels would be extending their hands saying: Give up your souls; today you will be punished with humiliation for what you wrongfully said about God, and for rejecting His revelations arrogantly.

6:94. God will say: You have come to Us alone as We created you at first, leaving behind what We gave you. We do not see your defenders with you whom you claimed to be equal to God. Certainly, their ties with you are now cut off and what you asserted is gone from you.

6:95. It is God who germinates the seeds of grain and fruit. He brings the living from the dead and the dead from the living. That is God Who does all that. How can you turn away from Him?

6:96. He brings the dawn from the night. He has made the night for rest, and the sun and the moon for measuring time. This is predetermined by God and He is the almighty and all-knowing.

6:97. It is He who created the stars to guide you in the darkness of the land and the sea. We have made plain Our revelations for a people who have wisdom.

6:98. It is He who created you from a single soul, and gave you the earth for living and resting. We have explained Our revelations in detail to people who understand.

6:99. It is He Who sends down rain from the sky for producing vegetation of all kinds. From these, We produce green crops for grain, palm-trees laden with clusters of dates, and gardens of grapes, olives, and pomegranates, each similar in kind but different in variety. See their fruits when they ripen. In these, surely are signs for people who believe.

6:100. Yet the people consider jinns equal to God, while He created them, and they falsely assign sons and daughters to Him. Glory is to Him; He is above what they attribute to Him.

6:101. He is the creator of the heavens and the earth. How can He have children when He has no wife? He created all things and knows everything.

6:102. Such is God, your Lord. There is no God except Him, the creator of all things. So worship Him. He takes care of all things.

6:103. Human eyes cannot see Him, though He sees all eyes. He is subtle and well acquainted with all things.

6:104. Clear proofs have come to you from your Lord. Whoever will see them have much to gain and whoever will be blind to them will lose much. Prophet Muhammad is not your guardian.

6:105. We explain Our revelations in different ways so that:

- The disbelievers might say: You, Prophet Muhammad, have studied them deeply.
- The reality becomes clear to the people who understand.

6:106. O Muhammad, follow what has been revealed to you from your Lord. There is no god except Him. Turn away from the idolaters.

6:107. If God wanted, they would not have been idolaters. We have not made you their keeper or guardian.

6:108. Believers, do not insult the idols, lest the disbelievers ignorantly insult God in their anger. We have made pleasing to every community their deeds. In the end, they will return to their Lord, and then He will tell them about what they used to do.

6:109. They swear a solemn oath by God that if a sign be given to them, they would believe in Muhammad's Prophethood. Tell them: God alone can show signs. How would you, O Muhammad, tell that if a sign be given them, they will indeed believe in it?

6:110. We are turning their hearts and eyes away from guidance since they refused to believe in it at first. We leave them blundering and wandering blindly.

6:111. Even if We had sent down the angels to them, made the dead speak to them, and brought together all things before them, they still would not have believed unless God willed it. But most of them are ignorant.

6:112. Thus, for every prophet, We appointed enemies, the devils from among men and jinns, who inspire one another with deceptive falsehoods. If your Lord had willed, they would not have done it. Therefore, leave them to their fabrications.

6:113. The hearts of those who disbelieve in the hereafter, let them remain inclined to it, and being satisfied, let them continue in their sinful ways.

6:114. Say: Shall I, Muhammad, seek a judge other than God while it is He who has revealed to you the Qur'an, containing detailed explanations? Those to whom We previously revealed the Scriptures (Jews and Christians) know that it is sent down from your Lord in truth. So have no doubt.

6:115. Your Lord's words have been perfected in truth and justice. No one can change them. He hears and knows all.

6:116. If you obey most of mankind, they will lead you away from God's way. They follow nothing but conjectures, and do nothing but lie.

6:117. Surely, your Lord knows best who strays from His way and who follows the right course.

6:118. If you are believers in His revelations, eat the meat on which His name has been pronounced.

6:119. Why should you not eat the meat on which God's name has been invoked while He has explained to you in detail what is forbidden to you, except under compulsion or necessity? Surely, many lead mankind off the right path by their own desires through lack of knowledge. Certainly, your Lord knows best those who break the limits.

6:120. Do not sin openly or in secret. The sinners will be punished for their sins.

6:121. Do not eat any meat upon which God's name has not been invoked, because that is sinful. The devils inspire their allies to argue with you. If you were to obey them, you will become an idolater.

6:122. Can the dead man, whom we gave life and a light for his guidance among men, be equal to the one who is in the depths of darkness, from which he will never come out? Thus to the disbelievers their own deeds seem pleasing.

6:123. We have placed within every city the greatest of its criminals to conspire there. But they conspire only against themselves, though they are not aware of it.

6:124. When a sign is revealed to them, they say: We will not believe till we are given what God's Messengers have been given. God knows best whom to entrust His message. God will humiliate and punish them for their scheming.

6:125. If God wants to guide someone, He opens his breast to Islam (to surrender); and whoever He wants to misguide, He makes his breast small and narrow as though he was climbing up to the sky. Thus God punishes the disbelievers.

6:126. This is your Lord's straight path. We have detailed the revelations for thinking people.

6:127. They shall have the home of peace, paradise, with their Lord. He will be their protector because of what they used to do.

6:128. On the day when God will gather them all and say: O you assembly of jinn, you have mislead many human beings. Their allies among humans will say: Lord, we benefited from one another, but now we have reached our appointed term which You appointed for us. God will say: The fire is your home; you will live there forever unless God wills otherwise. Certainly, your Lord is all-wise and all-knowing.

6:129. Thus We will make the wrongdoers allies of one another as a punishment for their sins.

6:130. Thus God will ask: O company of jinns and men, did Messengers not come to you from among you, who explained My revelations to you and warned you of this Day's meeting? They will reply: Yes, they did. We bear witness against ourselves. Indeed, the worldly life seduced them. They will bear witness against themselves that they were disbelievers.

6:131. This is because your Lord would not destroy the cities arbitrarily while their people were unaware.

6:132. All shall be ranked according to their actions. Your Lord is not unaware of what they do.

6:133. Your Lord is self-sufficient and merciful. If He pleases, He can destroy you and replace you with others as He raised you from the offspring of other people.

6:134. Surely, what you have been threatened with is coming. You will not escape it.

6:135. O Muhammad, say: O people, you may do whatever you like and I will do my part. Soon you will know who gains the reward in the hereafter. Certainly, the wrongdoers will not prosper.

6:136. The disbelievers assign a share to God from the crops and the cattle He created. They say and pretend: This is for God, and this is for our idol-gods. Then the share of their idol-gods does not reach God, while God's share is wholly given to their idol-gods. Evil is the way they judge.

6:137. Their idol-gods have induced many disbelievers to kill their children so that they may destroy them and confuse them in their religion. If God had willed, they would not have done so. So leave them with their false inventions.

6:138. The disbelievers say: Such and such cattle and crops are forbidden; no one may eat them except whom we allow. They have made this restriction on their own. There are other animals which are forbidden for riding, and also others upon which God's name is not pronounced. They commit a sin against God. He will punish them for their inventions.

6:139. They also say: The offspring of the cattle is exclusively for our males and not for our females. But if it is born dead, they all have share in it. God will punish them for attributing falsehoods to Him. Indeed, He is wise and knowing.

6:140. Lost indeed are those who kill their children foolishly without knowledge, and make unlawful what God has given them, forging lies against God. They have indeed gone off the right path, and are not the followers of the right course.

6:141. It is God who grows gardens, both vine-type and tree-type, palm trees, crops, olives and pomegranates, looking alike but dissimilar in taste. Eat their fruit when ripen but give the due share to charity on the day of their harvest. Do not waste by excess. Indeed, God does not like those who waste by excess.

6:142. Some of the cattle are for carrying loads and some are for slaughter. Eat of what God has provided for you. Do not follow Satan's footsteps. Indeed, he is your clear enemy.

6:143. From the eight kinds of livestock, first take a pair each of sheep and goats, and ask them: Has He forbidden you their males, females, or offspring in their wombs? Tell me if you are knowledgeable and truthful.

6:144. Then take a pair each of camels and oxen, and ask: Has He forbidden you their males, females, or offspring in their wombs, or were you present when God gave you these instructions? If not, who is more unjust than the one who in ignorance invents a lie about God to mislead the people? Indeed, God does not guide the wrongdoers.

6:145. O Muhammad, tell them: I do not find anything in what has been revealed to me that forbids eating any food except meat of a dead animal, running blood, and flesh of swine, for they are unclean, or meat on which a name other than God's name has been invoked. But whoever is driven to eat these by necessity and not by desire exceeding the limit, will surely find God forgiving and merciful.

6:146. We forbade the Jews every animal with claws, and the fat of oxen and sheep, except that on their backs and intestines or mixed with bones. We penalized them for their bad deeds. We are truthful.

6:147. If the Jews disbelieve you O Muhammad, say: Your Lord is merciful and generous; but His punishment cannot be averted from the evildoers.

6:148. The idolaters will say: If God wanted, neither we nor our fathers would have worshiped gods besides Him; nor we would have prohibited anything. Like them, their ancestors denied the truth until they tasted Our punishment. Ask them: Do you have any proof you can show us in support of your claim? You believe nothing except unproven things and falsifications.

6:149. Then say: God alone has the conclusive proof. If He wanted, He

certainly would have guided you all.
6:150. Say: Bring your witnesses to prove that God forbade this. If their witnesses testify, do not testify with them, nor follow the vain desires of those who deny Our revelations, do not believe in the life hereafter, and associate other gods with Me.
6:151. O Muhammad, say to them: Come, I will tell you what your Lord has prohibited for you: Do not:

- Worship other gods except Him.
- Be disrespectful to your parents.
- Kill your children because of poverty, God provides both for you and them.
- Commit shameful sins, openly or secretly.
- Kill anyone whom God has forbidden, except for a just cause.

He has given you these commandments that you may understand.
6:152. Do not tamper with orphans' property, but try to improve it until they reach maturity. Give full measure and weight justly. We do not burden any person beyond its capacity. Speak justly even if it affects a relative. Fulfill your duty to God. He has commanded you that you may follow the right path.
6:153. This is God's straight path. Follow it and do not follow other paths, for they will take you off the right path. Thus God has instructed you that you may become righteous.
6:154. We gave Moses the Torah, a complete code for the righteous, containing explanation of all important things, and a guidance and mercy, so that perhaps his people would believe in meeting with their Lord.
6:155. We have revealed this blessed book (the Qur'an ). Follow it and be righteous that you may receive mercy.
6:156. You, the followers of Islam, cannot say: The Scriptures were only sent down to Jews and Christians before us, and for our part, we were unaware of what they studied.
6:157. You cannot even say: If the Scriptures had been revealed to us, we would certainly have been better guided than they. A clear proof of guidance and mercy (the Qur'an ) has come to you from your Lord. Who then is more unjust than he
who rejects God's revelations and turns away from them? We will severely punish those who turn away from Our revelations because of their indifference.

6:158. Are they waiting for the angels or God Himself or some of His signs to come down? The day when your Lord's signs do come, to believe then will do no good to a person, if he did not believe earlier, or did not do good deeds through his faith. O Muhammad, say: Wait, as we too are waiting.

6:159. You have nothing to do with those who have split their religion into sects. Their affair is left to God, Who will tell them about what they used to do.

6:160. He that does a good action will have ten-time credit; but He that does evil will only be punished for it. No one will be wronged.

6:161. O Muhammad, say: My Lord has guided me to a straight path, a right religion, the faith of Abraham, who was not an idolater.

6:162. Say: My prayers, sacrifice, living, and dying are for God, Who is the Lord of the universe.

6:163. He has no partner. I have been commanded for that, and I am the first one to bow to His will to be a Muslim.

6:164. Say: Should I seek my Lord other than God while He is the Lord of all things? Every person earns the reward of its deeds for itself, and will not carry another's burden. In the end, you all will return to your Lord, and He will resolve your differences.

6:165. It is He who gave you authority on the earth. He has given some of you a higher rank than others so that He may test you through what He has given you. Indeed, your Lord is swift in punishment, but He is the forgiving and merciful.

# CHAPTER 7

# THE HEIGHTS

**Name:** From Verse 46.

**Verses:** 206

**Summary:**

- Theme: Invitation to the divine message sent down to mankind through Prophet Muhammad. The message has been expressed as a warning to the disbelievers.
- Questioning of the Messengers and their people on the Day of Resurrection, and establishing the scale of justice.
- Adam's story; Satan's seduction of Adam and Eve; God's acceptance of their repentance; contrast between God's and Satan's instructions, and their consequences; and mankind's testimony of Adam's creation.
- God's:
    - command to wear decent and proper dress, and to eat good food.
    - creation of the universe and its system.
- Dialogue between the residents of paradise and hell, and those in between.
- Events from the lives of Prophets Noah, Houd, Saleh, Lot, Shuaib, Moses, and their people.
- Moses' confrontation with Pharaoh and the magicians; Pharaoh's revenge against the people of Moses; and God's punishment to Pharaoh and his chiefs.
- Rescue of Israel's children; Prophet Moses' communication with God; the Torah's tablets; worshipping of calf; provision of food and water in desert; violation of Saturday/Sabbath; and Jews' belief about God's forgiveness.

Prophet Muhammad's:

- description in the Torah and the Gospel.
- powers.

- Proper use of faculties to understand the message.
- Reality of idol gods.
- Instructions to Prophet Muhammad and his followers to show

forgiveness, speak for justice, avoid the ignorant, and listen to the Qur'an's recitation in silence.

## By Verse

In the name of God, the compassionate, the merciful:

7:1. Alif, Lam, Meem, Sad (are Arabic letters).
7:2. This book, the Qur'an, has been revealed to you, O Muhammad. Let there be no doubt in your heart about it. It has been revealed to you for warning disbelievers and reminding believers.
7:3. Follow what has been revealed to you from your Lord and do not follow other masters beside Him. But you seldom pay attention to the warning.
7:4. We have destroyed many cities. Our punishment came to them suddenly at night or while they were sleeping for their afternoon rest.
7:5. When Our punishment came to them, their only cry was: Surely we have been wrongdoers.
7:6. On the Day of Judgment, We will question those to whom Our message was sent, and also question Our Messengers.
7:7. With Our knowledge, We, God, shall tell them what they did as We were watching over them.
7:8. That day, their deeds shall be weighed justly. Those, whose scales shall be heavy, will be successful.
7:9. And whose scale will be light, their souls will suffer because they disbelieved in Our revelations.
7:10. It is God Who has placed you on the earth with authority and provided you with livelihood, but you are least grateful.
7:11. We created you humans and gave you shape. Then We asked the angels to bow down to Adam. They bowed down except Satan.
7:12. God said: What prevented you from bowing down when I commanded you? Satan replied: I am better than Adam. You created me from fire and him from clay.
7:13. God said: Get out of here, the heaven. There is no place for your arrogance here. So get out because you are disgraced.
7:14. Satan said: Postpone my punishment till they are raised up on the Day of Resurrection.
7:15. God said: Your punishment is postponed.
7:16. He said: Because you have judged me to be at fault, I will ambush them on Your straight way.

7:17. I shall attack them from their front, behind, right, and left. You will find most of them ungrateful.

7:18. God said: Get out from here, disgraced and expelled. If any of them will follow you, I shall fill hell with all of you.

7:19. God said to Adam: Live in paradise with your wife, Eve, eat whatever you like, but do not go near this tree, or you both will become wrongdoers.

7:20. Satan tempted them, so that he might show them their nakedness, which was hidden from them before. He said: Your Lord forbade you from this tree only to prevent you from becoming angels or becoming immortals.

7:21. Then Satan swore to them that he was their sincere adviser.

7:22. By deceit, Satan brought their fall. When they ate from the tree, their nakedness became visible to them, and they covered themselves with garden leaves. Their Lord called them: Did I not forbid you to go near that tree, and told you that Satan was your sworn enemy?

7:23. They said: Our Lord, we have wronged ourselves. Forgive us and have mercy on us, otherwise we will surely be among the losers.

7:24. God said: Get down from here. There will be enmity among your offspring. For a time, you will live on earth and have livelihood there.

7:25. He said: You shall live and die there. Then, you shall be raised to life.

7:26. O Adam's children, We, God, have given you clothing to cover your nakedness and to beautify yourselves. But the clothing of righteousness is the best. This is from God's revelations that perhaps they will pay attention.

7:27. O Adam's children, let Satan not deceive you as he deceived your parents to leave paradise, stripping them of their clothing to show them their nakedness. He and his tribe see you from where you cannot see them. We have made these devils allies to the disbelievers.

7:28. When the disbelievers commit an immorality, they say: We found our fathers doing it, and God has ordered us to do it. Say: God surely does not order immorality. Do you say about God what you do not know?

7:29. O Muhammad, say to them: My Lord has ordered you to act justly. When praying, turn to Him with devotion. As He created you, He will bring you back to life on the Day of

Resurrection.

7:30. He has guided some but let others err to go off the right path. Because, instead of God, they chose the evil ones for their friends and protectors, and thought that they received guidance.

7:31. O Adam's children, dress well when you worship. Eat and drink, but do not waste. God does not like the wasters.

7:32. O Muhammad, ask them: Who has forbidden you from wearing the decent clothes and eating the good things that God has provided for His servants? Say: They are for believers' enjoyment in this life though used by disbelievers also, but for them alone on the Day of Judgment. Thus, We explain Our revelations to those who understand.

7:33. O Muhammad, say to them: My Lord has forbidden immoralities, whether committed openly or privately, sins, wrongful oppression, joining partners with God for which He has given no authority, and saying things about God of which you have no knowledge.

7:34. Every nation has been given a fixed term. When their term is reached, neither they can delay it by an hour nor advance it.

7:35. O Adam's children, if there come to you My Messengers from among you narrating My verses, then whoever shall guard against evil and act right shall have no fear and grief.

7:36. Those who deny Our revelations and scorn them are companions of the hellfire. They will live in it forever.

7:37. Who is more unjust than the one who invents a lie about God or denies His verses? They will have their destined time until Our angels will come to them to make them die and ask: Where are those you used to worship beside God? They will reply: They have deserted us. They will bear witness against themselves that they were disbelievers.

7:38. God will say: Enter into hellfire among nations of jinns and humans that had passed on before you. Every time a nation will enter, it will curse its sister nation until they all have entered into it. When all have entered, every nation will say about the one previous to it: Lord, it misled us, give it double punishment of the hellfire. He will say: For each is double punishment, but you do not know.

7:39. The previous nation will say to the next nation: You were not better than us. Taste the punishment for all that you did.

7:40. Who reject Our verses and scorn them, the gates of the heaven will not be opened for them. Their entry into paradise will be as impossible as the passing of a camel through a needle's eye. Such is Our punishment for the sinners.

7:41. Hell will be their bed and sheets of fire will cover them. Such will be the wrongdoers' reward.

7:42. The believers, who do good deeds, will live in paradise forever. We do not burden anyone beyond a person's capacity.

7:43. We shall remove all hatred from the believers' hearts. Rivers shall flow beneath their feet and they shall say: Praise is to God, who has guided us to this; we would never have been guided if God had not guided us. Certainly, our Lord's Messengers had come with truth. They shall hear a voice saying: This is paradise, which you have inherited for your good deeds.

7:44. The dwellers of the paradise will call out to the dwellers of the hellfire: We have found what our Lord promised us to be true. Have you found what your Lord promised to be true? They will say: Yes. Then an announcer among them will announce: God's curse shall be upon the wrongdoers,

7:45. who prevented others from God's path, sought to make it crooked, and had no faith in the life to come.

7:46. There will be a partition between the two groups of the dwellers of paradise and hell. On its heights, some people will stand who will recognize the dwellers by their looks. They shall call out to the dwellers of the paradise: Peace be upon you. The people on the heights will not have entered the paradise yet, but long to do so.

7:47. When their eyes will be turned toward the dwellers of the hellfire, they will say: Lord, do not place us with the wrongdoers.

7:48. The dwellers on the heights will call to those in hell, whom they will recognize by their looks: Your riches and arrogance were of no benefit to you.

7:49. Are these the ones whom you, the dwellers of hell, swore that God would never offer them mercy? Today, the same ones have been welcomed to enter paradise, with nothing to fear and grieve.

7:50. The dwellers of hell shall call out to the dwellers of paradise: Pour on us some water or what God has given you. They shall reply: God has prohibited both things for the disbelievers,

7:51. who took their religion for a sport and a pastime, and the life of the world deceived them. That day, We, God, will forget them as they forgot the meeting of that day and denied Our verses.

7:52. We have brought them a book, the Qur'an, which contains detailed knowledge, as a guidance and mercy to the believers.

7:53. Are they waiting for the fulfillment of the book's warning? On that day, when the warning's results would come, those who had ignored it will say: Our Lord's Messengers had come with the truth. Will no one now plead for us? If we could be sent back to live our lives again, we would not do as we did earlier. They will have lost themselves and their inventions will have failed them.

7:54. Your Lord is God, Who created the heavens and the earth in six days, and then mounted the throne. He draws the night as a veil over the day, each follows the other. He created the sun, moon, and stars. All are governed by His command. His is the creation and the command. Blessed be God, the Lord of the universe.

7:55. Call on your Lord humbly and privately. He does not love those who exceed the limits.

7:56. Do not do mischief on the earth after it has been set right. Call on Him with fear and hope. God's mercy is always near to those who do good.

7:57. It is God Who sends the winds as the forerunner of His mercy's happy news. When they have carried the heavy water-laden clouds, We drive them to a land that is dead, make rain on it, and produce every kind of harvest. Like that, We shall raise up the dead, perhaps you may take heed.

7:58. By Lord's permission, the good land yields harvest, but the barren one yields sparsely with difficulty. Thus We diversify the signs for a people who are grateful.

7:59. We sent Noah to his people. He said: O my people, worship God. You have no other god but Him. I fear for you a dreadful day's punishment.

7:60. The chiefs of his people said: Surely, we see you in clear error.

7:61. Noah replied: O my people, I am not in error, but a Messenger sent by the Lord of the universe.

7:62. I convey to you my Lord's messages and advise you sincerely because I know from God what you do not know.

7:63. Do you wonder that a warning has come to you from your Lord through a man from among you, so that he may warn you and you may fear God and receive His mercy?

7:64. They rejected him. So We saved Noah and those with him in the boat. We drowned those who denied Our verses. They were indeed a blind people.

7:65. To Aad's people, We sent their brother Houd. He said: O my people, worship God; you have no god but Him. Will you then not guard against evil?

7:66. The disbelievers' leaders among his people said: We can see that you are a fool and a liar.

7:67. Houd replied: O my people, I am not foolish, but a Messenger from the Lord of the universe.

7:68. I convey to you my Lord's message, and am your honest adviser.

7:69. Do you wonder that your Lord's message has come to you through a man from your own people to warn you? Remember God made you successors after Noah's people, and increased your stature. Remember God's favors that you may prosper.

7:70. They replied: Have you come to us that we worship God alone and leave what our forefathers have worshipped? Then bring us the punishment you have threatened us with, if you are truthful.

7:71. Prophet Houd said: Your Lord's punishment and anger have already come upon you. Do you dispute with me about the names which you and your fathers have invented like gods of wind, rain, wealth, health, etc., without God's authority? Then wait as I am waiting.

7:72. We saved Houd and his companions by Our mercy. We eliminated those who denied Our verses and were disbelievers.

7:73. To Thamoud, We sent their brother Saleh. He said: O my people, worship God, you have no other god but Him. A clear sign has come to you from your Lord. This she-camel of God is a sign for you. Leave her to graze in God's land, do not harm her, or you shall be punished severely.

7:74. Remember when God made you successors after Aad's people and settled you in the land. You built palaces in its plains and carved homes in its mountains. Remember God's favors and do not spread corruption on earth.

7:75. His tribe's proud chiefs said to the oppressed believers: Do you really believe that God has sent Saleh? They said: Surely, we believe in his message.

7:76. The arrogant ones said: We reject what you believe in.

7:77. They killed the she-camel, revolted against their Lord's commandment, and said: O Saleh, bring upon us the threatened punishment, if you are one of God's Messengers.

7:78. Thereupon, an earthquake overtook them, and they lay face down lifeless in their homes in the morning.

7:79. Saleh left them saying: O my people, I conveyed to you my Lord's message and advised you, but you do not like advisors.

7:80. Remember Lot, who said to his people: Have you become so shameless that you commit the worst sin which no one before you have committed?

7:81. You lust after men than women. Truly you are a people exceeding the limits of decency.

7:82. Their only answer was: Drive Lot and his people from your city because they show off to be pure.

7:83. We saved him and his family, except his wife, who stayed behind with the evildoers.

7:84. We rained stones upon them. See the end of the criminals.

7:85. We sent to the Midian people their brother Shuaib. He said: O my people, worship God. You have no god but Him. A clear proof has come to you from your Lord. Give full measure and weight and do not defraud others of their possessions. Do not make mischief in the land after it has been set right. This is better for you if you are believers.

7:86. Do not sit on every path, threatening and hindering the believers from God's way, and seeking to make it crooked. Remember when you were a few and He increased you in number. See the end of the trouble makers.

7:87. If there are some among you who believe in the message with which I have been sent, and others who do not believe in it, be patient until God decides between us. He is the best judge to decide.

7:88. The arrogant elders among his people said to him: We will drive you and your followers out of our city unless you will return to our religion. He said: Even if we hate your religion?

7:89. We would have invented a lie against God if we returned to your religion after God had saved us from it. It is not for us to return to it except by the will of God, our Lord. He has knowledge of all things. We have relied upon God. Our Lord, decide rightly between us and our people. You are the best judge.

7:90. The disbelieving chiefs said to their people: If you would follow Shuaib, surely, you would be losers.

7:91. Thereupon, an earthquake overtook them, and they lay face down in their homes in the morning.

7:92. Those who denied Shuaib became as if they had never lived there. They were losers for disbelieving him.

7:93. He turned away from them saying: O my people, I certainly conveyed to you my Lord's message and advised you. How can I grieve for a disbelieving people?

7:94. Whenever We sent a prophet to a city, We gave its people poverty and hardship to humble them.

7:95. Then We changed their suffering into prosperity, until they grew and multiplied, and began saying: Our fathers were also touched by suffering and joys. We punished them suddenly, when they were unaware.

7:96. If the people of those cities had believed and feared God, We would have opened upon them blessings from the heaven and the earth. But they denied the Messengers, so We punished them for their bad deeds.

7:97. Do the cities' people feel secure from Our punishment that it will not come to them by night while they are asleep?

7:98. Do they feel secure from Our punishment that it will not come in the broad daylight while they were playing?

7:99. Do they feel secure from God's plan? No one feels secure from God's plan except the losers.

7:100. Is it not clear to the current occupants of the earth that had We, God, willed, We would have punished them for their sins and sealed their hearts so that they could not hear?

7:101. Those were the towns whose story We have related to you, O Muhammad. The Messengers indeed came to them with clear proofs, but they persisted in their disbelief. Thus God seals up the hearts of the disbelievers.

7:102. We found most of them untrue to their agreement, rebellious and disobedient.

7:103. After them, We sent Moses with Our signs to Pharaoh and his chiefs, but they wrongfully rejected them. Consider the end of the mischief-makers.

7:104. Moses said: O Pharaoh, I am a Messenger from the Lord of the universe.

7:105. It is proper for me to say nothing about God but the truth. I have come to you with a clear proof from your Lord. Let Israel's children depart with me.

7:106. Pharaoh said: Show us your sign, if you are truthful.
7:107. Moses threw his stick down and it became a big snake.
7:108. He drew out his hand. It was radiating white to all who saw it.
7:109. The chiefs of Pharaoh's people said: This man is a skilled magician.
7:110. He would expel you from your land. What would you like us to do?
7:111. They said: Put him and his brother off for a while, and send Messengers into towns.
7:112. They will bring every skilled magician for you.
7:113. The magicians came to Pharaoh. They said: Will there be a reward for us if we win?
7:114. He answered: Yes, and you will become my close associates.
7:115. They said: O Moses, will you throw your staff first or should we?
7:116. Moses said: Throw. When they threw, they cast a spell upon the people's eyes, overawed them, and produced a mighty spell.
7:117. We inspired Moses to throw his stick. At once, it swallowed their false devices.
7:118. Thus the truth was established and what they did was proved in vain.
7:119. Pharaoh and his people were defeated and ashamed.
7:120. The magicians bowed down.
7:121. They said: We believe in the Lord of the universe;
7:122. the Lord of Moses and Aaron.
7:123. Pharaoh said: You have believed in Moses before I permitted you. This is your planned plot to drive people out of the city. But you will see.
7:124. I shall cut off your hands and feet on opposite sides and then crucify you all.
7:125. They said: Surely, we shall return to our Lord.
7:126. You would punish us because we have believed in our Lord's signs when they came to us. Lord, give us patience and make us die in submission to You.
7:127. The chiefs of Pharaoh's people said: Will you allow Moses and his people to spread mischief in the land and to abandon you and your gods? He said: We will slay their sons but not daughters. We have power over them.
7:128. Moses said to his people: Pray for God's help and be patient. The earth is God's. He gives it to His chosen servants. The best

end shall be for the righteous.

7:129. They said: We have suffered, both before and after you came to us. He said: May be your Lord will destroy your enemy and make you inheritors on the earth, so that He may see how you act.

7:130. We punished Pharaoh's people with famine and drought so that they might pay attention.

7:131. But when good fortune came to them, they said: This is our due. If a bad fortune struck them, they said that it was due to the ill-luck of Moses and those with him. Unquestionably, God decides their ill-luck, but most of them do not know.

7:132. They said to Moses: Whatever signs you may bring to us to charm us, we shall not believe you.

7:133. So We sent upon Pharaoh's people the flood, locusts, lice, frogs, and rain of blood as clear signs, but they were arrogant and criminal people.

7:134. When the punishment came upon them, they said: O Moses, call your Lord for us because of His promise to you. If you can remove the punishment from us, we will believe you, and let Israel's children go with you.

7:135. When We removed the punishment from them for a fixed time in which they were to fulfill their pledge, they broke their promise.

7:136. So We, God, took revenge from them and drowned them in sea because they had denied Our signs and failed to take warning from them.

7:137. We made the oppressed people inherit the eastern and western lands, which We had blessed. Your Lord's gracious promise was fulfilled for Israel's children because they had suffered with patience. We destroyed Pharaoh and his people's great works and buildings.

7:138. We took Israel's children across sea. They came upon a people who worshipped idols. They said: O Moses, make a god for us just as they have gods. He said: Indeed, you are ignorant.

7:139. Surely, these people will be destroyed and what they are doing is in vain.

7:140. Moses said: Should I seek for you a god other than Him, Who has preferred you over other nations?

7:141. Remember when We, God, saved you from Pharaoh's people, who were oppressing you cruelly by killing your sons and keeping your daughters alive. That was a great trial from your

Lord.

7:142. We made an appointment with Moses at Mount Sinai for 30 nights and added 10 more. He completed the term appointed by his Lord. Moses said to his brother Aaron: Take my place among my people, do right, and do not follow the wrongdoers' way.

7:143. When Moses came at the appointed time and his Lord spoke to him, he said: My Lord, show Yourself to me so that I may look upon you. The Lord said: You cannot see Me but look at the mountain. If it remains firm in its place, you will be able to see Me. But when his Lord appeared on the mountain, it crumbled and Moses fell down unconscious. When he recovered, he said: Glory be to You, I repent, and I am the first of the believers.

7:144. God said: O Moses, I have chosen you over mankind to spread the message I have given you and the words I have spoken to you. So take what I have given you and be grateful.

7:145. We wrote instructions and explanations for all things on the tablets for him, and said: Hold these firmly and order your people to follow to the best of them. I shall show you the ruined home of the wicked for you to learn from their examples.

7:146. I shall turn them away from My signs who behave arrogantly on the earth in defiance of right. Even if they see all the signs, they will not believe in them; and if they see the way of the right conduct, they will not adopt it. But if they see the way of error, they will adopt it. That is because they have rejected Our signs, and failed to take warning from them.

7:147. The deeds of those who denied Our signs and the meeting of the hereafter have become worthless. Will they not be rewarded for what they used to do?

7:148. In his absence, the people of Moses made from their ornaments an image of a calf with a hollow sound. Did they not see that it could neither speak to them nor guide them? They took it for worship and did wrong.

7:149. When regret overcame them and they saw that they had gone off the right path, they said: If our Lord does not have mercy upon us and forgive us, we surely shall be losers.

7:150. When Moses came back to his people, angry and grieved, he said: You have done evil in my absence. Did you make haste to bring on your Lord's judgment? He put down the tablets, caught his brother by the hairs of his head, and pulled him towards himself. Aaron said: My mother's son, the people overpowered me and almost killed me. Let not my enemies rejoice over my misfortune, and do not consider me amongst the sinners.

7:151. Moses said: My Lord, forgive my brother and me and admit us into Your mercy, for You are the most merciful.

7:152. Those who worshipped the calf will get God's anger and humiliation in this life. Thus, We punish those who invent lies.

7:153. For those who committed bad deeds, then repented and believed, will find their Lord forgiving and merciful.

7:154. When Moses' anger subsided, he took up the tablets. In their writing was guidance and mercy for those who fear their Lord.

7:155. Moses chose 70 people for Our meeting. When earthquake shook them, he said: My Lord, if You had willed, You could have destroyed us earlier. Would You destroy us for what the foolish among us have done? This is Your trial to send off the right path whom You will and guide whom You will. You are our protector, so forgive us and have mercy upon us. You are the best forgiver.

7:156. Grant us what is good in this world and the hereafter. We have returned to You. God said: My punishment is for whom I will, but My mercy extends to all things. I, God, will show mercy to those who stay away from evil, give charity and believe in Our verses.

7:157. The mercy is for those who follow the unschooled Prophet Muhammad, who is mentioned in the Torah and the Gospel, and he enjoins upon them what is right, and forbids them what is wrong. He makes good things lawful for them and prohibits the bad ones. He relieves them of their burdens and frees them from their shackles. Those who believe in him, honor, and help him, and follow the light that has been sent down with him will be successful.

7:158. Say: O mankind, I have been sent to you as the Messenger of God, Who has The kingdom of the heavens and earth. There is no god but Him. He gives life and death. Therefore, believe in God and His Messenger, who cannot read or write, but believes in God and His word. Follow him so you may be guided.

7:159. Among the people of Moses, some were guided by truth and established justice.

7:160. We divided them into twelve 12 tribes. When his people asked Moses for drinking water, We told him to strike the rock with his stick. Twelve 12 springs gushed from it and each tribe knew its drinking place. We provided them shade with clouds and sent down upon them manna* and quails*, saying: Eat the good things We have provided for you. By doing what they did afterwards, they did Us no wrong, but wronged themselves.

**Manna is the miraculous food God provided to the Israelites in the wilderness. Quail is a small, migratory game bird.*

7:161. Remember when it was said to them: Live in this city, eat whatever you like, pray for forgiveness, and enter the gate bowing humbly. We will forgive your sins and increase the reward of the righteous.

7:162. But the wrongdoers among them changed the words of what they have been told. So We, God, sent upon them a punishment from the sky for their wrongdoing.

7:163. Ask them about the town by the sea* and what happened to its people when they broke God's commands on Saturday. The fish came to them floating on water each Saturday/Sabbath, but not on other days. Thus We tried them with temptation because they were defiantly disobedient.

**Eylat on the Red Sea.*

7:164. When some asked the others: Why do you warn a people whom God will destroy with a severe punishment? They replied: To be free from blame before Lord and perhaps they may guard themselves against evil.

7:165. When they disregarded the given warnings, We saved those who forbade evil but punished the wrongdoers because they were defiantly disobeying.

7:166. When they revoltingly persisted in what they had been forbidden, We changed them into hated monkeys.

7:167. Remember when your Lord declared that, until the Day of Resurrection, He would send against them those who would punish them severely. Your Lord is quick in punishing, but is forgiving and merciful.

7:168. We, God, dispersed them into nations throughout the earth. Some of them were righteous and some were not. We tested them with good and bad times, perhaps they would return from their wrongdoing.

7:169. Their successors inherited the Scriptures and took the pleasures of this life saying: We shall be forgiven for our sins. If similar things were to come their way, they will take them again. Was not the promise of the Scriptures, which they had studied, taken from them that they would not say untruths about God? Surely, the home of the hereafter is better for those who fear God. Why do not you understand?

7:170. The reward of those who follow the Scriptures and establish prayer will not be lost.

7:171. Remember when We, God, raised the mountain over them as a canopy and they thought that it was going to fall on them. We said: Hold firmly to what We have given you, the Torah, and remember what is in it, so that you may fear God and obey Him.

7:172. Remember when your Lord created descendants from the offspring of Adam's children and made them testify against themselves saying: Am I not your Lord? They said: Yes, we testify that You are. He, God, did this, lest you would say on the Day of Resurrection that we were unaware of that.

7:173. Or you would say: Our forefathers were idolaters; but will You destroy us, their descendants, for what the wrongdoers did?

7:174. Thus We, God, explain the verses in detail, so that they return to the right path.

7:175. O Muhammad, tell them the story of the person whom we gave knowledge of Our signs, but he turned away from them; how Satan pursued him and he was led off the right path.

7:176. If We, God, had willed, We could have raised his rank with Our signs, but he preferred the earthly life and followed his desires. He is like the dog that pants whether you chase it away or leave it alone. That is the example of the people who denied Our signs. So tell them these stories that perhaps they may give thought.

7:177. Dreadful is the example of those who reject Our signs and wrong their own souls.

7:178. Whom God guides is rightly guided; and whom He sends off the right path is the loser.

7:179. We have created many jinns and humans for hell. They have hearts with which they do not understand, eyes with which they do not see, and ears with which they do not hear. They are like livestock, but more off the right path. They pay no attention.

7:180. God has the most beautiful names. Call Him by them. Keep away from those who use profanity in His names. They will be punished for what they do.

7:181. Among those whom We, God, have created are some who guide by truth and establish justice.

7:182. Slowly, We will destroy those who deny Our verses but they do not know.

7:183. I will give them time, but My plan is firm.

7:184. Have they never thought that their companion Muhammad is not a madman, but he clearly warns?

7:185. Do not they consider The kingdom of the heavens and earth, all that God has created, and the end of their lives may be near? After this, in what signs would they believe in?

7:186. No one can guide those whom God leads off the right path. He leaves them wandering aimlessly.

7:187. O Muhammad, they ask you about the arrival of the Day of Resurrection. Say: God only has its knowledge. He will reveal it at the proper time. It will be heavy upon the heavens and the earth and will come unexpectedly. They ask you as if you are familiar with it. Say: Its knowledge is only with God, but most of the people do not know.

7:188. O Muhammad, say: I have no power of benefitting or averting harm from myself except what God has willed. Had I known the unseen, I could have acquired much wealth, and no harm would have come to me. I only warn and give good news to those who believe.

7:189. It is God Who created mankind from a single soul, and then its mate so that you may enjoy the pleasure of living with her. When you had sexual intercourse with her, she became pregnant and carried the child for a while when it was light. When it became heavy, you both prayed to God saying: If You, God, give us a good child, we shall be grateful.

7:190. When He gave them a good child, they associated other partners with Him for what He gave them. God is above their idols.

7:191. Do they worship idols who cannot create anything, but are created themselves?

7:192. The idols can help neither them nor themselves.

7:193. If Prophet Muhammad invite the idol-worshippers to guidance, they will not follow you. It is the same whether you invite them or keep quite.

7:194. The idols you call beside God are His servants like you. Call on them and let them answer you, if you are truthful.

7:195. Do they have feet to walk, hands to strike, eyes to see, or ears to hear? O Muhammad say: Call on your false gods to conspire against me and give me no relief.

7:196. God is My protector. He has sent down the Qur'an and is an ally of the righteous.

7:197. Those you call upon besides Him are unable to help neither them nor you.

7:198. If you invite them to guidance, they do not hear you. They appear to be looking at you but they cannot see you.

7:199. O Prophet, show forgiveness, tell what is right, and avoid the ignorant.

7:200. If Satan tempts you, seek refuge in God. He hears and knows all.

7:201. Those who fear God, when tempted by Satan, remember Him and see the right path.

7:202. The Satan's evil brothers shall keep them in error and shall not let go.

7:203. O Prophet, if you do not bring them a revelation, they say: Why have you not created it? Say: I follow only what my Lord reveals to me. This book, the Qur'an, is a clear proof from your Lord for guidance and a blessing for the believers.

7:204. When The Qur'an is recited, listen to it with attention so that you may receive God's mercy.

7:205. O Prophet, remember your Lord in your heart with humility and respect without speaking loudly. Remember Him in the mornings and evenings, and do not be negligent.

7:206. The angels, who are near to your Lord, are not too proud to worship Him, praise Him, and bow down before Him.

# CHAPTER 8

# THE SPOILS OF WAR

**Name:** From Verse One.

**Verses:** 75

**Background:**

The chapter was revealed after the first battle between Muslims and the disbelievers at Badr. It:

- Reviews the battle.
- States principles of war and peace for training of Muslims.

This chapter tells that God would give a great victory to Muslims, and their enemies' property and possessions would fall into their hands.

**Summary:**

- Nature and distribution of war-spoils.
- Why God ordained the Battle of Badr?
- Why and how the Muslims won the battle?
- What should be the Muslims' aim of war; how should they prepare for and fight it?
- Lesson for the unbelievers, hypocrites, Jews, and the prisoners of this war.
- Why and when God changes His blessings?
- Sanctity of treaties.
- Treatment of the prisoners.
- Muslims should have cordial relations with one another for success against their enemies.
- Duties and obligations of the Islamic State towards Muslims living in non-Muslim countries.

## By Verse

In the name of God, the compassionate, the merciful:

8:1. The believers ask Prophet Muhammad about war-spoils. Say: The spoils belong to God and the Messenger. So fear God and keep relations between yourselves straight. Obey God and His Messenger, if you are true believers.

8:2. The true believers are those whose hearts feel fear when God is mentioned; their faith is increased when His verses are recited to them; and they rely upon their Lord;

8:3. who establish regular prayers and spend from what We have provided them.

8:4. Such are true believers. God will raise their ranks, forgive their sins, and provide generously for their living.

8:5. Your Lord brought you, the believers, out of your homes to fight at Badr for justice, when some believers were unwilling.

8:6. They argued with Prophet Muhammad about the truth after it had been made clear, as if they were being driven to certain death.

8:7. Remember when God promised that you will be victorious over one of the two groups, the Meccan trade caravan or the army. You wished to fight the unarmed caravan. But God intended to establish the truth by His words and to eliminate the disbelievers;

8:8. so that truth should triumph and the falsehood be proven false, though it may be unpleasant to the guilty.

8:9. Remember when you, the believers, requested your Lord's help. He answered you saying: I will assist you with 1,000 angels rank upon rank.

8:10. By giving you good news, God assured your hearts. Help only comes from God. He is powerful and wise.

8:11. Remember when sleep overcame you as a security from Him. He caused rain to fall on you to clean you and purify you from the Satan's filth, strengthen your hearts, and make your feet firm.

8:12. Remember when your Lord inspired the angels saying: I am with you; give courage to the believers; I will put fear into the disbelievers' hearts; strike off their necks, and hit their joints.

8:13. That is because they have opposed God and His Messenger. Whoever opposes God and His Messenger shall be punished severely.

8:14. We said to the disbelievers: Taste the punishment. The hellfire is the disbelievers' punishment.

8:15. Believers, when you meet the disbelievers in battle, do not turn your backs to them.

8:16. On the day of the battle, whoever will turn his back to the disbelievers, unless it is for tactical reasons or to join another company of his own, will incur God's anger and live in hell, which is an evil destination.

8:17. You believers did not kill the disbelievers, God did. It was not you O Muhammad, who threw dust towards the enemy, but God threw it to reward the believers with a great favor from Himself. Indeed,

God hears and knows all.
8:18. That is a gift for you, and God will weaken the disbelievers' plot.
8:19. If you, the disbelievers:

- Sought the decision between you and the Muslims, the decision of defeat has come to you.
- Stop hostilities, it will be best for you.
- Return to war against the faithful, We shall return to assist them. Your forces may be large in number, but will avail you nothing because God is with the believers.

8:20. Believers, obey God and His Messenger. Do not turn away from him when he speaks.
8:21. Do not be like those who say that they have heard, but pay no attention.
8:22. The worst beasts in God's sight are people who are deaf, dumb, and have no sense.
8:23. Had God known any good in them, He would have made them hear. But if He had made them hear, they would still have turned away and refused to listen.
8:24. Believers, obey God and the Messenger when he calls you to that which gives you life. Know that God comes between a man and his heart and you will be gathered before Him.
8:25. Guard yourselves against a suffering which will not fall exclusively on the wrongdoers. Know that God is severe in punishment.
8:26. Remember when you were a few, were persecuted in the land, and feared that your enemies might overpower you. But God sheltered you, strengthened you with His help, and provided you with good things so that you might be grateful.
8:27. Believers, do not betray God and His Messenger, and your trust knowingly.
8:28. Know that your possessions and children are a test and God's reward is great.
8:29. Believers, if you fear God, He will guide you, remove your sins, and forgive you. God's generosity is great.
8:30. Remember O Muhammad, when the disbelievers plotted against you to keep you captive, kill you, or evict you. They planned, but God planned too. God is the best planner.
8:31. When Our verses are read to them, they say: We have heard them. If we disbelievers wanted, we could invent verses like these. These are old stories.

8:32. When they said: O God, if this is the truth from You, then rain down stones from the sky upon us or bring us a painful punishment.

8:33. But God would neither punish them while you O Muhammad were among them, nor punish them while they could seek forgiveness.

8:34. But why should God not punish them while they keep out people from the sacred mosque at Mecca and they are not its legitimate guardians. Its only guardians are the righteous, but most of the disbelievers do not understand.

8:35. Their prayers at the sacred mosque are nothing but whistling and handclapping.
Therefore, they shall be punished for their disbelief.

8:36. Those who disbelieve, spend their wealth to keep people away from God's way.
They will keep on spending, but they will regret it and in the end will be overcome. Those who disbelieve shall be gathered into hell.

8:37. God will separate the wicked from the righteous, place the wicked one upon another and heap them into hell. It is those who are the losers.

8:38. O Prophet, tell the disbelievers that if they reform, their past will be forgiven. But if they persist in sin, let them know the fate of their forefathers.

8:39. O believers, fight the disbelievers till there is no more oppression, and faith in God is established. If they stop oppression, God sees all that they do.

8:40. If the disbelievers pay no attention, then know that God is your protector. He is the best protector and the helper.

8:41. Know that a fifth from the war-spoils is for God, the Messenger, his relatives, orphans, needy, and travelers. That is if you believe in God and what We revealed to Our servant on the day of the victory, when the two armies met. God has power over all things.

8:42. Remember when you were on the near side of the valley, the enemy was on the farther side, and its caravan was on the lower ground than you towards the sea shore. If you had fixed an appointed time to fight, you would have missed it. But God wanted to accomplish what He had already decided; that whoever had to die should perish with a clear sign and whoever deserved to live, should live with a clear sign. God hears and knows everything.

8:43. God showed the enemy to you, the believers, in your dream as few in number. Had He shown them to you as many, you would have been discouraged and there would have been dispute among the believers about whether to fight or not, but God saved you from that. Indeed, God knows what is within the hearts.

8:44. When you met the enemy, He made them appear to you small in number, so that He might accomplish what He had already decided. All matters return to God for decision.

8:45. Believers, when you meet an enemy force, stand firm, and pray to God more that you may be successful.

8:46. Obey God and His Messenger, and do not dispute with one another, lest you lose heart and your strength. Be patient. God is with the patient.

8:47. Do not be like those who came by leaving their homes boastfully, to be seen by people, and to prevent others from God's way. God knows all about what they do.

8:48. Satan made their deeds pleasing to the disbelievers and said: No one can conquer you today; I am your protector. But when the two armies sighted each other, he turned on his heels and said: I am not with you, because I can see what you cannot. I fear God. God is severe in punishment.

8:49. The hypocrites and those with diseased hearts said: The believers' religion has deceived them. But whoever relies upon God will find that God is mighty and wise.

8:50. If you could see the angels taking the disbelievers' souls, striking their faces and backs, saying: Taste the punishment of the hellfire.

8:51. That is your punishment for what your hands earned. Otherwise, God is not unjust to His servants.

8:52. Like Pharaoh's people and those before them, they disbelieved in God's verses. Therefore, God destroyed them because of their faults. God is mighty and severe in punishment.

8:53. God does not change favors which He bestowed upon a people until they change what is in their hearts. God hears and knows all.

8:54. Like Pharaoh's people and those before them, they disbelieved God's signs. Therefore, God destroyed them because of their faults as We drowned Pharaoh's people. All were evildoers.

8:55. The worst creatures in God's sight are the faithless who will not believe;

8:56. they are those with whom you made a treaty; but they break it time after time, and have no fear of God.

8:57. If you meet them in a battle, scatter them utterly to strike fear in their followers, so that they may learn a lesson.

8:58. If you fear treachery from any group, withdraw from that treaty in a just way. God does not like the treacherous.

8:59. Let not the disbelievers think that they have won. They will never be able to save themselves from God's punishment.

8:60. Prepare against them with your full power, including the war horses, for striking terror in the enemies of God and yours, and others beside them whom you do not know, but God does. Whatever you, the believers, spend in God's cause will be repaid to you, and you will not be wronged.

8:61. If the enemy shows willingness for peace, you should also do so by relying upon God. Indeed, He hears all and knows all.

8:62. If the enemy intends to deceive you, God is sufficient for you. He has supported you with His help and rallied the believers around you.

8:63. God reconciled the believers' hearts. If you had spent all the riches on the earth, you could not have brought their hearts together; but God brought them together. Indeed, He is mighty and wise.

8:64. O Prophet, God is sufficient for you and your believing followers.

8:65. O Prophet, urge the believers to fight. In future, your 20 steadfast men will overcome 200 disbelievers, and your 100 steadfast men will overcome 1,000 disbelievers, because they do not understand.

8:66. For the present, God has lightened the believers' burden for He knows that you are weak. Now, your 100 steadfast men will overcome 200 of the enemy and 1,000 will overcome 2,000 by permission of God. God is with the steadfast.

8:67. It is not fit for a prophet that he should take prisoners unless he has fought and triumphed in the land. You, the believers, desire the worldly gain*, but God desires for you the gain in the hereafter. God is mighty and wise.

**The Meccans fled at the end of the battle of Badr. The Muslims, instead of chasing the enemy to surrender, started taking prisoners and collecting the war-spoils.*

8:68. Had it not been for an earlier ordinance from God allowing taking war-spoils and prisoners, you would have been severely punished.

8:69. Enjoy the good and lawful war-spoils you have gotten and fear God. He is the forgiving and merciful.

8:70. O Prophet, say to the prisoners you have taken: If God finds goodness in your hearts, He will give you something better than what has been taken from you, and He will forgive your sins. God is forgiving and merciful.

8:71. If they intend to betray you, know that they already have betrayed God. That is why He gave you victory over them. God is the all-knowing and the wise.

8:72. Those who believed and emigrated, and fought with their wealth and life in God's cause, and those who gave them shelter and help, are allies of one another. But for those who believed and did not emigrate, you have no responsibility for their protection until they emigrate. If they seek your help for the religion, you must help them, except against a people with whom you have a treaty. God sees what you do.

8:73. The disbelievers help one another. If believers do not do the same, there will be great mischief and corruption on the earth.

8:74. Those who have believed and emigrated and fought in God's cause and those who gave them shelter and help are true believers. They shall receive forgiveness and a great reward.

8:75. Those who believed afterwards and emigrated (from Mecca to Medina)* and fought the enemy with you, they too are your people. But, according to the book of God, those with blood relationship are only entitled to inheritance. Indeed, God has knowledge of all things.

**The emigrants and their host families thought they will share their properties as inheritance. This verse clarified that the inheritance was only for the blood relations.*

# CHAPTER 9

# THE REPENTANCE

**Name:** From Verse 104.

**Verses:** 129

**Summary:**

- Theme: Issues of war and peace based on the Tabuk Expedition. Prophet Muhammad travelled towards Syria with 30,000 fighters to fight with the Romans and their allies. Arriving at Tabuk, the Prophet learnt that the enemy had withdrawn its troops from the frontier and there was no enemy to fight with. The Muslims won a victory without a fight that increased Islam's prestige.
- Topics:
    1. Preparations for the Tabuk campaign.
    2. Dealings with those who did not participate in the Tabuk campaign.
    3. Declaration of the new policy towards the disbelievers.
- Obligations and breaking of treaties.
- Urging the Muslims to fight in God's cause and its reward.
- Warning to the disbelievers, and prohibiting them from taking care of the mosques and entering the sacred mosque at Mecca.
- Islamic months and their sacredness.
- Hypocrites' characteristics, categories, and punishment, including not offering their funeral prayer.
- Collection and distribution of Zakat (mandatory charity).
- Exemptions from the battlefront and God's forgiveness.
- Guidance to the believers: Prefer prophet's life over your own, obtain understanding of the religion, fight the disbelievers, and be aware that God is with the pious, and the Qur'an ic verses increase faith.
- The Prophet's character: Gentle, compassionate, well-wisher, and trusts God.

**By Verse**

This chapter does not begin with the verse: In the name of God, the compassionate, the merciful. Commentators have differed about the reasons. Looks like, Prophet Muhammad forgot to dictate it at the beginning of the chapter.

9:1. This is a declaration of treaty annulment from God and His Messenger that the believers have made with the idolaters.

9:2. O disbelievers, for four more months* you can travel freely in the land, but know that you cannot frustrate God's will and He will disgrace you.

**Starting from the date of declaration on the 10th day of Dhul-Hijjah (the Islamic calendar's 12th month), in the 9th year of the Islamic calendar.*

9:3. This is God and His Messenger's announcement to all on the day of the greater pilgrimage* that God and His Messenger are free from the treaty obligations to idolaters. If the idolaters repent, it will be better for you; but if you do not, know that you cannot frustrate God's will. O Muhammad, declare a painful punishment to the disbelievers;

**The yearly pilgrimage to the grand mosque at Mecca is on the 10th day of the Islamic lunar calendar's 12th month, Dhul-Hijjah. The pilgrimage on the 10th Dhul-Hijjah is called greater pilgrimage and on other days is called smaller pilgrimage.*

9:4. except for the idolaters with whom you have made a treaty, which they have honored and have not helped your enemies against you. Fulfill the treaty with them for its term. God loves the righteous.

9:5. When the declared four months have passed, kill the idolaters* wherever you find them, capture them, besiege them, and ambush them everywhere. But if they repent, establish prayer, and give Zakat (mandatory charity), let them go their way. God is forgiving and merciful.

**who has broken treaties with the believers, and has started hostilities.*

9:6. If an idolater seeks your protection, give it to him so that he may hear God's words, and then escort him to safety. Idolaters are ignorant.

9:7. How can God and His Messenger trust idolaters, except those with whom you made a treaty at the sacred mosque at Mecca? As long as they remain true to you, you should deal with them fairly. God loves righteous.

9:8. How can you trust other idolaters? If they overpower you, they will respect neither kinship nor treaty. They please you with their words, but their hearts are against you. Most of them are defiantly disobedient.

9:9. They have traded God's verses for a meager worldly gain and hinder others from His way. They do evil.

9:10. They do not care for any ties of kinship or respect for a treaty made with the believers. They go beyond the limits.

9:11. If they repent, establish prayer, and give Zakat (mandatory charity), they will become your brothers in religion. We explain the verses for those who understand.

9:12. If they breach their oaths after coming to terms with you and assault your religion, fight with the leaders of disbelief. They have no regard for their oaths, and your fighting with them might restrain them.

9:13. Will you not fight with those who broke their oaths, plotted to expel the Messenger, and attacked you first? Do you fear them? It is God that you should fear, if you are believers.

9:14. Fight the disbelievers. God will punish them with your hands, disgrace them, give you victory over them, and heal the hurt feelings of the believers.

9:15. God will remove anger from the believers' hearts. He shows mercy to whom He pleases. God is all-knowing and all-wise.

9:16. Do you think that you will be abandoned as if God does not know who strive for His cause and take no friends other than God, His Messenger, and believers? God is aware of what you do.

9:17. It is not for idolaters to maintain God's mosques as they are the self-confessed disbelievers. Their deeds have become worthless, and they will live in the hellfire forever.

9:18. God's mosques are only to be maintained by those who believe in God, the last day, establish prayer, give Zakat (mandatory charity), and fear none other than God. They shall be rightly guided.

9:19. Do you consider the providing of drinking water to the pilgrims and maintenance of the sacred mosque are as worthy as believing in God and the last day, and striving in God's cause? They are not equal before God. He does not guide the wrongdoers.

9:20. Those who have believed, left their homes, and striven with their wealth and lives in God's way, are in His higher regard. They are successful.

9:21. Their Lord gives them good news of His mercy, approval, and gardens for them where there will be joys forever.

9:22. They will live there forever. Indeed, God has a lot for reward.

9:23. Believers, do not befriend your fathers or brothers if they have preferred disbelief over belief. Doing so is wrong.

9:24. O Prophet tell them: If your fathers, sons, brothers, wives, relatives, your acquired property, the merchandise you fear may not be sold, and the homes you like, are dearer to you than God, His cause, and the Messenger, then wait till God fulfils His command. God does not guide the wrongdoers.

9:25. God has given you victory on many battlefields. In the battle of Hunain*, you rejoiced at your great numbers, but it availed you nothing; and earth, vast as it is, seemed to close in on you and you turned your backs and fled.

**Hunain is between Mecca and Taif.*

9:26. God sent His tranquility on His Messenger and the believers, and also sent the invisible angel-soldiers to punish the disbelievers. Such is the disbelievers' reward.

9:27. Even after that, God will accept repentance from whom He wills. He is the forgiving and merciful.

9:28. Believers, the idolaters are unclean. Do not allow them to come near the sacred mosque after this year of their pilgrimage. If you fear poverty from the loss of their merchandise, God, if He pleases, will enrich you from His bounty. God is all-knowing and all-wise.

9:29. Fight with those people of the Scriptures, Jews and Christians, who do not believe in God or the last day, consider unlawful what God and His Messenger have made unlawful, and do not adopt the religion of truth, until they give the protection-tax* willingly for being subdued.

**the tax will protect them and allow them to practice their religion.*

9:30. The Jews say Ezra is God's son, while the Christians say the Messiah is God's son. By saying these words they repeat only what the earlier disbelievers used to say. God's curse is on them. How willfully misled they are?

9:31. The Jews worship their rabbis, and Christians their monks and the Messiah, the son of Mary, as gods beside God, when they were ordered to worship one God only. There is no God except Him. He is above their gods.

9:32. They would extinguish God's light with their mouths, but God will not allow it. He would perfect His light, though the disbelievers hate it.

9:33. It is God who has sent His Messenger with guidance and the religion of truth to make it prevail over all religions, though the idolaters dislike it.

9:34. Believers, many priests and monks defraud people of their wealth and prevent them from God's way. Give news of a painful punishment to those who hoard gold and silver and do not spend them in God's way.

9:35. The day will come when their wealth will be heated in the hellfire and their foreheads, sides, and backs will be branded with it saying: This is what you hoarded for yourselves, so taste the punishment for it.

9:36. When God created the heavens and earth, He decreed the months to be 12. Four months are sacred* according to the true faith. So do not wrong yourselves by violating them. However, if the disbelievers fight against you in these months, you may fight with them. Know that God is with the righteous.

**of the Islamic (lunar) calendar: the 1st month (Muharram), the 7th (Rajab), the 11th (Dhul-Qadah) and the 12th (Dhul-Hijjah).*

9:37. The postponement of the sacred months is grossly wrong*, in doing that the disbelievers are misguided. They allow it one year and disallow it the next year to correspond to the number made lawful by God. By doing so, they make lawful what God has forbidden. Their evil deeds seem pleasing to them. God does not guide the disbelievers.

**Year to year, the disbelievers changed the sacred months to serve their needs. For example, for taking revenge from an enemy, they used to change the sacred month to a non-sacred month and vice versa, for keeping the number of the sacred months same. Sometimes, they increased the yearly months to 13 for the Hajj to fall in the same season.*

9:38. Believers, what is the matter with you that when you are asked to march in God's cause, you move lazily? Do you prefer this worldly life to the hereafter? This life compared to the hereafter has few blessings.

9:39. If you do not march out to fight, God will punish you with a grievous penalty. He will replace you with others. In no way, you will harm Him, for God has power over all things.

9:40. If you do not help the Prophet, God will help him as He did when the disbelievers drove him out of Mecca with one companion (Abu-Bakr, later the first caliph). In the cave, the Prophet said to his companion: Have no fear, God is with us. God sent down His tranquility upon him, strengthened him with invisible forces, and defeated the disbelievers' plan to kill him. But God's plan is always superior. God is the mighty and wise.

9:41. Whether light or heavy*, march on and fight for God's cause, with your wealth and lives. That is best for you, if you only knew.

**Light or heavy has multiple meanings: Unarmed or well-equipped; healthy, young, and wealthy or ill, old, and poor; willingly or unwillingly; and in favorable or unfavorable circumstances.*

9:42. If there had been an immediate gain and the journey short*, the hypocrites would have followed you O Prophet, but the distance appeared too long to them. Yet they would swear by God: If we only could, we would have accompanied you. They destroy their own souls. God knows that they are lying.

**Medina to Tabuk for fighting with the Romans.*

9:43. God forgives you O Muhammad. Why did you give the hypocrites permission to remain behind before you knew who were truthful and who were the liars?

9:44. Those who believe in God and the last day would not ask you to excuse them from fighting with their wealth and lives. God knows best who do their duty.

9:45. Only those ask for exemption who do not believe in God and the last day and their hearts have doubt. They hesitate in their doubt.

9:46. If they had intended to accompany you, they would have prepared for it. But God disliked their accompanying you and kept them back, by telling them to remain with those who stayed behind.

9:47. Had they gone with you, they would not have added to your strength, but had caused confusion by actively sowing discord among your ranks. There are those among you who would have listened to them. God knows the wrongdoers.

9:48. Earlier, they sowed dissension, and plotted against you, until the truth came, and God prevailed, though they disliked it.

9:49. There are many among them who say: Permit us to remain behind and do not put us to trial. Unquestionably, they are in trial already. The hellfire will surround disbelievers.

9:50. If you have good fortune, it distresses them. If you have misfortune, they say: We took our precautions; and turn away rejoicing.

9:51. Say: Nothing will happen to us except what God has decreed for us. He is our protector. In God, let the believers put their trust.

9:52. Say: Are you expecting for us a fate other than that of martyrdom or victory? For you, we are expecting God's direct punishment or by our hands. So wait, we too are waiting.

9:53. Say: Whether you spend willingly or unwillingly in God's cause, it will not be accepted, for you are defiantly disobedient people.

9:54. The only reasons for their contributions not to be accepted are: They reject God and His Messenger; come to prayer without earnestness; and offer contributions unwillingly.

9:55. Let not their wealth or children impress you. God intends to punish them through these in this life, so that they shall die disbelievers.

9:56. They swear by God that they are believers like you, but they are not. They are afraid of you.

9:57. If they could find a shelter, a cave, or a hiding place, they would run to it in a hurry.

9:58. There are some among them who criticize you concerning charity distribution. If they are given a part from it, they approve; but if they are not given, they become angry.

9:59. It would have been better for them if they had been satisfied with what God and His Messenger gave them and said: God is sufficient for us; God will give us from His bounty, so will His Messenger; and to God we submit.

9:60. The charitable donations shall be used only for the poor, needy, debtors, collectors of charity, converts to Islam, freeing slaves, God's cause, and traveler. This is an obligation decided by God. God is all-knowing and all-wise.

9:61 And there are some among them who hurt the Prophet and say: He believes everything he hears. Say: He hears what is good for you, believes in God, trusts the faithful, and is a blessing for believers among you. God shall punish those severely who hurt His Messenger.

9:62. They swear in God's name to please you, the believers. But it is more fitting that they should please God and His Messenger, if they are believers.

9:63. Do the believers not know that whoever opposes God and His Messenger will live in the hellfire forever? That is the great disgrace.

9:64. The hypocrites are afraid that a chapter of the Qur'an may be revealed about them, telling what is in their hearts. Say: Keep on mocking, but God will surely bring out what you are afraid of.

9:65. If you ask the hypocrites, they will say: We were only talking and joking. Say: Was it God, His verses, and His Messenger that you were joking about?

9:66. Make no excuses. You have rejected faith after accepting it. We may pardon some of you; but We will punish others, for they are guilty of committing evil.

9:67. The hypocritical men and women are all alike. They impose evil, forbid good, and withhold their hands from charity. They have left God and God has left them. Surely, the hypocrites are sinners.

9:68. God has promised the hypocrites, both men and women, and the disbelievers the hellfire. They will live there forever as a suitable repayment. God has cursed them for a lasting punishment.

9:69. You, the hypocrites, are like the disbelievers before you. They were mightier than you, and had more wealth and children. They had their enjoyment as you have yours. Like them, you indulged in idle talk. Their works were fruitless in this world and shall be useless in the hereafter. They will be losers.

9:70. Have they not heard the stories of those before them: the people of Noah, Aad, Thamoud, and Abraham, and that of the Midians*, and the ruined cities? Their Messengers came to them with clear proofs. God did not wrong them, but they wronged themselves.

**lived in the northwest Arabian Peninsula, on the east shore of the Gulf of Aqaba on the Red Sea*

9:71. The believing men and women are allies of one another. They urge what is right, forbid what is wrong, establish prayer, give Zakat (mandatory charity), and obey God and His Messenger. God will have mercy upon them. God is mighty and wise.

9:72. God has promised the believing men and women gardens, watered by running streams, for living there forever. There will be beautiful mansions in the gardens. In addition, they would have God's grace upon them, a great success.

9:73. O Prophet, fight against the disbelievers and the hypocrites, and be firm with them. They shall live in hell, an evil destination.

9:74. They swear by God that they said nothing evil, but they uttered lies after accepting Islam. They planned to do what they could not do*. God and His Messenger had enriched them with the bounty, but their response was an evil plan. If they repent, it will be best for them. But if they return to their evil ways, God will punish them with a grievous penalty in this life and the hereafter.

They shall have no one to protect or help them on the earth.

**Kill Prophet Muhammad.*

9:75. Some of them made a promise with God, saying: If He would make us rich; we will spend in charity, and be among the righteous.

9:76. But when God gave them from His bounty, they became miserly, turned away from their promise, and refused to fulfill the promise.

9:77. Because the hypocrites broke their promise with God and lied, God penalized them with hypocrisy in their hearts until the day they will meet Him.

9:78. Do they not know that God knows their secrets and private conversations and the unseen?

9:79. God will ridicule those who criticize the believers for giving charity freely and the ones who find nothing for giving charity except their effort. The criticizers will have a painful punishment.

9:80. It does not matter whether O Muhammad, you ask forgiveness for the hypocrites or not. Even if you ask forgiveness for them 70 times, God will not forgive them, because they have disbelieved in God and His Messenger. God does not guide the defiantly disobedient people.

9:81. Those who remained behind from the Tabuk expedition rejoiced that God's Messenger left them behind, because they disliked to strive in God's cause with their wealth and lives. They said: Do not go to war in the fierce heat. Say to them: The hellfire is hotter. If only they could understand.

9:82. Let them laugh a little, but they will weep a lot in return for their evil deeds.

9:83 If God brings you Prophet Muhammad back in safety and a party of the hypocrites asks your permission to march with you, say: You shall neither march with me, nor fight an enemy with me. You decided to stay behind on the first occasion, therefore, now stay with those who remained behind.

9:84. O Muhammad, neither offer funeral prayer nor attend the hypocrites' burials. They disbelieved in God and His Messenger and they died as evildoers.

9:85. Let not their wealth and children impress you. God intends to punish them thereby in this life and they shall die as disbelievers.

9:86. When a chapter was revealed saying: Believe in God and join His Messenger in fighting the enemy, the wealthy among them asked your permission to stay back saying: Leave us with those who are to stay behind.

9:87. They preferred to be with those who stayed behind. A seal was set on their hearts to deprive them of understanding.

9:88. But the Messenger and those who believed with him fought with their wealth and lives. They shall be rewarded with good things and be successful.

9:89. God has prepared for them gardens, watered by running streams, to live there forever. That is the great achievement.

9:90. Some Desert-Arabs came with excuses begging to stay behind; while those who lied to God and His Messenger sat at home. The disbelievers among them will be severely punished.

9:91. There is no blame on those who are weak or ill or find no resources to contribute to the fighting, as long as they are sincere and true to God and His Messenger. There can be no ground for complaint against those who do good works. God is forgiving and merciful.

9:92. Nor there is blame upon those who came to you asking for battle-horses to ride, and you said: I cannot find anything for you to ride upon. They turned back with eyes overflowing with tears of grief that they could not take part in the battle.

9:93. The cause of disapproval is only against those who ask your permission while they are wealthy. They are satisfied to be with those who stay behind. God has sealed their hearts to deprive them of understanding.

9:94. When you return, the hypocrites will present their excuses to you. Say to them: Make no excuses, we shall not believe you. God has already revealed the truth to us about you. God and His Messenger are seeing your deeds. In the end, you will be brought back to God Who knows the seen and unseen, and He will tell you about what you used to do.

9:95. When you return, they will request your pardon in God's name. So leave them alone, they are evil. Their living place will be hell as a punishment for their evil deeds.

9:96. The hypocrites will swear to you to please you. But if you will accept their excuses, certainly, God will not be pleased with such rebellious people.

9:97. The Desert-Arabs are the worst in disbelief and hypocrisy, and more likely will remain ignorant of what God has revealed to His Messenger. God is all-knowing and all-wise.

9:98. Some Desert-Arabs consider their payments in God's cause or charity as a fine, and watch for some misfortune to befall you. But ill-fortune may befall them. God hears and knows all.

9:99. But some of the Desert-Arabs believe in God and the last day, and consider their payments as gifts for bringing them nearer to God and obtaining the Messenger's prayers. Yes, indeed, these bring them nearer to God; soon God will admit them to His mercy. God is forgiving and merciful.

9:100. God is pleased with those who led the way among the Muhadjirs*, the Ansar**, and who followed them with good conduct, and they are pleased with Him. He has prepared for them gardens, watered by running streams, wherein they will live forever. That is the great achievement.

**The Muhadjirs were the Meccans who left for Medina to avoid persecution of the Meccan-disbelievers.*

***The Ansar were supporters of the Muhadjirs living in Medina.*

9:101. Some of the Desert-Arabs around you and some citizens of Medina are hypocrites, who have become adamant in hypocrisy. You do not know them, but We do. We shall punish them twice, and in addition, a grievous penalty shall be sent upon them.

9:102. There are others, who have acknowledged their wrong-doings. They have a mixed record of their good and bad deeds. Perhaps God will forgive them. He is the forgiving and merciful.

9:103. O Prophet, take charity from them to clean and purify them, and pray for them. Your prayers will comfort them. God hears and knows all.

9:104. Do they not know that it is God who accepts repentance from His servants, receives charities, and is forgiving and merciful?

9:105. Tell them: Do as you will; God, His Messenger, and the believers will watch over your deeds, then you will return to Him Who knows both the visible and invisible, and He will tell you of what you did.

9:106. There are others who await God's decision. He will either punish them or forgive them. God is all-knowing and all-wise.

9:107. And there are those hypocrites who built a mosque to cause harm by spreading disbelief and disunity among the believers, and by preparing an outpost for him* who earlier made war against God and His Messenger. They will certainly swear of their good intentions, but God bears witness that they are liars.

**Abu Amir, a Christian. His religious business was affected by Prophet Muhammad's arrival at Medina. He schemed with the enemies of Islam for its destruction.*

9:108. Do not pray in that mosque. A mosque founded on righteousness from the first day is more worthy for you to pray in. In it, you will find men who love to purify themselves. God loves those who purify themselves.

9:109. Who is better between the one who founded his building upon duty to God and His good pleasure, and the one who founded his building on the brink of a crumbling, overhanging cliff, so that it will topple with him into the hellfire? God does not guide the wrongdoers.

9:110. The building they have built will continue to be a source of skepticism in their hearts until their hearts are cut into pieces. God is all-knowing and all-wise.

9:111. God has purchased from believers their lives and properties. In exchange, they will have paradise. They fight in God's cause; kill and are killed. It is a true binding promise which He has made in the Torah, the Gospel, and the Qur'an. And who is more truthful to his promise than God? So rejoice in your bargain you have made with God. That is the great achievement.

9:112. Those believers are rewarded who repent to God, worship Him, praise Him, travel in His cause, bow down in prayer, urge what is right, forbid what is wrong, and observe the limits set by God. So give the good news to these believers.

9:113. It is not for Prophet Muhammad and the believers to ask forgiveness for the idolaters, even if they are relatives, after it has become clear to them that they are the hellfire's companions.

9:114. Prophet Abraham prayed for his father's forgiveness only because of a promise he had made to him. But when it became clear to him that he was God's enemy, he dissociated himself from him. Abraham was most tender-hearted and compassionate.

9:115. God would not let a people off the right path after He has guided them until He makes clear to them what they should avoid. God knows all things.

9:116. God is the king of the heavens and the earth. He gives life and death. You have no protector or helper beside God.

9:117. God has certainly turned with mercy to Prophet Muhammad, the emigrants (Muhadjirs), and the locals of Madinah (Ansar), who followed him in the hour of difficulty (of the Tabuk expedition), when some of them were losing heart. He forgave them. Indeed, He was kind and merciful to them.

9:118. He also forgave the three* who were left behind. They felt so bad that the earth, despite its vastness, and their souls appeared to close on them. They were certain that there was no refuge from God except in Him. Therefore, He turned to them with mercy so they could repent. God is the acceptor of repentance and is the merciful.

**Kaab bin Malik, Hilal bin Umayyah, and Murarah bin Ar-Rabi were believers, but failed to join the Tabuk expedition without any excuse.*

9:119. Believers, fear God and be with those who are truthful.

9:120. It was not proper for the People of Medina and the surrounding Desert-Arabs to remain behind after the departure of God's Messenger for battle, and to prefer themselves over him. If they bear thirst or fatigue or hunger in God's cause, or tread on any ground enraging disbelievers, or hurt an enemy, then it is not possible that such of their deeds are not written down as righteous actions for them. God will not allow the loss of reward for the good-doers.

9:121. Whatever they spend, small or large, or each journey they make in God's cause, shall be registered for them, so that God may reward them for their best deeds.

9:122. It is not required that all believers go to battle. Some people from each community should leave their community to study the religion, and, upon return, warn their people to guard against evil.

9:123. Believers, fight the disbelievers who live around you. Deal firmly with them. Know that God is with those who fear Him.

9:124. Whenever a chapter of the Qur'an is revealed some hypocrites ask Muslims: Whose faith it increases? It surely increases the faith of believers and gives them joy.

9:125. As for those whose hearts are diseased, it will increase their disbelief, and they will die as disbelievers.

9:126. Do they not see that they are tried once or twice with a calamity every year? But they neither repent nor pay attention.

9:127. Whenever a chapter of the Qur'an is revealed, they glance at one another asking: Is anyone watching? Then they turn away. God has turned away their hearts because they do not understand.

9:128. A Messenger has come to you from among you. He grieves over your sinfulness, is concerned about you, and is kind and merciful to the believers.

9:129. If they pay no attention to you O Muhammad, say: God is sufficient for me; there is no god beside Him; I have put my trust in Him; and He is the Lord of the great throne.

# CHAPTER 10

## JONAH

**Name:** From Verse 98.

**Verses:** 109

**Summary:**

- Theme: Invitation to God's message, and admonition and warning to the disbelievers.
- The Qur'an's characteristics as the book of wisdom, mercy, blessing, cure for problems of mankind, and God's revelation. Its disbelievers shall be losers in the hereafter.
- God's:
    - Oneness and the proofs and misunderstandings about the life-after-death.
    - Signs in the creation of the universe, including the heaven, earth, sun, moon, day, and night.
- The doubts and objections about Muhammad's Prophethood.
- Test of the worldly life. God watches what humans do.
- Comparison of God and idols.
- The wrongdoers' behavior of inventing different creeds. Calling upon God when suffering but plotting against Him when comfortable. Following conjecture and preaching falsehood.
- Stories of Prophets Noah, Moses, and their people.
- Invitation to the disbelievers to believe for their good and disbelieve at their own peril.
- Forcing someone to convert to Islam is prohibited.

**By Verse**

In the name of God, the compassionate, the merciful:

10:1. Alif, Lam, Ra (are Arabic letters). These are verses of the book of wisdom, the Qur'an.

10:2. Why is it a surprise to people that We, God, have revealed to a man among them that he should warn people, and give good news to the believers that their good deeds will be rewarded by their Lord? The disbelievers say: This man is clearly a magician.

10:3. Your Lord is God who created the heavens and earth in six days, then sat over His throne, and began governing everything. There is no one that can intervene with Him without His permission. Such is God, your Lord, so worship Him. Will you not pay attention?

10:4. You all shall return to Him; that is God's true promise. He created you in the first place, and in the end will bring you back to life, so that He may justly reward the believers who did good deeds. But the disbelievers will drink boiling water and be punished severely, because they disbelieved.

10:5. It is He who gave the sun its brightness and the moon its light and phases so that you may calculate years and dates from it. God did not create all these without a serious truthful purpose. He explains His signs to those who understand.

10:6. For the god-fearing people, there are signs in succession of the day and the night, and what God has created in the heavens and on earth.

10:7. There are those who:

- do not expect to meet God;
- are pleased and content with the worldly life; and
- are paying no attention to Our signs.

10:8. They shall live in hellfire because of their bad deeds.

10:9. As for those who believe and do good deeds, their Lord will guide them because of their faith. Streams will flow at their feet in the gardens of delight in paradise.

10:10. There, their prayer will be: Glory to You, O God; and greeting will be: Peace. In the end, they will say: Praise be to God, the Lord of the universe.

10:11. If the Lord had punished them in proportion to their deep involvement in the worldly affairs, their time would have been up a long time ago. I, God, let those, who do not believe in their meeting with Me, wander blindly in their excesses.

10:12. When a misfortune befalls a man, he calls on God, whether lying on his side, sitting, or standing. But when We take away his troubles, he behaves as though he had never called on Us for help. In the same way, the sinners' behavior seems fair and justified to them.

10:13. We destroyed generations before you when they did wrong. Their Messengers brought them clear signs, but they never believed. That is how We punish evildoers.

10:14. Then, We made you their successors in the land, to see how you would perform.

10:15. When Our clear signs are recited to those who do not expect to meet Us, they say: Bring another Qur'an or change it. Prophet Muhammad, say: It is not for me to change it on my own. I only follow what is revealed to me. Was I to disobey my Lord, I fear the punishment of a dreadful day.

10:16. Say: If God had willed, neither I would have recited it to you, nor He would have brought it to your knowledge. I have lived a lifetime among you before the Qur'an was revealed to me. Will you not then understand?

10:17. Who could be more wicked than the one who invents lies against God or denies His revelations? The sinners will never prosper.

10:18. They worship others than God who neither can benefit nor harm them. They say: These are our mediators with God. Say: Do you want to inform God of things in the heavens and on earth He does not know? Glory is to God, who is above their idols.

10:19. People were once a community of one faith, but they differed. If it had been that God postponed their punishment, their differences would have been resolved.

10:20. The disbelievers say: Why no sign has been sent down to Prophet Muhammad from his Lord? Say: Only God knows the unseen; so wait, as I am waiting.

10:21. When We let people taste mercy after hardship has visited them, they start plotting against our revelations. Say: God is swifter at plotting. Our angels are recording your plots.

10:22. It is God who enables you to travel on the land and sea. You board ships, which sail in a favorable wind and you rejoice; then comes a stormy wind and the waves come to you from all sides, and you fear that you will die. You pray to God sincerely saying: If You save us from this, we shall truly be grateful.

10:23. Yet, when He has saved you, you rebel on earth wrongfully. O mankind, your rebellion is only against yourself. Enjoy this life, but you will return to Us in the end, and We, God, shall show you what you used to do.

10:24. The example of the worldly life is like rain which We send down from the sky to be absorbed by the plants on earth that humans and animals eat. When the earth takes its adoring shape and looks beautiful and its inhabitants expect a rich harvest, Our punishment comes by the night or the day, making the land a wasteland, even though it was flourishing the day before. That is the way We, God, clarify the revelations to the thoughtful men.

10:25. God invites you to the home of peace, paradise, and guides whoever He wills to a straight path.

10:26. Those who do good deeds shall be rewarded immensely. Neither darkness nor shame will cover their faces. They will live in paradise forever.

10:27. For those who earned evil shall be punished for it. They will be covered with shame, and no one will protect them from God. Their faces shall be covered as though with patches of the black dark night. They will live in hell forever.

10:28. The day, We, God, shall gather them all together, We shall say to the idolaters: Take your stand with the idols you worshipped. We shall then separate them from one another, and the idols will say to them: You did not worship us.

10:29. God is our sufficient witness; we were not aware of your worship.

10:30. Then, every soul will realize what it did. They will be returned to God, their rightful Lord, and the idols they invented will desert them.

10:31. Prophet Muhammad, ask them: Who:

- provides for you from the sky and earth?
- controls the hearing and the sight?
- brings out the living from the dead and the dead from the living?
- governs everything?

They are sure to say: God. Then say: So why do you not pay attention to Him?

10:32. That is God, your true Lord. What is there other than the truth but falsehood? How then can you turn away from Him?

10:33. Your Lord's verdict will be confirmed against those who rebel, because they do not believe.

10:34. Ask them: Can any of your idols originate creation, and then repeat it? Say: It is God that originates creation, and then repeats it. So how can you be misled?

10:35. Ask: Can any of your idols guide you to truth? Say: God can guide you to truth. Then who has more right to be followed, one who guides you to truth, or the one who cannot guide unless he is guided? What is the matter with you that you cannot judge?

10:36. Most of them follow nothing but mere conjecture, which can be of no value against truth. God is well aware of what they do.

10:37. This Qur'an could not have been formulated by anyone other than God. It confirms what was revealed before it and explains the Scriptures. Let there be no doubt that it is from the Lord of the universe.

10:38. If they say: You, Prophet Muhammad, have forged the Qur'an; say: Then produce a chapter like it. Call on your idols to help you, if you are telling truth.

10:39. In fact, they are denying what they cannot understand, and whose explanation has not yet come to them. Likewise, those before them denied. But see what the wrongdoers' fate was.

10:40. Some of them believe in it and some do not. But your Lord knows the wrongdoers.

10:41. If they do not believe you, say: My deeds are mine and your deeds are yours. Neither one of us is responsible for the other.

10:42. Some of them listen to you Prophet Muhammad. But, can you make the deaf hear you when they are incapable of understanding?

10:43. Some of them look at you. But, can you guide the blind when they cannot see?

10:44. God does not wrong people; they wrong themselves.

10:45. The day God will gather them together, it will appear to them as if they had lived in the world but an hour of a day. They will recognize each other. Surely, those who deny meeting with God will be lost, and not find the way.

10:46. Whether We let Prophet Muhammad see some of the punishment We have threatened the disbelievers with, or cause you to die before that, they will return to Us. God is witness to what they do.

10:47. A Messenger is sent to every community. When its Messenger comes, they are judged justly and are not wronged.

10:48. They ask: When will this promise be fulfilled, if what you say is true?

10:49. Say: I do not have the power to benefit or avoid harm for myself, except as God wills. There is an appointed term for every community, and when it arrives, they can neither delay nor hasten it, even for a moment.

10:50. Say: Tell me, if His punishment were to come to you during the night or the day, what part of it would the guilty like to hasten?

10:51. Will you believe it when it comes to pass? Indeed, you will believe it then. How impatient you were to hasten it.

10:52. It will be said to the evildoers: Taste the lasting punishment. What else did you expect to earn for your evil deeds?

10:53. They ask you Prophet Muhammad if what you say is true. Say to them: Yes, by my Lord it is true, and you cannot escape it.

10:54. If every soul that has sinned possessed all that is on earth, it would gladly offer it to ransom itself, and feel repentant on seeing the punishment. Yet, the sentence would be passed justly, and no one will be wronged.

10:55. Everything in the heavens and on earth belongs to God. His promise is true, but most people do not realize it.

10:56. It is God who gives life and death, and you all will return to Him.

10:57. People, a warning from your Lord has come to you, a healing for what is in your hearts, and a guidance and mercy for the believers.

10:58. Say: Let them rejoice in God's grace and mercy, which are better than the worldly riches they accumulate.

10:59. Say: Have you, the humans, considered the provisions God has sent down for you, some of which you have made unlawful and some lawful? Ask: Has God given you permission to do that, or are you inventing lies about God?

10:60. What will those, who invent lies about God, think on the Day of Resurrection? God is gracious towards people, but most of them do not give thanks.

10:61. We are witnessing whatever you are engaged in, including whatever portion of the Qur'an you are reciting, and whatever you are doing. Not even the weight of a speck of dust on earth or in the sky escapes your Lord. Everything, smaller or greater, is recorded in a clear book.

10:62. The God's servants have nothing to fear and to grieve about.

10:63. Those who believe and obey God,

10:64. for them are good news in this life and in the life to come. There can be no change in God's words. That is the greatest success.

10:65. Do not let the disbelievers' words grieve you O Prophet. Honor belongs entirely to God. He hears all and knows all.

10:66. Know that all creatures in the heavens and on earth belong to God. Those, who worship others beside God, follow nothing but their assumptions and falsehoods.

10:67. It is He who made for you the night to rest and the daylight to see. There truly are signs in this for those who think.

10:68. The disbelievers say: God has fathered a son. Glory is to Him, He is self-sufficient. Everything in the heavens and on earth belongs to Him. You have no authority to say this. How dare you say things about God without any knowledge?

10:69. Say O Prophet: Those who invent lies about God will not prosper.

10:70. After enjoyment in this world, they will return to Us and will be severely punished for their disbelief.

10:71. Tell them Noah's story, who said to his people: If my presence among you and reminding you of God's revelations are too hard for you to bear, I put my trust in God. You and your associates should agree on the action against me, without being secretive about it, and carry it out without any delay.

10:72. Do not turn away from me. I have not asked for any reward from you. My reward is from God alone. I have been ordered to devote myself to Him.

10:73. But they rejected him. We saved Noah and those with him on the boat and let them survive the flood. We drowned those who denied Our revelations. See the fate of those who were forewarned.

10:74. After that, We sent Messengers to their people, and they brought them clear signs, but they were never going to believe in something they had previously denied. That is how We seal the hearts of those who overstep the limits.

10:75. Then We sent Moses and Aaron with Our signs to Pharaoh and his chiefs, but they acted arrogantly. They were wicked people.

10:76. When Our truth came to them, they said: This is plain magic.

10:77. Moses said: Do you call the truth magic? Magicians are never successful.

10:78. They said: Have you come to turn us away from our forefathers' faith, so that you two can rule this land? We will never believe in you.

10:79. Then Pharaoh said to his chiefs: Bring me every expert magician.

10:80. When the magicians arrived, Moses said to them: Cast your

spell.
10:81. When they had cast their spell, Moses said: What you have cast is only magic which God will surely nullify. God does not approve evildoers' deeds.
10:82. He will uphold the truth with His words, even if the evildoers may hate it.
10:83. And none of Pharaoh's people believed in Moses save some youth, because they feared that Pharaoh and his chiefs would punish them. Pharaoh was a cruel ruler in the land, exceeding all limits of evil.
10:84. Moses said: My people, if you have faith in God and are devoted to Him, put your trust in Him.
10:85. They said: We have put our trust in God. Our Lord, do not make us a target of these wrongdoing people.
10:86. Save us by Your mercy from the disbelievers.
10:87. We revealed to Moses and his brother to live in Egypt with their people, to make
their houses places of worship, to establish regular prayers, and to give good news to the believers.
10:88. And Moses said: Lord, You have given Pharaoh and his chiefs splendor and wealth in this life and they are leading others away from Your path. Lord, destroy their wealth and harden their hearts so that they do not believe until they see the agonizing punishment.
10:89. God said: Your prayers are accepted. Stay on the right course, and do not follow the path of the ignorant.
10:90. We took Israel's children across the sea. Pharaoh and his army pursued them in arrogance and aggression. But as Pharaoh was drowning, he cried: I believe there is no God except the one Israel's children believe in. I submit to Him.
10:91. God said to Pharaoh: Now you believe, but earlier, you were a disbeliever and a wrongdoer.
10:92. We shall preserve your dead body so that you may become a lesson for those who come after you; as most people do not pay attention to Our signs.
10:93. We settled Israel's children in a blessed land and provided them with good things. They did not differ until knowledge was given to them. Your Lord will settle their differences on the Day of Resurrection.
10:94. If you, the readers of the Qur'an, are in doubt about what We have revealed to you, ask those who have been reading the

Scriptures before you. The truth has come to you from your Lord, so do not doubt it.

10:95. Do not be among those who deny God's signs, or you will be among the losers.

10:96. Those against whom your Lord's verdict of punishment has been confirmed will not believe.

10:97. They will not believe even if every sign comes to them, until they see the agonizing punishment.

10:98. Had they believed, they would have benefited from it. Only Jonah's people believed, and when they did, We relieved them from the punishment of disgrace in this life, and let them enjoy life for a time.

10:99. Had your Lord willed, all people on earth would have believed. So can you O Prophet compel people to believe?

10:100. No soul can believe except by God's will, and He brings disgrace on those who do not use their brains.

10:101. Say to them: Look at what is in the heavens and on earth. But signs and warnings are of no use to those who will not believe.

10:102. Are they waiting for the fateful punishment that came to those before them? Say: Wait then, I am waiting too.

10:103. We shall save Our Messengers and believers. We have made it binding upon Ourself to save the believers.

10:104. O Prophet say: People, if you have doubt about my faith, then know that I do not worship your idols; I worship God, who will make you die. I am commanded to be a believer.

10:105. I have been commanded to dedicate myself to the faith uprightly and not be among idolaters.

10:106. Do not pray to idols which can neither benefit nor harm you. If you do, you will be among the evildoers.

10:107. If God harms you; no one can save you from it but Him. If He gives you something good, no one can take it away from you. He grants His reward to anyone He wills. He is the most forgiving and merciful.

10:108. O Muhammad say to people: The truth has come to you from your Lord. Whoever follows the right path follows it for his own good, and whoever goes off does so for his own loss. I am not your guardian.

10:109. O Prophet, follow what is revealed to you, and be steadfast until God decides. He is the best decision maker.

# CHAPTER 11

## HOUD – HUD

Name: From Verse 50-60.

Verses: 123

Summary:

- Theme: The same as of Chapter 10, Jonah – invitation to God's message, advice, and firm warning.
    - Invitation: Obey God's Messenger, Prophet Muhammad, discard idol worship, worship God alone, and live the worldly life on the belief that there shall be a life in the hereafter, which will be based on deeds in the worldly life.
    - Advice: Do not follow the people who put their faith in enjoyment of this worldly life, rejected the Prophets' message, and met destruction.
    - Warning: Do not depend upon the delay in the coming of God's punishment, because God is giving you more time to mend your ways. If you will not, God will punish you severely except believers.
- For achieving the theme's objectives, the Qur'an has used the stories of the people of Prophets Noah, Houd, Saleh, Lot, Shuaib and Moses for drawing the disbelievers' attention. The prominent in their stories is that when God punishes the wrongdoing people, He does not even spare the Prophets' relatives. The faith demands to disregard the relationships of blood and race; and it was demonstrated by the Muslims in the Battle of Badr by fighting with their disbelieving relatives and friends from Mecca.
- Prophet Muhammad did not forge the Qur'an's teachings.
- God is the sustainer of all creatures, but most are ungrateful except believers. Virtues remove evils. God does not waste the reward of righteous. God has given freedom of choice to mankind.
- Some Jews and Christians have seen truth, but not all. Differences arose about the Torah for Jews' lack of belief.
- Address of:
    - Prophet Noah to his people and their response. God's command to Noah to build the boat and to gather on board the believers and a pair each from all species. Dialogue

between Noah and his son, and between Noah and God regarding his son.
    - Prophets Houd, Saleh, Lot, and Shuaib to their people, their disbelief, and its consequences.

- Good news for Prophet Abraham of having a son and a grandson.
- The fate of Pharaoh and his associates.

**By Verse**

In the name of God, the compassionate, the merciful:

11:1. ALR (Alif, Lam, Ra are Arabic letters). The Qur'an is a book whose verses have been perfected and explained in detail by God who is wise and all-knowing.

11:2. Do not worship anyone except God. God has sent me, Prophet Muhammad, to warn you and give good news.

11:3. Ask forgiveness from your Lord and repent to Him. He will let you enjoy the worldly life for a period and reward the righteous. But if you turn away, I fear for you the punishment of a fateful day.

11:4. You shall all return to God. God has power over all things.

11:5. The disbelievers cover up their chests to hide their thoughts from God. But even when they cover themselves with garments, He knows what they conceal and reveal. He knows the innermost secrets of their hearts.

11:6. There is no creature on earth whose livelihood is not provided by God. He knows its places of dwelling and storage. All is recorded in a clear book.

11:7. God's throne was upon water, and He created the heavens and earth in six days to test you for who is noble in conduct. When you, Prophet Muhammad, say: After death you will be brought to life; the disbelievers say: This is nothing but clear magic.

11:8. And if We hold back their punishment for a stated period, they ask: Why is it delayed? The day it will come to them, it shall not be turned away, and it shall surround them as they used to ridicule it.

11:9. If We give man a taste of Our mercy and then withdraw it, he despairs and becomes ungrateful.

11:10. If We give him a taste of favor after hardship, he says: Bad times have left me. He feels joyful and boastful.

11:11. Except those who are patient and do good deeds; they shall have forgiveness and a great reward.

11:12. So the disbelievers vainly hope that you, Prophet Muhammad, may omit, by chance, some part of what has been revealed to you and your heart feels heavy for it because they say: Why has not a treasure been sent for him or an angel come with him? But you are only a warner. God is custodian of all things.

11:13. If they say: You, Prophet Muhammad, has invented the Qur'an. Say to them: Then invent 10 chapters like it and call upon your idols for assistance, if what you say is true.

11:14. But if your idols do not answer you, then know that it is revealed by God's knowledge and that there is no god but Him. Will you then submit to God?

11:15. Those, who desire the worldly life and its attractions, will be rewarded for their deeds here and they will not be deprived of anything.

11:16. For them, there is nothing in the hereafter but fire; their deeds are fruitless and works are useless.

11:17. Are they comparable to those that have received a clear proof from their Lord, recited by a witness from Him, and preceded by the book of Moses (the Torah), a guide and a mercy? They believe in it; but those who deny it will be put to the hellfire. So do not doubt it. It is the truth from your Lord, but most men do not believe.

11:18. Who is more unjust than he who invents a lie about God? Men like him will be presented before their Lord, and the witnesses will say: These are the ones who lied against their Lord. Unquestionably, God's curse is upon the wrongdoers;

11:19. who prevent others from God's way, would like to make it crooked, and disbelieve in the hereafter.

11:20. They shall not escape in this life and there is no one to protect them beside God. Their punishment will be doubled, for they would neither hear the truth from others nor see it themselves.

11:21. They have lost their souls, and what they forged is gone from them.

11:22. Certainly, the wrongdoers will be the greatest losers in the hereafter.

11:23. Those who have believed, do good deeds, and humble themselves before their Lord, will live in paradise forever.

11:24. Can the blind and deaf be compared to those that can see and hear? Will you not then pay attention?

11:25. We sent Noah to his people, who said to them: I have come to you with a clear warning.

11:26. Do not worship anyone but God. I fear for you the punishment of a painful day.

11:27. The chiefs of the disbelievers among his people said: We consider you but a man like ourselves, we see the lowest among us following you without thinking, you are not better than us, in fact, we think you are lying.

11:28. Noah said to his people: If I have a clear sign from my Lord and He has given me His mercy which is hidden from you, can I force it upon you while you are against it?

11:29. O my people, I do not ask you to believe for giving me any wealth for it. My reward is only from God. I will not drive away the believers who will meet their Lord. But I see that you are ignorant.

11:30. O my people, if I drove away the believers, who would protect me from God? Will you not pay attention?

11:31. I, Noah, do not tell you that I have God's treasures, know the unseen, am an angel, and I do not say about those whom you look down upon that God will never grant them any good. By saying so, I would be among the wrongdoers. God knows what is in their hearts.

11:32. They said: O Noah, you have argued with us for too long. So bring down upon us the punishment you have been threatening us with, if you are truthful.

11:33. Noah replied: Only God will bring the punishment upon you when He will like, and you will not be able to escape from it.

11:34. I wish to advise you, but my advice will not benefit you if God intends to mislead you. He is your Lord, and to Him you will return.

11:35. If they say O Muhammad: Have you invented Noah's story? Reply to them: If I have invented it, I will be punished for my guilt; but I am not responsible for what you commit.

11:36. God revealed to Noah: No more of your people will believe you except those who have already believed. So do not be distressed by their misdeeds.

11:37. Build a boat under Our eyes and according to Our revelation, and do not plead with Me for the wrongdoers; they shall be drowned.

11:38. Noah started building the boat. Whenever the chiefs of his people passed by the boat, they ridiculed him. He said: Ridicule us if you will, a time will come when we will ridicule you.

11:39. You will know who will get a disgraceful and everlasting punishment.

11:40. At last, Our order came and water gushed from the earth. We said to Noah: Load the boat with two of each kind, a male and a female, your family, except the already declared disbelievers, and load the believers. But only a few were believers.

11:41. Noah said: Board the boat in God's name Who will be its sailor and anchor. My Lord is forgiving and merciful.

11:42. The boat floated on the mountainous waves, and Noah called to his son who was at a distance: O my son, come aboard with us and do not be with the disbelievers.

11:43. The son replied: I will go to a mountain that will save me from the water. Noah said: This day no one will be saved from God's punishment except upon whom will be His mercy. And a wave came between them and the son drowned.

11:44. God ordered the earth to swallow its water and the sky to stop its rain. The flood subsided, God's punishment was completed, the boat came to rest on the mountain of Judi, and it was said: The wrongdoers are gone.

11:45. Noah cried to his Lord and said: My Lord, my son is of my family, please save him. However, Your promise is true, and You are the most just judge.

11:46. God said: O Noah, your son is not of your family; his conduct is evil. Do not ask Me about which you have no knowledge. I advise you against being ignorant.

11:47. Noah said: My Lord, forgive me asking for something about which I have no knowledge. Unless You forgive me and have mercy upon me, I will be among the losers.

11:48. God said to Noah: Come down from the boat in peace with Our blessings upon you and those with you. To others, We will grant enjoyment in the worldly life, but in the end will punish them severely.

11:49. What We have revealed to you, O Muhammad, is ancient history, which neither you nor your people knew. Be patient, the end will be joyful for the righteous.

11:50. To Aad, We sent their brother Houd. He said to them: O my people! worship God; you have no god but Him; you have invented other false gods.

11:51. O my people, I do not ask you any reward for it. My reward is only from God who created me. Will you not pay attention?

11:52. O my people, ask forgiveness of your Lord and repent to Him. He will send rain from the sky and increase your strength. Do not turn away from Him being wrongdoers.

11:53. They said: O Houd, you have not brought us any clear evidence; we will not leave our gods on your word; and we will not believe you.

11:54. It appears that some of our gods have possessed you with madness. He replied: I call God and you to witness that I have nothing to do with your idol-gods.

11:55. You are welcome to plot against me and grant me no respite.

11:56. I have put my trust in God who is your and my Lord. There is not a creature whose destiny God does not control. My Lord's path is straight.

11:57. If you turn away, I have conveyed the message for which I was sent to you. My Lord will replace you with others. You cannot harm Him. He is watching over all things.

11:58. When Our order came, We saved Houd and those who believed with him by Our mercy. We saved them from a harsh punishment.

11:59. Such were Aad. They rejected their Lord's revelations, disobeyed His Messengers, and followed the command of every wicked leader.

11:60. They were cursed in this world and will also be cursed on the Day of Resurrection. Aad denied their Lord. Gone are the Aad, the people of Houd.

11:61. And to Thamoud, We sent their brother Saleh. He said: O my people, worship God, you have no other god but Him. He made you from the earth and settled you on it. Ask for His forgiveness and repent to Him. My Lord is near and responds to prayers.

11:62. They said: O Saleh, before this you were a man of promise among us. Do you forbid us to worship what our forefathers worshipped? We have strong doubt about the faith you are inviting us to.

11:63. He said: O my people, have you considered that if I have clear evidence from my Lord and He has bestowed His mercy upon me, who would protect me from God if I disobeyed Him? You certainly would ruin me.

11:64. O my people, this is God's she-camel as a sign to you. Let her graze freely on God's earth, do not harm her, or you will be swiftly punished.

11:65. They killed the she-camel. So Saleh said to them: Enjoy yourselves in your houses for three days. Then promise of the punishment will be fulfilled.

11:66. When Our order of punishment came, We saved Saleh and the believers with him from the disgrace of that day with Our mercy. Your Lord is powerful and mighty.

11:67. A mighty explosion struck the wrongdoers, and killed them in their homes before morning.

11:68. As if they had never lived there. Thamoud disbelieved their Lord. So they were discarded.
11:69. Our Messengers came to Abraham with good news. They said to him: Peace be upon you. He answered: Peace be upon you also. Then he hastened to entertain them with a roasted calf.
11:70. When he saw that they did not touch the roasted calf, he found it strange on their part and was afraid of them. They said: Do not be afraid; we have been sent to Lot's people.
11:71. Upon that, his wife who was standing there, was also struck with awe. We gave her good news of giving birth to Isaac, who will have a son, Jacob.
11:72. She was astonished and said: Shall I bear a child while I am an old woman, and my husband is old too? This is surely a strange thing.
11:73. They said: Are you amazed at God's command? May God's mercy and blessings be upon you, O people of this house. Indeed, He is praiseworthy and glorious.
11:74. When fear left Abraham and he heard the good news, he started pleading with Us for Lot's people.
11:75. Abraham was a gracious, compassionate, and kind-hearted person.
11:76. The angels said to Abraham: Please stop pleading. God has ordered a punishment for them, which cannot be stopped.
11:77. When Our Messengers came to Lot, he was worried about them as he lacked strength to protect them. He said: This is an awful day.
11:78. His people, who were used to doing bad sexual acts, rushed to him. He said: O my people, these are my daughters, more lawful for you to marry. So fear God and do not disgrace me concerning my guests. Is there not a thoughtful man among you?
11:79. They said: You know we have no need of your daughters. You certainly know what we want.
11:80. He said: I wish that I had the strength to overpower you or take refuge with some powerful man.
11:81. The angels said: O Lot, we are your Lord's Messengers. Your enemies will not be able to touch you. Leave with your family, except your wife, during the remaining portion of the night, and no one should look back. Your wife will be punished with others. They will be punished in the morning. Is not the morning near?
11:82. When Our order came, We destroyed their town by raining upon them the stones of baked clay, layer upon layer.
11:83. Your Lord targeted every stone. God's punishment is never far from the wrongdoers.
11:84. To the Midian* people, We sent their brother Shuaib. He said: O

my people worship God; you have no god other than Him. Do not give short measure and weight. I see you are prosperous, but I fear that a punishment will surround you on an awful day.

**they lived in the northwest Arabian Peninsula, on the east shore of the Gulf of Aqaba on the Red Sea.*

11:85. O my people, give full measure and weight in fairness, do not defraud people of their possessions, and do not spread mischief on earth.

11:86. God's reward is best for you, if you are believers. I am not your guardian.

11:87. They said: O Shuaib, does your prayer command you that we should not worship what our forefathers worshipped, or not use our property as we please? Indeed, you are a gracious wise man.

11:88. He said: O my people, have you considered that if I have clear orders from my Lord and He has provided me with good livelihood, should I not guide you? I do not do what I forbid you to do. I only intend to reform you as much as I can. God will help me. I rely upon Him and look to Him for forgiveness.

11:89. O my people! Let your differences with me not cause you to suffer a fate similar to that of the people of Prophets Noah, Houd, and Saleh. Not long ago, Lot's people were punished.

11:90. Ask your Lord's forgiveness and repent to Him. My Lord is merciful and loving.

11:91. They replied: O Shuaib, we do not understand much of what you say. We consider you weak. If it was not for your tribe, we would have stoned you to death. You shall not be able to prevail upon us.

11:92. He said: O my people, you consider my tribe more powerful than God? You have turned away from Him. My Lord watches all that you do.

11:93. My people, do whatever you will, and so will I. Soon, you will know who will be punished disgracefully and who is a liar. You wait; I am waiting too.

11:94. When God's order came, We saved Shuaib and the believers with him by Our mercy. A mighty blast hit the wrongdoers, and they died in their homes.

11:95. As if they had never lived there. Like the Thamoud, the Midians* were cast away.

**they lived in the northwest Arabian Peninsula, on the east shore of the Gulf of Aqaba on the Red Sea*

11:96. We sent Moses with Our signs and a clear authority,

11:97. to Pharaoh and his chiefs. But they followed Pharaoh's wrong orders.
11:98. Pharaoh will lead his people on the Day of Judgment to the hellfire; which is a dreadful place to be led into.
11:99. A curse has fallen on Pharaoh's people in this world and will also fall on them on the Day of Resurrection. They will be given a wretched gift.
11:100. We have given you an account of the fate of the towns and their people; some of which survived and others were destroyed.
11:101. We did not wrong the disbelievers, they wronged themselves. When the order of your Lord came, their false gods did not benefit them. Rather they increased their ruin.
11:102. Such is the punishment of your Lord when He punishes the sinful people. His punishment is painful and severe.
11:103. In this, surely there is a sign for those who fear the punishment of the hereafter. That day, the mankind will be gathered for witnessing everyone's fate.
11:104. We shall defer the Day of Judgment to an appointed time.
11:105. The day it comes, no person will speak except by God's permission. Some will be doomed, others blessed.
11:106. The doomed ones will be put in the hellfire. There, they will groan and wail.
11:107. They will live there as long as the heavens and earth will endure, unless Your Lord decides otherwise. Your Lord does what He pleases.
11:108. The blessed ones will live in paradise as long as the heavens and earth will endure, unless your Lord will decide otherwise. Their reward will be endless.
11:109. O Muhammad, have no doubt about what the disbelievers worship. They worship what their forefathers worshipped before them. We shall punish them in full.
11:110. We gave Moses the Torah, but his people disagreed about it. Had your Lord not deferred their punishment, their fate would have been decided long ago. Similarly, the disbelievers doubt the Qur'an.
11:111. Your Lord will compensate all for their deeds. He is aware of what everyone does.
11:112. O Muhammad, as ordered, remain on the right course with your companions who have asked God's forgiveness with you. Do not go away from the right course. God is seeing what you do.
11:113. Do not associate with the wrongdoers, otherwise you will be

punished by the hellfire. You would have no protector and helper other than God.

11:114. Establish prayer morning, evening, and in the early part of the night. Good deeds do away the bad ones. That is a reminder for those who remember.

11:115. Be patient. God does not waste the reward of the righteous.

11:116. Among the generations before you, why persons of good understanding were not there for prohibiting people from doing mischief on the earth except a few whom We saved from harm? The wrongdoers pursued the enjoyment of life's good things and persisted in sin.

11:117. Your Lord would not have destroyed the towns unjustly if their people were righteous.

11:118. If your Lord willed, He could have made mankind one community; but they will not stop to differ.

11:119. Except those on whom your Lord has shown mercy and for the mercy He created them. But the promise of your Lord to fill hell with jinns and men shall be fulfilled.

11:120. In revealing the Messengers' stories to you, the objective is to make your heart strong. Through these, the truth has come to you, as well as a warning and a reminder for the believers.

11:121. Say to the disbelievers: Do whatever you like, so will we.

11:122. Wait for the result as we are waiting too.

11:123. God knows the secrets of the heavens and the earth, and every affair goes to Him for decision. Worship Him, and put your trust in Him. Your Lord is watching over what you do.

# CHAPTER 12

# JOSEPH

**Name:** Joseph was Prophet Jacob's son, Prophet Isaac's grandson, and Prophet Abraham's great grandson.

**Verses:** 111

**Background:**

Some disbelievers, on the instigation of Jews, asked Prophet Muhammad: Why did Israelites go to Egypt? Jews knew that their story was not known to Arabs. They expected that Prophet Muhammad would not be able to give an answer to the question and would be exposed. But, the tables were turned on them. God revealed the story of Prophet Joseph to Prophet Muhammad and he recited it on the spot.

Prophet Joseph was born around 1906 B. C. He was 17 years old when the story began.

**Summary:**

- Joseph's stepbrothers threw him into a well. A caravan found him, brought him to Egypt, and sold him.
- The wife of the Egyptian, who bought Joseph, tried to seduce him but failed. Joseph was jailed.
- Joseph interpreted the dreams of inmates and the king.
- The king heard Joseph's seduction case, declared him innocent, and appointed him to his cabinet.
- Joseph's brothers came to Egypt to get food and grain. Joseph disclosed his identity. He forgave his brothers and sent for his family.

## By Verse

In the name of God, the compassionate, the merciful:

12:1. ALR (Alif, Lam, Ra are Arabic letters). These are verses of the Qur'an that makes its objective perfectly clear.

12:2. We, God, have revealed the Qur'an in Arabic so that you may understand it.

12:3. In revealing the Qur'an, We tell you, Prophet Muhammad, the historical events in the best manner, about which you do not know.

12:4. This is an event when Joseph said to his father: O father, in my

dream I saw seven stars, the sun and the moon bowing to me.
12:5. The father said: Son, do not tell about your dream to your brothers, lest they will plot against you. Satan is mankind's sworn enemy.
12:6. Your Lord will choose you, teach you the interpretation of dreams, and complete His favor upon you and Jacob's family, as He completed it upon your forefathers, Prophets Abraham and Isaac. Your Lord is all-knowing and all-wise.
12:7. Certainly in the story of Joseph and his brothers are signs for those who look for the truth.
12:8. Joseph's stepbrothers* said to each other: Our father loves Joseph and his brother more than us, though we are more in number. Indeed, our father is clearly mistaken.

**Prophet Jacob had 12 sons from four wives. Prophet Joseph and his younger brother Benjamin were from one wife and other 10 were from other wives.*

12:9. Let us kill Joseph or leave him in a far-off land, so our father's love will only be for us, and after that we will be honorable men.
12:10. One of them said: Do not kill Joseph. If you must do something, throw him into a well. Some caravan will take him out.
12:11. They said to their father: Why do you not trust us with Joseph? Surely, we are his well-wishers.
12:12. Send him with us tomorrow for him to play and enjoy himself. We will take good care of him.
12:13. He said: It saddens me to send him with you; I fear that a wolf would eat him when you are off guard.
12:14. They replied: If a wolf would eat him while we are quite a few, we, indeed, would be losers.
12:15. When they took Joseph with them, they decided to throw him into a well. We told Prophet Joseph: You will tell them about it when they will not know your identity.
12:16. At nightfall, they came weeping to their father.
12:17. They said: Father, we went racing and left Joseph with our possessions. A wolf ate him. But you would not believe us, even if we were truthful.
12:18. They showed him Joseph's shirt deceptively stained with blood. He cried saying: No, you have made up a story. But I shall be patient. God will help me to bear what you have told me.
12:19. There came a caravan, who sent its waterman to the well. He let down his bucket in the well and cried: Good news! Here is a boy! They concealed Joseph in their merchandise. But God knew of what they did.
12:20. They sold him for a few pieces of silver. They did not care much

for him.
12:21. The Egyptian who bought Joseph said to his wife: Treat him nicely. He may prove useful for us, or we may adopt him as a son. Thus, We established Joseph in the land and taught him interpretation of mysteries. God is the master of His affairs, but most people do not know it.
12:22. When Joseph reached maturity, We gave him wisdom and knowledge. Thus we reward the righteous.
12:23. His master's wife tried to seduce him. She closed the doors and said: Come. He replied: God protect me. Your husband, my master, has been kind to me. The wrongdoers never succeed.
12:24. She certainly was determined to seduce him, and he would have been seduced had he not seen his Lord's sign. We warded off evil and immorality from him as he was one of Our chosen servants.
12:25. He raced to the door, and she tore his shirt from the back. They found her husband at the door. She said: Should the person who intended evil for your wife not be imprisoned or severely punished?
12:26. Joseph said: It was she who tried to seduce me. One of her family members testified: If his shirt is torn from the front, she has told the truth, and he is lying.
12:27. If his shirt is torn from the back, he is telling the truth, and she is lying.
12:28. When her husband saw Joseph's shirt torn from the back, he said to her: Indeed, it is your (his wife's) cunning trick.
12:29. O Joseph, forget this mischief. O woman, you ask for forgiveness for your sin. Certainly you have done wrong.
12:30. The women in the city started gossiping: The chief's wife has tried to seduce her servant. She is infatuated in his love. Surely, she is wrong.
12:31. When she heard about their gossip, she sent for them and prepared a banquet for them. She gave each of them a knife, and ordered Joseph to come before them. When they saw him, they were amazed at his beauty, and cut their hands exclaiming: God protect us, he is not a human, but a noble angel.
12:32. She said: That is the one about whom you blamed me. I certainly tried to seduce him, but he refused. If he will not do what I order him, he will be imprisoned and disgraced.
12:33. Joseph said: My Lord, I prefer prison than to what they invite me to. If You will not protect me from their plan, I might yield to them and become sinful.

12:34. His Lord accepted his prayer and protected him from their plan. He hears all and knows all.

12:35. Though the chiefs were convinced of Joseph's innocence, but to preserve their reputation, they preferred to imprison him for a while.

12:36. Two young men came to prison with Joseph. One of them said: In my dream, I pressed grapes. The other said: I dreamed of carrying bread upon my head, which birds were eating. Interpret our dreams for us as we see you a knowledgeable man.

12:37. Joseph replied: Before any food is served to you, based on the knowledge my Lord has taught me, I will interpret your dreams for you. I have abandoned the ways of those who do not believe in God and the life hereafter.

12:38. I, Joseph, follow the religion of my forefathers, Abraham, Isaac, and Jacob. We should never attribute any partners with God. That is God's grace to us and mankind, but most human beings are not grateful.

12:39. Fellow-prisoners! Are many gods better than one God, who is almighty?

12:40. Those you worship besides God are names which you and your fathers have invented, but God has not sanctioned them. God is the only judge. He has commanded that you worship none but Him. That is the right religion, but most people do not know.

12:41. My prison-companions, one of you will serve wine to his master. The other will be crucified, and the birds will peck at his head. That is the interpretation of your dreams.

12:42. Joseph said to the prisoner he knew would be freed: Talk to your master about freeing me. But Satan made him forget that, and Joseph remained in prison several more years.

12:43. One day, the king said: In a dream, I have seen seven lean cows eating seven fat cows, and seven green ears of corn and seven others dry. O nobles, explain to me my vision, if you could interpret visions.

12:44. They said: It appears to be a false dream; but we cannot interpret dreams.

12:45. The prisoner, who had been freed, remembered Joseph after all these years. He said: I will get it interpreted for you. Allow me to go.

12:46 The king said to Joseph: O man of truth, interpret for me the meaning of the seven lean cows eating seven fat cows, and seven green ears of corn and seven others dry, so I could explain it to the

king.
12:47. Joseph said: You will plant for seven consecutive years, but leave corn in its ears, except a little which you can eat.
12:48. Then, there will come seven difficult years which will consume all what you had saved for them, except a little.
12:49. Then, a year of abundant rain will come, in which people will press olives and grapes.
12:50. The king said: Bring him to me. When the Messenger came to Joseph, he said to him: Return to the king and ask him about the women who cut their hands. My Lord knows their plot.
12:51. The king asked the women: What took place when you tried to seduce Joseph? They replied: God forbid, we know no evil about him. The wife of the noble said: Now, the truth has come out. It was I who tried to seduce him, but he has told the truth.
12:52. Joseph said: From this, I would like my master to know that I did not betray him in his absence and that God does not guide the betrayers' plan.
12:53. I do not absolve myself from sin as humans are prone to evil, except to whom God shows His Mercy. My Lord is forgiving and merciful.
12:54. The king said: Bring him to me. I shall appoint him to serve me exclusively. And when the king spoke to Joseph, the king said: You will live with us as honored and trusted.
12:55. Joseph said: Appoint me over the land's storehouses. I shall guard them wisely.
12:56. Thus, We gave power to Joseph to live wherever he willed in the land. We bestow Our mercy to whom We will and do not deny the reward to the virtuous.
12:57. The reward of hereafter is better for those who believe in God and ward off evil.
12:58. Joseph's brothers came and presented themselves to him. He recognized them, but they did not recognize him.
12:59. When he had given them their provisions, he said to them: Bring to me a brother of yours from your father. Do you not see that I give full measure and am the best host?
12:60. If you do not bring him to me, there will be no provisions for you, and you will not come to see me again.
12:61. They replied: We will request our father to let him come with us. We will surely do it.
12:62. Joseph said to his servants: Put their money into their bags so they might find it when they return to their people. Perhaps, they will

come again.

12:63. Upon return, they said to their father: We shall not get any more provisions unless we take our brother with us. So send him with us for us to get more provisions. We will take good care of him.

12:64. He replied: Am I to trust you with him as I earlier entrusted you with his brother? But God is the best guardian, and He is the most merciful of those who show mercy.

12:65. When they opened their bags, they found their money returned to them. They said: Father, what more could we wish for? Our money has been returned to us. We will obtain provisions for our family and take good care of our brother. We shall buy an extra camel-load and that should not be hard to get.

12:66. He said: I will not send him with you until you swear in God's name that you will bring him back to me unless you are overpowered by enemies. And when they had sworn their solemn oath, he said: God is witness over what you have said.

12:67. He said: My sons do not enter the city from one gate but enter from different gates. I cannot help you against God's will. God is the only decision-maker. I have put my trust in God. The believers should put their trust in Him too.

12:68. When they entered the city the way their father had advised them, it was not against God's will. Jacob's wish was fulfilled. He was a possessor of knowledge which We had taught him, but most people did not know of it.

12:69. When they presented themselves to Joseph, he embraced his brother and said to him: I am your brother. Do not grieve at what they did to me.

12:70. When he had given them their supplies, he hid a bowl into the bag of his brother. Then, an announcer called out: O caravan, you are thieves.

12:71. They turned back and asked: What have we stolen?

12:72. Joseph said: King's bowl is missing. Who will find it will have a reward of a camel's load. I pledge for it.

12:73. They said: By God, you know we did not come to do evil in the land, and we are not thieves.

12:74. The Egyptians said: What shall be the penalty for it if you prove to be liars?

12:75. Joseph's brothers said: In whose bag the cup is found will be punished. Thus, we punish the wrongdoers.

12:76. Joseph began the search of their bags before the bag of his brother. He found the cup in his brother's bag. Thus, We planned for

Joseph. He could not seize his brother by the king's law, but God willed otherwise. We increase the knowledge of whom We will, but over every possessor of knowledge is the One, God, knowing more.

12:77. They said: If he has stolen, you should know that his brother* stole before. But Joseph kept it within himself and did not reveal it to them. He said in his heart: You crime was worse, and God knows that you are lying.

**It has been said that Joseph stole his maternal grandfather's idol and broke it. So that he would not worship it.*

12:78. They said: Nobleman, he has an old father. Take one of us in his place. We can see that you are a generous man.

12:79. He replied: God forbids me to seize someone other than the one who stole our property, otherwise it would be unjust.

12:80. When they failed to get him released, they consulted among themselves. The eldest said: Do you not know that we gave our father a pledge in God's name and earlier we broke our father's trust regarding Joseph? So, I will not leave this land until our father permits me or God decides for me, as He is the best judge.

12:81. Return to your father and say to him: Your son stole. We could testify only to what we know. We could not guard against the unseen.

12:82. You, our father, can ask the people of the city in which we stayed and the caravan with which we travelled. We are telling the truth.

12:83. Jacob said: No, you have made up a story. I will be patient. May be, God will bring them all to me. God indeed is full of knowledge and wisdom.

12:84. He turned away from them and said: How great is my grief for Joseph! And he lost his sight because of the sorrow he had been suppressing.

12:85. His sons said: By God, you will not stop remembering Joseph until you ruin your health or die.

12:86. He replied: I only complain of my suffering and grief to God. He has told me about things which you do not know.

12:87. My sons, go and search for Joseph and his brother. Never give up hope of God's mercy. Except disbelievers, no one despairs of God's mercy.

12:88. When they presented themselves to Joseph, they said: Nobleman, misfortune has fallen upon us and our family, and we have little money. But give us some provisions and be charitable to us. Indeed, God rewards the charitable.

12:89. He asked: Do you know what you did with Joseph and his brother in your ignorance?
12:90. His brothers inquired: Are you indeed Joseph? He replied: Yes, I am Joseph and this is my brother Benjamin. God has been gracious to us. Those who fear God and endure with patience, God does not deny their reward.
12:91. They said: God has preferred you over us. Indeed, we have been sinners.
12:92. He said: No one is blaming you today. God may forgive you. He is the most merciful of those who show mercy.
12:93. Take my shirt and touch my father's face with it. He will recover his sight. Then return to me with your entire family.
12:94. When the caravan departed, their father said: I smell Joseph's scent, though you may not believe me.
12:95. They said: By God that is your old illusion.
12:96. When the bearer of good news arrived, he touched Jacob's face with Joseph's shirt. Jacob regained his sight. He said: Did I not tell you that God has given me knowledge of things about which you do not know?
12:97. The sons said: Father, ask God's forgiveness for our sins. Indeed, we have been sinners.
12:98. He replied: I will ask God for your forgiveness. He is the forgiving and merciful.
12:99. When they presented themselves to Joseph, he embraced his parents and said: Welcome to Egypt, God willing, you will live in peace.
12:100. He placed his parents on a throne and they all bowed to him. He said: Father, this is my old dream's fulfillment. My Lord has fulfilled it. He has been kind to me. He took me out of the prison, have brought you from the desert, after Satan had made strife between my brothers and me. My Lord is gracious to whom He wills. He is the all-knowing and all-wise.
12:101. My Lord You have given me power and taught me interpretation of dreams. You are the creator of the heavens and earth. You are my guardian in this world and the hereafter. Make me die in submission to you and join the righteous.
12:102. What We have revealed to you, O Muhammad, is ancient history. You were not with Joseph's brothers when they plotted and conspired against him.
12:103. Regardless how much you may desire, most will not believe.
12:104. You do not ask any reward for it. The Qur'an is but a reminder to

mankind.

12:105. There are many a sign in the heavens and the earth, which they pass by but pay no attention to them.

12:106. Most of them do not believe in God without associating idol-gods with Him.

12:107. Do they then feel secure that God will not punish them or the hour of doom will not come upon them suddenly without warning?

12:108. O Muhammad, say to them: This is my way. My followers and I invite you to God with sure knowledge. Glory is to God. I am not an idolater.

12:109. We sent Messengers before you who were humans and were chosen from the people of their towns. We sent revelations to them. Have the disbelievers not travelled in the land and seen what was the end of those before them? Certainly, life of the hereafter is better for those who guard against evil. Can you not then understand?

12:110. When Our Messengers despaired and thought that no one will believe in them, Our help came to them, saving whom we pleased. The guilty did not escape from Our punishment.

12:111. There is a lesson in their stories for people of understanding. The Qur'an is not a fabricated account, but a confirmation of the previous Scriptures, and contains an explanation of all things. It is a guidance and blessing for the believers.

# CHAPTER 13

## THUNDER

**Name:** From Verse 13.

**Verses:** 43

**Summary:**

- Theme: Prophet Muhammad's message is the truth, but it is people's fault that they are rejecting it.
- God:
    - has revealed the Qur'an in Arabic for easy understanding.
    - watches every soul minutely. When God commands, there is none to reverse it. God is the master of all planning.
- God's signs are trees, fruits, vegetables and their tastes.
- There is no God but Him. All things are subject to His command. Pray to God alone. Deities beside God have no control over any harm or benefit. It is God's remembrance that provides tranquility to hearts.
- Those who do not respond to their Lord's call will have no way to escape. Those who fulfill their pledge with God will have an excellent abode in the hereafter. Those who break their pledge will have the curse and a terrible home.
- God sent a Messenger for every nation. God never changes the condition of people unless they change what is in their hearts.
- Prophet Muhammad has no power to show any miracle without God's approval.

### By Verse

In the name of God, the compassionate, the merciful:

13:1. Alif, Lam, Meem, Ra (are Arabic letters). These are verses of the Qur'an. What your Lord has revealed to you, O Muhammad, is the truth, but most people do not believe it.

13:2. It is God who erected the heavens without visible pillars. Then He sat on His throne. He subjected the sun and the moon to service, each running its course for a specified term. He directs all affairs. He reveals signs that you may be convinced of meeting your Lord.

13:3. It is He who spread the earth and placed firmly standing mountains and rivers on it. He made fruits in pairs, and the night to cover the day. Indeed, there are signs in these for the thinkers.

13:4. There are adjoining plots in the land with grapevines, crops, and palm-trees, grown as single or multiple stems. They are watered with the same water, but We give each a different taste. Indeed, in that are signs for people of understanding.

13:5. O Muhammad, if you are astonished, then astonishing is their saying: When we have become dust, shall we be raised to life again? Those are the ones who have disbelieved in their Lord. They will have chains around their necks, and will live in the hellfire forever.

13:6. They urge you to bring evil sooner than good. Yet many were punished before them. Despite their sins, your Lord is merciful to people, but He is severe in punishment.

13:7. The disbelievers say: Why a sign has not been sent down to Prophet Muhammad from his Lord? But you are only a warner. Every people have a guide.

13:8. God knows what every female's womb carries and the time it falls short or exceeds. He plans everything.

13:9. He knows the seen and the unseen. He is the supreme and most high.

13:10. It is the same whether you conceal or say aloud, hide in the darkness of the night or walk freely in the daylight.

13:11. Each human being has angels before and behind him, who guard him by God's command. God does not change the fate of people until they change what is in their hearts. If God intends punishment for people, no one can ward it off. They have no protector beside God.

13:12. It is God who flashes lightening upon you, causing fear and hope, as he gathers the heavy clouds.

13:13. The thunder declares His glory with praise, and the angels declare it too for His awe. He sends the thunderbolts and strikes with them whom He pleases. The disbelievers dispute about God. He is severe in punishment.

13:14. The true prayer is to God alone. The disbelievers pray to the idols, who give them no answer. They are like the one who stretches his hands toward water, calling it to reach his mouth, but water never reaches his mouth. The disbelievers' prayers are useless.

13:15. Whoever is in the heavens and on earth bows to God, willingly or unwillingly, as their shadows bow to Him in the mornings and afternoons.

13:16. O Muhammad, ask them: Who is the Lord of the heavens and the earth? Then, tell them: It is God. Ask: Why then have you chosen other gods besides Him, who can neither benefit nor harm themselves? Are the blind and the seeing alike? Or can the darkness and the light be equal? Have their gods created anything like His creation, so that both creations look alike to them? Say: God is the creator of all things. He is the one, the supreme.

13:17. God sends down rain from the clouds, streams overflow, and their rapid flow carry the rising foam. Similarly, when ore is smelted for making ornaments and tools, the foam rises. Thus God presents truth and falsehood. The foam is cast away, but what remains is useful to mankind. Thus God presents His moral lessons.

13:18. The reward of those who have responded to their Lord is rich. The ones who have not responded to Him, even if they had all that is on earth and even more, and offered it as ransom for themselves, they will be severely punished and live in hell, a miserable place.

13:19. Then the one, who knows what has been revealed to you from your Lord is truth, be equal to the one who is blind to this fact? But only men of understanding pay attention.

13:20. Those are the ones who fulfill their promise to God and do not break their pledge.

13:21. They keep the ties of love and relations that God has commanded them to be kept intact, and fear both their Lord and the terrible accounting.

13:22. They are patient, seek their Lord's pleasure, establish prayer, and give charity in private and in public out of what We have given them, and repel evil with good. They shall have a happy end.

13:23. They shall enter paradise together with the righteous among their fathers, spouses, and children. From every side, the angels will come to them saying:

13:24. Peace be upon you for what you patiently endured. Excellent is your final home.

13:25. As for those who break the promise with God after agreeing to it, and also break the ties which God has ordered be kept together, and spread evil on the earth, will be cursed and will have the worst home.

13:26. God increases and decreases the livelihood for anyone He pleases. The disbelievers rejoice in this life, but this life is a brief comfort compared with the hereafter.

13:27. The disbelievers ask: Why has a sign not been sent down to him from his Lord? O Muhammad, Say: God lets them off the right path whom He wills and guides those who repent and turn to Him.

13:28. Those who have believed, their hearts find comfort in God's remembrance. Unquestionably, in remembering God, hearts are assured.

13:29. Those who have believed and do righteous deeds will have a joyful end.

13:30. Thus, We have send you, O Muhammad, to a nation, before which many other nations have passed away. You may recite to them Our revelations, but they disbelieve in the beneficent God. Say: He is my Lord. There is no God, but Him. I have put my trust in Him and shall return to Him.

13:31. What if this Qur'an was to move mountains, break the earth apart, and make the dead speak? All affairs belong to God. Do the believers not accept that had God willed, He would have guided mankind? As for the disbelievers, because of their misdeeds, they will continue to be punished and misfortune will continue to be at their doorstep till God's promise is fulfilled. Indeed, God does not fail in His promise.

13:32. Other Messengers before you were ridiculed, but I extended the disbelievers' time. Ultimately, I seized them with terrible punishment.

13:33. Will God, Who watches over every soul and its deeds, let the disbelievers go unpunished? Yet they associate other idol-gods with God. Say: Name them. Do you mean to inform Him of what He does not know on the earth, or are your words empty? Rather, the disbelievers' plans appear fair to them, for they are kept back from the right path. No one can guide whom God leads off the right path.

13:34. They will be punished in this life, but the punishment of the hereafter is more severe. They will not have any protector from God.

13:35. Paradise, which the righteous have been promised, will have flowing rivers and its fruits and shades will be everlasting. That is the reward of the righteous, and the disbelievers' reward is the hellfire.

13:36. Those to whom We have given the Scriptures rejoice at what has been revealed to you O Muhammad, but some factions deny part of it. Say: I have been commanded to worship God and not to associate anyone with Him. I obey Him and shall return to Him.

13:37. Thus We have revealed the Qur'an in Arabic as a code of conduct. If you were to follow their desires after all knowledge has been given to you, you would have neither protector nor defender against God.

13:38. We sent Messengers before you and gave them wives and children. It was not for a Messenger to come with a sign except by God's permission, and for every era there is a divinely fixed term.

13:39. God eliminates or confirms what He pleases. He has the eternal book.

13:40. Whether We show you a part of the punishment We have threatened the disbelievers with or let you die before it is fulfilled, your duty is only to give the message, and calling them to account is Our responsibility.

13:41. Have the disbelievers not seen that We have been reducing their land from its borders? If God decides, no one can reverse His decision. He is swift in decision-making.

13:42. Those before them plotted, but God is the master planner. He knows what every soul earns, and the disbelievers will know for whom reward of the paradise is.

13:43. The disbelievers say: You, O Muhammad, are not God's Messenger. Say: God and those who know the Scriptures are sufficient witnesses between you and me.

# CHAPTER 14

# ABRAHAM

**Name:** From Verse 35

**Verses:** 52

**Summary:**

- Warning to the disbelievers who were rejecting Prophet Muhammad's message and devising schemes to defeat his mission.
- The Qur'an is revealed to bring mankind out of darkness into light.
- God:
    - has created the heavens and the earth on truth.
    - is the one and the only God.
    - is aware of the unjust.
- Satan has no power over humans. He only invites and people follow.
- All Prophets spoke their people's language. The Prophets' dialogue with their people and their response. God will never break His promise made to His Prophets.
- Prophet Moses was sent to lead his people out of darkness into light.
- Prophet Abraham's prayer.
- If all mankind becomes nonbelievers, it makes no difference to God.
- The believers should put their trust in God. God punishes the wrongdoers and blesses those who fear Him. God has given you countless favors. Those who show ingratitude shall be cast into hell.
- Greetings in paradise will be: Peace.
- Example of a good and a bad word.

**By Verse**

In the name of God, the compassionate, the merciful:

14:1. ALR (Alif, Lam, Ra are Arabic letters). O Muhammad, We have revealed the Qur'an to you so that you may lead mankind from darkness to light by the command of their Lord, and to the path of the mighty and praiseworthy God.

14:2. Whatever is in the heavens and on earth belongs to God. There will be severe punishment for the disbelievers.

14:3. Those who prefer this life over life of the hereafter, prevent people from God's path, and seek to make it crooked, have gone far away

from the right path.
14:4. Our every Messengers spoke to his people in their language to make them understand his message clearly. God sends off the right path whom He wills and guides whom He wills. God is mighty and wise.
14:5. We sent Moses with Our signs for bringing out his people from darkness to light and remind them of Our favors. Indeed, there are signs in that for everyone patient and grateful.
14:6. Moses said to His people: Remember God's favor upon you when He saved you from Pharaoh's people, who were oppressing you, were killing your sons and letting your daughters live. That was a great trial from your Lord.
14:7. Remember when your Lord said: If you are grateful, I will surely increase my favors upon you, but if you deny them, I will punish you severely.
14:8. And Moses said: If you and all others on earth prove thankless, God does not need your thanks, but He deserves your praise.
14:9. Has not the history of those who came before you reached you, for example, the people of Noah, Aad, and Thamoud, and those who came after them? None except God knows their number. Their Messengers came to them with clear proofs, but they put their hands to their mouths and said: We disbelieve you, and indeed, we gravely doubt to which you call us.
14:10. Their Messengers said: Do you have doubt about God, Who is the creator of the heavens and the earth? He invites you so that He may forgive your sins, and grant you respite till an appointed term. They said: You are but humans like us. You wish to turn us away from what our forefathers worshipped. Bring us a clear proof.
14:11. Their Messengers replied: True, we are human like you, but God grants His grace to His chosen servants as He pleases. It is not for us to bring you an authoritative proof except as God wills. True believers should put their trust in God.
14:12. Why would we not trust God, when He has already guided us to the right path? We will bear your persecution patiently. The believers should rely on God.
14:13. The disbelievers said to their Messengers: We will drive you out from our land, unless you return to our religion. Then Lord said to His Messengers: We shall destroy the wrongdoers.
14:14. And We will let you live in the land after them. Let those take notice who fear standing before Me to answer and heed My threats.

14:15. When the Messengers requested help from God, every obstinate sinner was destroyed.
14:16. Hell lies before every obstinate sinner. He will drink stinking water.
14:17. He will sip it, but will not be able to swallow it. Death will come to him from every side, but he will not die. A severe punishment awaits him.
14:18. The disbelievers' works are like ashes which wind blows away on a stormy day. They shall gain nothing from what they have earned. That is the extreme failure.
14:19. Have you not seen that God created the heavens and the earth with truth? If He wills, He can replace you with a new creation.
14:20. And that is not difficult for God to do.
14:21. All will come before God for judgment. The weak will say to those who were arrogant: We were your followers; can you save us from God's punishment? They will reply: If God had guided us, we would have guided you. Neither anger nor patience will help us now. There is nowhere to escape.
14:22. When God's judgment has been passed, Satan will say: It was God Who promised the wrongdoers truth; I promised you too, but failed you. I had no authority over you except to call you, and you followed me. Do not blame me, but blame yourselves. Neither I can help you, nor you can help me. I never said that I was equal to God. The wrongdoers shall be severely punished.
14:23. The believers who did righteous deeds will be admitted to gardens with running streams. They will live there forever by their Lord's permission. Their greeting will be: Peace.
14:24. Have you not seen that God presents an example that a good word is like a good tree, whose roots are firm and its branches reach the sky?
14:25. It produces fruit in all seasons by its Lord's permission. God gives examples for people that perhaps they will pay attention.
14:26. The example of a bad word is like a bad tree, uprooted from the ground having no stability.
14:27. God will help the believers to be steadfast with His firm word, in this life and the hereafter. God leads the wrongdoers off the right path. God does what He wills.
14:28. Have you not seen those who exchanged God's favor with disbelief and drove their people into hell?
14:29. They will burn in hell, an evil place.
14:30. They set up idol-gods as equal to God for misleading others. Say

to them: Enjoy yourselves, but you are destined for hell.

14:31. O Muhammad, tell My believing servants to establish prayer and give charity in private and in public from what We have provided them, before a day comes in which there will be no trading and friendship.

14:32. It is God who created the heavens and the earth. He sent down rain from the sky to produce fruits to feed you. He subjected ships to you to sail through the sea by His command and subjected rivers for you.

14:33. And He subjected for you the sun and the moon, orbiting continuously, and the night and the day.

14:34. He gave you all you asked for. If you counted God's favors, you could not count them. Indeed, man is unjust and ungrateful.

14:35. Abraham said: Lord, make this city Mecca a city of peace and protect me and my descendants from worshipping idols.

14:36. Lord, they have led many people off the right path. Whoever follows me shall be with me, and whoever disobeys me, You are indeed forgiving and merciful.

14:37. Lord, I have settled some of my children in a barren valley near Your sacred house (Kabah at Mecca), so that they may establish prayer. Put kindness in people's hearts for them and provide them fruits, so that they may be grateful.

14:38. Lord, certainly, You know what we conceal and reveal. Nothing on earth or in heaven is hidden from You.

14:39. Praise is to God, who has given me Ishmael and Isaac in old age. God hears all prayers.

14:40. Lord, make me and my descendants establish prayer, and accept my prayer.

14:41. Lord, forgive me, my parents, and the believers on the Day of Accounting.

14:42. Do not think that God is unaware of what the wrongdoers do. He only delays their punishment to the day when eyes will stare in horror.

14:43. They shall rush in fear with their heads raised, gazing but not seeing anything, with empty hearts.

14:44. O Muhammad, warn people of the day when punishment will come to them and the wrongdoers will say: Lord, please delay the punishment for a while. We will obey Your call and follow the Messengers. But it will be said to the disbelievers: Had you not sworn that you will never have a downfall?

14:45. You lived among the dwellings of those who wronged themselves.

You knew how We dealt with them because We gave you many examples about them.

14:46. The disbelievers plotted, but even if their plots could move mountains, God stopped them.

14:47. Do not think that God will fail in His promise to His Messengers. God is mighty and revengeful.

14:48. On the day the earth will be replaced by another earth and so will the heavens, all will come before God, the one, almighty.

14:49. On that day, you will see the guilty in chains.

14:50. Their garments will be black like tar coal and their faces will be covered by fire.

14:51. God will reward every one for what it earned. God is swift in taking account.

14:52. This is a warning to mankind to know that He is but one God. Let the wise pay attention.

# CHAPTER 15

# THE ROCKY PATH

**Name:** From Verse 80

**Verses:** 99

**Summary:**

- Theme: Warning to the disbelievers who rejected Prophet Muhammad's message, and encouragement to him.
- The Qur'an is a divine book. God has taken the responsibility for its preservation.
- God created the heavens and everything on earth for the human life.
- Adam's creation; angel's bowing before him, and Satan refusal to bow. Satan and his followers are destined for hell.
- On the Day of Judgment, the disbelievers will wish that they were Muslims. Righteous will be awarded paradise.
- Two angels gave good news of a son to Prophet Abraham. The same angels came to Prophet Lot and executed God's decree of stoning to death his nation of homosexuals.
- Punishment to the people of al-Hijr (The Rocky Path) for their disbelief.
- The seven verses of Chapter 1, the Opening, are worthy of recitation often.
- Prophet Muhammad, proclaim God's commandments publicly and turn away from the disbelievers.

## By Verse

In the name of God, the compassionate, the merciful:

15:1. Alif, Lam, Ra (are Arabic alphabets). These are verses of the Qur'an that makes things clear.

15:2. The day will come when the disbelievers will wish that they were Muslims.

15:3. Let them feast and enjoy and be deceived by the false hope. Soon, they will know the truth.

15:4. Never did We destroy a population whose term of life was not decided beforehand.

15:5. Neither people can hasten their doom nor they can postpone it.

15:6. The disbelievers say: You, Prophet Muhammad, to whom the divine message has been revealed, are a madman.

15:7. They say: Bring down the angels, if what you say is true.
15:8. We, God, only send down angels for a just cause. If they were to come, the disbelievers will not be spared punishment.
15:9. Indeed, We have sent down the divine message (the Qur'an) and We are its guardian.
15:10. We sent Messengers before you to the previous nations.
15:11. They ridiculed each Messenger We sent them.
15:12. Thus, We inserted disbelief into the criminals' hearts.
15:13. They will not believe in their Messenger despite the example of the previous people.
15:14. Even if We, God, opened a gate in the heaven for the disbelievers and they continued ascending through it;
15:15. they would say: Our eyes have been dazzled and we have been bewitched.
15:16. We have placed stars in the heaven and beautified it for the observers.
15:17. And We guard them from every cursed devil.
15:18. The eavesdroppers are pursued by burning flames.
15:19. We have spread out the earth with firm mountains and have grown seasonal fruits and crops in it.
15:20. We have provided subsistence for you and for those earthly creatures that you are not responsible for providing.
15:21. We, God, keep everything in store and sent it down in a known quantity.
15:22. We sent down the fertilizing winds and bring down water from the sky for you to drink. But you are not its store keeper.
15:23. We give life and death, and are the inheritor of everything.
15:24. We know who have gone before you and who will come after you.
15:25. Certainly, your Lord will gather them all before Him. He is wise and knowledgeable.
15:26. We created man from dry, black clay.
15:27. Earlier, We, God, created jinns from the smokeless fire.
15:28. Remember when your Lord said to the angels: I will create a human being from dry, black clay.
15:29. When I have made him and breathed My spirit into him, kneel down and bow to him.
15:30. So all the angels bowed before Adam,
15:31. except Satan, who refused to bow.
15:32. God asked Satan, why did you not bow?
15:33. He replied: I will not bow to a human whom You have created from dry, black clay.

15:34. God said: Then get out, you are cursed.
15:35. You are cursed till the Day of Judgment.
15:36. He said: Lord, delay my punishment till the Day of Resurrection.
15:37. God replied: Your request is approved,
15:38. until the appointed day.
15:39. Satan said: Lord, because You have declared me misguided, I will surely make disobedience attractive to mankind on the earth, and I will mislead them,
15:40. except those who are faithful to you.
15:41. God said: This faithfulness is the path that leads to Me.
15:42. You will have no authority over My servants, except those sinners who will follow you.
15:43. They will all live in hell.
15:44. The hell has seven gates. A separate class of sinners will come through each gate.
15:45. But the righteous shall live in gardens with fountains.
15:46. They shall enter there in peace and security.
15:47. We shall remove hatred from their hearts and they will sit on couches, face to face, like brothers.
15:48. No fatigue will touch them, and they will never leave paradise.
15:49. O Muhammad, tell My servants that I am most forgiving and merciful.
15:50. But My punishment is severe indeed.
15:51. Tell them about Abraham's guests.
15:52. They came to him and said: Peace be upon you. Abraham replied: I am afraid of you.
15:53. The angels replied: Do not be afraid. We give you good news of a son blessed with wisdom.
15:54. He said: Do you give me good news of a son in old age? How could that be?
15:55. They said: We have given you the good news truthfully. Do not despair.
15:56. Abraham said: No one despairs of his Lord's mercy except the one who has gone off the right path.
15:57. Messengers, what has brought you here?
15:58. They said: We have been sent to a guilty nation.
15:59. Lot's household will be saved, except his wife.
15:60. God has ordered that she be with those who stay behind.
15:61. When the Messengers came to Lot's house,
15:62. he said: I do not know you.
15:63. They said: No, but we have come to you with the punishment

about which the disbelievers have been disputing.
15:64. We have come to you with truth and we are sincere.
15:65. Go out with your family late at night. You should walk in the rear and no one should look back. Go where you are commanded.
15:66. We gave him God's orders, because the sinners were to be completely destroyed by morning.
15:67. People of the city came to Lot rejoicing.
15:68 Lot said: These are my guests, so do not put me to shame.
15:69. Fear God and do not disgrace me.
15:70. They said: Have we not forbidden you from protecting strangers?
15:71. Lot said: Here are my daughters, take them to marry, if you are bent upon doing evil.
15:72. By your life, O Prophet Muhammad, they were intoxicated wandering blindly.
15:73. A mighty blast overtook them at sunrise.
15:74. We destroyed their city and rained upon them stones of hard clay.
15:75. There are signs in this for those who think.
15:76. Their city is on the road between Mecca and Syria, near the Dead Sea.
15:77. There is a sign in this for the believers.
15:78. And dwellers of the forest (Prophet Shuaib's people, Midians*) were also wrongdoers.

**they lived in the northwest Arabian Peninsula, on the east shore of the Gulf of Aqaba on the Red Sea*

15:79. We punished them too. Both cities are on a highway still used.
15:80. The people of Al-Hijr* denied Messengers.

**The rocky path, north of Medina, where Thamoud lived.*

15:81. We gave them signs, but they ignored them.
15:82. They carved their houses in mountains and lived there in security.
15:83. But one morning, a mighty blast brought them death.
15:84. Nothing benefited them from what they earned.
15:85. We created the heavens and earth, and all that is between the two, to reveal truth. Surely, the hour of judgment is coming; so O Muhammad, overlook their faults graciously.
15:86. Surely, your Lord is the all-knowing creator.
15:87. We have given you seven of the oft-repeated verses of the First Chapter and the glorious Qur'an.
15:88. Do not envy what We have given some others for enjoyment and do not grieve over them. Show kindness to the believers.
15:89. And say to the disbelievers: My responsibility is to warn you

clearly.
15:90. We will surely punish those,
15:91. who have split the Qur'an into pieces pronouncing it to be a pack of lies.
15:92. By your Lord, We will surely question them,
15:93. about their deeds.
15:94. Proclaim what you have been commanded to, and avoid idolaters.
15:95. We will defend you from those who mock you,
15:96. who serve gods other than God. Before long, they will know the truth.
15:97. We know that you are distressed from what they say.
15:98. Praise your Lord and bow to Him.
15:99. Worship your Lord till you die.

# CHAPTER 16

# THE BEE

**Name:** From Verse 68.

**Verses:** 128

**Summary:**

- Theme: Refutation of idolatry, proof of God's oneness, and warning to the disbelievers for rejection of Prophet Muhammad's message.
- God's:
    - Favors like the creation of humans, honeybees, birds, cattle and the milk-producing animals for the benefit of humans, sending down water from the sky for drinking and agriculture, and setting mountains to stabilize the earth.
    - Commands: Do justice, do good to others, give charity; do not:
        - be indecent, wicked, and rebellious.
        - break agreements.
        - declare what is lawful and unlawful against God's decision.
    - Rewards to those who migrate for God's sake.
- The disbelievers' excuse for not worshiping God, and call to God during distress and their conduct afterwards.
- The Day of Judgment: Witnesses and rewards.
- Prophet Abraham was a model believer. O Muhammad, call the disbelievers courteously to God's way with wisdom, advice, and reason.
- Advice to Prophet Muhammad and his companions in face of the disbelievers' antagonism and persecution.
- If God was to punish mankind for its wrong doings, He would not leave anyone alive.
- Benefits of the Qur'an's recitation and the disbelievers' accusation of Prophet Muhammad for his non-Arab teacher of the Qur'an.
- What is with you is transitory; and what is with God is everlasting.

## By Verse

In the name of God, the compassionate, the merciful:

16:1. God's judgment will surely come; do not be impatient for it. Glory is to God, Who is high above the disbelievers' idols.

16:2. God sends down angels, with revelations by His command, to those of His servants whom He chooses to proclaim: There is no God except Me; so fear Me.

16:3. God created the heavens and the earth to reveal the truth. He is high above the idol-gods that they associate with Him.

16:4. God created man from a sperm-drop; but man has become an adversary.

16:5. God created livestock which provide you warm clothing of their hides, food, and other benefits.

16:6. You have a sense of pride and beauty in the livestock as you drive them home or to a highway pasture.

16:7. The livestock carry your loads to distant-lands where you could not have reached without difficulty. Your Lord is kind and merciful.

16:8. Your Lord has created horses, mules, and donkeys for you to ride and show as ornaments or parade them in processions or exhibitions; and He has created other things of which you have no knowledge.

16:9. God alone can lead you to the right path, but some go off the right path. If He willed, He could have guided you all to the right path.

16:10. God sends down rain from the sky for you to drink and grow pasture to feed the animals.

16:11. With rainwater, God produces crops, olives, date-palms, grapes, and every kind of fruit for you. Certainly, in this is a sign for those who think.

16:12. By His command, He has subjected the night, day, sun, moon, and stars to you. Surely, in this are proofs for people who understand.

16:13. On the earth, God has made objects in varying colors for you. Indeed, in this is a sign for those who pay attention.

16:14. God has made the sea subservient to you for eating fresh fish from it, bringing up ornaments from it to wear, and seeing ships sailing through it. He has created all this that you might seek His bounty and be grateful to Him.

16:15. God has set up mountains on earth to stabilize it for minimizing the effects of earthquakes, lest it should shake with you; and rivers and pathways to guide you.

16:16. And set up landmarks. Stars guide people too.

16:17. Is then God, Who has created everything, equal to the idol-god, who has created nothing? So, will you not pay attention?

16:18. If you were to count God's favors, you would not succeed. God, indeed, is forgiving and merciful.

16:19. God knows what you conceal and reveal.

16:20. The disbelievers call on idols which have not created anything while they themselves have been created.

16:21. The idols are dead, lifeless, and do not know when they will be raised up.

16:22. Your god is one God. Those who do not believe in the life to come have disbelieving hearts and they are arrogant.

16:23. God surely knows what they conceal and reveal. He does not like the arrogant.

16:24. When the arrogant disbelievers are asked: What do you think of that your Lord has revealed? They reply: Old stories.

16:25. They shall bear their own burden on the Day of Resurrection, and also the burden of those whom they misled because they were ignorant. Evil indeed is what they shall bear.

16:26. The disbelievers before them also plotted, but God uprooted their buildings from the foundations and the roofs fell upon them. The punishment came upon them from directions they did not perceive.

16:27. On the Day of Resurrection, God will disgrace them and ask: Where are your idols for which you used to argue with the believers? The knowledgeable believers will say: Indeed, today there is disgrace and misery for the disbelievers.

16:28. Those wrongdoers, whose lives angel would take away, after submitting to the angels would say: We did not do any wrong. Angels will reply: No, God surely knows what you used to do.

16:29. Enter the gates of hell to live there forever. It is a wretched place to live for the arrogant.

16:30. Those who feared God will be asked: What did your Lord send down? They will say: That which is good. The reward for those who do good in this world is good; but better is the reward in the life to come. The home of the righteous will be excellent.

16:31. They shall enter paradise where rivers flow. There, they will have whatever they would wish. Thus the righteous shall be rewarded.

16:32. The angels will take the lives of the righteous saying: Peace be upon you; enter paradise for the reward of your good deeds.

16:33. Are the ungodly waiting for angels to take their lives or for the

Lord's command for their punishment to be fulfilled? Those who went before them also waited. God did not wrong them, they wronged themselves.

16:34. They were punished for their evilness and mockery.

16:35. The idolaters say: Had God willed, neither we nor our forefathers would have worshipped anyone beside Him, nor we would have made anything unlawful without His permission. Those were also excuses of those before them. Yet, what is the Messengers' responsibility but to give the message clearly?

16:36. We sent a Messenger to every nation saying: Serve God and avoid false gods. God guided some and some went off the right path. Roam the earth and see the sinners' end.

16:37. O Muhammad, if you desire for their guidance, God will not guide those whom He leads off the right path. They shall have no helper.

16:38. The disbelievers solemnly swear by God that He will not raise up the dead. No, God's promise to raise the dead will be fulfilled, but most of mankind may not know it.

16:39. He will show them the truth of what they disputed about, and rejecters shall realize their falsehood.

16:40. For anything to happen, We only say: Be, and it happens.

16:41. As for those who, after suffering oppression, emigrated in God's cause, God will certainly look after them in this world, but better will be their reward in the life to come, if they only knew.

16:42. Those are the people who remained patient and put their trust in their Lord.

16:43. The Messengers We sent before you were men too. We sent down revelations to them. Ask the people of the Scriptures (Jews and Christians), if you do not know this.

16:44. We sent the Messengers with clear proofs and books. We have revealed the Qur'an to you that you may make clear to people what has been sent down for them, so that they might think.

16:45. Are those who plot evil deeds feel secure that God will not cause the earth to swallow them or that punishment will not come upon them unexpectedly?

16:46. Or that He may not punish them during their journeys when they will be helpless to escape it?

16:47. Or that He would not destroy them slowly? Indeed, your Lord is kind and merciful.

16:48. Do they not see the things God has created, that cast their shadows right and left and bow to God in humility?

16:49. Angels and all creatures of the heavens and the earth bow to God,

and none is arrogant.
16:50. They fear their Lord, high above them, and do as they are directed.
16:51. God has said: Do not serve two gods, as I am the only God; so fear Me alone.
16:52. To Him belongs whatever is in the heavens and on earth. Duty is always due to Him. Is it then other than God that you fear?
16:53. Whatever you have is God's favor. When an adversity touches you, you cry to Him for help.
16:54. When He removes your adversity, some of you associate others with your Lord.
16:55. They deny Our favors. Enjoy yourselves, but before long you will know the truth.
16:56. They assign some of Our favors to their idol-gods. By God, you shall certainly be questioned about your false fabrications.
16:57. They assign daughters to God – Holy is He – while they have sons whom they desire for themselves. Glory is to Him.
16:58. When news of a daughter's birth is given to one of them, his face darkens, and he grieves.
16:59. He hides himself from people because of the bad news he got, contemplating whether he should keep her alive despite his disgrace, or bury her in the ground? Certainly, their decision is evil.
16:60. Those, who do not believe in the life to come, have evil character and God has the loftiest character. He is the mighty and the wise.
16:61. If God were to punish people for their wrong-doings, no creature on earth will be left alive. But He defers their punishment for a specified period. When the period expires, they would neither be able to delay it or hasten it.
16:62. The disbelievers attribute to God what they hate for themselves. They lie that all good things are for them. Surely, hellfire awaits them, and they will be driven to it first.
16:63. By God, We sent Messengers to nations before you, but Satan made their ill deeds seem attractive to them and to this day he is their patron. They shall be severely punished.
16:64. We have revealed the Qur'an to you for the express purpose of making clear to them the things they differ about. It is a guide and blessing for the believers.
16:65. God sends down rain from the sky to revive the lifeless earth. Indeed, this is a sign for those who ponder.
16:66. There is an instructive sign in the cattle too. For your drinking, We produce milk in their bodies between bowls and bloodstreams.

Milk is an enjoyable drink.
16:67. From date-palm and grapevines, from which you derive intoxicating drink and healthy food. Indeed, this is a sign for those who are wise.
16:68. Your Lord inspired bees saying: Build your homes in mountains, trees, and the man-made hives.
16:69. Feast on all kinds of fruits and follow the paths your Lord has laid down for you. Honey of various colors comes from their bellies for use as a medicine by people. Indeed, this is a sign for those who give thought.
16:70. God creates you and causes your death. Some of you live long, reaching the weakest age, when you will not remember what you knew once. God is the all-knowing and all-powerful.
16:71. God has given more riches to some than others. Those with more riches deny their slaves an equal share. Is it then God's grace they are denying?
16:72. God has given you wives from among yourselves, children and grandchildren from them, and provided you good things. Then do they believe in false gods and deny His blessings;
16:73. worship helpless gods, who can provide them no livelihood from the heavens or the earth, and have no such power?
16:74. Compare none with God. He has knowledge and you do not.
16:75. God gives example of two men: One a slave, the other his master. The slave has no power, but his master, on whom We have bestowed Our favors, spends freely in private and public. Are the two equal? No, they are not. Praise is to God, but most do not understand this simple thing.
16:76. God presents another example of two men, one is a helpless dumb, who is a burden on his guardian. Wherever he sends him, he comes back empty handed. Is he equal to the one who commands justice and follows the straight path?
16:77. God alone knows the secrets of the heavens and the earth. The coming of the final hour will be completed in the twinkling of an eye, or even quicker. God has power over all things.
16:78. God brought you out from your mothers' wombs while you had no knowledge. He gave you hearing, sight, and hearts that you might give thanks.
16:79. Do they not see birds flying in the sky? None holds them there but God. Surely, in this are signs for people who believe.
16:80. God has given you houses to live in, and tents of the animal skins which are light to carry during travel and easy to pitch for shelter.

He has given you their wool, fur, and hair for comfort and household goods.

16:81. From His creations, God has given you shelters, mountains for retreat, garments to preserve you from heat and cold, and body armor to preserve you in fighting. Thus, He completes His favors upon you, so that you may submit to Him.

16:82. If the disbelievers turn away, your duty O Muhammad is only to convey the message in a clear way.

16:83. The disbelievers recognize God's favors, yet they deny them. Most of them are ungrateful.

16:84. On the Day of Judgment, We shall call a witness from every nation. The disbelievers will neither be allowed to offer excuses nor repent.

16:85. When disbelievers will face their punishment, it will not be made light or delayed for them.

16:86. When disbelievers will see their idols, they shall say: Lord, these are the idols we prayed to. But the idols will reply: Most surely you are liars.

16:87. The disbelievers shall submit to God on that Day (of Judgment) and their idols shall abandon them.

16:88. Those who rejected God and prevented others from God's path will have increased punishment for spreading mischief.

16:89. On the Day of Judgment, We shall call a witness from every nation to testify against it. We shall call you O Muhammad to testify against your nation. We have revealed the Qur'an to you for clarifying all things, and giving guidance, mercy, and good news to the believers.

16:90. God orders justice, good conduct, and giving charity to relatives, and forbids immorality, bad conduct, and oppression. He scolds you so that you may pay attention.

16:91. Fulfill the agreement with God when you have made it. Do not break your sworn oaths as you have made God your witness. Indeed, God knows what you do.

16:92. Do not be like the woman who worked hard to spin the yarn and then broke it into pieces. Do not make your oaths for deceit when you are stronger than others in numbers. God tests you by this. He will certainly make clear to you on the Day of Resurrection about which you disputed.

16:93. If God willed, He could have made you all one nation. But He leads off the right path or guides whom He pleases. You shall certainly be called to account for all your deeds.

16:94. Do not take oaths to deceive one another, lest your foot should slip after being rightly guided and evil should befall you for debarring others from God's way. Then you will have an awful punishment.
16:95. Do not exchange the agreement with God for a small price. God's reward is best for you, if only you knew.
16:96. That which is with you will end; but that which is with God will be everlasting. We will most certainly reward the ones with patience for their good deeds.
16:97. Whether male or female, We will give a happy life to whoever does good and is a believer, and reward them for their good deeds.
16:98. When you read the Qur'an, seek God's protection from Satan, the rejected one.
16:99. Satan has no power over those who believe and put their trust in their Lord.
16:100. Satan's authority is only over those who befriend him and who associate other gods with God.
16:101. When We substitute a sign by another, they say: O Muhammad, you are a forger. God knows best what He reveals, but most of them do not understand.
16:102. Say, the Holy Spirit (Angel Gabriel) has brought the revelation from your Lord in truth, to strengthen the believers, and to guide and give good news to those who submit to God.
16:103. We certainly know that they say: A human teaches Prophet (Muhammad). But, the one to whom they allude to, speaks a foreign language, and the Qur'an is clearly in Arabic language.
16:104. God will not guide those who disbelieve in His revelations. They will be punished severely.
16:105. Those who do not believe in God's verses, invent falsehood and are liars.
16:106. Anyone, after accepting faith, opens his heart to disbelief except under compulsion but his heart remaining firm in faith, will not be punished. But all those who open their hearts to disbelief will incur God's wrath, and will have a dreadful punishment.
16:107. That is because they love the worldly life over the life to come. God does not guide the disbelieving people.
16:108. They are those whose hearts, hearing, and vision God has sealed. It is those who are heedless.
16:109. Certainly, they will be losers in the life to come.
16:110. However, your Lord will be forgiving and merciful to those who left their homes because of persecution, and they struggled hard and were patient.

16:111. Remember the day when every soul will come pleading for itself, and it will be repaid for what it did. No one will be wronged.

16:112. God presents an example of a city which once was safe and secure. Provisions came to it in abundance from every quarter, but it denied God's favors. So God made it taste hunger and fear for what they had been doing.

16:113. A Messenger came to them from among themselves, but they denied him. So they were punished for their wrongdoing.

16:114. Eat the lawful and the good things God has provided you and be grateful for His favors, if it is He whom you worship.

16:115. God has forbidden for you dead animals, blood, pork, and that on which a name other than that of God has been invoked. But whoever is driven by necessity to eat these without desire and not exceeding the limit, surely will find God forgiving and merciful.

16:116. Do not say that this is lawful and that is not to invent falsehood about God. Indeed, those who invent falsehood about God will not succeed.

16:117. They can have brief enjoyment in this life, but will have a painful punishment.

16:118. We forbade Jews foods We have forbidden you. We did not wrong Jews, but they wronged themselves.

16:119. Those who have done wrong out of ignorance, then repent and correct themselves, will indeed find their Lord forgiving and merciful.

16:120. Abraham was a model, devoutly obedient to God, true in faith, and a non-idolater.

16:121. Abraham was grateful to God for His favors. God chose him to be a prophet and guided him to a straight path.

16:122. We blessed him in this world and he will be among the righteous in the life to come.

16:123. We have revealed to you O Muhammad to follow Abraham's religion. He was truthful in faith and was not an idolater.

16:124. God ordained the punishment for profaning Saturday* only for those Jews who differed about it. On the Day of Resurrection, your Lord will judge between them concerning their differences.

**Saturday, week's seventh day, is the day of rest and religious observance among Jews and some Christians.*

16:125. Invite non-believers to your Lord's way with wisdom and meaningful preaching, and reason with them courteously. Your Lord knows best who have strayed from His path, and who is rightly guided.

16:126. O believers, if you punish an enemy, punish proportional to the wrong the enemy has done to you. But if you endure patiently, it is better for you.

16:127. O Muhammad, be patient with God's help. Do not grieve for the disbelievers and do not distress yourself at their evil designs.

16:128. God surely is with those who guard against evil and do good deeds.

# CHAPTER 17

# CHILDREN OF ISRAEL

**Name:** From Verse Two.

**Verses:** 111

**Summary:**

- Theme: A combination of warning and instruction:
    - The success or failure depends upon the correct understanding of God's oneness, the life-after-death, and the Prophethood.
    - The Qur'an is God's book and its teachings are true and genuine. The disbelievers' doubts about these basic realities have been removed and they have been warned against their ignorance.
    - Prophet Muhammad has been instructed to stand firm against the disbelievers and never to compromise with them.
    - Muslims have been instructed to face adversity with patience and keep control over their feelings.
    - Five daily prayers have been prescribed for reforming and purifying the believers' souls.
- God:
    - took Prophet Muhammad on a tour of the universe at night.
    - has provided conveyance for humans on the land and the sea.
    - sent a human-Messenger to humans. If dwellers of the earth had been angels, God would have sent an angel as a Messenger.
- Israelites: Two prophecies of their corruption; Prophet Moses' nine signs, and peoples' disbelief in him.
- Hereafter: Belief in it is necessary to understand the Qur'an; the disbelievers' questions and doubts; disbelievers will be resurrected as deaf and blind; each individual shall be given the book of his own deeds. He that seeks guidance does so to his own good and he who goes off the right path does so to his own loss. The reward in this life and the life to come.
- Commandments for proper behavior with parents, relatives, and the community. The believers should speak only good words.

- If there were other gods beside God, they would have tried to dethrone Him. The invented gods have no power to relieve you from any distress.
- Why signs are not sent to Prophet Muhammad like prior prophets?
- Satan's enmity with humans, and his vow to seduce them.
- Accountability of every community and its leaders.
- No compromise is allowed in matters of the Islamic law and principles.
- Five daily obligatory prayers for believers.
- For Prophet Muhammad only, the Tahujudd prayer in the small hours of the morning.
- Offer prayers neither too loud nor in too low a voice, adopt the middle course.
- The soul is at God's command.

**By Verse**

In the name of God, the compassionate, the merciful:

17:1. Glory is to God who took His servant Prophet Muhammad on a night journey from the sacred mosque to the distant mosque*, whose surroundings We have blessed, to show him some of Our signs. Indeed, God hears all and sees all.

**The Arabic name of the sacred mosque at Mecca is al-Masjid al-Haram; and the distant mosque is the Solomon's Temple built by Prophet Solomon in Jerusalem.*

17:2. We gave Moses the Scriptures and made them a guide for Israel's children saying: Do not take a guardian other than Me.

17:3. You are offspring of those whom We carried in Noah's boat. He surely was a grateful servant.

17:4. We gave a clear warning to Israel's children in the Scriptures that twice they would do mischief on the earth and would become great tyrants.

17:5. So when time came for fulfilling first of the two prophesies, We sent Our mighty servants, the Assyrians, against you. They ravaged your country. That completed Our threatened punishment for you.

17:6. Then, We gave you victory over them and multiplied your riches and offspring to increase your manpower.

17:7. We said: Your doing good or bad is for yourselves. When time came for fulfilling the second prophesy, We permitted your enemies, the Romans, to disfigure your faces and to enter your temple, as they had entered it before, to destroy it completely.

17:8. If you repent, your Lord will have mercy upon you. But if you return to sin, We will punish you again. We have made hell a prison-house for the disbelievers.

17:9. The Qur'an guides to the perfectly right way and gives good news to the believers, who do righteous deeds and will have a great reward.

17:10. We have prepared a painful punishment for those who do not believe in the life to come.

17:11. Man prays both for evil and good. Man is ever hasty.

17:12. We have made the night and the day two signs. We made the night dark and gave light to the day, so that you may seek bounty from your Lord and count the number of days and years. We have explained all things in detail.

17:13. We have tied every man's fate with his neck. On the Day of Resurrection, We will show him his record as an open book.

17:14. It will be said: Read your record and judge it for yourself.

17:15. Whoever seeks guidance is doing it for his own benefit, and whoever goes off the right path is doing it for his own loss. No one will bear another's burden. We never punish a nation until We have sent a Messenger to warn it.

17:16. When We decide to destroy a nation, first We warn those who are affluent. If they persist in doing evil, then we decide and destroy them completely.

17:17. How many generations have We destroyed after Noah? Your Lord is aware of His servants' sins. He observes them all.

17:18. Whoever desires the transitory things of this life, We readily give him what We want and to whom We want. However, We have prepared hell for him and he will burn in it disgraced and rejected.

17:19. Whosoever desires the hereafter, diligently works for it, and is a believer, God will reward his efforts.

17:20. Your Lord's gifts are given to all without restriction.

17:21. See how We have given more to some than others in this life, but rewards in the hereafter will be superior.

17:22. Do not worship other gods, but God alone. Otherwise, you will be disgraced and abandoned.

17:23. Your Lord has ordered that you worship none but Him, and show kindness to your parents. If one or both of them attain old age in your lifetime, say neither a word of disrespect to them, nor rebuke them, but address them in kind words.

17:24. Treat the parents with humility and compassion, and pray: Lord, be merciful to them. They raised me when I was an infant.

17:25. Your Lord knows best what is in your hearts and whether you do good deeds. He surely forgives those who turn to Him again and again.

17:26. Give their due to the relative, the poor, and the traveler, and do not spend wastefully.

17:27. The wasteful are Satan's brothers, and he is ever ungrateful to his Lord.

17:28. But if you do not have the means to assist the relative, the poor, and the traveler and are waiting for God to provide you with the means, at least speak to them kindly.

17:29. Do not be miserly, or so much spendthrift that you yourself may become insolvent poor.

17:30. Your Lord provides abundantly to whom He wants and poorly to whom He wants. He knows and sees all His servants.

17:31. Do not kill your children for fear of poverty. We provide for them and you. Killing them is a great sin.

17:32. Do not commit adultery. It is immoral and evil.

17:33. Do not kill anyone because God has forbidden it, except for a just cause. If someone is killed unjustly, We have given his heir the right to demand justice. But let him not exceed limits in taking a life, as the victim has rights too.

17:34. Do not squander an orphan's property, but preserve it until the orphan reaches maturity. Fulfill your commitment, about which you will be questioned.

17:35. Give full measure when you measure, and weigh with an even scale. That is most fitting and better in the end.

17:36. Do not follow what you do not know. Surely, your ears, eyes, and hearts shall be questioned.

17:37. Do not walk on earth arrogantly. You can neither split the earth, nor attain a mountain like stature.

17:38. Your Lord hates the bad aspects of the above (as explained in 17:29-37).

17:39. This is a part of the wisdom with which your Lord has inspired you, O Muhammad. Do not worship gods other than God alone, otherwise you will be thrown in hell, blamed and rejected.

17:40. What! Has your Lord preferred to give the disbelievers sons, and take for Himself daughters from among the angels? What you are saying is awful.

17:41. We have explained Our revelations in the Qur'an in various ways, so that the disbelievers may pay attention, but it has only increased their disbelief.

17:42. O Muhammad, tell them: Were there other gods beside God, as the disbelievers claim, they would have tried to dethrone Him.

17:43. Glory is to God, Who is way high above what they say.

17:44. The seven heavens, the earth, and what they contain glorify God. There is not a thing that does not praise Him. But you do not understand their praising. He indeed is ever kind and forgiving.

17:45. When you recite the Qur'an, We, God, put an invisible curtain between you and those who do not believe in the life to come.

17:46. We seal their hearts and make them hard of hearing, so they understand nothing. That is why when you mention about your Lord's oneness, they turn back in dislike.

17:47. We fully know what the disbelievers wish to hear when they listen to you and what they say in private. The wrongdoers say: The man (Prophet Muhammad), whom you follow, is affected by magic.

17:48. See what contemptuous phrases they utter about you O Muhammad. They have gone off the right path and cannot find the right path.

17:49. They say: When we are reduced to bones and dust, would we be raised up to a new life?

17:50. Tell them: Whether you become stones or iron,

17:51. or something which you think may not be given life even then you shall be raised up. They will ask: Who will restore us? Say: God Who created you the first time. Then, they will shake their heads and ask: When will that be? Reply: Perhaps, it will be soon.

17:52. On that Day (of Resurrection), God will call you. You will respond by praising Him and thinking that you were in the world for a little while.

17:53. Tell My servants to speak courteously. Satan creates discord among them. Satan indeed is mankind's clear enemy.

17:54. Your Lord knows you best. If He wills, He will be merciful to you; or if He wills, He will punish you. We have not sent you O Muhammad as their guardian.

17:55. Your Lord knows best what is in the heavens and on earth. We gave higher rank to some Prophets, and We gave the book of Psalms to David.

17:56. Say: Call on those you worship beside God. They have neither the power to remove your troubles nor to change them.

17:57. Those, to whom they pray, themselves seek access to their Lord, competing with each other to be near Him. They hope for His mercy and fear His punishment. The punishment of your Lord indeed is severe.

17:58. There is no community that We will not destroy before the Day of Resurrection or punish it severely. That has been written in Our book of orders.

17:59. Nothing prevents God from sending signs even though the former nations denied them. We gave Thamoud the she-camel as a visible sign, but they wronged her. We send signs for warning.

17:60. We have told you Prophet Muhammad that your Lord encompasses mankind. We showed you our granted vision as a trial for people's faith, and also the cursed tree (the Zaqqum in hell). We continue to warn them, but it only increases their evilness.

17:61. Remember when We said to the angels: Bow down to Adam. They bowed except Satan, who replied: Shall I bow down to the one You have created from clay?

17:62. The Satan said: Do You God see the one You have honored above me? If You delay my punishment until the Day of Resurrection, I will surely lead his descendants off the right path, except a few.

17:63. God said: Be gone. You and whoever will follow you will earn hell. That will be full repayment.

17:64. Lead to destruction those you can with your seductive voice. Make assault on them with your forces. Be their partner in wealth and children, and make promises to them. But Satan promises them nothing but deceit.

17:65. You will have no power over My faithful servants. Your Lord will be their sufficient guardian.

17:66. It is your Lord who sails humans' ships through the sea, so that you may seek His reward. Your Lord is merciful to you.

17:67. When disaster befalls you at sea, all those whom you pray except God abandon you. But, when He brings you back to land safely, you turn away from Him. Humans are very ungrateful.

17:68. Do you feel secure that God will not cave the earth under you or send a violent sandstorm upon you? Then, you will find no one to protect you.

17:69. Are you confident that when you return to sea, God will not send a hurricane against you and drown you for your thanklessness? Then you will find no one to help you.

17:70. We have honored Adam's children and provided them transport on land and sea. We have provided them good things and have given them higher status over Our other creations.

17:71. The day will come when We shall call together all nations with their Messengers. Those who will be given their record in their right hand will read it with pleasure, and they will not be dealt unjustly in the least.

17:72. Whosoever is living blindly here will be blind in the hereafter, and farther away from the right path.

17:73. O Muhammad, the Meccan-Disbelievers tried hard to entice you from Our revelations, that you might invent other revelations to their liking. Then they would have accepted you as a friend.

17:74. Had We not strengthened you in your faith, you may have compromised with them a bit.

17:75. Then, you would have incurred a double punishment in this life and the life to come. You would have no protector against Our punishment.

17:76. Their purpose was to scare and expel you from the land. In that case, they would not have been able to live there, except for a little while.

17:77. That was Our way with the Messengers We sent before you. You will find no change in Our way.

17:78. Perform prayers* from mid-day till night darkness, and recite the Qur'an at dawn, which is especially witnessed by angels.

**Five prayers: Fajr (at dawn), Zuhr (at afternoon), Asr (at late afternoon), Maghrib (at sunset), and Isha (about an hour after sunset/early night).*

17:79. Prophet Muhammad, in the small hours of the morning, pray an additional prayer (Tahujudd). The time is not far when God will raise you, Prophet Muhammad, to a position of honor.

17:80. Say: My Lord, give me an honorable exit and entry, and grant me Your support.

17:81. And declare: Truth has come and falsehood has departed. Falsehood was bound to be defeated.

17:82. What We have revealed in the Qur'an is a healing and a mercy for the believers, though it increases the ruin of the evildoers.

17:83. When We bestow favor upon man, he turns away arrogantly. When misfortune befalls him, he despairs.

17:84. Tell them: Everyone acts according to one's liking. But your Lord knows best who is on the right path.

17:85. They ask you about the soul. Say: The soul is under my Lord's command. But mankind has been given a little knowledge.

17:86. Had God willed, He could take away what He has revealed to you. Then, you would have no one to plead with Us for you.

17:87. But your Lord is merciful and always kind to you.

17:88. Say: If humans and jinns were to collaborate to produce the like of this Qur'an, they would not succeed.

17:89. We have given various arguments in the Qur'an, but most people refuse to believe.

17:90. They say: We shall not believe you O Muhammad, until you cause a spring to gush from the earth for us.

17:91. Or you cause rivers to flow through a garden of palms and grapes.

17:92. Or, as you have threatened us, make the sky fall upon us in pieces, or bring God and angels before us.

17:93. Or you build a house of gold or ascend to the sky. Even then, we will not believe in your ascension until you would have sent down a book for us to read. Say: Glory is to my Lord; I am a human sent as a Messenger.

17:94. Nothing kept humans from belief when guidance came to them, except the excuse: Could God send a human to be His Messenger?

17:95. Say: If there were angels living and walking on the earth safely, We would have sent down to them from heaven an angel as a Messenger.

17:96. Say: God is sufficient as a judge between you and me. Indeed He knows and sees everything.

17:97. Whomever God guides follows the right path, and whomever He misleads shall not find another guardian beside Him. We shall gather the disbelievers on the Day of Resurrection lying on their faces, blind, dumb, and deaf. Their abode will be hell. Whenever its flames will die down, We will rekindle them to increase their burning.

17:98. That is their reward because they disbelieved Our revelations and said: When we are reduced to bones and dust, shall we be raised to life again?

17:99. Do they not see that God created the heavens and the earth and is able to create others like them? Beyond doubt, He has ordained a fixed duration for them. But the wrongdoers refuse to believe.

17:100. O Muhammad, say to them: If you had possessed the treasures of Lord's mercy, you would have greedily hoarded them. Humans have always been stingy.

17:101. We gave Moses nine clear signs. Ask Israel's children about what Pharaoh said to him when Moses came to him. He said: Moses, you are bewitched.

17:102. Moses replied: You know full well that none except the Lord of the heavens and the earth has sent down these clear signs. Pharaoh, you are destined for destruction.

17:103. Pharaoh wanted to drive the Israelites from the land, but We drowned him and those with him.

17:104. After Pharaoh, we said to the Israelites: Live in the land, and when the time to fulfill the promise of the hereafter will come, We shall gather you all together.

17:105. We have revealed the Qur'an with truth, and it has come down with truth. We have sent you to give good news to the believers and to warn the disbelievers.

17:106. We have divided the Qur'an into chapters so that that you may recite it to people at intervals. We have revealed it in stages.

17:107. Say: To believe or not to believe in the Qur'an is up to you. When it is recited to Jews and Christians, who were given its knowledge before its revelation, they bow down and fall upon their faces.

17:108. They say: Glory is to our Lord. His promise has been fulfilled.

17:109. They fall down on their faces weeping and it adds to their humility.

17:110. (O Prophet), say: Whether you call upon God or the merciful is the same. God has the best names. Pray neither with a loud voice nor in silence but seek a way between these.

17:111. Say: Praise is to God, who has no son and no partner in His kingdom, and does not need any protector because of any weakness in Him. Glorify His greatness.

# CHAPTER 18

# THE CAVE

**Name:** From Verse Nine

**Verses:** 110

**Summary:**

- Background: The chapter was revealed to Prophet Muhammad to answer three questions the Meccan-Disbelievers put to him:

    1. Who were the dwellers of the cave?
    2. What is the story of Khidr and Prophet Moses as his companion?
    3. What do you know about Dhul-Qarnain?

  The questions were prepared in consultation with the Jews and Christians. The questions involved the history of Jews and Christians, and this particular aspect of the history was unknown. Accordingly, choice of the questions was made to test whether Prophet Muhammad possessed any source of knowledge for unknown things.
- Theme:

    - The dwellers of the cave believed in God's oneness which has been put forward in the Qur'an.
    - The sleepers were persecuted as Meccan-Muslims were being persecuted.
    - Even if a believer is persecuted by a cruel society, he should not bow down before falsehood but emigrate from the place with trust in God.
    - God brought the dwellers of the cave out after a long hiding of 300 years. God has power to end the universe and raise everyone to life at the Day of Judgment.

- Those who say God has begotten a son are uttering a monstrous lie.
- God has given examples in the Qur'an for people to understand His message.
- God's words are countless and all cannot be recorded.
- Whenever you promise to do something in future, always say: If God wills (Insha Allah).
- No one is authorized to change God's word.

- O Muhammad, be content with those who call upon their Lord. Proclaim: Truth from God has come, choice is yours to believe or disbelieve.
- Prophet Muhammad is a human.
- An example of:
    - Two gardens to show difference between a believer and a disbeliever.
    - The worldly life and its relationship with the life of hereafter.
- Fate of:
    - those who follow Satan and commit to idol worship.
    - the believers and the disbelievers on the Day of Judgment.

**By Verse**

In the name of God, the compassionate, the merciful:

18:1. All praise is for God, Who revealed the Qur'an to His servant Prophet Muhammad and it does not contain any falsehood.

18:2. God made the Qur'an plain and clear to warn the disbelievers of His severe punishment and give good news to the believers who do righteous deeds. They will have a good reward of paradise.

18:3. They will live in paradise forever.

18:4. Warn those who say: God has fathered a son.

18:5. Their forefathers and they have no knowledge of it. What they are saying is a dreadful lie.

18:6. O Muhammad, if they do not believe in this message, you would torment yourself with grief.

18:7. We have decorated the earth with all kind of ornaments to test mankind as to who is best in deeds.

18:9. Have you thought that companions of the cave and writings at the cave were a wonder of Our signs?

18:10. When the young men fled to the cave for refuge, they said: Lord, have mercy upon us, and help us in our difficulty.

18:11. We put them to sleep in the cave for a number of years.

18:12. We awakened them to find out which of their two groups could best estimate the length of their sleep.

18:13. We tell you their story in truth. They were youths who believed in their Lord, and We advanced them in guidance.

18:14. We strengthened their hearts. They stood up and said: Our Lord is the Lord of the heavens and the earth. We will not call upon any god beside Him. Otherwise, we would have done an evil deed.

18:15. Our people worship gods other than Him. Do they have a convincing proof of their divinity? Who is more evil than the one who fabricates a lie against God?

18:16. They were told: When you leave your people and their worship of idol-gods than God, seek refuge in the cave. Your Lord will show His mercy upon you and take care of you.

18:17. Had you been present, you would have seen the rising sun passed to the right of the cave, and passed to the left for sunset, while they slept in the cave. That was God's sign. Whom God guides is rightly guided; but whom God leaves to go off the right path, no one can lead him to the right path.

18:18. You would have thought that they were awake while they were sleeping. We changed their sides from right to left and vice versa, while their dog stretched his forelegs at the entrance. If you had looked at them, you would have run away from them in fear.

18:19. We awakened them that they might question one another. One of them asked: How long have we been here? Some replied: May be a day or part of a day; the others said: Our Lord knows best how long we have remained here. One of us should go to the city with this silver coin to bring some good food and provisions. He hould be cautious not to let anyone know our whereabouts.

18:20. If the people were to find us, they will stone us to death or force us to return to their religion. Then we surely will be ruined.

18:21. We let people know about the cavemen's secret so that people might know that God's promise was true, and that the hour of judgment was sure to come. The later people argued what to do with the remains of their dead saints. Some said: Let us construct a monument over them; their Lord knows best who they were. Those who won the argument said: Let us build a house of worship over them.

18:22. Some will say: There were three cavemen, the fourth was their dog. Others, guessing the unseen, will say: There were five, the sixth was their dog. Some others will say: There were seven, the eighth was their dog. O Muhammad, say: Except My Lord, not very many people know of their number. Do not argue about them except what has been revealed and do not ask about them from anyone.

18:23. Do not say about anything: I will surely do it tomorrow.

18:24. Except by adding: If God wills (Insha Allah). If you forget, remember your Lord and say: I hope my Lord will guide me to what is nearer to the right conduct.

18:25. Some people say they slept in the cave for 300 years and some add nine years.

18:26. Say: God knows best how long they slept. He has the knowledge of the secrets of the heavens and the earth. He sees clearly and hears keenly. There is no protector except Him. He does not share His command with anyone.

18:27. O Muhammad, recite what has been revealed to you in the Qur'an. No one can change His words, and you will find no protector besides Him.

18:28. Associate yourself with those who call on their Lord in the morning and the evening desiring His goodwill. Do not turn your eyes away from them desiring the riches of this life. Do not follow the disbeliever whose heart We have made unmindful to Our remembrance. He follows his low desires and exceeds limits.

18:29. Say: The truth is from your Lord. Let him believe, whoever wills, and disbelieve, whoever wills. For the wrongdoers, We have prepared a fire whose walls will surround them. If they call for a drink, they will be given water with hot molten metal, which will scald their faces. Wretched will be the drink, and evil will be their resting place.

18:30. Reward of the believers, who have acted rightly, will not be lost.

18:31. They will live in paradise forever, where rivers will be flowing. They will wear gold bracelets, green garments of fine silk and brocade, and recline on decorated couches. Their reward and the resting place will be excellent.

18:32. O Muhammad, give them an example of two men. To one, We granted two gardens of grapevines, which were surrounded by palm-trees, and had crop fields between them.

18:33. Each of the two gardens produced abundant crop. A river flowed through the gardens.

18:34. After the abundant harvest, he said to his companion: I am richer than you and have more manpower.

18:35. Having wronged his soul with pride, he went into his garden and said: I do not think that this will ever perish.

18:36. I do not think that the Hour of Judgment will ever come. Even if I am brought back to my Lord, I shall surely find there a better place than this.

18:37. His companion said to him: Do you disbelieve in He Who created you from dust and a sperm-drop and then grew you to be a man?

18:38. For me, God is my Lord, and I do not associate anyone with Him.

18:39. When you entered your garden, why did you not say: What God wills happens and there is no power greater than God? Though you see me poorer than you in wealth and children,

18:40. but my Lord may give me a garden better than your garden and will send upon your garden a calamity from the sky, and it will become barren land.

18:41. Or its water will drain deep into the earth and you would never be able to find it.

18:42. His garden of grapevines was destroyed. He wrung his hands in sorrow for all that he had spent upon it, because it was all ruined on its grapevine supports. He said: I should not have served other gods except my Lord.

18:43. There was no one to help him except God and he could not protect himself.

18:44. In such cases, protection only comes from God, the true Lord. His reward is the best, and He is the best in giving success.

18:45. Present to them an example from this life. Rain makes earth's vegetation green, but soon it turns into stubble, which winds scatter. It is only God who prevails over all things.

18:46. The wealth and children are ornaments of this life. But lasting good deeds are better in your Lord 's sight for reward, and are a better hope for salvation.

18:47. One day, We, God, shall remove mountains, and you will see the earth as a level plain. We shall gather all mankind, leaving no one behind.

18:48. They shall be presented before your Lord in rows, and He will say to them: You have returned to Us just as We created you the first time. But, you thought that you will never meet your Lord.

18:49. Record of their deeds will be placed before them. You will see criminals fearful of its contents, saying: Woe to us! What kind of book is this that leaves out nothing; all small or great acts are written in it? They will find all their deeds recorded there. Your Lord will not do injustice to anyone.

18:50. Remember when We said to angels: Bow down before Adam; they did, but not Satan. He was one of the jinns. He disobeyed his Lord's command. Would you then take him and his offspring as protectors and helpers than God while they are your enemies? What an evil exchange the wrongdoers have chosen.

18:51. I, God, did not call the Satan and his offspring to witness the creation of the heavens and the earth or their own creation. I would not ask them for assistance as they were to lead mankind off the right path.

18:52. Remember the day when your Lord will say: Call on those idols whom you considered to be My associates. They shall call the idols, but shall not have any response. We will cause a separation between them.
18:53. The sinners shall see the fire of hell and know that they shall be thrown into it. They will find no way of escape from it.
18:54. We have given many examples in the Qur'an for the benefit of mankind, but man is overly contentious.
18:55. Nothing prevents mankind from believing and asking forgiveness from their Lord when guidance has come to them, unless they are waiting for the calamity which overtook previous nations, or to see Our punishment with their own eyes.
18:56. We send Messengers only for giving good news and warnings. Those who disbelieve refute truth with falsehood by mocking Our revelations and warnings.
18:57. Who is more unjust than the one who is reminded of his Lord's revelations, but turns away from them and forgets what his hands have done? We have sealed their hearts, lest they understand Our revelations, and made them hard of hearing. If you will call them to guidance, they will never be guided.
18:58. Your Lord is most forgiving and merciful. If He were to take them to task for what they have earned, He would have hastened their punishment. But He has set an appointed term for them, from which they will not escape.
18:59. We destroyed such people when they did wrong. But We had fixed time for their destruction.
18:60. Moses said to his servant: We will keep on traveling until we reach the junction of the two rivers, even if we have to travel a long time.
18:61. When they reached the junction, they forgot about their fish. It slipped into water and swam freely.
18:62. When they had travelled some more, Moses said to his servant: Let us eat; this journey has tired us.
18:63. The servant said: I forgot the fish where we rested on the rock. Satan made me forget to tell you. The fish slipped into the water miraculously.
18:64. That is what we have been searching. They went back the way they came.
18:65. They found one of Our servants (Khidr) whom We had granted Our mercy and had given knowledge.
18:66. Moses said to him: May I follow you to guide me by what God has taught you?

18:67. He said: You will not have patience in accompanying me.

18:68. He also said: How can you have patience about which you have no knowledge?

18:69. Moses replied: God willing (Insha Allah), I shall be patient, and obey you.

18:70. He said: If you are to follow me, do not ask me about anything until I talk to you about it myself.

18:71. They both proceeded and boarded a boat. Moses' companion made a hole in the bottom of the boat. Moses said: Have you made a hole to drown the people in the boat? You have done a strange thing.

18:72. He replied: Did I not tell you that you would not bear with me?

18:73. Moses said: I forgot and am sorry. Please do not be angry with me because of this.

18:74. They moved on until they met a boy. Moses' companion killed him. Moses said: You have killed an innocent person who did no wrong. Certainly you have done an evil thing.

18:75. He replied: Did I not tell you that you would not bear with me?

18:76. Moses said: If I ask you about anything after this, do not keep me as a companion. You would have justification for that.

18:77. They moved on and came to a town. They asked its people for food, but the people refused. They found a wall about to collapse. Moses' companion (Khidr) repaired it. Moses said: If you wished, you could have asked a payment for it.

18:78. Moses' companion replied: We must go our separate ways, but I will explain to you my deeds about which you had no patience.

18:79. As for the boat, it belonged to poor fishermen. I damaged it because behind them was a king who was seizing every boat by force.

18:80. As for the boy, his parents were believers. I was afraid that he would oppress them by rebellion and disbelief.

18:81. I wished that their Lord would give them another son, righteous and affectionate.

18:82. As for the wall, it belonged to two orphans. There was a treasure beneath it. Their father was a righteous man. Your Lord, in His mercy, decreed that they should reach maturity and dig out their treasure. I did not repair the wall of my own accord. Those are interpretation of the things about which you could not have patience.

18:83. O Muhammad, they ask you about Dhul-Qarnain*. Say: I shall tell you about him.

**To be either Alexander the Great, or Cyrus - the king of Persia.*

18:84. We gave him power on the earth, and means to accomplish everything.
18:85. He journeyed on a road,
18:86. till he reached a muddy pond where the sun was setting. Nearby he found people. We said: Dhul-Qarnain, either you punish them or show them kindness.
18:87. He replied: I will punish those who have done wrong. Then, they will return to their Lord, Who will punish them severely.
18:88. As for those who have faith and have done good acts, they will have good reward, and I (Dhul-Qarnain) will speak to them kindly.
18:89. Then, he followed another road.
18:90. He came to a place where the sun was rising on a people who had no shelter.
18:91. He left them and moved on. We had full knowledge of all his resources.
18:92. Then, he followed another road,
18:93. till he reached between two mountains. There he found a people who could hardly understand a word of what he said to them.
18:94. They said: Dhul-Qarnain, Gog and Magog* are ravaging the land. We will honor you if you will build us a wall between them and us.

**wild tribes of Central Asia.*

18:95. He replied: The power my Lord has given me is far greater than what you attribute to me. Only provide me with material and labor; and I will build a strong wall between them and you.
18:96. Bring me iron sheets. When he erected them to close the gap between the two mountains, he said: Make fire by blowing with your bellows. When the iron sheets became red hot, he asked that molten copper be brought to pour on the iron wall.
18:97. Gog and Magog could neither scale the wall nor penetrate through it.
18:98. He said: This is a mercy from my Lord. But when my Lord's promise is fulfilled, He will level the wall to ground. The promise of my Lord is ever true.
18:99. On that Day (of Resurrection), We shall allow them to come in crowds. The trumpet will be blown, and We shall gather them all.
18:100. On that Day (of Resurrection), We, God, shall show hell to the disbelievers.
18:101. They had turned a blind eye to My advice and a deaf ear to My

warning.

18:102. Do the disbelievers think that they can take My servants as their guardians besides Me? We, God, have prepared hell for the disbelievers to live.

18:103. O Muhammad, tell them: Shall We tell you of the greatest losers because of their deeds?

18:104. They are those whose efforts are lost in the worldly life, while they think that they are acting righteously.

18:105. They are those who disbelieve in their Lord's revelations and in meeting with Him. Therefore, their deeds are useless, and We will not give them any consideration on the Day of Resurrection.

18:106. Their reward is hell, because they rejected faith, and ridiculed My revelations and Messengers.

18:107. The believers who have acted righteously will live in paradise.

18:108. They will live there forever desiring no change.

18:109. O Muhammad, tell them: If the ocean was ink to write my Lord's words, the ocean would be consumed before my Lord's words were finished, even if We were to bring another ocean to add to it.

18:110. Tell them: I, Prophet Muhammad, am a human like you. It has been revealed to me that your god is one God. So whoever hopes to meet his Lord should act righteously and not worship anyone except Him.

# CHAPTER 19

## MARY

**Name:** From Verse 16.

**Verses:** 98

**Historical Significance:**

This chapter has played a significant role in Islam's early history. It was revealed to Prophet Muhammad very early at Mecca, towards the end of the fourth year of his Prophethood.

Some Muslims migrated to Abyssinia, the Christian King Negus' country, because of their increased persecution by the Quraysh (Tribe of Mecca). The Quraysh approached the king to return the Muslims. The king asked the Muslims to explain their faith. They said: O king, because of our ignorance, we became corrupt. Prophet Muhammad, God's Messenger, has reformed us. The Quraysh began to persecute his followers, so we have come to your country to be free from the persecution.

Hearing that, the king asked the Muslims to recite a piece of the revelation which God has sent to Prophet Muhammad. The Muslims recited parts of this chapter that relate the story of Prophets Jesus and Yahya (John). The king wept and said: Surely, this revelation and Jesus' message have come from the same source. I will not force you to go back.

The next day, the Quraysh returned to the king and said: The Muslims say a horrible thing about Jesus, the son of Mary. The king sent for the migrants and asked them to explain about Jesus. The Muslims replied: Jesus was God's servant and a Messenger. He was a spirit and God's word which was sent to Virgin Mary. The king was satisfied and allowed the Muslims to stay in his kingdom in peace.

**Summary:**

- The story of:
    - Prophets Zacharias, and Yahya's (John's) birth and youth.
    - Mary, and Jesus' miraculous birth. Dialogue between Mary and God's angel. Baby Jesus spoke from the cradle to defend his mother and to proclaim to be a prophet.
    - Prophet Abraham, and his idol-worshipping father.
- It is a huge lie that Jesus is God's son. It is not befitting to God's

majesty to father a son.
- The Prophethood of Moses, Ishmael and Idris (Enoch, Cain's son).
- The believers' and disbelievers' lives in this world and the hereafter.
- No god other than God will be able to save humans on the Day of Judgment.
- God has revealed the Qur'an in Arabic to make it easier for Prophet Muhammad's community to understand it.

**By Verse**

In the name of God, the compassionate, the merciful:

19:1. Kaf, Ha, Ya, Ain, Suad (are Arabic letters).
19:2. This is a description of your Lord's mercy to His servant Zacharias,
19:3. when he prayed to his Lord privately.
19:4. He prayed: Lord, my bones have weakened, grey hair has grown on my head with age, and I have never been unsuccessful in my prayer to You.
19:5. I fear about what my relatives will do after me, because my wife is barren. Bless me with a heir,
19:6. who will be my heir and heir of Jacob's family. Make him to please You.
19:7. God answered his prayer: O Zacharias, We give you good news of a son whose name will be Yahya (John). We have not given this name to anyone before.
19:8. He asked: Lord, how will I have a son when my wife is barren and I am quite old?
19:9. God replied: That will be so. Your Lord says that it is easy for Me as I created you before, while you were nothing.
19:10. Zacharias said: Lord, give me a sign. God replied: You shall not talk to people for three successive days and nights.
19:11. Zacharias came out from his chamber and signaled to his people to celebrate God's praises in the morning and the evening.
19:12. God said: John, follow the Scriptures firmly. We blessed him with wisdom in his childhood.
19:13. And We gave him affection, purity from sins, and he grew up to be righteous.
19:14. And obedient to his parents, and not arrogant.
19:15. He was blessed the day he was born, the day he will die, and the day he will be raised to life.
19:16. O Muhammad, point to Mary's story in the Qur'an, when she

withdrew from her family to her chamber to the east.

19:17. She went into seclusion behind a curtain. We sent Our angel to her in the form of a man.

19:18. She said: I seek refuge with the gracious God from you if indeed you fear Him.

19:19. He replied: I am your Lord's Messenger to give you news of a righteous son.

19:20. She said: How can I give birth to a child when I am a virgin and no man has touched me?

19:21. The angel replied: That will be so. Lord says: It is easy for Him; We will make him a sign to the people and a blessing from Us. This has already been decided.

19:22. She conceived him, and retired to a remote place.

19:23. When she started to have childbirth pangs, she lay down by the trunk of a palm-tree, and cried: I wish I had died before this and was forgotten.

19:24. But a voice spoke to her from under the tree: Do not lose heart, your Lord has provided you a stream running at your feet.

19:25. And if you will shake the palm-tree trunk, it will drop fresh, ripe dates for you.

19:26. So eat, drink, and be happy. Should you see any human being, say: I have vowed a fast to God, the most gracious, and will not talk to anyone today.

19:27. Then she brought the baby to her people, who said: O Mary, you have certainly done a strange thing.

19:28. O Aaron's sister*, your father was not adulterous, and your mother was not a prostitute.

**Aaron was a prophet. "O Aaron's sister" is not literally, but as a "virtuous woman."*

19:29. She pointed to the baby. They said: How can we speak to a child in the cradle?

19:30. The baby Jesus spoke: I am a servant of God, Who has given me the Gospel and made me a prophet.

19:31. He has blessed me wherever I may be, and has directed me to establish prayer and give charity to the poor as long as I live.

19:32. God has told me to be kind to my mother, and not be arrogant.

19:33. I was blessed the day I was born, and may peace be upon me on the day I die, and on the day I will be raised to life.

19:34. That was Jesus, the son of Mary. That is the truth which they are disputing.

19:35. It is not suitable for God to father a son. Glory is to Him. When

He orders something to happen, it happens.
19:36. Jesus said: God is my Lord and your Lord. Worship Him. That is the right path.
19:37. But people are divided about Jesus. The disbelievers are warned about the Day of Resurrection.
19:38. The disbelievers will hear and see clearly the day they will come before Us. The wrongdoers today are in clear error.
19:39. O Muhammad, warn them about the Day of Regret, when their fate will be decided. They are negligent and persist in disbelief.
19:40. We, God, will inherit the earth and all those who are on it. They will return to Us.
19:41. Abraham's story is in the Qur'an. He was a truthful person and a prophet.
19:42. Abraham said to his father: Why do you worship an idol which can neither hear nor see, and will not benefit you at all?
19:43. Father, truth has been revealed to me, not you. Therefore, follow me; I will guide you to a right path.
19:44. Father, do not worship Satan. He has rebelled against God.
19:45. Father, I fear that God will punish you and you will become Satan's follower.
19:46. His father replied: Do you hate my gods, O Abraham? If you do not stop, I will stone you. Go away from me forever.
19:47. Abraham said: Peace be upon you. I will ask God to forgive you. Indeed, He has been gracious to me.
19:48. I will leave you and your idols. I will pray to God and hope that He will not ignore my prayers.
19:49. When Abraham left them and the idols they worshipped, We gave him Isaac and Jacob, and made each a prophet.
19:50. We blessed them with Our mercy, and gave them high honor.
19:51. Moses' story is in the Qur'an. He was chosen to be a Messenger and a prophet.
19:52. We called Moses from the right side of the Mount Sinai, and when he came near, We talked to him intimately.
19:53. Out of Our mercy, We made his brother Aaron a prophet to help him.
19:54. Ishmael's story is in the Qur'an. He was truthful in his promise, and he was a Messenger and a prophet.
19:55. He used to direct his people for prayer and almsgiving and his Lord was pleased with him.
19:56. The story of Idris* is in the Qur'an. He was a man of truth and a prophet.

**Enoch, son of Cain.*

19:57. We gave him high honor.
19:58. God has been gracious upon prophets from:

- Adam's descendants,
- those We carried in Noah boat,
- Prophets Abraham and Israel's descendants, and
- those We guided and chose.

When God's verses were recited to them, they fell on their knees in prayer and wept.
19:59. But their descendants neglected their prayers and followed sensual desires. They will meet their destruction.
19:60. Except those who repent, believe, and act righteously. They will enter paradise and will not be wronged at all.
19:61. They will enter into gardens of perpetual residence, which the merciful God has promised His servants and are yet hidden from their eyes. His promise shall be surely fulfilled.
19:62. There, they will not hear any idle talk, but hear only the words of peace. Their sustenance will be provided, morning and evening.
19:63. That is paradise, which Our righteous servants will inherit.
19:64. The angels say: O Muhammad, we do not come down except by your Lord's command. To Him belongs what is before us, behind us, and in between. Your Lord does not forget.
19:65. He is the Lord of the heavens and the earth and whatever is in between them. So worship Him steadfastly. Do you know any other like Him?
19:66. The man asks: When I am dead, shall I be raised to life?
19:67. Does the man not remember that We created him out of nothing?
19:68. By Lord, We will surely gather them and also the devils; and bring them around hell upon their knees.
19:69. From every sect, We shall draw out their most obstinate rebels against God.
19:70. We, God, alone know best who deserve most to be burned in hell.
19:71. Every one of you will pass over hell; this is an unavoidable decree of your Lord.
19:72. We shall save those who guarded against evil, but leave the wrongdoers there to suffer on their knees.
19:73. When Our clear revelations are recited to the disbelievers, they say to the believers: Which of our two parties is better in position and company?

19:74. How many generations have We destroyed before them who were better in possessions and glitter?

19:75. Say: God will put up with the disbelievers until they see that God's promise of either punishment or the Hour of Resurrection is fulfilled. Then, they will come to know who is in a worst position and smaller in following.

19:76. God increases the guidance of those who do right. The lasting good works are better for earning Lord's reward and a good end.

19:77. Have you seen who disbelieved in God's verses and yet said: I will surely be given wealth and children?

19:78. Has the disbeliever seen future, or has he taken a promise from God?

19:79. By no means! We will record what he says and lengthen his punishment.

19:80. He will leave behind what he talks about and will appear before Us alone.

19:81. The disbelievers have taken other gods to be a source of strength.

19:82. Idol-gods shall deny their worship, and turn against them.

19:83. Do you not see that We have sent devils to allure the disbelievers to do evil?

19:84. Have patience. Their days are numbered.

19:85. The day will surely come when We shall gather the groups of righteous before the most gracious God.

19:86. And drive the sinners to the hell thirsty.

19:87. None will have the power of intercession without permission from the most merciful God.

19:88. They say: The most merciful God has fathered a son.

19:89. They have said an atrocious lie.

19:90. Because of that the heavens might burst open, the earth split apart, and the mountains crumble to dust.

19:91. That they should assign a son to the most merciful God.

19:92. It is not befitting for the most merciful God to father a son.

19:93. There is no one in the heavens and on earth that will not come to the most merciful God as a servant.

19:94. God knows all His creatures and has their exact count.

19:95. Every one of them will come to Him alone on the Day of Resurrection.

19:96. God will bless the faithful and the righteous with love.

19:97. O Muhammad, We have revealed the Qur'an in your own language so that you may give good news to the righteous and warn the contentious people.

19:98. We have destroyed many generations before them. Can you find one of them or hear a sound of them?

# CHAPTER 20

## TA-HA

**Name:** From Verse One

**Verses:** 135

**Summary:**

- God revealed the Qur'an in Arabic to teach and remind those who fear God. Those who do not read the Qur'an and follow its guidance shall be raised blind on the Day of Resurrection. The Qur'an is a sign from God so there can be no excuse for the disbelievers on the Day of Judgment.
- A scene from the Day of Judgment. What will happen to the criminals and the believers on the Day of Judgment?
- Do not envy others in worldly benefits; rather seek God's pleasure if you want to attain the blessed end.
- The story of:
    - God's:
        - Creation of Adam and Satan's temptation. God forgave Adam's forgetfulness, chose him for His service, and guided him to the right path.
        - Selection of Prophet Moses and his brother Aaron as His Messengers, and revelations of His miracles to Moses.
    - Prophet Moses':
        - Invitation to Pharaoh to believe in God. Pharaoh's refusal and challenge to Prophet Moses to confront his magicians in public. After witnessing Prophet Moses' miracle, the magicians' acceptance of his God. Dialogue between Pharaoh and the magicians.
        - Communion with God on the mountain. Israelites' worshipping of the calf in absence of Prophet Moses. Prophet Moses' inquiry about idol worshipping, his decision about Samiri (a rebellious follower) and the golden calf, and his address to his people.
    - Deliverance of Israel's children from Pharaoh's bondage. Drowning of Pharaoh and his soldiers in the sea.

## By Verse

In the name of God, the compassionate, the merciful:

20:1. Ta-Ha (is an Arabic word).
20:2. O Muhammad, We have not revealed the Qur'an to distress you.
20:3. But to advise the God-fearing.
20:4. The Qur'an is God's revelation. God created the earth and the high heavens.
20:5. God, the merciful, is sitting on the throne of authority.
20:6. To God belongs what is in the heavens, on earth, between them, and beneath the surface of ground.
20:7. You do not need to speak aloud because God knows the secrets and what is hidden.
20:8. He is God. There is no god but Him. The most beautiful names belong to Him.
20:9. Have you heard Moses' story?
20:10. When Moses saw the fire, he said to his family: Wait; I see a fire. Perhaps, I can bring you a torch of light or find guidance for the way.
20:11. When he came to the fire, a voice called him: O Moses,
20:12. I am your Lord; remove your shoes; you are in Towah's sacred valley.
20:13. I have chosen you. So listen to what shall be revealed to you.
20:14. I am God. There is no god except Me. Worship Me and establish prayer for My remembrance.
20:15. Surely, the Hour of Judgment is to come, but I am concealing it so that everyone may be rewarded for its deeds.
20:16. Let not those, who do not believe in it and follow their desires, turn you away from it for you to perish.
20:17. What is in your right hand, Moses?
20:18. Moses replied: It is my stick; I lean on it, bring down leaves with it for my sheep, and have other uses for it.
20:19. God said: Throw it down, Moses.
20:20. Moses threw down his stick. It became quickly a moving snake.
20:21. God said: Take hold of it and do not fear; We will restore it to its former state, the stick.
20:22. Put your hand under your armpit. It will come out white without harm. This will be another sign.
20:23. We shall show you Our greater signs.
20:24. Go to Pharaoh; he has exceeded all limits.
20:25. Moses said: Lord, give me courage.

20:26. And make my task easy for me.
20:27. Untie the knot from my tongue.
20:28. So that they may understand my speech,
20:29. and appoint a helper for me from my family,
20:30. my brother, Aaron.
20:31. Increase my strength with him,
20:32. and let him share my task.
20:33. So that we may glorify You.
20:34. And remember You always.
20:35. You are surely looking after us.
20:36. God replied: Moses, your request is granted.
20:37. We favored you another time,
20:38. when We revealed to your mother,
20:39. saying: Place the child (Moses) into a chest and cast it into the river. The river shall throw it on the bank. There, his and My enemy will pick him up. I placed you (Moses) under My love to raise you before My eyes.
20:40. Recall when your sister went to them and said: Shall I bring you someone who will nurse him? So We brought you back to your mother to put her at ease and not to grieve. You slew a man, but We saved you from the trouble, but tried you in various ways. Then you lived for a number of years with the Midians* and came here as I ordained.

**they lived in the northwest Arabian Peninsula, on the east shore of the Gulf of Aqaba on the Red Sea*

20:41. I, God, have chosen you for My mission.
20:42. Your brother and you should go with My signs and do not forget to remember Me.
20:43. Both of you should go to Pharaoh, who has transgressed.
20:44. Speak to him gently; he may pay attention and fear God.
20:45. They said: Lord, we are afraid that he will punish us severely.
20:46. God replied: Do not be afraid. I am with you. I hear and see everything.
20:47. Go to Pharaoh and say to him: We are your Lord's Messengers. Let Israel's children go with us and do not oppress them anymore. We have come to you with your Lord's sign. Peace will be on him who follows his Lord's guidance.
20:48. It has been revealed to us that God will punish those who deny His signs and turn away from Him.
20:49. Pharaoh said: O Moses, who is your Lord?
20:50. Moses replied: Our Lord is He who created everything in their

distinctive forms and then determined their function.

20:51. Pharaoh asked: Then what is the status of earlier generations?

20:52. Moses replied: The knowledge of that is with my Lord, duly recorded. My Lord neither errs, nor forgets.

20:53. It is God Who has made the earth like a bedspread for you; has enabled you to travel in it; and has sent down water from the sky to produce diverse plants,

20:54. saying: Eat and feed your cattle. Surely, there are signs in that for those who are thoughtful.

20:55. We created you from earth, you will return to it, and We will bring you back to life from it.

20:56. We showed Pharaoh Our signs, but he rejected them and refused to pay attention.

20:57. Pharaoh said: Moses, have you come to drive us out of our land with your magic?

20:58. We can surely produce magic like yours. Let us agree upon when and where to meet, and neither one of us shall fail to keep the agreement. Let us meet in an open field.

20:59. Moses replied: Let us meet on the festival day when people assemble at mid-morning.

20:60. Pharaoh went away, and came back with his magicians.

20:61. Moses said to Pharaoh's magicians: Woe to you. Do not invent a lie against God or He will destroy you. Whoever invents falsehood fails.

20:62. In private, the magicians debated with one another about what to do.

20:63. The magicians said to Pharaoh: These are two magicians who want to drive you out of your land with their magic and do away with your way of life.

20:64. So, solidify your plan, and come forward in ranks. Whosoever will win this day will surely be successful.

20:65. The magicians asked Moses: Will you make your move first or should we?

20:66 Moses replied: You be the first. Because of the magicians' magic, it appeared to Moses that their ropes and staffs were moving like snakes.

20:67. Moses was alarmed.

20:68. But We, God, said to Moses: Do not be afraid; you will have the upper hand.

20:69. Throw down what is in your right hand. It will swallow up what they have made. What they have made is but a magic trick, and the magicians will not succeed regardless how skillful they may be.

20:70. The magicians prostrated saying: We believe in the Lord of Prophets Aaron and Moses.

20:71. Pharaoh said: How dare you believe in God of Moses without my approval? Moses must be your leader who has taught you magic. I will cut off your hands and feet on the opposite sides, and crucify you on the trunks of palm-trees. You will know whose punishment is more severe and lasting.

20:72. They replied: We will not follow you because of the clear evidence that has come to us from God Who created us. Therefore, you can punish us if you like, but only in this life.

20:73. We have put our trust in our Lord so that He may forgive our sins and the magic you compelled us to practice. God's reward is better and more lasting.

20:74. Whoever comes to his Lord as a sinner will be thrown in hell, where he will neither live nor die.

20:75. But whoever comes to Him as a believer having acted rightly will be raised to the highest rank.

20:76. He will live in paradise forever, where rivers flow. That will be the reward of those who purify themselves.

20:77. We revealed to Moses to travel by night with My servants and to strike a dry path through the sea for them. There was no need to fear for being overtaken by Pharaoh or for drowning.

20:78. Pharaoh pursued them with his soldiers, but Pharaoh and his soldiers drowned in the sea.

20:79. Pharaoh misled his people and did not guide them.

20:80. O Children of Israel, We saved you from your enemy, and made an agreement with you at the right side of Mount Sinai. We sent down to you manna (miraculous food) and quails,

20:81. saying: Eat the good things We have provided you and do not transgress, lest God's anger should fall upon you. And upon whom My anger falls has certainly perished.

20:82. But I, God, forgive whoever repents, believes in Me, acts rightly, and follows the right path.

20:83. God asked Moses: Why have you come in haste from your people?

20:84. Moses replied: They are close behind. I hastened to please You.

20:85. God said: We have tested your people in your absence. The Samiri (a rebellious follower) has led them off the right path.

20:86. Moses returned to his people angry and sad. He said to them: Did God not made a good promise with you? Was my absence too long for you, or you wanted God's displeasure that you broke your promise to me?

20:87. They replied: We did not break our promise to you intentionally. We were made to carry people's ornaments. We throw them into fire, and Samiri did the same.

20:88. Then he forged a calf for them, which had a hollow sound. Then Samiri and his companions said: This is your god, and the god of Moses, whom he has forgotten.

20:89. Could they not see that it could not answer a word for them, and could neither benefit nor harm them?

20:90. Aaron told them: My people, you are being tested by it. Your Lord is most merciful. Follow me and obey my orders.

20:91. They replied: We will worship it till Moses returns.

20:92. Moses asked: Aaron, when they were going off the right path, what prevented you,

20:93. from following me? Why did you disobey me?

20:94. Aaron replied: O my mother's son, do not grab me by my beard or by the hair of my head. I was afraid that you would say: I caused division among the Children of Israel, and did not obey you.

20:95. Moses asked Samiri: Why did you do it?

20:96. Samiri replied: I saw what they did not see. I took a handful of dust from the footsteps of the Messenger and threw it on the calf. That is what my soul enticed me to do.

20:97. Moses said: Go away. You will be an outcast in this life and will not escape your punishment in the life to come. Look at your god to whom you are devoted; we will burn it and scatter its ashes over sea.

20:98. O people, your god is the one God. There is no god but Him. He has knowledge of all things.

20:99. O Muhammad, We have given you history of the previous times and the Qur'an.

20:100. Whoever turns away from it will bear a heavy burden on the Day of Resurrection.

20:101. They will carry the burden forever, an evil burden on the Day of Resurrection.

20:102. On that Day (of Resurrection), the trumpet will be blown and the sinners will be gathered with terrified eyes.

20:103. They will murmur among themselves: You lingered but only for 10 days.

20:104. We know well what they will say. The most righteous among them will say: You stayed away no longer than a day.

20:105. They ask you about mountains. Say: My Lord will break them into dust.
20:106. He will leave the earth a level field.
20:107. You will not see there a depression or a mound.
20:108. On that Day (of Resurrection), mankind will follow the truthful caller. Their voices will be humbled before God, the most merciful. You shall hear nothing except the low voice of their footsteps.
20:109. On that Day (of Resurrection), no one will be able to intercede for them except the one permitted by the most merciful God and whose word is acceptable to Him.
20:110. God knows what is before them and behind them, but they do not know about it.
20:111. All faces will be humbled before God, the ever-living, and ever-sustaining. The sinner who carried injustice will have failed.
20:112. The believer who acts rightly will neither fear injustice nor loss of his reward.
20:113. We have revealed the Qur'an in Arabic and have given warnings in it so that they may avoid sin or it may cause them to pay attention.
20:114. Praise is to God, the true king. O Muhammad, do not hasten in reciting the Qur'an before its revelation is completed to you, but say: Lord, increase my knowledge.
20:115. We had taken a promise from Adam, but he forgot it. We found no resolve in him to disobey Us.
20:116. When We, God, said to angels: Bow down to Adam. They did, but Satan refused.
20:117. We said to Adam: He is an enemy to you and your wife Eve. Let him not remove you from paradise to suffer.
20:118. In paradise, you will not be hungry and naked.
20:119. You will not be thirsty and feel the sun's heat.
20:120. But Satan whispered to Adam: Shall I show you the tree of eternity and the everlasting kingdom?
20:121. Adam and his wife Eve ate the tree's fruit. They saw their nakedness and covered themselves with leaves from paradise. Thus, Adam forgot to obey his Lord and went off the right path.
20:122. Then, his Lord chose him for His service, forgave him, and guided him.
20:123. God said: Go forth, both of you, from here. Your descendants will be enemy to one another. When My guidance comes to you, those who follow it will neither go off the right path nor suffer.

20:124. But whosoever turns away from My message will have a troubled life, and We shall raise him blind on the Day of Judgment.
20:125. He will say: Lord, why have you raised me blind while I had sight when I lived?
20:126. God will answer: Because Our signs came to you, and you ignored them. Thus you are being ignored this Day of Judgment.
20:127. Like that We, God, repay him who exceeds all limits and does not believe in his Lord's signs. But punishment of the hereafter is more severe and lasting.
20:128. Has it not become clear to them that how many generations We have destroyed before them as they walk among their dwellings? In that are signs for the thoughtful.
20:129. Had your Lord not fixed and deferred the term of their punishment, they would have been punished in this life.
20:130. Be patient with what they say. Glorify your Lord before sunrise and sunset, and during the day and the night, and you will find comfort.
20:131. Do not long for what We have given to some of them to test them. Your Lord's reward is better and more lasting.
20:132. Prescribe prayer to your people and establish it steadfastly. We do not ask you to provide Us anything, but We provide for you. The best outcome will be for the righteous.
20:133. They say: Why does Prophet Muhammad not bring us a proof from his Lord? Have they not been given enough evidence in the former Scriptures?
20:134. If We had punished the disbelievers before this, they would have said: Lord, if You would have sent us a Messenger, we would certainly have followed Your revelations before we were humbled and put to shame.
20:135. Say: Everyone is waiting; so you wait too. You will know who have been on the right path and have been rightly guided.

# CHAPTER 21

# THE PROPHETS

**Name:** Not from a Verse.

**Verses:** 112

**Summary:**

- The conflict between Prophet Muhammad and the Meccan-disbelieving chiefs:
    - Objection that Prophet Muhammad, being a human, could not be a Messenger.
    - Wrong conception that life was merely a sport and pastime and had no accountability after it.
    - Insistence on idol-worship and antagonism to God's oneness.
    - Misunderstanding that Prophet Muhammad's warnings of God's punishment were empty threats in spite of their persistent rejection of the Prophet.
- The chapter has stories of Prophets Moses, Aaron, Abraham, Isaac, Jacob, Noah, David, Solomon, Job, Ishmael, Zachariah, and Jesus. They had human characteristics except those which were exclusive to the Prophethood. They had no share in the godhood and had to request God for fulfilling their needs. All Prophets had to face difficulties. Despite fierce opposition from the disbelievers, they became successful because of God's help.
- All Prophets and Prophet Muhammad had one and the same way of life. Their followers will come out successful in God's final judgment and those who reject the Prophets shall meet the worst consequences. The people have been told that it is God's blessing that He has sent Prophet Muhammad to inform them beforehand of the worst consequences.

**By Verse**

In the name of God, the compassionate, the merciful:

21:1. The Day of Reckoning is coming near, but the disbelievers are turning away from the faith carelessly.

21:2. They listen to every new warning from their Lord playfully.

21:3. Their hearts are preoccupied. They confer privately saying: Is

Prophet Muhammad not a human like you? Will you submit to magic when you are seeing it?

21:4. Prophet Muhammad replied: My Lord knows whatever is said throughout the heavens and the earth. He hears and knows everything.

21:5. The disbelievers say: His revelations are dreams; he has invented them; and he is a poet. Let Prophet Muhammad bring us a sign just as the previous Messengers brought.

21:6. We showed the signs to the people We destroyed but they did not believe them. Will the disbelievers believe in them?

21:7. O Muhammad, the Messengers We sent before you were humans. We inspired them. If the disbelievers do not know it, let them ask the people of the Scriptures (Jews and Christians).

21:8. We gave them bodies; they ate; and were not immortal.

21:9. Then, We fulfilled Our promise with them, and saved them and others We wanted, and destroyed the transgressors.

21:10. We have revealed the Qur'an with a message for mankind. Will you pay no attention?

21:11. We have destroyed many sinful nations and replaced them with others.

21:12. When they saw Our punishment coming, they tried to flee from it.

21:13. They were told: Do not flee. Return to your life of luxury and homes. You shall be questioned.

21:14. They said: Woe to us. We were wrongdoers.

21:15. Their crying did not stop till We destroyed and extinguished them.

21:16. We did not create the heavens and the earth and what is between them just for play.

21:17. Had We, God, needed a pastime, We could have done it close to Us, but We did not wish any such thing.

21:18. We will make the truth prevail over the falsehood to destroy it. Woe to you the disbelievers for all falsehoods you have invented.

21:19. Whatever is in the heavens and the earth belongs to God. Angels are in His presence. They are neither too proud to worship Him nor are tired of doing so.

21:20. Without tiredness, they praise Him day and night.

21:21. Have the disbelievers' earthly gods power to bring the dead back to life?

21:22. Had there been other gods in the heavens and on earth beside God, both the heavens and the earth would have been ruined. God is exalted. He is the king of the throne and is above what they associate with Him.

21:23. No one can question God for what He does, but the disbelievers will be questioned for their deeds.

21:24. Have they chosen other gods beside Him? O Muhammad, say: Produce your proof. The Qur'an and the earlier Scriptures have proof. But most disbelievers do not know the truth, so they are turning away.

21:25. We sent the Messengers before you with the revelation: There is no deity except Me (God), so worship Me.

21:26. The disbelievers say: God has fathered angels. God forbid, they are His honored servants.

21:27. They do not speak unless God has spoken to them, but they act on His command.

21:28. God knows what is before and behind them. They do not intercede for anyone without His approval. They tremble for His fear.

21:29. If anyone of the angels would say: I am a god besides Him; We would repay him with hell. That is how We will reward the wrongdoers.

21:30. Have the disbelievers not known that heavens and the earth were a closed up one piece; then We separated the heavens and the earth? We made everything from water. Will they not then believe?

21:31. God set mountains on the earth to stabilize it, lest it should shake beneath them. We made passes in the mountains to pass through so that they might be guided.

21:32. We have made the sky a protected ceiling, but they are not paying attention to the signs it contains.

21:33. It is God who created the night, day, sun, and moon. They all move in their orbits.

21:34. O Muhammad, We did not make any man immortal before you. If you are to die, will the disbelievers live forever?

21:35. Everyone will die. We test you with good and bad. You will return to Us.

21:36. When the disbelievers see you Prophet Muhammad, they ridicule you and say: Is this he who speaks against the disbelievers' gods? They lie and slander while mentioning the beneficent God.

21:37. Man, by nature, is impatient. Soon, I will show you My signs. You need not ask Me to hasten them.

21:38. They say: When will the promise be fulfilled if what you say is true?

21:39. If only the disbelievers knew the day when they will not be able to save their faces and backs from the fire of hell, and nobody will

help them.
21:40. It will come to them unexpectedly and bewilder them. They will neither be able to repel it nor defer it.
21:41. The Messengers before you were ridiculed, but the ridiculers themselves were engulfed by it.
21:42. O Muhammad, say to them: Who can protect you, by night and day, from the most merciful God? Yet, they are turning away from remembering their Lord.
21:43. Do the disbelievers have other gods to defend them? Their gods will neither be able to defend nor protect themselves from Our punishment.
21:44. We gave this life's luxuries to these men and their forefathers and prolonged their lives. Can they not see that We gradually reduce the land under their control by shrinking its borders? Is it then they who will be victors?
21:45. O Muhammad, say: I warn you according to the revelation. But, the deaf will not hear the warning.
21:46. If a breath of your Lord's punishment should touch them, they would say: Woe to us, we have been wrongdoers.
21:47. We shall set up scales of justice on the Day of Judgment, so that no one will be wronged in the least. Deeds as small as a grain of mustard seed shall be weighed out. Our accounting will be comprehensive.
21:48. We gave Prophets Moses and Aaron the judgment of the right and wrong, a light, and a reminder for the righteous.
21:49. The righteous fear their Lord without seeing Him and are afraid of the Day of Judgment.
21:50. We have revealed a blessed message in the Qur'an. Will you then not accept it?
21:51. Earlier, We blessed Abraham with guidance, because We knew him well.
21:52. He said to his father and the people: What are these images to which you are so devoted?
21:53. They replied: Our forefathers worshipped them.
21:54. He said: Certainly your forefathers and you are in great error.
21:55. They asked: Are you preaching the truth, or is it just a joke?
21:56. He replied: Your Lord is the Lord of the heavens and the earth. He created them, and I am a witness to that truth.
21:57. By God, I will destroy your idols as soon as you have gone away.
21:58. He broke them to pieces, except the supreme god, so that they might turn to it.

21:59. They said: Who have done this to our gods? Surely, he must be an evil person.
21:60. Some said: We heard Abraham, a young man, talk about them.
21:61. They said: Then bring him here before people, so that they may testify against him.
21:62. They asked: Abraham, have you done this to our gods?
21:63. He replied: The supreme god has done it. Ask the idols, if they can speak.
21:64. They turned to one another and said: Indeed, we are wrongdoers.
21:65. They were confused and said to Abraham: You know they cannot speak.
21:66. Abraham replied: Would you then worship these idols besides God, when idols can neither benefit nor harm you?
21:67. Shame on you and those you worship instead of God. Have you no sense?
21:68. They said: Let us burn him in avenging our gods, if we must do something.
21:69. God ordered the fire to be cool to keep Abraham safe.
21:70. The disbelievers intended to harm Abraham, but We made them the greatest losers.
21:71. We brought Prophets Abraham and Lot to the land which We blessed for all people.
21:72. We gave Abraham Isaac and Jacob, a grandson, and We made all of them righteous.
21:73. We made them leaders for guiding mankind by Our command. We inspired them to do good deeds, establish prayer, and give charity. They worshipped none but Us.
21:74. We gave wisdom and knowledge to Lot, and saved him from the city of wicked deeds. Its people were evil and rebellious.
21:75. We admitted him to Our mercy. He was one of the righteous.
21:76. Before Lot, Noah prayed to Us. We accepted his prayer and saved him and his family from the great flood.
21:77. We saved him from the people who denied Our revelations. They were evil people. We drowned them all.
21:78. Mention the decision of Prophets David and Solomon in the case of the field where sheep strayed and grazed. We were witness to their decision.
21:79. We gave understanding of the case to Solomon; gave wisdom and knowledge to each; and We subjected the mountains and the birds who celebrated Our glory along with David. We did all that.
21:80. We taught Prophet David the art of making the coat of armors to

protect you from the enemy in battle. Will you not then be grateful?

21:81. We put the raging wind under Solomon's command to go to the land which We had blessed. We have knowledge of everything.

21:82. We subjected to him deep divers, who dived in the sea for him and did other tasks. We kept an eye over them.

21:83. Mention Job's calling to his Lord: Adversity has overpowered me. You are the most merciful of the merciful.

21:84. We accepted his prayer; removed his suffering; and gave him his lost household and more people to double their number. That was a blessing from Us and a reminder for those who worship Us.

21:85. Also mention about Ishmael, Idris (Enoch), and Dhul-Kifl (a historic pious person). They all were patiently persevering.

21:86. We admitted them to Our mercy, because they were righteous.

21:87. Remember Jonah, who departed in anger from his people thinking that We would not cause him any distress. But when We did, he cried out in the midst of his afflictions*: There is no god but You; glory to You; I was Indeed wrong.

**In the darkness of the fish's belly, he prayed to God.*

21:88. We accepted his prayer and saved him from his suffering. That is how We shall save believers too.

21:89. And mention Zechariah, when he called to his Lord: Lord, do not leave me childless, though You are the best heir.

21:90. We accepted his prayer; cured his wife's infertility; and gave them a son, John. They were ever quick in doing good works; and called on Us with love, reverence, and humbleness.

21:91. Remember Mary, who guarded her virginity. We breathed Our spirit into her; and made her and her son Jesus a sign for mankind.

21:92. Your religion is one religion. I am your only Lord, so worship Me.

21:93. But later people have divided their religion into sects, but they all will return to Us.

21:94. The good works of a believer will not be lost. We record them.

21:95. There is unchangeable law for a township which We have destroyed that it shall never rise again.

21:96. Until Gog and Magog (see Verse 18:94) are set free by breaking their barrier to swarm from every hill.

21:97. When true promise of the Day of Resurrection shall draw near, the disbelievers with staring eyes will say: Woe to us. We did not pay attention to this. We have done wrong.

21:98. You and the idols you worship other than God are hell's firewood. You

will go into it.
21:99. Had your idols been true gods, they would not have gone to hell, but they will live there forever.
21:100. They shall groan there with pain, but will be deprived of hearing.
21:101. But those we have already favored will be far removed from hell.
21:102. They will not hear the slightest sound of hell, but will enjoy forever in what their souls desire.
21:103. The great fear of the Day of Resurrection will not grieve them, but angels will greet them saying: This is the day you were promised.
21:104. That Day (of Resurrection), We shall roll up the heavens like the rolling up of written scrolls. We will bring the man to life as We first created him. That is a promise binding upon Us and We will fulfill it.
21:105. Before the Qur'an, We wrote in the Psalms (the book of Prophet David), after the message had been given earlier to Prophet Moses, that My righteous servants shall inherit the earth.
21:106. This is a message for those who worship Us.
21:107. O Muhammad, We have sent you as a mercy for mankind.
21:108. Say: It has been revealed to me that your god is but one God. Will you submit to Him?
21:109. But, if they pay no attention, then tell them: I have warned you all alike, but I do not know whether your threatened punishment is near or far.
21:110. God surely knows what you speak and what you hide.
21:111. I do not know whether this is a trial for you or is an enjoyment for a while.
21:112. Say: Lord, judge us with justice. Our Lord is the merciful, whose help we seek against all your lies.

# CHAPTER 22

# THE PILGRIMAGE

**Name:** From Verse 27.

**Verses:** 78

**Summary:**

- Theme: Address to the Meccan-disbelievers, wavering Muslims, and true believers.
    - The disbelievers have been warned against following their idol-gods and rejecting Prophet Muhammad.
    - The wavering Muslims have been warned that when they meet hardship in God's way, they discard their Lord and cease to remain His servants.
    - For counteracting the tyranny of Meccan-disbelievers, Muslims were allowed to fight with them.
    - The believers:
        - have been told that the Meccan-Disbelievers had no right to debar the believers from visiting the holy mosque. It was built by Prophet Abraham by God's command. He invited all people, locals and visitors alike, to perform pilgrimage there.
        - were given instructions to adopt the right and just attitude when they acquired power to rule the land.
        - have been officially given the name of Muslims, as the real heirs to Prophet Abraham, and chosen to become witnesses of truth before mankind. Therefore, they should establish prayer, pay Zakat (mandatory charity) for becoming the best models of the righteous life, and strive for propagating God's word.
- In the hereafter, the disbelievers will have garments of fire, boiling water to drink, and maces of iron to lash them with.
- On the Day of Judgment, God will:
    - Be the judge for all.
    - Judge the matters in which humans differed.
    - Forgive those who accepted the truth, and punish the others.

- God:
    - Has given humans life, makes you to die, and will bring you back to life for His judgment. All dwellers of the heavens and earth prostrate before God.
    - Always helps His Messengers. The disbelievers denied Prophet Muhammad and the Prophets before him.
- People invoke deities other than God, without knowledge and guidance. The deities have no power to create even a fly.
- It is not meat or blood of the sacrificed animals that reaches God; it is your piety that reaches Him.
- God's one day is equal to human 1,000 years.
- Satan tampered with the wishes of all Messengers but God repealed such interjections.
- Those who migrated for God's sake shall be generously rewarded.

**By Verse**

In the name of God, the compassionate, the merciful:

22:1. O mankind, fear your Lord. The earthquake of the Hour of Judgment will be a terrible thing.

22:2. That day, you will see that every nursing mother will forget her baby, every pregnant woman will abort her pregnancy, and people will be like drunkards although not drunk. But God's punishment will be severe.

22:3. There are some who dispute about God without knowledge and follow every rebellious devil.

22:4. Every devil has been destined to misguide his followers and lead them to punishment of the hellfire.

22:5. O mankind, if you have doubt about the Resurrection, remember:

- We created you first from dust, then from a sperm, a clot of blood, and a partly formed piece of flesh, so that We may make you aware of our power.
- We cause whom We will to stay in the womb for an appointed term, then give birth to a baby and make it grow up to its prime.
- Some die young, and some live to old age even to forget what they knew once.
- When We pour down rain on the barren and lifeless earth, it comes to life to grow every kind of beautiful growth.

22:6. This is so, because God is real. It is He who gives life to the dead, and has power over all things.

22:7. Surely, the hour of reckoning is coming, when God will raise those in graves to life.

22:8. There are some among mankind who dispute about God without knowledge, guidance, or a revelation from God.

22:9. Such a person turns his back in arrogance and misleads others from God's way. He will be disgraced in this world, and will taste punishment of the burning fire on the Day of Resurrection.

22:10. That will be the reward of his deeds. God is not ever unjust to His servants.

22:11. There is someone who serves God on the edge. If good fortune befalls him, he is content; but if a trial comes to him, he turns on his back, losing both this world and the hereafter. Evidently, that is a loss.

22:12. He calls on others beside God, but they can neither harm nor help him. That is a blunder.

22:13. He calls on the one whose harm is much more likely than his good. He is an evil patron and an evil friend.

22:14. God will admit the believers who do righteous deeds to gardens, watered by streams. God does what He intends.

22:15. If anyone thinks that God will not help Prophet Muhammad in this world and the hereafter, let that person tie a rope to the ceiling and hang himself. Then let him see whether his plan has removed what enraged him.

22:16. We have revealed the Qur'an in clear verses. God guides those whom He intends.

22:17. On the Day of Resurrection, God will judge the true believers, Jews, Sabaeans*, Christians, Magians**, and pagans. God is witness to all things.

**an ancient South Arabian people, modern-day Yemen, believed to be the biblical land of Sheba.*
*** of the Zoroastrian religion in Persia.*

22:18. Do you not see that everything in the heavens and on earth bow down to God, including the sun, moon, stars, hills, trees, animals, a great number of people, and even those who deserve His punishment? No one can honor whom God disgraces. God carries out all that He wills.

22:19. The believers and the disbelievers dispute about their Lord. Garments of fire have been prepared for the disbelievers. Boiling water shall be poured over their heads.

22:20. It will melt their skins and what is in their bellies.
22:21. They will be beaten with iron rods.
22:22. Whenever they would want to get away from suffering of the hellfire, they will be pushed back saying: Taste the torment of the burning fire.
22:23. God will admit the believers who did righteous deeds to gardens watered by streams. They will wear there gold bracelets, pearls, and silk garments.
22:24. They were inspired to speak noble words and guided to the path of the praiseworthy Lord.
22:25. The disbelievers will be severely punished:

- Who hinder people from God's way,
- And bar them from visiting the sacred mosque at Mecca, which We have opened for all mankind, be they the local residents or outside visitors,
- And commit evil in it.

22:26. When We prepared the site of the sacred mosque for Abraham, We said: Do not worship anyone except Me, keep My house clean for those who walk around it, and for those who stand in prayer and bow down is worship.
22:27. Urge mankind to perform pilgrimage. They will come to you from every distant quarter on foot and on camels, turned lean because of travel.
22:28. That they may see the benefits provided to them, and mention God's name on appointed days over the sacrificial animals He has provided for them. They can eat their meat and feed the distressed and the poor.
22:29. Then let them complete the cleansing rites* prescribed for them, make their vows, and walk around the ancient house.

**changing clothes, cutting hair, shaving, and taking a bath.*

22:30. That is God's command. Whoever honors God's sacred rites will be better in his Lord's sight. The grazing animals are permitted to you, except what was prohibited earlier. Avoid the filth of the idols and falsehoods.
22:31. Be faithful to God, and worship none but Him. The one who worships gods other than God is like the one who falls from the sky, is snatched up by birds, or is carried to a far off place by wind.
22:32. Those are God's commandments. Whoever honors the symbols prescribed by God does so from the piety of heart.

22:33. You can benefit from the sacrificial animals for an appointed term till they are brought for sacrifice to the ancient house.
22:34. For every nation, We have appointed a rite of sacrifice that they may mention God's name over the sacrificial animals We have provided for them. Your God is one God, submit to Him. O Muhammad, give good news to the humble,
22:35. whose hearts are filled with fear when God is mentioned; and who bear their misfortunes patiently, perform payers, and give charity from what We have provided them.
22:36. We have included the sacrificial camels among God's rites. They are of much use to you. Recite God's name over them as they line up for sacrifice. When they have fallen down, eat their meat, and feed the poor and beggars with it. We have subjected the animals to your service, so that you may be grateful.
22:37. Their meat and blood does not reach God; it is your piety that reaches Him. He has thus made them subject to you, that you may glorify God for His guidance to you. O Muhammad, give good news to the righteous.
22:38. God protects the believers from evil. God does not like unfaithful and ungrateful.
22:39. Permission to fight has been given to those who are being attacked and wronged. God has power to give them victory.
22:40. They are those who have been expelled from their homes for no cause except they said: Our Lord is God. If God would not have protected some by means of others, the monasteries, churches, synagogues, and mosques, in which God's name is glorified, would have been destroyed. God will certainly help those who help Him. God is powerful and mighty.
22:41. They are those God fearing who, if We give them authority in the land, establish prayer, give Zakat (mandatory charity), and direct others to do what is right and forbid what is wrong. God decides all matters.
22:42. O Muhammad, if they reject you, you should know that the people of Noah, Aad, and Thamoud rejected their prophets too.
22:43. Also the people of Prophets Abraham and Lot,
22:44. and the Midians* did the same. Moses was denied. I, God, prolonged enjoyment for the disbelievers; then I seized them. My punishment was terrible.

**they lived in the northwest Arabian Peninsula, on the east shore of the Gulf of Aqaba on the Red Sea*

22:45. We have destroyed many sinful nations. Their cities are ruins, palaces are deserted, and wells are unused.

22:46. Have the disbelievers not traveled through the land, and have no hearts to feel and ears to hear? It is their hearts, not eyes that are blind.

22:47. They urge you to hasten the punishment. God will never fail in His promise. A day of your Lord is like your 1,000 years.

22:48. For many sinful nations, I, God. prolonged their enjoyment. Then I punished them. All will return to Me.

22:49. O Muhammad, say to mankind: I have been sent to warn you clearly.

22:50. Those believers who do righteous deeds will be forgiven and given plentiful livelihood.

22:51. But those who reject our revelations will be companions of the hellfire.

22:52. We have never sent any Messenger or a prophet before you whose wishes were not tempered by Satan. But God negated Satan's tempering and confirmed His revelations. God is all-knowing and all-wise.

22:53. God makes Satan's interjections a trial for those whose hearts are diseased and hardened. That is why the wrongdoers are in dissension.

22:54. And to those whom knowledge has been given may realize that the Qur'an is the truth from their Lord for them to believe in it, and submit their hearts to Him humbly. Surely, God will guide the believers to a straight path.

22:55. The disbelievers will not cease to be in doubt concerning the Qur'an until the Hour of Judgment will come upon them suddenly, or the punishment on the Day of Disaster will fall upon them.

22:56. On that day, God shall be the king. He will judge them all. The believers who did righteous deeds will enter gardens of pleasure.

22:57. But the disbelievers who have denied Our revelations will have a humiliating punishment.

22:58. God will provide for those who emigrated for God's cause and were killed or died. God is the best provider.

22:59. God will admit them to a place with which they will be well pleased. God is all-knowing and most patient.

22:60. That will be so. If one retaliates to no greater than the injury he received, and is harmed again, God will help him. God is the One who wipes out sins and forgives again and again.

22:61. God makes the night and the day to come after each other. God hears and sees all.

22:62. That is because God is the truth, and those they call upon other than Him are false gods. God is the most high and great.

22:63. Do you not see that God sends down rain from the sky and the earth becomes green with vegetation? God understands the finest mysteries, and is well-acquainted with them.

22:64. To God belongs what is in the heavens and on earth. God is free of need and is praiseworthy.

22:65. Do you not see that God has made whatever is on earth to serve you, including the ships which sail through the sea by His command? He restrains the heavenly bodies from falling upon the earth without His permission. God is kind and merciful to mankind.

22:66. It is God who has given you life, will make you die, and will raise you again to life on the Day of Resurrection. However, mankind is ungrateful indeed.

22:67. For every nation, We have prescribed religious ceremonies to follow. So O Muhammad, let the disbelievers not contend with you over that. But invite them to your Lord. You are upon straight guidance.

22:68. If they argue with you, say: God knows best of what you do.

22:69. On the Day of Resurrection, God will judge your disputes.

22:70. Do you not know that God knows what is in the heavens and on earth? All is recorded in a book. That is easy for God to do.

22:71. The disbelievers worship others beside God for which He has not sent down authority and about which they have no knowledge. There will not be anyone to help the wrongdoers.

22:72. When Our verses are recited to disbelievers, you can see denial on their faces. It is hard for them to restrain from assaulting those who recite Our verses to them. Tell them: Shall I inform you of what is worse than that? God has promised fire to the disbelievers, an evil destination.

22:73. O mankind, listen to the example of those who call upon others than God, that even if their gods join together to create a fly they will never be able to do that. And if the fly took something away from them, they cannot get it back from it. Weak are both, the unbelieving seekers and whom they seek.

22:74. They have not paid the respect due to God. Indeed, God is powerful and mighty.

22:75. God chooses His Messengers from the angels and the humans. God hears and sees all.

22:76. God knows what is before them and behind them. All matters return to God for decision.

22:77. Those of you, who believe, should bow, prostrate, and worship your Lord, and do good that you may succeed.

22:78. Strive hard for God's faith with devotion due to Him. He has chosen you and has not laid upon you any hardship in practicing your faith, the faith of your father Abraham. God has named you Muslims in this and earlier Scriptures, so that His Messenger may be a witness for you, and you may be a witness for other people. Therefore, keep up the prayer, pay Zakat (mandatory charity), and hold fast onto God, who is your guardian. He is an excellent guardian and a helper.

# CHAPTER 23

## THE BELIEVERS

**Name:** From Verse One.

**Verses:** 118

**Summary:**

- Theme: Invitation to people to accept and follow Prophet Muhammad's message. Various proofs have been given in this regard.
- The believers' true characteristics.
- Evidence of the message's truth: The creation of the humans and the universe, and stories of Prophets Noah and Moses and their communities.
- God's statements:
    - The success and prosperity or the poverty and adversity in the worldly life are not a criterion of success in God's sight. The real criterion is faith or lack of it.
    - God has:
        - not charged any soul with more than it can bear.
        - given humans ears, eyes, and hearts, but they seldom show gratitude.
        - neither taken a son, nor is there another god beside Him.
    - Those who do not believe in the hereafter will stray from the right path.
    - Even the disbelievers recognize God's existence.
    - Prophet Muhammad should not adopt any wrong way to counteract enemies' evil ways and to guard against Satan's incitement.
    - The enemies of truth have to render an account in the hereafter and bear the consequences of their persecution of the believers; therefore, they should mend their ways.
    - Repel evil with good and seek refuge with God against Satan's temptations.
    - The wrongdoers will wish that they could be sent back to this world to adopt the right way, but it will be too late.
    - On the Day of Judgment, it will appear as if the worldly life was less than a day.
    - The disbelievers will never attain salvation.

## By Verse

In the name of God, the compassionate, the merciful:

23:1. Successful are the believers,
23:2. who are humble in their prayer,
23:3. avoid profane talk,
23:4. pay Zakat (mandatory charity),
23:5. and who guard their private parts,
23:6. save from those with whom they are married, either free women or bondwomen. For that, there is no blame on them.
23:8. Those who are faithful to their trusts and promises,
23:9. and do not neglect their prayers.
23:10. They are heirs of
23:11. paradise, where they will live forever.
23:12. We first created man from an extract of clay.
23:13. Then, We placed him as a sperm-drop in womb's safe lodging.
23:14. We made the sperm-drop into a clot of blood, then turned the clot into a lump of flesh, the lump into bones, and covered the bones with flesh, and developed it into another creation. God is blessed, the best creator.
23:15. After that, you shall surely die.
23:16. On the Day of Resurrection, you shall be raised.
23:17. We, God, have created seven heavens above you, and have never been unmindful of Our creation.
23:18. We rain water from the sky in a measured quantity to soak the earth, and certainly are able to drain it off.
23:19. With it We grow gardens of date-palms and grapes to produce abundant fruit for you to eat.
23:20. The olive tree that grows at Mount Sinai, produces oil to flavor the food.
23:21. There is a lesson for you in the livestock. We produce milk in their bellies for you to drink. They have other benefits for you. You eat their meat.
23:22. The animals and the ships carry you from place to place.
23:23. We sent Noah to his people, who said to them: Worship God; you have no god but Him. Will you not pay attention?
23:24. The disbelievers' chiefs among his people said: He is a human like you; he seeks superiority over you. Had God willed, He could have sent down angels. We never heard such a thing from our forefathers.
23:25. He, Prophet Noah, is a madman; therefore, bear with him for a

while.
23:26. Noah said: Lord, help me because they have denied me.
23:27. We inspired him saying: Construct the boat under Our supervision and guidance. When Our command comes, and the earth gushes out water, take on board a pair of a male and a female of every specie, and your family, except those who have already been doomed. Do not plead with Me for those who have done wrong. They surely are to be drowned.
23:28. When you and others with you have embarked on the boat, say: Praise is to God, Who has saved us from the sinful people.
23:29. Lord, land us at a blessed place. You alone can land us safely.
23:30. Surely, there are signs in this, and We have always brought people to trial.
23:31. After them, We raised another generation.
23:32 We sent them a Messenger from themselves, who said: Worship God; you have no god but Him. Will you not pay attention?
23:33. The disbelieving chiefs of his people, who denied the life to come and on whom We had bestowed the good things of this life, said: He is a human like you, he eats and drinks like you.
23:34. If you obey a human like yourselves, certainly you will be losers.
23:35. Does he promise you that when you have died and become dust and bones, you will be raised to life?
23:36. What he has promised is far away from the truth.
23:37. There is no other life than this worldly life. We will live and die, but will never be raised again.
23:38. He is but a human who has invented a lie about God. We will never believe him.
23:39. He said: Lord, help me because they have denied me.
23:40. God replied: Before long, they will surely regret.
23:41. Our punishment that overtook them was justified, and We made them a heap of dead leaves. Gone are the sinners.
23:42. After them, We, God, raised other generations.
23:43. No nation can hasten its appointed term, nor delay it.
23:44. We sent Our Messengers one after the other. Time after time, the disbelievers denied them. So We destroyed them one by one and made them the stories of the past. Gone are the disbelievers.
23:45. Then, We sent Moses and his brother Aaron with Our signs and a clear authority
23:46. to Pharaoh and his establishment, but they were scornful and arrogant people.
23:47. They said: Should we believe two humans like us while their

people are our servants?
23:48. Pharaoh and his establishment denied Moses and Aaron. Pharaoh and his establishment were destroyed.
23:49. We gave Moses the Torah to guide his people.
23:50. We made Mary and his son Jesus a sign for mankind and sheltered them on a peaceful hillside with a spring of flowing water.
23:51. O Messengers, eat good things, and do right. I am aware of what you do.
23:52. Your religion is one religion, and I am your Lord, so fear Me.
23:53. But people have divided themselves into sects, each rejoicing in its beliefs.
23:54. Leave them in their error for a time.
23:55. Do they think that We have given them wealth and children
23:56 for seeking their welfare? No, they do not understand.
23:57. Surely, those who live in their Lord's fear,
23:58. who believe in His signs,
23:59. who worship none other than their Lord,
23:60. who give charity with their hearts full of fear, because they will return to their Lord,
23:61 are those who hasten to do good deeds, and are the first ones to do them.
23:62. We do not place a burden on anyone more than it can bear. We record the truth. None will be wronged.
23:63. But the disbelievers do not understand this; they will continue doing evil deeds.
23:64. When We, God, would punish their rich, they will cry for help.
23:65. We shall say: Do not cry out today; We will not help you.
23:66. My verses were recited to you, but you turned back on your heels
23:67. scornfully, and talked bad about them day and night.
23:68. Do they not ponder over the Qur'an, or has anything been revealed to them that was not revealed to their forefathers?
23:69. Or is it that they do not know their Messenger, so they deny him?
23:70. Or do they say: He is possessed? No, he has brought them the truth, but most of them hate the truth.
23:71. If the truth had followed their desires, the heavens and the earth and what is between them would have been corrupted. We have brought them their reminder for their own good, but they have turned away from it.
23:72. O Muhammad, are you asking for a reward from them? Your Lord's reward is better. He is the best provider.
23:73. You have called them to a straight path.

23:74. Those who do not believe in the life to come are straying away from the right path.
23:75. Even if We showed them mercy and removed their distress, they would still persist in breaking limits and wandering blindly.
23:76. We punished them, but they did not submit to their Lord humbly.
23:77. And when We will punish them severely, they will despair.
23:78. It is God who gave you ears, eyes, and hearts; but you are least thankful.
23:79. It is He who has multiplied you on the earth. You will be gathered before Him.
23:80. It is He who gives life and death. He brings night after day. Then why do not you pay attention?
23:81. But rather than trying to understand, they say what former people had said.
23:82. They say: When we are dead and become dust and bones, shall we be raised to life?
23:83. We and our forefathers have been promised this earlier. Decidedly, these are nothing except ancient myths.
23:84. O Muhammad, ask them: To whom belongs the earth and what it contains? Answer if you know.
23:85. They will say: To God. Then ask: Why do not you pay attention?
23:86. Ask: Who is Lord of the seven heavens and the great throne?
23:87. They will reply: God. Then ask: Will you not guard against evil?
23:88. Ask: In whose hands is the governance of all things; who protects all, but is not protected by anyone? Answer if you know.
23:89. They will say: In God's hands. Then ask: Why are you so deceived?
23:90. We have revealed them the truth, but they are practicing lies.
23:91. God has neither taken a son, nor there is another god beside Him. Had this been otherwise, each god would have governed what he created, and tried to overcome others. God is glorified above all that they allege.
23:92. God knows what is visible and invisible. He is high above the gods they serve beside Him.
23:93. O Muhammad, pray: Lord, if you let me witness the punishment You have threatened them with,
23:94. do not include me among the sinful people.
23:95. Certainly, We have the power to show you the punishment We have threatened them with.
23:96. O Muhammad, repel evil with good. We fully know their allegations.

23:97. And pray: Lord, I seek refuge in You from the incitements of the evil ones,
23:98. and I seek refuge in You from their presence.
23:99. When death comes to a wrongdoer, he says: Lord, send me back,
23:100. so that I may do good in the life I have left behind. No, these are just words he is saying. Behind them is a barrier until the Day of Resurrection.
23:101. The day the trumpet will be blown, their ties of kinship shall cease to exist, and they will not ask about one another.
23:102. Those whose scales are heavy with good deeds will be successful.
23:103. But those whose scales are light are the ones who have ruined their souls and live in hell forever.
23:104. The fire shall burn their faces, and they shall twist in severe pain.
23:105. They will be asked: Were My verses not recited to you and did you not deny them?
23:106. They will reply: Lord, our misfortune overcame us, and we went off the right path.
23:107. Lord, take us out of hell. If we were to return to evil, we would indeed be sinners.
23:108. God will say: Remain there in shame and do not plead with Me.
23:109. Among My servants were those who said: Lord, we have believed in You. Please forgive us and have mercy upon us. You are the most merciful.
23:110. But you mocked them to the point of forgetting to remember God, and you used to laugh at them.
23:111. Today, I have rewarded the believers for their patience and they are successful.
23:112. God will ask the disbelievers: How many years did you stay on the earth?
23:113. They will reply: A day or part of a day. Please ask those who have kept account.
23:114. God will say: You stayed but a little, if only you had known.
23:115. Did you think that We created you in vain and you would not return to Us?
23:116. Honor is to God, the true king. There is no god except Him, Lord of the glorious throne.
23:117. If a human worships another god beside God, without proof of the other god's godhood, the Lord will bring that human to account. The disbelievers will not succeed.
23:118. O Muhammad, say: Lord, forgive and have mercy. You are the most merciful.

# CHAPTER 24

# THE LIGHT

**Name:** From Verse 35.

**Verses:** 64

**Summary:**

- Punishment for adultery, false witnessing, and accusing one's wife when there was no witness.
- A slander against Prophet Muhammad's wife Aisha and God's declaration of her innocence.
- God's orders for:
    - marriage to an adulterer, adulterous, idolater, and idolatress.
    - the believers not to follow Satan, not to take part in false accusations and slanders, and to grant liberty to slaves who seek to buy their freedom.
    - Singles to marry.
- Etiquettes for:
    - entering and eating at houses of others.
    - seeking permission to enter a married couple's room.
    - attending meetings that require collective action.
- God's characterization:
    - God is the light of the heavens and earth. His light is found in places of worship which His devotees build for His remembrance.
    - Everything in the heavens and the earth glorifies and praises God.
    - God has created every living creature from water.
- The disbelievers' characterization: Their deeds are like a mirage in a desert.
- The believers' characterization:
    - The believers who do not demonstrate their belief through deeds are not true believers.
    - The true believers when called towards God and His Messenger say: We hear and obey.

**By Verse**

In the name of God, the compassionate, the merciful:

24:1. We have revealed this chapter and made its communications clear and obligatory for you to follow.

24:2. A hundred lashes should be given to an adulterer and an adulteress. No pity for them should make you disobey God, if you believe in God and the last day. And let the believers witness their punishment.

24:3. An adulterer may marry only an adulteress or an idolatress, and an adulteress may marry only an adulterer or an idolater. Such marriages are forbidden to the believers.

24:4. Give 80 lashes to those who accuse honorable women without bringing out four witnesses, and never ever accept their testimony. They indeed are evildoers.

24:5. Except those who repent and mend their ways. God is forgiving and merciful.

24:6. If a man accuses his wife of adultery, but has no witness, he should testify four times in God's name that he is telling the truth.

24:7. He should testify a fifth time for God's curse to be on him should he be lying.

24:8. She will not be punished if she would testify four times in God's name that her husband was lying.

24:9. Her fifth testimony should be for God's wrath to be upon her if she was lying.

24:10. This has been told to you because of God's grace and mercy on you. God is forgiving and wise.

24:11. Those who spread the slander* are Prophet Muhammad's own people. Do not consider it to be a misfortune for you; rather, it is good for you. Every one of them will be punished for its sin. As for the one who had the greater share in it will be punished severely.

**Prophet Muhammad's wife, Aisha, had committed adultery.*

24:12. When the believers heard about the slander, why did they not believe their own people and said: This is obviously a lie?

24:13. Why did the slanderers not produce four witnesses? Because they did not produce the witnesses, they were liars in God's sight.

24:14. Had it not been for God's favor and mercy upon the believers in this world and the hereafter, you would have been severely punished for what you did.

24:15. You spread it with your tongues, and uttered it with your mouths, though you had no knowledge of it. You may have thought it to be a trifle, but it was a serious matter in God's sight.

24:16. When you heard it, why did you not say: It is not appropriate for us to talk about it; glory is to God, this is sheer slander?

24:17. God forbids you to repeat the like of it forever, if you are believers.

24:18. God makes His revelations clear to you. He is all-knowing and all-wise.

24:19. Those who like that slander be spread among the believers will be severely punished in this world and the hereafter. God knows them, but you do not.

24:20. Had it not been for God's favor and mercy upon you, because God is kind and merciful, you would have been punished.

24:21. Believers, do not follow Satan's footsteps. Whoever follows his footsteps, spreads immorality and wrongdoing. Had it not been for God's favor and mercy upon you, none of you would have been cleansed of sin. God cleans whom He wills, and He hears and knows all.

24:22. The honorable and rich among you should not pledge against helping their relatives, the needy, and those who have emigrated in God's cause. Forgive and overlook their faults. Do not you wish that God forgives you? God is forgiving and merciful.

24:23. Those who defame believing, but virtuous and simple women are cursed in this world and the hereafter. They will be severely punished

24:24. on the day when their tongues, hands, and feet would testify against them as to what they did.

24:25. That day, God will repay them for what they deserved. They will know that God is the perfect truth.

24:26. Unchaste women are for unchaste men, and unchaste men are for unchaste women. Chaste women are for chaste men, and chaste men are for chaste women. They shall be cleared of slander, pardoned, and given a bountiful provision.

24:27. Believers, do not enter houses other than your own until you have asked their owners' permission and saluted them. That is better for you. Perhaps you will pay attention to it.

24:28. If you find no one in the house, do not enter until permitted. If you are asked to go back, it is appropriate for you to go back. God knows about all that you do.

24:29. It shall not be wrong for you to enter the empty houses that may benefit you. God knows what you reveal and hide.

24:30. O Prophet, tell the believing men to lower their gaze, and protect their private parts. That will purify them. God is aware of what they do.

24:31. O Prophet, tell the believing women:

- to lower their gaze,
- to protect their private parts,
- not to show off their adornments except what is normally visible,
- to draw their head-covers on their chests, and
- not to display their adornment except to their:
    - husbands,
    - fathers,
    - father-in-laws,
    - sons,
    - step-sons,
    - brothers,
    - brother's sons,
    - sister's sons,
    - sisters in Islam,
    - slave-girls, and
    - male servants who lack sexual desire and children who have no knowledge of woman's private parts.

In addition, they should not stamp their feet while walking to reveal their hidden adornments. O believers, turn to God for forgiveness that you may be successful.

24:32. Arrange marriages between single men and women among you and between virtuous male and female slaves. If they are poor, God will enrich them from His grace. God is generous and all-knowing.

24:33. Those who find no means for marriage should stay away from sexual relations, until God enriches them out of His grace. Free your slaves who want to buy their freedom, if they are trustworthy. Give them a part of your riches which God has given you. Do not force your slave-girls into prostitution for you to earn money if they desire to keep themselves out of it. But if anyone would compel them, God will forgive the slave-girls and be merciful to them.

24:34. We have sent you revelations for making things clear. We have given you examples of those who have passed away before you as a warning to those who fear God.

24:35. God is the light of the heavens and the earth. His light is that of a lamp in a niche, the lamp being enclosed in a star-like brightly shining glass, lit from the oil of a blessed olive-tree, which is neither eastern nor western. The oil gives perpetual light though fire has not touched it. God guides anyone He likes to His light. God gives examples to mankind and has knowledge of all things.

24:36. God's light is found in the houses of worship, which He has permitted to be built for His remembrance in the mornings and evenings,

24:37. by those whom neither buying nor selling distracts from God's remembrance, praying, and giving Zakat (mandatory charity). They fear the Day of Judgment when hearts and eyes will be distressed with agony.

24:38. They hope that God will reward them according to their best deeds, and even give it more from His grace. God provides to whom He wills, without measure.

24:39. The disbelievers' deeds are like a desert-mirage. The thirsty one thinks it to be water. But, when he comes up to it, he finds it to be nothing, but finds God there, Who pays the human its due. God is fast in accounting.

24:40. Or the disbelievers' deeds are like darkness in a deep ocean covered by wave after wave, overcast by clouds in darkness over darkness. When one puts out one's hand, one can hardly see it. And the one to whom God has not granted light will have no light.

24:41. Do you not see that God is praised by all those in the heavens and the earth? God is praised by flying birds. Everyone knows its prayer and praise. God knows about all their deeds.

24:42. Kingdom of the heavens and the earth belongs to God. All will return to Him.

24:43. Do you not see that God drives clouds? God brings them together, makes them into a mass, and makes rain from it. And God sends down hail from massive clouds, He strikes with it whom He wills, and saves from it whom He wills. The flash of God's lightening almost takes away the eyesight.

24:44. God brings night after day. Certainly, there is a lesson in it for the thoughtful.

24:45. And God has created every animal from water; some creep on their bellies; and some walk on two legs and some on four legs. God creates what God wills. God has power over all things.

24:46. We have sent down revelations that explain the truth. God guides whom God wills to a straight path.

24:47. The hypocrites say: We have believed in God and the Messenger and obey them. Thereafter, some of them turn away. Those are not the believers.

24:48. When they are called to God and His Messenger that he may judge between them, some of them go away.

24:49. Had the truth been on their side, they would have come to him obediently.

24:50. Is there a disease in their hearts or they have doubts? Do they fear that God and His Messenger will be unjust to them? Surely they are wrongdoers.

24:51. When true believers are called to God and His Messenger that he may judge between them, they say: We hear and obey. Those will be successful.

24:52. Those, who obey God and His Messenger, fear God, and discharge their duty to God, will triumph.

24:53. They swear by God solemnly that if you would order them to fight they will do so. Tell them: Do not swear, because only obedience counts. God is aware of all your deeds.

24:54. Say: Obey God and His Messenger. But, if you do not, The Messenger's only responsibility is for the duty placed on him, and your responsibility is for the duty placed on you. If you obey him, you shall be guided. The Messenger's duty is only to convey the message clearly.

24:55. God promised the believers who do good deeds that God:

- will make them rulers on earth as God made their ancestors,
- will establish the religion God has chosen for them, and
- change their fear to safety.

They should worship Me and serve no god beside Me. Whoever disbelieves after this will be a wrongdoer.

24:56. Establish prayer, give Zakat (mandatory charity), and obey the Messenger so that you may receive God's mercy.

24:57. Never think that the disbelievers will escape God's punishment on earth. They will live in hell, an evil refuge.

24:58. Believers, let your slaves and children, who have not reached puberty, ask your permission at three occasions before they come into your presence: Before the dawn-prayer, at noon when you have laid aside your clothes because of the heat, and after the night-prayer. These are occasions of your privacy. At other times, when you go around seeing each other, it will be permissible to come into each other's presence without permission. Thus God makes God's revelations clear to you. God is wise and knows all.

24:59. And when children have reached puberty, let them ask your permission as theirs elders do. Thus, God makes His revelations clear to you. God is wise and knows all.

24:60. For women who have passed the menstrual age and have no desire for marriage, there will be no offence for removing their cloaks without showing their adornments. However, it will be better if they do not remove their cloaks. God hears all and knows all.

24:61. There is no offence if the blind, lame, and sick eat at someone's house. Similarly, there is no offence for you to eat at the houses of your children, fathers, mothers, brothers, sisters, paternal uncles, paternal aunts, maternal uncles, maternal aunts, and friends, or at the houses whose keys have been entrusted to you. Also, there is no offence whether you eat together or separately. When you enter a house, greet each other in God's name for God's blessings and kindness. Thus, God makes His revelations clear to you so that you may understand.

24:62. Those who have faith in God and His Messenger are true believers. When they are with him for consultation on a communal matter, they do not leave until they have asked for his permission. Those who ask for your permission truly believe in God and His Messenger. When they ask for your permission to attend to their own business, give permission to whomever you please and ask God for their forgiveness. God is forgiving and merciful.

24:63. Do not equate the Messenger's summons to you with your summons to one another. God knows those of you who slip away with some excuse. Let those, who disobey his orders be aware that some misfortune or severe punishment may fall on them.

24:64. Whatever is in the heavens and on earth certainly belongs to God. He knows your thoughts and deeds. On the day when you will be brought back to God, God will tell you all about what you did. God has knowledge of everything.

# CHAPTER 25

# THE CRITERION

**Name:** From Verse One.

**Verses:** 77

**Summary:**

- Theme: Answering disbelievers' doubts about the Qur'an, Muhammad's Prophethood, and his teachings.
- People have been warned of the consequences of rejecting the truth.
- A clear picture of the moral superiority of the believers has been given.

**By Verse**

In the name of God, the compassionate, the merciful:

25:1. Blessed is God who has sent down the criterion of right and wrong upon His Messenger for warning people.

25:2. The kingdom of the heavens and earth belongs to God. He has fathered no son, has no partner in the kingdom, and has created everything and determined their destinies.

25:3. Yet, the disbelievers worship, beside God, other gods. They can create nothing. They were created themselves; can neither benefit nor harm themselves, and possess no power of life, death or resurrection.

25:4. The disbelievers say: It the Qur'an is a lie that Prophet Muhammad has forged with the assistance of others. In fact, it is the disbelievers who have committed an injustice and a lie.

25:5. The disbelievers say: He has written stories of old times, dictated to him by others morning and evening.

25:6. O Muhammad, say: God:

- has revealed the Qur'an.
- knows the secrets of the heavens and the earth.
- is forgiving and merciful.

25:7. The disbelievers say: What kind of a Messenger is this who eats and walks through the streets? Why an angel has not been sent down with him to warn people?

25:8. Why has no treasure been given to him, or a garden for his livelihood? And the wrongdoers say: You are following someone who is bewitched.

25:9. See what kind of degrading comparisons they coin for you! But they have gone off the right path, and will never be able to find the true path.

25:10. God is blessed, and if He wills, can give you better than that, palaces and gardens with running streams.

25:11. The disbelievers deny the Hour of Resurrection. We have prepared a blazing fire for those who deny the hour.

25:12. When they will see it from a distance, they will hear its rage and roar.

25:13. When, chained together, they will be thrown into a narrow place, they will cry for death.

25:14. They will be told: Do not cry for one death, call for many deaths.

25:15. Ask them: Is this better or the garden of eternity in paradise, which has been promised to the righteous? The garden is their reward and destination.

25:16. They will find there everything they desire and will live there forever. It is a promise that God will fulfill.

25:17. On that Day (of Judgment), God will gather the disbelievers and their idol-gods. God will ask them: Did you mislead My servants, or did they themselves go away from the way?

25:18. The idol-gods will say: Glory is to God, it was not for us to choose guardians other than You. You gave the disbelievers and their ancestors comforts, but they forgot Your message and earned punishment.

25:19. Then God will address the disbelievers: Your idols have proved you wrong. They can neither avert your punishment nor help you. Those of you who have committed injustice will be severely punished.

25:20. O Muhammad, the Messengers We sent before you were all humans who ate food and walked through the streets. We test you through one another. Will you not have patience? God sees all things.

25:21. Those who do not expect to meet Us say: Why angels have not been sent to us, or why cannot we see our Lord? Indeed, they think too highly of themselves, and are scornful with great pride.

25:22. The day the disbelievers will see angels, there will be no joy for the sinner, who will say: We wish there were a great barrier between us and our punishment.

25:23. We shall consider their deeds and scatter them as meaningless dust.

25:24. That Day (of Judgment), dwellers of paradise shall be in a better living and resting place.

25:25. On that day, the heaven with its clouds will be opened, and angels will be sent down successively.

25:26. On that day, God will be king and the disbelievers will be doomed.

25:27. On that day, the wrongdoer will bite his hands and say: I wish I had followed the Messenger.

25:28. Woe to me, I wish I had never taken so-and-so as a friend.

25:29. It was that person who led me away from God's message after it had come to me. Satan is ever a traitor to humans.

25:30. The Messenger, Prophet Muhammad, will say: Lord, my people denied the Qur'an.

25:31. Thus, for every Prophet, We made enemies from among the sinners. But, you do not need anyone other than your Lord as a guide and a helper.

25:32. The disbelievers ask: Why was the Qur'an not revealed to him all at once? We have revealed it to you in parts to strengthen your heart.

25:33. Whenever they came to you with an argument, We revealed you the truth and explained it properly.

25:34. Those who will be thrown headlong into hell will live in an evil place for going away from the straight path.

25:35. We gave Moses the Torah and his brother Aaron as an assistant.

25:36. We sent them to the people who had denied Our signs, and destroyed those people completely.

25:37. We drowned Noah's people for denying the Messengers and made them an example for mankind. We have prepared a painful punishment for the wrongdoers.

25:38. And also God destroyed the tribes of Aad and Thamoud, the people who lived at al-Rass*, and many generations between them.

**al-Rass was the town where a tribe of Thamoud lived.*

25:39. To each of them, We warned by examples, and destroyed each one of them.

25:40. Have they not seen the ruins of the city they have passed by which was destroyed with an evil rain? But, they are not expecting resurrection.

25:41. O Muhammad, whenever they see you, they ridicule you saying: Is this the one whom God has sent as a Messenger?

25:42. He would have misled us from our gods had we not been steadfast in worshiping them. But, when they will see their punishment they will know who have been misled the farthest.

25:43. Have you seen those who have made their desires their gods? Would you be their guardian?

25:44. Do you think that they can hear or reason? They are like animals, more off the right path.

25:45. Have you not seen how your Lord lengthens the shadow? If God had willed, He could have made it standing still. God made it dependent on the position of the sun.

25:46. As the sun rises, We reduce the shadows little by little towards Ourselves.

25:47. It is God who has made the night a garment for you, sleep for rest, and the day to rise up again.

25:48. It is God who sends winds as His mercy's forerunner, and sends down clean water from the sky.

25:49. So that, We may give life to the dead land, and quench the thirst of humans and animals.

25:50. We have explained it to them in diverse ways so that they may reflect, but most humans are ungrateful.

25:51. If We, God, had willed, We could have sent into every city a warner.

25:52. Do not listen to the disbelievers, but strive hard against them with the Qur'an.

25:53. It is God Who has let free the two bodies of flowing water: One drinkable and sweet, the other salty and bitter. Yet, God has created an un-crossable barrier between them.

25:54. It is God Who created humans from water, made them related to each other through descent and marriage. Your Lord is powerful.

25:55. Yet, the disbelievers worship idol-gods instead of God. But, idol-gods can neither benefit nor harm them. The disbeliever has become a helper of every rebel against his Lord.

25:56. O Muhammad, We have sent you for giving good news and warnings.

25:57. Tell them: I do not ask any reward from you for it, except that you may take the right path to your Lord.

25:58. O Muhammad, put your trust in the ever-living God, Who does not die. Celebrate God's praise. God knows the sins of God's servants.

25:59. God created the heavens and the earth and what is between them in six days. Then God settled Himself firmly on the throne. God is most merciful. Ask anyone knowledgeable about God.

25:60. When they are asked to bow down to the most merciful God, they say: Who is the most merciful? Should you make us worship anyone you like? And it increases their rebelliousness.
25:61. Blessed is God Who has placed galaxies in the sky, a lamp (the sun), and a shining moon.
25:62. It is God Who has made night and day to follow each other. It is a sign for those who pay attention and be thankful.
25:63. Servants of the most gracious God are those who walk on the earth humbly, and when the ignorant address them harshly, they respond by words of peace.
25:64. Those who spend the night in kneeling down to their Lord and standing in prayer.
25:65. And they say: Lord, save us from the punishment of hell, the lasting punishment.
25:66. The hell is an evil place to be put in and live.
25:67. When they spend, they are neither extravagant nor miser, but moderate.
25:68. Who do not pray to any other god but God, do not kill anyone God has forbidden, except for just cause, nor commit adultery. Whoever does that shall be punished.
25:69. His punishment will be doubled on the Day of Resurrection and he will live in disgrace forever.
25:70. Except for those who repent, believe and do good deeds. God will change their evil deeds with good deeds. God is ever forgiving and merciful.
25:71. The one who repents and do good deeds truly returns to God.
25:72. And those who do not testify falsely, and keep their dignity by avoiding listening to profanity.
25:73. When reminded of their Lord's revelations, they do not turn a blind eye and a deaf ear to them.
25:74. Who say: Lord, give us joy in our wives and children and make us an example for the righteous.
25:75. They shall be rewarded with paradise because of their patience. They shall be met there with greetings and the word of peace and respect.
25:76. They shall live there forever in a place of blessings and comfort.
25:77. O Muhammad, say to the disbelievers: My Lord would not care for you if you do not pray to Him. But you have rejected Him, for which you will be punished.

# CHAPTER 26

# THE POETS

**Name:** From Verse 224.

**Verses:** 227

**Summary:**

- Background: The Meccan-Disbelievers were persistently refusing to accept Prophet Muhammad's message of Islam. This was causing anguish and grief to the Prophet.
- Consolation to the Prophet that if these people have not believed in him, it is not because they have not seen any sign, but because they are stubborn.
- The earth has signs that can guide a seeker of truth to reality, but the misguided people have never believed even after seeing the signs.
- The history of seven Prophets Moses, Abraham, Noah, Houd, Saleh, Lot, and Shuaib and their tribes has been told.
- It has been pointed out that instead of seeing those horrible signs of the doomed communities of the past, why not to see the sign that the Qur'an is presenting in their own Arabic language.

### By Verse

In the name of God, the compassionate, the merciful:

26:1. Ta, Seen, Meem (are Arabic letters).
26:2. These are verses of the Qur'an that clarifies things.
26:3. O Muhammad, perhaps, you would worry yourself to death because they will not believe.
26:4. If We, God, like, We could reveal a sign to them from heaven, to bow their heads to the sign in humility.
26:5. They turn away from every new warning they get from the merciful God.
26:6. Before long, the truth, upon which they have laughed scornfully, will dawn upon them.
26:7. Do they not look at earth, where We have produced all kinds of beneficial things?
26:8. Surely, there is a sign in that, but most of them will not believe.
26:9. Your Lord indeed is mighty and merciful.
26:10. Your Lord told Moses to go to the wrongdoing people
26:11. of Pharaoh. Will they not fear God?

26:12. Moses said: My Lord, I fear that they will deny me.
26:13. My breast tightens and my speech is not fluent, so send my brother Aaron to help me.
26:14. The disbelievers have a charge of crime against me*, and I fear they will kill me.

**An Egyptian was fighting with an Israelite. Moses punched him, and he died. Moses was afraid and left Egypt.*

26:15. God said: Do not fear; both of you go with Our signs. We will be with you listening.
26:16. Go to Pharaoh and say: We are Messengers from the Lord of the universe.
26:17. Let Israel's children go with us.
26:18. Pharaoh said to Moses: Did we not raise you as a child, and you lived many years among us?
26:19. And you killed a man; surely, you are ungrateful.
26:20. Moses replied: I did that wrongful act unintentionally.
26:21. I fled because I was afraid of you. But my Lord has given me wisdom and has made me His Messenger.
26:22. You have reminded me of the favor, but have enslaved the children of Israel.
26:23. Pharaoh asked: Who is this Lord of the universe?
26:24. Moses replied: God is the Lord of the heavens and the earth and what is between them. If only you would have faith.
26:25. Pharaoh said to those around him: Have you heard what Moses said?
26:26. Moses continued: He is your forefathers' and your Lord.
26:27. Pharaoh said: The Messenger who has been sent to you is surely a madman.
26:28. Moses said: He is the Lord of the east and the west and what is between them. If you could only understand.
26:29. Pharaoh said: If you serve a god other than me, I shall surely imprison you.
26:30. Moses said: Even if I show you a convincing proof?
26:31. Pharaoh replied: Show it if you are truthful.
26:32. Moses threw down his staff, and suddenly it became a visible snake.
26:33. Then, Moses drew out his hand; it appeared white to all who saw it.
26:34. Pharaoh said to the chiefs around him: He surely is a skilled magician.
26:35. He wants to drive you out of your land by his magic. So what is

your advice?
26:36. They replied: Put him and his brother off for a while and send Messengers to the cities,
26:37. who will bring you every skilled magician.
26:38. The magicians were gathered on an appointed day.
26:39. And the people were told to gather too.
26:40. The people said: We would follow the magicians if they win.
26:41. And when the magicians arrived, they asked Pharaoh: Will we be rewarded if we win?
26:42. Pharaoh replied: Yes, and you will then be my favored ones.
26:43. Moses said to them: Throw whatever you like.
26:44. They threw down their ropes and staffs and said: By Pharaoh's power, we will surely win.
26:45. Then, Moses threw down his staff, and it swallowed their false devices.
26:46. The magicians bowed down in adoration.
26:47. The magicians said: We believe in the Lord of the universe,
26:48. the Lord of Prophets Moses and Aaron.
26:49. Pharaoh said: You have believed in Moses without my permission! Indeed, he is your leader who has taught you magic. But, you will see that I shall cut off your hands and feet on the opposite sides, and crucify you all.
26:50. They replied: It does not matter, we shall return to our Lord.
26:51. We trust that our Lord will forgive our sins because we are the first ones to believe.
26:52. We told Moses to travel by night with My servants because he surely was going to be pursued.
26:53. Pharaoh sent callers to the cities, saying:
26:54. These Israelites are a small group of people,
26:55. who have enraged us,
26:56. but we are vigilant and great in number.
26:57. God took away the Egyptian-disbelievers' gardens, springs,
26:58. treasures and comfortable houses,
26:59. and gave like these to the Israelites.
26:60. The Egyptians pursued the Israelites at sunrise.
26:61. When the Egyptians and the Israelites saw one another, the companions of Moses said: We surely have been overtaken.
26:62. Moses said: No, my Lord is with me; He will guide me.
26:63. We told Moses to strike the sea with his staff. The sea parted. Each part was like a towering mountain.
26:64. We brought Pharaoh and his army to that place.

26:65. We saved Moses and those with him,
26:66. but drowned Pharaoh and his army.
26:67. Surely, there is a sign in that, but most disbelievers would not believe.
26:68. Certainly, your Lord is mighty and merciful.
26:69. Tell them Abraham's story.
26:70. He asked his father and his people: Who do you worship?
26:71. They replied: We worship idols and are devoted to them.
26:72. He asked: Do they hear you when you call on them?
26:73. Can they benefit or harm you?
26:74. They replied: But, we found our forefathers calling on idols.
26:75. He said: Have you considered what you have been worshipping,
26:76. and your forefathers before you?
26:77. The idols are enemies to me, except the Lord of the universe,
26:78. Who created me, guides me,
26:79 gives me food and drink,
26:80. cures me, when I am sick;
26:81. will cause me to die and bring me to the life hereafter;
26:82. and God, I hope, will forgive my faults on the Day of Judgment.
26:83. Lord, give me wisdom, and join me with the righteous.
26:84. Grant me honor in the generations to come,
26:85. and place me among the inheritors of paradise.
26:86. Forgive my father, who has gone off the right path.
26:87. Do not disgrace me on the Day of Resurrection.
26:88. That day, wealth and children will avail nothing.
26:89. Except the one who brings a clean heart to God.
26:90. That Day (of Judgment), the paradise will be brought near to the righteous,
26:91. and the hell will be brought near to the sinners.
26:92. The sinners will be asked: Where are those you used to worship
26:93. other than God? Can they help you or themselves?
26:94. They will be thrown into the hell with those who misled them,
26:95. and with Satan's soldiers.
26:96. They will quarrel with their idols and say:
26:97. By God, we were obviously wrong
26:98. in equating you with the Lord of the universe.
26:99. It was the evildoers who misled us.
26:100. So now we have no one to plead for us before God,
26:101. and no loving friend.
26:102. If we could live our lives again, we would be believers.
26:103. Surely, there is a sign in that; but most disbelievers would not

believe.
26:104. Your Lord is mighty and merciful.
26:105. The people of Noah rejected the Messengers.
26:106. Their brother Noah said to them: Will you not fear God?
26:107. I am indeed a trustworthy Messenger.
26:108. Fear God and follow me.
26:109. I do not ask you for any reward for it; my reward is only from the Lord of the universe.
26:110. Have fear of God and follow me!
26:111. They replied: Should we believe in you while you are followed by the lowest-class people?
26:112. Noah said: I have no knowledge of what they may have done in the past.
26:113. My Lord alone can bring them to account. I wish if you could understand that.
26:114. I will not drive away the believers.
26:115. I have been sent to give plain warning.
26:116. They replied: Noah, desist, or you shall be stoned to death.
26:117. Noah said: Lord, my people have rejected me.
26:118. Therefore, judge between us, and save me and the believers.
26:119. So, We saved him and his companions in the loaded boat, Noah built.
26:120. We drowned others.
26:121. Surely, there is a sign in that, but most disbelievers would not believe.
26:122. Your Lord is mighty and merciful.
26:123. Aad's people rejected their Messengers.
26:124. Their brother Houd said to them: Will you not fear God?
26:125. I am indeed your trustworthy Messenger.
26:126. Fear God and follow me.
26:127. I do not ask you for any reward for it. My reward is only from the Lord of the universe.
26:128. Will you build a monument on every high place for the sake of vain glory?
26:129. You build fortresses in hope of living there forever.
26:130. And when you assault, you assault as cruel tyrants.
26:131. Fear God and follow me.
26:132. Fear God Who has bestowed upon you all that you know.
26:133. Have given you livestock, children,
26:134. gardens and springs.
26:135. I fear for you the punishment of a terrible day.

26:136. They replied: It does not matter whether you preach to us or not.
26:137. Your threats are a usual story of the past.
26:138. We shall surely not be punished.
26:139. They denied him and We destroyed them. There is a sign in that, but most disbelievers would not believe.
26:140. Your Lord is mighty and merciful.
26:141. Thamoud denied their Messengers too.
26:142. Their brother Saleh said to them: Will you not fear God?
26:143. Indeed, I am your trustworthy Messenger.
26:144. Fear God and follow me.
26:145. I do not ask you for any reward for it. My reward is from the Lord of the universe.
26:146. Will you be left here safe
26:147. amid gardens, springs,
26:148. crop fields and palm-trees laden with fine fruit,
26:149. and skillfully carving houses out of the mountains?
26:150. Fear God and follow me.
26:151. Do not follow the transgressors,
26:152. who make mischief on earth and have no concern to reform it.
26:153. They replied: Magic has affected you;
26:154. you are a human like us; show us a sign, if you are truthful.
26:155. He replied: Your sign is this she-camel. She will drink water on an appointed day, and you will drink water on an appointed day.
26:156. Do not harm her, otherwise, you will be punished on a terrible day.
26:157. But they hamstrung her, and then they became remorseful.
26:158. They were punished. Surely, there is a sign in that, but most disbelievers would not believe.
26:159. Your Lord is all-mighty and most merciful.
26:160. Lot's people rejected their Messengers too.
26:161. Their brother Lot said to them: Will you not fear God?
26:162. I am your trustworthy Messenger.
26:163. Fear God and follow me.
26:164. I do not ask any reward from you for it. My reward is only from the Lord of the universe.
26:165. Will you have sex with males,
26:166. and leave your wives aside, whom Lord has created for you? You are indeed exceedingly transgressors.
26:167. They replied: Lot, desist, or we will drive you out.
26:168. He said: I hate your conduct.
26:169. Lord, protect my family and me from what they do.
26:170. We saved him and his followers,

26:171. except an old woman, Lot's wife, who stayed behind.
26:172. We destroyed others.
26:173. We rained stones on them. The rain was severe which fell on those who were warned.
26:174. Surely, there is a sign in that, but most disbelievers would not believe.
26:175. Your Lord is mighty and merciful.
26:176. Midians*, the dwellers of the forest rejected their Messengers too.

**they lived in the northwest Arabian Peninsula, on the east shore of the Gulf of Aqaba on the Red Sea*

26:177. Shuaib said to them: Will you not fear God?
26:178. I am indeed your trustworthy Messenger.
26:179. Fear God and follow me.
26:180. I do not ask any reward from you for it. My reward is only from the Lord of the universe.
26:181. Give full measure and do not defraud anyone.
26:182. Weigh with even scales.
26:183. Do not cheat people of their due, do not behave wickedly on the earth spreading corruption.
26:184. Fear God Who created you and the generations before you.
26:185. They replied: You are under the influence of magic.
26:186. You are a human like us. Indeed, we think you are lying.
26:187. Make a part of sky fall upon us, if you are truthful.
26:188. He replied: My Lord knows what you do.
26:189. They disbelieved him, and were punished with the day of dark gloom. Indeed, it was the punishment of a terrible day.
26:190. That indeed was a sign, but most disbelievers would not believe.
26:191. Your Lord is mighty and merciful.
26:192. The Lord of the universe has revealed the Qur'an.
26:193. Angel Gabriel, the faithful spirit, has brought it down
26:194. into your heart O Muhammad that you may warn mankind
26:195. in plain Arabic language.
26:196. The revelation of the Qur'an was mentioned in the Scriptures (Torah and Gospel) of the earlier generations.
26:197. Is it not sufficient proof for them that the Israelite-scholars recognize it?
26:198. Had We revealed it to a non-Arab,
26:199. and he had recited it to them; they still would not have believed it.
26:200. Thus We place disbelief into the hearts of the guilty.
26:201. They will not believe it until they see the painful punishment.
26:202. The punishment will come to them unexpectedly.

26:203. They will ask: Shall we have no relief from it?
26:204. Do they ask to hasten Our punishment?
26:205. Have you considered that if We let them enjoy this life for years,
26:206. and then they were punished as promised,
26:207. what benefit will they have for enjoying this life?
26:208. We, God, have never destroyed any nation without warning it beforehand.
26:209. We are never unjust.
26:210. The devils did not bring the Qur'an down.
26:211. They are neither allowed, nor are capable of doing so.
26:212. They indeed are kept away from hearing it.
26:213. Call on no other god beside God, otherwise you will be punished.
26:214. Warn your nearest relatives.
26:215. And be kind to the believers who follow you.
26:216. If they disobey you, say: I am not responsible for what you do.
26:217. Put trust in God, the all-mighty, the most merciful.
26:218. We see you when you stand up to pray,
26:219. and when you walk among the worshippers.
26:220. God indeed hears and knows all.
26:221. O people, shall I tell you upon whom the devils descend?
26:222. They descend upon every lying sinner.
26:223. They listen eagerly, but most of them are liars.
26:224. And as for the poets, the erring ones follow them.
26:225. Do you not see that poets roam in every valley,
26:226. and preach what they do not practice?
26:227. Except those poets who believe, do good deeds, remember God, and defend themselves if oppressed. Those who act unjustly shall know their fate.

# CHAPTER 27

# THE ANTS

**Name:** From Verse 18.

**Verses:** 93

**Summary:**

- Theme:
    1. The people who can benefit from the Qur'an's guidance accept the realities of the universe, and live their lives under its guidance.
    2. The greatest hindrance for humans to follow this way is denial of the hereafter.
- Pharaoh, Thamoud's chiefs, and Prophet Lot's people did not believe in the hereafter and had become slaves of the world.
- God blessed Prophet Solomon with wealth and kingdom. He ruled over jinns, humans, birds, and winds. He was obedient to God and there was no vanity in his character.
- The Queen of Sheba ruled over a wealthy and well-known nation. She was a disbeliever because of her ancestral way of life. But, when Prophet Solomon made the truth known to her, she and her people submitted to God.
- The attention of the Meccan-Disbelievers has been drawn to the realities of the universe and its creator and asked to distinguish between their disbelief and the truth of God's oneness to which the Qur'an invited them.
- Reality of the hereafter and the consequences of being heedless to it.
- The Qur'an clarifies the matters in which the Israelites differ and gives signs of the doomsday. The disbelievers have been warned not to deny God's revelations without gaining their comprehensive knowledge.

### By Verse

In the name of God, the compassionate, the merciful:

27:1. Ta, Seen (are Arabic letters). These are verses of the Qur'an that makes things clear.

27:2. The Qur'an is guidance and good news for the believers,

27:3. who perform prayers, pay Zakat (mandatory charity), and are sure of the hereafter.
27:4. For those who do not believe in the hereafter, We have made their deeds seem fair to them, but they wander on blindly.
27:5. They shall be punished severely and shall be the greatest losers in the hereafter.
27:6. O Muhammad, you have received the Qur'an from Him who is wise and all-knowing.
27:7. Tell disbelievers about Moses who said to his household: I see fire. I shall bring you information about it or a lighted torch from it to burn our own fire so that you may warm yourselves with it.
27:8. When he came to the fire, a voice called him saying: Blessed are those in and around the fire; glory be to God, the Lord of universe;
27:9. Moses, I am God, the mighty and wise;
27:10. throw down your staff. When Moses saw it writhing like a snake, he ran away, and did not see back. God said: Moses, do not be afraid. My Messengers are not afraid in My presence.
27:11. But those who sin and then do good instead of wrong, I forgive them, and I am merciful to them.
27:12. Put your hand into your robe at the chest. It will come out white without stain. These are among the nine signs you will take to Pharaoh and his people. Indeed, they are defiantly disobedient.
27:13. When Our signs appeared before them, they said: This is plain magic.
27:14. They rejected the signs unjustly with arrogance, though their hearts acknowledged them. Consider the end of those wrongdoers.
27:15. We gave knowledge to Prophets David and Solomon. They said: Praise is to God, Who has favored us over many of His believing servants.
27:16. Solomon succeeded David. He said: O people, I have been taught the birds' language, and been blessed with many good things. Surely, this is God's favor.
27:17. For Solomon, his armies of jinns, men and birds were gathered in a battle formation.
27:18. When they came upon an ants' valley, an ant said: O ants, go to your houses so that Solomon and his soldiers may not crush you under their feet unknowingly.
27:19. Solomon smiled at her speech, and said: Lord, enable me to be grateful for Your favor which You have bestowed upon me and my parents, and to do good deeds that will please You. By Your mercy admit me into ranks of Your righteous servants.

27:20. Solomon took birds' attendance and said: I do not see the hoopoe. Is he absent deliberately?
27:21. I will punish him or kill him unless he would give me a genuine excuse.
27:22. Soon after, the hoopoe appeared and said: I have seen about which you have no knowledge. I have come to you with news from Sheba.
27:23. I have found a woman ruling over her people. She has everything in abundance and has a grand throne.
27:24. I found her and her people worshiping sun instead of God. Satan has made their deeds pleasing to them and averted them from God's way, so they are not guided.
27:25. They do not worship God, Who brings to light what is hidden in the heavens and the earth, and knows what you hide and reveal.
27:26. There is no god but Him, the Lord of the glorious throne.
27:27. Solomon replied: We will see whether what you say is true or false.
27:28. Take my letter and deliver it to them. Then, turn aside and wait for their reply.
27:29. The Queen of Sheba said: Chiefs, I have received a noble letter.
27:30. It is from Solomon and reads: In the name of God, the compassionate, the merciful,
27:31. do not be arrogant, submit to God, and come to me.
27:32. She said: Chiefs, advise me, as I never decide without your counsel.
27:33. They replied: We are men of strength and military might, but decision is yours to make. We will wait for your decision.
27:34. She said: When kings enter a city, they ruin it and enslave its chiefs. These people will do the same.
27:35. I will send them a present, and see what answer my Messengers will bring.
27:36. When they came to Solomon, he said: Are you giving me wealth? What God has given me is better than what He has given you. You keep your present.
27:37. Go back to your people. We will invade them with our armies against which they will not be able to defend. We will expel them from their land in humiliation and disgrace.
27:38. Solomon asked his chiefs: Which one of you will bring me her throne before they come to me to surrender?
27:39. A powerful jinn replied: I will bring it to you before you rise from your seat. I am strong and trustworthy.

27:40. One with the knowledge of the Scriptures said: I will bring it to you within the twinkling of an eye. When Solomon saw it placed before him, he said: By my Lord's grace, this is to test me whether I am grateful or ungrateful. Whoever is grateful, it is for his good, and whoever is ungrateful, it is only for his loss. Certainly, my Lord is free of all wants and is generous.

27:41. Solomon said: Modify the throne and let us see whether she will recognize it or not. Let us see if she could reach the truth or would be among those who cannot be guided.

27:42. Upon her arrival, she was asked: Is your throne like this? Yes, it looks the same. Solomon said: We are given knowledge and have submitted to God.

27:43. Her worship of idol-gods barred her from belief in God, because she was from disbelieving people.

27:44. She was asked to enter the palace. When she saw it, she thought it was a pool of water and pulled her skirt up her legs. Solomon said: It is a palace paved with glass. She said: Lord, I have sinned and surrender with Solomon to You, the Lord of the universe.

27:45. To Thamoud, We sent their brother Saleh. He said: Worship God. But they differed and divided themselves into two quarreling groups.

27:46. He said: My people, why do you hasten to evil instead of good? Why do you not seek God's forgiveness for receiving His mercy?

27:47. They replied: We have met with ill-luck on account of you and your companions. He said: The cause of your evil fortune is with God; you are being tested.

27:48. There were nine persons in the city that made mischief in the land and did not act right.

27:49. They said: Let us swear by God to kill Saleh and his family at night. Then, we will say to his relatives that we were not present at the killings. We are telling the truth.

27:50. They plotted, so did We, God, without their knowledge.

27:51. Look at the outcome of their plan. We destroyed them and their people.

27:52. Because they sinned, their houses are in ruin and deserted. Surely, there is a sign in that for those who think.

27:53. But We saved those who believed and acted rightly.

27:54. Mention Lot, who said to his people: Why do you commit immorality knowingly?

27:55. You approach men lustfully instead of women? Surely, you are ignorant.

27:56. But, his people's answer was: Expel Lot's family from your city; they pose to be pure.

27:57. We saved him and his followers, except his wife. We made her to stay behind.

27:58. We rained stones on those who stayed behind. The rain was evil for those who were warned.

27:59. O Muhammad, say: Praise is to God and peace is upon His servants whom He has chosen. Who is better, God or the false gods they associate with Him?

27:60. Surely, He is God Who created the heavens and the earth; sends down rain from the sky; and grows beautiful gardens. It is impossible for you to grow such trees. Is there another god beside God? Yet they set up equals with Him.

27:61. Is He not the best Who made the earth, put rivers and mountains on it, and placed a barrier between two bodies of salty and sweet water? Is there another god beside God? No, but most of them do not know.

27:62. Is He God not the best, Who responds to the desperate when they call upon Him and removes their distress? He has given you the earth to inherit. Is there another god beside God? Little do you know!

27:63. Is He not the best Who guides you through darkness of the land and the sea, and sends winds as harbingers of His mercy? Is there another god beside God? God is higher than their idol-gods.

27:64. Is He not the best Who created the universe and keeps it going, and provides your sustenance from the heaven and the earth? Is there another god beside God? Show your proof, if you are truthful.

27:65. O Muhammad, tell the disbelievers: Except God, no one in the heavens and on earth knows the unseen. And no one shall ever know when they will be raised to life again.

27:66. They have no knowledge of the hereafter. They are in doubt and blind about it.

27:67. The disbelievers ask: When we and our forefathers have become dust, shall we be raised to life?

27:68. We and our forefathers before us have been told this, but these are ancient stories.

27:69. O Muhammad, tell them: Travel through the earth and see the sinners' end.

27:70. Do not worry about them, nor distress yourself because of their plots.

27:71. The disbelievers say: When will this threat be fulfilled, if what you say is true?
27:72. Say: Perhaps what you are asking to hasten may be near at hand.
27:73. Your Lord is generous to people, but most are not thankful.
27:74. Your Lord knows what their breasts conceal and what they reveal.
27:75. There is nothing secret in the heaven and on earth that is not recorded in a clear book.
27:76. This Qur'an explains to the Israelites most of the matters in which they disagree.
27:77. It is a guide and a blessing for the believers.
27:78. Your Lord will rightly judge them. He is the mighty, all-knowing.
27:79. O Muhammad, put your trust in God; the truth is on your side.
27:80. You can neither make the dead nor the deaf to hear you, when they have turned their backs to flee.
27:81. You cannot guide the blind out of their error. None will hear you except those who believe in Our verses and have submitted to Us.
27:82. When Our judgment will be passed against them, We will bring from the earth an insect* which shall wound them, because humans did not believe in Our verses.

**the fleas that feed on bacteria (Yesinia Pestis) and bite humans to spread the contagious disease of plague that kills millions.*

27:83. And warn of the day when We will gather, from every nation, those who denied Our signs. They will be driven in rows,
27:84. before God, Who will ask: Did you reject My revelations while you had no knowledge of them? What did you do?
27:85. They will be punished for doing wrong and will be speechless.
27:86. Do they not see that We made the night for them to rest and the day to give them light? Surely, there are signs in that for believers.
27:87. Warn of the day when the trumpet will be blown, and whoever is in the heavens and on earth will be terrified except whom God will exempt. All will come to God humbly.
27:88. The mountains, though firm, will pass away like clouds. Such is the artistry of God, Who disposes all things in perfect order. He is well acquainted with all that you do.
27:89. Whoever has done good will be rewarded better than it, and will be saved from the terror of that day.
27:90. Whoever comes with an evil deed will be tossed headlong into fire, and will be asked: Are you not rewarded for your doings?
27:91. O Muhammad say: I have been directed to worship the Lord of this city Mecca, Who has made it sacred. All things belong to Him. I have been directed to submit to Him,

27:92. and to proclaim the Qur'an. Whoever is guided is only for his benefit. Whoever strays, say: I have warned you.
27:93. Say to them: All praise is for God. He will show you His signs and you will recognize them. Your Lord is watching your deeds.

# CHAPTER 28

## THE STORY

**Name:** From Verse 25.

**Verses:** 88

**Summary:**

- Theme: Prophet Moses' story to remove the disbelievers' objections against Muhammad's Prophethood. The story impresses the following points:

    1. God:

        - does whatever He wills to do. For example, God arranged for Prophet Moses to be brought up in Pharaoh's house to destroy Pharaoh of Egypt.
        - does not grant Prophethood to a person with festivities as is done in the case of a king. Muhammad was blessed with Prophethood unexpectedly as was Moses while on a journey.
        - uses His Messengers without armies to rout much stronger and better equipped opponents. For example, Prophet Moses was weaker than Pharaoh, and Muhammad was weaker than the Meccan Quraysh. But Prophets Moses and Muhammad came out victorious in the end.

    2. The Meccan-Disbelievers said: Why was Muhammad not given the same miracles which were given to Prophet Moses, for example, the miracles of the staff and the shining hand? Pharaoh and his people did not believe in those miracles and were destroyed. Do the Meccans wish to meet the same doom by asking for the miracles in their stubbornness?
    3. Prophet Muhammad narrated a 2,000 year old historical event in detail. That was a proof of his Prophethood as he was un-lettered and had no access to such information.
    4. What the Meccans' feared most was that if they gave up the idol-worship and accepted God's oneness, it will put an end to their supremacy in the land.

- Pharaoh's plot to kill Israelites' sons to save his kingship, and God's plan to bring up one of them (Moses) in Pharaoh's own household.

- Moses, in his youth, accidentally killed a man, but escaped from Pharaoh's punishment.
- Moses' arrival at:
    - Midian*, his acceptance of the employment term, and the marriage.

      **they lived in the northwest Arabian Peninsula, on the east shore of the Gulf of Aqaba on the Red Sea*

    - a mountain, seeing a fire, conversation with God, and his appointment as a Messenger to Pharaoh and his chiefs.
- Pharaoh and his chiefs' disbelief; God destroyed them but saved the Israelites.
- The destruction of prior generations to teach them a lesson.
- Truth has been conveyed; the true people of the book (Jews and Christians) believe in it.
- Righteous Jews and Christians can recognize the Qur'an's truth and feel that they were Muslims even before hearing it.
- Prophets cannot succeed in guiding anyone they like; it is God Who blesses someone with guidance.
- On the Day of Judgment, the disbelievers will wish that they had accepted guidance.
- God has not allowed the disbelievers to assign His powers to whomever they want.
- The rich man Korah's story. He was from Prophet Moses' people but rebelled against God's guidance.
- The Qur'an's revelation is God's mercy. O Muhammad, let no one turn you away from it.

**By Verse**

In the name of God, the compassionate, the merciful:

28:1. Ta. Sin. Mim. (These are Arabic letters).

28:2. These are verses of the Qur'an that makes things clear.

28:3. We, God, shall tell you the true story of Moses and Pharaoh for the believers' benefit.

28:4. Pharaoh made himself a cruel ruler in his land. He divided people into factions. He oppressed a faction of Israelites, slaughtered their sons, and spared their daughters. Indeed, he was a tyrant.

28:5. We wished to favor the oppressed, make them leaders and heirs,

28:6. grant them power in the land, and inflict Pharaoh, his minister Haman and their army with the same punishment that they feared.

28:7. We inspired Moses' mother saying: Suckle him, but if you are afraid for his safety, put him into the river. Do not be afraid, nor grieve; We will surely bring him back to you and make him one of the Messengers.

28:8. It was decided that Pharaoh's family would pick him up, so that he would become an enemy and a cause of grief for them. Indeed, Pharaoh, Haman and their soldiers were sinners.

28:9. Pharaoh's wife said to him: He would bring us joy. Do not kill him. He may benefit us, or we may adopt him as a son. They did not know what they were doing.

28:10. The heart of Moses' mother was troubled. She would have disclosed his secret had We not strengthened her heart for her to have faith in Our promise.

28:11. She said to his sister: Follow him. She watched him from a distance while they were not aware.

28. 12. We had decreed that he would refuse to suck a foster-mother. His sister said to them: Shall I tell you of a household who will rear him for you and take care of him?

28. 13. So We restored him to his mother so that she might be comforted, not grieve, and know that God's promise was true. But most humans do not know that.

28. 14. When Moses reached the age of maturity and was full grown, We granted him wisdom and knowledge. That is how We reward the righteous.

28. 15. One day, Moses entered the city unnoticed and found two men fighting. One was from his group, and the other an enemy. The man from Moses' group appealed to him for help against his foe. Moses struck the enemy with his fist and caused his death. Moses said: This is Satan's work, which is an enemy and misleads.

28. 16. Moses prayed: Lord, I have wronged my soul; forgive me. God forgave him, because He is oft-forgiving and most merciful.

28. 17. Moses said: Lord, because of Your favor, I shall never help a sinner.

28.18. Next morning, when Moses was walking in the city afraid, the man he had helped the day before asked for his help again. Moses said to him: You are quarrelsome.

28. 19. When Moses was about to hit the enemy, he said: Moses, would you kill me as you killed a person yesterday. You are surely becoming a tyrant in the land, and not a peacemaker.

28. 20. A man came running from the city's other end. He said: Moses: The chiefs are planning to kill you; run away immediately; I am giving you sincere advice.

28. 21. Moses ran away afraid, but was vigilant and praying: Lord, save me from the wrongdoing people.

28. 22. When Moses started towards the land of Midian*, he prayed: Lord, guide me to the straight path.

**they lived in the northwest Arabian Peninsula, on the east shore of the Gulf of Aqaba on the Red Sea*

28. 23. When Moses arrived at the well of Midian, he found a group of men watering their flock and beside them two women keeping back their flock. He asked them: What is the matter? They replied: We cannot water our flock until the shepherds have taken back their flock. Our father is an old man.

28. 24. Moses watered their flock, retired to the shade, and said: Lord, I need Your blessing.

28. 25. Then, one of the women walked to him bashfully. She said: My father invites you to reward you for watering our flock. When Moses came to him and told him his story, he said: Moses, do not be afraid, you are safe from the unjust people.

28. 26. One of the women said: Father, hire him. Surely, he is the best man you can hire. He is strong and trustworthy.

28. 27. He said: I shall wed one of my daughters to you, provided you would serve me for eight years. But if you, on your own will extend this period to 10 years, it will be an act of grace on your part. I do not intend to treat you harshly. God willing, you will find me righteous.

28. 28. Moses replied: That is an agreement between us. Neither of the two terms that I would fulfill shall be unjust to me. God is a witness between us.

28. 29. After fulfilling the term, he journeyed with his family. On a side of the mountain, he saw a fire. He said to his family: Wait, I have seen a fire, maybe I will bring to you useful information or a lighted torch from it to warm yourselves.

28. 30. When Moses came to the fire, He heard a voice from a bush on the right side of the blessed valley: Moses, I am God, the Lord of the universe,

28:31. throw down your staff. When he saw it moving like a snake, he ran away, not to return. God said: Moses, come back and do not be afraid. You are safe.

28:32. Through the opening of your shirt, put your hand on your breast.

It will become white without any flaw. And draw in your arm close to you as protection from fear. Those are two signs from your Lord for Pharaoh and his people. Indeed, they are defiantly disobedient.

28:33. Moses said: Lord, I have killed one of their men. I am afraid they will kill me.

28:34. My brother Aaron speaks more fluently than me. Send him with me to help and confirm what I say. I am afraid that they would deny me.

28:35. God said: We will give you your brother to help you and grant to both of you power so that they will not be able to harm you. Because of Our signs, you and your followers will be victorious.

28:36. When Moses came to Pharaoh and his people with Our clear signs, they said: This is nothing but invented magic. We have not heard of this from the time of our forefathers.

28:37. Moses said: My Lord knows best who brings guidance from Him and who will be rewarded paradise. The wrongdoers will not prosper.

28:38. Pharaoh said: Chiefs, I know that you have no god other than me. Haman, bake bricks of clay and build me a lofty tower for me to see Moses' god. Surely, Moses is lying.

28:39. Pharaoh and his soldiers were arrogant beyond reason. They thought that they would not return to Us.

28:40. We punished Pharaoh and his army by drowning them into sea. See the wrongdoers' end.

28:41. We made them guides who invited others to the hellfire. No one will help them on the Day of Judgment.

28:42. In this world, We made it a curse to follow them, and, on the Day of Judgment, they will be hated.

28:43. After We had destroyed the former generations, We gave Moses the Scriptures as enlightenment, and a guidance and mercy for people to be thoughtful.

28:44. O Muhammad, you were not on the western side of the mountain when We revealed the commandment to Moses, and you did not witness the event.

28:45. We raised many generations after Moses, and prolonged their lives. O Muhammad, you did not live among the Midians*, nor did you recite to them Our verses, but We sent them other Messengers.

**they lived in the northwest Arabian Peninsula, on the east shore of the Gulf of Aqaba on the Red Sea*

28:46. O Muhammad, you were not at the side of the mountain when We called Moses. Yet, as a mercy from your Lord, We have sent you to warn a people to whom no warner has been sent, so that they may pay attention.

28:47. Otherwise, if disaster were to fall on them because of their sinning, they might say: Lord, why did You not send us a Messenger? We would have followed Your revelations and believed in them.

28:48. Now, when the truth has come to them from Us, they say: Why the signs that were sent to Moses have not been sent to him Prophet Muhammad? But, have they not rejected the signs which were sent to Moses? They say: The Torah and the Qur'an are two works of magic that assist each other, and we reject them both.

28:49. Say: Then, bring a book from God which gives better guidance than either one of them so that I may follow it, if you are truthful.

28:50. If they do not answer you, then know that they only follow their desires. And who is more off the right path than the one who follows his desires without God's guidance? God does not guide the wrongdoers.

28:51. We have sent the Qur'an to them so that they might think.

28:52. Those to whom We gave the Scriptures (Jews and Christians) before it believe in the Qur'an.

28:53. When it is recited to them, they say: We believe in it because it is the truth from our Lord. Indeed, we surrendered ourselves to God even before it.

28:54. They will be rewarded twice for what they have endured patiently by averting evil with good; and giving in charity from what We have provided them.

28:55. When they hear idle talk, they turn away from it saying: We have our deeds and you have yours; peace be upon you, we do not associate with the ignorant.

28:56. You cannot guide whom you like, but God guides whom He pleases. He knows best who will follow the right way.

28:57. The Meccan-Disbelievers say: If we were to follow Prophet Muhammad's guidance, we shall lose our land. But, have We, God, not settled them in a safe, sacred territory in which We provide fruits of every kind for their living? However, most of them do not understand that.

28:58. We have destroyed many nations who were thankless for their means of livelihood. Their houses, save for a few, have been rarely lived after them. After all We, God, are the inheritor.

28:59. Never your Lord has destroyed towns until He had sent Messengers to them reciting Our verses. We only destroyed them because they sinned.

28:60. Whatever you have been given is just a passing enjoyment of the present life and temporary pomp and show. But God's reward is better and everlasting. Will you not pay attention?

28:61. Are the two alike, one to whom We have promised an excellent reward which he will get and the one whom We have provided enjoyment of the worldly life, but who will be punished on the Day of Resurrection?

28:62. On that day, God will ask them: Where are the gods you associated with Me?

28:63. The idol-gods, who are to be punished, will say: Lord, these are the ones whom we misled. We misled them, as we ourselves were misled. We disassociate from them in Your presence; they did not worship us.

28:64. It will be said to the disbelievers: Call on to your idol-gods. They will call them; but will get no response. They will see Our punishment and wish that they had followed the guidance.

28:65. That day, God will ask them: What was your answer to the Messengers?

28:66. That day, they will be confused to be able to ask any question to one another.

28:67. But those who repent, have faith, and do righteous deeds, may hope to achieve salvation.

28:68. Your Lord creates and chooses for mankind as He pleases. Their idol-gods have no power of choice. Glory is to God; He is above their idol-gods.

28:69. Your Lord knows what their hearts hide and reveal.

28:70. He is God; there is no god but Him. All praise is to Him in this life and in the hereafter. He has the final say. All will return to Him.

28:71. O Muhammad, ask them: If God was to continue the night till the Day of Resurrection, who beside Him could bring you light? Will you not then listen?

28:72. Ask: Have you considered that if God was to continue the day till the Day of Resurrection, what deity other than God could bring you a night to rest? Have you no eyes to see?"

28:73. Because of His mercy, God has made the night for you to rest and the day to seek His bounty for you to be grateful.

28:74. Warn of the day when God will call them and ask: Where are those you claimed to be My partners?

28:75. God will call a witness from every nation and ask them: Produce your proof. Then, they will know that the truth belongs to God, and the idol-gods they invented will leave them.

28:76. Korah was one of Moses' people. But he oppressed them. We gave him so much treasure that its keys would have been a burden for a troop of mighty men to carry. His people said to him: Do not rejoice; God does not like the jubilant.

28:77. But seek, through what God has given you, the home in the hereafter. Do not neglect your responsibility in this world. Do good to others as God has done good to you. Do not make mischief in the land, for God does not like the mischief-makers.

28:78. He replied: I have been given this only because of the knowledge I possess. Did he not know that God destroyed generations before him who were mightier and richer than him? The guilty shall not be questioned about their sins but punished.

28:79. So when Korah came out to his people in his glitter, those who desired the worldly life said: We wish we had what Korah has; indeed, he is a lucky man.

28:80. But the knowledgeable said: Shame on you! God's reward is better for those who believe and do good deeds, but none are granted it except the patient.

28:81. We caused the earth to swallow him and his house. He had no helper against God; nor was he able to help himself.

28:82. The very same people who had desired Korah's position the day before, began to say: Ah! God gives abundance to whom He wills and sparingly to whom He pleases. If God had not favored us, He would have caused the earth to swallow us. Ah, the disbelievers will not succeed.

28:83. We shall assign paradise to those believers who neither desire glory nor corrupt the earth. The best outcome will be for the righteous.

28:84. The one who does good will be rewarded better than that; but the one who does evil will be only punished for that.

28:85. O Muhammad, God, Who has made the teachings of the Qur'an binding on you, shall bring you back to your ordained place of Mecca, the place of your birth and pilgrimage. Say: My Lord knows best who brings guidance and who is in clear error.

28:86. You did not expect that the Qur'an would be revealed to you. But, through your Lord's mercy, you have received it. Therefore, never help the disbelievers.

28:87. Let no one turn you away from God's revelations, now that they have been revealed to you. Call people to your Lord and do not associate anyone with God.

28:88. Do not call upon another god beside God. There is no god but Him. Everything will perish except Him. He is the judge. You all will return to Him.

# CHAPTER 29

# THE SPIDER

**Name:** From Verse 41.

**Verses:** 69

**Background:**

The chapter was revealed:

- During extreme persecution of Muslims at Mecca. The disbelievers were opposing and fighting Islam tooth and nail, and new converts were subjected to the severest oppression.
- To encourage Muslims, and to shame those who were showing weakness of the faith.
- To instruct Muslims:
    - To be kind to their parents, but not to follow their disbelieving faith.
    - To migrate if the persecution had become unbearable for them. They should give up their homes, instead of giving up their faith.
    - To establish prayer, because it keeps one away from shameful acts.
    - Not to follow the disbelievers who were saying to the believers that if God was to punish them for abandoning the faith, the disbelievers will take their punishment.
    - Not to argue with the people of the book (Jews and Christians) except in good taste.

**Summary:**

- There are creatures who do not carry their provisions with them. God provides them as He provides humans.
- The worldly life is a short lived pastime. The real life is in the hereafter.
- Those who strive in God's cause, God guides them to His ways.
- The stories of ancient Prophets Noah, Abraham, Lot, Moses, and Shuaib. They suffered hardships for long periods. But, God helped them at last. Undergoing a period of trial was God's test for them.
- Warning to the disbelievers that God's delayed punishment does not mean that they will never be punished. The signs of the doomed

nations of the past are before them.
- The disbelievers should understand God's oneness and the hereafter by drawing their attention towards the signs in the universe.

**By Verse**

In the name of God, the compassionate, the merciful:

29:1. Alif, Lam, Meem (are Arabic letters).
29:2. Do people think that when they say: We believe; they will be left alone and not tested?
29:3. We, God, tested those who have gone before them. God certainly knows those who are truthful and those who are liars.
29:4. Those who do evil acts, do they think they can escape Our punishment? They are wrong in their judgment.
29:5. Whoever hopes to meet God must know that God's appointed time will surely come. God hears all and knows all.
29:6. Whoever strives for God's cause only strives for his own benefit. God does not need His creatures' help.
29:7. As for those who believe and do good deeds, We will do away with their evil deeds and reward them for their good deeds.
29:8. We, God, have directed humans to be kind to their parents. But if they ask you to associate with Me other gods about whom you have no knowledge, do not obey them. All will return to Me and I will tell them about what they used to do.
29:9. Those who believe and do good deeds, We, God, shall admit them to the company of the righteous.
29:10. Some say: We believe in God. But, when they suffer in God's cause, they consider it God's punishment. When victory comes from your Lord, they say: We were with you. Does God not know what is in all creatures' hearts?
29:11. God knows the believers and the hypocrites.
29:12. The disbelievers say to the believers: Follow us, and we will carry your sins. But, they will not carry their sins. Indeed, they are lying.
29:13. They shall bear their own burdens and the burdens of leading others astray. They shall be questioned on the Day of Resurrection about their fabrications.
29:14. We sent Noah to his people. He lived among them 950 years, and the flood overtook them for their wrongdoing.
29:15. We saved him and his companions in the boat, and We made it a sign for mankind.
29:16. We sent Abraham, who said to his people: Worship God and fear Him. That is best for you, if you knew it.

29:17. You worship idols beside God and create a lie. Those you serve beside God cannot give you your living. Therefore, seek your livelihood from God and worship Him. Be grateful to Him; you shall return to Him.

29:18. If you deny the message, then other nations have done the same before you. The duty of a Messenger is to convey the message clearly.

29:19. Have they not considered how God creates and then repeats it? That is easy for God.

29:20. Say to them: Travel through the land and see how God created. Then God will recreate. God has power over all things.

29:21. God punishes whom He wills and shows mercy to whom He pleases. You will return to Him.

29:22. You will not be able to escape God upon the earth or in the heaven. Beside God, you have no other protector or helper.

29:23. Those who disbelieve in God's revelations and meeting with Him shall despair of God's mercy. They will have a painful punishment.

29:24. Abraham's people replied: Kill him or rather burn him. But God saved him from the fire. Surely, there are signs in that for the believers.

29:25. Abraham said: You have chosen idols instead of God, but your love for them will only last in this worldly life. On the Day of Resurrection, you will deny and curse one another. You will live in hell, and no one will help you.

29:26. Lot believed Abraham and said: I shall leave my home in my Lord's service. He is mighty and all wise.

29:27. We gave Abraham Isaac and Jacob, son of Isaac, and gave his descendants Prophethood and the Scriptures. We rewarded him in this life; and he will live in the company of the righteous in the life to come.

29:28. Lot said to his people: You commit immorality which no other nation has committed before you.

29:29. You have sex with men and commit highway robbery! You turn your meetings into orgies. And the answer of his people was: Bring God's punishment on us, if you are truthful.

29:30. Lot said: Lord, help me against the corrupt people.

29:31. Our Messengers brought good news to Abraham and said: We will destroy the people of this city. Its people are wrongdoers.

29:32. Abraham said: Lot lives there. They said: We know who lives there. We will save him and his followers, except his wife. She is to remain behind.

29:33. When Our Messengers came to Lot, he was concerned about their safety from his people. But they said: Do not be afraid and concerned. We will save you and your followers except your wife. She is to stay behind.

29:34. We will bring down heavenly punishment on the people of this city because they have been defiantly disobedient.

29:35. Surely, the city ruins are a clear sign for those who ponder.

29:36. We sent their brother Shuaib to Midians*. He said: O my people, serve God, and look forward to the last day. Do not corrupt the earth with mischief.

**they lived in the northwest Arabian Peninsula, on the east shore of the Gulf of Aqaba on the Red Sea*

29:37. They denied him. An earthquake overtook them, and they became corpses in their homes.

29:38. We destroyed Aad and Thamoud. That is visible from their ruins. Satan made their deeds pleasing to them and averted them from the right path, though they were intelligent.

29:39. We destroyed Korah, Pharaoh, and Haman, though Moses came to them with clear signs, but they were arrogant. They could not escape Our punishment.

29:40. We punished them for their sins. To some, We sent a storm of stones, some were seized by a blast, some were swallowed by the earth, and some were drowned. God did not wrong them, but they wronged themselves.

29:41. The example of those who take allies beside God is like that of the spider that makes a cobweb. Indeed, the spider's home is the weakest, if they only knew.

29:42. God knows whoever they call upon beside Him. He is the all-mighty and all-wise.

29:43. We present these examples for mankind, but none will grasp their meaning except the wise.

29:44. God has created the heavens and the earth in truth. Indeed, there is a sign in that for the believers.

29:45. O Muhammad, recite the Qur'an that has been revealed to you and establish prayer. Prayer prohibits immorality and wrongdoing. God's remembrance is the greatest virtue. God knows all that you do.

29:46. Be courteous in arguing with the people of the book (Jews and Christians) except those who act unjustly. Say: We both believe in what has been revealed to you and us. Your and our God is one.

We surrender to Him.

29:47. Thus We have revealed the Qur'an to you Prophet Muhammad. Those to whom We gave the Scriptures (Jews and Christians) believe in it, and so do some of your own people, the Meccans. Only the disbelievers deny Our revelations.

29:48. O Muhammad, before this, you have neither read a book nor written one with your hand. Otherwise, the disbelievers would have doubted you.

29:49. The Qur'anic verses are clear signs for those who have been given knowledge. Only wrongdoers reject Our verses.

29:50. They ask: Why his Lord has not sent down signs to him? Say: The signs are in God's control; I am only a clear warner.

29:51. Is it not enough for them that We have revealed the Qur'an to you for reciting to them? Surely, it is a blessing and a reminder for the believers.

29:52. Say: God is a sufficient witness between us. He knows what is in the heavens and on earth. Those who believe in falsehood and disbelieve in God are the losers.

29:53. They ask you to hasten their punishment. Had a time not been fixed for it, the punishment would certainly have come to them. It will suddenly come to them when they would not be expecting it.

29:54. They urge you to hasten the punishment. But hell will surely surround the disbelievers.

29:55. The day the punishment will cover them from above and below, they will be told: Taste the result of what you used to do.

29:56. My earth is large for My believing servants. They should worship Me alone.

29:57. Everyone shall taste death. Then you shall return to Us.

29:58. The believers who do good will live in mansions of paradise where streams flow. They will live there forever. That will be an excellent reward for the virtuous,

29:59. who are patient, and put their trust in their Lord.

29:60. A lot of creatures cannot provide for themselves. God provides for them as He provides for the humans. He hears and knows all.

29:61. If you asked the disbelievers: Who created the heavens and the earth and subjected the sun and the moon? They would surely say: God. Then, how can they turn away from Him?

29:62. God provides abundantly to whom He wills and sparingly to whom He pleases. He knows all things.

29:63. If you were to ask them: Who sends down rain from the sky and revives the lifeless earth? They surely would say: God. Say: Praise is to God. But, most of them have no sense.

29:64. This worldly life is a short lived pastime. The eternal life will be in the hereafter, if only they knew.

29:65. When they go on a ship, they pray to God with devotion, but when He brings them safe to land, they worship other gods beside Him.

29:66. They show ingratitude for Our favors and enjoy the worldly life. But they will know soon.

29:67. Do they not see that We have given them a safe sanctuary at Mecca, while there is terror all around them? Then, why do they believe in falsehood, and reject God's blessing?

29:68. Who is more unjust than the one who invents a lie about God and denies the truth when it has come to him? Is hell not the place for such disbelievers?

29:69. Those who strive hard in Our cause, We will certainly guide them to Our ways. God is with the doers of good.

# CHAPTER 30

# THE ROMANS

**Name:** From Verse Two.

**Verses:** 60

**Background:**

The chapter predicts that the Romans will be victorious over the Persians and the Muslims will be victorious over the Meccan-disbelievers. This is an evidence of the Qur'an being God's word and Prophet Muhammad being God's Messenger.

**Summary:**

- It is God Who:
    - originates the creation and then repeats it, and everyone will be brought to Him for final judgment.
    - has created you and shall bring you to justice on the Day of Judgment.
    - commands the believers to give their due to the relatives, poor, and travelers.
    - sent His Messengers to guide people; some believed while others rejected. God punished the guilty and helped the believers. God said: O Muhammad, you cannot make the dead and the deaf to hear you.
- God's signs: The creation of men, their wives, heavens, earth, languages, colors, sleep, quest for work, lightening, rain, and growth of vegetation.
- The wrongdoers are led by their own desires without knowledge.
- When a punishment befalls upon people, they call upon God, but when He relieves them, they revert to disbelief.
- Mischief in the land is the result of man's own misdeeds. That is how God lets them taste the fruit of their deeds.

**By Verse**

In the name of God, the compassionate, the merciful:

30:1. Alif, Lam, Meem (are Arabic letters).
30:2. The Romans have been defeated,
30:3. in a land close by. But they will overcome their defeat and be

victorious,

30:4. within a few years. God made the decisions before and after these events. On the Day of Judgment, the believers shall rejoice,

30:5. with God's help. He gives victory to whom He wills. He is mighty and merciful.

30:6. That is God's promise to give victory to the Romans against the Persians. God does not fail in His promise, but most humans do not know it.

30:7. People care about what they see in the worldly life, but are unaware of the life to come.

30:8. Have they not pondered that God created the heavens and the earth and what is between them with truth for a destined end. But most humans do not believe that they will meet their Lord.

30:9. Have they not traveled through the land and seen the end of those before them? They were more powerful than them. They plowed the land and built on it more than them. Their Messengers came to them with clear signs. God did not wrong them, they wronged themselves.

30:10. Evil was the wrongdoers' end, because they denied and ridiculed God's revelations.

30:11. God creates and keeps on repeating it. All will return to Him.

30:12. On the Day of Judgment when the hour of punishment will come, the guilty will despair.

30:13. Their idol-gods will not plead with God for them, though they will reject their idols.

30:14. On the Day of Judgment, when the hour of punishment will arrive, the mankind will be divided into believers and disbelievers.

30:15. Those who believed and did good works will be made happy in a garden.

30:16. But the disbelievers who denied Our verses and the meeting in the hereafter will be punished.

30:17. Praise God morning and evening.

30:18. Praise is due to God alone in the heavens and on earth, and in the late afternoon and when the day begins to decline at noon.

30:19. God brings the dead to life, the living to death, and the lifeless earth to life. Likewise, you will be raised to life.

30:20. One of God's signs is that He created you from dust; you became humans and multiplied.

30:21. Another of His signs is that He created your wives from among yourselves so that you may live with them in peace. He planted love and kindness between you. Indeed, there are signs in it for those who think.

30:22. Among His other signs are the creation of the heavens and the earth and the diversity of your languages and colors. Surely, there are signs in this for the knowledgeable.

30:23. Among His other signs is that you sleep at night and during the day, you seek His bounty. Indeed, in that are signs for a people who listen.

30:24. Lightening, a cause of fear and hope, is another of His signs. He sends down rain from the sky to revive the lifeless earth. Indeed, there are signs for those who reason.

30:25. Among His other signs is that the heaven and the earth remain firm by His command. Then, when He would call you with a single call, you would come out from the earth.

30:26. Whatever is in the heavens and the earth belongs to Him. All are obedient to Him.

30:27. It is He Who creates and repeats it. That is easy for Him. He has the loftiest attributes in the heavens and the earth. He is mighty and wise.

30:28. He gives you an example from your own lives. Do your slaves share equally the riches we have given you? Do you fear them as you fear one another? Thus, We make Our verses clear to those who reason.

30:29. The wrongdoers follow their desires without knowledge. And who can guide those whom God leads off the right path? There will be no helpers for them.

30:30. Therefore, follow your religion firmly. God has created it to suit the natural requirements of mankind. God's creation cannot be changed. This is the right religion, but most humans do not know.

30:31. Repent and turn to God. Fear Him. Establish prayer and do not worship anyone but God.

30:32. Do not divide your religion into sects, each rejoicing in its own beliefs.

30:33. When adversity touches people, they call upon their Lord and repent. Then, when He shows them kindness, some of them go back to idol-worship.

30:34. They show no gratitude for Our favors. They can enjoy for a while, but soon they will know their folly.

30:35. Have We, God, authorized them to worship idols?

30:36. When We show kindness to people, they rejoice in it, but if evil befalls them because of their own fault, they despair.

30:37. Do they not see that God provides abundantly for whom He wills, and sparingly for whom He pleases? Indeed, there are signs in that for the believers.

30:38. Give their due to the relatives, needy, and travelers. That is best for those who desire God's pleasure; they will surely be successful.

30:39. Whatever usury you take to increase your wealth will not be blessed by God, but whatever alms you give will please God and He will reward you manifold for it.

30:40. God created you, provided for you, will cause you to die, and then will bring you to life. Can any of your idol-gods do anything like that? Praise is to God. He is high above their idol-gods.

30:41. Corruption has appeared on the land and the sea because of the mankind's misdeeds. God may let them taste some of what they have done, so that they may return to Him.

30:42. O Muhammad, say to the disbelievers: Travel through the land and see the end of those before you. Most of them worshipped idol-gods.

30:43. So follow the correct religion before the day comes from God which could not be avoided. That day, the mankind will be divided into disbelievers and believers.

30:44. The disbelievers will suffer because of their disbelief. The righteous will gain access to paradise because of their good deeds.

30:45. God, out of his kindness, may reward the believers who did righteous deeds. God does not like disbelievers.

30:46. One of His signs is that He sends winds bearing good news so that you may enjoy His kindness, your ships may sail by His command, and you may seek His reward to be grateful.

30:47. O Muhammad, before you, We sent Messengers to their people with clear signs. We punished the guilty; and duly helped the believers.

30:48. It is God Who sends winds that raise clouds. He spreads them in the sky as He wills, and breaks them up so you can see the rain-drops falling from their midst. When He sends them down on his servants they rejoice.

30:49. Though before the rain-drops came down upon them, they were in despair.

30:50. Observe the effects of God's kindness; how He gives life to the lifeless earth. Likewise, He will bring back the dead to life. He has power over all things.

30:51. But if We send a wind that turns their crops to yellow, they return to disbelief.

30:52. O Muhammad, you can neither make the dead hear you, nor make the deaf hear your call when they turn their backs and walk away.
30:53. Nor you can guide the blind away from their error. Only those will hear you who believe in Our verses and submit to Us.
30:54. God creates you weak, then gives you strength, and turns strength into infirmity and grey hair. He creates what He wills. He is all-knowing and all-powerful.
30:55. When the hour of reckoning will come, the guilty will swear that they dwelled no more than an hour. Thus, they were ever deceived.
30:56. But those who have been given knowledge and faith will say: Certainly you stayed away till the Day of Resurrection as decreed by God. This is the Day of Resurrection, but you did not know it.
30:57. That Day (of Resurrection), the wrongdoers' excuses will neither benefit them, nor will they be allowed to make amends.
30:58. We have given every kind of argument in the Qur'an. But, if you would show any sign to the disbelievers, they would certainly say: You are preaching lies.
30:59. Thus, God seals the hearts of those who are ignorant.
30:60. Therefore, have patience O Muhammad. God's promise is true. Let not those who doubt the faith make you impatient.

# CHAPTER 31

# LUQMAN

**Name:** From Verse 12.

**Verses:** 34

**Summary :**

- The Qur'an is the book of wisdom, a guide and a blessing for the righteous.
- If all trees were pens and oceans were ink, God's words could not be put into writing.
- Luqman's advice to his son about:
  - worshipping no one except God.
  - moral behavior and interaction.
- Rights of mother and parents. Obey your parents but not in matter against faith.
- Main reason for being misguided is blindly following one's forefathers.
- God is real, all others idol-gods are false.
- Mankind, fear that day when neither a father shall help his child nor the child shall help the father.
- Let Satan not deceive you about God.

**By Verse**

In the name of God, the compassionate, the merciful:

31:1. Alif, Lam, Meem (are Arabic letters).
31:2. These are verses of the wise book, the Qur'an,
31:3. a guide and a blessing to those who do good,
31:4. establish prayer, give Zakat (mandatory charity), and firmly believe in the life to come.
31:5. They are rightly guided by their Lord, and will surely be successful.
31:6. There are some who engage in useless talk, lead people off the right path from God's path without knowledge, and make fun of it. They shall be severely punished.
31:7. When Our verses are recited to them, they turn away arrogantly as if they had not heard them and were deaf. Give them news of a painful punishment.

31:8. The believers who do go deeds will enter gardens of pleasure in paradise.

31:9. They will live there forever. It is God's firm promise. He is the mighty and wise.

31:10. God created the heaven without visible pillars. He set firm mountains on earth lest it should shake with you. He scattered all kinds of animals on earth, and sends down rain from the sky to grow all kinds of useful plants.

31:11. That is God's creation. Now show Me what your other gods have created. The wrongdoers are truly in clear error.

31:12. We blessed Luqman with wisdom, saying: Be grateful to God. Whoever is grateful, that is for his own good; but if someone is ungrateful, surely God is self-sufficient and praiseworthy.

31:13. Remember when Luqman advised his son: Worship no other god except God. Worshipping idol-gods is a great sin.

31:14. We have directed humans to be kind to their parents. A mother bears a child in weakness and pain, and her weaning the child takes two years. You should be grateful to God and to your parents. In the end all will return to Me.

31:15. If your parents insist that you should worship others than Me about which you have no knowledge, do not obey them. Be kind to them in this world, but follow the one devoted to Me. All will return to Me and I shall tell you what you have done.

31:16. Luqman said to his son: Even if there is something as small as a mustard seed in a rock or anywhere else in heavens or on earth, God will bring it out. God understands the finest mysteries and knows everything.

31:17. My son, establish prayer, direct what is right, forbid what is wrong, and bear with patience what befalls you. These matters require determination.

31:18. Do not treat people with contempt and do not walk on earth proudly. God does not like the arrogant and the boastful.

31:19. Be modest in your walking and lower your voice. A donkey's voice is the most repugnant.

31:20. Do you not see that God has subjected to you whatever is in the heavens and on earth and has blessed upon you His visible and non-visible favors? But there are some who dispute about God without knowledge, guidance or an enlightening book.

31:21. When it is said to them: Follow what God has revealed, they reply: We will only follow our forefathers' faith. Will they follow them even if Satan was inviting them to the punishment of hell?

31:22. Whoever submits to God completely and does good deeds has held the most trustworthy hand. God is the ultimate decision maker of all matters.

31:23. O Muhammad, the disbelievers' disbelief should not grieve you. They will return to Us, and We will tell them of what they did. God has knowledge of what is in their hearts.

31:24. We are letting the disbelievers enjoy the worldly life for a while; but then will punish them severely.

31:25. O Muhammad, if you ask them: Who created the heavens and the earth? Surely, they will reply: God. Say: All praise is to God; but most of them do not understand.

31:26. Whatever is in the heavens and on earth belongs to God. God is free of all needs and is praiseworthy.

31:27. If all trees on earth were pens, and the ocean, with seven more oceans to replenish it, was ink, the writing of God's words could not be finished. God is mighty, full of wisdom.

31:28. The creation and resurrection of all of you are like the creation and resurrection of a single person. God hears and sees all.

31:29. Do you not see that God makes the night and day follow one another, and He has subjected the sun and the moon to follow their orbits till an appointed time? God is aware of what you do.

31:30. That is because God is for real, and others they partner with Him are false. God is the most high and great.

31:31. Do you not see that ships sail through the sea by God's blessing so that He may show you His signs? There are signs in that for everyone patient and grateful.

31:32. When waves come over them like canopies, they pray to God with devotion. But when He brings them safely to land, there are some who start doubting the faith. No one rejects Our signs except those who are deceitful and ungrateful.

31:33. O mankind, fear your Lord and the day when no father will be able to help his child, and no child will be able to help his father. God's promise is true. Neither the worldly life nor the deceiver Satan should be able to deceive you about God.

31:34. God alone knows the hour of punishment. He sends down rain and knows what is in the wombs. No one knows what he will accomplish tomorrow, and where he will die. God knows about and is aware of everything.

# CHAPTER 32

# THE PROSTRATION

**Name:** From Verse 15.

**Verses:** 30

**Summary:**

- Theme: Removal of peoples' doubts about God's oneness, the hereafter, and Muhammad's Prophethood. It invites people to these three realities.
- The Qur'an contains no doubts. It has been revealed to Prophet Muhammad, so that he may warn people to whom no warner has come earlier.
- The disbelievers have been asked to use their common sense to judge for themselves which things presented by the Qur'an are strange and novel? For example, look at the administration of the heavens and the earth; consider your own creation and structure; see how rain revives the lifeless earth. Don't these things testify to Prophet Muhammad's teachings?
- A scene from the hereafter has been described. The fruits of belief and the evil consequences of disbelief have been mentioned. The people have been urged to give up disbelief and to accept the Qur'an's teachings before they meet their punishment. That will be to their advantage in the hereafter.
- On the Day of Judgment, the disbelievers shall believe, but that belief will be of no benefit to them.
- Humans have been told that it is God's mercy that He does not seize them immediately for their errors but warns them beforehand by punishing them lightly in this world so that they may wake up and change.
- This is not the first time that God has sent down a book upon a human. Before this, as you all know, the book had been sent down upon Moses also.
- The Meccan-Disbelievers have been admonished to the effect that the disbelieving communities of the past, whose ruined dwellings they see, were destroyed. Will they like to meet the same fate themselves?
- There is a special reward for those who get up from their sleeping beds, call upon their Lord with fear and hope, and spend in charity.

## By Verse

In the name of God, the compassionate, the merciful:

32:1. Alif, Lam, Meem (are Arabic letters).

32:2. There is no doubt that Lord of the universe has revealed the Qur'an.

32:3. Do they say: He Prophet Muhammad has invented it? In fact, it is the truth from your Lord, so that you Prophet Muhammad may warn people to whom no warner has come earlier and perhaps they may be guided.

32:4. God created the heavens and the earth, and what is between them, in six days. Then He sat on the throne. Beside Him, you have no protector or mediator. Will you then not pay attention?

32:5. God directs the affairs from the heavens to the earth; then its report goes to Him in a day, which is equal to your 1,000 years.

32:6. God knows the seen and the unseen. He is the all-mighty and merciful.

32:7. God perfected everything He created. First, He created a human from clay.

32:8. Then, He made the human race from the insignificant semen from male and female intercourse.

32:9. God molded you, the humans, breathed His spirit into you, and gave you hearing, vision, and heart; yet, you are seldom grateful.

32:10. The disbelievers ask: When we are dead and decomposed in the earth, how can we be re-created? Indeed, they deny that they will ever meet their Lord.

32:11. Prophet Muhammad, tell them: The angel of death, who has been put in-charge of you, will gather you, and you will return to your Lord.

32:12. If you could see when the criminals would bow their heads before their Lord, and say: Lord, we have seen and heard. Please return us to the world; we will do good deeds; we are now certain in our faith.

32:13. If God had willed, He could have guided every human. But God's promise of filling hell with jinns and humans will be fulfilled.

32:14. So taste the punishment because you forgot the meeting of this day. We will forget you too. Taste the punishment forever for what you did.

32:15. Those who believe in Our verses, when they are reminded of them, they bow down in prostration, praise their Lord, and are humble.

32:16. They rise from their sleeping beds; pray to their Lord in fear and

hope; and give charity from what We have provided for them.
32:17. No person knows what reward is in store for them for their good deeds.
32:18. Are a believer and a disbeliever equal? No, they are not.
32:19. The believers who did righteous deeds will be rewarded the gardens of paradise for their good deeds.
32:20. For those who defiantly disobeyed, their refuge will be hellfire. Every time they would wish to get away from it, they will be pushed back and told: Taste the punishment of the fire you used to deny.
32:21. We will let them taste the light punishment in this world before the greater punishment in the life to come, so that they may return to the right path.
32:22. And who is more unjust than the one who is reminded of his Lord's verses, and he turns away from them? We will indeed punish the guilty.
32:23. We gave the Scripture to Moses. There should be no doubt about his receiving that. We made the Torah guidance for Israel's children.
32:24. When they became steadfast and believed firmly in Our revelations, We raised leaders from among them who guided them by Our command.
32:25. On the Day of Resurrection, your Lord will resolve their differences.
32:26. By walking around the ruined dwellings, do they not see how many generations We have destroyed before them? These indeed are visible signs. Then, why do they not listen?
32:27. Do they not see that We drive rain to the barren land by which We bring forth crops for them and their livestock to eat? Do they not have eyes to see that?
32:28. They ask: When will the judgment come, if you are truthful?
32:29. O Muhammad, tell them: On the Day of Judgment, the disbelievers' conversion to belief neither will benefit them, nor they will be given any relief.
32:30. Therefore, pay no attention to them, and wait as they are waiting.

# CHAPTER 33

# THE ALLIES

**Name:** From Verses 20 and 22.

**Verses:** 73

**Background:**

The Islamic army's setback in the battle of Uhud boosted the morale of Pagan-Arabs, Jews, and hypocrites. They started hoping that they would exterminate Islam and Muslims. The battle of Trench was a combined raid by many Arab tribes. They numbered 10,000-12,000 men.

Had it been a sudden attack, it would have been disastrous. Prophet Muhammad got a trench dug out on the north-west of Medina in six days. The disbelievers were not aware that they would encounter a trench outside Medina. They had to lay a siege in winter for which they had not come prepared. After this, the only alternative they had was to incite the Jewish Tribe of Bani Quraizah to rebellion, who inhabited the southeastern part of the city. The Bani Quraizah, who had a treaty with Muslims, was persuaded to break the treaty. The siege was prolonged for more than 25 days in winter. Then, suddenly one night a severe windstorm with thunder and lightning hit the camp. The enemy left the battleground during the night and returned to their homes.

This was the time when the Islamic social laws were complemented, for example, the question of a son's adoption. He got share in inheritance and was treated like a real son and a real brother by the adopted mother and the sister respectively. He could not marry the daughter of his adopted father and his widow after his death. And the same was the case if the adopted son died or divorced a wife. The adopted father regarded the woman as his real daughter-in-law and could not marry her. To correct the situation, a little before the battle of Trench, God allowed the Prophet through revelation to marry the divorced wife Zainab of his adopted son, Zaid bin Harithah. The fact that the tales invented by the enemies also became topics of conversation among the Muslims was a clear sign that the element of sensuality in society had crossed all limits. This was precisely the occasion when the reformative commandments pertaining to the law of women's dress were introduced in this chapter.

There were two other problems of the Prophet's domestic life which needed attention. The first problem was that at that time the Prophet was not well off financially. The other problem was, that before marrying Zainab, he already had four wives. The opponents and the Muslims started doubting that why the Prophet himself had taken a fifth wife, while only four were allowed.

These were the questions that were engaging the attention of the Prophet and the Muslims when this chapter was revealed.

**Summary:**

- Theme: The battle of Trench, raid on the Jewish Tribe of Bani Quraizah, and Prophet Muhammad's marriage with Zainab, his cousin, who was the divorced wife of his adopted son, Zaid bin Harithah.
- Fear God and do not obey the disbelievers and the hypocrites.
- By your declaration, neither your wives become your mothers nor adopted sons your real sons.
- The Prophet's wives are like believers' mothers.
- Blood relations have greater claims than others in the Qur'an.
- God:
    - favored the believers during the Battle of Trench.
    - helped Muslims gain victory over the disbelievers and the Jewish tribes in Medina and Khyber.
    - ordered Prophet Muhammad to marry the divorced wife of his adopted son, Zaid.
    - clarified that Muhammad is not the father of any man but the last Prophet.
    - gave permission to Prophet Muhammad to marry more than four wives, but restricted him not to marry or divorce one and marry another one after this commandment.
    - and His angels send blessings on the Prophet; the believers should do the same.
- The hypocrites, who discouraged others from participating in the fight against the disbelievers and did not participate in such a war themselves, had no faith and all their acts would be void.
- The Prophet's life is the best model for humans.
- God's admonition and orders to the Prophet's wives.
- It is not proper for the believers to take exceptions in what has been decided by God and His Messenger.
- The Prophet has been sent to give good news, warn, and spread light of guidance as a lamp.

- If, after marriage, there is no sexual intercourse between a couple, then there is no waiting period for divorce and remarriage.
- Do not enter prophet's houses without permission. If invited, do not seek long conversation. Do not marry prophet's wives after his death.
- Commandment for women's dress code.
- Punishment for the hypocrites and the scandal mongers.
- In hell, the disbelievers shall ask for double punishment for their leaders.
- The believers fear God and always say the right thing.
- The heavens, earth, and mountains refused to take the burden of God's trust but humans took it.

**By Verse**

In the name of God, the compassionate, the merciful:

33:1. O Prophet, fear God and do not obey the disbelievers and the hypocrites. God is ever knowing and wise.

33:2. Follow what your Lord has revealed to you. God knows what you do.

33:3. Put your trust in God. He is sufficient as your protector.

33:4. God has not given two hearts to a human. He considers neither the wives you divorce your mothers, nor your adopted sons your sons. These are just your utterances. But, God tells you the truth, and guides you to the right path.

33:5. Call your adopted sons by their fathers' names. That is more just in God's sight. But, if you do not know their fathers, consider them your religious brothers and friends. There is no blame upon you for your unintentional mistakes, but not for your intentional ones. God is forgiving and merciful.

33:6. The Prophet is more worthy of the believers' love than they love themselves, and his wives are like their mothers. God has decreed that the blood relations are entitled to more inheritance than other believers and emigrants. But, you may show kindness to your close associates through a will. God has decreed it in the Qur'an.

33:7. We have made an agreement with you as We made with other prophets, for example, Noah, Abraham, Moses, and Jesus, the son of Mary. We took a solemn promise from them,

33:8. so that God may question their truthfulness about following His orders. God has prepared a painful punishment for the disbelievers.

33:9. Believers, remember God's favor to you when your enemies attacked you. We sent upon them a windstorm and armies of invisible angels. God was watching what you were doing.
33:10. Your enemies attacked you from above and below. That blurred your eyes, sank your hearts, and shook your faith in God.
33:11. The believers were tested and shocked.
33:12. The hypocrites and the weak-hearted said: God and His Messenger have deceived us.
33:13. Others said: O people of Medina, you cannot stand the enemy-attack; so go back. Some of them asked for Prophet's leave, saying: Our houses are unprotected; but that was not true. Their only intention was to run away.
33:14. If the enemy had entered the city from all sides and asked them to rebel, they would have done so without much hesitation.
33:15. They had promised with God not to turn their backs and flee. They shall be questioned about their promise with God.
33:16. O Muhammad, tell them: Your running away will not benefit you. If you flee from death or killing, you would only enjoy this life for a little while.
33:17. Say: Who can protect you if God intends to punish you; and who can stop Him if He intends to show you kindness? They will have no protector or helper beside God.
33:18. God knows those who keep others from fighting in God's cause and say to their brothers: Join us. They seldom take part in fighting.
33:19. Some Muslims are reluctant to help you. When danger comes, they look to you for help with their eyes fearful of death. But when the danger departs, they talk to you with sharp tongues greedily demanding major part of the booty. They are not believers. God will render their deeds worthless, and that is easy for God to do.
33:20. They think the attacking allies may not have gone away. If the attackers were to come again, the hypocrites would rather be sitting among the desert-nomads, waiting for the news of what happened to you. If they were with you, they would not fight much.
33:21. The God's Messenger is certainly a good example for those who look to God and the last day and remember God often.
33:22. When the believers saw the enemy and its allies, they said: This is what God and His Messenger had promised us. God and His Messenger spoke the truth. It increased their faith and obedience.
33:23. Among the believers are those who have been true to their promise

with God. Some of them have died, and others are waiting, but they have not changed their determination in the least.

33:24. God will reward the truthful for their faith and punish the hypocrites or accept their repentance if He wills. Indeed, God is ever forgiving and merciful.

33:25. God repelled the disbelievers in their rage. They went back without any advantage. God was sufficient to help the believers in the battle. God is all-powerful and all-mighty.

33:26. God drove down, from their fortresses, the Jews of Beni Qurayza, who backed the allies of your enemy. He casted terror into their hearts; you killed some and captured some.

33:27. God gave you their land, homes, and wealth, and also a land which you have never visited*. God is able to do all things.

**Khaybar, 90 miles north of Medina.*

33:28. O Prophet, tell your wives: If you desire the worldly life and its glitter, then come, I shall provide for you and graciously divorce you.

33:29. But if you seek God, His Messenger, and the hereafter, God has prepared a great reward for those who do good deeds.

33:30. O Prophet's wives, whoever among you would commit an evident indecency, your punishment would be double. That is easy for God to do.

33:31. Whoever is obedient to God and His Messenger and does good deeds, her reward will be double. And We have provided a generous living for her.

33:32. O Prophet's wives, you are not like other women. If you fear God, do not be mellow in your speech, so that a lust-hearted person may not long for you. Speak in firm voice.

33:33. Live in your houses. Do not display yourselves as was done in days of ignorance. Establish prayer, give Zakat (mandatory charity), and obey God and His Messenger. O Prophet's household, God intends only to remove all impurities from you, and to purify you.

33:34. Remember God's revelations and His wisdom recited in your homes. God understands the finest mysteries and is well-acquainted with them.

33:35. God will forgive and reward, both men and women, who:

- submit to God,
- are believers, obedient, truthful, patient, and humble, and
- give charity, fast, guard their private parts, and remember

God often.

33:36. When a matter has been decided by God and His Messenger, it is not fitting for a believing man or woman to have an option about their decision. Anyone who disobeys God and His Messenger is indeed clearly on a wrong path.

33:37. O Muhammad, remember when you said to Zaid, whom you and I had favored: Keep your wife and fear God. You hid in your heart what God wanted to disclose. You feared people, while God has more right that you fear Him. So when Zaid divorced her, We married her to you so that the believers would have no reason not to marry the wives of their adopted sons when they have divorced them. God's orders must be carried out.

33:38. There is no blame on the Prophet for what God has ordered him to do. That has been God's way with previous Prophets. God's commands are predetermined.

33:39. That has been God's way for those who convey God's message, fear Him, and do not fear anyone but God. God is sufficient to take account.

33:40. Muhammad is not the father of any man among you. He is God's Messenger and the seal of the Prophets. God knows all things.

33:41. Believers, remember God frequently.

33:42. Glorify God morning and evening.

33:43. It is God who sends blessings on you, as do His angels, so that He may bring you out from the depths of darkness into light. God is merciful to the believers.

33:44. The day they meet Him, their greeting will be: Peace. He has prepared a rich reward for them.

33:45. O Prophet, We have sent you as a witness, a bearer of good news, and a warner.

33:46. And as the one who invites people to God by His permission, and guides them as a lamp spreading light.

33:47. Give good news to the believers that they will have a great reward from God.

33:48. Do not obey the disbelievers and the hypocrites. Ignore them but rely upon God. God is sufficient as your guardian.

33:49. Believers, when you marry believing women and then divorce them before you have intercourse with them, then there is no waiting period to complete the divorce. Provide for them and give them a gracious release.

33:50. O Prophet, We have made lawful to you:

- the wives to whom you have paid their dowries;
- the slave-girls We have assigned to you from the prisoners of war;
- the daughters of your paternal uncles and aunts;
- the daughters of your maternal uncles and aunts, who migrated from Mecca to Medina with you; and
- any other believing women who dedicated themselves to you if you wish to marry them.

This privilege is only for you and not for other believers. We know the duties We have decreed for the believers regarding their wives and the slave-girls. We have clarified this so that there should be no difficulty for you. God is oft-forgiving and most merciful.

33:51. O Muhammad, you may defer taking to bed any of your wives or take anyone you please. There is no blame upon you if you take anyone from those whom you have temporarily set aside. That is more suitable for them to be content and not grieve, and be satisfied with what you give them. God knows what is in your hearts. God is the all-knowing and the most patient.

33:52. O Muhammad, it is not lawful for you to take additional wives or to exchange the present ones with other women, even if their beauty attracts you, except the slave-girls. God observes all things.

33:53. Believers! You should not enter prophet's houses without permission, nor stay waiting for the mealtime. But when invited to eat, do come. When you have eaten, depart without engaging in lengthy conversation, because it will cause inconvenience to the Prophet, but he would be shy of dismissing you. However, God is not shy of telling you the truth. When you ask his wives for something, ask them from behind a curtain. That is more virtuous for their and your hearts. You are not allowed to trouble God's Messenger or to marry his wives after his death. That would be a great sin in God's sight.

33:54. Whether you reveal or conceal anything, God has knowledge of all things.

33:55. There is no blame on prophet's wives to appear without veil before:

- their fathers,
- sons,
- brothers,
- brother's sons,
- sisters' sons,

- familiar women, and
- slave-girls.

Ladies, fear God, He observes all things.

33:56. God and His angels send blessings on the Prophet. Believers send blessing on him, and salute him with all respect.

33:57. Those who annoy God and His Messenger, God has cursed them in this world and the hereafter. He has prepared a disgraceful punishment for them.

33:58. Those who slander believing men and women unduly, they are guilty of a false accusation and a gross sin.

33:59. O Prophet, tell your wives, daughters, and believing women to bring down a part of their outer garment over their faces. That is more suitable for their recognition and to avoid lustful gaze. God is forgiving and merciful.

33:60. If hypocrites, and those who have diseased hearts, and the scandal-mongers in Medina, will not stop their mischievous actions, We shall authorize you to overpower them and they will not be able to stay in the city for long.

33:61. They will be cursed wherever they are found, seized and killed.

33:62. This has been God's practice with those who lived before them. You will find no change in God's practice.

33:63. People ask you about when the world will end. Say: Only God knows. Who knows, the end may just be at hand.

33:64. God has cursed the disbelievers and prepared a blazing fire for them.

33:65. They will live there forever and will have no protector or helper.

33:66. On that day when their faces will be turned over in the hellfire, they will say: Had we obeyed God and His Messenger!

33:67. And they shall say: Lord, we obeyed our leaders and dignitaries, but they led us off the right path.

33:68. Lord, give them double punishment and curse them greatly.

33:69. Believers, do not be like those who abused Moses. God saved him from their abuse and honored him.

33:70. Believers, fear God and speak the truth.

33:71. God will bless your deeds and forgive your sins. Whoever obeys God and His Messenger shall achieve a great victory.

33:72. We offered the trust of duty and responsibility to the heavens, earth, and mountains. They declined because they were afraid to bear it. Humans undertook to bear it, but have proven to be unjust and ignorant.

33:73. God will punish the hypocrites and idolaters, both men and women, and will pardon the true believers, both men and women. God is ever forgiving and merciful.

# CHAPTER 34

## SHEBA

**Name:** From Verse 15.

**Verses:** 54

**Summary:**

- Theme: Answering the disbelievers' objections against Prophet Muhammad's Prophethood, God's oneness, and the hereafter.
- The disbelievers' objections have been answered by the stories of the Sabaeans* and those of Prophets David and Solomon. God blessed both prophets with great powers and such grandeur and glory as had been granted to hardly anyone before them. In spite of that, they were not proud and arrogant. On the other hand, God blessed the Sabaeans, but they became proud. They were destroyed and remembered only in stories. With these precedents, the disbelievers could judge for themselves between faith and disbelief in God, the hereafter, and Muhammad's Prophethood.

  **an ancient South Arabian people, modern-day Yemen, believed to be the biblical land of Sheba.*

- The hour of punishment is surely to come and the Day of Judgment shall be established to reward the believers and punish those who discredit God's revelations. Those who do not believe in the hereafter are doomed.
- The mountains and birds used to sing God's hymns with Prophet David. God subjected winds and jinns to Solomon. The people's claim that jinns know the unseen is wrong. The people of Sheba rejected God's blessings and disbelieved in the hereafter, so God made them merely a tale of the past.
- No one can plead before God for anyone except for whom He permits it. Prophet Muhammad is the Messenger for the entire mankind.
- Those who disbelieve in the Qur'an and prior Scriptures will have chains placed around their necks before being tossed into hell.
- Wealth and children are not the indications of God's pleasure, but faith and righteousness are. Whatever you spend in charity, God will pay you back.
- The disbelievers:

  - denied Prophet Muhammad and the Qur'an.
  - who are Prophet Muhammad's enemies are asked to ponder upon their wrong statements because the truth has come and the falsehood has vanished and shall not return.

- On the Day of Judgment, the disbelievers will want to believe but it will be too late.

**By Verse**

In the name of God, the compassionate, the merciful:

34:1. Praise be to God:

- Who owns all that is in the heavens and on earth.
- In the hereafter.

He is full of wisdom and all-aware.

34:2. God knows what:

- goes into the earth and what springs from it, and
- what comes down from the heaven and what goes up to it.

God is merciful and ever forgiving.

34:3. The disbelievers say: The hour of punishment will never come to us. Say: By my Lord, Who knows the unseen, it will surely come to you. Neither an atom's weight is hidden from Him in the heavens or on earth; nor is anything smaller or greater that is not recorded in a clear book.

34:4. So that God may reward those who believe and act righteously. Forgiveness will be their lot and they will be provided generous sustenance.

34:5. But, those who try to prove Our revelations false shall be punished severely.

34:6. Those who have been given knowledge can see that what is revealed to you O Muhammad from your Lord is the truth, and it guides to a path of the almighty, the praiseworthy God.

34:7. The disbelievers say: Should we show you a man, Muhammad, who says that when your body has been completely disintegrated, you shall be raised to life again?

34:8. Has he, Muhammad, invented a lie about God or is he mad? Those who do not believe in the hereafter will be punished and are for astray.

34:9. Do they not then see what is before them and behind them in the heaven and on the earth? If We want, We could let the earth swallow them or a piece of the sky fall upon them. Indeed, there is a sign in that for every one turning to God.

34:10. We blessed David by saying: O mountains and birds, sing My praises with him. We made iron soft for him,

34:11. saying: Make coats of armor of interlinked balanced rings. Do what is right. I am watching over all what you do.

34:12. We made the wind obedient to Solomon. The wind traveled a month's journey in a morning and a month's journey in an evening. We made a spring of molten brass flow for him; and jinns worked for him, by his Lord's leave. If anyone of them did not obey Our orders, We punished him in blazing fire.

34:13. Jinns made for him what he willed: Elevated chambers, images, basins like reservoirs, and huge cooking vessels built into the ground. O David's family, give thanks; but few of My servants are thankful.

34:14. When We decreed death for Solomon, Jinns did not know that he was dead till they saw a worm eating away his staff. When his corpse fell down, the jinns came to know that if they had known the unseen, they would not have continued in humiliating torment.

34:15. For the people of Sheba, there was a sign in their homeland, a garden on their right and a garden on their left. We had said to them: Eat from what your Lord has given you and be grateful to Him. Your land is good and your Lord is ever forgiving.

34:16. But, they turned away from God. So, We sent upon them a devastating flood, and reduced their two gardens with gardens of bitter fruit and sparse shrubs.

34:17. We punished them for their disbelief. We never punish any except the ever ungrateful?

34:18. Between them and the cities We blessed, We located villages at measured distances, and said: Travel through them by day and night in safety.

34:19. But they said: Lord, lengthen distances between stages of our journeys. They wronged themselves, so We made their fate a tale by disintegrating them in the land. Indeed, there is a sign in that for everyone most patient and ever grateful.

34:20. And Satan surely did confirm his idea about them; they all followed him, except a group of true believers.

34:21. Satan absolutely had no power over them, except that We wanted to make distinction between those who believed in the hereafter and those who had doubt about it. Your Lord ever watches over all things.

34:22. O Muhammad, say: Call upon those you claim as deities beside God. They neither possess an atom's weight of power in heaven or on earth, nor have any partnership with Him. God has absolutely no helpers among them.

34:23. No intercession benefits with God except for the one He gives permission. When fear shall be removed from their hearts, they shall ask one another: What has the Lord said? Some of them shall reply: The truth. God is the most high, the great.

34:24. O Prophet, ask them: Who provides for you from the heaven and the earth? Tell them: God. Either we, the believers, or you, the unbelievers, are on clear guidance or in manifest error.

34:25. Say: You will not be questioned what sins we committed nor shall we be questioned about what you did.

34:26. Say: Our Lord will bring us together on the Day of Resurrection and will judge between us justly. He is the all-knowing judge.

34:27. Ask them: Show me those whom you have joined to be partners with God. No, He alone is God. He is the all mighty and all wise.

34:28. O Prophet, We, God, have sent you to all mankind as a universal Messenger to give good news and to warn, but most men do not know.

34:29. The disbelievers ask: When will this promise of the Day of Resurrection be fulfilled if you are truthful?

34:30. Reply: The coming of the day is fixed for you, neither you can delay it nor hasten it by an hour.

34:31. The disbelievers say: We shall neither believe in the Qur'an nor any Scriptures before it. If you could see when the wrongdoers will stand before their Lord, they will blame one another. Those who were powerless will say to the arrogant: Had it not been for you, we would certainly have believed.

34:32. The arrogant will say to the powerless: Did we keep you away from guidance after it had come to you? No, you yourselves were the wrongdoers.

34:33. The powerless will say to the arrogant: You conspired day and night and ordered us to disbelieve in God and worship other gods. But they will all hide regret on seeing the punishment. We will put chains on the disbelievers' necks. Will they not be punished for what they used to do?

34:34. It has never happened that We sent a warner to a city and his message was not denied by its effluent.

34:35. They said: We have more wealth and children than the believers.

Surely, we shall never be punished.

34:36. Say: My Lord provides abundantly or sparingly to whom He pleases, but most of the people do not know it.

34:37. Neither your wealth nor your children will bring you near to God, except faith and righteousness. The faithful and the righteous will be given double reward and they will live in peace in chambers of paradise.

34:38. Those who oppose Our revelations shall be punished.

34:39. O Prophet, say to them: My Lord increases or decreases the livelihood of his servants as He pleases. Whatever you spend in His cause, He will compensate you for it. He is the best giver.

34:40. The day God will gather all humans, He will ask the angels: Did they used to worship you?

34:41. The angels will reply: Glory is to God, You are our protector, not them. They worshipped the jinns; most of them believed in them.

34:42. That day no one will have power to help or harm anyone. God shall say to the wrongdoers: Taste the punishment of the hellfire, which you used to deny.

34:43. When Our clear revelations are recited to them, they say: This man desires to turn you away from what your forefathers worshipped. Some say: This is an invented lie. And others, who disbelieved the truth when it was first told to them, say: This is clearly magic.

34:44. We have neither given them any Scriptures to study, nor sent a warner before you.

34:45. Those who have gone before them also denied our revelations. They were 10 times more effluent and powerful. But they denied My Messengers, how terrible was My punishment!

34:46. O Prophet, say to them: I only advise you of one thing in God's name that you should think individually and in groups about what makes you believe your companion the Prophet is mad. He is only warning you before a severe punishment.

34:47. Say: I do not ask any reward from you, keep it for yourself. My reward is only from God. He watches over all things.

34:48. Say: My Lord reveals the truth. He knows about all the unseen.

34:49. Say: The truth has come; the falsehood has vanished and shall not return.

34:50. Say: If I am in error, the loss is my own alone, but if I am rightly guided, it is because of what my Lord has revealed to me. God hears all and is near.

34:51. If you could see when the disbelievers will be terrified, but there will be no escape, and they will be seized immediately.

34:52. They will say: We do believe in God now. But how could that be possible for them to have faith when they had wandered so far away from having faith!

34:53. They had in the past disbelieved and mocked at the unseen when they were far away in the world.

34:54. They shall be prevented from achieving their desire as was done for others like them before them, who disbelieved and doubted.

# CHAPTER 35

# THE CREATOR

**Name:** From Verse One.

**Verses:** 45

**Summary:**

- Theme. To:
    - warn the Meccans for their antagonistic attitude towards Prophet Muhammad's message of God's oneness.
    - console the Prophet against Meccans' opposition.
    - encourage the believers to remain steadfast.
- No one can withhold or award God's blessings.
- Satan is humans' enemy. Anyone who considers his evil deeds to be good cannot be guided to the right path.
- Those who seek honor should know that real honor is in God's obedience.
- For the benefit of the humans, God has created water, day, night, sun, and moon.
- Deities other than God can neither hear nor respond. They have no power at all.
- Mankind needs God, while God does not need anyone and anything.
- The living and the dead are not alike. Prophet Muhammad, you cannot make those who are buried in the graves hear you.
- Those who recite the Qur'an, establish prayer, and give charity may hope for God's blessings and rewards. The disbelievers will be punished in the hellfire forever.
- God has not sent any book which has a provision for worshipping anyone other than God.
- Plotting evil harms none but its plotter. If God was to punish people for their wrong doings, He would not have left a human around.

## By Verse

In the name of God, the compassionate, the merciful:

35:1. Praise is to God, the creator of the heavens and earth. He made angels His Messengers, with two, three and four pair of wings. He increases creatures with His will. God is able to do all things.

35:2. No one can withhold or release God's blessings on mankind. God is almighty and all-wise.

35:3. O mankind, remember God's favor upon you. Is there a creator other than God who provides for you from the heaven and the earth? There is no god except Him. So how can you turn away from Him?

35:4. O Muhammad, if the disbelievers deny you, other Messengers before you were denied too. All matters return to God for decision.

35:5. O mankind, God's promise is true. Let this worldly life not deceive you, nor let Satan deceive you about God.

35:6. Satan is your enemy; therefore treat him as an enemy. He only invites his followers to follow him so they may become companions of the hellfire.

35:7. The disbelievers will have severe punishment, and the believers who do good works will have forgiveness and great reward.

35:8. Is there a limit to the wickedness of the person whose evil conduct seems fair to him and he considers it good? God sends him off the right path whom He wills and guides whom He wills. O Muhammad, do not worry yourself to death for the disbelievers. God knows all what they do.

35:9. It is God who sends winds, which raise clouds. We drive them to a dead land and give life to the lifeless earth. The resurrection will be like that.

35:10. Whosoever desires glory should know that glory is God's alone. God hears the good words, and exalts the good deeds. Those who plan evil deeds will be severely punished. Their evil plan shall perish.

35:11. God created you from dust, then from a sperm-drop. He divided you into pairs of male and female. No female conceives or gives birth without God's knowledge. No person grows old or has his lifespan lessened but as prerecorded in God's book. All this is easy for God to do.

35:12. The two seas are not alike. One is fresh, sweet, and pleasant to drink. The other is salty and bitter. But from both, you get fresh fish and ornaments to wear. You see the ships sailing through them for you to seek God's bounty so that you may be thankful.

35:13. God makes the night and the day follow each other, and has ordered the sun and the moon to follow their course for a specified time. That is God, your Lord; the kingdom belongs to Him. The idol-gods whom you claim partners with God have no power at all.

35:14. If you pray to your idol-gods, they cannot hear you; even if they were to hear you, they cannot respond to you. On the Day of Resurrection, they will deny your association. None can guide you like God Who knows it all.

35:15. O mankind, you are in need of God, while God is free of need and is praiseworthy.

35:16. If God wills, He can do away with you and replace you with a new creation.

35:17. That is not difficult for God to do.

35:18. No one will carry another's burden. If a heavily laden soul will call another to carry some of its burden, even a close relative will not do it. O Muhammad, you can only warn those who fear their Lord without seeing Him and have established prayer. Whoever purifies oneself only purifies for one's own benefit. All things shall return to God.

35:19. The blind and those who can see are not alike.

35:20. Nor are the darkness and the light.

35:21. Nor are the shade and the sun's heat.

35:22. Nor are the living and the dead. God can cause anyone and anything to hear Him, but O Muhammad you cannot make those buried in graves hear you.

35:23. You are but a warner.

35:24. We have sent you with truth to give good news and to warn your people. There has never been a nation that has not been warned by a warner.

35:25. If they deny you, those before them did the same. Their Messengers came to them with clear proofs, Scriptures, and the enlightening book.

35:26. In the end, I, God, punished the disbelievers; and My punishment was terrible.

35:27. Do you not see that God sends down rain from the sky, which grows fruits of varying colors? The mountains have rocks of varying shades, white, red, and dark black.

35:28. Similarly, humans, beasts, and livestock have various colors. Among God's servants, only those who fear God know God is all-mighty and all-forgiving.

35:29. Those who recite God's book, the Qur'an, establish prayer, and give charity in private and in public from what We have provided them, may expect a non-perishable profit.

35:30. God will give them their reward and enrich them from His abundance. He is forgiving and appreciative.

35:31. What We have revealed to you O Muhammad in the Qur'an is the truth confirming what was revealed in previous Scriptures. God knows and watches over His servants.

35:32. We have given the Qur'an as inheritance to Our chosen ones. Some of them wrong themselves, some are lukewarm, and some lead in good deeds, by God's leave. That is the great blessing.

35:33. They will enter the gardens of paradise. There, they will be adorned with bracelets of gold and pearls, and silk clothes.

35:34. They will say: Praise is to God, who has removed all our sorrows. Our Lord is forgiving and appreciative.

35:35. God has settled us in the everlasting home by His blessing. There, we will have no toil and fatigue.

35:36. The hellfire will be for the disbelievers. Neither the time for their death shall be fixed, nor shall punishment be lightened for them. That is how We shall repay every disbeliever.

35:37. They will cry for help: Lord, please release us; we will do good deeds, not the sins we used to do. We will ask: Did We not grant you a life long enough for you to reflect on the warnings that came to you from Our Messenger? Now taste the punishment of your deeds. There will be no helper for the evildoers.

35:38. God knows what is hidden in the heaven and on the earth. God has full knowledge of all that is in the hearts of humans.

35:39. It is God Who made you inherit the earth. Whoever disbelieves increases one's own burden. Their disbelief earns God's displeasure for them. Their disbelief increases their loss.

35:40. O Prophet, ask them: Have you seen your idol-gods to whom you pray beside God? Show me what they have created on earth? Do they have a share in the heavens? Has God given idolaters a book to prove their idol worship? No, the evildoers promise one another only deception.

35:41. It is God who keeps the heavens and the earth from falling. If they were to fall, no one could hold them except God. God is patient and forgiving.

35:42. They swore by God earnestly that if a warner had come to them, they would have been better guided than any of the previous nations. But when a warner came to them, it increased their dislike.

35:43. They behaved arrogantly in the land and plotted evil. But the evil plots only harm the plotters. Are they waiting to be treated as the ancients were treated? There will never be any change or alteration in God's treatment.

35:44. Have they not travelled through the land and seen the end of the nations who came before them, while those nations were stronger than them? There is nothing in the heaven or on the earth that frustrates God. God is all-knowing and all-powerful.

35:45. If God took humans to task for what they deserve, He would not leave a human on the earth. But He gives them relief for an appointed time, and when their time comes, they will know that God has been watching over His servants.

# CHAPTER 36

## YA SIN

**Name:** From Verse One.

**Verses:** 83

**Summary:**

- Theme: Warning to the Meccan-Quraysh about the consequences of not believing in God's oneness, hereafter, and Prophet Muhammad's Prophethood.
- Special Feature: According to Prophet Muhammad, this chapter is the heart of the Qur'an because it presents the Qur'an's message in a forceful manner. This is similar to the first chapter, Al Fatiha, the Qur'an's core, because it contains the sum and substance of the Qur'an's teachings. According to scholars, the Prophet has said: Recite this chapter to the dying one to refresh the Islamic creed in the mind of the dying person, and to bring before him a complete picture of the hereafter. So that, he may know the stages he would pass through after this worldly life. For a non-Arabic person, its translation should be read in the dying person's language so that the objective is fulfilled.
- God:
    - revealed the Qur'an to warn people, but only to those who have God's fear.
    - sent three Messengers to a city. The people denied them except one person. People killed him, but God blessed him with paradise and destroyed the disbelievers.
    - has created all things in pairs.
    - regulates the day, night, sun, and moon.
    - Who has created humans, shall give them life again for accountability on the Day of Judgment.
- God's:
    - Address to the sinners.
    - Greeting to the residents of paradise.
- The disbeliever's attitude towards spending in God's way.
- A scene from the Day of Judgment. The hands and the feet shall testify that day.

- The Qur'an warns those who are alive, and blames the disbelievers for falsehood.

**By Verse**

In the name of God, the compassionate, the merciful:

36:1. Ya Sin (are Arabic letters).
36:2. I, God, swear by the wise Qur'an,
36:3. that you Muhammad are one of the Messengers,
36:4. on a straight path.
36:5. The Qur'an has been revealed by the almighty and merciful God,
36:6. so that you Prophet Muhammad may warn a nation that is unaware because its forefathers were not warned.
36:7. Most of the disbelievers deserve Our punishment because they do not believe.
36:8. We have put metallic chains on their necks up to their chins so that they cannot bow their heads.
36:9. We have put barriers in front of them and behind them. We have covered them so that they cannot see.
36:10. It does not matter whether you warn them or not, they will not believe.
36:11. You can only warn those believers who follow the guidance and fear the merciful God unseen. Give them good news of forgiveness and a great reward.
36:12. It is We Who brings the dead to life and record clearly in a book their deeds they have sent forward and which they leave behind.
36:13. Tell them the story of a city, where we sent Our Messengers.
36:14. At first, We sent two Messengers to them, but they denied them. Then, We sent a third one to help them, and they said: God has sent us to you the people of the city.
36:15. The people said: You are humans like us. The merciful God has revealed nothing, you are lying.
36:16. They replied: Lord knows that we are His Messengers.
36:17. Our duty is to warn you clearly.
36:18. The people said: You are a bad omen. If you do not stop, we will stone you, and punish you severely.
36:19. The Messengers replied: You are your bad omen. Will you not pay attention? You are exceeding the limits.
36:20. There came a man running from the farthest part of the city, who said: My people follow the Messengers.
36:21. Follow those who do not ask any reward from you and are rightly guided.

36:22. Why should I not worship God who has created me and to whom you all will return?
36:23. Should I worship other gods than Him? If the merciful God intends harm for me, the pleading of other gods will neither benefit me, nor they can save me.
36:24. I would then certainly be in clear error.
36:25. People, I have believed in your Lord, so please listen to me.
36:26. The disbelievers killed him, but God told him: Enter paradise. He replied: I wish my people knew,
36:27. why my Lord has forgiven me and honored me.
36:28. After they killed him, We did not send down soldiers from the heaven to his people. We did not have to.
36:29. With a single blast, they were all killed.
36:30. It is bad for the people who ridiculed every Messenger who came to them.
36:31. Do they not see how many generations We have destroyed before them? After that, they never returned to their places and nothing is left of them.
36:32. All will be brought before Us.
36:33. For the disbelievers, the dead earth is a sign. We brought it to life and produced grain from it for them to eat.
36:34. We produced orchards of date-palms and vines, and watered them from gushing springs,
36:35. so that they may eat their fruit. Their disbelievers' hands have not produced any of that. Should they not be grateful?
36:36. Glory is to God who created pairs of what is grown on earth, including humans and other creatures about which humans do not know.
36:37. Another sign for them is the night. We remove the daylight from it, so they get darkness.
36:38. The sun runs on its course for the term determined by God, the mighty and all-knowing.
36:39. For the moon, We have ordered it to go through stages till it becomes again like an old dry palm branch.
36:40. The sun is not allowed to overtake the moon, nor does the night overtake the day. Each runs in its orbit.
36:41. And another sign for them is that We carried their progeny in Noah's loaded boat.
36:42. And We have made similar vessels for the disbelievers' journey.
36:43. If We please, We can drown them. No one would help or save them,

36:44. except Our mercy, and We allow them to prolong their life for a while.
36:45. When it is said to them: Have fear of the punishment in front of you and what has been for others before you so that you may receive mercy, they pay no attention.
36:46. They have turned away from their Lord's every sign.
36:47. When it is said to them: Give in charity from what God has given you, the disbelievers say to the believers: Should we feed those whom God can feed, if He wants to? Disbelievers, you are clearly in error.
36:48. They ask: When the threat of resurrection will be fulfilled, if you are truthful?
36:49. What they are waiting for will be just a blast which will seize them while they would be disputing about their worldly affairs.
36:50. They will not be able to make any will, nor return to their homes.
36:51. When the trumpet shall be blown, they shall rise from their graves and quickly run to their Lord.
36:52. They will say: Woe to us! Who has roused us from our sleep? This is what the merciful God had promised, and the Messengers told about truthfully.
36:53. With one blast, they will gather before Us.
36:54. That Day (of Judgement), no one will be wronged unjustly. You will be compensated only for what you did.
36:55. That day, those in paradise will be happy.
36:56. They and their wives shall sit in shade on couches.
36:57. There, they shall have fruit and whatever they shall desire.
36:58. God will say to them: Peace is upon you.
36:59. God will say to the sinners: Stay away.
36:60. O Adam's children, did I not tell you not to serve Satan, who was your sworn enemy?
36:61. But to worship Me alone? That is the straight path.
36:62. Despite that Satan led many of you off the right path. Did you have no sense?
36:63. This is the hell about which you were repeatedly warned.
36:64. Burn there today because you disbelieved.
36:65. That day, We God will seal the disbelievers mouths. Their hands will speak to Us, and their feet will testify about what they did.
36:66. Had We willed, We could have taken out their eyesight and they would have floundered to find the path. How could they see the path?
36:67. Had We willed, We could have fixed them in place to be unable

to go forward or turn back.

36:68. We cause to regress the growth of those whom We grant long life. Why cannot they understand?

36:69. We have neither taught Prophet Muhammad poetry, nor is it suitable for him. This is a warning, a clear message of the Qur'an,

36:70. to warn the living and to establish proof against the disbelievers.

36:71. Do they not see that We Ourselves have created livestock for them to own?

36:72. We have subjected the livestock for them to ride and to eat their flesh.

36:73. They drink their milk and use them for other benefits. Will they not then be grateful?

36:74. They worship other gods beside God, hoping they would help them.

36:75. The other gods cannot help their worshippers; though their worshipers be ready like soldiers to defend them.

36:76. O Muhammad, what they say should not bother you. We know what they hide and what they show.

36:77. Does man not consider that We created him from a mere sperm-drop, yet he has become a clear adversary?

36:78. He presents an example to Us and forgets his own creation. He says: Who will give life to rotten bones?

36:79. O Muhammad, tell them: He will give them life that produced them the first time. He has knowledge of every creature.

36:80. It is God who gives you fire from the green tree so that you could ignite your fuel.

36:81. Has God, who created the heavens and the earth, no power to create more like them? Yes, He has. He is the all-knowing creator.

36:82. When He intends something to happen, He commands it to be, and it happens.

36:83. Glory is to God who controls everything. We all will be brought back to Him.

# CHAPTER 37

# THE RANKS

**Name:** From Verse One.

**Verses:** 182

**Summary:**

- Theme: Warning to the Meccan-Disbelievers for their attitude of mockery toward Prophet Muhammad's message of God's oneness, the hereafter, and his claim to Prophethood. They have been warned plainly that the Prophet would overwhelm them in spite of their power.
- Impressive arguments about God's oneness and the hereafter. Precedents from history have been cited to show how God has been favoring God's faithful servants and punishing the disbelievers. The most instructive of the historical narratives is the event in which Prophet Abraham became ready to sacrifice his only son when he received an inspiration from God.
- God:
    - testifies that your God is one God and devils do not have access to the angel's exalted assembly.
    - bestowed His favors on Prophets Moses and Aaron.
    - has promised to help His Prophets and devotees.
- The reality of life in the hereafter and the Day of Judgment.
- A scene from the:
    - Day of Judgment and a treat for the wrongdoers.
    - Paradise. A conversation of a resident of paradise with the one in hell.
    - Hell.
- A dialogue between the followers and the leaders who misled them.
- Prophet Noah prayed and God responded to his prayers.
- The story of God's friend, Prophet Abraham.
- Prophets Elias and Lot were God's Messengers.
- Prophet Jonah's story. A fish swallowed him, but God rescued him.
- The disbelievers' claim of angels being God's daughters and jinns having blood relations with God are utterly false.

## By Verse

In the name of God, the compassionate, the merciful:

37:1. I, God, swear by the angels, who line up in ranks,
37:2. drive away the wicked vigorously,
37:3. and recite Our message
37:4. that your God is one.
37:5. He is the Lord of the heavens and the earth, what is between them, and of the variable locations where the sun rises in the east.
37:6. We have beautified the nearest heaven with stars,
37:7. who guard against rebellious devils.
37:8. They cannot listen to the assembly of the angels and are pelted from every side,
37:9. then repelled, and are punished forever.
37:10. The eavesdroppers are pursued by the flaming stars.
37:11. O Muhammad, ask the disbelievers: Was it more difficult to create the disbelievers than Our other creatures? We created the disbelievers from the sticky clay.
37:12. You marvel at God's powers, while they mock.
37:13. When they are warned, they pay no attention.
37:14. When they are shown a sign, they ridicule it,
37:15. and say: Obviously, this is magic.
37:16. When we have died and become dust and bones, shall we be raised to life;
37:17. and our forefathers as well?
37:18. O Muhammad, say: Yes. And you shall be humiliated.
37:19. With only one shout, they will come to life at once.
37:20. They will say: Woe to us! This is the Day of Judgment.
37:21. They will be told: This is the Day you used to deny.
37:22. The angels will be told to gather the wrongdoers, their wives, and the idols they worshipped
37:23. other than God, and lead them to the path of hell,
37:24. but stop them for questioning.
37:25. They will be asked: What is the matter with you that you do not help each other?
37:26. But that Day, they shall surrender.
37:27. They will turn to one another and question one another.
37:28. They will say to their leaders: You used to tell us with confidence.
37:29. They will reply: No, you yourselves had no faith.
37:30. We had no authority over you. You were rebellious.
37:31. Our Lord has justly sentenced us and we will taste the punishment.

37:32. We misled you, because we ourselves were off the right path.
37:33. That Day (of Judgement), they all will share the punishment.
37:34. That is how We shall deal with the guilty.
37:35. When they were told that there was no god except God, they scornfully used to say:
37:36. Are we to leave our gods for a mad poet Prophet Muhammad?
37:37. He has come with the truth and confirmed the previous Messengers.
37:38. You shall be severely punished.
37:39. You shall be paid for your deeds.
37:40. But the true servants of God
37:41. will be given predetermined provisions,
37:42. fruits, and honored
37:43. in the gardens of paradise.
37:44. They will sit on couches facing one another.
37:45. They will be served, from a flowing spring, cups of wine,
37:46. sparkling, delicious to drink.
37:47. It will have no bad effect on them, nor will it intoxicate them.
37:48. They will sit with bashful women, with beautiful eyes,
37:49. and delicate like protected ostrich eggs.
37:50. They will turn to one another and talk.
37:51. One of them will say: I had a friend,
37:52. who would ask: Are you a believer;
37:53. when we have died and become dust and bones, will we indeed be judged?
37:54. Would you like to know where my friend is?
37:55. On looking down, he will see his friend in the midst of hell.
37:56. He will say to his friend: By God, you almost ruined me.
37:57. Had it not been for my Lord's favor, I would have been in hell.
37:58. The favored one will say: Well, we shall not die again;
37:59. we have already died once; and we will not be punished.
37:60. Indeed, this is the great achievement!
37:61. Everyone should work for it.
37:62. Is this not a better welcome in paradise than the tree of Zaqqum* in hell?

**Bitter in taste, bad in smell, and its milky fluid wounds if it touches the human body.*

37:63. We have made this tree a punishment for the wrongdoers.
37:64. This tree grows in the hell's lowest part.
37:65. Its shoots are like devils' heads.
37:66. The wrongdoers will eat it and fill their bellies with it.

37:67. They will drink boiling water.
37:68. Then, they shall return to the hellfire.
37:69. They found their forefathers off the right path.
37:70. They eagerly followed in their footsteps.
37:71. Most of the ancients before them went off the right path,
37:72. though We sent Messengers to warn them.
37:73. Look at the end of those who were warned,
37:74. except God's true servants.
37:75. Noah prayed to Us, and We, God, graciously answered his prayer.
37:76. We saved him and his followers from the great calamity.
37:77. We made his descendants the survivors.
37:78. We blessed him with praise of the later generations.
37:79. Peace be upon Noah among all people.
37:80. Thus We reward those who do right.
37:81. He was one of our believing servants.
37:82. We drowned the disbelievers.
37:83. Abraham followed Noah's way.
37:84. He came to his Lord with pure heart.
37:85. He asked his father and people: What are these that you worship?
37:86. Would you worship false gods other than God?
37:87. What do you think about the Lord of the universe?
37:88. He looked at the stars,
37:89. and said: I feel sick.
37:90. The people left him and departed.
37:91. Then he turned to their idol-gods and asked: Why do not you eat your offerings?
37:92. Why do not you speak?
37:93. Then he destroyed them with his right hand.
37:94. The people came running to Abraham.
37:95. He said: Why do you worship that you have carved yourself,
37:96. while God created you and those you have carved?
37:97. They said: Build a furnace and throw him into the blazing fire.
37:98. They plotted against Abraham, but We foiled their plan.
37:99. Abraham said: I will follow my Lord. He will guide me.
37:100. Lord, give me a righteous son.
37:101. We gave him good news of a patient son.
37:102. When the son reached the working age, Abraham said to him: I have dreamed that I was slaughtering you for sacrifice. Please tell me what you think? The son replied: Father, do as you have been commanded. God willing, you will find me steadfast.
37:103. When they both submitted to God's will and Abraham laid his son

face down for slaughtering;
37:104. We, God, called out to Abraham saying:
37:105. You have fulfilled your vision. That is how We reward those who do good.
37:106. Indeed, that was clearly a test.
37:107. We ransomed his son with a great sacrifice*.

**An angel brought a ram for Abraham to slaughter for sacrifice. God made it a yearly custom that on the day of Hajj, the pilgrims sacrifice animals.*

37:108. We blessed Abraham for praise of the later generations:
37:109. Peace be upon Abraham.
37:110. Thus, We reward those who do good.
37:111. Abraham was one of our believing servants.
37:112. We gave Abraham good news of giving him his son, Isaac, a righteous prophet.
37:113. We blessed Abraham and Isaac. Among their descendants, some did good and others sinned.
37:114. We favored Prophets Moses and Aaron.
37:115. We delivered them and their people from their great calamity of Pharaoh's tyranny.
37:116. We helped them to be victorious.
37:117. We gave them the Scriptures that made things clear.
37:118. We guided them to the right path.
37:119. We, God, blessed them with kind remembrance by the later generations:
37:120. Peace be upon Prophets Moses and Aaron.
37:121. Thus We reward who do good.
37:122. Indeed, they were Our believing servants.
37:123. Elias was one of the Messengers.
37:124. He asked his people: Do you not fear God?
37:125. Why do you worship Baal, your idol-god, and not the best creator,
37:126 God, who is your and your forefathers' Lord?
37:127. But they denied Elias, so they will certainly be punished,
37:128. except God's true servants.
37:129. We blessed him with praise from the later generations:
37:130. Peace be upon Elias.
37:131. That is how We reward those who do good.
37:132. He was one of Our believing servant.
37:133. Lot was a Messenger too.
37:134. We saved him and his followers,
37:135. except an old woman, his wife, who stayed behind.
37:136. We destroyed the others including his wife.

37:137. You pass by their ruins morning,
37:138. and evening. Why do not you pay attention?
37:139. Jonah too was Our Messenger.
37:140. Remember, he ran to a loaded ship.
37:141. He cast lots with the crew and lost.

**There were more people on the ship than it could carry. So lots were cast and Prophet Jonah was thrown into the sea.*

37:142. A fish swallowed him while he was reproaching himself for leaving his people without God's approval.
37:143. Had he not prayed to God,
37:144. he would have remained in fish's belly till the Day of Resurrection.
37:145. We cast him on a barren shore while he was ill.
37:146. We caused a ground vine grow near him for shade.
37:147. We sent him to a nation of 100,000 or more people of Nineveh* who had repented.

**the ancient capital of Assyria, on the River Tigris opposite the present-day city of Mosul (north Iraq)*

37:148. The people believed in Jonah, so We let them live in peace for a while.
37:149. O Muhammad, ask the disbelievers: Do they think that God has daughters while they have sons?
37:150. Or, did they see God creating the angels as females?
37:151. Unquestionably, they falsify when they say:
37:152. God has fathered children. They are liars.
37:153. Would He choose daughters over sons?
37:154. What is wrong with you? How can you be that stupid?
37:155. Will you not pay attention?
37:156. Do you have proof?
37:157. Show us your proof, if what you say is true.
37:158. The disbelievers claim that there is a relationship between God and the jinns. But certainly the jinns know that they shall be brought before God on account of their deeds.
37:159. Praise be to God. God is free from what they attribute to God,
37:160. except God's chosen servants, who do not attribute falsehoods to God.
37:161. You and your idol-gods,
37:162. cannot lead anyone away from God,
37:163. except who is destined for the hellfire.
37:164. The angels say: Everyone among us knows our appointed position,

37:165. we line up for prayer,
37:166. and glorify God.
37:167. The disbelievers say:
37:168. Had we received the message which was given to the former people,
37:169. we would have become God's true servants.
37:170. But they have disbelieved in it, so they shall soon know the truth.
37:171. We had promised with Our Messengers
37:172. that they would be helped,
37:173. and Our forces would be victorious.
37:174. Therefore, O Muhammad, pay no attention to the disbelievers for a while.
37:175. Watch, they shall soon see your triumph and their punishment.
37:176. Do they wish to hurry our punishment?
37:177. When the punishment will come in their courtyards, it will be a bad day for them who were warned about it beforehand.
37:178. Leave them for a while,
37:179. and watch, they shall soon see your triumph and their punishment.
37:180. Glorified is your Lord, who is the Lord of honor and is above what they attribute to Him.
37:181. And peace be upon the Messengers.
37:182. Praise is only for God, the Lord of the universe.

# CHAPTER 38

## SUAD

**Name:** From Verse One.

**Verses:** 88

**Summary:**

- Review of the meeting between Prophet Muhammad and the Meccan-chiefs. God says that the reason for their denial is not any defect in Islam's message but their own arrogance, jealousy, and insistence on following their ancestors' faith. They are not prepared to follow one of their own as God's Prophet. God warns the disbelievers that the Prophet will overpower them.
- Description of nine prophets, but with greater details of Prophets David and Solomon. God's law of justice is impartial and objective, and only the right attitude is acceptable to Him.
- Two clarifications about the hereafter. The disbelievers' leaders will have reached the hell before their followers and the two groups will be cursing each other. The disbelievers will be amazed to see that there is no trace in hell of the believers they used to regard wicked.
- Contains the story of Prophet Adam and Satan. It tells the Meccan-Disbelievers that the same arrogance and vanity, which were preventing them from following Prophet Muhammad, had prevented Satan from bowing before Prophet Adam, whom God created. Therefore, their fate will be that of Satan to live in the hellfire forever.

### By Verse

In the name of God, the compassionate, the merciful:

38:1. Suad (is an Arabic letter). I swear by the renowned Qur'an,

38:2. that those who disbelieve are doing so because of their pride and stubbornness.

38:3. Before them, We have destroyed many generations like them. They cried out for mercy, but it was too late for escape.

38:4. The disbelievers wonder that a warner has come to them from among themselves. They say: He is a magician and a liar.

38:5. Has he made all gods to be one God? That is surely strange.

38:6. The disbelievers' leaders left saying: Leave and stay firm in worshiping your gods. What he, Prophet Muhammad, is saying is

designed against you.
38:7. We have never heard about it from the earlier people. This is nothing but a forgery.
38:8. Why, among us all, he alone has been given this message? So, they are in doubt about My message, because they have not yet tasted My punishment.
38:9. Do they possess the treasures of the mercy of your Lord, the mighty and the giver?
38:10. Or do they have the kingdom of the heavens and earth and what is between them? Then, let them climb to the heaven by any means.
38:11. Their faction, like the disbelievers before them, will be defeated.
38:12. Before them, the people of Prophets Noah, Aad, and Pharaoh, who punished his victims with stakes,
38:13. Thamoud's tribe, Lot's people, and those who lived in the forest (Midians*), were the disbelievers' factions.

**they lived in the northwest Arabian Peninsula, on the east shore of the Gulf of Aqaba on the Red Sea*

38:14. They all denied the Messengers, so My punishment was justified.
38:15. These disbelievers are waiting for just one blast; because there will be no delay in it.
38:16. They are saying: Lord, hasten our punishment before the Day of Accounting comes.
38:17. O Muhammad, be patient with what the disbelievers say and remember Our servant, David, who was strong and turned to God in all matters.
38:18. We, God, made the mountains join him in praising God in the morning and evening.
38:19. The birds assembled and joined in singing with him.
38:20. We strengthened his kingdom, and gave him wisdom and sound judgment in speaking and decision making.
38:21. Have you heard the story of two disputants, who climbed over the wall and entered David's chamber?
38:22. When they reached David, he was alarmed. They said: Do not be afraid, we are two disputants; one of us has wronged the other. Judge between us with truth and do not be unjust, and guide us to the right path.
38:23. Prophet David, my brother has 99 sheep, and I have one. He has asked me to give it to him, and he has overpowered me in the dispute.
38:24. David replied: He has certainly wronged you in asking for your sheep to add to his. Many partners are unjust to one another except

those who have faith and do good deeds, but they are few indeed. David realized that God had tested him. He asked forgiveness of his Lord and bowed down in repentance.

38:25. We forgave David for that. In the life to come, nearness unto Us shall be his, a beautiful resort.

38:26. We said: David, We have made you a ruler on the earth. Judge between the people justly and do not follow your desire*, as it will lead you off the right path from God's way. Those who go off the right path from God's way will be severely punished for forgetting the Day of Accounting.

**Prophet David was interested in someone else's wife.*

38:27. We did not create the heavens and the earth and what is between them for nothing. That is what the disbelievers think. Woe to the disbelievers from the hellfire.

38:28. Are We to treat the believers who do good works like those who corrupt the land with wickedness? Are We to treat those who fear God like those who are wicked?

38:29. O Muhammad, We have revealed the blessed book the Qur'an to you, so that they might reflect upon its verses and those of understanding learn from it.

38:30. We gave David a son, Solomon, who was a good servant and often repented to Us.

38:31. One evening, his trained racehorses were presented to him.

38:32. He said: I love the good things of life including the horses because of my Lord's glory. When the sun went down,

38:33. he asked that the horses be brought back to him. Then, he passed his hand over their legs and necks.

38:34. We tested Solomon by placing a dead-body on his throne*, but Solomon repented to Us.

**Solomon saw in a vision that a dead-body was placed on his throne. It meant that his kingdom will be inherited by his son who was incapable to rule his vast and powerful empire.*

38:35. He said: Lord, please forgive me and give me such a kingdom which You will not give to anyone after me. You are the great bestower.

38:36. We put the wind under his command. It blew softly to wherever he directed it.

38:37. We also put under his command the devils, all kinds of builders, divers,

38:38. and others bound in chains.

38:39. We said to Solomon, this is Our gift. There will be no accounting whether you give it to someone or withhold it from someone.
38:40. In the life to come, We will honor him and place him in paradise.
38:41. And tell about Our servant Job. He called to his Lord saying: Satan has harmed me with pain and suffering.
38:42. God told him: Strike the ground with your foot; there will be a spring of water to wash and drink.
38:43. We gave him his family and as many more people as a mercy from Us and a reminder to those who understand.
38:44. We said: Take a twigs-bunch and strike with it your wife to comply with your oath (to beat her for being impatient/critiquing God), and do not incline towards falsehood by making compromise with idol-worshippers. We found him patient and an excellent servant. He repeatedly turned to God.
38:45. And tell about Our servants Prophets Abraham, Isaac and Jacob. They all had strength and vision.
38:46. We chose them for their exclusive quality of remembering the hereafter.
38:47. They surely are among our chosen noblemen.
38:48. Tell the disbelievers about Ishmael, Elisha and Dhul-Kifl. They were among the virtuous.
38:49. This is a reminder. The righteous will return to a blessed place,
38:50. the gardens of Eden/paradise. Their gates will be opened for them.
38:51. They shall recline on couches and feast on abundant fruit and drinks.
38:52. Their companions will be bashful virgins of their age.
38:53. We have promised to give you all this on the Day of Reckoning.
38:54. Our promise to provide you all this will not fail.
38:55. This is for the righteous, but the transgressors will return to an evil end.
38:56. They shall burn in hell, a wretched place to be in.
38:57. This is for the transgressors. They will taste boiling water, dirty blood, and pus.
38:58. They will have similar other punishments.
38:59. The leaders of the faithless seeing their followers coming towards hell will say to one another: This is a group rushing to be with us. There is no welcome for them. They will burn in fire.
38:60. The followers will say to their leaders: No welcome for you either. It is you who brought this upon us. This is an evil place to live.
38:61. Then they will say: Lord, give double punishment to those who brought this upon us.

38:62. And they will also say: Why do not we see those whom we considered to be wicked?
38:63. We ridiculed them. Have our eyes missed them?
38:64. Indeed, that is the truth that those living in hell will dispute.
38:65. O Muhammad, say to them: I am only a warner. There is no one worthy of worship except God, the one, and the almighty.
38:66. He is the Lord of the heavens and the earth and what is between them. He is almighty and oft-forgiving.
38:67. Say: It is an important message,
38:68. but you are not paying attention to it.
38:69. Tell them: You had no knowledge of the discussion of the exalted assembly*.

**The discussion among angels when God told them that He was to create His vicegerent on earth.*

38:70. It has been revealed to me to warn you clearly.
38:71. Your Lord said to the angels: I am going to create a human from clay.
38:72. When I have made him and breathed My spirit into him, you should kneel down and prostrate to him.
38:73. All angels prostrated,
38:74. except Satan. He was proud and a disbeliever.
38:75. God asked Satan: What has prevented you from prostrating to whom I have created with My hands? Are you too proud or consider yourself among the higher rank?
38:76. He replied: I am better than him. You created him from clay and me from fire.
38:77. God said: Then get out from here; you are an outcast.
38:78. I have cursed you till the Day of Judgment.
38:79. He replied: Lord, give me reprieve till the Day of Resurrection.
38:80. God said: You request is approved,
38:81. till the appointed day.
38:82. He said: I swear by Your honor that I will mislead them all,
38:83. except Your faithful servants.
38:84. God said: You should know the truth and I only speak the truth that
38:85. I will fill hell with you and your followers.
38:86. O Muhammad, tell them: I do not ask any reward from you for it; nor I am a pretender.
38:87. It is but a warning to mankind.
38:88. Before long, you shall know its truth.

# CHAPTER 39

# THE CROWDS

**Name:** From Verses 71 and 73.

**Verses:** 75

**Summary:**

- The disbelievers justify their worship of saints by saying that it may bring them close to God.
- The real losers are those who shall lose their souls and families on the Day of Judgment. That day, no one will bear another's burden. The book of deeds will be laid open and justice will be done with all fairness. After judgment, the disbelievers will be driven to hell and the righteous will be led to paradise.
- The believers who cannot practice their faith should migrate to other places where they can do so.
- No one can rescue the one against whom God's punishment has been decreed.
- The Qur'an is consistent in its revelations and it repeats its teachings in different ways. God has cited every kind of example in the Qur'an so that people may learn a lesson.
- Who can be wicked more than the one who invents a lie against God? If God intends to harm you, no one can save you and if He intends to bless you, no one can withhold it.
- It is God who recalls people's souls upon their death and of the living during their sleep.
- If the wrongdoers possess all the treasures of the earth and much more, they will gladly offer it as a ransom to redeem them on the Day of Judgment.
- Those who have sinned against their souls should not despair of God's mercy. They should repent while they can.
- Worship God and be among His thankful servants.

**By Verse**

In the name of God, the compassionate, the merciful:

39:1. God, the mighty and the wise, has revealed this book the Qur'an.
39:2. We have revealed the book to you Prophet Muhammad in truth. Therefore, serve God and worship Him alone.
39:3. True worship and obedience is for God alone. As for those who

take guardians beside God saying: We only serve them that they may bring us nearer to God, God will judge their differences. He does not guide the liar and the disbeliever.

39:4. Had God wanted to take a son, He could have chosen whom He pleased from those He created. But He is above such things. He is God, the one, the almighty.

39:5. God created the heavens and the earth in accordance with the requirements of wisdom. He made day and night to follow one another. He has subjected the sun and the moon to follow their course for a specified term. He is almighty and oft-forgiving.

39:6. He created you all from a single being (Prophet Adam), and from that He created his mate (Eve). He produced four pairs of livestock (camels, cows, sheep and goats) for you. He creates you in your mothers' wombs by stages in threefold darkness*. That is God, your Lord. To Him belongs the kingdom. There is no god except Him. How then can you turn away from Him?

**of abdomen, uterus, and the sack/membrane around the baby.*

39:7. If you are thankless to God, He does not need you. He is not pleased with His servants' thanklessness. If you are thankful He is pleased. No person will carry another's burden. You all will return to your Lord; and He will tell you what you used to do. He knows what is in your hearts.

39:8. When an adversity befalls a human, he cries to his Lord and repents. But, when God favors him, he forgets what he cried for; he worships other gods beside God to mislead others from God's path. Say: Enjoy your disbelief for a while; you shall be companions of the hellfire.

39:9. Is one who worships during the night by prostrating or standing, pays attention to the hereafter, and hopes for his Lord's mercy, to be compared to a disbeliever? Ask them: Are the wise and the ignorant equal? Only those with understanding will pay attention.

39:10. O Muhammad, say to My faithful servants: Fear your Lord. There will be good reward for those who do good deeds in this world. God's earth is spacious. Those who are patient will receive their reward without measure.

39:11. Say: I have been commanded to serve God with sincere devotion;

39:12. and I have been commanded to be the first to submit to God in Islam.

39:13. Say: Should I disobey my Lord, I am afraid of the punishment of a fateful day.

39:14. Say: I serve and worship God alone with sincere devotion.

39:15. As for you, you may worship whom you like beside God. Say: They will lose much who will lose their souls and families on the Day of Resurrection. Unquestionably, that will be a great loss.

39:16. Layers of fire shall cover them from above and below. That is how God warns his servants. Therefore, My servants fear Me, God.

39:17. There is good news for those who avoid worshipping false gods and repent to God. Give good news to My slaves,

39:18. who hear advice and follow the best of it. They are those whom God guides. They are wise.

39:19. Can you O Muhammad save those who have earned Our punishment and are destined to burn in hell?

39:20. But, for those who have feared their Lord, lofty mansions with flowing streams have been built for their living. That is God's promise. God will not fail in His promise.

39:21. Do you not see that God sends down rain from the sky and makes it flow as springs and streams on earth. Thereby, He produces crops of varying types. They dry, you see them turn yellow, and He crumbles them into chaff. Surely, in that is a reminder for those who understand.

39:22. Is the one whose heart God has opened to Islam and is following the path of enlightenment equal to the one who is a hard-hearted disbeliever? Woe to those whose hearts are hardened against remembering God. They are in clear error.

39:23. God has revealed the best book the Qur'an, consistent in style, repeating its teaching on various aspects. Those who fear their Lord tremble when they listen to its revelations and their hearts soften at God's remembrance. Such is God's guidance. He guides whom He pleases, but no one can guide whom God leaves to go off the right path.

39:24. Can the person who will face the worst of the punishment on the Day of Resurrection be compared to a believer? The wrongdoers shall be told to taste the punishment for what they have earned.

39:25. Others before them also denied their Messengers, therefore Our punishment came upon them unexpected.

39:26. God disgraced them in the worldly life, but punishment of the hereafter will be greater, if they only knew.

39:27. We have given mankind all kinds of arguments in the Qur'an so that they might pay attention.

39:28. We have revealed the Qur'an in Arabic, free from fault, so that they might become righteous.

39:29. God compares two slaves, one owned by quarreling partners and another exclusively by one person. Are they equal? God forbid. Praise is to God. But most of them do not know.
39:30. You O Muhammad and they shall die.
39:31. Then, on the Day of Judgment, you all shall settle your disputes in presence of your Lord.
39:32. Who is more unjust than one who lies about God and denies the truth when it has come to him? Is there not a home in hell for the disbelievers?
39:33. The one who has brought the truth and those who believed in it are the righteous.
39:34. Their Lord will give them whatever they will desire. That will be the reward of those who do good deeds.
39:35. God will do away with their worst deeds they did prior to becoming believers and reward them for their best deeds.
39:36. Is God not enough for his servant Muhammad? Yet, they try to frighten you with their idol-gods. No one can guide those whom God leaves to go off the right path.
39:37. No one can mislead whom God guides. Is God not almighty and capable of retribution?
39:38. If you were to ask them: Who created the heavens and the earth? They would most certainly say: God. Say: Have you then considered that if God was to punish me, your idol-gods could save me from it, or if God was to show me mercy, they could withhold that? Say: God is sufficient for me. Let the faithful put their trust in Him.
39:39. O Muhammad, say: My people, do as you like and so will I. Before long, you are going to know that
39:40. who will get a shameful and everlasting punishment.
39:41. O Muhammad, We have revealed the book the Qur'an to you in truth, for instructing mankind. The person who receives guidance benefits himself; and the one who goes off the right path hurts oneself. You are not responsible for their affairs.
39:42. God takes the souls at the time of death, but for the living He takes during their sleep. He withholds those souls for which He has decreed death, and sends back the others for a specific time. Surely, there are signs in it for those who think.
39:43. Have they chosen others beside God to intercede for them? Say: Even though they have neither power nor intelligence?
39:44. The power to intercede entirely belongs to God. He is the king of the heavens and the earth. You will all return to Him.

39:45. When God alone is mentioned, hearts of the disbelievers, who do not believe in the hereafter, are filled with hate, and when their idol-gods are mentioned, they rejoice.
39:46. O Muhammad, say: God, creator of the heavens and the earth and knower of the visible and invisible, You alone will judge the disputes of your servants.
39:47. Even if the wrongdoers had all the treasures of the earth and much more, they would offer these to exchange for avoiding the punishment on the Day of Judgment. But, God will show them what they never thought of.
39:48. Their evil deeds will confront them and what they used to mock at will encircle them.
39:49. When adversity befalls a person, he calls upon Us, God; then, when We favor him by taking it away, he says: I have been favored because of my knowledge. No, it is but a test, but most humans do not know.
39:50. Those before them said the same, but they got nothing from what they did,
39:51. and the evil consequences of their deeds overtook them. The wrongdoers among the Meccans will also be penalized for their sins; and they will not escape Our punishment.
39:52. Do they not know that God increases the livelihood for whom He wills and reduces it for whom He pleases? Indeed, there are signs in that for the believers.
39:53. O Muhammad, say to My servants who have sinned against themselves: Do not despair of God's mercy, because He forgives all sins of believers. He is the forgiving, the merciful.
39:54. Repent to your Lord and submit to Him before His punishment comes upon you; then you will not be helped.
39:55. Follow the best teaching that has been revealed to you from your Lord before the punishment comes upon you suddenly while you do not expect it,
39:56. lest a human should say: Alas! I neglected my duty to God and mocked his revelations;
39:57. or should say: If God had guided me, I would have been pious;
39:58. or should say upon seeing the punishment: Oh, had I a second chance, I would be among the righteous.
39:59. But, God will say to him: My revelations came to you, but you denied them. You were arrogant and a disbeliever.
39:60. On the Day of Resurrection, you will see those who lied about God with their faces darkened. Is there not in hell an abode for the

arrogant?
39:61. God will save those who feared Him, and will confer success upon them; no harm will touch them, nor they will grieve.
39:62. God is creator and guardian of all things.
39:63. God has the treasures of the heavens and the earth. Those who disbelieve in His revelations are the losers.
39:64. O Muhammad, say: O ignorant ones, is it someone other than God that you ask me to worship?
39:65. It has already been told to you and to those before you that if you would worship someone other than God, your deeds would become worthless, and you would be losers.
39:66. Therefore, worship God alone and be grateful to Him.
39:67. They have not made a just estimate of God's power. On the Day of Judgment, the whole earth will be in His grasp, and the heavens will be rolled up in His right hand. Glory is to Him; He is above the partners they associate with Him.
39:68. The trumpet will be blown and all in the heavens and on earth will fall dead except whom God will spare. Then, it will be blown again, and all will stand awaiting judgment.
39:69. The earth will shine with its Lord's light. The record of deeds will be opened. The Prophets and the witnesses will be brought in and all shall be judged justly, and none shall be wronged.
39:70. Each person will be paid for what the person did, because God knows about all their deeds.
39:71. The disbelievers will be driven to hell in crowds. When they will reach it, its gates will be opened and the keepers will say: Did your own Messengers not come to you who recited your Lord's revelations and warned you about this Day (of Judgement)? They will reply: Yes. Thus, the promise of punishment to the disbelievers will be fulfilled.
39:72. They will be told to enter the gates of hell to live there forever. Wretched is the residence of the arrogant.
39:73. Those who feared their Lord will be taken to paradise in crowds. When they will reach it, its gates will be opened and its keepers will say: Peace is upon you; you have been good. Please enter paradise and live in it forever.
39:74. They will say: Praise is to God, who has fulfilled the promise He made to us, and gave us this land to inherit, so that we may live in paradise wherever we like. Excellent is the reward of the righteous.
39:75. You will see the angels surrounding God's throne, praising their

Lord. Mankind will be judged justly, and all will say: Praise is to God, the lord of the universe.

# CHAPTER 40

## THE BELIEVER

**Name:** From Verse 28

**Verses:** 85

**Background:**

The chapter was revealed when the Meccan-Disbelievers were engaged in creating suspicions about the Qur'anic teachings and were preparing to kill Prophet Muhammad. God warns the disbelievers that they will not succeed as Pharaoh did not succeed against Prophet Moses.

**Summary:**

- God's characteristics.
- God:
    - saved the believers from Pharaoh's plots and destroyed his people.
    - helps His Messengers and the believers in this life and will help them in the hereafter.
    - says: Call Me; I will answer your prayers.
    - sent many Messengers before Muhammad; some are mentioned in the Qur'an and some are not.
- No one disputes God's revelations except the disbelievers. The angels pray to God for those who repent and follow the right way.
- A preview of the Day of Judgment and the hell.
- Those who denied God's Prophets and His revelations were all destroyed.
- One of Pharaoh's relatives, who was a believer, speaks in favor of Prophet Moses.
- No one has the right to be worshipped except God, the creator and the lord of the universe.
- Those who argue about God's revelations will soon find out the truth.
- Livestock are God's signs for the people of understanding.
- Belief after seeing God's punishment will be of no avail to the disbelievers.

## By Verse

In the name of God, the compassionate, the merciful:

40:1. Ha-Meem (are Arabic letters).

40:2. God, the mighty and the all-knowing, has revealed this book (the Qur'an).

40:3. God forgives sin and accepts repentance. He is severe in punishment and is Lord of abundance. There is no God except Him. All shall return to Him.

40:4. No one, except the disbelievers, dispute God's revelations. Do not be deceived by their prosperity in the land.

40:5. Before these disbelievers, the people of Noah and the generations after them denied God's revelations. Every nation plotted to kill its Messenger, and use falsehood to invalidate the truth. So God seized them, and God's punishment was terrible.

40:6. Thus, your Lord's decision will be fulfilled for the disbelievers. They are companions of the hellfire.

40:7. The angels who carry God's throne and those around it praise their Lord, believe in Him, and ask forgiveness for the believers saying: Lord, Your mercy and knowledge reach all things. Forgive those who have repented and have followed Your way. Protect them from punishment of the hellfire.

40:8. Lord, admit them to paradise to live there forever as You have promised them, together with the righteous among their fathers, spouses and offspring. You are the almighty and the wise.

40:9. Protect them from all evil. Those You will protect from evil that day will have earned Your mercy. That will be the great achievement.

40:10. Those who disbelieved will be told: When you were invited to faith but you refused, God's hatred for you was greater than your hatred of yourself today.

40:11. They will say: Lord, You made us die twice and gave us life twice*. We have confessed our sins. Is there a way to get out of the hell?

**The first death is when a human is lifeless dust or a sperm-drop. The second death is when a human dies. The first life is when the sperm-drop develops into the birth of a child. The second life will be when God will make the humans rise from their graves on the Day of Judgment.*

40:12. The disbelievers will be told: You are in this situation because when you were called upon to serve God alone, you disbelieved; but if others were associated with God, you believed. So now it is

God's decision, who is the most high and the majestic.
40:13. It is God who shows you His signs and sends down your livelihood from the sky (rain to grow crops). But no one pays attention except who repents.
40:14. So worship God alone with sincere devotion to Him, even though the disbelievers dislike it.
40:15. God has the highest rank and the throne. He selects for Prophethood anyone He likes from His servants to warn mankind about the day for meeting Him.
40:16. That Day (of Resurrection), when all humans will come out from their graves, nothing will be hidden from God. They will be asked: Who is the king this day? It is God, the one, the almighty.
40:17. That Day (of Judgement), every person shall be rewarded for what the person has earned. No injustice shall be done. God is quick in taking account.
40:18. O Muhammad, warn them of the day that is drawing near, when the hearts will come right up to the throats to choke them; the wrongdoers will have no friend and no pleader who will be heard.
40:19. God knows the stealthy looks and the secret thoughts.
40:20. God will judge justly, but the idols whom they associate with Him cannot judge anything at all. God hears all and sees everything.
40:21. Have the disbelievers not travelled in the land to see the end of those who disbelieved before them? They were mightier than them and have left bigger signs of their splendor on earth. God punished them for their sins, and they had no protector from God.
40:22. That was because their Messengers came to them with clear proofs, but they disbelieved. So God punished them. God is powerful and severe in punishment.
40:23. We sent Moses with Our signs and a clear authority
40:24. to Pharaoh, Haman and Korah*. But they said: Moses is a magician and a liar.

**Pharaoh was king, Haman was a minister and advisor, and Korah was the richest man.*

40:25. When Moses brought them God's truth, they said: Kill the sons of those who have believed in him and spare their daughters. But the plan of the disbelievers was useless.
40:26. Pharaoh said: Let me kill Moses and let him call his Lord. I am afraid that he will change your religion or cause mischief in the land.
40:27. Moses said: I take refuge with your and my Lord from every proud person who denies the Day of Reckoning.

40:28. One of Pharaoh's relatives, who was a believer in secret, said: Would you kill a person just for saying that his Lord is God? He has brought you clear proofs from your Lord. If he is lying, let it be on his head; but if he is speaking the truth, some of his threats will strike you. God does not guide a lying sinner.

40:29. O my people, yours is the kingdom today, and you are dominant in the land. But who would protect us from God's punishment if it were to come to us? Pharaoh said: I have told you what I think. I guide you to the right path.

40:30. The person who was a believer said: My people, indeed I fear for you a fate like that of the earlier disbelievers,

40:31. for example, the people of Noah, Aad, and Thamoud, and those after them. God does not want to do any injustice to His servants.

40:32. My people, I fear for you the day when you will call one another for help,

40:33. turn your backs and flee. There will be none to protect you from God. Whom God leaves off the right path, there is none to guide him.

40:34. Earlier Joseph came to you with clear proofs, but you doubted him. When he died, you said: God will never send another Messenger after him. Thus, God misleads the doubting sinner.

40:35. Those who dispute God's revelations without proof are hated by God and the believers. Thus, God seals the heart of every arrogant oppressor.

40:36. Pharaoh said to Haman: Construct me a tower to reach the paths

40:37. of heaven to look at the god of Moses. I think Moses is a liar. Thus, Pharaoh's evilness was made attractive to him and he was turned away from the right path. His plan was ruined.

40:38. The person, who was a believer, said: My people, follow me, I will guide you to the right path.

40:39. O my people, this worldly life is of passing enjoyment, but, the life to come will be the permanent home.

40:40. Whoever does an evil action will receive an equal return; but whoever does a righteous deed, whether male or female and is a believer, will enter paradise, and will be given limitless livelihood.

40:41. O my people, how is it that I invite you to salvation while you invite me to the hellfire?

40:42. You invite me to disbelieve in God and worship other gods of whom I have no knowledge, while I invite you to serve the almighty, the most forgiving.

40:43. Certainly, the idols you invite me to pray cannot be called upon in this world or in the life to come. Our return is to God. Those who break the limits will be companions of the hellfire.

40:44. Remember what I, God, have told you. I entrust my affair to God. He looks after His servants.

40:45. God protected the believer from their evil plots, and the people of Pharaoh were punished severely.

40:46. They are brought to the fire morning and evening. On the Day of Judgment, it will be said to the angels: Give the people of Pharaoh the severest punishment.

40:47. They will argue in the hellfire. The weak will say to those who were arrogant: We followed you, so will you save us from a part of the hellfire?

40:48. The arrogant will say: All of us are in the hellfire. God has judged His servants.

40:49. Those in hell will say to its keepers: Request your Lord to lighten our punishment for a day.

40:50. The keepers will ask: Did the Messengers not come to you with clear proofs? They will answer: Yes. And the keepers will reply: Then pray as you like, but the disbelievers' prayer is useless.

40:51. God shall help His Messengers and believers during this worldly life and on the Day of Judgment when the witnesses will stand to testify.

40:52. That day, no excuse will help the wrongdoers. They will have the curse and the worst home to live.

40:53. God gave Moses guidance and to Israel's children the Scriptures to inherit,

40:54. for guidance and a message to those who understand.

40:55. O Muhammad, be patient. God's promise is true. Request God to forgive them their sins committed against you. Praise your Lord morning and evening.

40:56. Those who dispute God's signs without proof have nothing in their hearts except ambition which they shall never achieve. Therefore, request God's protection. He hears all and sees all.

40:57. The creation of the heavens and the earth is greater than the creation of mankind, yet most of mankind does not know it.

40:58. The blind and the seeing are not alike, nor are the believers, who do good, and the wrongdoers. But humans seldom think.

40:59. There is no doubt that the Hour of Judgment is to come, but most people do not believe that.

40:60. Your Lord says: Pray to Me; I will answer your prayer. Those who are too arrogant to serve Me will enter hell, disgraced.

40:61. It is God who has made for you the night to rest and the day to give you light to see. God is graceful to mankind, but most of mankind is not thankful to Him.

40:62. Such is God, your Lord, the creator of all things. There is no god except Him. Then, how can you turn away from Him?

40:63. Like you, there were others before you who rejected God's signs.

40:64. It is God who made for you the earth to live and the sky a ceiling. He gave you an attractive body and provided you with good things. That is God, your Lord. Blessed be God, the Lord of the universe.

40:65. God is living. There is no god except Him. So pray to Him with devotion. All praise is due to God, the Lord of the universe.

40:66. O Muhammad, say: I have been forbidden to worship your idols as I have been given clear proofs from my Lord. I have been commanded to submit to the Lord of the universe.

40:67. It is God who has created you from dust to a sperm-drop, and then to a clot. Then He brings you out of womb as a child; develops you to maturity, makes you grow old to complete your appointed term and become wise, though some of you die young.

40:68. God gives life and death. When He decides to do something, He says it to happen, and it happens.

40:69. Do you not see those who dispute God' revelations turn away from the right path?

40:70. Those who deny the Qur'an and the revelations with which God sent His Messengers, they will ultimately know the truth

40:71. when they will have shackles and chains around their necks and will be dragged

40:72. through the boiling water and burn in the hellfire.

40:73. They will be asked: Where are your idol-gods whom you used to worship

40:74. beside God? They will reply: They have abandoned us. In fact, those we prayed to were nothing. Thus, God let the disbelievers off the right path.

40:75. They will be told: You shall be punished because you rejoiced on earth wickedly and behaved rudely.

40:76. Enter the gates of hell to live there forever. Wretched is the home of the arrogant.

40:77. O Muhammad, have patience. God's promise is true. Whether We show you some part of what We have threatened the disbelievers with or make you die before that, they shall all return to Us.

40:78. Before you, We have sent Messengers. We have told you about some but not others. Without God's approval, no Messenger could show a sign. But when God decided, justice was done, and those who made wrong claims perished.

40:79. It is God who has made livestock for you to ride on some and to eat the flesh of others.

40:80. They give you other benefits. They take you wherever you desire, by carrying you on land as ships carry you by the sea.

40:81. God shows you His signs. Which of God's signs will you deny?

40:82. Have the disbelievers not travelled through the land to see the end of those before them? They were more numerous than them, mightier in strength, and have left bigger landmarks of their splendor on earth, but, all that was of no use to them.

40:83. When the disbelievers' Messengers came to them with clear proofs, they boastfully rejoiced in their knowledge, but they were punished for what they ridiculed.

40:84. And when they saw God's punishment, they said: We believe in God alone. We disbelieve in the idols we used to worship beside Him.

40:85. But, their new faith could not benefit them when they saw God's punishment. That is how God dealt the previous generations. The disbelievers were the losers.

# CHAPTER 41

## THE DETAILED EXPLANATION

**Name:** From Verse Three.

**Verses:** 54

**Summary:**

- Background: A chief from Prophet Muhammad's tribe Quraysh went to him and offered him wealth, chiefdom and kingship if he would stop preaching his message. Prophet Muhammad responded by reciting parts of this chapter. The chief was disappointed, but impressed from what he heard, and advised his people to leave Prophet Muhammad alone.
- The Qur'an gives good news and a warning. It is a guide and healing for the believers.
- The disbelievers' response to Prophet Muhammad's message.
- Woe to those who deny the hereafter and do not pay Zakat (mandatory charity).
- Story of the creation of the earth, mountains and heavens.
- Warning to the disbelievers and the example of God's punishment upon the nations of Aad and Thamoud.
- On the Day of Judgment:
    - Human beings' ears, eyes and skins will bear witness against them for their sins.
    - The idol-gods, people worshipped beside God, will disappear.
- Those who do not listen to the Qur'an will be severely punished.
- The angels are assigned for protection of those who say our Lord is God and stay firm on it.
- The best speaker calls people towards God, does good deeds and says: I am a Muslim.
- Repel evil with good, remain patient and steadfast, and your enemy will become your dear friend.
- Example of God's signs.
- Nothing is said to Prophet Muhammad which was not said to earlier Prophets.
- The book given to Prophet Moses was similar to the Qur'an.
- Have the disbelievers ever considered that if the Qur'an is really

from God and they deny it, what will happen to them?

## By Verse

In the name of God, the compassionate, the merciful:

41:1. Ha Meem (are Arabic letters).

41:2. This book, the Qur'an, is revealed by God, who is most gracious and most merciful.

41:3. This is a book of revelations which have been explained in detail. This is a Qur'an in Arabic for knowledgeable people.

41:4. It gives good news and a warning; but most of the disbelievers turn away from it and pay no attention.

41:5. The disbelievers say: Our hearts are protected from what O Muhammad are inviting us to, our ears are plugged, and there is a curtain between us. Do what you like and we will do what we like.

41:6. O Muhammad, say: I am a human like you. It has been revealed to me that your god is one God. Therefore, take a straight path to Him and ask for His forgiveness. Woe to those who worship gods other than Him,

41:7. and do not pay Zakat (mandatory charity) and do not believe in the hereafter.

41:8. The believers who do good deeds will have a lasting reward.

41:9. O Muhammad, ask them: Do you disbelieve in God Who created the earth in two days, and you join idol-gods with Him? He is the Lord of the universe.

41:10. God placed on earth the firmly standing mountains. He blessed the earth and in four days provided livelihood for all alike.

41:11. Then, God turned to the heaven when it was a cloud of vapor, and said to it and the earth: Will you obey Me willingly or unwillingly? They replied: Willingly.

41:12. In two days, God completed the seven heavens and assigned each one its function. God installed the lowest heaven with stars and guardian comets. Such is the plan of the almighty and the all-knowing.

41:13. O Muhammad, if the disbelievers do not pay attention, tell them: I have warned you of the punishment that struck Aad and Thamoud.

41:14. When the Messengers came to them from all directions saying: Worship no one except God, they replied: If our Lord had willed, He would have sent down the angels. We will not believe in your message.

41:15. Aad were unjustly proud in the land. They said: Who is mightier than us? Did they not remember that God Who created them was mightier than them? They denied God's revelations.

41:16. God sent upon them furious wind in their misfortune days so that they might taste a disgraceful punishment in this life; but more severe will be punishment of the hereafter. They will have no one to help.

41:17. God guided Thamoud, but they preferred ignorance over guidance. So, a humiliating punishment seized them for their sins.

41:18. God saved the believers and those who feared God.

41:19. O Muhammad, mention the day when God's enemies shall be gathered into groups and brought together to hell.

41:20. When they will reach it, their ears, eyes, and skins will testify against them to their wrong-doings.

41:21. They will ask their skins: Why have you testified against us? They will reply: God has made us speak as He has made everything speak; He created you in the beginning, and to Him you all shall return.

41:22. In doing wrong, you did not hide yourselves from your eyes, ears and skins. You thought that God did not know of what you were doing.

41:23. It is that thought of yours about your Lord that has destroyed you, and you are among the losers.

41:24. Whether they accept their situation or not, the hell shall still be their home. If they beg for pardon, their begging will not be accepted.

41:25. God gave them companions who made everything around them attractive to them. They deserve the fate of jinns and humans who have passed before them. They were all losers.

41:26. The disbelievers say: Do not listen to the Qur'an. Make noise during its recitation, so that you may subdue it.

41:27. God will surely punish the disbelievers, and repay them for their evil acts.

41:28. The hellfire shall be the recompense of God's enemies. They shall live there forever for rejecting God's revelations.

41:29. The disbelievers will say: Lord, show us those jinns and humans who led us off the right path. We shall crush them under our feet, so that they become the lowest.

41:30. Those who say: Our Lord is God, and then remain steadfast on the right course, the angels will descend upon them saying: Do not fear and grieve but enjoy the good news of paradise you have been promised.

41:31. We, angels, are your allies in this world and the hereafter. There, you will have whatever you will desire and ask for,
41:32. as a hospitable gift from a forgiving and merciful Lord.
41:33. Who is a better speaker than the one who invites people to God, does what is right, and says: I am a Muslim?
41:34. Good and bad deeds are not equal. Repel evil by good, and your enemy will become your dearest friend.
41:35. But no one will achieve such goodness except those who exercise patience and self-restraint and are favored by God.
41:36. If Satan tempts you, seek protection from God. God hears all and knows all.
41:37. God's signs are the night, day, sun, and moon. Do not prostrate to the sun or to the moon, but prostate to God, who created them, if you worship Him truly.
41:38. If the disbelievers are too proud to worship God, then there are angels with your Lord who glorify Him day and night, and are never tired.
41:39. Among God's signs is the barren earth. When He sends down rain on it, it stirs to life and swells. He Who gives the earth life will raise the dead to life. He is able to do all things.
41:40. Those, who distort God's revelations are not hidden from Him. Is the one who will be thrown into the hellfire better or the one who will be safe on the Day of Resurrection? Do what you like; God is seeing what you do.
41:41. Those who disbelieved in God's message, the Qur'an, when it came to them, shall receive punishment. This is a powerful book.
41:42. Falsehood cannot approach the Qur'an from any direction. It is revealed by a wise and praiseworthy God.
41:43. Nothing is said in opposition to you O Muhammad that has not been said to other Messengers before you. Your Lord is forgiving, but severe in giving painful punishment.
41:44. If God had revealed the Qur'an in a foreign language, they would have said: Why its verses are not explained in detail? Why is it in a foreign language while the Messenger is an Arab? Say: For the believers, it is a guide and a cure. But the disbelievers are deaf and blind. As if they are being called from a distance.
41:45. God gave Moses the Scriptures, but the disbelievers differed about it. Had God not decided to defer their punishment, God would have punished them in this life. The disbelievers are in great doubt about the Qur'an.
41:46. Whoever does right, it is for his own soul; whoever does evil, it is

for his own harm. Your Lord is never unjust to His servants.

41:47. God alone has the knowledge of the Hour of Judgment. Without His knowledge, no fruit comes out from its sheath and no female conceives or gives birth. On the Day of Judgment, God will ask the disbelievers: Where are My partners? They will reply: We confess that no one among us can attest for them.

41:48. The idol-gods, the disbelievers used to pray, will abandon them. The disbelievers will know that they have no place of escape.

41:49. Man is never tired of praying for good things, but if evil touches him, he despairs and loses hope.

41:50. If God lets the man taste God's mercy after an adversity, he says: I deserve it. I do not think the Hour of Judgment will come. Even if, I return to my Lord, He will reward me well. But, God will surely tell the disbelievers about what they did, and will punish them severely.

41:51. When God shows favor to man, he turns away and distances himself; but, when evil touches him he prays extensively.

41:52. O Muhammad, ask them: Have you considered that if the Qur'an is from God and you disbelieve in it, who would be more off the right path than the one who has gone far in its opposition?

41:53. God will soon show them God's signs in the universe and in their own souls, until it will become clear to them that it is the truth. Is it not sufficient that your Lord is watching over all things?

41:54. Yet, they still doubt about the meeting with their Lord. Unquestionably, He surrounds all things.

# CHAPTER 42

# CONSULTATION

**Name:** From Verse 38.

**Verses:** 53

**Summary:**

- Theme: Truth of Prophet Muhammad's message.
- The heavens may break apart from God's glory, and angels glorify Him and ask forgiveness for those on earth.
- Islam is the same religion that was prescribed to Prophets Noah, Abraham, Moses and Jesus. They were all ordered to establish the religion and not to create division in it.
- He who desires reward in the hereafter shall be given many folds, but he who desires reward in this life shall be given here but shall have no share in the hereafter.
- Whatever misfortunes befall upon people are the result of their own misdeeds.
- True believers are those who establish prayer, give charity, and defend themselves when oppressed.
- The real losers are those who will lose on the Day of Resurrection.
- It is God Who gives daughters and sons to some and nothing to others.
- It is not suitable for a human that God should speak to him face to face.
- Social and administrative affairs are to be resolved through mutual consultation.
- The basis of Islamic criminal punishment laws is laid down.
- Prophet Muhammad has done his duty of warning the people and he is not a guardian over them.
- Various forms of revelations are identified.

**By Verse**

In the name of God, the compassionate, the merciful:

42:1. Ha Meem (are Arabic letters).

42:2. Ain Sin Qaf (are Arabic letters).

42:3. Thus, God the almighty, the wise, sends revelation to you O Muhammad as He did to others before you.

42:4. God owns all that is in the heavens and on earth. He is the highest, the greatest.

42:5. The heavens may break apart from God's glory as angels glorify God and ask forgiveness for those on earth. God is the forgiving, the merciful.

42:6. God watches over those who choose guardians other than Him. O Muhammad, you are not accountable for what they do.

42:7. We have revealed the Qur'an to you in Arabic, so that you may warn the residents of the central city Mecca and those around it about the Day of Gathering, which is sure to come, for some to go to paradise and others to hell.

42:8. If God wanted, He could have made them all of one religion, but He is merciful to whom He wills. The wrongdoers have no protector or helper.

42:9. Have they taken protectors beside God? He alone is the protector. He gives life to the dead, and has power over all things.

42:10. In whatever you differ its decision is in God's hand. That is God, my Lord; I rely on Him and turn to Him time after time.

42:11. God is the creator of the heavens and earth. He has given you wives from yourselves to multiply you, and also male and female cattle. There is no one like Him. He hears and sees all.

42:12. God has the keys of the heavens and earth. He increases and decreases livelihood for anyone He pleases. He knows all things.

42:13. O Muhammad, God has ordained the religion He has revealed to you, and earlier to Prophets Noah, Abraham, Moses and Jesus, saying: Establish the religion and stay united. It is difficult for those who associate others with God to accept your invitation. God chooses for Himself whom He wills and guides those who turn to Him.

42:14. They only differed after knowledge had come to them because of rivalry between them. Had God not postponed their punishment for a specified time, they would have been punished in this life. Those who inherited the Scriptures after them have great doubts too.

42:15. Thus Prophet Muhammad invite them to God's religion and stay on the right course steadfastly as you are commanded. Do not follow the disbelievers desires, but say: I believe in the Scriptures God has revealed. I am commanded to do justice between you. God is your and our Lord. We have your deeds and we have our deeds. There is no argument between us. God will gather us together, and we shall return to Him.

42:16. Those who argue about God after accepting obedience to Him, their arguments are useless with their Lord. His wrath will fall upon them and they shall be severely punished.

42:17. It is God who has sent down the Qur'an with truth and justice. And who knows the Hour of Justice may be near.

42:18. Those who deny the Hour of Justice want to hasten it, but the believers are fearful and know it is the truth. Indeed, those who doubt about the hour are in great error.

42:19. God is gracious to His servants. He provides for whom He wills. He is most powerful, the almighty.

42:20. Whoever desires reward of the hereafter, God increases his reward. And whoever desires reward of this world, God gives it to him, but there will be no share for him in the hereafter.

42:21. Do they have partners with God who have established a religion for them without God's permission? Had God not decided already to defer their punishment, their fate would have been decided in this life. The wrongdoers will be greatly punished.

42:22. On the Day of Resurrection, you will see the wrongdoers fearful of what they have earned, but they will surely be punished. However, the believers who did righteous deeds will be in lush gardens of paradise having their desires fulfilled by their Lord. That would be a great gift.

42:23. That is God's promise to His servants who believe and do good deeds. O Muhammad, say: I do not ask any reward for my effort but ask for love of kinship. Whoever does good will be rewarded more. God is forgiving and appreciative.

42:24. Do they say: Muhammad has forged a lie against God? But if God wanted, He could seal your heart. God will end falsehood and confirm the truth with His words. He knows hearts' secrets.

42:25. God accepts repentance from His servants and forgives sins. He knows what you do.

42:26. God answers the prayers of the believers who do good deeds, and gives them more out of His grace. The disbelievers will have a severe punishment.

42:27. If God had given abundantly to His servants, they would have rebelled on the earth. But He gives them what He wills in proportion. God is well acquainted with and sees His servants.

42:28. It is God who sends down rain after they had lost all hope and spreads out His mercy. He is the protector, the praiseworthy.

42:29. Among God's signs is the creation of the heavens and earth, and the living creatures that He has spread through them. He has power to gather them together when He wills.

42:30. Whatever misfortune befalls you, it is because of what you have done. God forgives much.
42:31. You cannot frustrate God's plan upon earth. Beside God, you have no protector or helper.
42:32. And among God's signs are the ships sailing through the ocean like mountains.
42:33. If God wills, He could still the wind, and the ships would remain motionless on ocean surface. Indeed, there are signs in that for everyone patient and grateful.
42:34. Or God could destroy the ships for the sins of those who sail in them. But, He pardons much.
42:35. Those who dispute about God's revelations may know that they have no escape.
42:36. Whatever you have been given is for passing enjoyment of the worldly life. But, what is with God is better and more lasting for the believers who rely upon their Lord,
42:37. and avoid gross sins and indecencies. When they are angry, they forgive,
42:38. respond to their Lord, establish prayer, conduct theirs affairs by consultation, give alms from what We have provided them,
42:39. and defend themselves when oppressed.
42:40. Repayment for an injury is an equal injury, but whoever pardons and reconciles, God rewards him. God does not like the wrongdoers.
42:41. There is no blame on who defends himself after having been wronged.
42:42. The blame is only on those who oppress others and wrongly rebel on earth. They will be severely punished.
42:43. But whosoever shows patience and forgives, he surely acts courageously.
42:44. Whom God sends off the right path, no one can protect him beside God. When the wrongdoers will see the punishment, you will see them saying: Is there a way back?
42:45. You will see them being brought to the hellfire, humbled with shame, and looking with stealthy glance. The believers will say: The true losers are the ones who lost themselves and their families on the Day of Resurrection. Unquestionably, the wrongdoers will be punished forever.
42:46. They shall have no friend to help them beside God. To whom God leads off the right path shall be lost.
42:47. Answer the call of your Lord before a day comes from God that

cannot be averted. That day you will have no refuge and will not be able to deny your sins.

42:48. O Muhammad, if they pay no attention, you are not their guardian. Your duty is only to notify them. When God blesses a person, he enjoys it; but if an evil befalls him because of his own wrongdoing, he is ungrateful.

42:49. God has the kingdom of the heavens and earth. He creates what He wills. He gives daughters or sons to whom He wills.

42:50. God gives both sons and daughters to some, and nothing to others. God is the all-knowing and powerful.

42:51. It is not fitting for a man that God should speak to him except by inspiration, or from behind a veil, or through an angel to reveal with God's permission what God wills. God is most high, most wise.

42:52. O Muhammad, We have inspired you by Our command. You knew nothing of the Qur'an or the faith. We have made it a light by which We guide those of Our servants whom We please. You shall guide them to a right path,

42:53. God's path. God owns whatever is in the heavens and on earth. Unquestionably, all things in the end shall return to God.

# CHAPTER 43

## THE GOLD ORNAMENTS

**Name:** From Verse 35.

**Verses:** 89

**Summary:**

- The Qur'an is from God's original book, truly outstanding, full of wisdom. The original book is the source from which God has sent revelations to Prophets at various locations and times in different languages. But God's message throughout has been the same.
- Hold fast to the Qur'an if you want to be rightly guided.
- Even the disbelievers believe that the heavens, the earth, and everything between them are created by God.
- Some disbelievers consider the angels to be God's daughters.
- Prophet Abraham recognized God's oneness and rejected associating someone else with God.
- If it were not that by removing the social and financial inequality, all mankind would become one type, and human society would have ceased to function, God would have provided the disbelievers houses made with silver and gold.
- He who turns away from God's remembrance, God appoints a devil to be his intimate friend.
- Prophet Moses was sent to Pharaoh and his chiefs with signs, but they ridiculed the signs and him; as a result, God drowned them.
- Prophet Jesus was no more than a human being whom God favored and made him an example for Israel's children.
- On the Day of Judgment, the believers will have no fear or regret; they will be awarded paradise and made happy.
- O Prophet, tell the Christians that if God had a son, I would have been the first one to worship him.
- A brief but very convincing discourse is given on the unity of God.

### By Verse

In the name of God, the compassionate, the merciful:

43:1. Ha Meem (are Arabic letters).
43:2. I swear by the Qur'an that makes things clear.
43:3. We, God, have revealed the Qur'an in Arabic so that you may

understand its meaning.
43:4. The Qur'an is from God's original book*, truly outstanding, full of wisdom.

**is the source from which God has sent revelations to Prophets at various locations and times in different languages. But God's message throughout has been the same.*

43:5. Should We, God, take the message away from you because you are an extravagant people?
43:6. We sent many prophets among the earlier people,
43:7. but they ridiculed every Prophet.
43:8. We destroyed stronger people than these Meccan-disbelievers, as there are examples of those who have passed before them.
43:9. If you ask the disbelievers: Who has created the heavens and the earth? They will surely say: The all-mighty, the all-knowing God created them.
43:10. It is God who has made the earth a resting-place for you, and has provided routes of roads, rivers, and oceans for you to find your way.
43:11. God sends down rain from the sky in measured amounts to revive the dead land. Similarly, you will be raised to life.
43:12. God has created all living things in pairs and has made ships and animals for you to ride.
43:13. By riding on their backs, you may remember the favor of your Lord and say: Glory is to God who has put them under our control, otherwise we could not have controlled them.
43:14. We shall surely return to our Lord.
43:15. Despite that, they assign some of God's servants to be a part of Him. Indeed, man is openly ungrateful.
43:16. Would God choose daughters* for Himself and sons for you?

**The pagan-Arabs believed that their goddesses and angels were God's daughters.*

43:17. When one of them is given news of the birth of a daughter like what he assigns to the most merciful God, his face darkens, and he grieves.
43:18. Would you assign to God the idols decorated with ornaments and incoherent in disputes?
43:19. The disbelievers say that the angels, who are servants of the merciful God, are females. Did they witness their creation? Their testimony will be recorded, and they will be questioned.
43:20. They say: If God had willed, we should never have worshipped

the idol-gods. They have no knowledge of that; they are lying.
43:21. Or, have We given them a book before the Qur'an to which they are holding fast?
43:22. Rather, they say: We found our forefathers practicing this religion, and we are following in their footsteps.
43:23. Thus, whenever We sent a Messenger before you to any people, its wealthy people said: We found our forefathers following a certain religion, and we will certainly follow in their footsteps.
43:24. Each Messenger said: Even if I brought you a better religion than what your forefathers practiced? They replied: We deny your religion.
43:25. So We punished them. See the end of those who rejected faith.
43:26. O Muhammad, tell about Prophet Abraham, who said to his father and people: I disassociate from those you worship,
43:27. except Him who created me. He will guide me.
43:28. And he left it as a lasting message among his offspring so that they may turn back to God.
43:29. I, God, gave enjoyable life to these people and their forefathers until truth and a Messenger came to them to guide them.
43:30. But when the truth came to them, they said: This is magic and we reject it.
43:31. They also said: Why this Qur'an has not been sent down to a great man from the two cities of Mecca and Taif?
43:32. Is it they who would distribute your Lord's mercy? It is We, Who give them their livelihood in this world and has raised some of them above others in rank so that they may serve one another. The mercy of your Lord is better than their accumulated treasures.
43:33. If it were not a concern that all mankind would become one community, We would have made the disbelievers' house ceilings and stairs of silver,
43:34. and their doors and couches, upon which they recline,
43:35. of gold ornaments. But, all that is for enjoyment in the worldly life. The life of the hereafter with your Lord is for the righteous.
43:36. Whoever neglects the remembrance of the merciful God, We appoint a devil for his companion.
43:37. The devils turn the disbelievers away from the right path, though they think themselves rightly guided.
43:38. When a disbeliever will come before Us, he will say to his devil companion: I wish we were as far apart as the distance between the east and the west. Satan is a miserable companion.
43:39. Since you were unjust, it will not benefit you that your devils will

share your punishment that day.

43:40. O Muhammad, can you make the deaf to hear, or guide the blind and those who are in clear error?

43:41. Either We shall take you away, and We avenge them,

43:42. or let you live to see Our promise of punishment to them fulfilled. We have complete power over them.

43:43. So, hold fast to what is revealed to you in the Qur'an. You are on the right path.

43:44. The Qur'an is a reminder for you and your people, and you all will be questioned about it.

43:45. Ask those of Our Messengers whom We sent before you if We ever appointed gods to be worshipped beside the gracious God?

43:46. We sent Moses with Our signs to Pharaoh and his chiefs. Moses said to them: I am the Messenger of the Lord of the universe.

43:47. When Moses showed them Our signs, they laughed.

43:48. We showed them sign after sign, each greater than the previous one. We punished them so that they might turn to Us.

43:49. They said to Moses: O magician, pray to your Lord for us for the promise He has made to you. We shall accept guidance.

43:50. But, whenever We removed their punishment, they broke their promise.

43:51. One day, Pharaoh announced among his people: My people, does not the kingdom of Egypt and the streams flowing beneath my palace belong to me? Do you not see?

43:52. Am I not better than this undignified miserable person Moses, who can hardly speak clearly because of his stammer.

43:53. Why bracelets of gold have not been given to him or angels have not been sent down with him?

43:54. Pharaoh misled his people, and they obeyed him. They were disobedient to God.

43:55. When they angered Us, We punished them and drowned them.

43:56. We made them a precedent and an example for those who succeeded them.

43:57. When Mary's son Jesus is cited as an example, your people laughed

43:58. saying: Is he better than our gods? They raise the question just to argue with you. They are contentious people.

43:59. Jesus was a human being whom We favored, and made him an example for Israel's children.

43:60. If We pleased, We could have sent angels to be your successors on earth.

43:61. And Jesus is a sign* of the Hour of Judgment. So do not doubt it; follow Me; this is the right path.

**Some scholars say it to be his second coming on earth and some refer it to his birth without a human father.*

43:62. Let Satan not mislead you, because he is your sworn enemy.
43:63. When Jesus brought clear proofs, he said: I have come to you with wisdom to resolve some of your differences, so fear God and obey me.
43:64. God is my and your Lord, so worship Him. This is the right path.
43:65. But, the factions among them differed. Woe to the wrongdoers for the punishment of a painful day.
43:66. Are they waiting for the hour of doom to come upon them suddenly without warning?
43:67. That day, friends will become enemies, except the righteous.
43:68. God will say to them: My servants, this day you need not fear and grieve,
43:69. because you believed in Our revelations and submitted yourselves;
43:70. enter paradise with your spouses happily.
43:71. You will be served with golden plates and cups. There, you will have all that you will desire and delight your eyes. You will live there forever.
43:72. You will inherit paradise as a reward for your good deeds in the world.
43:73. There will be abundant fruit for you to eat.
43:74. The guilty shall live forever in the punishment of hell.
43:75. Their punishment will not be lightened, and they will despair.
43:76. We did not wrong them; they wronged themselves.
43:77. They will call out: O keeper of the hell, let your Lord cause us to perish. He will reply: You shall live here forever.
43:78. We brought you the truth, but most of you hated the truth.
43:79. Have the Meccan-Disbelievers plotted against the Prophet? We are also devising our plan.
43:80. Do they think We cannot hear their secret talks and private conversations? We hear everything. Our angels are with them recording.
43:81. O Muhammad, say: If the most merciful God had a son, I would have been the first to worship him.
43:82. Glory is to the Lord of the heavens, the earth, and the throne. He is free from what they attribute to Him.
43:83. Let them talk falsely and amuse until they meet the day they have been threatened with.

43:84. He is the only God in the heavens and on earth; and He is the wise, the all-knowing.

43:85. Blessed is God who has the kingdom of the heavens and earth and whatever is between them. He has the knowledge of the hour of doom. You all will return to Him.

43:86. The idols you call upon beside God do not possess power to plead for you. No one can plead except who knows the truth and testifies to it.

43:87. If you ask the disbelievers who created them, they would surely say: God. So how can they turn away from the truth?

43:88. The Prophet said: Lord, they are a people who would not believe.

43:89. O Muhammad, turn away from them by wishing them peace. Before long, they shall know their blunder.

# CHAPTER 44

# THE SMOKE

**Name:** From Verse 10.

**Verses:** 59

**Summary:**

- Theme:
    1. Humbling of the worldly pride and power.
    2. Recompensing the evil and good deeds in the hereafter.
- The Meccans were wrong in thinking that instead of God, Prophet Muhammad was composing the Qur'an. God revealed the Qur'an in a blessed night, in which all matters were decided wisely by His command.
- The disbelievers were wrong in thinking that they will fight with the Prophet and the Qur'an, and win.
- There are lessons to be learned from the story of Prophet Moses and the people of Pharaoh.
- The Israelites' escape and the drowning of Pharaoh and his army.
- God delivered Israel's children and chose them over the nations of the world in spite of their weaknesses.
- The Day of Judgment is the time appointed for the Resurrection.
- The sinners' food and drink in hell.
- The righteous' food and entertainment in paradise.

### By Verse

In the name of God, the compassionate, the merciful:

44:1. Ha Meem (are Arabic letters).
44:2. We God swear by the Qur'an that makes things clear.
44:3. We revealed it to warn mankind
44:4. on a night when We made decisions wisely
44:5. by Our command. We send it down
44:6. as a blessing from your Lord. He indeed hears all and knows all.
44:7. He is the Lord of the heavens, the earth, and all that is between them. Make a note of it if you truly believe.
44:8. There is no god but Him. He gives life and death. He is your Lord and the Lord of your forefathers.
44:9. Yet, in their doubt, they amuse themselves.

44:10. Wait for the day when a visible smoke from the sky will
44:11. cover the people as a painful punishment.
44:12. Then they will say: Lord, remove this punishment from us; we are now believers.
44:13. How will their new faith help them, when a Messenger already came to them to explain things?
44:14. They denied him saying: He is a madman taught by others.
44:15. If We remove the punishment for a while, you will return to disbelief.
44:16. One day, We shall hit you hard and punish you.
44:17. Before these disbelievers, We tested Pharaoh's people. A noble Messenger Prophet Moses came to them,
44:18. who said: Give me God's servants. I am a truthful Messenger.
44:19. Do not be arrogant against God. I give you clear proofs.
44:20. I seek protection from your and my Lord against you for hurting me.
44:21. If you do not believe me, then leave me alone.
44:22. Then Moses cried to his Lord, saying: They are sinful people.
44:23. God answered: Go with My servants by night; you will be pursued.
44:24. Cross the parted sea. Pharaoh's army shall be drowned.
44:25. How many gardens and springs they left behind,
44:26. including crop-fields, grand palaces,
44:27. and enjoyable good things.
44:28. We made other people inherit their things.
44:29. Neither the heaven nor the earth wept for them; nor their punishment was delayed.
44:30. We saved Israel's children from humiliating punishment
44:31. from Pharaoh. He was the most excessive oppressor.
44:32. And knowing Israelites' strengths and weaknesses, We preferred them over other nations.
44:33. We showed them signs to test them.
44:34. The disbelievers are saying:
44:35. We will die only once and we will not be resurrected.
44:36. Bring back our forefathers, if what you say is true.
44:37. Are they better than the people of Tobba* and those before them? We destroyed them all because they were sinners.

*Tobba was the title of the kings of Hamyar. They were Sabaeans (*an ancient South Arabian people, modern-day Yemen, believed to be the biblical land of Sheba*).

44:38. We did not create the heavens and the earth and what is between

them for amusement.
44:39. We created them to reveal the truth, but most people do not know it.
44:40. The Day of Judgment has been fixed for all.
44:41. That day, no one will help a friend, nor receive help from anyone else,
44:42. except those on whom God will have mercy. God is the almighty, the merciful.
44:43. The tree of Zaqqum
44:44. will be the sinner's food.
44:45. Like oil sediment, it shall boil in disbeliever's belly
44:46. like steaming water.
44:47. It will be said to the angles: Seize the sinner and drag him into the midst of the blazing hellfire.
44:48. Then pour boiling water over his head, saying:
44:49. Taste this you claimant of power and honor.
44:50. This is the punishment for what you doubted.
44:51. The righteous will be in a safe place
44:52. with gardens and springs.
44:53. They shall wear fine silk and rich brocade, and sit with each other.
44:54. We shall marry them to fair color women with large, beautiful eyes.
44:55. There, they would be able to ask for every kind of fruit in peace and security.
44:56. Having died once, they will not die again. God will save them from the hellfire
44:57. through His mercy. That will be the great achievement.
44:58. We have revealed the Qur'an in your language Arabic so that the disbelievers might pay attention.
44:59. So you and the disbelievers should wait for the result.

# CHAPTER 45

# THE KNEELING

**Name:** From Verse 28.

**Verses:** 37

**Summary:**

- Theme: Answering the doubts and objections of the Meccan-Disbelievers about God's oneness and the hereafter, and warning them against their hostile attitude towards the Qur'an's message.
- Food for thought for those who are seeking God's signs. The signs are all around. If they do not believe in God and His revelations, then in what fact will they believe?
- God has subjected the seas and all that is between the heavens and earth to serve humans.
- The Israelites made sects in their religion after the knowledge had come to them through the Torah.
- The wrongdoers are protectors of one another while the protector of the righteous is God Himself.
- He who has made his own desires his god, God lets him go off the right path and sets a seal upon his hearing and heart, and covers his eyes.
- God's address to the disbelievers on the Day of Judgment.

**By Verse**

In the name of God, the compassionate, the merciful:

45:1. Ha Meem (are Arabic letters).
45:2. God, the almighty and the wise, has revealed the Qur'an.
45:3. The heavens and the earth have signs for the believers.
45:4. God's creation of the mankind and scattering of animals through the earth are signs for the faithful.
45:5. Alternations of the night and the day, God's sending down of livelihood from the sky, giving life to the lifeless earth, and directing winds, are signs for people of understanding.
45:6. O Muhammad, these are God's revelations which We recite to you in truth. In what discourse will they believe, if they are denying God and His revelations?
45:7. Woe is to every sinful liar.
45:8. He hears God's revelations recited to him, but persists arrogantly

as if he had not heard them. Give him news of a painful punishment.

45:9. When he comes to know about any of Our revelations, he ridicules them. Such people will have humiliating punishment.

45:10. In front of them is hell. Whatever they have earned in this worldly life will not benefit them; neither will the idol-gods they serve beside God. There will be a great punishment for them.

45:11. This Qur'an is guidance. The disbelievers in the revelations of their Lord will have a painful and severe punishment.

45:12. God has subjected the sea to serve you so that the ships may sail by His command, and you may seek His reward and be thankful.

45:13. God has made whatever is in the heavens and on earth to serve you. It is all from Him. Surely, there are signs in that for those who reflect.

45:14. O Muhammad, tell the believers to forgive those who do not expect God's days of punishment; so that He may reward people for what they earned.

45:15. Whoever does good or bad is for oneself. You all will return to your Lord.

45:16. We gave Israel's children the Scriptures, wisdom, and Prophethood. We provided them with good things and preferred them over other nations.

45:17. We gave them clear religious instructions. They did not differ till knowledge came to them. They differed because of rivalry among them. On the Day of Resurrection, your Lord will judge their differences.

45:18. O Muhammad, We have put you on the right path of religion. Follow it. Do not follow the desires of those who have no knowledge.

45:19. In no way, they can benefit you against God. The wrongdoers are allies of one another; but God is the protector of the righteous.

45:20. This Qur'an is an enlightenment for the mankind. It is guidance and a blessing for the true believers.

45:21. Do the evildoers think that God shall make them equal to the believers who do good deeds, and their lives and deaths shall be alike? Bad is their judgment.

45:22. God has created the heavens and earth to reveal the truth and to reward each person according to his deeds. No one will be wronged.

45:23. Have you thought about the person who has made his desires his god? God knowingly has set a seal upon his hearing and heart, and put a cover on his eyes. Who can guide him beside God? Will you not pay attention?

45:24. The disbelievers say: There is no other life than this worldly life. We live and die here and nothing but time destroys us. They have no knowledge of what they are saying. They are guessing.

45:25. When Our clear revelations are recited to them, their only argument is: Bring back our forefathers, if what you say is true.

45:26. O Muhammad, tell them: God gives you life and death. He will gather you all on the Day of Judgment. There is no doubt about that, but most people do not know.

45:27. The kingdom of the heavens and earth belongs to God. When the Hour of Judgment will arrive, the followers of falsehood will lose.

45:28. That day, you shall see all nations kneeling down. Every nation shall be called to see its record and told that it will be rewarded for what it did.

45:29. Your record speaks truthfully about you. We wrote what you did.

45:30. Lord will admit the believers into His mercy who did righteous deeds. That clearly would be the success.

45:31. The disbelievers will be asked: Were Our revelations not recited to you? Did you not scorn them and committed sins?

45:32. When you were told: God's promise is true; the Hour of Judgment is sure to come, you replied: We know nothing about the hour. It is just a guess, and we are not convinced about it.

45:33. The evil consequences of what they did will become clear to them, and they will be surrounded by what they used to ridicule.

45:34. They will be told: God will forget you today as you forgot the meeting of this day. You will live in hell, and no one will help you.

45:35. That is because you ridiculed God's revelations and the worldly life enticed you. That Day (of Judgement) they will have no way out and will not be asked to make amends.

45:36. All praise is for God, Who is the Lord of the heavens and the earth, and the creator of the universe.

45:37. He has the glory throughout the heavens and the earth; and He is all-powerful and all-knowing.

# CHAPTER 46

# THE WINDING SAND-TRACTS

**Name:** From Verse 21.

**Verses:** 35

**Summary:**

- Prominent Feature: A group of jinns listened the Qur'an. They believed in it, and returned to their people to preach Islam.
- Warning the disbelievers for their errors in resisting the faith arrogantly, and condemning Prophet Muhammad who was trying to redeem them. Their errors have been refuted, and they have been warned that if they would irrationally reject the Qur'an's invitation and Muhammad's Prophethood, they would be preparing for their doom.
- God created the heavens, the earth, and all that lies between them to reveal the truth.
- The idol-gods to whom the disbelievers call upon are not aware that they are being called upon. They cannot save people from God's wrath.
- The Qur'an :
    - o is God's word, not of Prophet Muhammad. The Prophet is but a plain warner.
    - o confirms the Torah, which was revealed to Prophet Moses.
- Those who treat their parents with kindness shall be rewarded and those who mistreat their parents shall be punished.
- Aad's nation rejected God's message. As a result, it faced destruction.
- God advised Prophet Muhammad to keep on passing His message and bear the disbelievers with patience.

## By Verse

In the name of God, the compassionate, the merciful:

46:1. Ha Meem (are Arabic letters).

46:2. The revelation of the Qur'an is from God, the almighty, the all-wise.

46:3. We created the heavens and the earth and what is between them for a specified duration to reveal the truth. But, the disbelievers do not pay attention to the truth about which they are warned.

46:4. O Muhammad, ask the disbelievers: Have you thought about those you call upon beside God? Show me what they have created on earth, or the share they have in creation of the heavens? Bring me a book revealed before this, or some evidence of divine knowledge, if you are truthful.

46:5. Who is more off the right path than the one who calls upon those beside God, who cannot answer him till the Day of Resurrection? They are unaware of his prayers to them.

46:6. When the mankind will be gathered on the Day of Judgment, their idols will be their enemies and will deny their worship.

46:7. When Our clear revelations are recited to them and the truth is told to them, the disbelievers say: This is plain magic.

46:8. Do they say: Prophet Muhammad has invented it? Say to them: If I have invented it, you can do nothing to protect me from God's wrath. He knows what you are saying. He is sufficient witness between us. He is the forgiving, the merciful.

46:9. Say: I have neither brought a new faith different from other Messengers, nor I know what will happen to you and me. I follow only what is revealed to me. I am but a plain warner.

46:10. Ask the disbelievers: Have you considered that if the Qur'an is from God, and you reject it while a witness from Israel's children has testified to its similarity with earlier Scriptures and has accepted Islam, but you arrogantly deny it? God does not guide the wrongdoers.

46:11. The disbelievers say about the believers: If there had been any good in the Qur'an, the believers would not have believed in it before us. And since the disbelievers are not guided by it, they will say: This is an ancient falsehood.

46:12. Before the Qur'an, the book of Moses, Torah, was revealed for guidance and as a blessing. The Qur'an has been revealed in Arabic language to confirm the Scriptures, to warn the wrongdoers, and to give good news to the righteous.

46:13. Those who say that our Lord is God and remain firm on that path shall have neither fear nor grief.

46:14. They are habitants of paradise. They will live there forever as a reward for what they did.

46:15. We have directed man to be kind to his parents. Mother carries a child during pregnancy with hardship and gives birth to the child with hardship. From conception to weaning it takes 30 months. When the child grows to maturity and reaches the age of 40 years, let him say: Lord, enable me to be grateful for Your favors, which You have bestowed upon me and my parents, and to do good work that will please you. Give me good offspring. I ask Your forgiveness and surrender to You.

46:16. Those are the ones whose best deeds We will accept and overlook their misdeeds. They will be among the dwellers of paradise. That is a truthful promise which they have been given.

46:17. But, there is one who rebukes his parents saying: Shame on you. Do you threaten me with the Resurrection when generations before me have passed away? They cry to God for help: Woe to you; have faith; God's promise is true. But he says: These are stories of the ancient.

46:18. He is like the earlier generations of jinns and mankind against whom the decision of punishment is justified. Surely, they are losers.

46:19. They will be ranked according to what they did, so that God may pay them for their deeds. They will not be wronged.

46:20. That Day (of Judgment) when the disbelievers will be brought before the hellfire, they will be told: You squandered your good things in the worldly life in taking pleasure from them. Now you will have humiliating punishment because you were unjustly proud on the earth and behaved sinfully.

46:21. O Muhammad, tell about Houd, the brother of Aad, who warned his people in the winding sand-tracts of the Valley of Al-Ahqaf saying: Do not worship anyone except God. I fear for you the punishment of a terrible day. There have been other warners before and after him.

46:22. They replied: Have you come to turn us away from our gods? Bring down upon us the calamity with which you have been threatening us, if you are telling the truth.

46:23. He said: God alone knows when the calamity will come. I am here to give you the message. But I can see you are ignorant.

46:24. When they saw a cloud approaching their valley, they said: This cloud will bring us rain. He replied: No, it is that for which you were impatient; a hurricane for a painful punishment

46:25. that will destroy everything by its Lord's command. There was nothing left except their ruined dwellings. That is how We punish the criminals.

46:26. We had given them prosperity and power which We have not given the Meccans. We gave them faculties of hearing, seeing, and feelings, but these were of no use to them as they went on rejecting

God's revelations. The punishment, they used to ridicule, overtook them.

46:27. We destroyed the cities around you because We repeatedly sent our revelations to their people that they might return from disbelief.

46:28. Why the gods they choose to reach God did not help them? But their gods abandoned them. Those were their false concoctions.

46:29. O Muhammad, remember when We sent towards you a group of jinns to listen to the Qur'an. They said to one another: Listen quietly. When the recitation ended, they went back to their people as warners.

46:30. They said to their people: We have heard recitation of a book revealed after Moses that confirms what came before it. It guides to the truth and the right path.

46:31. O our people, respond to God's Messenger and believe in him. God will forgive your sins and protect you from a painful punishment.

46:32. He who does not respond to God's Messenger will neither escape God's judgment on the earth, nor will he have any protector beside Him. Such people are in great error.

46:33. Do they not see that God, Who created the heavens and the earth and was not tired by their creation, is able to give life to the dead? Yes, He has power over all things.

46:34. The Day (of Judgement), when the disbelievers will be brought to the hellfire, they will be asked: Is this not the truth? They will reply: Yes Lord, it is. He will say: Then, taste the punishment because you disbelieved.

46:35. O Muhammad, be patient, as were the steadfast Messengers before you. Do not be impatient for the punishment to the disbelievers. The day, they will face the punishment they have been promised, their life on the earth would appear to them like an hour. You have warned them. Will anyone be destroyed other than the defiantly disobedient people?

# CHAPTER 47

## MUHAMMAD

**Name:** From Verse Two.

**Verses:** 38

**Background:**

Muslims were target of persecution and tyranny in Mecca. Because of that, they immigrated to Medina. The disbelieving Quraysh of Mecca were not prepared to leave them alone and let them live in peace even there. Such were the conditions when this chapter was revealed.

**Summary:**

- Theme: To prepare the believers for war and to give them preliminary instructions.
- God:
    - Will void the disbelievers' deeds who turn others away from God's path.
    - Curses the vain promise of obedience and good talk which is not followed by action.
    - Put the believers to test in order to identify the brave and the resolute.
    - Will help and protect you, if you help God's cause.
    - Has put a seal on the hypocrites' hearts.
- In war:
    - Thoroughly subdue the disbelievers before taking them as prisoners of war.
    - God is on the believers' side.
- The believers do not follow their own desires.
- A parable of paradise and hell.
- Do not be stingy if you are asked to give in God's cause.

### By Verse

47:1. God will void the deeds of disbelievers who turn others away from God's path.

47:2. God will remove the misdeeds and improve the condition of the believers who do righteous deeds and believe in what has been revealed to Muhammad, which is the truth from their Lord.

47:3. That is because the disbelievers follow falsehood, and the believers follow the truth from their Lord. Thus God tells people what is their classification.

47:4. When you meet the disbelievers in battle, strike off their heads until you have overpowered them, and tie the prisoners firmly. Then, free them as a favor or let them pay ransom when the war ends. That is what you should do. If God wanted, He could have punished them Himself, but He wanted to test you by one another. Those who are killed in God's cause, He will not allow their deeds to be wasted.

47:5. God will guide them and improve their condition,

47:6. admit them to paradise, about which He has already told them.

47:7. Believers, if you help God, He will help you and make you strong.

47:8. For the disbelievers is misery. God will void their good deeds.

47:9. Because they disliked God's revelations, He made their deeds worthless.

47:10. Have they not traveled through the land and seen the end of those before them? God destroyed them completely. The disbelievers' fate will be similar,

47:11. because God is the believers' protector and the disbelievers have no protector.

47:12. God will admit the believers who do righteous deeds to gardens in paradise watered by streams. But the disbelievers, who enjoy themselves and eat as livestock eat, will live in hell.

47:13. O Muhammad, how many cities were stronger than your city Mecca, which drove you out? We destroyed them. There was no one to help them.

47:14. Can He who follows his Lord's guidance be compared to him whose evil deeds look attractive to him and he follows his desires?

47:15. Paradise, which has been promised to the righteous, will have rivers of unpolluted water, fresh milk, tasteful wine, and purified honey. They will eat there variety of fruits and receive their Lord's forgiveness. Can they be compared to those who will live in the hellfire forever and drink boiling water which will tear their intestines?

47:16. O Muhammad, some of them listen to you, but when they depart from you, they ask those who have knowledge: What did he say just now? God has sealed their hearts. They follow their own desires.

47:17. As for those who follow the right path, God increases their guidance and blesses them to guard against evil.

47:18. Are they waiting for the hour, when the world will end, to come upon them unexpectedly? Some of its signs have already come. When it will come, how would it benefit them to listen to the warnings? Then, it will be too late for them to ask for forgiveness.
47:19. O Muhammad, know that there is no one worthy of worship except God. Ask His forgiveness for your sins and those of believing men and women. God knows about your movements and homes.
47:20. The believers say: Why has a chapter not been sent down regarding fighting in God's cause? But when a decisive chapter is revealed in which fighting is mentioned, you see those in whose hearts is hypocrisy looking at you with fear of death. More appropriate for them would have been
47:21. obedience and words of acknowledgment. When the matter of fighting has been decided upon, it would be better for them to be loyal to God.
47:22. Would you the hypocrites then, if given the authority, do mischief in the land, and sever ties of kinship?
47:23. Those are the hypocrites God has cursed, made them deaf, and blinded their eyes.
47:24. Do they not reflect upon the Qur'an, or are their hearts locked up from understanding it?
47:25. Those who turn back to disbelief after guidance has been clearly shown to them, Satan enticed them and prolonged false hopes for them.
47:26. That is because they said to those who dislike what God revealed: We shall support you in some matters. God knows their secret talk.
47:27. What will they do when the angels will take their souls at death, and hit them on their faces and backs?
47:28. That will be because they follow what angers God, and they hate what pleases God. Therefore, God will make their deeds fruitless.
47:29. Do those, whose hearts are diseased, think that God will not expose their hypocrisy?
47:30. If God willed, God could point them out to you, and you would recognize them by their looks. But you will surely know them by the tone of their talking. God has knowledge of your actions.
47:31. God will surely test you until God knows who strives hard in God's cause with steadfastness. God will also check your character whether you are truthful or lying.
47:32. The disbelievers, who hinder others from God's path and oppose the Messenger after the guidance has been shown to them, cannot harm God in any way. Rather, God will make their deeds fruitless.

47:33. Believers, obey God and the Messenger, and do not make your deeds fruitless.

47:34. God shall not forgive the disbelievers who hindered others from God's path and died as disbelievers.

47:35. Do not show weakness, and call for peace when you are victorious. God is with you and will never deprive you from reward of your deeds.

47:36. This worldly life is but a play and a temporary pastime. God will reward you if you believe in God and avoid evil. He will not ask you to give up your wealth.

47:37. If God was to ask the hypocrites to give up your wealth and press you for that, you would become miser, and that will expose your animosity towards God and His Messenger.

47:38. You are invited to spend in God's cause. But some of you are misers. Whoever is miserly, his miserliness hurts him. God does not need you, but you need Him. If you turn away, He will replace you with another people, who will not be like you.

# CHAPTER 48

# THE VICTORY

**Name:** From Verse One.

**Verses:** 29

**Background:**

One day Prophet Muhammad dreamed that he had gone to Mecca with his companions for a visit to the sacred mosque there. Apparently, there was no possible way to act on this inspiration. The Meccan-Disbelievers had debarred Muslims from visiting the mosque for the past six years.

The Prophet informed his companions of his dream and began to make preparations for the journey. He made the announcement to other tribes also that he was proceeding for the visit and people could join him. Some thought that he and his companions were going into the jaws of death, because the Meccans would not allow the visit and fight to stop them. The Prophet went with 1,400 companions. Who wore pilgrims robes, took sacrifice-camels with them, and each one kept only a sword in sheath, which the pilgrims to the mosque were allowed to carry according to the custom.

The Quraysh were puzzled at the Prophet's bold step. The fighting during the month of prophet's journey was forbidden because it was considered sacred for pilgrimage for centuries. The Meccans wanted to provoke the Prophet's companions into fighting so that they may tell the Arabs that those people had actually come to fight on the pretext of pilgrimage.

The Prophet came to know of Meccans' intentions and stopped at Houdaybiyyah. Here, the negotiations between the Meccans and the Prophet were conducted for the Muslims to come to Mecca next year for the pilgrimage. Some terms of the negotiations were not liked by the Prophet's companions.

When their caravan was returning to Medina, feeling depressed and dejected at the truce of Houdaybiyyah, God revealed this chapter to Prophet Muhammad that the treaty his followers were regarding as their defeat was indeed a great victory. Though the believers were satisfied when they heard this divine revelation, but not much afterwards the advantages of the treaty began to appear one after the other. Therefore, to fully understand this chapter, it should be read with this historical background.

**Summary:**

- God granted the Muslims a clear victory through the treaty of Houdaybiyyah.
- Swearing allegiance to the Prophet is swearing allegiance to God.
- The Desert-Arabs, who did not go with the Prophet for the war between the Muslims and the disbelievers, are condemned for staying behind. Only the blind, the lame, and the sick are exempt from war.
- God was pleased with who swore allegiance to the Prophet before the treaty. Had there not been believers in Mecca, God would have allowed the Muslims to fight against the Quraysh. Prophet Muhammad was shown vision to conquer Mecca and to check the characteristics of his followers.

**By Verse**

In the name of God, the compassionate, the merciful:

48:1. O Muhammad, We have given you a clear victory,

48:2. so that God may forgive your past and future sins, complete His favor upon you, guide you to a straight path,

48:3. and bless you with a great victory.

48:4. It is God Who calmed the believers' hearts to strengthen their faith. God owns the soldiers of the heavens and the earth. God is all-knowing and all-wise.

48:5. That is done by God to admit the believing men and women to gardens of paradise, watered by running streams, to live there forever, and to forgive their sins. In the sight of God, that is a great achievement.

48:6. And God has done that also to punish the hypocrites and the idolatrous men and women who have doubts about God that He will help Prophet Muhammad and his followers. They will meet an evil end, because God is angry with them. He has cursed them and prepared for them hell, an evil destination.

48:7. The soldiers of the heavens and earth belong to God. God is all-knowing and all-wise.

48:8. O Muhammad, We have sent you as a witness and a giver of good news and warnings,

48:9. so that people may believe in God and His Messenger, help him, honor and respect him, and praise God morning and evening.

48:10. Those who pledged allegiance to you O Muhammad, actually pledged allegiance to God. God's hand is over their hands. He, who breaks his oath, breaks it for his own loss. He who fulfills his oath to God will be richly rewarded.

48:11. The Desert-Arabs who stayed behind from war will say to you O Muhammad: We were looking after our property and families. Request God to forgive us. What they say is not in their hearts. Tell them: Who has power to intervene with God, if His will is to punish or forgive you? God is well aware of your deeds.

48:12. But the Desert-Arabs thought that the Messenger and the believers would never return to their families. That thought pleased your hearts. Because of your evil thought, you were destined for destruction.

48:13. For the disbelievers in God and His Messenger, We have prepared a blazing fire.

48:14. The kingdom of the heavens and earth belongs to God. He forgives or punishes whom He wills. God is forgiving and merciful.

48:15. When O Muhammad you will go to take war booty from the next expedition against your enemies, those who stayed behind will say: Allow us to go with you. They would wish to change God's decision. Tell them: You will not join us; God has already decided that. They will reply: You are jealous of us. But they understand little.

48:16. Tell the Desert-Arabs who stayed behind: You will be called upon to fight a mighty nation till it submits. If you would obey to fight, God will give you a good reward. But if you would run away as before, God will punish you severely.

48:17. There will be no offense for the blind, the lame, and the sick not to go to war. Whoever obeys Gods and His Messenger will be admitted to gardens of paradise watered by streams. But whoever runs away will be punished severely.

48:18. God was pleased with the believers when they pledged allegiance to you O Muhammad under the tree*. He knew what was in their hearts. He calmed their hearts and rewarded them with a victory at hand,

**at Houdaybiyyah when the false rumors reached the Prophet that Uthman ibn Affan, his envoy of peace to the Meccans, was killed by the Meccans. The pledge of allegiance was taken under an acacia tree. It is known as the Pledge of Good Pleasure.*

48:19. and with the abundant war booty they were to get. God is mighty and wise.

48:20. God promised you rich booty, but has given you this victory at Khaybar promptly. God has protected you from your enemies, so that this victory may be a sign for the believers and He may guide

you to a straight path.
48:21. God foresees other victories for you to have. God has power over all things.
48:22. If the Meccan-Disbelievers had fought you, they would have run away. They would not find a protector or a helper.
48:23. Such has been God's practice in the past, and you will find no change in that.
48:24. It was God who made peace between you and the disbelievers in the Valley of Mecca after He had given you victory over them*. God was watching your deeds.

**at The Treaty of Houdaybiyyah.*

48:25. The disbelievers obstructed you from the sacred mosque in Mecca and prevented your sacrificial animals from reaching the place of sacrifice. If it was not that you will harm the believing men and women living in Mecca, whom you did not know and unknowingly would commit a sin, God would have allowed you to fight the Meccans. This was done so that God might admit to His mercy whom He willed. If the believers had been separate from the disbelievers, We would have punished the disbelievers severely.
48:26. When the disbelievers' hearts had pride due to ignorance, God gave calmness to His Messenger and the believers. God made them stick to the word of piety, because they were entitled and most worthy of it. God knows everything.
48:27. God has shown His Messenger the true vision: God willing, you will enter the sacred mosque in safety without fear, with hair shortened or shaved. God knew what you did not know and gave you a speedy victory.
48:28. It is God Who sent His Messenger with guidance and true religion to elevate it over all religions. God is a sufficient witness for Muhammad to be His Prophet and Islam to be the religion of truth.
48:29. Muhammad is God's Messenger. His followers are firm against the disbelievers, but compassionate with each other. You see them bowing down, prostrating, seeking God's grace and pleasure. Their marks of calmness are on their faces because of the effect of prostration. Their description is in the Torah and the Gospel. They are like the seed that sends forth its sprout and strengthens it, and makes its stem strong and firm, delighting its planters. Through the believers, God enrages the disbelievers. God has promised the believers, who do good deeds, forgiveness and a great reward.

# CHAPTER 49

# THE CHAMBERS

**Name:** From Verse Four.

**Verses:** 18

**Summary:**

- Theme: Teaching Muslims manners worthy of true believers.
- God commands the believers to lower one's voice in the presence of Prophet Muhammad, and not to call out to the Prophet from his chambers, rather to wait for him to come out.
- It is not right to believe in every news blindly and act on it without checking it out.
- Make peace between the believers if they fight among themselves.
- Safeguard against the evils that corrupt society and spoil relationships. Mocking and taunting each other, calling others by nicknames, creating suspicions, prying into other people's affairs and backbiting are the evils which are not only sins but corrupt society also. God has forbidden them.
- Mankind is created from a single male Adam and a female Eve, and the noblest is the one who is the most righteous.
- The difference between a true believer and someone who claims to be a Muslim.

**By Verse**

In the name of God, the compassionate, the merciful:

49:1. Believers, do not prefer your decisions to that of God and His Messenger, but fear God. God hears all and knows all.

49:2. Believers, neither raise your voice above the Prophet's voice, nor speak aloud to him as you may speak aloud to one another, lest your deeds become fruitless without your knowledge.

49:3. Those who speak softly in the presence of God's Messenger are the ones whose hearts God has tested for piety. God will forgive them and give great reward.

49:4. O Muhammad, those who call you out when you are in your chambers are mostly foolish.

49:5. It would be better for them to wait patiently until you come out to them. But God is forgiving and merciful.

49:6. Believers, if an evil-doer brings you news, check it out, lest you harm a people unknowingly, and then be sorry for what you have done.

49:7. Know that God's Messenger is among you. In many matters, had he followed you, you would be in difficulty. But God has endeared faith to you and has made it pleasing to your hearts, making disbelief, wrong-doing, and disobedience hateful to you. Such people are rightly guided,

49:8. by God's grace and favor. God is the all-knowing and all-wise.

49:9. If two believing groups fight, make peace between them. But if one oppresses the other, fight against the oppressor until it submits to God's judgment. If it submits, make settlement between them justly and fairly. God loves those who act justly.

49:10. The believers are in a brotherhood. Make peace among your brothers and fear God that you may receive mercy.

49:11. Believers, men should not ridicule other men, who may be better than them. Similarly, women should not ridicule other women, who may be better than them. Do not defame one another and call one another by offensive nicknames. To disobey after accepting faith is evilness. Those who do not repent for bad behavior are wrongdoers.

49:12. Believers, avoid excessive suspicion. In some cases suspicion is sinful. Neither spy nor backbite one another. Would anyone of you like to eat the flesh of his dead brother? You would hate it so hate backbiting. Fear God. He is the forgiving and the merciful.

49:13. O mankind, We, God, have created you from a pair of a male (Prophet Adam) and a female (Eve). We divided you into nations and tribes to know one another. The noblest of you in God's sight is the one most righteous. God is knowledgeable and aware.

49:14. The Desert-Arabs say: We have believed. O Muhammad, tell them: You have not. Rather say: You acknowledge Islam. Faith has not yet entered your hearts. If you obey God and His Messenger, God will not deprive you from the reward of your deeds. God is forgiving and merciful.

49:15. The true believers are those that have believed in God and His Messenger, never doubt, and fight in God's cause with their wealth and lives. It is those who are truthfully faithful.

49:16. O Muhammad, ask them: Would you tell God about your religion when He knows what the heavens and earth contain? He has knowledge of all things.

49:17. They consider it a favor to you that they have accepted Islam. Tell them: That is no favor to you. Rather, God has blessed you with a

favor in guiding you to the faith, if you are truthful in faith.
49:18. God knows the secrets of the heavens and earth. He is watching over all your deeds.

# CHAPTER 50

## QAF

**Name:** From Verse One.

**Verses:** 45

**Background:**

When Prophet Muhammad started preaching Islam, what surprised the people most was that they would be resurrected after death, and would have to render an account of their deeds. They said: That was impossible. How could it be possible when the body had become dust that it would be reassembled after hundreds of thousands of years, to be raised up as a living body? In response, God sent down this chapter.

**Summary:**

- Theme: The hereafter.
- Life after death is a reality and there is nothing strange about it.
- God:
    - has assigned two angels to each person for noting down every word he utters and every action he takes. Every stubborn disbeliever will be thrown into hell.
    - will ask the hell: Have you been filled? The hell will answer: Are there more to come?
- Advice to Prophet Muhammad: Warn the disbelievers, bear with them in patience, and warn them with the Qur'an.

### By Verse

In the name of God, the compassionate, the merciful:

50:1. Qaf (is an Arabic word). I, God, swear by the glorious Qur'an that Muhammad is God's Prophet.

50:2. The disbelievers wonder that a warner from among themselves has come to them. They say: This is strange that

50:3. when we will die and become dust, we will return to life? That is far-fetched.

50:4. We, God, know what the earth takes away from their dead bodies. Everything is recorded in Our book.

50:5. The Meccan-Disbelievers denied the truth when it came to them. That is why they are confused.

50:6. Have they not looked at the sky above them and noticed that how God made it and adorned it without flaws?
50:7. We spread out the earth, set upon it firmly standing mountains, and grow in it all kinds of beautiful plants.
50:8. All these things give an insight and a warning to every repenting person.
50:9. We send down blessed rain from the sky, grow gardens and grain for harvesting,
50:10. and tall palm-trees with clusters of dates,
50:11. as a livelihood for humans. That is how We give new life to the dead land. Such will be the resurrection.
50:12. Before the Meccans, Noah's people, the dwellers of Ar-Raas, Thamoud,
50:13. Aad, Pharaoh, Lot's people,
50:14. the dwellers of the forest (Midians*), and the people of Tubba**. They all denied their Messengers. Thus, they brought down My punishment.

**lived in the northwest Arabian Peninsula, on the east shore of the Gulf of Aqaba on the Red Sea*

***present Yemen.*

50:15. Were We, God, worn out by the first creation? Yet, they are in doubt about a new creation by the resurrection.
50:16. We created man, knows his heart's whisperings, and are closer to him than his jugular vein.
50:17. In addition, there are two writing angels, who sit on his right and left.
50:18. Each word he utters is recorded by a vigilant guardian.
50:19. The agony of death will bring out the truth that he was trying to avoid.
50:20. The trumpet will be blown. That will be the day about which you were warned.
50:21. Every person will be brought by an angel accompanied by another angel as a witness.
50:22. One angel will say: You never wanted to hear about the Day of Judgment. Now, we have removed your veil. You can see it clearly.
50:23. The other angel will say: I am ready to present his record.
50:24. God will order the angels to throw into hell everyone who was an obstinate disbeliever,
50:25. prevented good works, broke limits, doubted,

50:26. and set up other gods beside God to punish him severely.
50:27. His companion Satan will say: Lord, I did not mislead him. He himself erred to be off the right path.
50:28. God will say: Do not quarrel before Me. I had already warned you.
50:29. My sentence cannot be changed. I am not unjust to My servants.
50:30. That day We, God, will ask the hell: Have you been filled? It will reply: Are there more to come?
50:31. The paradise, which will not be far away, will be brought near to the righteous.
50:32. They will be told: This is what you were promised. It is for everyone who repented to God, was faithful,
50:33. feared the merciful God unseen, and came with a remorseful heart.
50:34. Enter paradise in peace. This is the day of the eternal life.
50:35. There, they will have whatever they will desire, and We shall give them more.
50:36. How many generations, mightier than them, We destroyed before them? They had spread throughout the land. But was there a place of escape for them?
50:37. Surely, there is a lesson in it for everyone who has a heart or pays attention.
50:38. We created the heavens and earth and what is between them in six days, and were not tired by that.
50:39. O Muhammad, be patient with what the disbelievers say. Glorify God before sunrise and before sunset.
50:40. Praise Him during the night and after prostration.
50:41. Listen! On the day when the caller will call out from a nearby place;
50:42. That day, when they will hear the call clearly, that will be the day of coming out of the graves.
50:43. It is God who gives life and death, and all shall return to Him.
50:44. That day, the earth will split and they will come out of it rapidly. To gather them all is easy for Us.
50:45. We are well aware of what they say. You cannot compel them to believe. Guide them with the Qur'an whoever fears My warning.

# CHAPTER 51

# THE WINDS

**Name:** From Verse One.

**Verses:** 60

**Summary:**

- The chapter deals with the hereafter, an invitation to God's oneness, and a warning that refusal to accept Prophet Muhammad's message and persistence in continuing the ignorance about faith have proved to be disastrous for previous nations.
- There are lessons in the stories of Prophet Abraham, and people of Pharaoh, Aad, Thamoud, and Prophet Noah.
- The people's differing beliefs about the hereafter are a proof that none of these beliefs is based on knowledge, but guess. It would be best to ponder about the hereafter based on the knowledge God's Prophet was conveying to humans. For example, God's creation of the earth, heavens, mankind, wind, rain, earth structure, and creatures in pairs are all evidence of God's power and competence to have the hereafter, which was to come for the eventual reward and retribution.
- Regarding invitation to God's oneness, it has been said: God has not created humans for servicing others but for His own service. He is not like idol-gods, which receive sustenance from humans. God is the sustainer of all, and does not need sustenance from anyone.
- God has assigned Prophet Muhammad to be a warner for mankind. God has instructed him not to bother about the rebels but to go on performing his mission because of its usefulness for the believers.

## By Verse

In the name of God, the compassionate, the merciful:

51:1. I, God, swear by the winds that scatter dust,
51:2. raise water-loaded clouds,
51:3. move swiftly,
51:4. distribute blessings of rain to mankind,
51:5. that what you are promised is true,
51:6. and the Day of Judgment will surely come.
51:7. I, God, swear by the sky of the differing starry pathways,
51:8. that you have contradicting views about the Day of Judgment.

51:9. Only the obstinate turn away from the truth.
51:10. The conjecturers are cursed,
51:11. for their ignorance and confusion about the hereafter.
51:12. They ask: When will the Day of Judgment come?
51:13. That day, they will be punished in the hellfire.
51:14. They will be told: Taste the punishment about which you asked to be hastened.
51:15. The righteous will live in gardens and springs of paradise.
51:16. They will happily receive what their Lord will give them. Before that day, they did good deeds.
51:17. They slept sparingly at night,
51:18. prayed for God's forgiveness before dawn,
51:19. and shared their wealth with the beggars and the needy.
51:20. For the faithful, there are signs on the earth
51:21. and in yourselves. Can you not see?
51:22. The heaven has your livelihood and whatever you are promised.
51:23. I swear by the Lord of the heaven and the earth that it is true that the last day will come, just as you are endowed with speech.
51:24. O Muhammad, have you heard the story of Abraham's honored guests?
51:25. The angels came to him and said: Peace be upon you. He answered: Peace be upon you too; you are unknown to me.
51:26. Then, he went to his family and came back with a fat roasted calf.
51:27. He set it before them and said: Will you not eat, please?
51:28. When they did not eat, he got afraid of them. They said: Do not be afraid. They gave him good news of the birth of a son blessed with knowledge.
51:29. His wife came out loudly crying, struck her forehead, and said: I am a barren old woman.
51:30. They said: That is your Lord's will. He is the wise, the all-knowing.
51:31. Abraham asked: What have you come for, O Messengers?
51:32. They replied: We have been sent to a sinful nation of Prophet Lot
51:33. to rain upon them stones of baked clay,
51:34. marked by your Lord for destruction of the sinful.
51:35. We, God, saved the faithful in the town.
51:36. But, We found only one house of faithful in it.
51:37. We, God, left there a sign for those who may fear the painful punishment.
51:38. In the story of Moses there is a sign too. We sent him to Pharaoh with clear authority.

51:39. But Pharaoh and his chiefs turned away saying: Moses is either a magician or a madman.
51:40. So We seized Pharaoh and his soldiers and threw them into the sea. He was blameful.
51:41. There is another sign in the story of Aad. We sent a dry wind upon them.
51:42. It destroyed everything in its path to dust.
51:43. And there is another sign in Thamoud's people. They were told to enjoy for a while.
51:44. But they disobeyed their Lord's orders. A thunderbolt struck them while they were looking on.
51:45. They were neither able to stand up nor save themselves.
51:46. Earlier, Noah's people were destroyed. They were defiantly disobedient.
51:47. With Our power, We built the heaven and gave it a vast extent.
51:48. We spread out the earth with excellence.
51:49. And We, God, have created all things in pairs, so that you may reflect.
51:50. Therefore, turn to God in haste. I, Prophet Muhammad, have come from Him to warn you clearly.
51:51. Do not set up other gods beside Him. I am His clear warner to you.
51:52. Similarly, no Messenger came to people before the Meccans who was not called a magician or a madman.
51:53. Have they passed on the legacy to their successors? No, but they are all arrogant people.
51:54. O Muhammad, leave them. There is no blame on you.
51:55. But keep on urging the believers. It will help them.
51:56. I, God, created the jinns and mankind to worship Me alone.
51:57. I want neither any livelihood nor feeding from them.
51:58. God alone is the generous provider. He is the all-mighty, the invincible.
51:59. Those who are doing wrong will be punished like those who came before them. Let them not urge Me, God, impatiently to hasten their punishment.
51:60. The disbelievers will face destruction on the day about which they are being warned.

# CHAPTER 52

# THE MOUNTAIN

**Name:** From Verse One.

**Verses:** 49

**Summary:**

- No one can prevent the occurrence of the hereafter. That day, the disbelievers will be punished and the believers rewarded.
- Opposition of the Meccan-chiefs towards Prophet Muhammad's message, and response to their arguments that he has invented the Qur'an. He is a magician, a madman, and a poet.
- Instructions to Prophet Muhammad to continue his mission and consolation that God has not abandoned him.

### By Verse

In the name of God, the compassionate, the merciful:

52:1. I, God, swear by the Mountain Sinai,
52:2. the Scriptures written,
52:3. on an unrolled parchment,
52:4. the frequently visited house, the grand mosque at Mecca,
52:5. the sky raised high,
52:6. and the swollen sea,
52:7. Your Lord's punishment will occur.
52:8. No one can prevent it.
52:9. That day, the sky will shake severely,
52:10. and the mountains will crumble and fly.
52:11. That day, there will be destruction for the disbelievers,
52:12. who now are involved in fruitless disputes.
52:13. That day, they will be pushed forcefully into the hellfire.
52:14. They will be told: This is the fire which you used to deny.
52:15. Is this magic, or do you not see?
52:16. Now burn in it. It does not matter whether you bear it patiently or impatiently. You are being paid only according to your deeds.
52:17. The righteous will be in gardens and pleasure (of paradise),
52:18. enjoying what their Lord will give them. Their Lord will protect them from the punishment of the hellfire.
52:19. They will be told: Eat and drink happily as a reward for your deeds.

52:20. They shall recline on couches arranged in rows. We shall wed them to fair color ladies with beautiful eyes.
52:21. We shall unite the believers with their descendants who followed them in faith. We shall not decrease the reward of their deeds, but every person is responsible for one's deeds.
52:22. We shall give them a variety of fruit and meat and whatever they will desire.
52:23. They will pass a cup of wine from one to the other, but it will not intoxicate them to talk uselessly and act sinfully.
52:24. Boy-servants, handsome like beautiful pearls, will serve them.
52:25. The righteous will talk to one another about their worldly lives.
52:26. They will say: When we were living with our families, we were afraid of displeasing God.
52:27. But God has been gracious to us and He has saved us from punishment of the hellfire.
52:28. In the worldly life, we prayed to Him. He, indeed, is the beneficent, the merciful.
52:29. O Muhammad, keep on warning the disbelievers. By your Lord's grace, you are neither a soothsayer nor a madman.
52:30. Do they say: He, Muhammad, is a poet; we are waiting for a misfortune to befall him?
52:31. Tell them: Wait; I am waiting too.
52:32. Does the disbelievers' reasoning make them say this, or are they wicked people?
52:33. Do they say: He, Muhammad, has invented the Qur'an ? The fact is they do not want to believe.
52:34. Let the disbelievers' produce a Scripture like it, if they are truthful.
52:35. Did a creator create them or they created themselves?
52:36. Did they create the heavens and the earth? The fact is that they have no faith.
52:37. Do they own the treasures of your Lord or manage them?
52:38. Do the disbelievers have a stairway to the heaven to overhear what goes on there? Let their eavesdropper produce a clear proof.
52:39. Is God to have daughters while you have sons?
52:40. Are you, O Muhammad, asking them for a payment that they are afraid to be burdened with debt?
52:41. Have they the knowledge of the unseen? Can they write it down?
52:42. Are they plotting against you? But they themselves shall be ruined.
52:43. Have they a god other than God? God is above what they associate with Him.
52:44. If they were to see a piece of the sky falling on them, they would

still say: It is a heap of clouds.
52:45. O Muhammad, leave them alone till they meet the day when they will be thunder-stricken.
52:46. That day, their plan will be of no use to them and no one will help them.
52:47. And besides that, there is punishment for the wrongdoers in the world, but most of them do not know it.
52:48. O Muhammad, wait patiently for your Lord's decision. We are watching over you. Glorify your Lord when you wake up,
52:49. and praise Him during the night and at the setting of the stars.

# CHAPTER 53

# THE STAR

**Name:** From Verse One.

**Verses:** 62

**Summary:**

- Theme: Warning to the Meccan-Disbelievers about the wrong attitude towards the Qur'an and Prophet Muhammad. They were telling people that Muhammad had gone off the right path and was misleading people. They were worshipping idol-goddesses, and calling the idols and angels God's daughters. The disbelievers have been warned that because of their similar wrong attitude, God destroyed the people of Aad, Thamoud, and of Prophets Noah and Lot. The Qur'an's message is the same as that of the books of Prophets Noah and Abraham.
- The scene of the first revelation, brought by Angel Gabriel to Prophet Muhammad. God gave Prophet Muhammad a tour of the heavens, paradise, and other great signs.
- The idols and angels have no share with God. They cannot intercede for anyone without God's permission.
- The actual cause of the disbelievers' wrong attitude is that they do not believe in the hereafter. Only this world is their goal.
- No human should claim piety, because God knows who is pious.
- No soul shall bear another's burden. People will be punished or rewarded for their own actions.
- The Hour of Judgment is approaching near, which no one can avert.

### By Verse

In the name of God, the compassionate, the merciful:

53:1. I, God, swear by the star that disappears because of the daylight that

53:2. your companion Prophet Muhammad is neither off the right path nor misled.

53:3. He does not speak out of his own desire.

53:4. A revelation is revealed to him.

53:5. It is taught to him by the one who is mighty powerful

53:6. and wise Angel Gabriel. He appeared

53:7. on the uppermost horizon;

53:8. came down
53:9. to a distance of two bow lengths or even closer.
53:10. He revealed to God's servant Prophet Muhammad what was to be revealed.
53:11. Prophet Muhammad's heart did not deny what he saw.
53:12. How can you the disbelievers then dispute what Prophet Muhammad saw?
53:13. Prophet Muhammad saw Angel Gabriel a second time
53:14. at the lote-tree, beyond which no one can pass,
53:15. near to the Paradise of Abode where believers whom God will reward with paradise will live.
53:16. At that time, the lote-tree was covered.
53:17. Prophet Muhammad's eyes neither wandered nor turned aside.
53:18. Prophet Muhammad saw some of the greatest signs of his Lord.
53:19. Have you thought about the reality of Al-Lat*, Al-Uzzah*,
53:20. and Manat*?

**Idol-goddesses of pagan Arabs.*

53:21. Are daughters for God and sons for you the disbelievers*?

**The disbelievers used to say that their three idol-goddesses were God's daughters. In their culture, it was degrading to have daughters. They always wanted to have sons.*

53:22. That would be an unjust division.
53:23. Your forefathers and you have invented the idols' names, but God has given no authority. The disbelievers follow their own assumptions and desires of their souls, even though their Lord's guidance has come to them.
53:24. Is it justified that a man should have all that he desires?
53:25. It is God who controls life on earth and in the hereafter.
53:26. There are numerous angels in the heavens whose pleading for anyone will not succeed unless God permits it in favor of whoever He chooses and is pleased with.
53:27. Those who disbelieve in the hereafter call the angels by female names,
53:28. although they have no knowledge about it. They guess, and a guess is not a substitute for truth.
53:29. O Muhammad, pay no attention to those who ignore Our message and desire only the worldly life.
53:30. That is the extent of their knowledge. Your Lord knows best who has strayed from His path and who is following the right path.
53:31. Whatever is in the heavens and on earth belongs to God. He would

punish the evildoers for their deeds, and reward those who do well for their good deeds with what is best for them.

53:32. Your Lord will show great mercy to those who avoid the major sins and immoralities, but may have committed minor offenses. God has known you well since He created you from clay and when you were fetuses in your mothers' wombs. So do not claim your piety; He knows best who is really pious.

53:33. Prophet Muhammad, have you thought about the person* who turned away from faith,

53:34. gave a little, and then withheld?

**Walid bin Mugeria, a Meccan chief, was inclined to accept Islam. But his friend convinced him not to accept Islam by saying: Do not leave your forefathers' faith. If you are afraid of punishment in the hereafter, give me money so that I, instead of you, will bear the punishment in the hereafter. Walid agreed to that, paid him some but stopped short of paying the full amount.*

53:35. Does he, Walid bin Mugeria, has knowledge of the unseen that he sees the reality?

53:36. Has he not heard of what was in the Scriptures of Prophets Moses

53:37. and Abraham, who fulfilled the commandments?

53:38. That no one will bear someone else's burden;

53:39. each person will be judged by his own deeds;

53:40. his deeds will be scrutinized;

53:41. and he will be justly rewarded for them;

53:42. in the end, all shall return to God;

53:43. it is God who makes one laugh and weep;

53:44. He gives life and death;

53:45. He created pairs of the male and female,

53:46. from a sperm-drop of ejected semen;

53:47. and He will create again by Resurrection;

53:48. it is God who enriches and gives property;

53:49. He is the Lord of Sirius, the Dog-Star, the brightest star in the sky, worshipped by the Pagan-Arabs.

53:50. He destroyed the ancient people of Aad

53:51. and Thamoud; sparing no one;

53:52. and before them the people of Noah, because they were more wicked and rebellious.

53:53. God destroyed the cities of Sodom and Gomorrah where Prophet Lot's people lived,

53:54. and covered them by the water of the Dead-Sea.

53:55. O humans, which favors of your Lord will you deny?

53:56. This is a warning like the previous warnings.

53:57. The Day of Judgment is drawing near.
53:58. Beside God, no one can delay it.
53:59. Are these the things you wonder about,
53:60. laugh, instead of weeping,
53:61. and lost in your frivolous amusement?
53:62. Rather, you should prostrate to God and worship Him.

# CHAPTER 54

# THE MOON

**Name:** From Verse One.

**Verses:** 55

**Summary:**

- Theme: Warning to the Meccan-Disbelievers for their stubbornness against Prophet Muhammad's invitation to faith.
- God's splitting of the moon and joining it back in front of the disbelievers' eyes. It was an obvious sign of the truth of resurrection. As God split the moon and joined it back, He would cause everything to die and raise it again.
- Stories of the people of Noah, Aad, Thamoud, Lot, and Pharaoh. They remind the disbelievers of the terrible punishments these nations suffered when they disregarded the warnings given by God's Prophets. After each story, it is pointed out that it is easy to learn the Qur'an for avoiding the pitfalls in everyday life.
- The disbelievers have been told that God does not need to make lengthy preparations to bring about the Resurrection. As soon as He gives a command, it happens immediately. Everything has a destiny and everything happens at its appointed time. Everything the humans do, big or small, is being recorded to be used as witness on the Day of Judgment.

**By Verse**

In the name of God, the compassionate, the merciful:

54:1. The Hour of Judgment has come near, and the moon has split in two parts.

54:2. Yet, when the disbelievers see a sign, they turn away and say: It is a clever magic trick.

54:3. The disbelievers deny the truth and follow their desires. But, in the end, every matter shall be settled.

54:4. From the stories of the previous nations, information to restrain the disbelievers from evil has already come to them,

54:5. that has profound wisdom, but they have not benefited from it.

54:6. O Muhammad, leave them alone. The day the crier will call them to a terrifying event,

54:7. they will come out from their graves with downcast eyes, like

scattered locusts,
54:8. and rush toward the crier. The disbelievers will say: This is a terrible day.
54:9. Earlier than these disbelievers, the people of Noah denied Our signs. They rejected Our servant Noah and called him a madman. Rejected badly,
54:10. he cried to his Lord saying: I have been overpowered, Lord please help me.
54:11. We opened the gates of the heaven with pouring rain
54:12. and caused the earth to burst with gushing springs, and the two waters from the sky and the earth met for a purpose that was predestined.
54:13. We carried Noah on the boat made of planks and nails.
54:14. It sailed under Our supervision, as a reward for the one who had been rejected.
54:15. We made the boat a sign, but will anyone pay attention?
54:16. I warned them, and then see how severe was My punishment.
54:17. We have made the Qur'an easy to understand and to remember, but will anyone learn from it?
54:18. Aad's people rejected their Prophet Houd. I warned them, and then see how dreadful was My punishment.
54:19. On a day of continuous misfortune, We sent upon them a furious wind,
54:20. which swept them as if they were trunks of uprooted palm-trees.
54:21. I warned them, and then see how dreadful was My punishment.
54:22. We have made the Qur'an easy to understand and to remember, but will anyone learn from it?
54:23. Thamoud's people rejected our warnings.
54:24. They said: Should we follow a human being, Prophet Saleh, who is one of us? That would be in error and madness.
54:25. Has God revealed His message to him alone among us? He is a bragging liar.
54:26. We told the Prophet: Tomorrow, they will know who the bragging liar is.
54:27. We are sending a she-camel to test them. Watch their end with patience.
54:28. Tell them: The water will be shared between the camel and them, and each share will be equitably proportioned.
54:29. They called their companion, who hamstrung the camel.
54:30. Then, see how dreadful My punishment was after I warned them.
54:31. We sent upon them a mighty blast, and they became like the dry

twigs used by a fence maker.
54:32. We have made the Qur'an easy to understand and to remember, but will anyone learn from it?
54:33. The people of Lot denied the warning.
54:34. We sent upon them a torrent of stones, which destroyed them, but We saved Lot's family except his wife before dawn,
54:35. with Our mercy. Thus We reward the grateful.
54:36. Lot had warned them of Our punishment, but they doubted the warning.
54:37. They demanded from Lot his guests to have sex with them, but We blinded their eyes and said: Taste My punishment, when you have been warned.
54:38. At daybreak, heavy punishment came upon them.
54:39. So, taste My punishment when you have been warned.
54:40. We have made the Qur'an easy to understand and to remember, but will anyone learn from it?
54:41. The warning also came to Pharaoh's people.
54:42. But they rejected Our signs. So, We hit them with the punishment of the mighty, the all-powerful God.
54:43. Are your Meccan-Disbelievers better than the former ones, the people of Noah, Lot, Saleh, and Pharaoh, or do you have immunity in the Scriptures?
54:44. Or, do they say: We are a victorious army to defend ourselves?
54:45. Their army will be defeated and they will turn their backs and flee.
54:46. The promised time for their punishment is the Hour of Judgment, a most disastrous and bitter hour.
54:47. The guilty are in misunderstanding and madness.
54:48. The day they will be dragged into the fire on their faces, they will be told: Taste the touch of hell.
54:49. We have created everything with a destiny.
54:50. We command once, and Our will is done in the twinkling of an eye.
54:51. We already have destroyed many like you. Will anyone pay attention?
54:52. Whatever they have done has been written,
54:53. every small and big thing.
54:54. The righteous will live in gardens with rivers flowing,
54:55. seated honorably in the presence of a mighty king, God.

# CHAPTER 55

# THE MERCIFUL

**Name:** From Verse One.

**Verses:** 78

**Summary:**

- Theme: God's attributes and favors, and asking the mankind and the jinns: Which rewards and blessings of your Lord will you deny?
- Unique: This is the only chapter of the Qur'an in which the jinns have been addressed. The jinns are another creation on the earth that has freedom of will and action. The Qur'an is meant both for the mankind and the jinns and Prophet Muhammad's Prophethood is for both.
- God:
  - created mankind, and taught it the Qur'an, and how to speak for expressing feelings and thoughts.
  - is the Lord of the east and the west, and regulates oceans and their products, including ships sailing in them.
- All that exists will perish except God, Who is busy in mighty tasks all the time.
- No one can run away from God's jurisdiction.
- The sinners will be punished in hell.
- The righteous will be rewarded in paradise with lush gardens, springs, fruits, bashful virgins, and much more.

## By Verse

In the name of God, the compassionate, the merciful:

55:1. God is the merciful.
55:2. God has taught the Qur'an.
55:3. God has created the mankind.
55:4. God has taught the mankind to speak.
55:5. The sun and the moon follow a predetermined course.
55:6. The stars and the trees prostrate to God.
55:7. God has raised the heaven and put everything in balance.
55:8. Therefore, you should not disturb the balance.
55:9. Weigh justly and do not give short weight.
55:10. God made the earth for His creatures.

55:11. The earth has all kind of fruits and date-palm trees.
55:12. The earth has husk-covered grain and scented herbs.
55:13. So, O mankind and jinns, which favors of your Lord would you deny?
55:14. God created man from the dry ringing clay, like the baked pottery.
55:15. And God created the jinns from the smokeless fire.
55:16. So, O mankind and jinns, which wonders of your Lord would you deny?
55:17. God is the Lord of two easts and two wests*.

**The two indicate different points at which the sun rises and sets in the summer and the winter.*

55:18. So, O mankind and jinns, which blessings of your Lord would you deny?
55:19. God has made two seas of the salt water and the sweet water join.
55:20. Yet, there is a barrier between them which they cannot cross.
55:21. So, O mankind and jinns, which miracles of your Lord would you deny?
55:22. The pearls and corals come from both seas.
55:23. So, O mankind and jinns, which wonders of your Lord would you deny?
55:24. The ships that sail in the sea, like mountains, belong to God.
55:25. So, O mankind and jinns, which favors of your Lord would you deny?
55:26. Everything on the earth will perish.
55:27. Only God, Who is majestic and glorified, will remain.
55:28. So, O mankind and jinns, which favors of your Lord would you deny?
55:29. All those in heaven and on earth beg God to fulfill their needs. Every day, He is exercising His universal power.
55:30. So, O mankind and jinns, which powers of your Lord would you deny?
55:31. O mankind and jinns, We, God, will attend to you in due course.
55:32. So, O mankind and jinns, which favors of your Lord would you deny?
55:33. O mankind and jinns, if you have the power to escape from the confines of the heaven and the earth, do it. But you will not be able to do so without God's approval.
55:34. So, O mankind and jinns, which powers of your Lord would you deny?
55:35. If you will try to escape, you will face a flame of fire and smoke. You will not be able to defend against them.

55:36. So, O mankind and jinns, which powers of your Lord would you deny?
55:37. When the heaven will split and become like red hide.
55:38. So, O mankind and jinns, which wonders of your Lord would you deny?
55:39. That day, there will be no need to ask the mankind and the jinns about their sins.
55:40. So, O mankind and jinns, which powers of your Lord would you deny?
55:41. The wrongdoers will be known by their looks. They will be caught by their forelocks and feet and dragged.
55:42. So, O mankind and jinns, which powers of your Lord would you deny?
55:43. They will be told: This is the hell you used to deny.
55:44. They will keep wandering between the hell and the boiling water to quench their thirst.
55:45. So, O mankind and jinns, which favors of your Lord would you deny?
55:46. There will be two gardens for anyone who fears to stand before his Lord for judgment.
55:47. So, O mankind and jinns, which rewards of your Lord would you deny?
55:48. The gardens will have shade trees.
55:49. So, O mankind and jinns, which blessings of your Lord would you deny?
55:50. Each garden will be watered by two flowing springs.
55:51. So, O mankind and jinns, which favors of your Lord would you deny?
55:52. Both gardens will have two kinds of every fruit.
55:53. So, O mankind and jinns, which wonders of your Lord would you deny?
55:54. The believers will recline on couches lined with silk brocade, and within their reach will be the hanging fruits of the two gardens.
55:55. So, O mankind and jinns, which rewards of your Lord would you deny?
55:56. Ladies with modest gaze will be in the gardens, whom neither a man nor a jinn will have touched before.
55:57. So, O mankind and jinns, which rewards of your Lord would you deny?
55:58. Their beauty will be like that of the rubies and the pearls.
55:59. So, O mankind and jinns, which rewards of your Lord would you

deny?
55:60. How could there be any other reward than a good reward for doing good in the worldly life?
55:61. So, O mankind and jinns, which blessings of your Lord would you deny?
55:62. Besides, there will be two other gardens (in paradise).
55:63. So, O mankind and jinns, which rewards of your Lord would you deny?
55:64. The two gardens will be lush-green.
55:65. So, O mankind and jinns, which rewards of your Lord would you deny?
55:66. Each garden will have two gushing springs.
55:67. So, O mankind and jinns, which wonders of your Lord would you deny?
55:68. Each garden will have fruit-trees, date-palms, and pomegranates.
55:69. So, O mankind and jinns, which blessings of your Lord would you deny?
55:70. In each garden there will be beautiful women of good character.
55:71. So, O mankind and jinns, which rewards of your Lord would you deny?
55:72. There will be fair-color, beautiful virgins ladies guarded in pavilions.
55:73. So, O mankind and jinns, which rewards of your Lord would you deny?
55:74. They will not have been touched before by a man or a jinn.
55:75. So, O mankind and jinns, which rewards of your Lord would you deny?
55:76. The believers will recline on green cushions and rich carpets.
55:77. So, O mankind and jinns, which rewards of your Lord would you deny?
55:78. Your Lord's name is blessed. He is mighty and glorious.

# CHAPTER 56

# THE INEVITABLE EVENT

**Name:** From Verse One.

**Verses:** 96

**Summary:**

- Theme: The hereafter, God's oneness, and refutation of the disbelievers' suspicions about the Qur'an.
- In response to the disbelievers' strong belief that resurrection would never take place, God says that it will definitely take place.
- At resurrection, all people will be divided into three classes:

    1. The foremost in rank and position.
    2. The common righteous people.
    3. Those that denied the hereafter, persisted in disbelief, and kept on committing major sins till the last.

  How the first two classes will be rewarded and the third punished have been described.
- The disbelievers' suspicions about the Qur'an have been refuted. They have been made to realize that instead of deriving benefit from it, they were treating it with scant attention. It has been mentioned that when God decrees death, the disbelievers cannot save anybody from it.

**By Verse**

In the name of God, the compassionate, the merciful:

56:1. When the inevitable event, the Day of Resurrection, will occur,
56:2. no one will be able to deny it.
56:3. It will destroy everything by bringing down the standing things and raising the fallen ones.
56:4. The earth will be shaken up.
56:5. The mountains will be broken down into pieces,
56:6. and scattered like dust.
56:7. The humans will be divided into three groups:
56:8. Those on the right hand will be blessed.
56:9. Those on the left hand will be wretched.
56:10. And those in the front will be foremost in faith and its practice.
56:11. They will be nearest to God.

56:12. They will live in the gardens of joy.
56:13. Most of them will be from the old generations,
56:14. and some will be from the later generations.
56:15. On decorated couches,
56:16. they will recline, facing each other.
56:17. Ever-young boys will serve them,
56:18. with bowls, jugs, and cups filled with wine from a flowing spring.
56:19. The wine will neither intoxicate them nor give them headache.
56:20. The boys will present them fruits of their choice,
56:21. and fowls' meat of their liking.
56:22. They will have the company of beautiful ladies with beautiful eyes.
56:23. Their beauty will be like that of the well-guarded pearls.
56:24. That will be the reward of their good deeds in the world.
56:25. There, they will hear neither idle talk, nor sinful speech,
56:26. but good talk only.
56:27. Those on the right hand, how happy they will be.
56:28. They will be among the lote-trees without thorns,
56:29. and clustered banana trees,
56:30. and extended shade,
56:31. and flowing water,
56:32. and plentiful fruits,
56:33. irrespective of the season, and limitless in quantity.
56:34. They will recline on couches raised high.
56:35. We will provide special ladies for them.
56:36. They will be virgins,
56:37. devoted to their husbands, equal in age.
56:38. All this will be for the people on the right.
56:39. Most of them will be from the earlier,
56:40. and the later generations.
56:41. Those on the left will be unfortunate.
56:42. They will be in scorching fire, boiling water,
56:43. and shade of black smoke,
56:44. which neither will be cool nor refreshing.
56:45. Earlier, they lived in comfort,
56:46. persisted in great sin,
56:47. saying: When we are dead and turn to dust and bones, shall we be raised to life again,
56:48. with our forefathers?
56:49. O Muhammad, tell them: Surely, the former and the later generations

56:50. will be gathered on an appointed Day of Judgment.
56:51. The sinners, who denied the truth,
56:52. will eat the fruit of the cursed Zaqqum tree,
56:53. fill their bellies with it,
56:54. and drink boiling water,
56:55. like thirsty camels.
56:56. That will be their fate on the Day of Judgment.
56:57. We have created you. Then why do not you believe?
56:58. Have you considered the semen you discharge?
56:59. Did you or We create the child from the semen?
56:60. We have decreed death for you. Nothing can prevent Us from
56:61. changing your figures and creating you in forms not known to you.
56:62. You certainly know of the first creation. So, why do not you reflect?
56:63. Have you thought about the seeds you sow?
56:64. Do you or We make them grow into crops?
56:65. If We willed, we could turn the crops into chaff for you to wonder
56:66. and say: We are burdened with debt,
56:67. and are ruined.
56:68. Have you thought about the water you drink?
56:69. Do you or We bring it down from the cloud as rain?
56:70. If We wanted, We could make it bitter. Why then are you not grateful?
56:71. Have you thought about the firewood you ignite?
56:72. Is it you or We Who grow the firewood tree?
56:73. We have made it a reminder for mankind and a provision for the needy.
56:74. Therefore, glorify the name of your Lord, the supreme one.
56:75. I, God, swear by the setting of the stars.
56:76. It is a great oath, if you knew
56:77. that this is the glorious Qur'an,
56:78. written in a book well-guarded in the heaven.
56:79. No one except the purified angels can touch it.
56:80. It is a revelation from the Lord of the universe.
56:81. Are you indifferent to this Scripture?
56:82. And make it your daily task, like earning a living, to deny it?
56:83. Why then, when the soul of a dying person is about to leave him,
56:84. you are helplessly watching him;
56:85. at that time, We are nearer to him than you, but you cannot see Us;
56:86. then why do not you, if you are excused from the judgment in the hereafter,

56:87. restore his soul, if you are truthful?
56:88. If the deceased is among the nearest to God,
56:89. there will be peacefulness, excellent livelihood, and a garden of pleasure for him.
56:90. If he is among those on the right hand,
56:91. they will greet him with: Peace be upon you.
56:92. But if he is among the disbelievers who has gone off the right path,
56:93. his welcome will be the boiling water
56:94. and he will burn in hell.
56:95. This is surely the absolute truth.
56:96. Therefore, glorify the name of your Lord, the supreme one.

# CHAPTER 57

# THE IRON

**Name:** From Verse 25.

**Verses:** 29

**Summary:**

- Theme: Persuading Muslims to make monetary sacrifices when they were engaged in a life and death struggle against the Arab-Paganism.
- All that is in the heavens and on earth glorifies God. He created the heavens and the earth in six days and has knowledge of everything.
- Those who spend in charity will be repaid manifold and in addition rewarded richly. God has sent down iron for the benefit of mankind.
- Those who sacrifice their lives and expend their wealth to promote Islam's cause, when it is already strong, cannot attain the rank of those who struggled with their lives and wealth to promote it when it was weak.
- On the Day of Judgment, the true believers will have their light shining before them while the hypocrites will have their fate no different than the disbelievers.
- The worldly life is but play, amusement and illusion. God has pre-ordained the good fortune and hardships in the world. Do not grieve for the things that you miss, and do not overjoy at what you gain.
- Prophets Noah, Abraham and Jesus were sent for guidance to the right way. People themselves have instituted the reclusive life of monks and nuns characterized by celibacy, poverty, and obedience.

### By Verse

In the name of God, the compassionate, the merciful:

57:1. Everything in the heavens and on earth glorifies God. He is the mighty, the wise.

57:2. He is the king of the heavens and the earth. He gives life and death and has power over all things.

57:3. He is the first and the last, the visible and the unseen. He has knowledge of all things.

57:4. God created the heavens and the earth in six days, then sat on His throne. He knows what enters into the earth and what comes out of it, what comes down from the heaven and what rises to it. He is with you wherever you are. God sees all your deeds.

57:5. His is the kingdom of the heavens and earth. All matters are referred to God for decision.

57:6. He makes the night to follow the day, and the day to follow the night. He knows the innermost thoughts of humans.

57:7. You should believe in God and His Messenger Prophet Muhammad. Give in charity from what He has entrusted you. There is a great reward for those who believe and give in charity.

57:8. Why do you not believe in God while the Messenger invites you to believe in your Lord, who has made an agreement with you, if you are true believers?

57:9. It is God who sends down clear revelations to His servant Muhammad, so that he may bring you out from darkness into light. God is kind and merciful to you.

57:10. Why do you not spend in God's cause, when everything in the heavens and the earth belongs to Him? Those who spent and fought, before the victory, are higher in honor than those who spent and fought afterwards. However, God has promised both a good reward. God knows all you do.

57:11. Who will give a good loan to God so that He may return it manifold with an additional rich reward?

57:12. On the Day of Judgment, you shall see the believing men and women with their light shining before them and by their right hands, and a voice saying to them: There is good news for you this day. You shall enter gardens watered by running streams to live there forever. That is indeed the highest achievement.

57:13. That day, the hypocrite men and women will say to the believers: Wait for us so that we may benefit from your light. But, they will be told: Go back and seek some other light. A wall, with a door, will be placed before them. There will be mercy inside the door and misery on the outside.

57:14. The hypocrites will call the believers: Were we not with you? The believers will reply: Yes, but you led yourselves into temptations, looked forward to our destruction, doubted faith, and were deceived by false desires, till God's will was done and Satan deceived you about God.

57:15. Today, no ransom will be accepted from you and the disbelievers. Your home is hell. You justly deserve it. It is an ignoble end.

57:16. Has the time not come for the believers to engage in God's remembrance and submit to the truth which has been revealed to them? So that they may not become like those who were given

Scriptures before this, but their hearts hardened with time? Many among them were wrongdoers.

57:17. You should know that God gives life to the earth after its lifelessness. We have made clear to you the signs; perhaps you will understand.

57:18. The men and women who give charity, and have given a good loan to God, shall be repaid many fold. They will have a noble reward.

57:19. Those who believe in God and His Messengers are truthful and will testify in their Lord's presence. They shall have their reward and their light. But those who reject God and deny Our revelations are the companions of hell.

57:20. You should know that the life of the world is but a sport and a pastime, for show and boasting among you, and a quest for greater wealth and children. It is like vegetation that grows after rain for farmers' pleasure, but afterward it dries up, turns yellow, and becomes straw. In contrast, in the hereafter, there is a severe punishment or God's forgiveness and pleasure. The worldly life is an illusion of enjoyment.

57:21. You should race toward your Lord's forgiveness and a garden whose width is like the width of the heavens and the earth, prepared for those who believe in God and His Messengers. That is God's blessing which He gives to whom He wills. God's grace is infinite.

57:22. No disaster befalls the earth or the humans without it being prerecorded in a register. That is easy for God to do.

57:23. The reason for that is that you should not despair over what you have failed to get and not boast over what He has given you. God does not like the prideful boasters, and

57:24. those who are miser and encourage others to be miserly. Anyone who pays no attention to it should know that God is free of all wants, and is worthy of praise.

57:25. We have sent Our Messengers with clear proofs, the Scriptures, and the scale of justice, so that humans could conduct themselves with justice. We sent down iron on earth, which has strength and beneficial uses for the people, so that God may know those who support Him unseen and His Messengers. God is powerful and mighty.

57:26. We sent Prophets Noah and Abraham, and gave their descendants Prophethood and Scriptures. Some of them were rightly guided, but many were disobedient.

57:27. After them, We sent other Messengers, followed by Jesus, the son of Mary. We gave him the Gospel and put compassion and mercy in the hearts of his followers. As for the reclusive life of monks and nuns, they invented it themselves for pleasing God, though We did not prescribe it for them. But they did not observe it faithfully. We rewarded only those who were true believers, but many were evildoers.

57:28. Believers, fear God and trust His Messenger Prophet Muhammad. God will give you His double mercy, a light for you to walk, and forgive you. God is forgiving and merciful.

57:29. Let the people of the Scriptures (Jews and Christians) know that they have no control over the grace of God, which is in His hands alone. He gives it to whom He wills. God's grace is infinite.

# CHAPTER 58

# THE PLEADING WOMAN

**Name:** From Verse One.

**Verses:** 22

**Summary:**

- Instructions to Muslims about the problems that confronted them at that time.
- The Arab-Pagans' practice of divorce, by calling one's wife like his mother, has been prohibited. A penalty has been prescribed for nullifying it.
- God is present whenever and wherever people converse in secret. The secret counsels except about virtue and piety are forbidden. Conspiring in secret is Satan's work.
- During meetings, room should be made for others and people should leave at the end of a meeting rather than lingering behind to cause difficulty for Prophet Muhammad.
- A Muslim should give charity before consulting the Prophet in private. Alternatives have been described for the one who cannot do so.
- People who befriend those with whom God is angry will be severely punished. True believers do not befriend those who oppose God and His Messenger.

## By Verse

In the name of God, the compassionate, the merciful:

58:1. God has heard the plea of the woman* who is pleading with you, Prophet Muhammad, about her husband and is complaining to God. God is hearing the dialogue between the two of you. God hears and sees everything.

**Khaula, Tha'alaba's daughter, was complaining about the divorce her husband, Owas, son of Samit, gave her on the ground that he called her "mother."*

58:2. Those who divorce their wives by declaring them to be like their mothers* should know that they are not like their mothers. Their mothers are only those who gave them birth. What they are saying is objectionable and false. But God is forgiving and merciful.

**God forbade the Arab-Pagans' custom.*

58:3. Those who divorce their wives by declaring them to be like their mothers and would like to retract what they have said should free a slave before touching their wives. That is your penalty. God is aware of your deeds.

58:4. He who does not have a slave to free will fast for two consecutive months before touching his wife. If he is unable to fast, he should feed 60 poor people. God has ordered that for the believers, so that you may believe in God and His Messenger. God has set these limits. There will be a painful punishment for the disbelievers.

58:5. Those who oppose God and His Messenger will be disgraced, as those before them were disgraced. We have sent down clear revelations. The disbelievers will have disgraceful punishment.

58:6. On the Day of Judgment, God will bring them back to life and tell them of what they did. They may have forgotten about their deeds, but God recorded them. God witnesses all things.

58:7. Do you not know that God knows what is in the heavens and on earth? In a private conversation among three persons, God is the fourth one; if there are five, God is the sixth one; and if there are fewer or more than that and wherever they may be, God is with them. On the Day of Resurrection, God will inform them of their deeds. God knows all things.

58:8. Have you not seen those who were forbidden to conspire, but they did? They plotted together sinfully for hostility and disobedience to the Messenger. When they come to you, they greet you with words with which God does not greet you, and they ask themselves: Why does God not punish us for what we say? Hell will suffice for them; they will burn in it and face a bad end.

58:9. Believers, when you converse privately, do not converse about sin, aggression, and disobedience to the Messenger, but converse about righteousness and piety. Fear God, before Whom you will be gathered.

58:10. Conspiracy is Satan's work, so that he may cause grief to the believers. But he cannot harm them without God's permission. The believers should put their trust in God.

58:11. Believers, make room in your assemblies when you are told to do so; God will make room for you. When it is said to get up to leave*, do so. God will raise the rank of those who have faith and knowledge among you. God is aware of what you do.

**Some people delayed leaving at the end of assembly with Prophet Muhammad. That caused difficulty for the Prophet.*

58:12. Believers, give charity before private consultation with the Prophet. That is better and purer for you. But, if you do not have the means for charity, know that God is forgiving and merciful.
58:13. Are you afraid to give charity before your private consultation with the Prophet? If that is the case, God forgives you, but at least establish prayer, give Zakat (mandatory charity), and obey God and His Messenger. God is aware of what you do.
58:14. Have you not seen the hypocrites who befriend a people* with whom God is angry? They are neither with you nor with them*. They knowingly are swearing falsely.

**The Jews of Medina.*

58:15. God has prepared severe punishment for them. Their deeds are evil.
58:16. They use their oaths as a cover to stop people from God's way. They will have a humiliating punishment.
58:17. Neither their wealth nor children will protect them from God. They are companions of the hell and will live there forever.
58:18. On the Day of Judgment, God will restore them to life, and they will swear to Him as they swear to you, thinking that it will help them. Unquestionably, they are liars.
58:19. Satan has overtaken them and made them forget God's remembrance. They are Satan's party, which surely will lose.
58:20. Those who oppose God and His Messenger will be humiliated.
58:21. God has decreed that He and His Messengers shall be victorious. God is powerful and mighty.
58:22. You will not find those who believe in God and the last day befriending the opponents of God and His Messenger, even if they were their fathers, sons, brothers, or relatives. God has given their hearts faith and strengthened them with His spirit. God will admit them to gardens watered by flowing streams, where they will live forever. God is pleased with them, and they are pleased with Him. They are God's party, which unquestionably will be successful.

# CHAPTER 59

# THE GATHERING

**Name:** From Verse Two.

**Verses:** 24

**Background:**

For understanding the subject of Muslims' battle against the Jewish tribe of Bani An-Nadhir, it would be useful to look at the history of the Jews in Medina. Per Syed Abu-Ala Maududi:

> In A. D. 132, the Romans expelled the Jews from Palestine. Many of the Jewish tribes fled to Hejaz along the Red Sea and the Gulf of Aqaba, contiguous to and south of Palestine. Among the tribes that settled in Medina, Bani Al-Nadhir and Bani Quraizah were prominent for being the priest class. About three centuries later, around A. D. 450, a great flood occurred in Yemen and its different tribes left. Among them were the pagan tribes of Aus and Khazraj, who settled in Medina.
>
> Before Prophet Muhammad's arrival at Medina, the following were the main features of the Jews' position in Hejaz in general and in Medina in particular:
>
> - For their survival, the Jews adopted the local language, dress, civilization and the way of life. But they kept their Jewish prejudice alive.
> - The Jews were more interested in their trade and business than in the preaching of their religion. That is why Judaism did not spread as a religion in the area.
> - The Jews were economically stronger than the Arabs, because they had emigrated from more civilized and culturally advanced countries of Palestine and Syria. They lent money to Arabs on high interest rates and charge them compound interest. They made Arabs economically hollow. That made them hate the Jews.
> - The demand of their trade and the economic interests made the Jews have alliances with other tribes. In Medina, Bani Quraizah and Bani An-Nadhir were allies of Aus while Bani Qainuqa was of Khazraj. A little before Prophet Muhammad's emigration to Medina, these Jewish tribes had fought each other in support of their respective allies in the bloody war that took place between

Aus and Khazraj.

Such were the conditions when Islam came to Medina. One of the first things that Prophet Muhammad accomplished soon after establishing the Muslim State was the unification of Aus, Khazraj, and the emigrant Muslims into a brotherhood.

The second thing was that he concluded a treaty between the Muslims and the Jews, in which it was pledged that neither party would encroach on the rights of the other and both would unite in a joint defense against the external enemies. However, not very long after, the Jews began showing hostility towards Prophet Muhammad and the Muslims. The Jews did not like:

1. Prophet Muhammad inviting them to believe in God, his Prophethood, and the Qur'an.
2. The Muslims emigrants, the tribes of Aus and Khazraj, and the Arab tribes of the surrounding areas were forming a brotherhood. The Jews were afraid that their policy of sowing discord among the Arab tribes for the promotion of their own wellbeing and interests would not work in the new system.
3. Prophet Muhammad putting an end to all unlawful methods in business and mutual dealings, including the taking of interest. In that, they saw their own economic disaster and death.

For these reasons, they made resistance and opposition to Prophet Muhammad their national ideal. They incited the Meccan-Disbelievers, against the Muslims in Medina, and helped the disbelievers in fighting with the Muslims. The Tribe of Bani An-Nadhir even plotted to kill Prophet Muhammad. Accordingly, there was no question of showing them any further concession. Prophet Muhammad sent to them the ultimatum that the treachery they had meditated against him had come to his knowledge. Therefore, they were to leave Medina within 10 days. Otherwise, they would be forced to leave.

The Arab tribes that were enemies of the Muslims told the Jewish Tribe of Bani An-Nadhir that they will help them and they should stand firm and not go. They responded to Prophet Muhammad's ultimatum saying that they would not leave Medina and he could do whatever was in his power. Consequently, Prophet Muhammad laid siege to them, and after a few days of the siege, they agreed to leave Medina on the condition that they could retain all their property which they could carry on their camels, except the armor. Thus, Medina was rid of another mischievous Jewish tribe.

**Summary:**

- Prophet Muhammad's order of exile given to the Jewish tribe of Bani An-Nadhir for their mutiny against the Islamic state.
- God's decree regarding the distribution of Bani An-Nadhir's belongings.
- Good qualities of the true immigrants and the residents of Medina.
- The hypocrites' conspiracy with the Jews.
- Satan's treacherous behavior with humans.
- What each person is sending for the hereafter.
- The stone-heartedness of the Arabian pagans.
- God's 15 exclusive attributes.

## By Verse

In the name of God, the compassionate, the merciful:

59:1. Everything in the heavens and on earth glorifies God. He is the mighty, the wise.

59:2. It was God Who drove the disbelievers among the Jews out of their homes at the first gathering of the forces. You did not think that they would go, and they also thought that their strongholds would protect them from God. But God's punishment came upon them from an unexpected place. It cast terror in their hearts so that their houses were ruined by their own hands and the hands of the believers. Learn from their example, O people of vision.

59:3. Had God not decreed exile for the Jews, He would certainly have punished them in this world. But in the hereafter, they shall be punished in the hellfire.

59:4. That is because they opposed God and His Messenger. Anyone who opposes God should know that God is severe in punishment.

59:5. It was God who gave you permission to cut down or spare their palm-trees, so that God could humiliate the evildoers.

59:6. God gave the enemy's spoils to His Messenger, for which you did not spur your horses and camels. God gives His Messenger authority over whom He wills. He has power over all things.

59:7. What God gives to His Messenger from the spoils of people of the towns, it is for God, the Messenger, his relatives, orphans, and travelers. It will not become the property of the rich among you. Accept whatever the Messenger gives or holds from you. Fear God, who is severe in punishment.

59:8. A share of the spoils is for the poor Muslim emigrants who were expelled from their homes and properties in Mecca, seek God's grace and pleasure, and support God and His Messenger. These are the true believers.

59:9. A part of the spoils is also for the residents of Medina, who accepted faith before arrival of the emigrants in Medina, love the emigrants, do not wish for what the emigrants are given, but give the emigrants preference over themselves, even though they are in need. Those who protect themselves from greed will be successful.

59:10. There is a share for those Muslims who came into Islam after them. They say: Lord:

- Forgive us and our brothers who preceded us in faith.
- Do not put any resentment in our hearts toward the believers.
- You are kind and merciful.

59:11. Have you not seen the hypocrites? They say to their fellow-disbelievers among the Jews: If you are expelled, we will go with you. We will not obey anyone, who will harm you. If you are attacked, we will surely help you. But God is witness that they are liars.

59:12. If the Jews are expelled, the hypocrites will not leave with them. If they are attacked, they will not help them. Even if they go to help them, they will turn their backs and run away, and leave them without help.

59:13. Within the hypocrites' hearts, they are afraid of you more than God. That is because they lack understanding.

59:14. The hypocrites will not fight with you in the open as a group except in fortified cities or from behind the walls. Their infighting is severe. You think they are united, but their hearts are divided. That is because they lack reasoning.

59:15. They are like those* who were punished shortly before them. They tasted the bad consequence of their deeds. A painful punishment is waiting for them.

**The Meccan-Disbelievers and the Jewish Tribe of Qainuqa.*

59:16. The hypocrites are like Satan, who asks man to disbelieve and when he does, says: I disassociate from you. I fear God, the Lord of the universe.

59:17. They both will end up in hell and live there forever.

59:18. Believers, fear God. Let every person consider what it has done for the Day of Judgment. Be careful of your duty to God, for He is aware of what you do.

59:19. Do not be like those who forgot God, so that He made them forget themselves. They are evildoers.

59:20. Those going to hell shall not be equal to those going to paradise. Those living in paradise alone will be successful.

59:21. Had We sent down this Qur'an upon a mountain, you would have seen it humbled and coming apart from God's fear. We present these examples to people so that they may think.

59:22. He is God, beside Him there is no other god. He knows the visible and the invisible. He is the compassionate, the merciful.

59:23. He is God, beside Him there is no other god. He is the king, the holy, the giver of peace, the keeper of faith, the guardian, the majestic, the enforcer of His decrees, and the most high. He is above the partners they associate with Him.

59:24. He is God, the creator, the inventor, and the modeler. He has the best names. Whatever is in the heavens and on earth is glorifying Him. He is the mighty, the wise.

# CHAPTER 60

# THE WOMAN TO BE EXAMINED

**Name:** From Verse 10.

**Verses:** 13

**Summary:**

- The immigrant women, who claim to be Muslims, should be examined for their faith. If found truthful, they should not be returned to their unbelieving husbands.
- God's instructions not to befriend the enemies of God and the Muslims. But, God does not forbid you to deal justly and kindly with those who did not fight with you because of religion and did not drive you out of your homes.
- Do not befriend anyone with whom God is angry.
- Prophet Abraham and his companions' conduct and prayer are excellent examples for the believers.

**By Verse**

In the name of God, the compassionate, the merciful:

60:1. Believers, do not befriend your and My enemies. Would you offer them love while they have denied the truth that has been revealed to you, and driven you and the Messenger out of your city Mecca because you believe in God, your Lord? If you strive for My cause and seek My pleasure, how can you love them? You send them friendly messages secretly*, whereas I know whatever you do secretly and openly. Anyone of you who does this will go off the straight path.

**Hatib bin Abi Baltahah sent a letter to the Meccan-Disbelievers that Prophet Muhammad was planning to invade their city.*

60:2. If they were to overpower you, they will be your enemies, and use their hands and tongues to harm you. They long to see you disbelieve.

60:3. On the Day of Resurrection, neither your relatives nor your children will benefit you. God will separate you from them. He sees what you do.

60:4. You have a good example in Prophet Abraham and those with him. They said to their people: We disassociate from you and the idols you worship beside God. We reject you. There will be animosity and hatred between us until you would believe in God alone. But what Prophet said to his father is exempt: I will ask God to forgive you, but I have no power to save you from God's punishment. Abraham and his companions prayed: Lord, we have put our trust in You, we will return to You, and You are our final destination.

60:5. Lord, do not make us a prey for the disbelievers, and forgive us. You are the mighty, the wise.

60:6. In the conduct of Prophet Abraham and his companions, there is a good example for you and those who look forward to meeting God and the last day. Whoever turns away from this should know that God is free of all wants and is worthy of all praise.

60:7. It is possible that God may make friendship between your enemies and you. God has power over all things. He is the forgiving and the merciful.

60:8. God does not forbid you to deal justly and kindly with those who did not fight with you because of religion and did not drive you out of your homes. God loves those who are just.

60:9. God forbids you to befriend those who fought against you because of religion, have driven you out of your homes, and have helped others to drive you out. Those who befriend them are wrongdoers.

60:10. Believers, when the believing women come to you as emigrants, examine their faith. God best knows their faith. If you find them to be believers, do not return them to the disbelievers; they are neither lawful wives for them, nor they are lawful husbands for them. But, give the disbelievers the dowries they gave them. There is no blame upon you if you marry them, provided you give them their dowries. Do not hold on to your marriage with the disbelieving women, but ask for the dowries you have given them and let the disbelievers do the same. That is God's decision. He judges between you. God is the all-knowing and the wise.

60:11. If any of the believers' wives have gone over to the disbelievers and afterward you triumph over them, and get some spoils from the disbelievers, then pay those believers whose wives have gone over equivalent of the dowries they had paid their wives. Fear God, if you are believers.

60:12. O Prophet, if believing women come to you for taking an oath of allegiance and pledge that they will not worship anyone but God, will not steal, commit adultery, kill their children, invent a lie, and disobey you for what is right, accept their oath and ask God to forgive them. God is forgiving and merciful.

60:13. Believers, do not befriend those with whom God is angry. They have lost hope of the life to come in the hereafter, just as the disbelievers lying in graves have lost hope.

# CHAPTER 61

# THE BATTLE FORMATION

**Name:** From Verse Four.

**Verses:** 14

**Summary:**

- Theme: Muslims should be sincere in faith and strive in God's cause with their wealth and lives. God:
    - addresses the Muslims of both the weak and strong faith, and the hypocrites.
    - warns Prophet Muhammad's community that their attitude towards him and Islam should not be like that of the Israelites towards Prophets Moses and Jesus.
- God's:
    - warning to the believers for saying something that they do not do.
    - proclamation that the Jews, Christians, and hypocrites may try hard to extinguish God's light, but it will shine. The religion brought by God's Messenger shall prevail over every other religion despite the disbelievers' dislike.
    - promise to the believers to give them paradise, help, and imminent victory over their enemies.
- Prophet Jesus gave good news of a Messenger coming after him whose name would be Ahmad, another name of Prophet Muhammad.

### By Verse

In the name of God, the compassionate, the merciful:

61:1. Everything in the heavens and on earth glorifies God. He is the all-mighty, the all-wise.

61:2. Believers, why do you say what you do not do?

61:3. God hates for you to say what you do not do.

61:4. God loves those who fight in His cause standing in battle formation, as if they were a solid structure.

61:5. Tell about Moses, who said to his people: Why do you hurt me, when you know that God has sent me to you? And when they went off the right path, God turned their hearts off the right path. God does not guide the rebellious people.

61:6. And tell about what Jesus, the son of Mary, said to Israelites: God has sent me to you to confirm the Torah, which has already been revealed to you, and to bring you good news of a Messenger to come after me, whose name is Ahmad, the praised one (another name of Prophet Muhammad). But when that Messenger came to them with clear signs, they said: This is plain magic.

61:7. Who is more unjust than the one who invents a lie about God when he is being invited to Islam? God does not guide the wrongdoers.

61:8. They want to blow out God's light with their mouths, but God will spread His light, even though the disbelievers may dislike it.

61:9. It is God, Who has sent His Messenger Muhammad with guidance and the religion of truth to make it victorious over all other religions even though the disbelievers may dislike it.

61:10. Believers, shall I lead you to a bargain that will save you from a grievous punishment?

61:11. Believe in God and His Messenger and strive in God's cause with your wealth and lives. That is best for you, if you knew.

61:12. God will forgive your sins and admit you to gardens watered by flowing rivers. There, He will provide you pleasant mansions to live there forever. That is the great achievement.

61:13. And God will give you another blessing which you desire: God's help and an imminent victory. O Prophet, give good news to the believers.

61:14. Believers, be God's helpers, like when Jesus, Mary's son, asked his disciples: Who are my helpers for God? The disciples replied: We are God's helpers. Some of the Israelites believed in him while others did not. We supported the believers against their enemy, and they triumphed over them.

# Chapter 62

## THE ASSEMBLY-PRAYER

**Name:** From Verse Nine.

**Verses:** 11

**Summary:**

- Theme: Refuting the Jews' claim to be God's favorites, and instructing Muslims about the etiquettes of the Friday assembly-prayer.
- Among the Meccan-Disbelievers, God has sent a Messenger of their own to purify them and teach them the Qur'an and wisdom.
- Jews claim to be favored alone by God, but they will never wish for death because of their deeds. They did not practice the law of Prophet Moses.
- When called for the Friday assembly-prayer, believers should hasten to God's remembrance and stop trading. When the prayer has ended, disperse and seek God's bounty.

**By Verse**

In the name of God, the compassionate, the merciful:

62:1. Everything in the heaven and on earth glorifies God. He is the king, holy, mighty, and wise.

62:2. It is God Who has sent among the unlettered people from among themselves, a Messenger of their own. He recites God's revelations to them, purifies them, and teaches them the Qur'an and wisdom. Before this, they have been in clear error.

62:3. And he is also the Prophet for those who have not yet joined in. God is all-mighty and all-wise.

62:4. That is God's blessing, which He gives to whom He wills. God's blessing is infinite.

62:5. The likeness of those who were entrusted with the law of Moses, but did not practice it, is that of a donkey carrying books, but learning nothing from them. Worse than that is the likeness of the people who deny God's revelations. God does not guide the wrongdoers.

62:6. O Muhammad, say to the Jews: If your claim is true that you alone are favored by God, then you should wish for death.

62:7. But, they will never wish for death because of their deeds. God knows the wrongdoers.

62:8. O Muhammad, tell them: The death from which you are running away will surely meet you. Then, you will be sent to God who knows the visible and the invisible. He will tell you what you used to do.

62:9. Believers, when you are called for the Friday assembly-prayer, hasten to God's remembrance and stop trading. That is better for you, if you only knew.

62:10. When the prayer has ended, disperse and seek God's bounty. Remember God often so that you may be successful.

62:11. When they see commercial merchandise and amusement, they rush to it eagerly, and leave you standing.* Prophet Muhammad, tell them: What God has is better than any merchandise and amusement. God is the most charitable provider.

**A commercial caravan came to sell its merchandise in Medina. It beat drums for people to know about the caravan. A lot of people left Prophet Muhammad's sermon to buy the merchandise.*

# CHAPTER 63

# THE HYPOCRITES

**Name:** From Verse One

**Verses:** 11

**Background:**

Before Prophet Muhammad's immigration to Medina, the tribes of Aus and Khazraj had agreed on the leadership of Abdullah bin Ubayy, the chief of the Khazraj. They were making preparations to crown him their king. However, before his crowning, a delegation from Medina went to Mecca and invited Prophet Muhammad to immigrate to Medina. When the Prophet arrived in Medina, Islam had penetrated every house of Medina. Abdullah bin Ubayy became helpless and to save his leadership became a Muslim himself. But his heart was burning with rage and filled with grief because the Prophet's arrival in Medina deprived him of his anticipated kingship. For several years, his hypocritical faith and grief resulted in harming Muslims in different ways. These were the circumstances under which God revealed this chapter.

**Summary:**

- Theme: The hypocrites' conduct and attitude.
- The hypocrites are such enemies of Islam and Muslims that even Prophet's prayer cannot obtain God's forgiveness for them.
- Do not let your riches or children distract you from God's remembrance, otherwise you become real losers.

**By Verse**

In the name of God, the compassionate, the merciful:

63:1. O Muhammad, when the hypocrites come to you, they say: We bear witness that you are indeed God's Messenger. God knows that you are indeed His Messenger, but God bears witness that the hypocrites are indeed liars.

63:2. They have made their faith a cover for their hypocrisy. They obstruct others from God's way. Evil is what they do.

63:3. That is because they first believed, then disbelieved. Their hearts have been sealed, so they do not understand.

63:4. When you look at the hypocrites, their appearances impress you, and when they speak, you listen to them. But, they are like propped-up wooden pieces clad in garments. They consider every battle cry is against them. They are the enemy. Therefore, beware of them. God may destroy them. How immoral they are?

63:5. When it is said to them: Come, God's Messenger will pray to God for your forgiveness; they turn aside their heads, and you see them turning away in arrogance.

63:6. Whether you pray for their forgiveness or not, is all the same for them. God will not forgive them. God does not guide the evildoers.

63:7. They are the ones who say: Give nothing to those who are with God's Messenger, so that they may desert him. The treasures of the heavens and the earth belong to God, but the hypocrites do not understand.

63:8. They say: If we return to Medina, the strong* will drive out the weak. But might belongs to God, His Messenger, and the believers; yet the hypocrites do not know it.

**Abdullah bin Ubayy, the chief of the Khazraj Tribe, said that. When Prophet Muhammad learnt of it, he asked him. He denied it. God revealed this verse to expose his lie.*

63:9. Believers, let neither your wealth nor children distract you from God's remembrance. Those who do so, they will be losers.

63:10. Give in charity from what We have provided you before death comes to you and you say: Lord, reprieve me for a while, so that I would give in charity and be among the righteous.

63:11. But God does not reprieve anyone when the person's term has expired. God is aware of what you do.

# CHAPTER 64

# THE MUTUAL LOSS AND GAIN

**Name:** From Verse Nine.

**Verses:** 18

**Summary:**

- Theme: An invitation to the faith, obedience to God and His Messenger, and teaching of good morals.
- The chapter contains four truths:
    1. The universe is not godless.
    2. The universe has a purpose.
    3. God has created humans for a purpose.
    4. Humans are responsible for their deeds and will ultimately return to their creator.
- The chapter addresses the disbelievers and the believers.
- The disbelievers have been told that the fundamental causes of the nations' destruction were their refusal to believe in God's Messengers, whom He sent for their guidance, and their rejection of the hereafter. Accordingly, the disbelievers have been admonished to wake up and believe in God, His Messenger, the Qur'an, and the hereafter.
- The believers have been given the following instructions:
    - No misfortune befalls a person without God's permission. Whoever remains steadfast to the faith, God guides him.
    - The believers should not only affirm the faith by tongue, but should obey God and His Messenger in their daily lives.
    - A believer should place his trust in God alone and not in his own power.
    - The worldly goods and children are a trial of distraction from the path of faith and obedience. Therefore, the believers should beware that some of their children and wives could be their enemies.
    - Every man is responsible only to the extent of his power and ability.

## By Verse

In the name of God, the compassionate, the merciful:

64:1. Everything in the heavens and on earth glorifies God. He is the king and praiseworthy. He has power over all things.

64:2. God created you. Some of you have become the disbelievers and some believers. God sees all that you do.

64:3. God created the heavens and the earth truthfully. He fashioned you in beautiful shape. You will return to Him.

64:4. God knows what:

- is in the heavens and on earth;
- you conceal and reveal; and
- what your innermost thoughts are.

64:5. Have you not heard of those who disbelieved before you? They tasted the evil result of their conduct, and yet a painful punishment awaits them in the hereafter.

64:6. That was because their Messengers brought them clear proofs, but they said: Shall humans guide us? They disbelieved and turned away from the truth. So God became indifferent to them. God is free of all needs and is praiseworthy.

64:7. The disbelievers deny the Resurrection. O Muhammad, tell them: By my Lord, you will surely be resurrected; then you will be told of what you did. That is easy for God to do.

64:8. Therefore, believe in God, His Messenger, and the Qur'an, which We have sent down. God is aware of what you do.

64:9. You will know of that when God will assemble you on the Day of Gathering. That will be the day of mutual loss and gain. Whoever believes in God and does good, God will forgive his sins and admit him to gardens, watered by flowing streams, to live there forever. That will be the great achievement.

64:10. But, those who have rejected faith and treated Our verses as false will be companions of hell. They will live there forever. Wretched will be their destination.

64:11. No misfortune befalls without God's permission. God guides the heart of those who believe in Him. God knows all things.

64:12. Obey God and His Messenger. If you turn away from Prophet Muhammad, his only duty is to give you the message clearly.

64:13. Except God, no one else has the right to be worshipped. The believers should put their trust in God.

64:14. Believers, some among your wives and children are your enemies.

Beware of them. But if you forgive them and overlook their faults, then know that God is forgiving and merciful.

64:15. Your wealth and children are a trial. God has a great reward.

64:16. Therefore, fear God as much as you can, be attentive, obedient and charitable. That is better for you. Those who protect themselves from their greed will be successful.

64:17. If you give God a generous loan, He will pay you back manifold and forgive your sins. God is most rewarding and generous.

64:18. God has knowledge of the visible and the invisible. He is the mighty, the wise.

# CHAPTER 65

# THE DIVORCE

**Name:** From Verse One.

**Verses:** 12

**Summary:**

- Theme: Laws of divorce; complementary to the laws in other chapters, like Verses 2:228-234 and 33:49.
- For a divorce to take effect, the waiting period is three menstruation periods, or three months, or the delivery of a child in case of pregnancy.
- Rebellion against God's commandments may bring stern punishment, so fear God and adhere to His laws.

**By Verse**

In the name of God, the compassionate, the merciful:

65:1. O Prophet and believers, when you divorce your wives, divorce them at the completion of their waiting period*. Count the period accurately and fear God, your Lord. Neither they should be turned out of their homes, nor should they leave themselves unless they have committed a clear indecency. Those are the limits set by God. Anyone who breaks the limits set by God wrongs his soul. You do not know that after this, God may bring about some new situation for reconciliation.

**the waiting period is three menstruation periods, or three months, or the delivery of a child in case of pregnancy.*

65:2. When their waiting period is completed, either take them back honorably or part from them honorably. Call to witness two honest persons for establishing your testimony before God. This is the instruction for him who believes in God and the last day. For those, who fear God, He will provide a way out from difficulties,

65:3. and will provide livelihood from sources one may not expect. God is sufficient for whoever puts his trust in Him. He accomplishes His purpose. God has predetermined a fate for all things.

65:4. If you are in doubt about the women who have passed the menstruation age, their waiting period is three months. For those who are pregnant, their period is until they give birth. God will ease the hardship for whoever fears Him.

65:5. That is God's order, which He has revealed to you. Whoever fears God, his sins will be forgiven and he will be richly rewarded.

65:6. Lodge the would-be divorced wives in your homes, according to your means. Do not harass them to make life miserable for them. Should they be pregnant, provide for them till they give birth. If they breastfeed your child, pay them the negotiated acceptable wage. If you cannot agree on the wage, let another woman breastfeed for you.

65:7. Let the rich man spend according to his means, and let the man with limited resources spend according to what God has given him. God does not burden anyone beyond what He has given him. It is possible that God will grant ease after hardship.

65:8. Many communities revolted against the ordinance of their Lord and His Messengers. We sternly called them to account and punished them severely.

65:9. They tasted the ill-effects of their conduct, and the consequence of their conduct was loss.

65:10. God has prepared for them a severe punishment in the hereafter. Therefore, fear God, O men of understanding and belief. God has sent down to you a warning.

65:11. God has sent you a Messenger, who recites God's revelations to you clearly, so that he may lead the believers, who do good deeds, from darkness to light. Whoever believes in God and does right, God will bring him into gardens watered by flowing rivers to live there forever. God has provided for him generously.

65:12. It is God who created seven heavens and similarly the earth like planets. His orders come down among them, so that you may know that God has power over all things, and has knowledge of all things.

# CHAPTER 66

# THE PROHIBITION

**Name:** From Verse One.

**Verses:** 12

**Summary:**

- Theme: What is lawful and unlawful; admonition to the Prophet's wives; and examples of disbelieving and pious women.
- God:
    - alone has the power to prescribe what is lawful and unlawful. He did not delegate that to His Prophets. That is why, in this chapter, God has said to Prophet Muhammad: Do not make something unlawful which God has made lawful.
    - closely supervised the Prophets' lives. Anything deviating from God's will was rectified immediately to make the Prophets' lives exemplary for the believers. That is why Prophet Muhammad's wives were admonished on their behavior with him.
    - cites an example of:
        - The disbelieving wives of Prophets Noah and Lot for the disbelievers.
        - Two pious women (Pharaoh's wife, and Prophet Jesus' mother Mary) for the believers.

**By Verse**

In the name of God, the compassionate, the merciful:

66:1. O Prophet, for pleasing your wives, why do you prohibit yourself from what God has made lawful for you? God is forgiving and merciful.

66:2. God has already prescribed the procedure for Muslims to get out of such oaths. God is your master. He is knowledgeable and wise.

66:3. It is noteworthy that Prophet Muhammad disclosed a matter in confidence to one of his wives (Hafsa), and she divulged it to another wife (Aisha). God made that known to him. He told her about a part of that but said nothing about the other. When he told her, she asked: Who told you this? He replied: The wise one, the all-knowing God, told me.

66:4. It will be better if you, the wives, repent to God, because your hearts have sinned. But, if you conspire against Prophet Muhammad, then know that God is his protector, and Gabriel, the righteous believers, and angels are his helpers.

66:5. If he were to divorce you (Prophet Muhammad's wives), may be, his Lord will give him wives better than you, who will be true Muslims, submissive to God, faithful, obedient, repentant, and given to fasting, previously widows or virgins.

66:6. Believers, protect yourselves and your families from the hellfire whose fuel is mankind and stones. Its keepers are strong and harsh angels, who do not disobey God's orders and do what they are told to do.

66:7. The angels will say to the disbelievers: Make no excuses this day. You will be repaid for what you did.

66:8. Believers, repent to God sincerely. He may forgive your sins and admit you to the gardens watered by flowing rivers. That Day (of Judgement), God will not disgrace the Prophet and those who believed with him. Their light will run before them and on their right hands, and they will say: Lord, perfect our light for us and forgive us. You are able to do all things.

66:9. O Prophet, strive hard against the disbelievers and the hypocrites and deal firmly with them. Their refuge is hell, a wretched destination.

66:10. For the disbelievers, God cites an example of Noah's wife and Lot's wife. They were married to two of Our righteous servants but betrayed them. Their husbands could not protect them from God. Both were told to enter the fire with others.

66:11. For the believers, God cites an example of Pharaoh's wife, who said: Lord, build me a house in Your paradise and save me from Pharaoh, his sins, and the wrongdoing people.

66:12. Another cited example is of Mary (Mother of Jesus), Imran's daughter, who guarded her virginity. We breathed into her Our spirit. She trusted the words of her Lord and His books. She was a pious servant.

# CHAPTER 67

# THE SUPREME POWER

**Name:** From Verse One.

**Verses:** 30

**Summary:**

- Theme: Introduction to Islam's teachings, and challenge to the disbelievers to think rationally about them.
- God:
    - o is the king of the universe.
    - o has decorated the lowest heaven with stars, which are used as missiles to ward off the devils.
    - o has warned that no one can help the disbelievers against God, provide them sustenance beside God, and save them from God's punishment.
- A conversation between hell's guards and its dwellers.

**By Verse**

In the name of God, the compassionate, the merciful:

67:1. God is blessed in Whose hand is the supreme power of the universe. He has power over all things.

67:2. He created life and death to test you as to which of you is best in conduct. He is the mighty and forgiving.

67:3. He created seven heavens, one above the other. The creation of the most gracious God is flawless. Look up, do you see any flaw?

67:4. Look again and again. Your eyes will be tired and unsuccessful in finding any flaw.

67:5. We have beautified the lowest heaven with stars, which are used as missiles for driving away devils. We have prepared for them the blazing fire's punishment.

67:6. The hell's punishment is for the disbelievers. That is a wretched place.

67:7. When they will be thrown into it, they will hear it roaring, boiling, and

67:8. bursting with rage. Every time, a group will be thrown into it, its keepers will ask: Did no one come to warn you?

67:9. They will reply: Yes, a warner did come to us, but we rejected him saying: God has revealed nothing; you are in great error.

67:10. And they will also say: If only we had listened or thought, we would not be among those living in hell.

67:11. They will admit their sins, but they will live in the blazing fire of the hell.

67:12. Those who fear their Lord without seeing Him will be forgiven and richly rewarded.

67:13. Whether you speak in private or in public, God knows what is in your hearts.

67:14. Will God not know what He created? He understands the subtle mysteries and is well aware.

67:15. It is God who has made the earth subservient to you. Travel through it and eat what God has provided. All shall return to Him at the Resurrection.

67:16. Do you feel confident that God, Who is in the heaven, will not cause you to be swallowed by the earth when it will shake like an earthquake?

67:17. Or, do you feel secure that He, Who is in the heaven, would not send against you a storm of stones? Then you would know what My warning means.

67:18. Those who have gone before you also denied their Messengers. Note that how terrible was My punishment for them.

67:19. Do they not see the birds above them, spreading and folding their wings? None can uphold them except the most gracious God. He watches over all things.

67:20. Do you have an army that can help you against the most gracious God? The disbelievers are in delusion.

67:21. Who will provide for you if God withholds His provision? Yet they persist in arrogance and rebellion.

67:22. Who is better guided, one who walks head down with the fearful face, or the one who walks upright on a straight path?

67:23. O Muhammad, tell them: It is God Who has created you, and given you the faculties of hearing, seeing, feeling and understanding. But you are seldom grateful.

67:24. Tell them: It is He who has increased your numbers on earth, and you will be gathered before Him.

67:25. They ask: When will this promise be fulfilled, if what you say is true?

67:26. O Muhammad, tell them: God alone knows that. My duty is only to warn you clearly.

67:27. But when the disbelievers will see it coming, their faces will be distressed. They will be told: This is it what you were asking for.

67:28. O Muhammad, ask them: Have you thought that if God was to destroy me and my followers, or have mercy on us, who will protect the disbelievers from a painful punishment?

67:29. Tell them: He is the most merciful; we have believed in Him, and have put our trust in Him. You will soon know who is in clear error.

67:30. Ask them: Have you thought that if all your water was to disappear into the earth, who then would bring you flowing water?

# CHAPTER 68

# THE PEN

**Name:** From Verse One.

**Verses:** 52

**Summary:**

- Theme: Replies to the disbelievers' objections, warns them, and advises Prophet Muhammad to be patient and steadfast.
- God:
    - has declared Prophet Muhammad to have a great moral character.
    - advises Prophet Muhammad not to yield to any disbelieving oath-monger, slanderer or wicked person.
    - is not going to treat Muslims as He will treat disbelievers. Why don't disbelievers understand this?
- The story of the arrogant and the stingy garden owners who did not want to give charity.
- Those who do not believe in God's revelations are led step by step towards destruction.

**By Verse**

In the name of God, the compassionate, the merciful:

68:1. Noon (is an Arabic letter). I, God, swear by the pen and the Qur'an, which the writers are writing, that
68:2. you O Muhammad, by your Lord's grace, are not a madman.
68:3. An endless reward is waiting for you.
68:4. You indeed have a great moral character.
68:5. Soon you and the disbelievers will see,
68:6. which of you is afflicted with madness.
68:7. Your Lord knows best who have strayed from His way, and who are rightly guided.
68:8. Give no attention to the disbelievers.
68:9. They desire you to compromise with them.
68:10. Do not pay attention to who swears often,
68:11. is a slanderer, gossiper,
68:12. preventer of good, transgressor, sinful,
68:13. ignoble and bastard.

68:14. Because of his wealth and children,

68:15. when Our verses are recited to him, he says: These are ancient stories.

68:16. We, God, shall brand him on his nose.

68:17. We have tested the Meccan-Disbelievers as We tested the garden owners, who had declared that they would pluck its fruit the next morning,

68:18. without saying: God willing (Insha Allah).

68:19. A calamity came upon the garden from your Lord while they were asleep.

68:20. The garden, by the morning, appeared to have been plucked.

68:21. At daybreak, they called one another, saying:

68:22. Go to the garden, if you would like to pluck the fruit.

68:23. They departed, talking in hushed voices, saying:

68:24. Today, no beggar shall be allowed to set foot in the garden.

68:25. Thus, they went out with determination to pluck the fruit.

68:26. But when they saw the garden, first they said: We have lost our way,

68:27. then said: We are utterly ruined.

68:28. The most upright person among them said: Did I not tell you to say God willing (Insha Allah) we will pluck the fruit.

68:29. They replied: Glory to Lord, we have been doing wrong.

68:30. Then they started blaming one another.

68:31. Finally, they said: Shame on us. We indeed broke the limits.

68:32. We hope that our Lord will give us a better garden than this. We repent to Him.

68:33. Such is the punishment in this life, but the punishment of the hereafter will be severer, if only they knew.

68:34. For the righteous, their Lord has the gardens of pleasure.

68:35. Will We treat the faithful like the disbelievers?

68:36. What is the matter with the disbelievers to think like that?

68:37. Do you have a book from which you learn

68:38. to choose whatever you like?

68:39. Or have We given you a sworn promise extending to the Day of Resurrection that you will surely have what you demand?

68:40. O Muhammad, ask the disbelievers if anyone of them will vouch for that.

68:41. Or, have they gods other than God? Then, let them bring their gods if they are truthful.

68:42. On the difficult Day of Judgment, the disbelievers will be invited to prostrate, but they will not be able to do so.

68:43. Their eyes will be cast down, they will be ashamed, because they used to be called to prostrate while they were healthy in the worldly life, but they did not.

68:44. O Muhammad, leave to Me, God, the fate of those who deny the Qur'an. We will punish them by degrees in ways they do not know.

68:45. I shall put up with them patiently, but My plan of punishment is firm.

68:46. O Muhammad, are you asking a reward of them that they feel weighed down by its burden?

68:47. Or, have they knowledge of the unseen, so that they can write it down?

68:48. Be patient for your Lord's decision, and do not act like Prophet Jonah who called to God in distress when he was swallowed by a whale.

68:49. Had God not favored him, he would have been cast off on a naked shore, in disgrace.

68:50. But his Lord chose him and made him righteous.

68:51. When the disbelievers hear Our revelations, they react as to strike you down with their angry looks, and say: Surely, he is a madman.

68:52. But it is a warning to mankind.

# CHAPTER 69

# THE INEVITABLE

**Name:** From Verse One

**Verses:** 52

**Summary:**

- Theme: The hereafter, and the Qur'an's revelation.
- Description of the Days of Resurrection and Judgment.
- Details of the reward for the righteous and the punishment for the sinners.
- The Qur'an is:
    - God's word, not of Prophet Muhammad's.
    - A reminder for those who fear God.

**By Verse**

In the name of God, the compassionate, the merciful:

69:1. The inevitable!
69:2. What is the inevitable?
69:3. And what do you know about it?
69:4. Thamoud and Aad denied the coming of the last judgment.
69:5. Thamoud were destroyed by the overpowering blast.
69:6. And Aad were destroyed by a violent wind.
69:7. God imposed the wind upon them for seven nights and eight days continuously. Had you been there, you would have seen them lying dead as if they were palm-trees' hollow trunks.
69:8. Do you see any of them alive?
69:9. Similarly, Pharaoh, those before him, and the overthrown cities of Prophet Lot's people who committed sins.
69:10. They disobeyed their Lord's Messenger, so God punished them severely.
69:11. When the floodwater rose high, We carried your ancestors, Prophet Noah's people, in the floating boat.
69:12. We made it a memorable warning for you and for the attentive ears to remember it.
69:13. When the trumpet will be blown,
69:14. the earth and the mountains shall be lifted up and crushed in one stroke.

69:15. That day, the inevitable event will occur.
69:16. That day, the heaven will split into pieces and it will be frail.
69:17. That day, the angels will be on the sides of your Lord's throne, and eight angels will carry it above them.
69:18. That day, you will be presented before God and none of your secrets will be hidden.
69:19. The one, whose record will be given in his right hand, will say to his companions: Take it and read it.
69:20. I knew that I will have to give my account.
69:21. He will pleasantly live,
69:22. in a lofty garden.
69:23. Its clusters of fruit will be within his reach.
69:24. People like him will be told: Eat and drink to your hearts' content for what you did in the worldly life.
69:25. But the one who will be given his record in his left hand will say: I wish I had not been given my record;
69:26. and not known what is in my account!
69:27. I wish my death would have been my final end.
69:28. My wealth has been of no use to me.
69:29. My power is gone.
69:30. God will say: Seize him and shackle him.
69:31. Throw him in hell.
69:32. Then chain him in a 70 arm-length chain.
69:33. He did not believe in God, the almighty.
69:34. Nor did he encourage others for feeding the poor.
69:35. Today, he is friendless.
69:36. Filth is his food,
69:37. which only the sinners eat.
69:38. I, God, swear by what you disbelievers see,
69:39. and what you do not see,
69:40. that the Qur'an is the word brought by a noble Messenger.
69:41. It is not the word of a poet, but you do not believe it.
69:42. It is not the word of a soothsayer, but you do not think much.
69:43. It has been revealed by the Lord of the universe.
69:44. Had Prophet Muhammad invented any sayings in Our name,
69:45. We would have caught him by the right hand,
69:46. and cut off his life-artery.
69:47. No one from you could have saved him from Us, God.
69:48. The Qur'an is a reminder for the righteous.
69:49. We know that some among disbelievers' deny it.
69:50. It is a cause of sorrow for the disbelievers.

69:51. It is the absolute truth.
69:52. O Muhammad, praise your Lord, the almighty.

# CHAPTER 70

# THE LADDERS

**Name:** From Verse Three.

**Verses:** 44

**Background:**

God revealed this chapter in response to the disbelievers' demand for their immediate punishment for making fun of Resurrection, hereafter, hell and heaven.

**Summary:**

God tells:

- Prophet Muhammad to be patient.
- The Day of Judgment will definitely come.
- That day, the disbelievers will wish to save themselves from the punishment at the expense of their children, wives, brothers, relatives, and all the people who lived on earth, but it will not happen. The disbelievers will have downcast eyes with shame.
- Believers' characteristics, and their going to paradise.

**By Verse**

In the name of God, the compassionate, the merciful:

70:1. A questioner has demanded that punishment be given
70:2. to the disbelievers. No one can prevent it.
70:3. The punishment is from God, who is the owner of the ladders.
70:4. The angels and Angel Gabriel ascend to God in a day, which is equal to human 50,000 years.
70:5. O Muhammad, be patient graciously.
70:6. The disbelievers think the Day of Judgment is far off.
70:7. But We, God, see it near.
70:8. That day, the sky will be like molten metal.
70:9. And the mountains will be like wool flakes.
70:10. The friends will not speak to one another.
70:11. Though they will meet one another. The sinner will desire to save himself from the punishment of that day by sacrificing his children,
70:12. his wife, his brother,

70:13. his relatives, who sheltered him,
70:14. and all the people on earth, if that would save him.
70:15. But the hellfire
70:16. will burn his flesh.
70:17. The hellfire will call him who turned his back from truth,
70:18. and collected wealth and hoarded it.
70:19. Indeed, man was created impatient.
70:20. He becomes despondent when faced with evil;
70:21. but miserly when he gets lucky.
70:22. But not believers, who are devoted to prayer;
70:23. are steadfast in prayer;
70:24. set aside a share of their wealth
70:25. for the beggar and the needy;
70:26. and those who believe in the Day of Judgment;
70:27. are fearful of their Lord's punishment;
70:28. no one is safe from their Lord's punishment;
70:29. and those who guard against their sexual desires,
70:30. except from their wives or the slave-girls they possess, because they are lawful to them.
70:31. But whoever seeks beyond that, breaks the limits.
70:32. And those who keep their trusts and promises;
70:33. and those who are honest witnesses;
70:34. and those who guard their prayer;
70:35. they will live in the gardens of paradise with honor.
70:36. O Muhammad, what is the matter with the disbelievers that they are rushing to you,
70:37. from the right and the left in groups?
70:38. Does every one of them desire to enter a garden of pleasure?
70:39. Not at all! They know from what We created them.
70:40. I, God, swear by the Lord of the east and the west that We have the power
70:41. to replace them with others better than them, and no one can stop Us from doing that.
70:42. Therefore, leave the disbelievers to talk uselessly and amuse themselves until they meet the promised day.
70:43. That day, they will come out of the graves racing to a goal-post,
70:44. with eyes cast down in disgrace. That is the day which they were threatened with.

# CHAPTER 71

# NOAH

**Name:** From Verse One.

**Verses:** 28

**Summary:**

Prophet Noah's:

- Preaching to the disbelievers and submission to God after exhausting all his efforts.
- Prayer to God for not leaving any disbeliever on earth and God granting his wish.

**By Verse**

In the name of God, the compassionate, the merciful:

71:1. We sent Noah to his people to warn them before a painful punishment comes to them.
71:2. He said: My people, I have come to warn you plainly.
71:3. Worship God, fear Him, and obey me, Noah.
71:4. God will forgive your sins and delay your punishment for a specified time. When the time set by God arrives, it cannot be delayed. Alas, if you only knew.
71:5. Prophet Noah said: Lord, I have invited my people to truth day and night.
71:6. But all my calling has increased their flight away from the truth.
71:7. Every time, I have called on them to seek Your forgiveness, they thrust their fingers into their ears, covered their faces with their garments, persisted in their refusal, and increased their arrogance.
71:8. I called out aloud to them.
71:9. I appealed to them in public and in private.
71:10. I said: Ask forgiveness from your Lord. He is ever forgiving.
71:11. He will send ample rain for you from the sky.
71:12. He will increase your wealth and children, and provide you gardens and rivers.
71:13. Why do you deny God's greatness,
71:14. when He has created you in stages?
71:15. Can you not see that God has created seven heavens one above the other?
71:16. He has placed in them the moon for light and the sun for a lamp.

71:17. God has grown you from the earth gradually like a plant.
71:18. He will cause you to return to earth, and raise you from it at the Day of Resurrection.
71:19. God has made the earth as a spread out carpet for you.
71:20. That you may travel on its spacious paths.
71:21. Noah said: Lord, they have disobeyed me and followed those whose wealth and children will increase their ruin.
71:22. They have devised a tremendous plot,
71:23. saying: Do not renounce your gods and do not leave Wad, Sowa, Yaghuth, Yauq, or Nasr*.

**Names of the idol-gods.*

71:24. They have misled many, and it only increased the disbelief of these wrongdoers.
71:25. Because of their sins, they were drowned and thrown into the fire. They found no one to help them beside God.
71:26. And Noah said: Lord, do not leave a single disbeliever on earth.
71:27. If You leave them, they will mislead Your devotees, and breed none but wicked and ungrateful ones.
71:28. Lord, forgive me, my parents, every believer who enters my house, and the believing men and women, and increase the destruction of the wrongdoers.

# CHAPTER 72

## THE JINN

**Name:** From Verse One.

**Verses:** 28

**Summary:**

- The jinns heard the Qur'an and returned to their people to preach Islam to them.
- The Satan is from the Jinns.
- Jinns:
    - o and mankind are separate creations. God created man from clay and jinns from fire. God created jinns before He created man.
    - o like mankind has the power of choice.
    - o can see the humans but the humans cannot see them.
    - o have been given certain extraordinary powers and abilities. But God has entrusted mankind with being God's deputy on earth and man is superior to the jinns.
    - o have different religions and sects; some are Muslims and some are not.
- The places of worship are for God's remembrance. So do not worship there anyone other than God.
- God's Messengers do not have the power to harm or benefit anyone. Their mission is just to convey God's message.
- Only God knows the unseen. He reveals it to His chosen Messengers.

### By Verse

In the name of God, the compassionate, the merciful:

72:1. O Muhammad, say: It has been revealed to me that a group of jinns listened to the recitation of the Qur'an and said that they have heard an amazing Qur'an.

72:2. It guides to the right course. We have believed in it and will not worship anyone other than our Lord.

72:3. Our Lord's majesty is unequaled. He has not taken a wife or a son.

72:4. The foolish among us have been saying atrocious lies about God.

72:5. We had thought that no man or jinn could speak a lie about God.

72:6. Some humans sought the help of the jinns, which increased the jinns' pride.
72:7. Like the jinns, the humans thought that God would never send anyone as a Messenger.
72:8. We, Jinns, tried to reach the heaven but found it filled with powerful guards and flaming comets.
72:9. Previously, we used to find a place to sit there and eavesdrop, but anyone trying that now finds a flaming comet waiting for him.
72:10. We, Jinns, do not know whether evil is intended for those on earth or their Lord intends to show them the right way.
72:11. Some of us are righteous, some are not; we follow different ways.
72:12. We know we cannot escape from God on earth, nor we can run away from His grasp.
72:13. When we, Jinns, heard the guidance, we believed in it. Whoever believes in his Lord will not be wronged or harmed.
72:14. Some of us have submitted to God and some have not. Those who have submitted to God are on the right path.
72:15. But, those who are wrongdoers will become hell's fuel.
72:16. O Muhammad, tell the disbelievers that if they follow the right path, We would give them ample rain.
72:17. This is a test for the disbelievers. Whoever turns away from his Lord's remembrance will be punished severely.
72:18. The places of worship are for God alone; so do not pray there to anyone other than God.
72:19. When God's servant Prophet Muhammad stood up to pray to God, the disbelievers were ready to assault him.
72:20. O Muhammad, say: I only pray to my Lord and do not associate anyone with Him.
72:21. Tell them: I, Muhammad, have no power to benefit or harm you.
72:22. Say: Neither anyone can protect me from God's punishment, nor I can find refuge with someone else.
72:23. My duty is only to give you God's message. Whoever disobeys God and His Messenger will live in hell's fire forever.
72:24. The disbelievers will continue in their disbelief until they would see the punishment they have been promised. Then they will know who are weaker in helpers and less in number.
72:25. Tell them: I do not know if the punishment you have been promised is near or my Lord has set a far-off day for it.
72:26. God alone has the knowledge of the unseen, which He does not disclose to anyone,
72:27. except to His selected Messengers. He sends guardians for the

Messengers, who walk in front and behind them,
72:28. so that He may know if they indeed have conveyed His messages.
He has knowledge of their deeds and takes account of everything.

# CHAPTER 73

## THE ENWRAPPED ONE

**Name:** From Verse One.

**Verses:** 20

**Summary:**

- God ordered Prophet Muhammad to stand in prayer for approximately half the night in preparation for carrying out the Prophethood's burden.
- Those who oppose the Prophet will be treated with shackles and a blazing fire.
- The Qur'an is a reminder for those who seek to find the right way.
- Read from the Qur'an as much as you easily can.
- Whatever you spend in God's way, you will find it in the hereafter.

**By Verse**

In the name of God, the compassionate, the merciful:

73:1. O Muhammad, who are wrapped in garments,
73:2. stand up in prayer all night, except for a few hours,
73:3. for half the night, or little less,
73:4. or more; and recite the Qur'an in slow measured tone.
73:5. We are about to reveal to you a burdensome message.
73:6. Rising by night is very useful for governing the self and most suitable effective speech.
73:7. During the day you are busy at work.
73:8. Remember your Lord's name and devote yourself to Him whole-heartedly.
73:9. He is the Lord of the east and the west. There is no god except Him. Accept Him as your protector.
73:10. Be patient with what the disbelievers say and leave their company graciously.
73:11. Leave to Me, God, to deal with the disbelievers, who are enjoying life's good things. Bear with them for a little while.
73:12. We have for them shackles and the burning fire,
73:13. chocking food, and painful punishment.
73:14. This will be their fate on the day when the earth and the mountains will shake and the mountains will become heaps of loose sand.
73:15. We have sent to you, the disbelievers, a Messenger to testify

against you as We sent a Messenger (Prophet Moses) to Pharaoh.

73:16. But, Pharaoh disobeyed the Messenger; so, We seized him with a heavy punishment.

73:17. If you persist in disbelief, how will you avoid the Day of Resurrection which will make the children grey-headed?

73:18. That day, the heaven will break apart. God's promise shall be fulfilled.

73:19. This is but a reminder. So, whoever likes, may take the path to his Lord.

73:20. O Muhammad, your Lord knows that you stand in prayer nearly for two thirds of the night, or half a night, or a third of it, and so does a group of your followers. God measures the hours of the night and the day. He knows that:

- you and the believers will not be able to do so precisely and is merciful to you. Recite the Qur'an as much as you easily can.
- among you there are sick, others are traveling through the land seeking God's bounty, and yet others are fighting for His cause. So recite the Qur'an as much as you easily can. Establish prayer, pay Zakat (mandatory charity), and give a good loan to God. Whatever good you do, you will find it with God. That is better and greater in reward. Seek God's forgiveness. He is the forgiving and the merciful.

# CHAPTER 74

# THE COVERED ONE

**Name:** From Verse One.

**Verses:** 56

**Summary:**

- Instructions to Prophet Muhammad for spreading God's message, cleanliness, and patience.
- The Day of Judgment will be very difficult for those who deny God's revelations and oppose His cause.
- Deeds that lead to the hellfire are: Not praying and feeding the poor, wasting time in vain talk, and denying the Day of Judgment.

### By Verse

In the name of God, the compassionate, the merciful:

74:1. O Muhammad, who is lying wrapped up in garments,
74:2. get up and warn;
74:3. glorify your Lord;
74:4. clean your clothes,
74:5. and avoid being unclean.
74:6. Do not do favors to others to expect more in return.
74:7. Be patient for the sake of your Lord.
74:8. When the trumpet will be blown,
74:9. it will be a difficult day,
74:10. far from easy, for the disbelievers.
74:11. Leave Me, God, alone to deal with the one I created,
74:12. gave him wealth,
74:13. and the children to be by his side.
74:14. Made his life smooth and comfortable.
74:15. Yet, he desires for more.
74:16. It will certainly not happen because he has been stubbornly denying our revelations.
74:17. Soon, I will impose on him a mountain of calamities.
74:18. He thought and plotted.
74:19. Let him be cursed for his plotting.
74:20. Again, he is cursed for his plotting.
74:21. Then, he looked around,
74:22. frowned, showed displeasure,

74:23. turned back arrogantly,
74:24. and said: This is nothing but old magic;
74:25. it is the word of a human being.
74:26. Soon, I, God, will throw him into the hellfire.
74:27. What do you know about the hellfire?
74:28. It leaves nothing, spares none.
74:29. It burns the skin.
74:30. It is guarded by 19 guards.
74:31. We have appointed no one other than angels to guard the hellfire and have fixed their number as a trial for the disbelievers. So, that those who were given the Scriptures will be convinced, the believers will be strengthened in faith, and the people of the Scriptures and the believers will not doubt, and those in whose hearts is disease and the disbelievers will say: What does God mean by this? God misleads whom He wills and guides whom He wills. No one knows the soldiers of your Lord except Him. The hellfire has been mentioned only as a reminder for mankind, not for a joke.
74:32. I, God, swear by the moon,
74:33. the departing night,
74:34. and the coming dawn,
74:35. that the hellfire is one of the greatest calamities,
74:36. a warning to mankind.
74:37. It is up to you to move forward in faith or stay behind in disbelief.
74:38. Every person is accountable for its deeds,
74:39. except those on the right,
74:40. who will be in the gardens of paradise.
74:41. They will ask the guilty:
74:42. What brought you to the hellfire?
74:43. They will reply: We did not pray,
74:44. and fed the poor.
74:45. We indulged in idle talk with those who talked against the faith,
74:46. and denied the Day of Judgment,
74:47. till death overtook us.
74:48. No one will plead for them.
74:49. Then what is wrong with the disbelievers that they are turning away from the warning,
74:50. like frightened donkeys,
74:51. fleeing from a lion?
74:52. Everyone among the disbelievers demands an open book to be brought to him saying that Muhammad is God's Prophet to be

obeyed.

74:53. No, their demand will not be granted. The reality is that they are not afraid of the hereafter.

74:54. No, their demand will not be granted. The Qur'an is an urgent advice.

74:55. Anyone who likes can benefit from it,

74:56. but only by God's will. He is the Lord of righteousness and forgiveness.

# CHAPTER 75

# THE RESURRECTION

**Name:** From Verse One.

**Verses:** 40

**Summary:**

- God has:
    - confirmed that the Day of Resurrection will come and there will be no escape from it.
    - taken the responsibility for explaining the Qur'an to Prophet Muhammad and to make him memorize it.
- The disbelievers' reasons for not believing in the Day of Resurrection.
- Description of the believers and the disbelievers on the Day of Resurrection.
- The last moments of a disbeliever's death.

**By Verse**

In the name of God, the compassionate, the merciful:

75:1. I, God, swear by the Day of Resurrection.
75:2. And I swear by the self-accusing soul.
75:3. Does man think that We shall not be able to assemble his bones?
75:4. Why not? We have even the power to remold his fingertips.
75:5. But, man desires to continue in sin.
75:6. He asks: When will the Day of Resurrection come?
75:7. When the eyes will be dazzled,
75:8. and the moon will become lightless,
75:9. and the moon and the sun will be joined to become one.
75:10. That day, man will ask: Where shall I flee?
75:11. No, there shall be no escape.
75:12. That day, all shall return to God.
75:13. That day, man will be told what he did and what he failed to do.
75:14. He will become his own witness,
75:15. despite all his pleas.
75:16. O Prophet, do not move your tongue in haste to memorize the revelation.

75:17. Its safe collection and recitation is Our responsibility.
75:18. When We are reading it through Angel Gabriel, pay attention.
75:19. Thereafter, to make you understand its meaning is Our responsibility.
75:20. The humans love the fleeing worldly life,
75:21. and neglect the life to come.
75:22. That day, there shall be some happy faces,
75:23. looking at their Lord;
75:24. and some gloomy faces,
75:25. thinking that some great calamity was about to fall on them.
75:26. No, you are wrong that there is no life hereafter. When the soul reaches the throat to exit,
75:27. and those around him say: Will no one save him from death?
75:28. And the dying person knows that it is the time of death,
75:29. and his legs rub each other under pangs of death.
75:30. That day, your journey will be to your Lord.
75:31. In this life, the disbeliever neither believed, nor prayed.
75:32. Instead, he denied the truth and turned away,
75:33. went to his people in pride.
75:34. Yes, this attitude is your destruction, and you deserve it.
75:35. Again, this attitude is your destruction, and you deserve it.
75:36. Does man think that he will be left alone without purpose?
75:37. Was he not an ejaculated semen drop?
75:38. Then, he became a blood-clot, and God made his body and proportioned his body parts,
75:39. and made two genders, male and female.
75:40. Does God then not have the power to raise the dead to life?

# CHAPTER 76

## THE PASSING TIME
## THE HUMAN

**Name:** From Verse One.

**Verses:** 31

**Summary:**

- Theme: Informing man of his true position in the world, and telling him that depending upon his attitude of doing good or bad, his end would be good or bad.
- The universe existed before God created man, provided him guidance, and gave him free will either to believe or to disbelieve.
- For the disbelievers, God has prepared chains, shackles, and a blazing fire. The real cause of their wrong attitude is their liking for the fleeting worldly life and forgetting the hereafter.
- The believers' exemplary life in paradise.
- God's advice to Prophet Muhammad.
- God revealed the Qur'an gradually according to the issues faced by mankind. It is a guide for those who want to adopt the right way to their Lord.

### By Verse

In the name of God, the compassionate, the merciful:

76:1. Has there not been a period during infinite time when man was not worth mentioning?

76:2. We have created man from the mixed semen of a man and a woman to test him. So We have given him hearing and sight.

76:3. We have shown him the right way. It is up to him to be grateful or ungrateful.

76:4. For the disbelievers we have prepared chains, shackles, and a blazing fire.

76:5. But the righteous will drink from cups of wine mixed with water from camphor.

76:6. It will be a gushing spring in paradise from which God's servants will drink wherever they would like.

76:7. They are those who fulfill their promises and fear the Day of Judgment whose terror will be widespread.

76:8. For God's love, they feed the needy, the orphan, and the captive,

76:9. saying: We feed you only for God's sake; we seek no reward or gratitude from you.
76:10. We fear from our Lord a day of painful suffering.
76:11. God will protect the believers from the dreadful Day of Judgment and make their faces radiate with happiness.
76:12. And God will reward them paradise and silk garments for their patience.
76:13. They will recline upon raised couches, and not bear the sun's heat or the bitter cold.
76:14. Trees will spread their shade on them and their hanging fruit will be within their reach.
76:15. They shall be served with silver dishes and glasses,
76:16. made of crystal-clear silver, filled according to their wishes.
76:17. They will be served with the cups of wine mixed with ginger,
76:18. from the fountain named Selsabil in paradise.
76:19. They will be attended by eternally young boys, who will look like scattered pearls.
76:20. Wherever you would look in paradise, you will see pleasure and workings of a great kingdom.
76:21. They will wear green color garments of fine silk and rich brocade, and silver bracelets. Their Lord will give them a purifying drink.
76:22. They will be told: This is your reward for God's appreciation of your efforts.
76:23. O Muhammad, We have revealed the Qur'an to you gradually.
76:24. Therefore, be patient with your Lord's judgment, and do not yield to the desires of the sinners or disbelievers.
76:25. Invoke the name of your Lord, morning and evening;
76:26. worship him at night; and praise Him all night long.
76:27. The disbelievers love the transitory worldly life, and neglect the heavy Day of Judgment to come.
76:28. We created the humans and made their limbs and joints strong. But if We want, We can replace them with others like them at any time.
76:29. This is an advice. Whoever likes can take the right path to his Lord.
76:30. But you cannot do that unless God wills. He is all-knowing, all-wise.
76:31. He is merciful to whom He pleases; but for the wrongdoers He has prepared a painful punishment.

# CHAPTER 77

# THOSE SENT FORTH

**Name:** From Verse One.

**Verses:** 50

**Summary:**

- Theme: God's affirmation of the Resurrection and the hereafter, and to warn people of the consequences for denying them.
- On the Day of Resurrection:
    - The disbelievers will be asked to walk towards hell which they used to deny.
    - There will be destruction for the disbelievers.
    - Righteous will be given all that they desire.

**By Verse**

In the name of God, the compassionate, the merciful:

77:1. I, God, swear by the winds sent one after the other,
77:2. which blow forcefully,
77:3. and spread the clouds;
77:4. then separate them from one another;
77:5. then spread a message,
77:6. to excuse some and warn others,
77:7. that what you have been promised will be fulfilled.
77:8. When the stars will lose their light,
77:9. the sky will be split,
77:10. the mountains will crumble into dust,
77:11. and the Messengers will be gathered at the appointed time;
77:12. when will all that be?
77:13. That will be upon the Day of Judgment.
77:14. What do you know about the Day of Judgment?
77:15. That day, there will be destruction for the disbelievers.
77:16. Did We not destroy the earlier people?
77:17. Similarly, We will destroy the generations that followed them.
77:18. That is how we deal with the guilty.
77:19. That day, there will be destruction for the disbelievers.
77:20. Did We, God, not create you from an unworthy fluid, semen,
77:21. and kept it in a safe place, womb,

77:22. for an appointed time?
77:23. We did that because We are capable of determining excellent arrangements.
77:24. That day, there will be destruction for those who deny the truth.
77:25. Did We not make the earth so as to hold
77:26: the living and the dead?
77:27. And have We not placed the high mountains on it, and have given you sweet drinking water?
77:28. That day, there will be destruction for the disbelievers.
77:29. They will be told: Go to hell that you used to deny.
77:30. Go to the shadow which has three columns;
77:31. it will give you neither cool shade nor shelter from the fire;
77:32. it will be throwing up spark as huge as towers,
77:33. as if they were yellow camels.
77:34. That day, there will be destruction for the disbelievers.
77:35. That day, they will neither speak,
77:36. nor their pleas will be accepted.
77:37. That day, there will be destruction for the disbelievers.
77:38. That will be the Day of Judgment. We will assemble you with the former people.
77:39. So if you have a trick, try it against Me, God.
77:40. That day, there will be destruction for the disbelievers.
77:41. The righteous will live among shades and springs,
77:42. and eat fruits of their liking.
77:43. We shall tell them: Eat and drink to your hearts content in return for what you did.
77:44. That is how We, God, reward who do good.
77:45. That day, there will be destruction for the disbelievers.
77:46. The disbelievers, you can eat and enjoy yourselves for a while in this worldly life. You are guilty.
77:47. That day, there will be destruction for the disbelievers.
77:48. When they are asked to kneel down before God, they do not do so.
77:49. That day, there will be destruction for the disbelievers.
77:50. In what discourse after the Qur'an will they believe?

# CHAPTER 78

# THE NEWS

**Name:** From Verse Two.

**Verses:** 40

**Summary:**

- Theme: The Resurrection and the hereafter.
- For the disbelievers, the acceptance of Resurrection and the hereafter were most difficult.
- God:
    - Asks the disbelievers that has God not:
        - spread the earth like a bed and raised the mountains like pillars;
        - created humans in pairs of male and female;
        - given you sleep for rest, made the night a cover of darkness for rest and the day for work;
        - built seven strong heavens above you, and placed a shining lamp (the sun) in them; and
        - sent down abundant rain from clouds to produce grain, vegetation, and lush gardens?
    - states that if He has done all that, He also has the power to recreate you, and reward hell to the disbelievers and paradise to the believers.

## By Verse

In the name of God, the compassionate, the merciful:

78:1. What are they asking one another?
78:2. Is it about the great news
78:3. they are disagreeing?
78:4. No, what they know about the Resurrection is wrong, but soon they will know the truth.
78:5. Again, no, what they know about it is wrong, but soon they will know the truth.
78:6. Have We not spread the earth like a bed?
78:7. And have We not raised the mountains like pillars?
78:8. And have We not created humans in pairs of male and female?
78:9. And have We not given you sleep for rest?

78:10. And have We not made the night as a cover of darkness for rest?
78:11. And have We not made the day for work?
78:12. And have We not built seven strong heavens above you?
78:13. And have We not placed a shining lamp, the sun, in them?
78:14. And have We not sent down abundant rain from the clouds,
78:15. to produce grain and vegetation,
78:16. and lush gardens?
78:17. The Day of Judgment is fixed.
78:18. That day, the trumpet will be blown, and you shall come out in crowds;
78:19. and the gates of the heaven shall be opened,
78:20. and the mountains shall be moved to become like dust.
78:21. The hell, in fact, is a place of ambush,
78:22. a home for the rebellious,
78:23. to live there for ages.
78:24. There, they will taste nothing cool and drinkable,
78:25. except boiling water, and filthy, stinking cold fluid.
78:26. That will be fitting recompense for their deeds.
78:27. They did not expect any accountability for their deeds,
78:28. and denied Our revelations emphatically.
78:29. But, We, God, recorded everything in a book.
78:30. We shall say: Taste the punishment of your deeds; We shall increase nothing for you except torment.
78:31. The righteous will certainly be successful.
78:32. They will have gardens and vineyards,
78:33. and company of maidens of equal age;
78:34. and the cups of wine filled to the brim.
78:35. There, they will not hear any trash-talk and lies.
78:36. That will be a generous reward from their Lord,
78:37. who is the Lord of the heavens, the earth, and whatever is between them, is most merciful, and no one has the power to address Him.
78:38. That day, Gabriel and the angels will stand in rows. No one will speak without the permission of the most merciful God, and who will speak only what is right.
78:39. That day is sure to come. So, whoever desires may follow the path to his Lord.
78:40. We have forewarned you of a punishment at hand, the day when a man will look at what he did and the disbeliever will say: I wish, I were dust!

# CHAPTER 79

# THE SOUL-SNATCHERS

**Name:** From Verse One.

**Verses:** 46

**Summary:**

- Theme: Confirmation of the Resurrection and the life hereafter. It also warns of the consequences of denying God's Messenger Prophet Muhammad.
- The story of Prophet Moses when he called Pharaoh to his Lord and Pharaoh denied God, Who punished him.
- For God, the creation of humans is not harder than the creation of the heavens, the earth and its contents.
- The punishment and the reward on the Day of Judgment.

**By Verse**

In the name of God, the compassionate, the merciful:

79:1. I, God, swear by the angels who violently snatch away the disbelievers' souls,
79:2. and by those who gently draw out the believers' souls;
79:3. and by those who float in space,
79:4. and by those who float with speed;
79:5. then per God's commands, they govern the affairs.
79:6. The day, when the trumpet will be blown for the first time like an earthquake,
79:7. followed by a second time,
79:8. the disbelievers' hearts will tremble that day,
79:9. and the eyes will be cast down with awe.
79:10. They are asking: Will we really be returned to life,
79:11. even after our bones would have decayed?
79:12. Then they say: That would be a useless return.
79:13. But with one blast,
79:14. they will appear upon the earth's surface.
79:15. Have you heard the story of Moses,
79:16. when his Lord called him in the sacred valley of Towa,
79:17. and told him to go to Pharaoh who had crossed all limits.
79:18. And say to him: Would you reform yourself?
79:19. I will guide you to your Lord, so that you may fear Him.

79:20. Then Moses showed Pharaoh the greatest miracle of the staff becoming a big snake.
79:21. But Pharaoh denied it and disobeyed.
79:22. He quickly went away,
79:23. gathered his people and said to them:
79:24. I am your supreme Lord.
79:25. God punished Pharaoh in this life and in the life to come.
79:26. Surely, there is a lesson in it for anyone who fears God.
79:27. Are you more difficult to create or the heaven that God built?
79:28. He, God, raised it high and fashioned it.
79:29. And made the night dark and the day bright.
79:30. After that, He spread the earth.
79:31. Drew water and vegetation from it.
79:32. And set the mountains,
79:33. as sustenance for you and your cattle.
79:34. But when the great catastrophe, the Day of Judgment, will come,
79:35. the day, when humans will remember what they did,
79:36. and the hellfire will be shown to all.
79:37. Those, who crossed the limits,
79:38. and preferred the worldly life,
79:39. will live in hell.
79:40. But those, who were afraid to stand before their Lord and had curbed their desires,
79:41. will live in paradise.
79:42. O Muhammad, they ask you: When will the Hour of Catastrophe come?
79:43. But, how can you know about it?
79:44. Your Lord only knows when it will come.
79:45. Your duty is only to warn those who fear it.
79:46. When they will see the hour that day, they will think that they have stayed away for one evening or one morning.

# CHAPTER 80

# HE FROWNED

**Name:** From Verse One.

**Verses:** 42

**Summary:**

- Theme:
    - To correct Prophet Muhammad in ignoring the blind man who wanted to be enlightened on some religious questions, but had intruded in Prophet's discussion with the chiefs of his community who were indifferent to God's message.
    - To warn the disbelievers of their arrogant attitude and indifference to God's message.
- On the Day of Judgment, no one shall care about his own brother, mother, father, wife or children because of his own burden.
- God draws attention to what God created man from and what He did to facilitate his life.

### By Verse

In the name of God, the compassionate, the merciful:

80:1. Prophet Muhammad frowned and turned away,
80:2. when the blind man* came to him.

**Abdullah bin Umm-Maktum.*

80:3. How could you tell that he might reform?
80:4. Or pay attention to the advice that might benefit him?
80:5. But, to the indifferent,
80:6. you pay attention,
80:7. though there would be no blame on you if he does not reform.
80:8. Yet, to the one who came to you earnestly,
80:9. with awe,
80:10. you neglected him.
80:11. That is not right, the Qur'an is a message of advice.
80:12. Whoever likes, can accept the Qur'an.
80:13. It is recorded on the honored sheets,
80:14. exalted and pure,
80:15. by the hands of angels,

80:16. noble and virtuous.
80:17. Cursed is the disbelieving man.
80:18. From what substance did God create him?
80:19. God created him from a sperm-drop and then proportioned him;
80:20. made the path of life smooth for him;
80:21. gave him death and provided a grave for him;
80:22. when God would like, He will raise him to life again.
80:23. No, man has not done the duty God assigned him.
80:24. Let the mankind look at the food it eats;
80:25. how We, God, pour down rain in abundance,
80:26. then split the earth apart,
80:27. to grow grain,
80:28. grapes and vegetables,
80:29. olive and palm-trees,
80:30. lush gardens,
80:31. fruit trees and pasture,
80:32. to be used by you and your livestock.
80:33. But when the deafening blast will be sounded, the second blowing of the trumpet on the Day of Judgment,
80:34. That day, every person will run away from his brother,
80:35. mother, father,
80:36. wife and children.
80:37. That day, every person will have enough of his own burden to forget about others.
80:38. That day, there will be some bright faces,
80:39. laughing and joyous.
80:40. That day, there will be some faces covered with dust,
80:41. and darkness.
80:42. Those will be the faces of the wicked disbelievers.

# CHAPTER 81

# THE FOLDING UP

**Name:** From Verse One.

**Verses:** 29

**Summary:**

- Theme: The hereafter and the Prophethood.
- The Resurrection's two stages.
- The Qur'an is God's word conveyed to Prophet Muhammad through Angel Gabriel, and its message is for all mankind.

**By Verse**

In the name of God, the compassionate, the merciful:

81:1. When the sun will be folded up not to shine;
81:2. when the stars will fall down;
81:3. when the mountains will crumble;
81:4. when the pregnant camels shall be neglected;
81:5. when the wild beasts will be gathered;
81:6. when the seas will be set on fire;
81:7. When various people shall be brought closer to each other;
81:8. when the infant girl buried alive by pagan-Arabs and others shall be asked,
81:9. for what crime she was killed;
81:10. when the written record of human deeds shall be laid open;
81:11. when the barrier to the heaven shall be removed;
81:12. when hellfire will be set ablaze;
81:13. and when paradise shall be brought near;
81:14. then, every person will know what it has done.
81:15. I, God, swear by the receding stars,
81:16. that rise and set;
81:17. and by the departing night;
81:18. and by the dawn of morning;
81:19. that the Qur'an is the word revealed to a noble Messenger Muhammad, by Angel Gabriel,
81:20. who is powerful and is honored by the Lord of the throne, God,
81:21. who is entitled to obedience, and is trustworthy.
81:22. No, O People of Mecca, your companion Muhammad is not a madman.

81:23. He has seen Gabriel on the clear horizon.
81:24. He does not purposely withhold any knowledge of the unseen;
81:25. and the Qur'an is not the word of the outcast Satan.
81:26. Where then are you going?
81:27. The Qur'an is but an advice for the mankind,
81:28. and for those who have the will to follow the straight path.
81:29. But you do not will, unless God, the Lord of the universe, wills it.

# CHAPTER 82

# THE SPLITTING APART

**Name:** From Verse One.

**Verses:** 19

**Summary:**

- Theme: Day of Resurrection. That day:
    - Every person will see what he did.
    - Mankind has been asked to ponder the question: What has misled you away from God, Who created you and provided generous living for you?
    - The righteous shall live happily in paradise; and the wicked shall be punished in hell.
    - No one shall be able to do anything for another person. God will have all power of judgment.

### By Verse

In the name of God, the compassionate, the merciful:

82:1. When the sky will split apart;
82:2. when the stars will scatter;
82:3. when the oceans will burst;
82:4. and when the graves will be opened;
82:5. then each person will know what it has done and what it failed to do.
82:6. O mankind, what has misled you away from your most generous Lord,
82:7. Who created you, fashioned you, proportioned you,
82:8. and molded your body by His will?
82:9. No, there is no plausible reason for you to be misled away from your Lord, but you still deny the final judgment.
82:10. Watching over you are guardians angels,
82:11. noble recorders,
82:12. who know about your deeds.
82:13. The righteous will surely live in pleasure in paradise,
82:14. and the wicked will certainly live in the hellfire.
82:15. They will enter into it on the Day of Judgment,
82:16. and they shall not escape from it.
82:17. What do you know about the Day of Judgment?

82:18. Oh, what would you know about the Day of Judgment?

82:19. It will be the day, when no person shall have power to do anything for another, and God will have absolute power.

# CHAPTER 83

# THE FRAUDULENT DEALING

**Name:** From Verse One.

**Verses:** 36

**Summary:**

- Theme: The hereafter.
- Those who defraud others, when measuring or weighing, will be called to account and punished in the hereafter; while the righteous will be rewarded with soft couches, choice wines, and special spring water.
- Today, the disbelievers laugh at the believers, but on the Day of Judgment, the believers will laugh at them.

### By Verse

In the name of God, the compassionate, the merciful:

83:1. Woe to the fraudulent dealers,
83:2. who take full measure from others,
83:3. but defraud them when they measure or weigh for them.
83:4. Do they not think that they shall be raised again to life,
83:5. on a fateful day,
83:6. the day, when mankind will stand before the Lord of the universe?
83:7. No, their thinking of no accountability is wrong. In fact, the record of the wicked is being kept in the prison register.
83:8. Do you know what the prison-register is?
83:9. It is a book of the written-record of the wicked.
83:10. That day, there will be destruction for the disbelievers,
83:11. who deny the last judgment.
83:12. No one denies it accept the sinner who exceeds all limits.
83:13. When Our verses are recited to him, he says: These are ancient stories.
83:14. Not at all; rather the rust of their sins has covered their hearts.
83:15. No. That day, they will not be able to see their Lord.
83:16. They will enter the hellfire.
83:17. They will be told: This is the punishment you used to deny.
83:18. No, your thinking of no accountability is wrong. Record of the righteous will be in the register of the honored ones.
83:19. Do you know what the register of the honored ones is?

83:20. It is a book of the written record of the righteous.
83:21. It is guarded by angels closest to God.
83:22. No doubt, the righteous will be in pleasure,
83:23. sitting on couches, enjoying the surroundings.
83:24. Their faces will be joyfully radiant.
83:25. They will drink pure wine, sealed
83:26. with musk. So for having it, let the contenders compete.
83:27. The wine will be mixed with Tasnim (the purest and the noblest heavenly drink), from
83:28. a spring where the favored by God will refresh themselves.
83:29. In the worldly life, the sinners used to laugh at the believers.
83:30. When they passed by them, they used to wink to one another.
83:31. And when they returned to their own people, they joked.
83:32. When they saw them, they said: These believers have gone off the right path.
83:33. But, the disbelievers were not sent as guardians of the believers.
83:34. On the Day of Resurrection, the believers will laugh at the disbelievers.
83:35. The believers will be sitting on couches enjoying the surroundings.
83:36. Should the disbelievers not be repaid for what they used to do?

# CHAPTER 84

# THE SPLITTING

**Name:** From Verse One.

**Verses:** 25

**Summary:**

- Theme: The Resurrection and the hereafter.
- On the doomsday, the:
    - heaven will split.
    - earth will be spread out.
    - books of deeds will be distributed.
    - righteous will be happy; the disbelievers will cry on their bad fate.
- People are asked to believe when there is still time.

**By Verse**

In the name of God, the compassionate, the merciful:

84:1. When the sky will split,
84:2. obeying its Lord in true submission;
84:3. and when the earth will be flattened out,
84:4. and will throw out all that it contains to become empty,
84:5. obeying its Lord in true submission.
84:6. O mankind, you have been moving towards your Lord, willy-nilly, you are about to meet Him.
84:7. He who is given his record in his right hand,
84:8. will be judged leniently,
84:9. and will return to his people in happiness.
84:10. But he who is given his record behind his back,
84:11. will cry on his bad luck,
84:12. he will enter into a blazing fire.
84:13. He lived happily among his people,
84:14. and thought that he would never return to God.
84:15. Why not; his Lord was always watching him.
84:16. So I, God, swear by the glow of sunset,
84:17. and by the night and all that it brings together,
84:18. and by the full moon,
84:19. that you shall pass through stages from birth to the hereafter.

84:20. Why then, the disbelievers do not believe,
84:21. and do not kneel in prayer when the Qur'an is read to them?
84:22. Instead, they reject it.
84:23. But, God knows best what they are hiding.
84:24. So, give them news of painful punishment,
84:25. except to those who believe and do good works; for them is an everlasting reward of paradise.

# CHAPTER 85

# THE CONSTELLATIONS

**Name:** From Verse One.

**Verses:** 22

**Summary:**

- Theme: Warning the disbelievers for their persecution of converts to Islam, and consoling the believers for remaining steadfast.
- God, Who created you, will bring you back to life for accountability.
- The stories of Pharaoh and Thamoud. They had strong armies but were punished for their disbelief.

**By Verse**

In the name of God, the compassionate, the merciful:

85:1. I, God, swear by the heaven with its constellations,
85:2. by the promised Day of Resurrection,
85:3. by the witnessing mankind and what is to be witnessed, the doomsday,
85:4. that the diggers of the trench are cursed,
85:5. who lighted the blazing fire,
85:6. they sat by it,
85:7. and watched the believers being tortured.
85:8. They tortured them for no other reason than believing in God,
85:9. who is the king of the heavens and the earth. God is watching over all things.
85:10. Those who have tortured the believing men and women and have not repented will have the punishment of hell and the burning fire.
85:11. But, those who have believed and do good will be rewarded with gardens watered by flowing streams. That is the great success.
85:12. Surely, your Lord's punishment is severe.
85:13. It is God who created first time and will resurrect also.
85:14. He is the forgiving, the loving,
85:15. He is the Lord of the glorious throne.
85:16. He does what He likes.
85:17. Have you not heard the story of the soldiers
85:18. of Pharaoh and Thamoud?
85:19. Yet, the disbelievers keep on denying the truth.
85:20. God has surrounded them.

85:21. But, this is the glorious Qur’an,
85:22. written on a preserved tablet.

# CHAPTER 86

# THE NIGHT-VISITOR

**Name:** From Verse One.

**Verses:** 17

**Summary:**

- Theme: Every human will appear before God after death for accountability.
- The Qur'an is a decisive word, which the disbelievers cannot defeat.
- There is a guardian over every human.
- The humans have been invited to reflect that God, Who has created them from a sperm-drop, has the power to raise them again after death.

**By Verse**

In the name of God, the compassionate, the merciful:

86:1. I, God, swear by the heaven and the visitor at night.
86:2. Do you know what the visitor at night is?
86:3. It is the bright shining star.
86:4. There is no human without a protector over him.
86:5. Let a human think from what he has been created.
86:6. He was created from an ejected fluid,
86:7. that comes from between the backbone and the ribs.
86:8. Certainly, God has the power to bring the human back to life.
86:9. That Day (of Resurrection), when his hidden thoughts shall be examined,
86:10. he will have no power or helper.
86:11. I, God, swear by the rain-giving heaven,
86:12. and by the earth that opens out with herbage,
86:13. that the Qur'an is a decisive word.
86:14. It is not a joke.
86:15. The disbelievers are plotting against you O Muhammad,
86:16. and I, God, am planning against them too.
86:17. So, grant the disbelievers respite for a while.

# CHAPTER 87

# THE MOST HIGH

**Name:** From Verse One.

**Verses:** 19

**Summary:**

- God has created all things with destiny.
- Instructions to Prophet Muhammad for reciting God's revelations, and giving people advice.
- The hereafter is better than the worldly life.

### By Verse

In the name of God, the compassionate, the merciful:

87:1. Praise the name of your Lord, the most high,
87:2. Who created all things, and proportioned them;
87:3. Who destined and guided them;
87:4. Who grows the pasture;
87:5. and then dries it to black stubble.
87:6. O Muhammad, We will enable you to recite Our revelations, so that you will not forget them,
87:7. except what God wills. He has knowledge of the visible and the invisible.
87:8. We, God, will make the path smooth for you.
87:9. Therefore, give people advice, if it will benefit them.
87:10. He who fears God will accept the advice,
87:11. but the wretched sinner will avoid it.
87:12. He will be thrown into the blazing fire,
87:13. where he will neither live nor die.
87:14. He who purifies himself will succeed, and
87:15. remembers the name of his Lord and prays to Him.
87:16. But you people prefer the worldly life,
87:17. Although, the hereafter is better and more lasting.
87:18. This has been revealed in the earlier Scriptures,
87:19. the Scriptures of Prophets Abraham and Moses.

# CHAPTER 88

# THE OVERWHELMING EVENT

**Name:** From Verse One.

**Verses:** 26

**Summary:**

- Theme: The Day of Resurrection, and the condition of disbelievers and believers that day.
- The disbelievers' attention has been drawn towards the wonders of nature, and the disbelievers' accountability.

**By Verse**

In the name of God, the compassionate, the merciful:

88:1. Have you heard of the overwhelming event of Resurrection?
88:2. That day, some faces will be downcast,
88:3. working hard but exhausted,
88:4. scorching by burning fire,
88:5. and drinking from a boiling spring.
88:6. There will be no food for them except from a thorny bitter plant.
88:7. This will neither nourish them nor satisfy their hunger.
88:8. That day, some faces will be radiant,
88:9. well-pleased because of their deeds in the world.
88:10. They will be in a lofty garden of paradise.
88:11. There, they will hear no useless talk,
88:12. and will have a gushing spring,
88:13. raised couches,
88:14. goblets placed before them,
88:15. cushions set in rows,
88:16. and rich carpets spread out.
88:17. Do the disbelievers not look at camels, how they were created?
88:18. And at sky, how it was raised high?
88:19. And at the mountains, how they were erected?
88:20. And at the earth, how it was spread out?
88:21. O Muhammad, keep on warning them. That is your only duty.
88:22. You are not their warden.
88:23. However, those who turn away and disbelieve,
88:24. will be severely punished by God.
88:25. They shall return to Us,
88:26. and We will bring them to account.

# CHAPTER 89

# THE DAWN

**Name:** From Verse One.

**Verses:** 30

**Summary:**

- Theme: Reward and punishment in the hereafter.
- Warning for social welfare through examples of prior nations.
- What should be avoided to do social welfare?
- The Day of Judgment will be too late to act on the warning.
- God's address to the believers for entering paradise.

**By Verse**

In the name of God, the compassionate, the merciful:

89:1. I, God, swear by the dawn,
89:2. by the ten nights*,

**of Dhul-Hijjah, Islamic calendar's 12th month for pilgrimage to Mecca.*

89:3. by the even and odd numbers*,

**Scholars differ about the explanation. It could be that out of the five daily obligatory prayers in Islam, four have even number of prayer cycles and the sun-set prayer has an odd number of prayer cycles.*

89:4. and by the departing night;
89:5. is this not a sufficient oath for a thinking person?
89:6. Have you not considered how your Lord dealt with Aad's people,
89:7. from the lofty-pillar city of Iram*,

**city in southeastern Arabia. The capital of the pre-Islamic people of Ad, whom God destroyed for their disbelief.*

89:8. the like of which was not build in any other land?
89:9. And with Thamoud, who carved out homes in the rocks of the valley?
89:10. And with Pharaoh, who tortured his victims with the stakes?
89:11. They all were rebellious in the lands,
89:12. and they increased wickedness.
89:13. Therefore, your Lord punished them.
89:14. The reality is that your Lord was watching them.
89:15. As for man, when his Lord tests him by being generous and

favorable to him, he says: My Lord has honored me.
89:16. But when He tests him by reducing his livelihood, he says: My Lord has humiliated me.
89:17. Not really! But you do not show kindness to the orphan,
89:18. and you do not encourage one another to feed the poor.
89:19. And you take away the inheritance with greed,
89:20. and you love wealth immensely.
89:21. No, your thinking is wrong! When the earth will be crushed to dust,
89:22. and your Lord will appear with the angels in rows,
89:23. and the hell will be brought near; that day, man will remember his deeds, but what good that will do for him?
89:24. He will say: Oh, I wish I had done some good for my life to come.
89:25. But that day, none will punish him as God will,
89:26. and none will bind him as God will.
89:27. The righteous will be told: O calm soul,
89:28. return to your Lord, joyfully, with His pleasure,
89:29. join my favored ones,
89:30. and enter My paradise.

# CHAPTER 90

## THE CITY

**Name:** From Verse One.

**Verses:** 20

**Summary:**

- God has created mankind to toil and strive, for which He has provided guidance, but mankind has a choice to follow it or not.
- The qualities of a righteous person and a wicked person.

### By Verse

In the name of God, the compassionate, the merciful:

90:1. I, God, swear by this city of Mecca,
90:2. and you O Muhammad are being troubled in this city.
90:3. And I, God, swear by the father Prophet Adam and his children,
90:4. We have created man to toil and to struggle.
90:5. Does he think that no one has power over him?
90:6. He says boastfully: I have wasted a lot of wealth.
90:7. Does he think that no one is watching him?
90:8. Have We, God, not given him two eyes,
90:9. and a tongue and two lips,
90:10. and shown him two paths of good and evil?
90:11. But, he would not attempt the uphill road of goodness.
90:12. And do you know what the attempting of the uphill road means?
90:13. It is the freeing a slave;
90:14. or feeding, on a day of hunger,
90:15. an orphaned relative,
90:16. or a poor hungry person;
90:17. and to be among those who believed and advised one another to be patient and show compassion.
90:18. Such people will stand on the right side.
90:19. But those who disbelieved Our revelations will stand on the left hand.
90:20. The hellfire would be surrounding them.

# CHAPTER 91

# THE SUN

**Name:** From Verse One.

**Verses:** 15

**Summary:**

- Distinction between good and evil.
- The distinction is explained by an example of Thamoud's people, who denied their prophet, hamstrung God's she-camel, and God punished them by razing their city to ground.

**By Verse**

In the name of God, the compassionate, the merciful:

91:1. I, God, swear by the sun and its brightness;
91:2. by the moon, which follows the sun;
91:3. by the day, which reveals the sun's glory;
91:4. by the night, which covers the sun;
91:5. by the sky and God who constructed it;
91:6. by the earth and Him who spread it;
91:7. by the soul and Him who molded it,
91:8. and inspired it to understand what is right and wrong,
91:9. that the person, who purifies his soul, will be successful,
91:10. and the one, who corrupts his soul, will be ruined.
91:11. Because of their rebellious pride, Thamoud's people denied their prophet.
91:12. When the worst sinner among them rose in rage,
91:13. God's Messenger said to them: This is God's she-camel; let her drink.
91:14. They called him a liar, and hamstrung and crippled her. So for that crime, their Lord punished them by razing their city to ground.
91:15. God was not afraid of the consequences.

# CHAPTER 92

# THE NIGHT

**Name:** From Verse One.

**Verses:** 21

**Summary:**

- Differentiation between two different ways of life and their end results:
    - First way: One spends one's wealth in charity, adopts God-consciousness and righteousness, and acknowledges the goodness.
    - Second way: One is miserly, does not care for God's pleasure or displeasure, and ignores what is good and right.
- God will facilitate the easy way for the good people and the hard way for the wicked. When a wicked person will die, his wealth will not benefit him.

**By Verse**

In the name of God, the compassionate, the merciful:

92:1. I, God, swear by the night that brings darkness;
92:2. by the shining day;
92:3. and by God, Who created male and female,
92:4. that your efforts are diverse.
92:5. For him, who gives charity and guards against evil,
92:6. and believes in goodness,
92:7. We, God, will smooth the path of goodness for him.
92:8. But for him, who is miserly and considers himself free from need of God,
92:9. and disbelieves in goodness,
92:10. We, God, shall ease his way to distress.
92:11. When he will die, his wealth will not benefit him.
92:12. Our responsibility is to guide.
92:13. Unto God belong the hereafter and this world.
92:14. Therefore, I, God, have warned you of the blazing fire.
92:15. No one will burn in it except the most wretched,
92:16. who denied the truth and turned away.
92:17. But, the righteous will be kept away from the blazing fire,

92:18. and also who purifies himself by giving his wealth in charity.
92:19. In doing so, he does not expect any favor from anyone.
92:20. He does so only to please his Lord, the most high.
92:21. God will indeed by happy with him.

# CHAPTER 93

# THE DAYLIGHT

**Name:** From Verse One.

**Verses:** 11

**Summary:**

- Consoling Prophet Muhammad by removing his anxiety and distress because there was delay in continuation of the revelation.
- God gives good news to the Prophet that the later period will be better for him than the earlier.

**By Verse**

In the name of God, the compassionate, the merciful:

93:1. I, God, swear by the light of day,
93:2. and by the fall of night,
93:3. that your Lord has neither abandoned you, nor is He displeased with you.
93:4. The time to come will be better for you than the present.
93:5. Soon your Lord will give you so much that you will be pleased with it.
93:6. Did God not find you an orphan and gave you refuge?
93:7. Did He not find you in search of guidance and guided you?
93:8. Did he not find you poor and enriched you?
93:9. Therefore, do not mistreat the orphan,
93:10. and do not scold the beggar,
93:11. and express gratitude for the blessings of your Lord.

# CHAPTER 94

# THE EXPANSION

**Name:** From Verse One.

**Verses:** Eight

**Summary:**

- Consoling and encouraging Prophet Muhammad for facing disbelievers' opposition from spreading Islam's message.
- God expanded the Prophet's chest, lightened his burden, increased his fame, and advised him to worship God exclusively.

### By Verse

In the name of God, the compassionate, the merciful:

94:1. O Muhammad, have we not expanded your breast for you,
94:2. and removed from you the burden,
94:3. which weighed down your back?
94:4. And have We not increased your reputation?
94:5. The reality is that ease follows hardship.
94:6. Surely, with difficulty comes ease.
94:7. Therefore, when you have finished your tasks, stand up for worship,
94:8. and turn to your Lord exclusively.

# CHAPTER 95

# THE FIG

**Name:** From Verse One.

**Verses:** Eight

**Summary:**

- Reward and punishment in the hereafter.
- God created the human as the best creature.

**By Verse**

In the name of God, the compassionate, the merciful:

95:1. I, God, swear by the fig and the olive,
95:2. by Mount Sinai,
95:3. and by this secure city of Mecca,
95:4. that We have created man in the best mold.
95:5. But, based on his deeds, have reduced him to the lowest of the low,
95:6. except those who have faith and do good deeds. They will have everlasting reward.
95:7. What then, after this, make the man deny the last judgment?
95:8. Is God not the best judge?

# CHAPTER 96

# THE BLOOD-CLOT

**Name:** From Verse Two.

**Verses:** 19

**Summary:**

- Start of revelation to Prophet Muhammad.
- The first five verses of this chapter are the first revelation that descended upon Prophet Muhammad in the cave of Hira, near Mecca.
- Threat of a disbeliever, Abu Jahl, to Prophet Muhammad against praying in the grand mosque at Mecca. God's advice to Prophet Muhammad to ignore the threat and worship Him.

**By Verse**

In the name of God, the compassionate, the merciful:

96:1. O Muhammad, read in the name of your Lord Who created,
96:2. created man from a blood-clot.
96:3. Read, your Lord is the most generous,
96:4. Who taught by the pen,
96:5. He taught man what he did not know.
96:6. Alas, but man breaks all limits.
96:7. Because, he considers himself independent.
96:8. Though, all shall return to your Lord.
96:9. Have you seen the disbeliever Abu Jahl who forbids
96:10. Our servant Muhammad when he prays at the Kabah – the great mosque at Mecca?
96:11. Have you seen if he does so out of guidance,
96:12. or he commands people to piety?
96:13. Do you think Abu Jahl denies the truth and turns away?
96:14. Does he not know that God is watching?
96:15. Not at all. Abu Jahl will not be able to carry out his threat against you, O Muhammad! If he does not stop, We will surely drag him by the forelock,
96:16. his lying, sinning forelock.
96:17. Then, let him call his helpers,
96:18. We too will call the guards of hell to punish him.
96:19. No, never! Do not yield to him; instead prostrate yourself and draw near to God.

# CHAPTER 97

## THE NIGHT OF HONOR

**Name:** From Verse One.

**Verses:** Five

**Summary:**

- The Qur'an was revealed during the honorable night of Ramadan, the Islamic calendar's 9th month.
- Importance of the night; and what happens during the night.

### By Verse

In the name of God, the compassionate, the merciful:

97:1. We revealed the Qur'an during the honorable night of Ramadhan*.

**Most Scholars consider it to be 27th Ramadhan.*

97:2. Do you know what the honorable night is?

97:3. The honorable night is better than a 1,000 months.

97:4. That night, the angels and the spirit, Angel Gabriel, by their Lord's permission, come down with His decree concerning every matter.

97:5. During that night, there is peace till dawn.

# CHAPTER 98

# THE CLEAR EVIDENCE

**Name:** From Verse One.

**Verses:** Eight

**Summary:**

- Prophet Muhammad's message for the people of the Scriptures (Jews and Christians).
- The sins of the disbelievers and the idolaters.
- God's rewards to the believers, and the punishment to the disbelievers from among the people of the Scriptures and the idolaters in the hereafter.

**By Verse**

In the name of God, the compassionate, the merciful:

98:1. The disbelievers among the people of the Scriptures (Jews and Christians) would not stop disbelieving till the clear proof would come to them,

98:2. a Messenger from God, who would recite them the holy Scriptures,

98:3. containing sound and correct writings.

98:4. The people of the Scriptures (Jews and Christians) were not divided until after the clear proof had come to them.

98:5. They were commanded only to worship God with devotion and faith, to establish prayer, and to give charity. That is the true religion.

98:6. The disbelievers among the people of the Scriptures (Jews and Christians) and the idolaters will burn in the hellfire forever. They are the worst of creatures.

98:7. The believers who have done good works are the best creatures.

98:8. God will reward them with gardens of paradise, watered by running streams, to live there forever. God is well pleased with them, and they with Him. That is for those who fear their Lord.

# CHAPTER 99

# THE EARTHQUAKE

**Name:** From Verse One.

**Verses:** Eight

**Summary:**

- Scene on the Day of Resurrection. The earth will throw up her burden of dead bodies and God will inspire her to expose the secrets of the people.
- Whoever would have done an atom's weight of good or evil will see it.

### By Verse

In the name of God, the compassionate, the merciful:

99:1. When the earth will be shaken up violently,
99:2. and the earth will throw up her burdens buried in it,
99:3. and man would say: What is the matter with the earth?
99:4. That day, the earth will report her news,
99:5. because, your Lord would have inspired her.
99:6. That day, the people will come in diverse groups to be shown their deeds.
99:7. Whoever would have done an atom's weight of good will see it,
99:8. and whoever would have done an atom's weight of evil will also see it.

# CHAPTER 100

# THE CHARGERS

**Name:** From Verse One.

**Verses:** 11

**Summary:**

Revealing man's ungratefulness to his Lord, his love for wealth, and what will happen to him on the Day of Resurrection.

**By Verse**

In the name of God, the compassionate, the merciful:

100:1. I, God, swear by the panting horses,
100:2. which strike sparks of fire with their hoofs,
100:3. raid the enemy camp at dawn,
100:4. raise the clouds of dust,
100:5. penetrate the ranks of enemy,
100:6. that man is ungrateful to his Lord,
100:7. and surely he is a witness to that by his behavior.
100:8. Man loves wealth intensely.
100:9. But, does he not know that when the dead from the graves will be raised,
100:10. and the secrets of the hearts will be made known,
100:11. that their Lord, that day, will be well aware of their deeds?

# CHAPTER 101

# THE DISASTER

**Name:** From Verse One.

**Verses:** 11

**Summary:**

On the Day of Judgment, those who did good deeds will live in paradise, and the sinners will live in hell.

### By Verse

In the name of God, the compassionate, the merciful:

101:1. The disaster!
101:2. What is the disaster?
101:3. What do you know the disaster is?
101:4. It is the day when people will be like scattered moths,
101:5. and the mountains will be like fluffed wool.
101:6. Then, whose scales will be heavy with good works,
101:7. he will live a pleasant life in paradise.
101:8. But, the one whose scales will be light,
101:9. he will live in a bottomless pit.
101:10. And do you know what that is?
101:11. It is a blazing fire of hell.

# CHAPTER 102

# THE WORLDLY GAIN

**Name:** From Verse One

**Verses:** Eight

**Summary:**

A warning to people about their competition in gaining worldly riches and not paying attention to doing good deeds. In the hereafter, they will be questioned about that.

**By Verse**

In the name of God, the compassionate, the merciful:

102:1. The competition in gaining the worldly riches diverts you from doing good deeds,
102:2. till you die.
102:3. No! You will soon come to know the truth.
102:4. Before long, you will know.
102:5. No! if you only knew the truth;
102:6. you would surely see the hell.
102:7. Yes! you would see it with your own eyes.
102:8. Then, that day, you will be questioned about the joys you indulged in.

# CHAPTER 103

# THE FLEETING TIME

**Name:** From Verse One.

**Verses:** Three

**Summary:**

Believers should profit from doing good deeds and advising each other to truth and patience.

**By Verse**

In the name of God, the compassionate, the merciful:

103:1. I, God, swear by the fleeting time,
103:2. that mankind is in loss,
103:3. except those who have believed, do good deeds, and urge each other to truth and patience.

# CHAPTER 104

# THE SLANDERER

**Name:** From Verse One.

**Verses:** Nine

**Summary:**

Every slanderer and backbiter, who hoards wealth, will be punished.

**By Verse**

In the name of God, the compassionate, the merciful:

104:1. Doomed is every slanderer and backbiter,
104:2. who amasses wealth and hoards it,
104:3. thinking that his wealth will make him immortal.
104:4. Not at all! He will surely be thrown into crushing torment.
104:5. Do you know what the crushing torment is?
104:6. It is God's kindled fire,
104:7. which rises to the hearts.
104:8. It will close upon the slanderers and backbiters from every side,
104:9. in high columns.

# CHAPTER 105

# THE ELEPHANT

**Name:** From Verse One.

**Verses:** Five

**Background:**

In 570 AD, the year of Prophet Muhammad's birth, a Yemeni Christian king, Abraha Al-Ashram, invaded the great mosque at Mecca. The Meccans could not defend it against the army containing elephants. They prayed to God to protect His mosque, and left the city.

**Summary:**

God sent flocks of birds, which pelted the army with clay-stones resulting into its destruction.

**By Verse**

In the name of God, the compassionate, the merciful:

105:1. Have you not seen how your Lord dealt with the companions of the elephant*?

**The army of the Yemeni Christian king, Abraha Al-Ashram.*

105:2 Did God not botch their plot?
105:3. He sent flocks of birds against them,
105:4. which pelted them with clay-stones,
105:5. and made them like straw eaten up by animals.

# CHAPTER 106

## QURAYSH

**Name:** From Verse One.

**Verses:** Four

**Summary:**

Prophet Muhammad's tribe, Quraysh in Mecca, looked after the grand mosque. The tribe is reminded about God's blessings for protecting their trading caravans, and providing them food during famine, and peace from the enemy fear. Therefore, they should show their gratitude to God by worshiping Him.

### By Verse

In the name of God, the compassionate, the merciful:

106:1. The Quraysh* are accustomed,

**Prophet Muhammad's tribe at Mecca.*

106:2. to their protection during their winter and summer journeys for trade.

106:3. Therefore, they should worship the Lord of the grand mosque at Mecca,

106:4. Who has provided them food against hunger, and security against fear.

# CHAPTER 107

# THE NEIGHBORLY NEEDS

**Name:** From Verse Seven.

**Verses:** Seven

**Summary:**

- Characteristics of the person who denies the last judgment.
- Warning to those who refuse small kindnesses to the neighbors.

**By Verse**

In the name of God, the compassionate, the merciful:

107:1. Have you thought of the person who denies the last judgment?
107:2. He is the one who drives away the orphan,
107:3. and does not encourage others to feed the poor.
107:4. So, this is a warning to the worshippers,
107:5. who are neglectful of their prayers.
107:6. They do good for show off,
107:7. but refuse small kindnesses to the neighbors.

# CHAPTER 108

# ABUNDANCE

**Name:** From Verse One.

**Verses:** Three

**Background:**

In Islam's early days, the whole nation was against Prophet Muhammad for preaching Islam. The disbelieving Quraysh of Mecca said:

- Muhammad is cut off from his community;
- he is a powerless and helpless individual;
- his sons have died; and
- when he dies, there will be no one to remember him.

**Summary:**

God:

- gives good news to Prophet Muhammad of giving him abundance.
- advises him to pray and offer sacrifice to God.
- predicts that his enemy will be cut off from the hope in the future.

**By Verse**

In the name of God, the compassionate, the merciful:

108:1. O Muhammad, We have given you abundance.
108:2. Therefore, pray only to your Lord and offer sacrifice to Him.
108:3. Your enemy shall be cut off from the hope in the future.

# CHAPTER 109

# THE DISBELIEVERS

**Name:** From Verse One

**Verses:** Six

**Background:**

When Prophet Muhammad started preaching Islam, the disbelievers came to him more than once with proposals to compromise:

- We can:
  - make you our chief;
  - give you a lot of wealth; and
  - marry you to any woman you like.
- You worship our gods and we will worship your God.

**Summary:**

God's commandment that Prophet Muhammad should not compromise with the disbelievers regarding religion.

**By Verse**

In the name of God, the compassionate, the merciful:

109:1. Say to the disbelievers:
109:2. I, Prophet Muhammad, do not worship whom you worship;
109:3. nor you worship whom I worship;
109:4. I shall never worship whom you worship;
109:5. nor you will worship whom I worship;
109:6. you have your religion and I have mine.

# CHAPTER 110

# THE HELP

**Name:** From Verse One.

**Verses:** Three

**Background:**

This chapter was the last complete chapter God revealed to Prophet Muhammad. Three months later, Prophet Muhammad passed away.

**Summary:**

God indicates that when Islam would achieve victory and people would start entering God's religion in great numbers, then Prophet Muhammad's mission would be fulfilled. His passing away will be near, and he should devote more time for the hereafter by glorifying God and asking for His forgiveness.

**By Verse**

In the name of God, the compassionate, the merciful:

110:1. When God's help comes and victory is achieved,
110:2. and you, O Muhammad, see people entering God's religion crowd after crowd,
110:3. glorify your Lord with His praise, and ask for His forgiveness. He is every-ready to be merciful.

# CHAPTER 111

# THE FLAME

**Name:** From Verse One

**Verses:** Five

**Background:**

Abu Lahab and his wife were diehard opponents of Prophet Muhammad. He was Prophet's neighbor and an uncle. Before proclamation of Prophethood, Prophet's two daughters were married to his sons.

**Summary:**

God curses Abu Lahab and his wife.

**By Verse**

In the name of God, the compassionate, the merciful:

111:1. May the hands of Abu Lahab perish, and may he perish.
111:2. His wealth and what he has earned will not benefit him.
111:3. He shall soon burn in a flaming fire,
111:4. and his wife, the carrier of firewood,
111:5. shall have a rope of palm-fibers around her neck.

# CHAPTER 112

# THE PURITY

**Name:** Does not appear in the chapter.

The recital of the chapter fosters deep appreciation of God's unity and uniqueness through the purity of one's heart.

**Verses:** Four

**Background:**

The chapter was revealed because the disbelievers were asking Prophet Muhammad about God's ancestry.

**Summary:**

God has unique attributes: Oneness, independence, and no human qualities of having children, fatherhood, and equality.

**By Verse**

In the name of God, the compassionate, the merciful:

112:1. Say: He is God, the one.
112:2. He is independent of all, but all depend on Him.
112:3. Neither He has fathered any children, nor has anyone fathered him.
112:4. No one is like Him.

# CHAPTER 113

## THE DAWN

**Name:** From Verse One.

**Verses:** Five

**Summary:**

Seeking refuge in God from the evil effects of all that exists, the darkness of the night, the mischief of those who cause discord and dissention, and the harms of jealousy.

### By Verse

In the name of God, the compassionate, the merciful:

113:1. O Prophet Muhammad say: I seek refuge with the Lord of daybreak,
113:2. from the mischief of God's creatures;
113:3. and from the mischief of the night when it spreads its darkness;
113:4. and from the mischief of those who break the knots of mutual relationships through magic;
113:5. and from the mischief of the envier, when he envies.

# CHAPTER 114

# MANKIND

**Name:** From Verse One.

**Verses:** Six

**Summary:**

Seeking God's refuge from sneaking whisperer's mischief.

**By Verse**

In the name of God, the compassionate, the merciful:

114:1. Prophet Muhammad Say: I seek refuge with the Lord of mankind,
114:2. the King of mankind,
114:3. the God of mankind;
114:4. from the mischief of the whisperer, who sneaks time after time;
114:5. who whispers to create doubt in the hearts of mankind;
114:6. whether the whisperer is from the jinns or the mankind.

# INDEX

## A

** 7:65 = Chapter 7, Verse 65.*

| | |
|---|---|
| | 2:282, 2:286, 3:13, 3:28, 3:49, 3:57, 3:68, 3:69, 3:72, 3:99, 3:100, 3:102, 3:110, 3:118, 3:121, 3:122, 3:124, 3:130, 3:139, 3:140, 3:141, 3:149, 3:152, 3:156, 3:160, 3:164, 3:166, 3:171, 3:175, 3:179, 3:200, 4:19, 4:29, 4:43, 4:45, 4:51, 4:57, 4:59, 4:71, 4:76, 4:84, 4:92, 4:93, 4:94, 4:95, 4:103, 4:115, 4:122, 4:135, 4:136, 4:139, 4:141, 4:144, 4:146, 4:173, 5:1, 5:2, 5:5, 5:6, 5:8, 5:9, 5:11, 5:23, 5:35, 5:43, 5:51, 5:53, 5:54, 5:55, 5:56, 5:57, 5:69, 5:82, 5:87, 5:90, 5:94, 5:95, 5:101, 5:105, 5:106, 5:112, 6:27, 6:75, 6:108, 6:118, 7:2, 7:32, 7:42, 7:43, 7:52, 7:75, 7:85, 7:86, 7:143, 7:203, 8:1, 8:2, 8:4, 8:5, 8:9, 8:12, 8:15, 8:17, 8:19, 8:20, 8:24, 8:27, 8:29, 8:39, 8:43, 8:45, 8:49, 8:62, 8:63, 8:65, 8:66, 8:67, 8:73, 8:74, 9:10, 9:13, 9:14, 9:15, 9:16, 9:23, 9:26, 9:28, 9:34, 9:38, 9:51, 9:56, 9:61, 9:62, 9:79, 9:105, 9:107, 9:111, 9:112, 9:113, 9:118, 9:119, 9:122, 9:123, 9:124, 9:128, 10:2, 10:4, 10:57, 10:87, 10:103, 10:104, 11:29, 11:30, 11:40, 11:66, 11:86, 11:94, 11:120, 12:67, 12:111, 13:31, 14:11, 14:12, 14:23, 14:27, 14:41, 15:77, 15:88, 16:27, 16:64, 6:89, 16:97, 16:102, 16:126, 17:9, 17:82, 17:105, 18:2, 18:30, 18:80, 18:107, 19:73, 20:75, 20:112, 21:88, 21:94, 22:14, 22:17, 22:19, 22:23, 22:38, 22:50, 22:54, 22:56, 23:1, 23:111, 24:2, 24:3, 24:12, 24:14, 24:17, 24:19, 24:21, 24:27, 24:31, 24:47, 24:51, 24:55, 24:58, 24:62, 26:102, 26:114, 26:118, 26:215, 27:2, 27:77, 27:86, 28:3, 29:11, 29:12, 29:24, 29:44, 29:51, 29:58, 30:4, 30:14, 30:37, 30:43, 30:45, 31:8, 32:18, 32:19, 33:6, 33:9, 33:11, 33:19, 33:22, 33:23, 33:25, 33:35, 33:37, 33:41, 33:43, 33:47, 33:49, 33:50, 33:56, 33:69, 33:70, 33:73, 34:20, 34:35, 35:7, 36:47, 37:52, 38:28, 39:24, 39:35, 39:52, 40:7, 40:28, 40:30, 40:35, 40:38, 40:40, 40:51, 40:58, 41:8, 41:44, 42:18, 42:22, 42:26, 42:36, 42:45, 44:12, 45:13, 45:14, 45:20, 45:21, 45:30, 46:11, 47:2, 47:3, 47:7, 47:11, 47:12, 47:20, 47:33, 48:4, 48:12, 48:18, 48:20, 48:25, 48:26, 48:29, 49:1, 49:2, 49:6, 49:10, 49:11, 49:12, 49:15, 49:18, 51:55, 52:21, 53:15, 55:54, 55:76, 57:8, 57:13, 57:14, 57:16, 57:27, 57:28, 58:9, 58:10, 58:11, 58:12, 58:22, 59:2, 59:8, 59:10, 59:18, 60:1, 60:10, 60:11, 60:13, 61:2, 61:10, 61:13, 61:14, 62:9, 63:8, 63:9, 64:2, 64:13, |

**C**

| Captive | 2:85, 4:24, 4:25, 8:30, 76:8. |
|---|---|
| Cattle | 3:14, 4:119, Chapter 6 Title, 6:144, 6:146, 16:66, 20:54,42:11, 79:33. |
| Cave | 9:40, 9:57, 17:68, Chapter 18 Title, 18:9, 18:10, 18:11, 18:17, 18:21, 18:22, 18:25. |
| Charity | 2:3, 2:43, 2:83, 2:110, 2:177, 2:215, 2:262, 2:263, 2:264, 2:267, 2:270, 2:271, 2:272, 2:274, 2:276, 2:277, 2:280, 3:92, 3:134, 4:77, 4:92, 4:114, 4:162, 5:12, 5:45, 5:55, 6:141, 7:156, 9:5, 9:11, 9:18, 9:58, 9:67, 9:71, 9:75, 9:79, 9:98, 9:103, 13:22, 14:31, 16:90, 19:31, 21:73, 22:35, 22:41, 22:78, 23:4, 23:60, 24:37, 24:56, 27:3, 28:54, 31:4, 32:16, 33:33, 33:35, 35:29, 36:47, 41:7, 57:7, 57:18, 58:12, 58:13, 63:10, 73:20, 92:5, 92:18, 98:5. |
| Children | 2:40, 2:47, 2:83, 2:122, 2:132, 2:133, 2:146, 2:211, 2:233, 2:246, 2:266, 3:10, 3:49, 3:52, 3:93, 3:116, 4:7, 4:11, 4:12, 4:54, 4:75, 4:98, 4:127, 5:18, 5:32, 5:70, 5:72, 5:110, 6:20, 6:101, 6:137, 6:140, 6:151, 7:26, 7:27, 7:31, 7:35, 7:105, 7:134, 7:137, 7:138, 7:172, 8:28, 9:55, 9:69, 9:85, 10:90, 10:93, 13:23, 13:37, 16:72, Chapter 17 Title, 17:2, 17:4, 17:31, 17:64, 17:70, 17:101, 18:39, 18:46, 19:77, 20:47, 20:80, 20:94, 21:26, 21:23, 21:55, 24:31, 24:58, 24:59, 24:61, 25:74, 26:17, 26:22, 26:88, 26:133, 32:33, 34:35, 34:37, 36:60, 37:152, 40:53, 43:59, 44:30, 45:16, 46:10, 57:20, 58:17, 60:3, 60:12, 63:9, 64:14, 64:15, 68:14, 70:11, 71:12, 71:21, 33:17, 74:13, 80:36, 90:3, 112:3. |
| Christ | 3:3, 3:53, 3:54, 5:17, 21:91, 26:196. |
| Christian | 2:62, 2:111, 2:113, 2:116, 2:120, 2:135, 2:136, 2:140, 3:19, 3:20, 3:64, 3:67, 3:98, 3:110, 4:47, 4:123, 4:131, 4:171, 5:5, 5:14, 5:15, 5:18, 5:51, 5:52, 5:69, 5:75, 5:82, 6:20, 6:114, 6:156, 9:30, 9:107, 16:43, 16:124, 17:107, 22:17, 38:7, 57:29, 98:1, 105:1. |
| City | 2:58, 2:61, 2:126, 7:82, 7:88, 7:94, 7:123, 7:161, 12:30, 12:67, 12:68, 12:82, 14:35, 15:67, 15:74, 15:76, 16:112, 18:19, 21:74, 25:40, 25:51, 27:34, 27:48, 27:56, 27:91, 28:15, 28:18, 28:20, 29:31, 29:34, 29:35, 33:14, 33:60, 34:34, 36:13, 36:14, 36:20, 42:7, 43:13, 60:1, 89:7, Chapter 90 Title:, 90:1, 90:2, 91:14, 95:3. |
| Clot | 22:5, 23:14, 23:40, 40:67, 75:38. Chapter 96 Title, |

**D**

| | |
|---|---|
| | 7:172, 7:187, 8:16, 8:41, 9:2, 9:3, 9:18, 9:19, 9:29, 9:35, 9:44, 9:45, 9:77, 9:99, 9:108, 10:3, 10:6, 10:15, 10:24, 10:28, 10:45, 10:50, 10:60, 10:93, 11:33, 11:7, 11:8, 11:26, 11:43, 11:60, 11:65, 11:66, 11:77, 11:84, 11:98, 11:99, 11:103, 11:104, 11:105, 12:43, 13:3, 14:8, 14:31, 14:33, 14:41, 14:42, 14:44, 14:48, 14:49, 15:2, 15:35, 15:36, 15:38, 16:12, 16:25, 16:27, 16:63, 16:84, 16:87, 16:89, 16:92, 16:111, 16:124, 17:12, 17:15, 17:52, 17:58, 17:62, 17:71, 17:78, 17:97, 18:19, 18:47, 18:52, 18:52, 18:99, 18:100, 18:105, 19:10, 19:15, 19:33, 19:37, 19:38,19:39, 19:84, 19:85, 19:95, 20:59, 20:64, 20:100, 20:101, 20:102, 20:103, 20:104, 20:108, 20:109, 20:124, 20:126, 20:130, 21:1, 21:20, 21:33, 21:39, 21:42, 21:47, 21:49, 21:97, 21:103, 21:104, 22:2, 22:9, 22:17, 22:28, 22:47, 22:55, 22:56, 22:61, 22:66, 22:69, 23:16, 23:67, 23:80, 23:100, 23:101, 23:111, 23:113, 24:2, 24:24, 24:25, 24:37, 24:44, 24:64, 25:17, 25:22, 25:24, 25:25, 25:26, 25:27, 25:47, 25:59, 25:62, 25:69, 26:38, 26:82, 26:87, 26:88, 26:90, 26:135, 26:155, 26:156, 26:189, 27:83, 27:86, 27:87, 27:89, 28:15, 28:18, 28:41, 28:42, 28:61, 28:62, 28:65, 28:66, 28:71, 28:72, 28:73, 28:74, 28:82, 29:13, 29:25, 29:36, 29:55, 30:4, 30:112, 30:14, 30:23, 30:43, 30:56, 30:57, 31:29, 31:33, 32:4, 32:5, 32:14, 32:25, 32:29, 34:18, 34:26, 34:29, 34:30, 34:33, 34:40, 34:42, 35:13, 35:14, 36:37, 36:40, 36:54, 36:55, 36:64, 36:65, 37:20, 37:21, 37:26, 37:33, 37:144, 37:177, 38:16, 38:26, 38:53, 38:78, 38:79, 38:81, 39:5, 39:13, 39:15, 39:24, 39:31, 39:47, 39:60, 39:67, 39:71, 40:9, 40:11, 40:15, 40:16, 40:17, 40:18, 40:27, 40:29, 40:32, 40:46, 40:49, 40:51, 40:52, 40:61, 41:9, 41:10, 41:12, 41:16, 41:19, 41:37, 41:38, 41:40, 41:47, 42:7, 42:22, 42:45, 42:47, 43:39, 43:51, 43:65, 43:67, 43:68, 43:83, 44:10, 44:16, 44:40, 44:41, 45:5, 45:14, 45:17, 45:26, 45:28, 45:34, 45:35, 46:5, 46:6, 46:20, 46:21, 46:34, 46:35, 50:20, 50:22, 50:30, 50:34, 50:38, 50:41, 50:42, 50:44, 51:6, 51:8, 51:12, 51:13, 51:16, 51:23, 51:60, 52:9, 52:11, 52:13, 52:45, 52:46, 53:57, 54:6, 54:8, 54:19, 54:48, 55:29, 55:39, 56:1, 56:50, 56:56, 57:6, 57:12, 57:13, 57:40, 58:6, 58:7, 58:18, 58:22, 59:2, 59:18, 60:3, 60:6, 64:9, 65:2, 66:7, 66:8, 68:39, 68:42, |

| | |
|---|---|
| | 69:7, 69:15, 69:16, 69:17, 69:18, 70:4, 70:6, 70:8, 70:11, 70:26, 70:42, 70:44, 71:5, 71:18, 72:25, 73:7, 73:14, 73:17, 73:20, 74:9, 74:46, 75:1, 75:6, 75:10, 75:12, 75:13, 75:22, 75:30, 76:7, 76:10, 76:11, 76:40, 76:45, 76:47, 76:49, 78:11, 78:17, 78:18, 78:38, 78:39, 78:40, 79:6, 79:8, 79:29, 79:34, 79:35, 79:46, 80:33, 80:34, 80:37, 80:38, 80:40, 82:15, 82:17, 82:18, 82:19, 83:5, 83:6, 83:10, 83:15, 83:34, 85:2, 85:3, 85:3, 86:9, 88:2, 88:8, 89:23, 89:25, 90:14, 91:3, 92:2, 93:1, 99:4, 99:6, 100:11, 101:4, 102:8. |
| Dead | 2:55, 2:73, 2:153, 2:139, 2:173, 2:259, 2:260, 3:27, 3:49, 3:169, 5:3, 5:31, 5:110, 6:36, 6:60, 6:95, 6:111, 6:122, 6:139, 6:145, 7:57, 10:31, 10:92, 13:31, 15:76, 16:21, 16:38, 16:115, 19:66, 21:21, 22:6, 23:41, 25:49, 27:80, 30:19, 30:15, 3052:, 32:10, 34:14, 35:9, 35:22, 36:12, 336:33, 39:68, 41:39, 42:9, 43:11, 46:33, 49:12, 50:4, 50:11, 51:37, 53:54, 56:47, 69:7, 75:40, 77:26, 100:9. |
| Death | 2:19, 2:94, 2:95, 2:133, 2:180, 2:234, 2:243, 2:246, 2:258, 3:143, 3:145, 3:154, 3:156, 3:168, 3:185, 4:18, 4:78, 4:159, 5:106, 6:61, 6:93, 7:158, 8:6, 9:116, 10:56, 11:7, 11:91, 14:10, 14:17, 15:23, 15:83, 16:70, 18:20, 23:80, 23:99, 25:3, 25:13, 25:14, 26:3, 26:116, 29:57, 30:19, 32:11, 33:16, 33:19, 33:53, 34:14, 35:8, 35:36, 39:42, 40:11, 40:68, 44:8, 45:21, 45:26, 47:20, 47:27, 50:19, 50:43, 53:44, 56:60, 57:20, 62:6, 62:7, 62:7, 62:8, 63:10, 67:2, 69:27, 74:47, 75:27, 75:28, 75:29, 80:21. |
| Debt | 2:282. |
| Decree | 4:24, 19:71. |
| Deed | 1:4, 2:82, 2:85, 2:139, 2:148, 2:167, 2:237, 3:57, 3:89, 3:134, 3:148, 3:193, 4:6, 4:16, 4:39, 4:40, 4:57, 4:122, 4:124, 4:125, 4:129, 4:147, 4:173, 5:9, 5:48, 5:53, 5:79, 5:85, 5:93, 5:95, 6:84, 6:88, 6:108, 6:122, 6:158, 6:160, 6:164, 7:42, 7:43, 9:17, 9:82, 9:102, 9:105, 9:120, 10:4, 10:9, 10:26, 10:52, 11:11, 13:29, 14:23, 16:32, 16:45, 16:63, 16:96, 16:97, 16:128, 17:9, 17:25, 18:2, 18:14, 18:105, 2173 21:74, 22:14, 22:23, 22:50, 22:56, 23:61, 23:63, 23:102, 24:38, 24:39, 24:40, 24:55, 25:70, 25:71, 26:227, 27:4, 27:19, 27:24, 27:90, 30:44, 30:45, 31:8, 31:22, 32:12, 32:17, 32:19, 33:29, |

**E**

| | |
|---|---|
| | 70:44, 75:7, 79:9, 90:8, 102:7. |
| Ezra | 9:30. |

**F**

| | |
|---|---|
| Face | 2:142, 2:143, 2:144, 2:145, 2:149, 2:150, 2:177, 2:214, 3:106, 3:107, 4:43, 4:47, 5:6, 6:79, 7:78, 7:91, 8:50, 10:26, 10:27, 12:93, 12:96, 14:50, 15:47, 16:58, 16:85, 17:7, 17:97, 17:107, 17:109, 18:29, 20:111, 21:39, 22:72, 23:104, 33:59, 33:66, 37:103, 39:24, 39:60, 43:17, 46:35, 47:27, 48:29, 51:60, 54:48, 55:35, 58:80, 67:22, 67:27, 70:20, 71:7, 75:22, 75:24, 75:24, 76:11, 80:38, 80:40, 80:42, 83:24, 88:2, 88:8. |
| Faith | 2:75, 2:90, 2:93, 2:108, 2:118, 2:132, 2:137, 2:143, 2:161, 2:217, 2:228, 2:249, 2:260, 3:86, 3:90, 3:91, 3:97, 3:101, 3:106, 3:137, 3:147, 3:173, 3:177, 3:193, 4:25, 4:42, 4:65, 4:66, 4:102, 4:124, 4:125, 4:136, 4:137, 4:168, 4:170, 5:5, 5:41, 5:50, 5:54, 5:102, 5:113, 5:158, 5:161, 7:45, 8:2, 8:19, 8:39, 8:55, 9:7, 9:8, 9:36,<br>9:61, 9:66, 9:124, 10:9, 10:19, 10:78, 10:84, 10:104, 10:105, 11:62, 15:40, 15:41, 16:52, 16:106, 16:120, 16:123, 17:19, 17:60, 17:65, 17:74, 18:88, 18:106, 19:96, 21:1, 22:31, 22:38, 22:78, 23:8, 24:62, 26:24, 26:193, 28:10, 28:67, 30:56, 30:60, 31:21, 31:32, 32:12, 33:10, 33:22, 33:24, 34:37, 34:52, 37:29, 38:24, 38:59, 38:83, 39:10, 39:38, 40:10, 40:85, 42:52, 43:25, 44:13, 45:4, 46:9, 46:17, 48:4, 49:7, 49:11, 49:14, 49:15, 49:17, 50:32, 51:20, 51:35, 51:36, 52:,21, 52:36, 53:33, 53:34, 56:10, 57:10, 57:14, 57:27, 58:11, 58:22, 59:9, 59:10, 59:23, 60:10, 63:2, 64:10, 66:5, 68:35, 74:31, 74:37, 74:45, 98:5. |
| False | 2:42, 2:56, 2:57, 3:71, 4:51, 4:60, 4:112, 4:156, 5:42, 5:60, 5:103, 6:81, 6:100, 6:112, 6:137, 6:139, 7:117, 7:195, 8:8, 10:32, 10:66, 11:50, 11:101, 12:18, 12:44, 13:17, 15:3, 16:36, 16:39, 16:56, 16:72, 16:105, 16:116, 17:81, 18:1, 18:56, 20:61, 21:18, 22:30, 22:62, 25:72, 26:45, 27:27, 27:59, 29:52, 29:67, 31:30, 33:58, 34:5, 34:49, 37:86, 37:160, 39:17, 40:5, 41:42, 42:24, 43:83, 45:27, 46:11, 46:28, 47:3, 47:25, 57:14, 58:2, 58:14, 64:10. |

| | |
|---|---|
| Famine | 7:130, 90:14. |
| Fasting | 2:183, 2:184, 2:187, 2:196, 66:5. |
| Fat | 6:146, 12:43, 51:26. |
| Fate | 2:210, 2:275, 3:11, 6:8, 6:10, 8:38, 9:52, 10:39, 10:73, 10:102, 11:3, 11:89, 11:100, 11:103, 11:110, 13:11, 17:13, 19:30, 26:227, 34:19, 39:13, 40:30, 41:25, 42:21, 47:10, 56:56, 65:3, 68:44, 73:14, 83:5. |
| Fear | 2:2, 2:19, 2:24, 2:38, 2:40, 2:41, 2:48, 2:62, 2:66, 2:74, 2:112, 2:114, 2:150, 2:155, 2:194, 2:197, 2:203, 2:206, 2:223, 2:229, 2:231, 2:233, 2:235, 2:239, 2:243, 2:262, 2:274, 2:277, 2:278, 2:281, 2:282, 2:283, 3:28, 3:30, 3:50, 3:102, 3:120, 3:123, 3:130, 3:131, 3:170, 3:173, 3:175, 3:179, 3:200, 4:1, 4:3, 4:9, 4:25, 4:34, 4:35, 4:77, 4:101, 4:128, 4:131, 5:2, 5:3, 5:7, 5:8, 5:11, 5:23, 5:28, 5:35, 5:44, 5:57, 5:65, 5:69, 5:88, 5:93, 5:94, 5:96, 5:108, 5:112, 6:15, 6:48, 6:51, 6:69, 6:72, 6:80, 6:81, 7:35, 7:49, 7:56, 7:59, 7:63, 7:96, 7:154, 7:169, 7:171, 7:201, 8:1, 8:2, 8:12, 8:26, 8:29, 8:48, 8:56, 8:57, 8:58, 8:69, 9:13, 9:18, 9:24, 9:28, 9:40, 9:119, 9:123, 10:6, 10:15, 10:22, 10:62, 10:83, 11:3, 11:26, 11:74, 11:78, 11:84, 11:102, 12:13, 12:90, 13:12, 13:21, 14:14, 14:43, 15:69, 16:2, 16:30, 16:50, 16:51, 16:52, 16:112, 17:31, 17:57, 17:60, 18:49, 19:5, 19:18, 19:45, 20:3, 20:21, 20:44, 20:77, 20:112, 21:28, 21:49, 21:103, 22:1, 22:35, 23:52, 23:57, 23:60, 24:34, 24:37, 24:50, 24:52, 24:55, 26:11, 26:12, 26:14, 26:15, 26:106, 26:108, 26:110, 26:124, 26:126, 26:131, 26:132, 26:135, 26:142, 26:144, 26:150, 26:161, 26:163, 26:177, 26:179, 26:184, 28:32, 29:16, 30:24, 30:28, 30:31, 30:33, 32:16, 33:1, 33:19, 33:32, 33:37, 33:39, 33:55, 33:70, 34:23, 35:18, 35:28, 36:11, 36:45, 37:124, 38:28, 39:10, 39:16, 39:20, 39:23, 39:61, 39:73, 40:30, 40:32, 41:18, 41:30, 42:18, 42:22, 43:63, 43:68, 46:13, 46:21, 47:20, 48:27, 49:1, 49:10, 49:12, 50:33, 50:45, 51:37, 55:46, 57:28, 58:9, 59:7, 59:16, 59:18, 59:21, 60:11, 64:16, 65:1, 65:2, 65:4, 65:5, 65:10, 67:12, 67:22, 70:27, 71:3, 76:7, 76:10, 79:19, 79:26, 79:45, 87:10, 98:8, 106:4. |
| Fig | Chapter 95 Title, 95:1. |

| | |
|---|---|
| Fighting | 2:194, 2:216, 2:217, 3:13, 3:156, 3:167, 4:77, 4:90, 9:12, 9:42, 9:44, 9:86, 9:91, 16:81, 26:14, 28:15, 33:18, 47:20, 47:21, 59:14, 73:20. |
| Fire | 2:17, 2:24, 2:174, 2:266, 3:103, 3:183, 4:10, 5:64, 6:128, 7:12, 7:41, 9:35, 11:16, 14:50, 15:27, 18:29, 18:53, 18:96, 20:10, 20:11, 20:87, 20:88, 21:39, 21:69, 21:98, 22:3, 22:9, 22:19, 22:22, 22:72, 23:104, 24:35, 25:11, 27:7, 27:8, 27:90, 28:29, 28:30, 29:24, 32:20, 33:64, 34:12, 36:80, 37:97, 38:59, 38:76, 39:16, 40:6, 48:13, 52:14, 54:48, 55:15, 55:35, 56:42, 56:71, 66:10, 67:5, 67:11, 70:15, 71:25, 72:23, 73:12, 76:4, 77:31, 81:6, 81:12, 84:12, 85:5, 85:10, 87:12, 88:4, 92:14, 92:17, 100:2, 101:11, 104:6, 113:3. |
| Fly | 2:260, 6:38, 22:73, 52:10. |
| Food | 2:61, 2:233, 2:259, 3:37, 3:93, 4:160, 5:5, 5:75, 5:96, 5:112, 5:114, 5:145, 7:160, 12:37, 16:5, 16:67, 16:118, 18:19, 18:77, 20:80, 23:20, 25:20, 26:79, 44:44, 69:36, 80:24, 88:6, 106:4. |
| Forbid | 2:85, 2:173, 2:275, 3:50, 3:104, 3:110, 3:114, 4:23, 4:31, 4:90, 4:161, 5:1, 5:3, 5:26, 5:42, 5:72, 5:87, 5:96, 6:28, 6:56, 6:119, 6:138, 6:143, 6:144, 6:145, 6:151, 7:22, 7:32, 7:33, 7:166, 9:37, 9:67, 9:71, 9:112, 11:62, 11:88, 12:51, 12:79, 15:70, 16:90, 16:115, 16:118, 17:33, 21:26, 22:41, 24:3, 24:17, 25:22, 25:68, 28:12, 31:17, 39:29, 40:66, 58:80, 60:8, 60:9, 96:9. |
| Forgive | 2:58, 2:109, 2:128, 2:175, 2:199, 2:221, 2:263, 2:268, 2:280, 2:284, 2:285, 2:286, 3:16, 3:17, 3:31, 3:128, 3:129, 3:133, 3:134, 3:135, 3:136, 3:147, 3:152, 3:155, 3:157, 3:159, 3:193, 3:195, 4:17, 4:18, 4:27, 4:31, 4:48, 4:64, 4:96, 4:106, 4:110, 4:116, 4:137, 4:168, 5:9, 5:12, 5:18, 5:39, 5:40, 5:74, 5:95, 5:101, 5:118, 7:23, 7:149, 7:151, 7:155, 7:161, 7:169, 7:199, 8:4, 8:29, 8:33, 8:38, 8:70, 8:74, 9:43, 9:80, 9:102, 9:106, 9:113, 9:114, 9:117, 11:3, 11:11, 11:47, 11:52, 11:61, 11:88, 11:90, 11:112, 12:29, 12:92, 12:97, 12:98, 14:10, 14:41, 15:85, 17:25, 18:55, 19:47, 20:73, 20:82, 22:50, 22:60, 23:109, 23:,118 24:22, 24:31, 24:33, 24:62, 26:51, 26:82, 26:86, 27:11, 27:46, 28:16, 33:35, 33:71, 34:4, 35:7, 36:11, 36:27, 38:24, 38:35, 39:53, 40:3, 40:7, 40:55, 41:6, 42:5, |

## G

| | 3:83, 3:84, 3:85, 3:86, 3:87, 3:89, 3:92, 3:94, 3:95, 3:97, 3:98, 3:99, 3:101, 3:102, 3:103, 3:107, 3:108, 3:109, 3:110, 3:112, 3:113, 3:114, 3:115, 3:116, 3:117, 3:119, 3:120, 3:121, 3:122, 3:123, 3:125, 3:126, 3:127, 3:128, 3:129, 3:130, 3:132, 3:134, 3:135, 3:136, 3:140, 3:141, 3:142, 3:144, 3:145, 3:146, 3:147, 3:148, 3:149, 3:150, 3:151, 3:152, 3:153, 3:154, 3:155, 3:156, 3:157, 3:158, 3:159, 3:160, 3:162, 3:163, 3:164, 3:165, 3:166, 3:167, 3:169, 3:170, 3:171, 3:172, 3:173, 3:174, 3:176, 3:177, 3:179, 3:180, 3:181, 3:182, 3:183, 3:187, 3:189, 3:191, 3:195, 3:198, 3:199, 3:200, 4:1, 4:5, 4:6, 4:9, 4:11, 4:12, 4:13, 4:14, 4:15, 4:16, 4:17, 4:18, 4:19, 4:23, 4:24, 4:25, 4:26, 4:27, 4:28, 4:29, 4:30, 4:32, 4:33, 4:34, 4:35, 4:36, 4:37, 4:38, 4:39, 4:40, 4:42, 4:43, 4:45, 4:468, 4:47, 4:48, 4:49, 4:50, 4:51, 4:52, 4:54, 4:56, 4:58, 4:59, 4:60, 4:61, 4:62, 4:63, 4:64, 4:69, 4:70, 4:72, 4:73, 4:74, 4:75, 4:76, 4:77, 4:78, 4:79, 4:80, 4:81, 4:82, 4:83, 4:84, 4:85, 4:86, 4:87, 4:88, 4:89, 4:90, 4:92, 4:93, 4:94, 4:95, 4:96, 4:97, 4:98, 4:99, 4:100, 4:102, 4:103, 4:104, 4:105, 4:106, 4:107, 4:10, 4:109, 4:110, 4:111, 4:113, 4:114, 4:116, 4:117, 4:118, 4:119, 4:122, 4:123, 4:125, 4:126, 4127, 4:128, 4:129, 4:130, 4:131, 4:132, 4:133, 4:134, 4:135, 4:136, 4:137, 4:139, 4:140, 4:141, 4:142, 4:143, 4:144, 4:146, 4:147, 4:148, 4:149, 4:150, 4:152, 4:153, 4:155, 4:157, 4:158, 4:160, 4:162, 4:165, 4:166, 4:167, 4:168, 4:169, 4:170, 4:171, 4:172, 4:173, 4:175, 4:176, 5:1, 5:2, 5:3, 5:4, 5:6, 5:7, 5:8, 5:9, 5:10, 5:11, 5:12, 5:13, 5:14, 5:15, 5:16, 5:17, 5:18, 5:19, 5:20, 5:21, 5:23, 5:26, 5:27, 5:28, 5:31, 5:33, 5:34, 5:35, 5:38, 5:39, 5:40, 5:41, 5:42, 5:43, 5:44, 5:45, 5:47, 5:48, 5:49, 5:50, 5:51, 5:52, 5:53, 5:54, 5:55, 5:56, 5:57, 5:59, 5:60, 5:61, 5:64, 5:65, 5:67, 5:69, 5:71, 5:72, 5:73, 5:74, 5:76, 5:80, 5:81, 5:82, 5:84, 5:85, 5:87, 5:88, 5:89, 5:91, 5:92, 5:93, 5:94, 5:95, 5:96, 5:97, 5:98, 5:99, 5:100, 5:101, 5:103, 5:104, 5:105, 5:106, 5:107, 5:108, 5:109, 5:110, 5:111, 5:112, 5:115, 5:116, 5:117, 5:119, 5:120, 6:1, 6:3, 6:12, 6:13, 6:14, 6:16, 6:17, 6:19, 6:20, 6:21, 6:22, 6:23, |

| | |
|---|---|
| | 6:24, 6:31, 6:33, 6:34, 6:35, 6:36, 6:37, 6:39, 6:40, 6:45, 6:46, 6:47, 6:50, 6:53, 6:54, 6:56, 6:57, 6:58, 6:64, 6:65, 6:69, 6:70, 6:71, 6:74, 6:76, 6:78, 6:80, 6:81, 6:88, 6:90, 6:91, 6:93, 6:94, 6:95, 6:96, 6:100, 6:102, 6:106, 6:107, 6:108, 6:109, 6:111, 6:114, 6:116, 6:119, 6:121, 6:124, 6:125, 6:128, 6:130, 6:136, 6:137, 6:138, 6:139, 6:140, 6:141, 6:142, 6:144, 6:145, 6:148, 6:149, 6:150, 6:151, 6:152, 6:153, 6:157, 6:158, 6:159, 6:162, 6:164, 7:10, 7:12, 7:13, 7:15, 7:18, 7:19, 7:24, 7:26, 7:28, 7:30, 7:32, 7:33, 7:37, 7:38, 7:43, 7:44, 7:45, 7:49, 7:50, 7:51, 7:54, 7:56, 7:57, 7:59, 7:62, 7:63, 7:65, 7:69, 7:70, 7:71, 7:73, 7:74, 7:75, 7:77, 7:85, 7:86, 7:87, 7:89, 7:96, 7:99, 7:101, 7:105, 7:127, 7:128, 7:131, 7:138, 7:140, 7:141, 7:144, 7:152, 7:156, 7:158, 7:160, 7:163, 7:164, 7:169, 7:171, 7:178, 7:180, 7:185, 7:186, 7:187, 7:188, 7:189, 7:190, 7:194, 7:195, 7:196, 7:200, 7:201, 7:204, 8:1, 8:2, 8:4, 8:7, 8:10, 8:13, 8:16, 8:17, 8:18, 8:19, 8:20, 8:22, 8:23, 8:24, 8:25, 8:27, 8:28, 8:29, 8:30, 8:32, 8:33, 8:34, 8:36, 8:37, 8:39, 8:40, 8:41, 8:42, 8:43, 8:44, 8:45, 8:46, 8:47, 8:48, 8:49, 8:51, 8:52, 8:53, 8:54, 8:55, 8:56, 8:58, 8:59, 8:60, 8:61, 8:62, 8:63, 8:64, 8:66, 8:67, 8:68, 8:69, 8:70, 8:71, 8:72, 8:74, 8:75, 9:1, 9:2, 9:3, 9:4, 9:5, 9:6, 9:7, 9:9, 9:13, 9:14, 9:15, 9:16, 9:17, 9:18, 9:19, 9:20, 9:22, 9:24, 9:25, 9:26, 9:27, 9:28, 9:29, 9:3, 9:31, 9:32, 9:33, 9:34, 9:36, 9:37, 9:38, 9:39, 9:40, 9:41, 9:42, 9:43, 9:44, 9:45, 9:46, 9:47, 9:48, 9:51, 9:52, 9:53, 9:54, 9:55, 9:56, 9:59, 9:60, 9:61, 9:62, 9:63, 9:64, 9:65, 9:67, 9:68, 9:70, 9:71, 9:72, 9:74, 9:75, 9:76, 9:77, 9:78, 9:79, 9:80, 9:81, 9:83, 9:84, 9:85, 9:86, 9:89, 9:91, 9:93, 9:94, 9:95, 9:96, 9:97, 9:98, 9:99, 9:100, 9:102, 9:103, 9:104, 9:105, 9:106, 9:107, 9:108, 9:109, 9:110, 9:111, 9:112, 9:114, 9:115, 9:116, 9:117, 9:118, 9:119, 9:120, 9:121, 9:123, 9:127, 9:129, 10:3, 10:4, 10:5, 10:6, 10:10, 10:11, 10:16, 10:17, 10:18, 10:19, 10:20, 10:21, 10:22, 10:25, 10:27, 10:29, 10:30, 10:31, 10:32, 10:34, 10:35, 10:36, 10:37, 10:44, 10:45, 10:46, 10:49, 10:55, 10:58, 10:59, 10:60, 10:62, 10:63, 10:64, 10:65, 10:66, 10:68, 10:69, |

| | |
|---|---|
| | 10:71, 10:72, 10:81, 10:84, 10:85, 10:89, 10:90, 10:91, 10:95, 10:100, 10:104, 10:107, 10:109, 11:1, 11:2, 11:3, 11:4, 11:5, 11:6, 11:7, 11:12, 11:14, 11:18, 11:19, 11:20, 11:26, 11:29, 11:31, 11:33, 11:34, 11:36, 11:41, 11:43, 11:44, 11:46, 11:48, 11:50, 11:51, 11:53, 11:54, 11:56, 11:61, 11:63, 11:64, 11:73, 11:76, 11:78, 11:83, 11:84, 11:86, 11:87, 11:88, 11:92, 11:94, 11:101, 11:105, 11:112, 11:113, 11:115, 11:123, 12:2, 12:18, 12:19, 12:21, 12:23, 12:31, 12:37, 12:38, 12:39, 12:40, 12:51, 12:52, 12:53, 12:57, 12:64, 12:66, 12:67, 12:68, 12:73, 12:76, 12:77, 12:79, 12:80, 12:83, 12:85, 12:86, 12:87, 12:88, 12:90, 12:91, 12:92, 12:95, 12:96,12:97, 12:98, 12:99, 12:106, 12:107, 12:108, 13:2, 13:8, 13:11, 13:13, 13:14, 13:15, 13:16, 13:17, 13:20, 13:21, 13:25, 13:26, 13:27, 13:28, 13:30, 13:31, 13:33, 13:34, 13:36, 13:37, 13:38, 13:39, 13:41, 13:42, 13:43, 14:1, 14:2, 14:3, 14:4, 14:6, 14:8, 14:9, 14:10, 14:11, 14:12, 14:15, 14:19, 14:20, 14:21, 14:22, 14:24, 14:25, 14:27, 14:28, 14:30, 14:32, 14:34, 14:39, 14:42, 14:46, 14:47, 14:48, 14:51, 14:52, 15:32, 15:34, 15:37, 15:41, 15:60, 15:66, 15:69, 15:96, 16:1, 16:2, 16:3, 16:4, 16:5, 16:9, 16:10, 16:11, 16:13, 16:14, 16:15, 16:17, 16:18, 16:19, 16:20, 16:23, 16:26, 16:27, 16:28, 16:30, 16:33, 16:35, 16:36, 16:37, 16:38, 16:41, 16:45, 16:48, 16:49, 16:51, 16:52, 16:53, 16:56, 16:57, 16:60, 16:61, 16:62, 16:63, 16:65, 16:70, 16:71, 16:72, 16:73, 16:74, 16:75, 16:76, 16:77, 16:78, 16:79, 16:80, 16:81, 16:83, 16:87, 16:88, 16:89, 16:90, 16:91, 16:92, 16:93, 16:94,16:95, 16:96, 16:98, 16:100, 16:101, 16:102, 16:104, 16:105, 16:106, 16:107, 16:108, 16:112, 16:114, 16:115, 16:116, 16:120, 16:121, 16:124, 16:127, 16:128, 17:1, 17:19, 17:22, 17:28, 17:33, 17:39, 17:42, 17:43, 17:44, 17:52, 17:56, 17:63, 17:67, 17:68, 17:69, 17:79, 17:86, 17:92, 17:94, 17:96, 17:97, 17:99, 17:100, 17:111,18:1, 18:2, 18:4, 18:14, 18:15, 18:16, 18:17, 18:21, 18:24, 18:26, 18:38, 18:39, 18:42, 18:43, 18:44, 18:45, 18:51, 18:66, 8:69, 18:110, 19:7, 19:9, 19:10, 19:11, 19:12, 19:18, |

| | |
|---|---|
| | 19:26, 19:30, 19:32, 19:35, 19:36, 19:40, 19:44, 19:45, 19:46, 19:47, 19:48, 19:58, 19:69, 19:75, 19:76, 19:78, 19:81, 19:82, 19:94, 19:96, 20:3, 20:4, 20:5, 20:6, 20:7, 20:8, 20:14, 20:19, 20:21, 20:36, 20:44, 20:46, 20:48, 20:61, 20:71, 20:72, 20:73, 20:83, 20:85, 20:86, 20:88, 20:97, 20:98, 20:108, 20:110, 20:111, 20:114, 20:123, 20:126, 21:19, 21:21, 21:22, 21:23, 21:24, 21:26, 21:27, 21:28, 21:29, 21:30, 21:31, 21:33, 21:36, 21:42, 21:43, 21:57, 21:58, 21:59, 21:62, 21:63, 21:66, 21:67, 21:68, 21:69, 21:87, 21:88, 21:98, 21:99, 21:108, 21:110, 22:2, 22:3, 22:6, 22:7, 22:8, 22:9, 22:10, 22:11, 22:12, 22:14, 22:15, 22:16, 22:17, 22:18, 22:23, 22:25, 22:28, 22:30, 22:31, 22:32, 22:34, 22:35, 22:36, 22:37, 22:38, 22:39, 22:40, 22:41, 22:47, 22:52, 22:53, 22:54, 22:56, 22:58, 22:59, 22:60, 22:61, 22:62, 22:63,22:64, 22:65, 22:66, 22:68, 22:69, 22:70, 22:71, 22:72, 22:73, 22:74, 22:75, 22:76, 22:78, 23:14, 23:23, 23:24, 23:28, 23:32, 23:38, 23:40, 23:85, 23:87, 23:89, 23:91, 23:92, 23:108, 23:112, 23:114, 23:116, 23:117, 24:2, 24:5, 24:6, 24:7, 24:8, 24:9, 24:10, 24:13, 24:14, 24:15, 24:16, 24:17, 24:18, 24:19, 24:20, 24:21, 24:22, 24:25, 24:28, 24:29, 24:30, 24:31, 24:32, 24:33, 24:34, 24:35, 24:36, 24:37, 24:38, 24:39, 24:40, 24:41, 24:42, 24:43, 24:44, 24:45, 24:46, 24:47, 24:48, 24:50, 24:51, 24:52, 24:53, 24:54, 24:55, 24:56, 24:57, 24:58, 24:59, 24:60, 24:61, 24:62, 24:63, 24:64, 25:1, 25:2, 25:3, 25:6, 25:10, 25:16, 25:17, 25:18, 25:19, 25:20, 25:26, 25:29, 25:41, 25:42, 25:43, 25:44, 25:45, 25:47, 25:48, 25:53, 25:54, 25:55, 25:58, 25:59, 25:61, 25:62, 25:63, 25:68, 25:70, 25:71. 26:5, 26:11, 26:15, 26:29, 26:57, 26:89, 26:93, 26:97, 26:100, 26:106, 26:108, 26:110, 26:124, 26:126, 26:131, 26:142, 26:144, 26:150, 26:161, 26:163, 6:177, 26:179, 26:184, 26:196, 26:213, 26:217, 26:220, 26:227, 27:8, 27:9, 27:10, 27:15, 27:16, 27:24, 27:25, 27:26, 27:30, 27:31, 27:36, 27:42, 27:43, 27:45, 27:46, 27:47, 27:49, 27:59, 27:60, 27:61, 27:62, 27:63, 27:64, 27:65, 27:79, 27:84, 27:87, 27:88, 27:93, |

| | |
|---|---|
| | 28:13, 28:16, 28:27, 28:28, 28:30, 28:31, 28:35, 28:38, 28:49, 28:50, 28:53, 28:56, 28:60, 28:62, 28:63, 28:64, 28:65, 28:68, 28:69, 28:70, 28:71, 28:72, 28:73, 28:74, 28:75, 28:76, 28:77, 28:78, 28:80, 28:82, 28:85, 28:87, 28:88, 29:3, 29:5, 29:6, 29:8, 29:10, 29:11, 29:16, 29:17, 29:19, 29:20, 29:21, 29:22, 29:23, 29:24, 29:25, 29:29, 29:36, 29:40, 29:41, 29:42, 29:44, 29:45, 29:46, 29:50, 29:52, 29:60, 29:61, 29:62, 29:63, 29:65, 29:67, 29:68, 29:69, 30:4, 30:5, 30:6, 30:8, 30:9, 30:10, 30:11, 30:13, 30:17, 30:18, 30:19, 30:20, 30:29, 30:30, 30:31, 30:37, 30:38, 30:39, 30:40, 30:41, 30:42, 30:43, 30:44, 30:45, 30:48, 30:50, 30:54, 30:56, 30:59, 30:60, 31:6, 31:9, 31:10, 31:11, 31:12, 31:13, 31:16, 31:18, 31:20, 31:21, 31:22, 31:23, 31:25, 31:26, 31:27, 31:28, 31:29, 31:30, 31:31, 31:32, 31:33, 31:34, 32:4, 32:5, 32:6, 32:7, 32:9, 32:13, 32:15, 33:1, 33:2, 33:3, 33:4, 33:5, 33:6, 33:7, 33:8, 33:9, 33:10, 33:12, 33:15, 33:17, 33:18, 33:19, 33:21, 33:22, 33:23, 33:24, 33:25, 33:26, 33:27, 33:29, 33:30, 33:31, 33:32, 33:33, 33:34, 33:35, 33:36, 33:37, 33:38, 33:39, 33:40, 33:41, 33:42, 33:43, 33:46, 33:47, 33:48, 33:50, 33:51, 33:52, 33:53, 33:54, 33:55, 33:56, 33:57, 33:59, 33:62, 33:63, 33:64, 33:66, 33:69, 33:70, 33:71, 33:73, 34:1, 34:2, 34:3, 34:4, 34:5, 34:6, 34:8, 34:9, 34:16, 34:22, 34:23, 34:24, 34:27, 34:33, 34:37, 34:40, 34:41, 34:42, 34:46, 34:47, 34:50, 34:52, 35:1, 35:2, 35:3, 35:4, 35:5, 35:8, 35:9, 35:10, 35:11, 35:12, 35:13, 35:14, 35:15, 35:17, 35:18, 35:22, 35:27, 35:28, 35:29, 35:30, 35:31, 35:32, 35:34, 35:35, 35:38, 35:39, 35:40, 35:41, 35:42, 35:43, 35:44, 35:45, 36:2, 36:5, 36:11, 36:14, 36:15, 36:22, 36:23, 36:26, 36:36, 36:38, 36:47, 36:52, 36:58, 36:59, 36:74, 36:75, 36:80, 36:81, 36:83, 37:1, 37:4, 37:12, 37:23, 37:35, 37:36, 37:40, 37:56, 37:74, 37:86, 37:91, 37:96, 37:102, 37:103, 37:107, 37:124, 37:125, 37:126, 37:128, 37:142, 37:143, 37:149, 37:150, 37:152, 37:158, 37:159, 37:160, 37:161, 37:162, 37:166, 37:169, 37:182, 38:5, 38:6, 38:17, 38:18, 38:24, 38:26, 38:28, 38:42, 38:44, 38:65, |

| | |
|---|---|
| | 38:69, 38:75, 38:77, 38:80, 38:84, 39:1, 39:2, 39:3, 39:4, 39:5, 39:6, 39:7, 39:8, 39:10, 39:11, 39:12, 39:14, 39:15, 39:16, 39:17, 39:18, 39:20, 39:21, 39:22, 39:23, 39:26, 39:29, 39:32, 39:35, 39:36, 39:37, 39:38, 39:42, 39:43, 39:44, 39:45, 39:46, 39:47, 39:52, 39:53, 39:56, 39:57, 39:59, 39:60, 39:61, 39:62, 39:63, 39:64, 39:65, 39:66, 39:67, 39:68, 39:70, 39:74, 39:75. 40:2, 40:3, 40:4, 40:5, 40:7, 40:10, 40:11, 40:12, 40:13, 40:14, 40:15, 40:16, 40:17, 40:19, 40:20, 40:21, 40:22, 40:25, 40:28, 40:29, 40:31, 40:33, 40:34, 40:35, 40:37, 40:42, 40:43, 40:44, 40:45, 40:48, 40:51, 40:53, 40:55, 40:56, 40:61, 40:62, 40:63, 40:64, 40:65, 40:67, 40:68, 40:69, 40:70, 40:73, 40:74, 40:77, 40:78, 40:79, 40:80, 40:81, 40:84, 40:85, 41:2, 41:6, 41:9, 41:10, 41:11, 41:12, 41:14, 41:15, 41:16, 41:17, 41:18, 41:19, 41:21, 41:22, 41:25, 41:27, 41:28, 41:30, 41:33, 41:35, 41:36, 41:37, 41:38, 41:39, 41:40, 41:42, 41:44, 41:45, 41:47, 41:48, 41:50, 41:51, 41:52, 41:53, 42:3, 42:4, 42:5, 42:6, 42:8, 42:9, 42:10, 42:11, 42:12, 42:13, 42:14, 42:15, 42:16, 42:17, 42:19, 42:20, 42:21, 42:23, 42:24, 42:25, 42:26, 42:27, 42:28, 42:29, 42:30, 42:31, 42:32, 42:33, 42:34, 42:35, 42:36, 42:40, 42:44, 42:46, 42:47, 42:48, 42:49, 42:50, 42:51, 42:53,43:3, 43:4, 43:5, 43:9, 43:10, 43:11, 43:12, 43:13, 43:15, 43:16, 43:17, 43:18, 43:19, 43:20, 43:28, 43:29, 43:36, 43:45, 43:54, 43:58, 43:63, 43:64, 43:68, 43:81, 43:84, 43:85, 43:86, 43:87, 44:2, 44:8, 44:18, 44:19, 44:23, 44:42, 44:56, 45:2, 45:4, 45:5, 45:6, 45:8, 45:10, 45:12, 45:13, 45:14, 45:19, 45:21, 45:22, 45:23, 45:26, 45:27, 45:32, 45:34, 45:35, 45:36, 46:2, 46:4, 46:5, 46:8, 46:10, 46:13, 46:17, 46:19, 46:21, 46:22, 46:23, 46:26, 46:28, 46:31, 46:32, 46:33, 47:1, 47:2, 47:3, 47:4, 47:5, 47:7, 47:8, 47:9, 47:10, 47:11, 47:12, 47:16, 47:17, 47:19, 47:20, 47:21, 47:23, 47:26, 47:28, 47:29, 47:30, 47:31, 47:32, 47:33, 47:34, 47:35, 47:36, 47:37, 413, 49:14, 49:15, 49:16, 49:17, 49:18, 50:1, 50:4, 50:6, 50:15, 50:24, 50:26, 50:28, 50:30, 50:32, 50:33, 50:39, 50:43, 51:1, 51:7, 51:18, 51:50, 51:51, 51:58, |

| | |
|---|---|
| | 52:1, 52:26, 52:27, 52:39, 52:43, 53:1, 53:10, 53:15, 53:20, 53:21, 53:23, 53:25, 53:26, 53:31, 53:32, 53:42, 53:43, 53:48, 53:58, 53:62, 54:25, 54:42, 54:55, 55:1, 55:2, 55:3, 55:4, 55:6, 55:7, 55:10, 55:14, 55:15, 55:17, 55:197:38, 48:2, 48:4, 48:5, 48:6, 48:7, 48:9, 48:10, 48:11, 48:13, 48:14, 48:15, 48:16, 48:17, 48:18, 48:19, 48:20, 48:21, 48:23, 48:24, 48:25, 48:26, 48:27, 48:28, 48:29, 49:1, 49:3, 49:5, 49:7, 49:8, 49:9, 49:10, 49:12, 49:, 55:24, 55:27, 55:29, 55:33, 56:11, 56:88, 57:1, 57:4, 57:7, 57:8, 57:9, 57:10, 57:11, 57:14, 57:16, 57:17, 57:18, 57:19, 57:20, 57:21, 57:22, 57:23, 57:24, 57:25, 57:27, 57:28, 57:29, 58:1, 58:2, 58:3, 58:4, 58:5, 58:6, 58:7, 58:8, 58:9, 58:10, 58:11, 58:12, 58:13, 58:14, 58:15, 58:16, 58:17, 58:18, 58:19, 58:20, 58:21, 58:22, 59:1, 59:2, 59:3, 61:9, 61:11, 61:12, 61:13, 61:14, 62:1, 62:2, 62:3, 62:4, 62:5, 62:6, 62:7, 62:8, 62:9, 62:10, 62:11, 63:1, 63:2, 63:4, 63:5, 63:6, 63:7, 63:8, 63:9, 63:11, 64:1, 64:2, 64:3, 64:4, 64:6, 64:7, 64:8, 64:9, 64:11, 64:12, 64:13, 64:14, 64:15, 64:16, 64:17, 64:18, 65:1, 65:2, 65:3, 65:4, 65:5, 65:7, 65:10, 65:11, 65:12, 66:1, 66:2, 66:3, 66:4, 66:5, 66:6, 66:8, 66:10, 66:11, 67:1, 67:3, 67:9, 67:13, 67:14, 67:15, 67:19, 67:20, 67:23, 67:26, 67:28, 68:1, 68:18, 68:28, 68:41, 68:48, 68:48, 69:7, 69:10, 69:18, 69:30, 69:33, 69:38, 70:3, 70:4, 70:40, 71:3, 71:4, 71:13, 71:15, 71:17, 71:19, 71:23, 71:25, 72:4, 72:5, 72:7, 72:12, 72:14, 72:18, 72:19, 72:22, 72:23, 72:26, 73:9, 73:18, 73:20, 74:26, 74:31, 74:32, 74:52, 74:56, 75:1, 75:12, 75:38, 75:40, 76:6, 76:8, 76:9, 76:11, 76:12, 76:22, 76:30, 77:1, 77:48, 79:1, 79:25, 79:26, 79:27, 80:18, 80:19, 80:22, 80:23, 81:15, 81:20, 81:29, 82:19, 82:21, 84:14, 84:16, 84:21, 84:23, 85:1, 85:8, 85:9, 85:13, 85:20, 86:1, 86:8, 86:11, 87:7, 87:10, 88:24, 89:1, 89:25, 89:26, 90:1, 90:3, 91:1, 91:13, 91:15, 92:1, 92:8, 92:21, 93:1, 95:1, 95:8, 96:14, 96:19, 98:2, 98:5, 98:8, 100:1, 103:1, 104:6, 105:2, 110:1, 110:2, 112:1, 141:3. |
| Good | 1:5, 2:25, 2:57, 2:58, 2:61, 2:62, 2:82, 2:83, 2:97, 2:105, 2:109, 2:112, 2:119, 2:148, 2:155, 2:158, |

| | |
|---|---|
| | 2:168, 2:172, 2:195, 2:197, 2:201, 2:213, 2:215, 2:216, 2:220, 2:223, 2:224, 2:271, 2:272, 2:277, 2:286, 3:26, 3:30, 3:37, 3:38, 3:39, 3:45, 3:104, 3:114, 3:115, 3:120, 3:134, 3:148, 3:170, 3:178, 3:179, 4:16, 4:19, 4:40, 4:62, 4:73, 4:79, 4:83, 4:85, 4:114, 4:124, 4:125, 4:127, 4:129, 4:147, 4:149, 4:160, 4:165, 4:173, 5:2, 5:4, 5:5, 5:9, 5:12, 5:13, 5:19, 5:48, 5:85, 5:87, 5:88, 5:93, 5:100, 6:17, 6:44, 6:48, 6:84, 6:158, 6:160, 7:32, 7:42, 7:43, 7:56, 7:58, 7:131, 7:156, 7:157, 7:160, 7:168, 7:188, 7:189, 7:190, 8:10, 8:17, 8:23, 8:26, 8:69, 8:70, 9:21, 9:50, 9:61, 9:67, 9:88, 9:91, 9:100, 9:102, 9:107, 9:109, 9:112, 9:120, 10:2, 10:4, 10:9, 10:26, 10:64, 10:87, 10:93, 10:107, 10:108, 11:2, 11:11, 11:23, 11:31, 11:69, 11:71, 11:74, 11:88, 11:114, 11:116, 12:12, 12:19, 12:63, 12:65, 12:96, 13:6, 13:22, 14:24, 15:53, 15:54, 15:55, 16:30, 16:32, 16:62, 16:72, 16:80, 16:89, 16:90, 16:96, 16:97, 16:102, 16:114, 16:128, 17:7, 17:9, 17:11, 17:25, 17:70, 17:105, 18:2, 18:19, 18:28, 18:46, 18:56, 18:88, 19:7, 19:76, 19:97, 20:81, 20:86, 21:35, 21:73, 21:90, 21:94, 22:11, 22:34, 522:37, 22:77, 23:33, 23:51, 23:61, 23:71, 23:96, 23:100, 23:102, 24:11, 24:55, 25:56, 25:70, 25:71, 26:227, 27:2, 27:11, 27:16, 27:19, 27:40, 27:46, 27:89, 28:54, 28:77, 28:80, 28:84, 29:7, 29:9, 29:31, 29:58, 29:69, 30:15, 30:44, 30:46, 31:3, 31:12, 31:22, 32:12, 32:17, 32:19, 33:21, 33:29, 33:31, 33:45, 33:47, 34:15, 34:28, 35:7, 35:8, 35:10, 35:24, 35:32, 35:37, 36:11, 37:101, 37:105, 37:110, 37:112, 37:113, 37:121, 37:131, 38:24, 38:28, 38:30, 38:32, 39:10, 39:17, 39:34, 39:73, 40:58, 40:64, 41:4, 41:8, 41:30, 41:34, 41:35, 41:49, 42:23, 42:26, 43:72, 44:27, 45:16, 45:21, 46:11, 46:12, 46:15, 46:20, 48:8, 48:16, 48:29, 50:25, 51:16, 51:28, 53:31, 55:60, 55:70, 56:24, 56:26, 57:10, 57:11, 57:12, 57:18, 60:4, 60:6, 61:6, 61:13, 64:9, 65:11, 68:12, 73:11, 73:20, 77:44, 84:25, 85:11, 89:23, 89:24, 90:10, 90:11, 92:6, 92:7, 92:9, 95:6, 98:7, 99:7, 101:6, 102:1, 103:3, 107:6. |
| Goliath | 2:249, 2:250, 2:251. |
| Golden | 43:71. |

| | |
|---|---|
| | 16:78, 16:106, 16:108, 17:25, 17:36, 17:46, 17:60, 18:14, 18:28, 18:57, 19:24, 21:3, 22:32, 22:35, 22:46, 22:53, 22:54, 23:60, 23:78, 24:37, 24:50, 25:32, 26:89, 26:194, 26:200, 27:14, 28:10, 28:69, 29:10, 30:59, 31:23, 32:9, 33:4, 33:10, 33:12, 33:26, 33:32, 33:37, 33:51, 33:53, 33:60, 34:23, 35:38, 37:84, 39:7, 39:22, 39:23, 39:45, 40:18, 40:35, 40:56, 41:5, 42:24, 45:23, 46:26, 47:16, 47:20, 47:24, 47:29, 48:4, 48:11, 48:12, 48:26, 49:2, 49:7, 49:14, 50:16, 50:16, 50:33, 50:37, 53:11, 57:16, 57:27, 58:22, 59:2, 59:10, 59:13, 59:14, 61:5, 63:3, 64:11, 66:4, 67:13, 69:24, 73:8, 77:43, 79:8, 83:14, 100:10, 104:7, 114:5. |
| Heaven | 2:29, 2:33, 2:107, 2:116, 2:117, 2:144, 2:164, 2:255, 2:284, 3:29, 3:83, 3:109, 3:129, 3:133, 3:180, 3:183, 3:189, 3:190, 3:191, 4:126, 4:131, 4:132, 4:153, 4:170, 4:171, 5:7, 5:18, 5:40, 5:97, 5:112, 5:114, 5:120, 6:1, 6:3, 6:12, 6:14, 6:73, 6:75, 6:79, 6:101, 7:13, 7:40, 7:54,7:96, 7:158, 7:185, 7:187, 9:36, 9:116, 10:3, 10:6, 10:18, 10:55, 10:66, 10:68, 10:101, 11:7, 11:107, 11:108, 11:123, 12:101, 12:105, 13:2, 13:15, 13:16, 14:2, 14:10, 14:19, 14:32, 14:38, 14:48, 15:14, 15:16, 15:85, 16:3, 16:49, 16:52, 16:73, 16:77, 17:44, 17:55, 17:95, 17:99, 17:102, 18:14, 18:26, 18:51, 19:65, 19:90, 19:93, 20:4, 20:6, 21:4, 21:16, 21:19, 21:22, 21:30, 21:56, 21:104, 22:18, 22:64, 22:70, 23:17, 23:71, 23:86, 24:35, 24:41, 24:42, 24:64, 25:2, 25:6, 25:25, 25:59, 26:4, 26:24, 27:25, 27:60, 27:64, 27:65, 27:75, 27:87, 29:22, 29:34, 29:44, 29:52, 29:61, 30:8, 30:18, 30:22, 30:25, 30:26, 30:27, 31:10, 31:16, 31:20, 31:25, 31:26, 32:4, 32:5, 33:72, 34:1, 34:2, 34:3, 34:9, 34:22, 34:24, 35:1, 35:3, 35:38, 35:40, 35:41, 35:44, 36:28, 36:81, 37:5, 37:6, 38:10, 38:27, 38:66, 39:5, 39:38, 39:44, 39:46, 39:63, 39:67, 39:68, 40:37, 40:57, 41:11, 41:12, 42:4, 42:5, 42:11, 42:12, 42:29, 42:49, 42:53, 43:9, 43:82, 43:84, 43:85, 44:7, 44:29, 44:38, 45:3, 45:13, 45:22, 45:27, 45:36, 45:37, 46:3, 46:4, 46:33, 48:4, 48:7, 48:14, 48:16, 48:18, 50:38, 51:22, 51:23, 51:47, 52:36, 52:38, 53:26, 53:31, 54:11, 55:7, 55:29, 55:33, 55:37, 56:78, 57:1, 57:2, 57:4, 57:5, 57:10, 57:21, 58:7, 59:1, 59:24, 61:1, 62:1, 63:7, 64:1, 64:3, 64:4, 64:12, 67:3, |

| | |
|---|---|
| | 67:5, 67:16, 67:17, 69:16, 71:15, 72:8, 73:18, 78:12, 78:19, 78:37, 79:27, 81:11, 85:1, 85:9, 86:1, 86:11. |
| Hell | 1:4, 2:206, 2:217, 3:12, 3:151, 3:162, 3:197, 4:10, 4:93, 4:97, 4:115, 4:121, 4:140, 4:145, 4:169, 5:29, 7:18, 7:41, 7:46, 7:48, 7:49, 7:50, 7:179, 8:16, 8:36, 8:37, 9:35, 9:73, 9:95, 10:27, 11:119, 13:18, 14:16, 14:28, 14:29, 14:30, 15:43, 15:44, 16:29, 17:8, 17:18, 17:39, 17:63, 17:97, 18:53, 18:100, 18:102, 18:106, 19:68, 19:70, 19:71, 19:86, 20:74, 21:29, 21:39, 21:98, 21:99, 21:101, 21:102, 23:103, 23:107, 24:57, 25:34, 25:65, 25:66, 26:91, 26:94, 29:25, 29:54, 29:68, 31:21, 32:13, 36:63, 37:23, 37:55, 37:57, 37:64, 38:56, 38:59, 38:64, 38:85, 39:19, 39:32, 39:60, 39:71, 39:72, 40:11, 40:49, 40:60, 40:76, 41:19, 41:24, 42:7, 43:74, 43:77, 45:10, 45:34, 47:12, 48:6, 50:24, 50:30, 54:48, 55:43, 55:44, 56:94, 57:15, 57:19, 58:8, 58:17, 59:17, 59:20, 64:10, 66:9, 67:6, 67:10, 67:11, 69:31, 70:15, 72:15, 72:23, 77:29, 78:21, 79:39, 81:12, 85:10, 89:23, 96:18, 101:11, 102:6, 104:4. |
| | 2:39, 2:80, 2:81, 2:119, 2:126, 2:167, 2:175, 2:201, 2:221, 2:257, 3:10, 3:16, 3:24, 3:116, 3:131, 3:181, 3:185, 3:191, 3:192, 4:14, 4:30, 4:55, 4:56, 5:10, 5:37, 5:72, 5:86, 6:27, 7:36, 7:38, 7:44, 7:47, 8:14, 8:50, 9:17, 9:49, 9:63, 9:68, 9:81, 9:109, 9:110, 10:8, 11:17, 11:98, 11:106, 11:113, 13:5, 13:35, 16:62, 21:98, 22:3, 22:51, 28:41, 33:66, 34:42, 35:6, 35:36, 37:68, 37:163, 38:27, 39:8, 40:6, 40:7, 40:41, 40:43, 40:47, 40:48, 40:72, 41:28,41:40, 42:45, 44:47, 44:56, 46:20, 46:34, 47:15, 51:13, 52:13, 52:18, 52:27, 59:3, 66:6, 70:17, 74:26, 74:27, 74:31, 74:35, 74:42, 79:36, 82:14, 83:16, 90:20, 113:4. |
| Hereafter | 2:86, 2:94, 2:102, 2:114, 2:130, 2:200, 2:201, 2:217, 2:220, 3:22, 3:45, 3:56, 3:77, 3:85, 3:145, 3:148, 3:152, 3:176, 4:74, 4:77, 4:134, 4:137, 5:5, 5:33, 5:41, 6:32, 6:113, 6:135, 6:150, 6:147, 6:156, 6:169, 8:67, 9:38, 9:69, 9:74, 11:16, 11:19, 11:22, 11:103, 12:37, 12:57, 12:101, 12:109, 13:26, 13:34, 14:3, 14:27, 17:19, 17:21, 17:72, 17:104, 20:127, 22:11, 22:15, 23:15, 24:14, 24:19, 24:23, 26:81, 27:3, 27:4, 27:5, 27:66, 28:70, 28:77, 29:64, 30:16, 33:29, 33:57, |

| | |
|---|---|
| | 34:11, 34:8, 34:21, 38:46, 39:9, 39:26, 39:45, 41:7, 41:16, 41:31, 42:20, 43:55, 51:11, 53:25, 53:27, 53:34, 56:86, 57:20, 59:3, 60:13, 64:5, 65:10, 68:33, 74:53, 75:19, 75:26, 84:19, 87:17. |
| Highway | 15:79, 16:6. |
| Home | 2:84, 2:85, 2:,94 2:196, 2:218, 2:243, 2:246, 3:151, 3:162, 3:168, 3:195, 4:66, 4:89, 4:95, 4:127, 4:128, 7:74, 7:78, 7:91, 7:145, 7:169, 8:5, 8:47, 9:20, 9:24, 9:90, 10:25, 11:67, 11:94, 13:24, 13:25, 16:6, 16:30, 16:68, 16:110, 21:13, 22:40, 28:77, 29:26, 29:37, 29:41, 33:27, 33:34, 34:15, 35:35, 36:50, 39:32, 39:60, 40:39, 40:52, 40:76, 41:24, 47:19, 57:15, 59:2, 59:8, 60:8, 60:9, 65:1, 65:6, 77:25, 78:22, 89:9. |
| Horse | 2:239, 3:14, 8:60, 9:92, 16:8, 38:31, 38:32, 38:33, 59:6, 100:1. |
| Hour | 2:238, 2:259, 6:31, 6:40, 7:34, 9:117, 10:45, 12:107, 15:85, 16:77, 17:79, 18:21, 18:36, 19:75, 20:15, 22:1, 22:7, 22:55, 25:11, 30:12, 30:14, 30:55, 31:34, 34:3, 34:30, 40:59, 41:47, 41:50, 42:17, 42:18, 43:61, 43:66, 43:85, 45:27, 45:32, 46:35, 47:18, 54:1, 54:46, 73:2, 3:20, 79:42, 79:46. |
| House | 2:125, 2:127, 2:158, 2:189, 2:196, 3:49, 3:96, 3:154, 4:15, 5:97, 10:87, 11:65, 11:73, 14:37, 15:61, 15:82, 16:80, 17:93, 18:21, 22:26, 22:29, 22:33, 24:27, 24:28, 24:29, 24:36, 24:61, 26:58, 26:149, 27:18, 27:52, 28:58, 28:81, 33:13, 33:33, 33:53, 43:33, 51:36, 52:4, 59:2, 66:11, 71:28, 106:3. |
| Houd | 7:65, 7:67, 7:72, Chapter 11 Title, 11:50, 11:53, 11:58, 11:60, 11:89, 26:124, 46:21, 54:18. |
| Hypocrisy | 5:52, 9:77, 9:97, 9:101, 47:20, 47:29, 63:2. |
| Hypocrite | 3:167, 3:173, 4:61, 4:88, 4:91, 4:138, 4:140, 4:141, 4:142, 4:145, 8:49, 9:42, 9:43, 9:64, 9:67, 9:68, 9:73, 9:80, 9:82, 9:84, 9:94, 9:96, 9:101, 9:107, 9:124, 24:47, 29:11, 33:1, 33:12, 33:20, 33:24, 33:48, 33:60, 33:73, 47:22, 48:6, 57:13, 57:14, 59:11, 59:12, 59:16, Chapter 63 Title, 63:1, 63:7, 63:8, 66:9, 74:31. |

**I**

| | |
|---|---|
| Satan | 2:34, 7:11, 15:31, 15:32, 17:61, 16:72, 18:50, 20:116, 26:95, 34:20, 38:74, 38:75. |
| Illegal | 3:61, 4:15. |

**J**

**K**

| | |
|---|---|
| Kind | 2:61, 2:83, 2:143, 2:164, 2:207, 2:229, 2:231, 2:237, 2:243, 2:251, 2:263, 3:286, 3:30, 3:171, 4:5, 4:8, 4:19, 4:36, 4:91, 5:13, 6:99, 6:143, 7:57, 9:117, 9:128, 11:75, 12:23, 12:100, 14:37, 15:88, 16:7, 16:11, 16:47, 16:69, 17:23, 17:28, 17:44, 17:88, 19:32, 22:5, 22:65, 24:20, 24:61, 25:7, 26:7, 26:215, 28:57, 29:8, 30:21, 30:33, 30:36, 30:45, 30:46, 30:50, 30:58, 31:10, 31:14, 31:15, 33:6, 33:17, 37:119, 38:37, 39:27, 44:55, 46:15, 50:7, 55:11, 55:52, 57:9, 59:12, 60:8, 89:17, 107:7. |
| Knowledge | 2:32, 2:53, 2:113, 2:120, 2:145, 2:247, 2:255, 3:7, 3:18, 3:19, 3:61, 3:66, 4:25, 4:32, 4:35, 4:39, 4:92, 4:104, 4:108, 4:157, 4:162, 4:166, 5:97, 5:109, 6:59, 6:80, 6:81, 6:119, 6:140, 6:143, 7:7, 7:33, 7:52, 7:69, 7:175, 7:187, 8:75, 10:16, 10:68, 10:93, 11:14, 11:46, 11:47, 12:22, 1236:, 1372:, 6812:,76 12:83, 12:96, 12:108, 13:37, 15:25, 16:8, 16:27, 16:74, 16:78, 17:85, 17:107, 18:5, 18:26, 18:65, 18:68, 18:91, 20:52, 20:98, 20:114, 21:74, 21:79, 21:81, 22:3, 22:8, 22:54, 22:71, 24:15, 24:31, 24:35, 24:64, 25:59, 26:112, 27:15, 27:22, 27:40, 27:42, 27:50, 27:66, 27:84, 28:14, 28:78, 28:80, 29:8, 29:49, 30:22, 30:29, 30:56, 31:6, 31:15, 31:20, 31:23, 33:54, 34:6, 35:11, 35:38, 36:79, 38:69, 39:49, 40:7, 40:42, 40:83, 41:3, 41:47, 42:14, 43:20, 43:85, 45:17, 45:24, 46:4, 47:16, 47:30, 49:2, 49:13, 49:16, 51:28, 52:41, 53:28, 53:30, 53:35, 57:3, 58:11, 64:18, 65:12, 66:2, 68:47, 772:26, 72:28, 81:24, 88:7. |

## L

| | |
|---|---|
| Lamp | 24:35, 25:61, 33:46, 71:16, 78:13. |
| Language | 14:4, 16:103, 19:97, 26:195, 27:16, 30:22, 41:44, 43:4, 44:58, 46:12. |
| Law | 2:168, 2:178, 2:179, 2:229, 2:232, 2:235, 3:50, 3:93, 4:4, 4:19, 4:23, 4:24, 4:160, 5:1, 5:3, 5:4, 5:5, 5:48, 5:50, 5:87, 5:88, 5:96, 5:107, 7:157, 8:69, 9:37, 10:59, 11:78, 12:76, 16:114, 16:116, 33:50, 33:52, 60:10, 62:5, 66:1, 70:30. |
| Liar | 2:87, 3:61, 6:28, 7:66, 9:43, 9:107, 11:93, 12:74, 16:86, 16:105, 24:13, 26:223, 29:3, 37:152, 38:4, 39:3, 40:24, 40:37, 45:7, 54:25, 54:26, 58:18, 59:11, 63:1. |
| Life | 1:4, 2:4, 2:28, 2:73, 2:85, 2:86, 2:96, 2:126, 2:154, 2:164, 2:179, 2:204, 2:207, 2:212, 2:217, 2:243, 2:258, 2:259, 2:260, 3:14, 3:49, 3:117, 3:156, 3:185, 4:74, |

| | |
|---|---|
| | 4:109, 5:32, 5:45, 5:48, 5:110, 6:2, 6:27, 6:29, 6:32, 6:36, 6:60, 6:70, 6:92, 6:122, 6:130, 6:150, 7:25, 7:29, 7:32, 7:45, 7:51, 7:78, 7:152, 7:158, 7:169, 7:176, 8:24, 9:38, 9:55, 9:74, 9:85, 9:116, 10:4, 10:7, 10:16, 10:23, 10:24, 10:56, 10:64, 10:88, 10:98, 11:3, 11:7, 11:15, 11:20, 11:48, 11:116, 12:37, 12:109, 13:5, 13:26, 13:34, 14:3, 14:27, 15:4, 15:23, 15:72, 16:21, 16:22, 16:30, 16:41, 16:60, 16:65, 16:97, 16:107, 16:109, 16:117, 16:122, 17:10, 17:18, 17:21, 17:23, 17:33, 17:45, 17:49, 17:49, 17:51, 17:75, 17:98, 18:28, 18:45, 18:46, 18:104, 19:15, 19:33, 19:66, 20:55, 20:63, 20:72, 20:97, 20:124, 20:129, 21:13, 21:21, 21:44, 21:104, 22:5, 22:6, 22:7, 22:66, 23:33, 23:35, 23:37, 23:74, 23:80, 23:82, 23:100, 25:3, 25:49, 26:81, 26:205, 26:207, 27:65, 27:67, 28:60, 28:61, 28:70, 28:79, 29:25, 29:27, 29:63, 29:64, 29:66, 30:7, 30:19, 30:24, 30:40, 30:50, 31:4, 31:24, 31:33, 32:21, 33:16, 33:28, 34:7, 35:5, 35:11, 35:37, 36:12, 36:33, 36:44, 36:68, 36:78, 36:79, 37:16, 37:19, 38:25, 38:32, 38:40, 39:26, 40:11, 40:39, 40:43, 40:51, 40:68, 41:66, 41:39, 41:45, 42:9, 42:14, 42:21, 42:36, 43:11, 43:29, 43:35, 44:8, 45:5, 45:10, 45:24, 45:26, 45:35, 46:20, 446:33, 46:35, 47:36, 50:3, 50:11, 50:34, 50:43, 52:28, 53:25, 53:29, 53:44, 55:60, 56:47, 57:2, 57:17, 57:20, 57:27, 58:6, 58:18, 65:6, 67:2, 68:33, 68:43, 69:24, 69:46, 73:11, 74:14, 75:20, 75:21, 75:26, 75:31, 75:40, 76:27, 77:46, 79:10, 79:25, 79:38, 80:20, 80:22, 83:4, 83:29, 86:8, 87:16, 88:24, 101:7. |
| Light | 2:17, 2:19, 2:20, 2:187, 2:257, 4:174, 5:15, 5:16, 5:44, 5:46, 6:1, 6:76, 6:91, 6:122, 7:9, 7:157, 7:189, 9:32, 9:41, 10:5, 13:16, 14:1, 14:5, 16:80, 16:85, 17:12, 20:10, 21:48, 23:103, Chapter 24 Title, 24:35, 24:36, 24:40, 24:43, 27:7, 27:25, 27:86, 28:29, 28:71, 30:24, 31:20, 32:21, 33:43, 33:46, 35:20, 36:37, 39:22, 39:69, 40:61, 42:52, 45:20, 57:9, 57:12, 57:13, 57:19, 57:28, 61:8, 65:11, 66:8, 71:16, 75:8, 77:8, 85:5, Chapter 93 Title, 9:, 101:8. |
| Limit | 2:61, 2:65, 2:173, 2:178, 2:187, 2:194, 2:229, 2:230, 2:282, 3:37, 3:112, 4:13, 4:14, 4:154, 4:171, 5:2, 5:3, 5:77, 5:78, 5:87, 5:94, 5:107, 6:119, 6:145, 7:55, 7:81, 9:10, 9:112, 10:74, 10:83, 16:115, 17:33, 18:28, 20:24, 20:127, 23:7, 23:75, 26:166, 35:8, 36:19, 40:40, 40:43, |

| | |
|---|---|
| | 17:23, 17:24, 17:25, 17:27, 17:30, 17:38, 17:39, 17:40, 17:46, 17:54, 17:55, 17:57, 17:60, 17:65, 17:66, 17:80, 17:84, 17:85, 17:87, 17:93, 17:100, 17:102, 17:108, 18:10, 18:13, 18:14, 18:16, 18:19, 18:21, 18:22, 18:24, 18:28, 18:29, 18:36, 18:38, 18:40, 18:42, 18:44, 18:46, 18:48, 18:49, 18:50, 18:52, 18:55, 18:57, 18:58, 18:81, 18:82, 18:87, 18:95, 18:98, 18:105, 18:109, 18:110, 19:2, 19:3, 19:4, 19:8, 19:9, 19:10, 19:19, 19:21, 19:24, 19:36, 19:55, 19:64, 19:65, 19:68, 19:71, 19:76, 20:12, 20:25, 20:45, 20:47, 20:49, 20:50, 20:52, 20:70, 20:73, 20:74, 20:90, 20:105, 20:114, 20:121, 20:122, 20:125, 20:127, 20:129, 20:130, 20:131, 20:133, 20:134, 21:2, 21:4, 21:42, 21:46, 21:49, 21:56, 21:83, 21:89, 21:92, 21:112, 22:1, 22:19, 22:24, 22:30, 22:40, 22:47, 22:54, 22:67, 22:77, 23:26, 23:29, 23:39, 23:52, 23:57, 23:59, 23:60, 23:72, 23:76, 23:86, 23:93, 23:97, 23:99, 23:106, 23:107, 23:109, 23:116, 23:117, 23:118, 25:21, 25:30, 25:31, 25:45, 25:54, 25:55, 25:57, 25:64, 25:65, 25:73, 25:74, 25:77, 26:9, 26:10, 26:12, 26:16, 26:21, 26:23, 26:24, 26:26, 26:28, 26:47, 26:48, 26:50, 26:51, 26:62, 26:68, 26:77, 26:83, 26:98, 26:104, 26:109, 26:113, 26:117, 26:122, 26:127, 26:140, 26:145, 26:159, 26:164, 26:166, 26:169, 26:175, 26:180, 26:188, 26:191, 26:192, 27:8, 27:19, 27:26, 27:40, 27:44, 27:73, 27:74, 27:78, 27:91, 27:93, 28:16, 28:17, 28:21, 28:22, 28:24, 28:30, 28:32, 28:33, 28:37, 28:46, 28:47, 28:53, 28:59, 28:63, 28:68, 28:69, 28:85, 28:86, 28:87, 29:10, 29:26, 29:30, 29:50, 29:59, 30:8, 30:33, 31:5, 31:33, 32:2, 32:3, 32:10, 32:11, 32:12, 32:15, 32:16, 32:22, 32:25, 33:2, 33:67, 33:68, 34:3, 34:6, 34:12, 34:15, 34:19, 34:21, 34:23, 34:26, 34:31, 34:36, 34:39, 34:39, 34:48, 35:50, 35:13, 35:18, 35:34, 36:37, 36:16, 36:25, 36:27, 36:46, 37:51, 37:5, 37:31, 37:57, 37:84, 37:87, 37:99, 37:100, 37:126, 37:180, 38:182, 38:9, 38:16, 38:24, 38:32, 38:35, 38:41, 38:61, 38:66, 38:71, 38:79, 39:6, 39:7, 39:8, 39:9, 39:10, 39:13, 39:20, 39:3, 39:31, 39:34, 39:54, 39:55, 39:69, 39:71, 39:73, 39:75, 40:3, 40:6, 40:7, 40:8, 40:11, 40:26, 40:27, 40:28, 40:49, 40:55, 40:60, 40:62, 40:64, 40:65, 40:66, 41:9, 41:14, 41:29, 41:30, 41:32, 41:38, 41:43, 41:46, 41:50, 41:53,<br>41:54, 42:10, 42:15, 42:16, 42:22, 42:36, 42:38, 42:47, |

**M**

| | |
|---|---|
| Mecca | 2:125, 2:127, 2:143, 2:144, 2:145, 2:149, 2:158, 2:191, 2:196, 2:198, 3:13, 3:96, 5:1, 5:95, 5:97, 6:92, 7:2, 8:7, 8:34, 8:67, 8:75, 9:3, 9:7, 9:25, 9:40, 9:100, 14:35, 14:37, 15:76, 17:1, 17:73, 22:25, 27:91, 28:57, 29:47, 29:67, 33:50, 39:51 42:7, 42:8, 43:8, 43:29, 43:31, 43:79, 46:26, 47:13, 48:22, 48:24, 48:25, 50:5, 50:12, 51:52, 52:4, 53:34, 54:43, 59:8, 59:15, 60:1, 62:2, 68:17, 81:22, 84:20, 89:2, 90:1, 95:3, 105:1, 106:1, 106:2. |
| Medina | 3:13, 3:121, 3:123, 8:75, 9:42, 9:100, 9:101, 9:107, 9:120, 15:80, 33:13, 33:27, 33:50, 33:60, 5:8,14 59:2, 59:9, 62:11, 63:8. |
| Midian | 7:85, 9:70, 11:84, 11:95, 15:78, 20:40, 22:44, 26:176, 28:22, 28:23, 28:45, 38:13, 50:14. |
| Man | 2:17, 2:72, 2:178, 2:207, 2:237, 2:259, 2:282, 3:47, 3:67, 3:79, 3:95, 3:195, 4:28, 4:77, 4:79, 4:112, 4:176, 5:41, 6:122, 7:63, 7:69, 7:109, 8:24, 10:2, 10:12, 11:9, 11:27, 11:62, 11:78, 11:80, 11:87, 12:36, 12:46, 12:78, 14:34, 15:26, 16:4, 16:68, 17:11, 17:13, 17:47, 17:83, 18:37, 18:54, 18:82, 19:17, 19:20, 19:56, 19:66, 19:67, 20:40, 21:34, 21:37, 21:60, 21:75, 21:104, 23:12, 24:6, 26:19, 28:15, 28:18, 28:20, 28:23, 28:26, 28:79, 33:35, 33:40, 34:7, 34:43, 36:20, 36:77, 40:24, 41:49, 41:50, 41:51, 42:51, 43:15, 43:31, 46:15, 49:11, 50:16, 53:24, 55:14, 55:56, 55:74, 59:16, 65:7, 70:19, 72:5, 75:3, 75:5, 75:10, 75:13, 75:36, Chapter 76 Title, 76:1, 76:2, 78:40, 80:2, 80:17, 80:23, 89:15, 89:23, 90:4, 95:4, 95:7, 96:2, 96:5, 96:6, 99:3, 100:6, 100:8. |
| Mankind | 2:21, 2:124, 2:125, 2:143, 2:161, 2:164, 2:168, 2:185, 2:213, 2:221, 2:243, 3:3, 3:9, 3:14, 3:21, 3:31, 3:87, 3:96, 3:110, 3:112, 3:138, 3:140, 3:187, 4:1, 4:79, 4:170, 4:174, 5:32, 5:109, 6:90, 6:91, 6:116, 6:119, 7:144, 7:158, 10:23, 11:103, 11:118, 12:5, 12:38, 12:104, 13:17, 13:31, 14:1, 14:52, 15:39, 16:38, 17:53, 17:60, 17:85, 18:7, 18:47, 18:51, 18:54, 18:55, 20:108, 21:10, 21:73, 21:91, 21:107, 22:1, 22:5, 22:8, 22:25, 22:27, 22:49, 22:65, 22:66, 23:73 23:30, 23:50, 24:35, 25:37, 26:194, 29:15, 29:43, 30:14, 30:30, 30:41, 30:43, 31:33, 34:28, 35:2, 35:3, 35:5, 35:15, 38:87, 39:27, 39:41, 39:75, 40:15, 40:57, 40:61, 43:33, 44:3, 45:4, 45:20, 46:6, 46:18, 49:13, 51:4, 51:56, 55:3, |

| | |
|---|---|
| | 6:48, 6:124, 6:130, 7:6, 7:35, 7:43, 7:53, 7:61, 7:67, 7:77, 7:96, 7:101, 7:104, 7:111, 7:157, 7:158, 8:1, 8:13, 8:20, 8:24, 8:27, 8:41, 8:46, 9:1, 9:3, 9:7, 9:13, 9:16, 9:24, 9:26, 9:29, 9:33, 9:54, 9:59, 9:61, 9:62, 9:63, 9:65, 9:70, 9:71, 9:74, 9:80, 9:81, 9:84, 9:86, 9:88, 9:90, 9:91, 9:94, 9:97, 9:99, 9:105, 9:107, 9:120, 9:128, 10:13, 10:47, 10:74, 10:103, 11:59, 11:69, 11:77, 11:81, 11:120, 12:50, 12:109, 12:110, 13:32, 13:38, 13:43, 14:4, 14:9, 14:10, 14:11, 14:13, 14:15, 14:44, 15:47, 15:10, 15:11, 15:13, 15:57, 15:61, 15:80, 16:35, 16:36, 16:43, 1644:, 16:63, 16:113, 17:15, 17:71, 17:77, 17:93, 17:94, 17:95, 18:56, 18:106, 19:19, 19:51, 19:54, 20:47, 20:96, 20:134, 21:5, 21:7, 21:25, 21:41, 22:52, 22:75, 22:78, 23:32, 23:44, 23:51, 23:69, 24:47, 24:48, 24:50, 24:51, 24:52, 24:54, 24:56, 24:62, 25:63, 25:1, 25:7, 25:20, 25:28, 25:30, 25:37, 26:41, 26:16, 26:21, 26:27, 26:36, 26:105, 26:107, 26:123, 26:125, 26:141, 26:143, 26:160, 26:162, 26:176, 26:178, 27:10, 27:35, 28:7, 28:45, 28:47, 28:59, 28:65, 29:18, 29:31, 29:33, 30:9, 30:47, 33:12, 33:21, 33:22, 33:29, 33:31, 33:33, 33:36, 33:40, 33:53, 33:57, 33:66, 33:71, 34:45, 35:1, 35:25, 35:37, 36:3, 36:13, 36:14, 36:16, 36:19, 36:20, 36:30, 36:52, 37:37, 37:72, 37:123, 37:133, 37:139, 37:171, 37:181, 38:14, 38:69, 39:25, 39:71, 40:5, 40:22, 40:34, 40:50, 40:51, 40:70, 40:78, 40:83, 41:14, 41:43, 41:44, 42:51, 43:23, 43:24, 43:29, 43:45, 43:46, 44:13, 44:17, 44:18, 46:9, 46:31, 46:32, 46:35, 47:32, 47:33, 48:9, 48:12, 48:13, 48:17, 48:26, 48:27, 48:28, 48:29, 49:1, 49:3, 49:7, 49:14, 49:15, 50:14, 51:31, 51:52, 57:7, 57:8, 57:19, 57:21, 57:25, 57:27, 57:28, 58:4, 58:5, 58:8, 58:9, 58:13, 58:20, 58:21, 58:22, 59:4, 59:6, 59:7, 59:8, 60:1, 61:6, 61:9, 61:11, 62:2, 63:1, 63:5, 63:7, 63:8, 64:6, 64:8, 64:12, 65:8, 65:11, 67:18, 69:10, 69:40, 72:7, 72:23, 72:27, 73:15, 73:16, 77:5, 77:11, 81:19, 91:13, 98:2. |
| Miracle | 2:253, 4:153, 55:21, 79:20. |
| Mirage | 24:39. |
| Mischief | 2:11, 2:12, 2:27, 2:30, 2:60, 2:205, 2:251, 3:63, 5:33, 5:64, 7:56, 7:85, 7:103, 7:127, 8:73, 11:85, 11:116, 16:88, 17:4, 26:152, 27:48, 28:77, 29:36, 40:26, 47:22, |

**N**

| | |
|---|---|
| | 6:151, 7:27, 12:99, 12:100, 14:41, 17:23, 18:80, 19:14, 27:19, 29:8, 31:14, 31:15, 46:15, 46:17, 71:28. |
| Paradise | 1:,4 2:35, 2:36, 2:82, 2:111, 2:214, 2:221, 3:133, 3:142, 3:185, 4:31, 4:57, 4:124, 5:72, 6:127, 7:19, 7:27, 7:40, 7:42, 7:43, 7:44, 7:46, 7:49, 7:50, 9:111, 10:9, 10:25, 10:26, 11:23, 11:108, 13:23, 13:35, 13:42, 15:48, 16:31, 16:32, 18:2, 18:3, 18:31, 18:107, 19:60, 19:63, 20:76, 20:117, 20:118, 20:121, 23:11, 25:24, 25:75, 26:85, 26:90, 28:37, 28:83, 29:58, 30:44, 32:19, 34:37, 35:33, 36:26, 36:55, 37:43, 37:43, 38:25, 38:40, 38:50, 39:73, 39:74, 40:8, 40:40, 41:30, 42:7, 42:22, 43:70, 43:72, 46:14, 46:16, 47:6, 47:12, 47:15, 50:31, 50:34, 51:15, 53:15, 55:46, 55:62, 59:20, 66:11, 70:35, 70:40, 76:6, 76:12, 76:18, 76:20, 79:41, 81:13, 82:13, 88:10, 89:30, 98:8, 101:7. |
| Patience | 2:45, 2:153, 3:200, 7:126, 7:137, 12:90, 14:21, 16:96, 18:67, 18:68, 18:78, 18:82, 21:85, 23:111, 25:20, 25:74, 30:60, 31:17, 40:77, 41:35, 42:43, 47:31, 54:27, 76:12, 103:3. |
| Peace | 2:11, 2:126, 2:194, 2:224, 4:90, 4:91, 4:94, 5:16, 6:54, 6:127, 7:46, 8:61, 9:26, 9:40, 10:10, 10:25, 11:48, 11:69, 12:99, 13:24, 14:23, 14:35, 15:45, 15:52, 16:32, 19:33, 19:47, 19:62, 20:47, 25:63, 25:75, 27:59, 28:55, 30:21, 33:44, 34:37, 36:58, 37:79, 37:109, 37:120, 37:130, 37:148, 37:181, 39:73, 43:89, 44:55, 47:35, 48:24, 49:9, 49:10, 50:34, 51:25, 56:91, 59:23, 97:5. |
| Pearl | 23:33, 35:33, 52:24, 55:22, 55:28, 56:23, 76:19. |
| Pen | 30:27, 54:31, Chapter 68 Title, 68:1, 96:4. |
| Penalty | 4:92, 5:60, 9:39, 9:74, 9:101, 12:74, 58:3. |
| People | 2:5, 2:49, 2:50, 2:54, 2:60, 2:62, 2:66, 2:67, 2:83, 2:94, 2:102, 2:105, 2:109, 2:114, 2:126, 2:134, 2:141, 2:146, 2:150, 2:164, 2:179, 2:189, 2:219, 2:224, 2:243, 2:259, 2:272, 2:273, 3:11, 3:33, 3:46, 3:64, 3:65, 3:69, 3:70, 3:71, 3:72, 3:75, 3:79, 3:86, 3:98, 3:104, 3:110, 3:113, 3:117, 3:118, 3:134, 3:187, 3:199, 4:26, 4:58, 4:75, 4:78, 4:90, 4:91, 4:105, 4:108, 4:114, 4:123, 4:127, 4:142, 4:153, 4:159, 4:165, 4:171, 5:5, 5:15, 5:19, 5:20, 5:21, 5:22, 5:25, 5:26, 5:44, 5:47, 5:50, 5:51, 5:59, 5:61, 5:65, 5:67, 5:68, 5:77, 5:84, 5:97, 5:102, 5:108, 5:110, 5:116, 6:25, 6:66, 6:68, 6:74, 6:78, 6:80, 6:83, 6:89, 6:92, 6:97, 6:98, 6:99, 6:100, 6:105, 6:126, 6:131, |

| | |
|---|---|
| | 6:133, 6:135, 6:144, 6:154, 6:156, 7:46, 7:58, 7:59, 7:60, 7:61, 7:64, 7:65, 7:66, 7:67, 7:69, 7:73, 7:74, 7:79, 7:80, 7:81, 7:82, 7:85, 7:88, 7:89, 7:90, 7:93, 7:94, 7:96, 7:97, 7:109, 7:116, 7:119, 7:123, 7:127, 7:128, 7:130, 7:133, 7:134, 7:137, 7:138, 7:139, 7:141, 7:142, 7:145, 7:148, 7:150, 7:155, 7:159, 7:160, 7:163, 7:164, 7:176, 7:187, 8:22, 8:34, 8:36, 8:47, 8:52, 8:53, 8:54, 8:72, 8:75, 9:29, 9:34, 9:53, 9:70, 9:80, 9:96, 9:115, 9:120, 9:122, 10:2, 10:6, 10:19, 10:21, 10:44, 10:55, 10:57, 10:60, 10:71, 10:74, 10:75, 10:83, 10:84, 10:85, 10:87, 10:92, 10:98, 10:99, 10:104, 10:108, 11:25, 11:27, 11:28, 11:29, 11:30, 11:36, 11:38, 11:49, 11:50, 11:51, 11:52, 11:60, 11:61, 11:63, 11:64, 11:70, 11:73, 11:74, 11:78, 11:84, 11:85, 11:88, 11:89, 11:92, 11:93, 11:98, 11:100, 11:102, 11:110, 11:116, 11:117, 12:21, 12:40, 12:49, 12:62, 12:68, 12:82, 12:109, 12:111, 13:1, 13:4, 13:6, 13:7, 13:11, 14:3, 14:4, 14:6, 14:9, 14:25, 14:28, 14:36, 14:37, 14:44, 15:5, 15:13, 15:67, 15:78, 15:80, 16:12, 16:16, 16:42, 16:43, 16:44, 16:59, 16:61, 16:69, 16:79, 16:107, 17:60, 17:89, 17:106, 17:107, 18:15, 18:16, 18:21, 18:22, 18:25, 18:59, 18:71, 18:77, 18:86, 18:90, 18:93, 19:10, 19:11, 19:21, 19:27, 19:37, 19:55, 19:97, 20:59, 20:79, 20:83, 20:85, 20:86, 20:87, 20:88, 20:90, 20:98, 20:132, 21:6, 21:7, 21:52, 21:61, 21:71, 21:74, 21:77, 21:84, 21:93, 22:2, 22:18, 22:25, 22:42, 22:43, 22:78, 23:23, 23:24, 23:28, 23:33, 23:46, 23:47, 23:49, 23:53, 23:94, 24:11, 24:12, 25:1, 25:7, 25:30, 25:36, 25:37, 25:38, 26:10, 26:39, 26:40, 26:54, 26:70, 26:105, 26:111, 26:117, 26:123, 26:160, 26:176, 26:183, 26:221, 27:12, 27:16, 27:23, 27:24, 27:34, 27:37, 27:44, 27:46, 27:51, 27:54, 27:56, 27:73, 28:4, 28:21, 28:25, 28:32, 28:36, 28:43, 28:46, 28:76, 28:79, 28:87, 29:2, 29:14, 29:16, 29:24, 29:28, 29:29, 29:30, 29:31, 29:33, 29:34, 29:36, 29:47, 30:7, 30:23, 30:33, 30:36, 30:47, 31:6, 31:18, 32:3, 33:13, 33:26, 33:37, 33:46, 33:63, 34:15, 34:36, 35:24, 36:14, 36:15, 36:18, 36:20, 36:25, 36:26, 36:28, 36:30, 37:39, 37:85, 37:90, 37:94, 37:115, 37:124, 37:141, 37:142, 37:147, 37:148, 37:168, 38:7, 38:12, 38:13, 38:26, 38:43, 39:39, 39:51, 40:5, 40:29, 40:30, 40:31, 40:32, 40:38, 40:39, 40:41, 40:45, 40:46, 40:59, 41:3, |

| | |
|---|---|
| | 32:13, 33:7, 33:15, 33:22, 33:23, 34:29, 35:5, 35:40, 36:52, 37:17, 38:53, 38:54, 39:20, 39:71, 39:74, 40:8, 40:55, 40:77, 41:30, 42:23, 43:42, 43:49, 43:50, 45:32, 46:16, 46:17, 46:35, 47:15, 48:20, 48:29, 50:32, 51:22, 54:46, 57:10, 66:1, 67:25,68:39, 70:32, 70:42, 72:24, 72:25, 73:18, 76:7, 77:7, 85:2. |
| Proof | 2:87, 2:92, 2:111, 2:159, 2:164, 2:209, 2:213, 2:253, 3:105, 3:184, 4:144, 5:110, 6:104, 6:148, 6:149, 6:157, 7:85, 7:101, 7:105, 7:203, 9:7, 11:17, 14:9, 14:10, 14:11, 16:12, 16:44, 18:15, 20:133, 21:24, 23:117, 52:38, 57:25, 64:6, 98:1, 98:4. |
| Property | 2:188, 4:2, 4:5, 4:6, 4:7, 4:10, 4:24, 4:29, 4:33, 4:161, 6:152, 9:24, 11:87, 12:79, 17:34, 48:11, 53:48, 59:6, 59:7. |
| Prophet | 2:4, 2:6, 2:61, 2:91, 2:104, 2:105, 2:108, 2:136, 2:139, 2:143, 2:177, 2:186, 2:213, 2:214, 2:215, 2:246, 2:247, 2:248, 3:21, 3:39, 3:68, 3:79, 3:80, 3:81, 3:84, 3:86, 3:101, 3:112, 3:132, 3:146, 3:152, 3:161, 3:181, 4:55, 4:69, 4:80, 4:105, 4:113, 4:155, 4:163, 5:19, 5:20, 5:44, 5:46, 5:81, 5:100, 6:89, 6:104, 6:105, 6:109, 6:112, 7:94, 7:157, 7:193, 7:199, 7:203, 7:205, 8:1, 8:7, 8:38, 8:64, 8:65, 8:67, 8:70, 9:24, 9:40, 9:42, 9:61, 9:73, 9:74, 9:103, 9:107, 9:113, 9:114, 9:117, 10:15, 10:31, 10:38, 10:46, 10:65, 10:69, 10:94, 10:99, 10:104, 10:109, 11:2, 11:7, 11:12, 11:13, 12:3, 12:8, 12:15, 13:7, 15:6, 15:72, 15:78, 16:103, 16:121, 17:1, 17:55, 17:79, 17:110, 18:1, 19:28, 19:30, 19:41, 19:49, 19:51, 19:53, 19:54, 19:56, 19:58, Chapter 21 Title; 21:3, 21:4, 21:112, 22:15, 22:42, 22:52, 24:11, 24:30, 24:31, 25:4, 25:31, 25:38, 26:196, 29:27, 32:2, 32:11, 33:1, 33:6, 33:7, 33:13, 33:28, 33:30, 33:33, 33:37, 33:38, 33:40, 33:45, 33:50, 33:53, 33:55, 33:56, 33:59, 34:24, 34:28, 34:39, 34:46, 35:40, 36:1, 36:69, 37:36, 37:112, 39:69, 40:15, 43:4, 43:6, 43:7, 43:79, 43:88, 45:16, 46:8, 48:6, 48:28, 49:2, 50:1, 51:50, 53:2, 53:10, 53:11, 53:12, 53:13, 53:17, 53:18, 53:33, 53:53, 54:18, 54:24, 54:26, 57:7, 57:26, 57:28, 58:1, 58:11, 58:12, 58:13, 59:2, 60:1, 60:12, 61:6, 61:13, 62:3, 62:11, 63:8, 64:12, 65:1, 66:1, 66:3, 66:4, 66:8, 66:9, 68:48, 69:9, 69:44, 72:19, 74:52, 75:16, 79:15, 80:1, 90:3, 91:11, 106:1, 111:1. |

| | |
|---|---|
| Race | 5:41, 12:25, 32:8, 36:41, 38:31, 57:21. |
| Rain | 2:19, 2:22, 2:164, 2:264, 2:265, 4:102, 6:99, 7:57, 7:84, 7:133, 8:11, 8:32, 10:24, 11:44, 11:52, 11:82, 12:49, 13:17, 14:32, 1574:, 16:10, 16:11, 16:65, 18:45, 22:5, 22:63, 23:18, 24:28, 25:40, 25:50, 26:173, 27:58, 27:60, 29:63, 30:24, 30:48, 31:10, 31:34, 32:27, 35:27, 39:21, 40:13, 41:39, 42:28, 43:11, 46:24, 50:9, 51:4, 51:33, 54:11, 56:69, 57:20, 71:11, 72:16, 77:3, 78:14, 80:25, 86:11. |
| Ramadan | 2:185. |
| Ransom | 2:48, 2:85, 3:91, 5:36, 6:70, 10:54, 13:18, 37:107, 47:57, 57:15. |
| Reality | 6:105, 53:19, 53:35, 74:53, 89:14, 94:5. |
| Reconciliation | 2:228, 4:35, 65:1. |
| Register | 5:83, 9:120, 9:121, 57:22, 83:7, 83:8, 83:18, 83:19. |
| Record | 4:81, 6:59, 9:102, 10:21, 10:61, 11:6, 17:13, 17:14, 17:71, 18:49, 19:79, 20:52, 21:94, 22:70, 23:62, 27:75, 34:3, 35:11, 36:12, 39:69, 43:19, 43:80, 45:28, 45:29, 50:4, 50:18, 50:23, 57:22, 58:6, 69:19, 69:25, 78:29, 80:13, 81:101, 82:11, 83:7, 83:9, 83:18, 83:20, 84:7, 84:10. |
| Relief | 2:162, 7:195, 26:203, 32:29, 35:45. |
| Religion | 2:120, 2:130, 2:135, 2:138, 2:256, 3:19, 3:24, 3:72, 3:73, 3:83, 3:85, 3:95, 4:46, 4:125, 4:146, 4:171, 5:3, 5:57, 5:77, 6:70, 6:137, 6:159, 6:161, 7:51, 7:88, 7:89, 8:49, 8:72, 9:11, 9:12, 9:29, 9:33, 9:122, 12:38, 12:40, 14:13, 16:123, 18:20, 21:92, 21:93, 23:52, 24:55, 28:15, 30:30, 30:32, 30:43, 40:26, 42:8, 42:13, 42:15, 42:21, 43:22, 43:23, 43:24, 45:18, 48:28, 49:16, 60:8, 60:9, 61:9, 98:5, 109:6, 110:2. |
| Rejoice | 3:120, 3:170, 3:171, 3:188, 7:150, 9:25, 9:81, 9:111, 10:22, 10:58, 13:26, 13:36, 28:76, 30:4, 30:36, 30:48, 39:45, 40:75, 40:83. |
| Remembrance | 5:91,13:28, 18:28, 20:14, 24:36, 24:37, 29:45, 37:119, 39:23, 43:36, 57:161, 58:19, 62:9, 63:9, 72:17, 75:17. |
| Repentance | 2:37, 2:54, 2:58, 2:160, 2:222, 3:9, 4:16, 4:17, 4:26, 4:92, 6:8, Chapter 9 Title; 9:27, 9:104, 9:118, 33:24, 38:24, 40:3, 45:25. |
| Resurrection | 2:85, 2:174, 2:212, 2:275, 3:55, 3:77, 3:106, 3:161, 3:180, 3:185, 3:194, 4:87, 4:109, 4:141, 4:159, 5:14, |

| | |
|---|---|
| | 12:90, 12:104, 13:18, 13:35, 13:42, 13:51, 16:30, 16:31,16:32, 16:41, 16:95, 16:96, 16:97, 17:9, 17:19, 17:21, 17:63, 17:66, 17:98, 18:2, 18:30, 18:31, 18:44, 18:46, 18:88, 18:106, 19:76, 20:15, 20:73, 20:76, 20:112, 20:131, 21:29, 22:10, 22:28, 22:58, 22:72, 23:111, 24:38, 25:15, 25:57, 25:75, 26:41, 26:109, 26:127, 26:145, 26:164, 26:180, 27:89, 27:90, 28:14, 28:25, 28:37, 28:54, 28:60, 28:80, 28:84, 29:7, 29:27, 29:58, 30:39, 30:45, 30:46, 32:17, 32:19, 33:24, 33:29, 33:31, 33:35, 33:44, 33:47, 34:4, 34:37, 34:47, 35:7, 35:12, 35:30, 35:36, 36:11, 36:21, 36:54, 37:39, 37:80, 37:105, 37:110, 37:121, 37:131, 38:86, 39:10, 39:34, 39:35, 39:75, 40:17, 40:40, 41:8, 41:27, 41:28, 41:50, 42:20, 42:23, 42:40, 43:72, 45:12, 45:14, 45:22, 45:28, 46:14, 47:35, 47:36, 48:10, 48:16, 48:18, 48:29, 49:3, 49:14, 52:19, 52:21, 53:41, 54:14, 54:35, 55:47, 55:55, 55:57, 55:59, 55:60, 55:63, 55:65, 55:71, 55:73, 55:75, 55:77, 56:24, 57:7, 57:10, 57:11, 57:18, 57:19, 57:27, 64:15, 64:17, 65:5, 66:7, 67:12, 68:3, 73:20, 76:9, 76:12, 76:22, 77:44, 78:26, 78:30, 78:36, 83:36, 84:25, 85:11, 95:6, 98:8. |
| Righteous | 2:21, 2:44, 2:130, 2:177, 2:189, 2:212, 2:236, 2:237, 2:241, 3:15, 3:39, 3:46, 3:57, 3:89, 3:114, 3:115, 3:133, 3:136, 3:140, 3:193, 3:198, 4:26, 4:34, 4:57, 4:69, 4:122, 5:27, 5:46, 5:69, 5:84, 6:32, 6:51, 6:85, 6:153, 6:154, 6:155, 7:26, 7:128, 7:161, 7:168, 7:196, 8:34, 8:37, 9:4, 9:7, 9:36, 9:75, 9:108, 9:120, 11:3, 11:49, 11:115, 11:117, 12:22, 12:101, 1323:, 13:29, 13:35, 14:23, 15:45, 16:30, 16:31, 16:32, 16:122, 17:9, 18:2, 18:81, 18:82, 18:104, 18:107, 18:110, 19:13, 19:60, 19:63, 19:85, 19:96, 19:97, 20:104, 20:132, 21:48, 21:49, 21:71, 21:75, 21:86, 21:105, 22:14, 22:23, 22:37, 22:50, 22:56, 25:15, 25:74, 26:83, 26:90, 26:152, 27:19, 28:14, 28:27, 28:67, 28:83, 29:9, 29:27, 30:44, 30:45, 32:19, 34:4, 34:37, 34:100, 34:112, 38:49, 38:55, 39:28, 39:33, 39:58, 39:74, 40:8, 40:40, 42:22, 43:35, 43:67, 44:51, 45:19, 45:30, 47:2, 47:12, 47:15, 49:13, 50:31, 51:15, 52:17, 54:54, 58:9, 63:10, 66:4, 66:10, 68:34, 68:50, 69:48, 72:11, 74:56, 76:5, 77:41, 78:31, 82:13, 83:18, 83:20, 83:22, 89:27, 92:17. |
| Road | 4:169, 15:76, 16:15, 18:85, 18:89, 18:92, 29:29, 43:10, |

**S**

| | |
|---|---|
| | 53:16, 54:20, 55:6, 55:11, 55:48, 55:68, 56:28, 56:29, 59:52, 69:7, 76:14, 80:29, 80:31. |
| Trial | 2:49, 2:214, 7:141, 7:155, 8:25, 9:49, 14:6, 17:60, 21:111, 22:11, 22:53, 64:15, 74:31. |
| Tribe | 7:75, 7:160, 25:38, 38:13, 49:13, 59:2, 59:3, 59:6, 59:15, 63:8, 106:1. |
| Trumpet | 6:73, 18:99, 20:102, 23:101, 27:87, 36:51, 39:68, 50:20, 69:13, 74:8, 78:18, 79:6, 80:33. |
| Trust | 2:283, 3:75, 3:122, 3:159, 3:160, 5:11, 5:44, 5:107, 6:89, 6:124, 8:27, 9:7, 9:51, 9:61, 9:129, 10:71, 10:84, 10:85, 11:56, 11:70, 11:123, 12:11, 12:54, 12:64, 12:67, 12:80, 13:30, 14:11, 14:12, 16:42, 16:99, 20:73, 23:8, 24:33, 24:61, 25:58, 26:51, 26:107, 26:125, 26:143, 26:162, 26:178, 26:217, 27:39, 27:79, 28:26, 29:59, 31:22, 33:3, 33:72, 39:38, 40:44, 57:7, 57:28, 58:10, 60:4, 62:5, 64:13, 65:3, 66:12, 67:29, 70:32, 81:21. |
| Truth | 2:23, 2:26, 2:42, 2:91, 2:100, 2:109, 2:111, 2:113, 2:119, 2:135, 2:144, 2:146, 2:147, 2:149, 2:176, 2:213, 2:252, 3:3, 3:17, 3:18, 3:60, 3:71, 3:93, 3:95, 3:108, 3:168, 3:183, 4:15, 4:105, 4:116, 4:122, 4:156, 4:167, 4:170, 4:171, 5:48, 5:75, 5:77, 5:83, 5:84, 5:113, 5:119, 6:5, 6:26, 6:33, 6:40, 6:57, 6:66, 6:73, 6:79, 6:114, 6:115, 6:143, 6:146, 7:148, 7:43, 7:53, 7:70, 7:104, 7:106, 7:118, 7:159, 7:169, 7:181, 7:194, 8:6, 8:7, 8:8, 8:32, 9:29, 9:33, 9:43, 9:48, 9:94, 9:119, 10:5, 10:32, 10:35, 10:36, 10:38, 10:76, 10:77, 10:82, 10:94, 11:108, 11:17, 11:20, 11:32, 11:120, 12:7, 12:17, 12:26, 12:27, 12:46, 12:51, 12:82, 13:1, 13:17, 13:19, 14:19, 14:22, 15:3, 15:55, 15:64, 15:85, 15:96, 16:3, 16:39, 16:55, 16:102, 16:123, 17:81, 17:105, 18:13, 18:29, 18:56, 19:34, 19:41, 19:43, 19:54, 19:56, 20:108, 21:18, 21:24, 21:55, 21:56, 22:54, 22:62, 23:62, 23:70, 23:71, 23:90, 24:6, 24:25, 24:46, 24:49, 25:33, 26:6, 26:31, 26:154, 26:187, 27:41, 27:49, 27:64, 27:79, 28:48, 28:49, 28:53, 28:75, 29:3, 29:29, 29:44, 29:68, 30:8, 30:30, 32:3, 32:28, 33:4, 33:8, 33:22, 33:24, 33:35, 33:53, 33:70, 34:6, 34:23, 34:29, 34:43, 34:48, 34:49, 35:24, 35:31, 36:48, 36:52, 37:37, 37:170, 38:22, 38:64, 38:84, 38:88, 39:2, 39:5, 39:32, 39:33, 39:41, 40:5, 40:25, 40:28, 40:70, 41:53, 42:17, 42:18, 42:24, 43:29, 43:30, 43:78, 43:86, 43:87, 44:18, 44:39, 45:6, 45:22, 45:29, 46:3, 46:4, 46:7, 46:16, 46:22, 46:30, 46:34, 47:2, 47:3, |

| | |
|---|---|
| | 9:107, 33:50, 47:4, 48:11, 48:15, 48:17, 48:19, 66:9, 100:1. |
| Waste | 3:171, 6:141, 7:31, 10:24, 11:115, 17:26, 17:27, 47:1, 47:4, 47:8, 90:6. |
| Warning | 4:165, 6:19, 6:44, 7:2, 7:3, 7:53, 7:63, 7:136, 7:146, 7:165, 10:57, 10:101, 11:25, 11:120, 12:107, 14:52, 17:4, 17:59, 18:56, 18:101, 20:113, 21:2, 21:45, 21:84, 24:34, 25:1, 25:56, 26:5, 26:115, 26:208, 34:46, 35:37, 36:69, 38:87, 41:4, 43:66, 47:18, 50:8, 50:45, 52:29, 53:56, 54:23, 54:33, 54:36, 54:41, 65:10, 67:17, 68:52, 69:12, 74:36, 74:49, 77:6, 88:21, 107:4. |
| Water | 2:25, 2:60, 2:74, 2:249, 2:266, 3:15, 3:136, 3:195, 3:198, 4:13, 4:43, 4:57, 4:122, 5:6, 5:12, 5:85, 5:119, 6:6, 6:70, 7:50, 7:57, 7:159, 7:163, 9:19, 9:72, 9:89, 9:100, 10:4, 11:7, 11:40, 11:43, 11:44, 12:19, 13:4, 13:14, 14:16, 15:22, 16:11, 18:,29 18:,41 18:61, 18:63, 20:53, 21:3, 22:14, 22:19, 23:18, 25:48, 26:155, 27:44, 28:2, 38:23, 40:72, 44:48, 47:15, 53:54, 54:28, 55:19, 55:44, 56:68, 56:93, 67:30, 69:11, 76:5, 79:31. |
| Way | 2:115, 2:128, 2:149, 2:150, 2:167, 2:194, 2:240, 2:261, 3:17, 3:99, 3:146, 4:3, 4:15, 4:22, 4:26, 4:27, 4:95, 4:125, 4:146, 4:150, 4:160, 5:16, 5:45, 5:48, 5:54, 6:48, 6:55, 6:65, 6:105, 6:113, 6:116, 6:,117 6:,136 7:16, 7:86, 7:142, 7:146, 7:169, 8:36, 8:47, 9:5, 9:9, 9:20, 9:34, 9:39, 9:74, 10:12, 10:24, 10:45, 11:19, 12:37, 12:68, 12:108, 16:82, 16:94, 16:125, 17:9, 17:41, 17:43, 17:77, 17:110, 18:53, 18:64, 18:78, 20:10, 20:40, 20:63, 22:9, 22:25, 24:5, 25:17, 27:24, 28:56, 29:69, 33:38, 33:39, 37:83, 38:26, 40:7, 40:11, 42:44, 43:10, 45:19, 45:35, 47:32, 58:16, 63:2, 65:2, 68:7, 68:26, 68:44, 72:10, 72:11, 76:3, 82:6. |
| Wealth | 2:155, 2:177, 2:180, 2:195, 2:236, 2:245, 2:261, 2:262, 2:264, 2:265, 2:267, 2:269, 3:10, 3:116, 4:34, 4:38, 4:95, 7:188, 8:36, 8:72, 9:20, 9:34, 9:35, 9:41, 9:44, 9:55, 9:69, 9:81, 9:85, 9:86, 9:88, 9:93, 10:88, 11:29, 17:64, 18:39, 18:46, 19:77, 23:55, 26:88, 27:36, 30:39, 33:27, 34:35, 34:37, 43:23, 47:36, 47:37, 49:15, 51:19, 57:20, 58:17, 61:11, 63:9, 64:15, 68:14, 69:28, 70:18, 70:24, 71:12, 71:21, 74:12, 89:20, 90:6, 92:11, 92:18, 1008:, 104:2, 104:3, 111:2. |
| Weight | 4:40, 6:152, 7:85, 10:61, 11:84, 11:85, 34:3, 34:22, 55:9, |

| | |
|---|---|
| | 5:83, 5:106, 5:108, 5:111, 5:113, 5:117, 6:19, 6:130, 6:150, 7:37, 9:107, 10:29, 10:46, 10:61, 11:17, 11:18, 11:54, 11:103, 12:35, 12:66, 13:43, 16:84, 16:89, 16:91, 17:78, 18:51, 21:56, 21:61, 21:78, 22:17, 22:78, 23:93, 24:2, 24:4, 24:6, 24:13, 27:49, 28:28, 28:44, 28:75, 29:52, 33:45, 39:69, 40:51, 43:19, 46:8, 46:10, 48:8, 48:28, 50:21, 58:6, 59:11, 63:1, 65:2, 70:33, 75:14, 85:3, 100:7. |
| Woman | 2:221, 2:230, 2:282, 4:25, 5:75, 11:72, 16:92, 19:28, 22:2, 24:31, 26:171, 27:23, 33:36, 37:135, 49:11, 51:29, Chapter 58 Title, 58:1, Chapter 60 Title, 65:6, 76:2. |
| Wood | 21:98, 56:72, 63:4, 111:4. |
| World | 1:4, 2:4, 2:86, 2:114, 2:130, 2:200, 2:201, 2:202, 2:204, 2:212, 2:220, 3:14, 3:22, 3:42, 3:45, 3:56, 3:145, 3:148, 3:152, 3:185, 4:74, 4:77, 4:94, 4:134, 5:33, 5:41, 6:2, 6:32, 6:70, 6:73, 6:130, 7:51, 7:54, 7:61, 7:156, 8:67, 9:9, 9:38, 9:69, 10:7, 10:11, 10:24, 10:45, 10:58, 10:70, 11:3, 11:15, 11:48, 11:60, 11:99, 12:101, 16:30, 16:41, 16:107, 16:122, 17:52, 18:104, 22:9, 22:11, 22:15, 23:37, 24:14, 24:19, 24:23, 28:42, 28:60, 28:61, 28:77, 28:79, 29:25, 29:64, 29:66, 30:7, 31:15, 31:24, 31:33, 32:12, 32:21, 33:28, 33:57, 33:63, 34:52, 34:53, 35:5, 36:49, 39:10, 39:26, 40:39, 40:43, 40:51, 41:31, 42:20, 42:36, 43:32, 43:35, 43:72, 45:10, 45:24, 45:35, 46:20, 47:18, 47:36, 52:25, 52:28, 52:47, 53:29, 55:60, 56:24, 56:80, 57:20, 59:3, 59:16, 68:43, 69:24, 75:20, 76:27, 77:46, 79:38, 83:29, 87:16, 88:9, 92:13, Chapter 102 Title, 102. 1. |
| Worship | 1:5, 2:21, 2:43, 2:51, 2:54, 2:65, 2:83, 2:92, 2:93, 2:114, 2:125, 2:128, 2:133, 2:138, 2:165, 2:172, 2:193, 3:43, 3:51, 3:62, 3:64, 3:79, 3:96, 3:151, 4:36, 4:48, 4:87, 4:117, 4:153, 4:172, 5:173, 5:55, 5:72, 5:76, 5:116, 6:117, 6:56, 6:76, 6:81, 6:88, 6:102, 6:148, 6:151, 7:31, 7:37, 7:59, 7:65, 7:70, 7:73, 7:85, 7:138, 7:148, 7:152, 7:191, 7:193, 7:206, 9:31, 9:112, 10:3, 10:18, 10:28, 10:29, 10:66, 10:87, 10:104, 11:2, 11:26, 11:26, 11:50, 11:61, 11:62, 11:84, 11:87, 11:109, 11:123, 12:40, 12:77, 13:36, 14:10, 14:35, 15:99, 16:35, 16:73, 16:114, 17:22, 17:23, 17:39, 17:56, 18:15, 18:16, 18:21, 18:110, 19:36, 19:42, 19:44, 19:49, 19:65, 19:82, 20:14, 20:91, 21:19, 21:25, 21:53, 21:66, 21:67, 21:73, 21:84, 21:92, 21:98, 21:106, 22:26, 22:31, 22:71, 22:77, 23:23, 23:32, 23:59, |

## Y



## Z

# BIBLIOGRAPHY


- Abdullah Yusuf Ali:
  - The Holy Qur'an: Text, Translation and Commentary.
  - The Meanings of the Illustrious Qur'an: Without Arabic Text.
- Dr. M. Taqi-Ud-Din Al-Hilali and Dr. M. Muhsin Khan: Noble Qur'an.
- Khaleel Mohd: Assessing English Translations of the Qur'an.
- Maulana Mufti Muhammad Shafi: Ma'ariful Qur'an.
- Marmaduke W. Pickthall: The Meaning of the Glorious Qur'an.
- M. H. Shakir: The Holy Qur'an.
- M. Farooq-i-Azam: Al-Qur'an, the Guidance for Mankind.
- N. J. Dawood: The Koran: Translated with Notes.
- Saudi Arabian Govt. : Qur'an Karim with Urdu Translation and Tafseer.
- Al Qur'an-ul-Karim, an Urdu translation with commentary.
- Syed Abu-Ala Maududi:
  - Tafhim-ul-Qur'an, an Urdu translation with commentary.
  - Tafhim al-Qur'an – The Meaning of the Qur'an.
- Dr. Feras Hamza (Translator): Tafsir al-Jalalayn.
- Thomas Cleary: The Essential Koran: The Heart of Islam.
- Professor (Dr. ) Syed Vickar Ahamed: The Glorious Qur'an.
- University of Southern California – Center for Muslim-Jewish Engagement:www.usc. edu/schools/college/crcc/engagement/resources/texts/muslim/Qur'an/ (Qur'anic translation by Yusuf Ali, Pickthal, Shakir, and Syed Abu-Ala Maududi).
- Yahiya Emerick: The Meaning of the Holy Qur'an.
- www. Qur'an. com: Qur'anic translations.
- http://readwithmeaning. WordPress. com/chapters
- http://www. Bangla Qur'an. co. UK/download/complete_surah_contents. pdf

## ABOUT THE AUTHOR

Akhtar A. Alvi, P. E. , is an International Management Consultant. He:

- Is a retired Civil and Environmental Engineer and a U. S. citizen of Pakistani heritage.
- Earned a Bachelor of Science and two Master of Science degrees in Civil Engineering and taught Civil Engineering at the University of Engineering and Technology, Lahore, Pakistan, and Louisiana State University, Baton Rouge, Louisiana, USA.
- Developed irrigation and hydropower projects for the government of Nigeria and managed engineering and environmental projects for oil and gas companies in the United States and for the U. S. government.
- Is an author and a public speaker.

Made in the USA
Las Vegas, NV
27 December 2025